A Dowry for the Sultan

A tale of the siege of Manzikert 1054

Lance Collins

First published in Australia in 2016
Reprinted with minor amendments August 2016

© Lance Collins 2016.

The right of Lance Collins to be identified as the author of this work has been asserted under the *Copyright Amendment (Moral Rights) Act 2000*.

Apart from any use as permitted under the *Copyright Act 1968*, no part may be reproduced, copied, scanned, stored in a retrieval system, recorded or transmitted, in any form or by any means, without prior written permission.

Requests and enquiries should be addressed to:
Lance Collins
PO Box 4079, Geelong VIC 3220
AUSTRALIA

National Library of Australia cataloguing in publication data

Creator:	Collins, Lance, author.
Title:	A Dowry for the Sultan: A tale of the seige of Manzikert 1054
ISBN:	9780994540904 (paperback)
	9780994540928 (epub ebook)
	9780994540911 (mobi ebook)
Subjects:	Historical fiction.
Dewey Number:	A823.4

Cover and internal design by DiZign Pty Ltd, Sydney
Cover artwork: *Flight from Archēsh*, by Jill Collins
Back cover artwork: *Nomad*, by Jill Collins
Maps by DiZign Pty Ltd, Sydney

Contents

Frontis Maps... IV
Main Characters... VIII
Acknowledgements IX
Prologue: Twenty Lifetimes Ago..X

✠ Book One: The Past is Small Place.. 1
    Chapter One: Empire Of Betrayals 2
    Chapter Two: How Frail The Time Of Man.................................31
    Chapter Three: A Skirmish..58
    Chapter Four: A Red Dress..79
    Chapter Five: The Fountains Of Manzikert 107
    Chapter Six: Irene...130
    Chapter Seven: The Fight At The Wadi 153
    Chapter Eight: A Gift...185
    Chapter Nine: From Archēsh...210

✠ Book Two: The Towers of Manzikert 243
    Chapter Ten: I Will Take As Wife The Most
    Beautiful Girl..245
    Chapter Eleven: Comes The Shepherd King 265
    Chapter Twelve: The Landscape of Fear...................................285
    Chapter Thirteen: Laced With Intimacy That Gesture 298
    Chapter Fourteen: The Dance Under Arms............................311
    Chapter Fifteen: One Love And One Death 333
    Chapter Sixteen: The Lonesome Dove......................................350
    Chapter Seventeen: Into The Breach 372
    Chapter Eighteen: Fairest Fame 388
    Chapter Nineteen: The Wrath of the Shepherd King.......405
    Chapter Twenty: A Draught of Cool Water............................429

Characters 448
Afterword 452
Glossary 454

All persons in this story are fictional, except where specified in the list of characters. Any resemblance of a fictional character to a person living or dead is entirely coincidental.

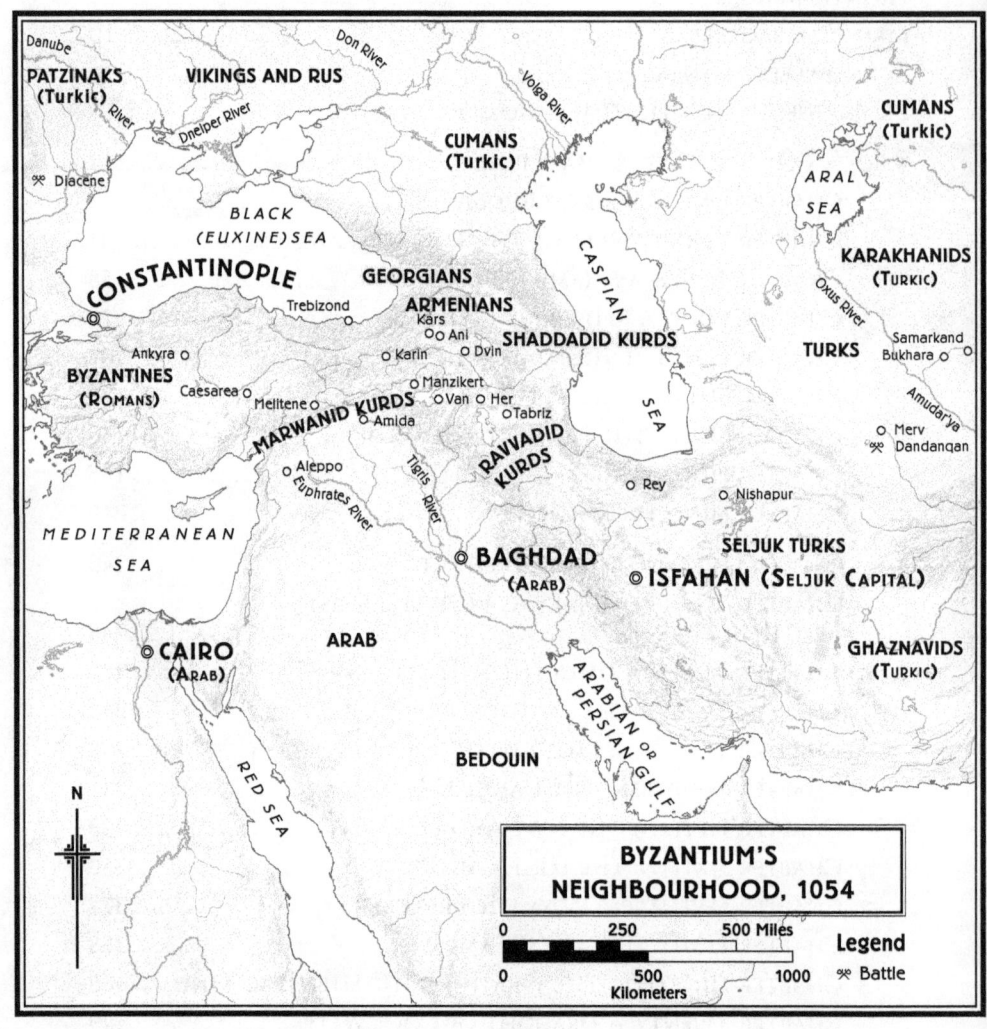

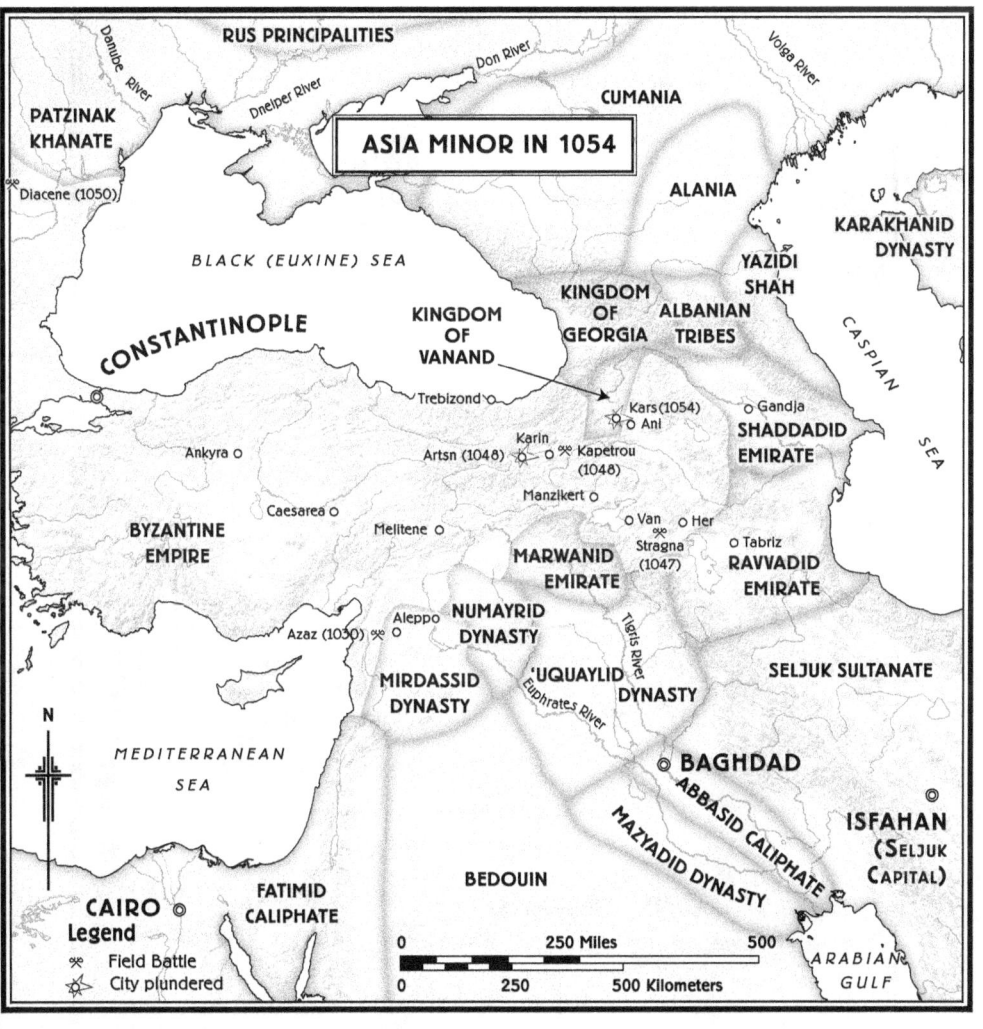

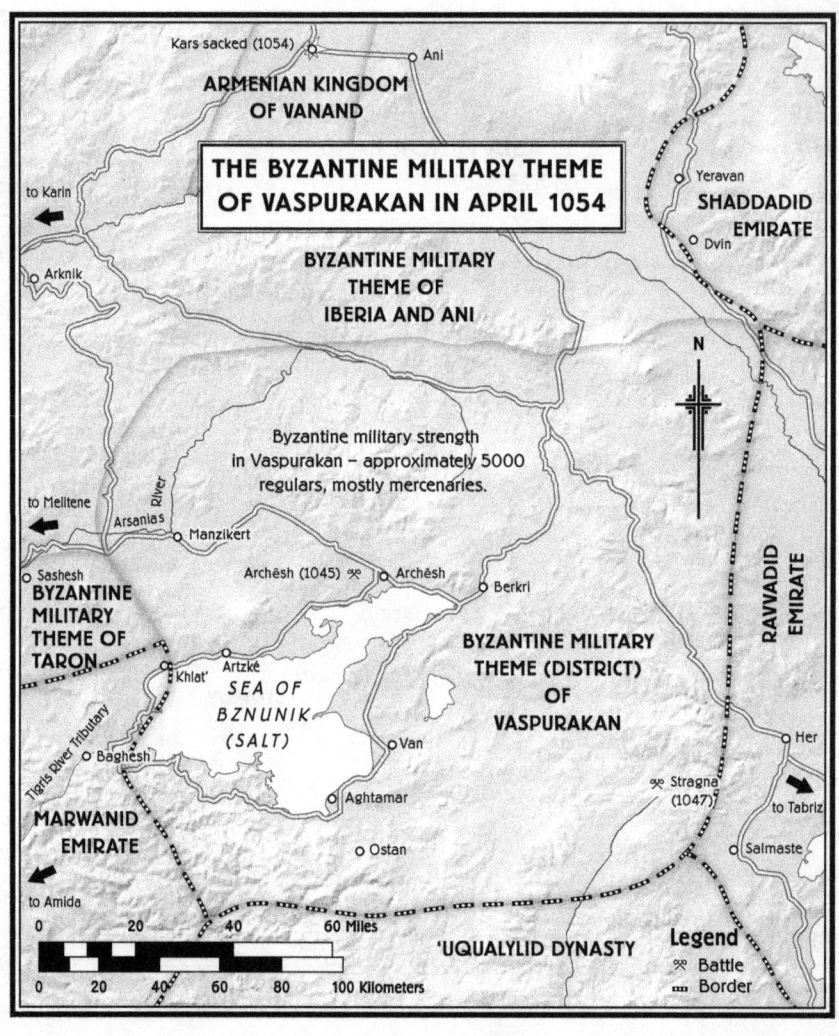

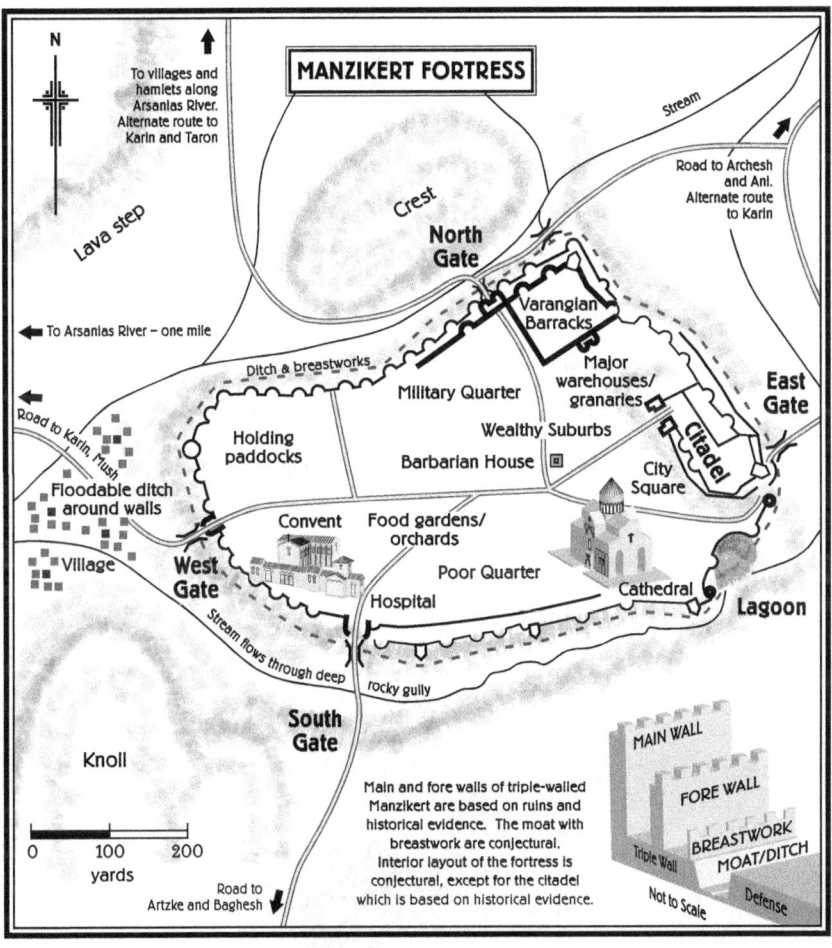

MAIN CHARACTERS

Guy d'Agiles	Frankish mercenary
Leo Bryennius	Byzantine officer
Basil Apocapes	Byzantine commander at Manzikert
Bardas Cydones	Byzantine bureaucrat
Bessas Phocas	Byzantine junior officer
Derar al-Adin	Arab mercenary in the Seljuk army
Irene Curticius	Greek-Armenian woman
Martina Cinnamus	Byzantine courier
Modestos Kamyates	Senior Byzantine official
Tughrul Bey	Sultan of the Seljuk Turks

ACKNOWLEDGEMENTS

This journey could not have been made without the kindness of friends and strangers. Paul A. Blaum, formerly of the University of Pennsylvania, an authority on 11th Century Byzantium's relations with its neighbours, was meticulous in checking the historical and biographical facts that underpin the story. His knowledge and enthusiasm for the subject were profoundly reassuring and encouraging. John Julius Norwich generously read a later draft and provided invaluable advice and support. A field trip to the fortress ruins and the surrounding region at Malazgird in eastern Turkey was enabled by my Turkish guide and the friendly interest and assistance of many local Turks and Kurds.

Warren Reed, Bob Breen, John Collins, formally of Jacaranda Press, and Rozamund Waring were generous with their time, knowledge and thoughtful suggestions during the early stages of the work. Louise Byrne, Patsy Thatcher, Annette Culley and Rebecca Langley together with Don and Cheryl Osborne, contributed markedly to the telling of this story with their timely editing of the final draft. Hilton Deakin, noted for his work for human rights in general, and Australian Aborigines, East Timorese and West Papuans in particular, very kindly took the time to read the work and speak at a pre-launch in Melbourne in December 2015.

My sister, Jill, researched and painted the cover illustration and Tommy Latupeirissa produced the cover photograph from her original oil painting.

Diana and Peter Murray, at DiZign in Sydney, with infinite patience and knowledge, undertook the design and layout, as well as drawing the maps and diagram.

The responsibility for any mistakes or oversight is mine alone.

PROLOGUE

Twenty lifetimes ago ...

They are times of fear and superstition, ignorance and suspicion rife as people attribute great powers to a deity and demons. The rich abuse the poor, the cunning exploit the just and the powerful prey upon the weak who brave famine, plague, attack from beyond and misrule within.

In the spring of 1054CE, Byzantium, the Eastern Roman Empire, languishes in fading glory as Western Europe shakes off the Dark Ages and ripples in the great whirlpool of Central Asia recast the Islamic world. Constantinople is in decline, the treasury looted and Roman Army weakened by neglect and ceaseless wars. Patzinak hordes ravage to the walls of the capital itself as Rus and Vikings prowl the Black Sea. Arabs and Kurds raid the desert borderlands while increasing numbers of mercenary Franks masquerade as friends.

Few in Constantinople recognise the greatest menace in the east, where the Seljuk Turks migrate in overwhelming numbers from the steppes by the Oxus River. With the legendary valour of the horse-people and the zeal of converts, the robber bands with their flocks are forged into armies under a Sultan, Tughrul Bey; risen from wanderer and prisoner to bestride an empire. Ageing and childless he plans to move on the Christian frontier seeking conquest and a captured wife.

As the Seljuk host prepares to engulf Byzantium's Armenian provinces, a woman with a warning, a Roman officer on a mission and a wandering Frank with nothing to lose, are despatched to meet the shepherd king at the crossroads of the world where the future for a thousand years will be decided.

~ BOOK ONE ~

THE PAST IS A SMALL PLACE

Chapter One

Empire Of Betrayals

The Great Palace, Constantinople,
Early morning, 18th April 1054

Though they may share a path, no souls make the same journey.

Martina's veil shrouded the outer world in mystery as she followed two nuns along a dark passage in the Great Palace. They had come for her after midnight and waited while she dressed. "You should look your best, dear."

A door loomed and swung open on oiled hinges. Martina could smell the dampness in the old stone and sensed the familiar iron-leather closeness of soldiers, but could hear only murmurs. She eased her wedding band and forced a composing breath into a bosom that felt crushed by the weight of her gown and cloak. By the light of a flaming torch she could make out an armed cavalryman take post either side of her. From their white cloaks and distinctive shield-emblem, she knew them as from the elite Scholae[1].

"Go with them, my child," said the older nun.

The troopers led her down a flight of stairs, torchlight reflecting orange on their cloaks as the sound of booted footsteps echoed off the walls. Tripping once, she admonished herself: people condemned horses for stumbling. Ascending flights of narrow stairs into another passageway, they halted before a stout door. She heard the knock, whispered challenge and password. A white-cloaked arm gestured towards the doorway. Martina stepped into the screened entrance of a large, lamp-lit room where an officer wearing a helmet and chainmail shirt took her cloak then left the room.

---

1 Cavalry brigade of the professional Byzantine Army.

"Come in. Come in, girl," a man said.

She stepped around the screen to face a veiled woman and two richly robed men, lounging on divans by a low table close to a fireplace. A desk covered with papers crowded the far corner where the wall was hidden by drapes and double-doors opened onto a balcony. Beyond that, first cock-crow stole over the battlements and tenements of the great city.

The older man motioned with an upward sweep of a hand across his face. "Let's see you."

Martina raised her veil and recognised, by reputation and association, the disfigured face his beard could not hide.

"D'you know me?"

"We all do, Strategos[2]. You're our most famous general, Catacalon Cecaumenus."

"No more than my colleague here, Commander of the Scholae."

The latter waved a deferential arm to Cecaumenus and nodded to her.

The woman remained silent.

From somewhere outside, not far away, came the sounds of a detachment of cavalry at mounted drill. Preparing for a change of the guard, she thought.

Cecaumenus rose, closed the balcony doors and strode to the fireplace, turning his back to the glow. "Martina Cinnamus, do you know why you're here?"

She felt her stomach knot. This was Constantinople, still called by its once village name, Byzantium, renowned capital of the Eastern Roman Empire. Though queen of cities, Christian and civilised, boasting a university and legal code; people were still murdered, blinded, disappeared and exiled on imperial whim. "Not really," she said.

Cecaumenus gave her a lingering look, then walked to stare through the window.

The quiet woman rose and approached, a sweep of gloved hand raising her own veil from a thin, plain face. "You've had a dream, child. Two, I'm told."

Martina did not know this obviously patrician woman and could not guess her age, something over fifty. She saw again the visions in her mind's eye and felt goose bumps on her arms, despite the warmth of her gown.

"You told a nun, the nun her abbess, the abbess informed me."

"Mistress?"

Cecaumenus turned from the window. "The Empress-Elector, Theodora."

"Augusta!" Martina made to lower herself but was prevented by the chaste old lady grasping her forearm with surprising strength.

"No longer an empress, child, so you need not address me by that title. But thank you."

"But you were," Martina protested, more aware her country accent contrasted with their crisp diction.

---

2 A Byzantine general.

Theodora, the Bulgarslayer's niece, last of the Macedonians, the virtuous "mother" of ordinary people, co-empress and force behind the throne until banished by her jealous sister, side-lined now by dead Zoe's husband—an emperor only by marriage—with his Georgian mistress. "All in the past," Theodora murmured as the tragedies of seventy-four years flitted across her face. "Tell us of your dreams, child?"

The three looked to Martina. She could read nothing on their faces. Did they think her sinner or saint, seer, sorceress or senseless? "I ... I had two. The same dream, twice. First when I was a child, the second, three nights ago. I didn't recognise the setting in the earliest for I was young and had never been to Constantinople. I don't know what they mean but I was ... puzzled ... and so told the nun." She looked to Theodora.

"Go on."

"I don't know, Mistress.' Perhaps I needed to know they meant nothing. They seemed too much to carry on my own and I knew the nun as her monastery is near where I work. I had no thought it would lead to this."

"What did you see, in your dreams?" Theodora asked gently.

Martina swallowed. "A blue mosque standing where the Great Palace should be."

"Both dreams the same?" the empress-in-waiting and the general asked in unison.

"A mosque?" Cecaumenus stared at her. "Here?"

Martina nodded mutely.

He again gazed intently at her. "Where were you, when you had your first dream?"

"When I was small, I grew up near the fortress of Abydos, by the ..."

Cecaumenus shook his head in disbelief or disquiet. "By the Hellespont, where Troy sleeps beneath olive trees and grazing goats! There Xerxes crossed the sea to attack the Greeks and Alexander traversed the narrows to subdue Babylon. The ancient Romans passed by to destroy the heirs of Alexander. We guard it still, for who holds the Hellespont owns the key to two worlds." He stared into nothing, seeing everything. "Sit down please," he said, guiding her to a divan. "Do you remember anything else? A sign or symbol?"

"I can't." She sat silently for what seemed like an eternity. "A host of dark riders ... and something else ... a crescent moon in the morning sky above the mosque."

"Crescent moon? You're sure?" Cecaumenus stooped over her, looking into her eyes.

"Yes. I'm certain."

He glanced at Theodora. "The Seljuk Turks!" His gaze returned to Martina. "Young woman, I'm a devout, some say overly zealous, Christian. In my time I've been approached by every manner of portent pedlar. Holy relics, icons, hermits, lizard's guts—I've seen them all, but you, ... you're different. For a start, you had to be brought here." The general rose, motioning his colleague and Martina to come with him.

Sensing his purpose, Theodora led them to the curtained wall, pulling the drapes back to reveal a swathe of colourful map: stylised, inaccurate and crowded with fanciful annotations, but nonetheless a representation of their world.

"Show me where we are?" Cecaumenus said.

"The city." Martina pointed to where Constantinople stood as a walled place at the confluence of the Sea of Marmara, the Golden Horn and the Bosphorus: the major crossing place and trade route between Europe, the Middle East and Asia.

"Very good. Your work with the Office of Barbarians stands you in good stead. Point out the Hellespont, where you grew up on the Asian side."

Martina met his look. The weather-beaten, battle-scarred face bespoke the wisdom of triumphs and disappointments, courage and fear. She felt a curious attraction and sensed he did also. With a flash of guilt she thought of her husband, a ranker in the Excubitores[3]. He had not come home last night—again. She pointed to the eastern shore of the narrow Hellespont.

"As the general says, you know your geography, Martina," Theodora broke in. "Our world has been dominated, with some Latin interruptions, by Greek-speaking peoples since the fall of Troy and her allies over two thousand years ago. The early Islamic invasions four hundred years past were a great and terrible threat. With God's help, we held and steadily regained many of our lost lands, but now, things are turning for the worse."

In a step, she was squinting at the western extremity of the map. "We're losing. The Pope in Rome wishes to take over our Church. Norman Kelts threaten Longobardia and Calabria. The populations of the Frankish-Keltic lands are warlike and growing rapidly. At present their armed and destitute younger sons come as mercenaries. Inevitably they will attempt to conquer us." She pointed to the Balkans. "Overwhelming numbers of barbarian Patzinaks[4], pressured by the Cumans[5] behind them, have moved southwest from north of the Black Sea, crossed the Danube River and ravaged Thrace. I do not need to tell you we are unable to expel them completely and must sue for peace. Vikings and their Rus offspring have settled along the great rivers north of the Black Sea. Our alliance with their prince at Kiev is one of religion and convenience only."

Cecaumenus took over. "The Muslim world to the south and east has been divided for centuries. The Shi'ite Fatimids of Cairo, with whom we've been friendly for some time, are enemies of the Sunni Abbasids of Baghdad. Fortunately, they've weakened each other and the other Arab states are too small to count. The Kurdish emirates—Ravvadids, Marwanids, Shaddadids—grouped like a horseshoe around the Armenian plateau, are torn by disunity. Further east, the Persians Buyids are a power no more. Beyond them, the Muslim

---

3   A brigade of cavalry in the Byzantine Army.
4   Turkic tribes from north east of the Black Sea.
5   Turkic people from western Central Asia.

Turkic Ghaznavids[6] are both, driven by the Seljuk Turks[7], and drawn by desire or destiny, southeast to Herat and Hind, away from us."

"That was all well and good. But now this Seljuk Sultan, Tughrul Bey, has united and inflamed Sunni Muslims from the Oxus to the Tigris. The multitude of his soldiers have occupied the strategic crossroads of the Iranian Plateau, subjugated the Ghaznavids and Kurds, enlisted the peoples of Transoxania and the Caspian hinterland. The Sunni Caliph in Baghdad is no more than a client. The Fatimids in Egypt are famine stricken and present no threat to him. Seljuk ambition and military strength have grown more powerful and sophisticated as their enemies crumpled. Byzantium is depleted by war and usury. We have nothing left to fight with, no men, no horses, no money. Our army destroyed a Seljuk incursion at Stragna River[8] and mauled another by Kapetrou fortress[9], six and seven years ago. I fear that was our high tide. Now the Seljuks are back and this time, if we falter, it might signal the last chukka."

"It is clear Armenia will be the battleground," said Theodora.

"But you're our most senior generals," Martina protested, wondering why they were confiding in her. "Can't you tell the Emperor?"

"We've tried and been rebuffed. He's surrounded by bureaucrats, was one himself, who have him thinking his agreement with the Sultan means something and there's no threat. He's too weak and sick to care anyway, a shell of a man since the death of the beautiful Sclerina—she, it's said, who could melt a heart of stone. Byzantium sleeps as the Seljuk wave prepares to fall on our eastern provinces. It'll be worse than the massacres around Artsn[10] six years ago."

Martina struggled to see her place in this. "And my ..."

"Your dreams," Theodora answered, "might mean nothing, or a very great deal. If they turn out to be prophetic, it is the end of everything. We, here, think this is very possibly our last chance, this summer, to stall the onslaught. Cecaumenus ..." She looked softly at him as though some old trouble between them was over. "Our Cecaumenus," she reeled off the sanguinary battles, "of Messina[11] and Diacene[12], of Kapetrou and of Stragna, believes, and he would be right, the weight of the Seljuk attack will fall on Vaspurakan[13], our most-exposed Armenian province in the southeast. The governor there has only about five thousand troops. A few years ago, sixty thousand defended the same frontier. If warned, he might be able to hold a fortress or two, shelter as many as he can, and delay the Turk just long enough for us to scratch an army together. If he cannot,

---

6 Turkic dynasty based in eastern Iran and Afghanistan.
7 Sunni Muslim Turkic sub-tribe of the Oghuz Turks.
8 Battle of Stragna (now the Great Zab River), spring 1047. See map page v.
9 Battle of Kapetrou (now Pasinler, eastern Turkey), 10 September 1048. See map page v.
10 Artsn—some ten miles north west of Karin; the first Armenian city to fall to the Seljuk Turks. See maps, glossary.
11 Defence of Messina, Sicily, against the Arabs in 1041.
12 Battle of Diacene, against the Patzinaks in 1049, see map page v.
13 Byzantine military province of Armenia, in which Manzikert (now Malazgird north of Lake Van) was a major fortress.

nothing lasts forever. The abbess tells me you have read some of the classics, so you will know collapses come very quickly. So! We brought you here because we wish you to carry despatches to Armenia and pass them to the patrician, Basil Apocapes, commander of the fortress at Manzikert, and effectively deputy commander of the Vaspurakan Theme."[14]

Martina held her breath.

"It will be dangerous," Theodora said. "If the Sultan's spies here get even a sniff of your mission they will surely hunt you down."

"But why me, to carry despatches to Armenia, I mean?"

Cecaumenus looked into her eyes. "You've chosen yourself. After all, you had the dreams and you come from restless stock, it seems. After the Hellespont, your mother took you to a border region near Syria, where you learned something of the Muslims, their religion and culture. We know you can read, write and converse in Arabic as well as our Greek, so you have a gift for languages. You're hardy and know horses. The translations you do for the Office of Barbarians give you knowledge and insight, without showing your face around too much. Nor, forgive me, will your accent describe you as from any particular place. In short, you do not look or sound like the usual military or diplomatic couriers, nor one of the merchants or priests we use for other little jobs. Our enemies know to look for them. We believe you can slip through unnoticed, pass your message and bring back Apocapes' despatches. An Armenian scout, a good fellow who knows the way, will accompany you—you can masquerade as a travelling couple. If you accept, you'll depart tomorrow night and make best speed, changing unbranded mounts at the military posts on the way."

"You can ride the distance, child?" Theodora looked almost fiercely at her.

"Yes, Mistress."

"It's well you know horses," the Empress-Elector turned, her gaze lingering on the map. "I don't. They are too big and frightening. For this, though, knowledge of them will stand you in good stead. Out there people depend on their horses for their very lives. Militarily, cavalry is our most important arm—our enemy's also, so your estimates of the relative strength of the armies and how they fight will be most useful for me." Theodora turned to her again. "To understand open warfare on the steppes, one needs to know horses."

"Yes, Mistress."

Cecaumenus allowed the moment between the women to pass. "We have this day, tonight and tomorrow to set in motion a cover plan to ensure you get away."

Martina stepped close to the map, what they asked becoming apparent. "Where is Strategos Apocapes?"

Cecaumenus thumped the fabric, the flat of his hand on Constantinople, then drew his reins-grimy paw eastward, past the famous cities of the Greeks, Macedonians, Romans and Persians, over the forgotten ruins of the Lydians, Cimmerians, of Midas the Phygrian, Trojans, Hittites and Assyrians. His hand

---

[14] Theme—a Byzantine civil and military province commanded by a strategos (the exact rank and function varied over time).

moved over the Euphrates and Tigris to the highlands of the Armenian plateau. "Karin, and several days' march beyond that, the fortress-city of Manzikert." The general tapped the map. "Vaspurakan is the province around the great lake. You see, virtually surrounding Vaspurakan, the Muslim world—Dvin, Her, Tabriz, Mosul, Baghdad: cities populated by Arabs, Kurds, Turks, others."

"Far away," Martina whispered, searching Cecaumenus' eyes. "Is the threat of which you speak not remote?"

"You had the dreams and as the Empress-Elector has said, every fallen civilisation has thought catastrophe far off."

Martina looked closely at the map a moment. "Why Strategos Apocapes at Manzikert? Van, at the eastern end of the great lake, is the capital of Vaspurakan?"

Cecaumenus glanced at Theodora. "You chose the right courier, Mistress." He stabbed Manzikert with a finger. "Nominally, yes. Van has a strong fortress and is the capital, with the Vaspurakan Theme commander, strategos, catepano, call him what you will, currently located there. But Van is too exposed to the frontier and too easily bypassed, strategically irrelevant if the Seljuks advance north of the lake. Manzikert, in contrast, is a powerful fortress well-sited to guard the invasion routes and has more secure routes back into the depth of the empire—hence its use at various times as the effective capital of Vaspurakan. Most importantly, although he is subordinate to the fellow at Van, I have faith in Basil Apocapes."

Three days ago her life had been fairly ordered and simple. "My husband?"

They glanced down and remained silent.

Martina struggled to remain composed as she read her fears into their gestures.

"Leave us please, gentlemen," Theodora said, "and complete your preparations."

The two men made for the screen, shrugging off their robes to reveal riding clothes. Cecaumenus turned to Theodora. "You understand that as soon as we set things in motion, the circle of knowledge grows?"

"Thus our deceptions and our prayers."

As the door closed, Martina sank to the divan, pinpricks of tears in her eyes. She looked up at Theodora.

"Don't ask me, child. I'm the last one that would know—another betrayal in an empire of betrayals."

Martina shook uncontrollably. At length, she steeled herself for the journey, to ride away and not look back. "I'll need some things."

"Of course. You'll go home now as you came. No messages to anyone. You will return here tonight, meet your guide, rest and leave tomorrow after dark. So that your husband does not draw attention to your absence, we have arranged a special duty for the troop he is in—a routine patrol for a few days—until you are well away."

"Is that where he was last night?"

Theodora shook her head slightly.

Martina looked down.

Advancing a step, Theodora placed a hand lightly on her shoulder. "The past is a small place. Try not to dwell on it."

Martina looked up to the older woman. "Is the future a small place also?"

Theodora turned and walked to the window. "The sun is just up. I have always loved this time of day."

"It's just ride there, deliver the message and bring back the answer?"

Theodora turned again to Martina. "When Apocapes sends it. You may need to wait awhile at Manzikert. I especially want you to go, Martina, because I need to know what feeling you get while there, what is in the air, and whether you have the same dream again. I have been too cloistered in my life. Like many city-dwellers, I do not know how to judge the seasons, tell the state of crops or ride a rough horse. Nor are we wise in the ways of dangers like serpents and wolves. You have these skills amongst many others, hence you will be able to tell me much. The whole thing has me uneasy. Cecaumenus also. I have just met you, but you seem to be a young woman of spirit and loyalty. You will be well paid and just perhaps, your husband will realise what he might lose if you disappear for a few weeks."

Martina knew for the moment anger sustained her. That would pass, then she would welcome the sedatives of fatigue and distracting danger.

It was as though Theodora read her thoughts.

"Mistress?"

"I fear for you, Martina, but also envy you. You will journey to our far frontier—the crossroads of the world where the very future for a thousand years is at stake. Strife, heroes and cowards, good and wicked will cross your path." She stepped close and placed a hand on the younger woman's shoulder. "Forgive me, child, I talk too much, once I like someone. I must trust Cecaumenus on this, but he has banned even my closest eunuch from knowledge of it." She sighed to herself. "The people need this. Can you do it?"

"I will."

In silence, they searched each other's eyes until Theodora said, "Beware of one man in particular, if his path crosses yours, though it should not. A courtier and diplomat named Michael Kamyates. Remember it. He is very powerful and dangerous. Some months ago he departed on an embassy to the Abbasids in Baghdad to determine the state of their relations with the Seljuks. He should have returned by now. If we, here, have heard rumours of trouble, then he surely must have. It is his bounden duty to hasten back and report what he knows, but we have heard nothing from him. We hear rumours he is alive and well, but anything else is a mystery. One of my advisors mistrusts the man, believing him to be too fond of the Seljuks."

"Mistress, who can I trust?"

"No-one!" Theodora's lips tightened. "You can only decide that for yourself." She stared far away. "But, I venture, Count Bryennius, of the Scholae. And it may be you will see him in Vaspurakan."

"Is he there now? Or should I meet him before I leave?" asked Martina, rising.

"He's here, but there will be no opportunity as he has much to do." Theodora again gripped her arm. "Tell no one of your dream, not even Apocapes. And get out in time. Make sure of it, any way you can. You do not need to experience for yourself that Roman girls are favoured for the harems, nor do we need them taking you and learning of your dreams. Also we hear the Sultan is childless and now intends a captured Roman bride to provide him an heir."

"Not me?"

Theodora smiled softly. "You undervalue yourself. You're quite lovely."

They stood and Theodora leaned forward and kissed her on the cheeks. "Go now, return as soon as you can and talk to me."

"Mistress." Martina bowed her head, moved to the door, drew down her veil and tapped the hardwood.

"Martina."

She turned.

"The future is a big place, Martina. God's speed."

The door swung open to reveal her escort. The officer, his face obscured beneath the helmet's low rim, smelled of iron, leather and horses like her husband, but he drew her cloak around her with surprising gentleness. Then Martina followed them into the passage of shadows, grateful the fine black netting of the veil concealed her tears from the world.

Constantinople,
Dusk, 19th April 1054

Another wrong road, thought Guy d'Agiles.

Distinguished by the two inns, a stable and a smithy amongst sparse houses and streets, this was a natural meeting place for those with swords, secrets or favours to sell. He turned in his saddle to face his two companions, also mounted on hired horses. "Charles, Jacques, I am sorry. I've dragged you both on another wasted day's search. It's getting dark and we should eat. Let's try this larger inn. It's perhaps better served than the other and I shall be glad to pay."

"One's as good as another and I'm hungry," agreed manly Charles Bertrum, looking around the crossroads not far from Byzantium's Golden Gate.

"There will be hitching-rails around the back," said Guy's servant, stubble-faced Jacques.

Turning down a side lane they entered a cobbled courtyard overlooked by the shadow-wreathed loft of the stables next door and hitched their horses to a rail. Guy cast an eye over the other six horses in the yard. Useful rather than well-bred, even these would be beyond his means to replace the mule he had ridden after the death of his old horse on the journey from Provence. Stepping past a wine-reeking barbarian sprawled by the doorway, they approached the inn's rear entrance.

Charles and Guy were childhood companions who had grown up playing, riding and training at arms together. Guy's servant, Jacques, followed them with the reserved dignity of his class and the less common authority of an experienced wayfarer. Guy and Charles were younger sons of the landed military class and stood to inherit nothing, birthright being the privilege of the eldest. Seven months earlier without so much as a parting note and carrying all they needed on their saddles, they had ridden from the estates of their sires: log-palisaded clusters of rude stone buildings dominating some miles of countryside and the peasants who lived there. Guy's ageing father held his lands with two elder sons, given their spurs and dubbed knights, a handful of paid men-at-arms and the local peasants, reinforced by an alliance with the nearby Bertrum estate.

Guy, Charles and Jacques entered the inn where oil lamps cast grotesque shadows across the ancient brick walls. A front door led directly to the street. The inn's other customers comprised two-dozen men, outwardly artisans, soldiers from the city's walls and labourers from the nearby orchards and fields. No one seemed to heed the three, for unemployed mercenaries were common here. Guy led them to a table with bench seats near the back door.

Jacques took in the scene. "We've chosen the wrong inn. There's something in the air."

Guy and Charles paid him cursory attention and tried to attract a serving woman. She approached, looking over their swords, rough-spun tunics, fitted riding pants and worn shoes. Patrician once, perhaps, she spoke Greek with an unfamiliar accent and wore a patched but clean dress covered by an apron. Guy noticed her lips move and the soft lines of her neck and arms where sleeves were immodestly rolled to the elbows for her work. They struggled with the order—stew, bread, wine.

Recalling Jacques warning, Guy's sweep of the room took in two men at the next table; a middle-aged priest of the Greek Church with a younger companion. Seated so they could observe both doors, their furtive study of the three Franks aroused Guy's attention. Jacques nudged him with a foot under the table and shook his head imperceptibly.

Charles, waving fair hair from his face, made light of their long day's ride in search of a suitable horse in the villages, monasteries and estates that nestled by the impregnable triple land-walls of Constantinople. "They all asked too much and there will be a better mount by and by. There always is. Though it has to be said, who seeks a wife or horse without blemish, for a mate or mount will surely famish."

Guy shot his friend an irritated glance. "My money runs low, Charles. I can't afford a mistake. We must soon find work as men-at-arms and for that I need a suitable horse. Constantinople is a worthy city, but it costs a fortune to live here idly."

"And heiresses are hard to impress from the back of a mule." Charles was disarmingly open about his desire to marry well. "For warring or wooing, a fellow needs a suitable horse."

"True enough." Guy stared at the bench top, struck by the sudden realisation there was no place to go back to without humility. A hollowness in his chest enveloped him. "If only I'd been more careful with the one I had."

"Your father made you horseman enough," said Jacques. The paunchy groom was twenty years older than Guy's nineteen. He had long ago vanished from the estate, to reappear only three years before, grey-haired, faced lined and so skilled a horseman Guy's father had employed him as head groom. They seemed close and often went on long hunts together. Jacques, on foot, had caught up with Guy and Charles on the road a week after they left. He travelled light: his bundle, a few gold coins, a cheap sword and crossbow with which he was very skilled.

Guy wondered, but never asked, if one of his parents had sent Jacques after him, or whether the groom had simply wished for adventure and the chance to improve his lot in foreign lands. He looked up as Jacques spoke and memory of his father returned. When the time comes—the old warrior had said—you will know when, you must go quickly and not look back.

Jacques waited until Guy re-focussed on him. "T'was no fault of yours the mare died of colic. Don't be ashamed of the mule, it was the best deal that could be done and the beast has carried you this far. I know of rough work in other lands where the mules outlasted the horses."

Guy suppressed an instinct to look sharply at Jacques, suspecting the peasant was speaking from more than hearsay.

The woman returned with bread and stew. "Kelts? Looking for work?"

Guy replied in halting Greek. "Yes, Franks. And work, if it's suitable."

"Come by the day after tomorrow. Some of the bands' recruiters will be here. Do you wish to go north or east?"

"Which is better?"

"Neither. In the north, the pagan Patzinaks of Tyrach, though there is a truce. To the east, Tughrul Bey's shepherd hordes. Muslims. False truce there."

The east seemed far away from Guy's present problems. "A shepherd king?"

"Don't mock me!" she snapped. "They're shepherds the like of which you've never seen in your lands. Two hundred thousand well-mounted and armed barbarians answer their Sultan's call. They are the wolves of the steppes, unwashed, unlettered, forever raiding, plundering and occupying the lands of Muslims and Christians alike, usurping the rule of any prince imprudent enough to employ them."

"We've come from the west," Charles said, spoon halfway to his lips. He fell silent at her stare.

Guy recounted the exchange for the benefit of his companions. A momentary seriousness crossed Charles Bertrum's handsome features.

The woman gave him a motherly look. "If you wish the north, a Flemish man is hiring, but is untrustworthy. If east, join the Norman band that picks up men here. And if you go to the east…" she leaned closer to them, "…and I wouldn't, do not go beyond Caesarea or Melitene, it's too dangerous."

The three looked blankly at her. "Why?" asked Guy.

"Haven't you heard of Artsn?"

"Artsn? A town?"

"A city, a beautiful Armenian city, now a ruin inhabited only by snakes and scorpions. And ghosts. Tughrul's half-brother destroyed it eight years ago."

Guy interpreted and there was an awkward silence.

"Was she there?" Charles kicked him under the table. "Was …"

"Yes! I was there."

"Wouldn't you want us to fight these infidels?" Charles regarded her with growing interest. A romantic, he loved stories of adventure, damsels in distress, poetry from such things and he loved women. "Surely they cannot defeat the great empires—Persian, Abbasid, Roman—we have heard of? Are they not simple herders—mere men after all?"

She looked to Guy, who duly interpreted.

"Alas that is their strength," she said, eyes on Charles. "All mounted with their mobile herds, they have no cities to capture. The Turk need only to move out of the way of the ponderous armies of the agricultural peoples, then attack again with their terrible bows. It's hopeless. The arrows of the infidels come like rain. You seem like decent enough young men. Don't throw your lives away." She hesitated a moment, looking at them all. "Go home."

Guy thanked the woman and answered the looks of the others.

They dined in silence until Jacques remarked, "Like rain, eh? Well, let's not go to Armenia, then!" Laughing, they got on with their meal.

Charles watched Jacques devour his portion and delve in for more. "I had a horse like you once, Jacques. He was literally starving to death when I bought him. Despite years of wanting for nothing, he could not stop eating. I had to lock him up much of the time or he would have died of the founder. Good horse though—as though he knew I saved him and always tried to repay me."

"Starving, you say?" said Jacques, still eating.

Four rough-looking men, bearded with hair over their ears like the Greeks, left the far end of the room and sat at a table beside the priest and his servant, though others were free. Soldiers hired for private purpose, Guy guessed, wondering if they owned any of the horses outside. He could understand some of their conversation and sensed tension between them and the priest.

"Four," whispered Jacques. "Daggers. One has a staff."

"Going far, god-botherer?" one of the thugs jeered.

"Where the Lord's work takes me," the priest smiled.

"To Armenia, no doubt, to warn the Seljuks are coming to destroy them?"

"The Armenians, though Christians, are misguided and need to be shown the true path."

"Important work," the thug rejoined, "for such a … new … priest." He paused. "Just last week, did you not carry sword and shield in the ranks of the Excubitores?"

"It's on," muttered Jacques, "and neither of you have your hauberks[15] nor helmets or shields. Stay out of it."

"You're mistaken," replied the priest evenly as the sound of three shod horses rung on the cobbled road outside.

One of the thugs rose, looked out of the door into the street and smirked over his shoulder, as though he recognised the riders. He lingered, blocking the doorway.

Guy and Jacques exchanged glances as they listened to the hoof beats enter the lane. "I can't afford to lose our hired horses. I'll go and check them." Shaking his head at Jacques' silent plea not to, Guy rose.

"You can't risk your life," muttered Charles.

"Stay here," Jacques hissed.

Ignoring them, Guy left the room and reached the shadows of their horses moments before three cloaked riders entered the yard.

"This is the place," said the first in cultured Greek. "Is it clear? Are your men ready?" The moonlight betrayed a drawn blade.

As his father had taught, Guy mentally ascribed a descriptive nickname—Swordleader.

"Yes," answered the second in gutter Greek, switching his lance to his right hand as he dismounted—Spearman. "They followed the Domestic's couriers here from the Palace. All's ready. We'll catch them and seize their despatches."

Guy understood the reference to one of the most senior of Byzantine military officers and sensed the high stakes of the game into which he and his companions had chanced.

"Make sure of it."

There was a moment's silence. "Are you certain about this?" asked Spearman.

"About what?" said Swordleader.

"Ah, murdering military couriers and stealing their despatches."

"Bah! The army has no power here. In any event, it's none of your concern. Shut up and do what you were paid for."

"Very well," Spearman acquiesced sourly.

Against the distant sounds of town dogs and the slow, shoe-scraping passage of some drunken rider, Guy held his breath, straining to discern the substance of their conversation. Despite the cool night, a prickle of perspiration touched his scalp beneath his shoulder-length red hair.

"And be sure of it." Swordleader said.

Guy tried to make out some detail of the third rider, who remained mounted, cloaked and silent, a shadow in the moonlight.

---

15 Hauberk—a knee/calf length chain-mail coat, split front and back for riding, with sleeves reaching at least to mid-forearm. It had either an integral mail hood protecting the head and neck, or a separate mail pullover coif serving the same purpose. It superseded, for those who could afford it, the earlier byrnie from the early 9th Century.

Spearman moved towards where Guy stood by his hired horse's head. "I'll let these beasts go. They'll be in the way and might be used by anyone pursuing us." Spearman made to untie Charles' mare.

Guy spoke darkly in Latin. "Leave it."

Spearman gasped in surprise, taking his weapon in both hands and leaping backwards to give himself space to use its length.

"What's up?" asked his companions in unison.

"A Kelt," replied Spearman over his shoulder as he brought up the point.

The third of their party moved his horse to menace Guy's right, easing back his cloak to draw an equestrian's strung bow from its shaped case on his left hip—Bowman.

"How much did he hear?" Swordleader asked.

"Or understand?" Bowman spoke for the first time in heavily accented Greek.

A mumbling man, seeming not to notice them, emerged from the inn door, tripped heavily over the drunken barbarian and felt along the wall, fumbling with his dress as though to urinate. Guy recognised Charles, sword concealed against his body.

There was uproar and the crash of a table overturned from within the inn, then the priest and his younger companion burst into the night, four thugs in pursuit.

Everyone froze for a moment until Guy broke the silence. "Three! Swordleader, mounted. Spearman, on foot, to my front. Bowman, under the cloak, mounted, on my right."

"Kill him! Kill them all!" screamed Swordleader as cavalry clattered along a nearby street.

Then all was confusion as men shouted and frightened horses pulled-back on their hitchings. Bowman threw back his cloak. Guy saw the long straight hair and brocade tunic over loose trousers as the man drew an arrow from the quiver at his right side. The apparently drunken barbarian in the threadbare coat sprang to his feet and struck down one of the thugs with his sabre. A thug grabbed the youth from behind as the priest, drawing a sword from under his mantle, turned back to help his companion. He was too late. The younger man screamed once and dropped to the ground as a thug knifed him savagely, before the priest ran-through his killer.

With the grind of steel on steel, Guy brushed aside Spearman's thrust, cut the haft in two and forced him back three paces.

Charles came up. "I'll take him!"

Guy, with the trained aggression of a confident swordsman advanced towards Swordleader, keeping his antagonist between himself and Bowman.

The man turned Guy's sword and forced him to retreat a few steps.

"They're the wrong ones. Fools!" Swordleader cried. "I told you one of the couriers was a woman. This is a trap."

Guy saw Bowman draw an arrow on him and stepped behind Swordleader's horse.

"Lookout!" shouted Jacques.

Guy risked a glance in time to see the threadbare barbarian hurl a war axe at Bowman, spoiling his aim. He heard Jacques say in Greek, "Thank you, friend."

At the clamour of approaching troops, one thug fled over a wall and was lost to the night. The last fell insensible to a blow from Jacques.

Guy seized Swordleader's bridle rein as the dark-cloaked rider spurred and wrenched his horse's mouth so it reared free. Against the night sky, Guy caught a glimpse of a blade that struck at his throat. Pulled off balance, he leapt back. "Cross me again, Kelt, and you die," the hooded shadow snarled before the two turned their horses and dashed into the lane, leaving Guy ashamed of the fear he had felt.

Spearman struggled to mount his skittish mare, but an arrow plunged into his lung. He collapsed, clutching at the shaft buried in his chest and losing his grip on the reins as his horse ran off. Disabled by shock and pain, he tried to turn on his side and look after his fleeing confederates.

Charles and Jacques, wild-eyed, weapons ready, approached him. Six armed men dressed as labourers appeared from the inn door but seemed uncertain what to do.

Jacques knelt by Spearman. "He's trying to tell us something. A name?"

A dozen mailed horsemen of the Scholae cantered down the lane and wheeled into the courtyard. Others raced into the night after the fugitives.

"Arrest them." The detachment commander wheeled his superb bay horse to take in the scene. "Arrest them all. Secure the area. Detain anyone still inside the inn. Clear those stables." Moonlight gleamed on his helmet and cast his eyes behind the burnished nasal into black shadows.

A trooper dismounted and knelt by Spearman as Jacques stood back. "He's dead, Count," the soldier said as others seized Guy and his companions.

The barbarian of the threadbare blue coat stood from carefully wiping his sabre on the tunic of a fallen thug and spoke to the count. "Horse-archer! These three didn't know."

"Very good, Togol. Arrest them." The helmet turned, peering after the tumult of the pursuit receding into the distance, then back to Guy. "Who're you?"

"I am Guy d'Agiles."

"Frankish mercenary?"

Guy was silent.

Togol stepped close to the count, sliding his long blade into the scabbard by his booted leg. "Their leader spoke Greek, a bit uppity. Sensed the trap—smart. Said one of the couriers is a woman."

"Did he now? Anyone get a look at him?"

"This Kelt," reported Togol, motioning at Guy. "Threatened to kill him."

"Who did?"

"The one you're after."

The count stepped his horse, slowly, deliberately, closer. The eyes hidden under the helmet looked down long on Guy. "Would you know him?"

"Perhaps. It was fleeting, only a glimpse and a few words."

"You spoke?" asked the count.

"No. He threatened me."

"Still, he'll recognise you, eh?"

"Perhaps."

"You're with us until I say otherwise." The count spoke without looking to a well-mounted officer behind him. "Bessas, see to it please." With his white cloak gleaming in the moonlight, he leaned forward a little and gave a light, caressing stroke to his horse's neck.

"Where're you taking us?" Guy demanded as he struggled against the troopers holding him.

The count turned his horse away. "Far away, I fancy," he said without a backward glance.

Constantinople,
Evening, 19th April 1054

"Everything's gone wrong," Byzantine imperial bureaucrat and traitor, Bardas Cydones, whined to his Seljuk handler as they paused in their flight from the inn near the Golden Gate. "How did they know?" he asked, sheathing his sword.

"Not everything," the Seljuk from their embassy to Constantinople responded in grim anger as he thrust his bow back into its case and swung his blowing horse into the shadows to better see behind them. "You planned our escape route well, your hirelings blocked the road with carts and cattle so the Emperor's soldiers cannot follow. As we left the inn, I saw your blundering go-between fall struck by an arrow from the men I secreted in the stable next door. That is what I like about this city, anything can be bought. At least one of the decoys paid with his life, and the thugs you hired presumably cannot lead anyone back to you. As you say, it's useful that we know they knew." A sinewy fifty and excellent rider, the Seljuk diplomat drew his hooded cloak about him to conceal his weapons and distinctive almond-eyed Turkic features.

The two men turned their horses into a canter and made their escape.

Cydones thought of the long-haired Kelt who had twice menaced him during the fight. He reasoned that while the man might recognise him if they met again, it was unlikely his path would again cross that of an itinerant foreign mercenary.

"We now know that someone's hunting us," the Seljuk continued. "We know also that the real couriers will be on their way to Armenia. All we … you … need do is intercept them on the road before they can deliver their message."

"Asia Minor. Armenia! So vast. Where'd they be? What if you can't find them?"

"You! You failed so you're going after them. Y'know where they started and where they're bound. They'll have left tonight so you need to hasten. Riding fast, it will take them seven days at the very least. Twice that probably." The handler glared at Cydones. "If you fail to prevent them reaching Manzikert, you can still be of use there. I have a message for you to give to a man called Kamyates, you know him, at Manzikert. You're to remain there and ensure the city falls to the Seljuk Sultan this summer."

Trepidation gripped Cydones. Michael Kamyates! There was ice-water in that man's veins. He was widely regarded as one of the foremost authorities on the Seljuk Turks and was currently on an embassy to the Caliph in Baghdad. Kamyates was too arrogant to bother hiding his sympathy for the Seljuks. His skill as a palace intriguer was evidenced by a string of blinded, exiled and disappeared victims. But Manzikert falling to the Sultan! Cydones had not expected this. A little well-renumerated scheming and murder on his home ground was one thing: riding to the far reaches of the empire and surviving a siege were another. "But I'd be missed."

"Don't concern yourself. You're senior enough to find an official reason to go there." The Seljuk looked directly at him. "And I will make sure your family is looked after."

Recognising the threat, Cydones took pains not to return a look at his companion. He suddenly realised the journey he was about to undertake began years ago, long before any hint of what course it might take. A minor official with a wife and four children, he was ambitious but without aristocratic birth. He had served two years with a regiment of theme cavalry—enough to gain some knowledge of horsemanship, weapons and military matters—while he studied the classics and finessed his diction in preparation to realise his ambition at court. A favour by an acquaintance of his father's secured him a post in the Office of Barbarians. It had been a start; his old contacts there still providing useful intelligence, such as the secret despatch of a pair of couriers to Manzikert.

Cydones, now an assistant to the Keeper of the Imperial Inkstand, had been diligent and learned that the way to advancement was to step in the shadows of powerful men without treading on their cloaks. He hid his minor military background in the army-hating bureaucracy while skill in Arabic, courtly affectations and graceful subservience to superiors brought him to notice. His first opportunity was a post with Kamyates, a senior diplomat charged with hosting an Arab delegation from Cairo. This had been an interesting and pleasant duty, the imperial aim being to incite the Shi'ite Fatimids against the weak Abbasid Caliph of Baghdad, commander of the Sunni faithful.

Cydones wondered now whether he could have, amongst the universal corruption and duplicity, remained aloof from the initially subtle Seljuk embrace. Turning a blind eye had become habitual and the constant flow of additional money indispensable. As they trotted now through the back streets, Cydones grappled with his dilemma: whether to continue with the treachery or throw himself on the mercy of the palace. He reasoned that there was still time to back out and betray his confederates, but it seemed easier to go along with them for the moment. Besides, the more deeply he was involved, the more precious the information he would have to bargain with.

The Seljuk emissary further instructed Cydones during the remaining hour of their journey, during which they abandoned their hired horses and hurried on foot through the city's crowded thoroughfares. Cydones was to find and kill the couriers and give their documents to Kamyates. He would hand other official despatches to the Roman governor after Kamyates read them. The imperial ambassador would receive a separate package, of which the military governor was not to know. "You should take a sturdy fellow with you. One that is handy with weapons," the handler advised. "You never know what can happen on the road."

Cydones had deduced most of the conspirators' broader plan. Through the disbandment of most Armenian troops, pruning of the Roman Army, the transfer west against the Patzinaks of many remaining eastern units and replacement of native Byzantine troops with fewer and cheaper mercenaries—the frontier fortresses that the Seljuk Sultan desired would be delivered to him. For the price of a few slain on the border, Sultan Tughrul Bey enhanced his prestige amongst Muslims and secured his frontier with Byzantium, enabling his campaign against the heretical Fatimids. For the Byzantine officials, the two rival caliphates would exhaust each other in war, thus securing the Romans from Muslim attack. The Byzantine military aristocracy would be further reduced in power and influence, ensuring the Emperor remained in the purple and continued his largesse to his friends—those of the court and church who ensured his survival. Not least, was the Sultan's payment to those, who delivered to him the Byzantine-Armenian frontier. Cydones would be rich with his influence at court in Constantinople assured.

Constantinople,
First light, 20th April 1054

It was not until first light that Count[16] Leo Bryennius made to leave the city barracks of the Scholae in the Imperial Palace cantonment. A highbred bay touched his muzzle to Leo's face and he lightly brushed the scar from a grazing Patzinak arrow on the Arabian's neck. "Sorry, Zarrar. Another night without rest."

The roving picket—two veteran cataphracts[17] of his Sixth Schola in pot helmets, mail hauberks and long riding boots—saluted him. Succeeding the disgraced Praetorian Guard of the ancients when the old Roman Empire had converted to Christianity, the proud regiments of the Scholae were now the finest field cavalry.

"The couriers are away and in the hands of fate," he whispered to the horse.

Disappointingly, the plan to decoy and arrest treacherous Romans in Seljuk pay had gone awry with three Kelts blundering into the trap and alerting the quarry. Worse, a loyal young man was dead and the traitors had escaped: even now probably hunting the couriers. Two days before, Leo had ushered the courier

---

16 Count—the commander of a regiment, of 300–450 men.
17 Cataphract—Byzantine cavalry trooper. .

into Cecaumenus' office and had later drawn her cloak around her as she left. Between her veil and his helmet they had remained as far apart as the stars.

Mounting, he rode to the gate and saluted two approaching riders: Cecaumenus, accompanied by Leo's commander, the Domestic of the Scholae. Their horses drew together, the riders looking as tired as Leo felt. With effort, he avoided staring at the horrifying wounds Cecaumenus had sustained four years before.

A jagged scar ran from the crown of the general's head to an eyebrow and another coursed his throat from the mouth to the back of the tongue. "How are you, Bryennius? And your father—forgot to ask last time I saw you. Too damn busy!"

Leo's father had fought with Cecaumenus through the Armenian and Thracian campaigns. The two had fallen under an avalanche of Patzinaks at Diacene, survivors of the lone unit to stand and cover the ignominious retreat. Both were left for dead until a Patzinak named Galinos had recognised Cecaumenus and nursed them from the brink of death. They were restored to the empire, though Michael Bryennius was unfit for further service.

"He's well, thank you."

"Good. Good. I've been hearing about your men, Bryennius. Making mounted archers of them, like the old days. You listened to your father then?"

Leo had drawn his own conclusions from the Patzinak wars, but there was no need to say it. "Indeed. It was good advice."

"Report," ordered the Domestic dryly when the civilities were complete.

Leo told them: the couriers were on their way, but the traitor and some of his contacts had escaped the trap.

"At least the young woman and that scouting fellow are away with our warning for Apocapes, but there'll be hell to pay here," the Domestic said. "The Army will be accused of undermining the bureaucracy. Palace eunuchs run the Empire to rack and ruin and there is little chance of undoing their influence."

Leo noticed that the Domestic was too cautious to personally criticise the weak and spendthrift Emperor. With informants operating everywhere, discretion had become habitual, especially in Constantinople. Nor was the army blameless, with provincial rebellions led by ambitious generals a common threat.

"The Treasury is nearly empty," the Domestic continued, "and a papal legation has just walked out on the Patriarch in a huff. The two churches are at impossible loggerheads. The bulk of our imperial armies of the East have been withdrawn to face the Patzinaks in Thrace, truce or not, and local troops in Armenia have been largely disbanded to farm and so better pay their taxes. More money for this secluded fantasy." He glared around at the domed rooves and vaulted arches of the palace.

They fell silent as an early morning passer-by gave them a look.

Satisfied the stranger was out of earshot, Cecaumenus cut in. "The eastern frontier is about to collapse, Leo, and there is nothing behind it. The emir, Kutlumush, supposedly fled from Tughrul two years ago and based himself at the city of Her[18], yet he took the walled Armenian city of Kars last January—through the snow, wouldn't you know. Massacred or enslaved all who were not fortuitously in the citadel. D'you believe it! The general slapped his pommel with emotion, so startling his horse it jerked its head and stepped a pace. "Kutlumush! We nearly had him seven years ago at Kapetrou, by damn! He and Ibrahim Inal both. A close thing, by damn! They're in and out of favour with the Sultan. Now they seem to be back, worse than ever."

Leo had heard various accounts of the vicious night battle in Armenia. By the most reliable the Seljuks, sated and widely dispersed after their destruction of Artsn, had been outmanoeuvred and brought to bay by the flying-columns of Cecaumenus and Aaron Vladislav, then the Roman military governor of Vaspurakan. Liparit, the neighbouring Georgian pretender, had joined them in a piecemeal night engagement from which the mauled Seljuks had escaped, many said, with a hundred thousand prisoners including Liparit and a great deal of booty.

The Domestic broached the efficacy of the Sultan's foreign policy, "Inal gave captured Liparit to Tughrul, who released him on parole not to fight the Seljuks again."

"Right," said Cecaumenus. "So the Georgians will be out of it this time. Liparit, the pretender to their throne, is exiled here and bounden by word to the Turkish sultan. The current Georgian king has nothing to thank us for since his gilded imprisonment here years ago. Those two are sworn enemies and divide Georgia as a result. Except for any of the heretical Armenians that want to throw in with us, we're on our own this time. War to the knife and ..."

"Someone," Leo returned the conversation to its point, "tries to stop us warning the frontier troops." He knew of the Seljuk spies attached to their embassy in Constantinople. After Artsn the Seljuks had sent emissaries to Constantinople, including educated Arabs and Persians whose dress they sometimes adopted. Their sultan received rich payments in return for peace.

Their efforts were assisted by increasingly powerful pro-Seljuk officials at court who suppressed any troublesome intelligence about the Sultan's expanding military capability. "You can buy peace more cheaply than pay for war," one courtier, Modestos Kamyates, had more than once lisped with his contemptuous dismissal of those who question dogma. "The Seljuks will not invade, so we needn't worry. We've got a plan for peace with them and can use their cavalry against others."

Leo could still picture Kamyates wielding the insidious menace of the bureaucrat, the campaign of whispers leading to banishment or blinding with the hot pin. Usually they preferred both, using the Emperor's name to dignify the settling of private scores. What plan with the Seljuks? And who were "we"?

---

18 Her—a city, now Khoy in Iran. See Map p. v.

"And the only one who might hold a clue is this Kelt you have in the cells?" the Domestic asked. The men were silent for a time, their horses' ears flicking back, sensing the feelings of their riders.

"Go there Bryennius." Cecaumenus glanced at the Domestic. "Take your regiment to Manzikert. I've spoken to Theodora, or rather she spoke to me. Take your Keltic bait as well. The main cities, Karin and Ani, are strongly fortified and should hold. There's nothing left to take from Kars—the Armenians can worry about it—it's theirs anyway. Manzikert's the strongest and best-sited fortress in the south. Tell 'em what we think. I'll organise ships to take you to Trebizond. We should send all three thousand Scholae, and thirty thousand others, but we don't have them to spare. You would be it! You and a few Kelts at Karin, already preparing to march. The palace eunuchs will be furious. It'll end your career." Cecaumenus paused. "You'll need to watch your eyes when you get back. Will you do it?"

"Is it an order?"

"No! Can't give you one. A mission without record—at stake, thousands of lives, perhaps the empire. But I cannot, will not, order you."

There was such a heavy silence that Zarrar bent his head to Leo's knee. "When do I leave?"

"God be with you, Bryennius. May God be with you. As soon as you can. A week, ten days? We, and Theodora, will do our utmost to protect you." Cecaumenus then looked long at Leo. "I have to ask though, why are you taking this on? It may end badly and there is nothing in it for you."

"They're our people out there."

The Domestic read Leo's face. "I can see you expected this. Be thankful you're out of the bureaucracy's malevolent gaze for a time. Be gone!" He rode into the grounds of the palace, then swung his horse around and returned. "You know how much depends on this. Good luck."

Cecaumenus kneed his mount close. "I'll send a man to you—a good one—a follower of Galinos when he saved your father and me. Patzinak father, Rus mother—part of no world but prepared to try ours. His name is Maniakh. When you get to Manzikert, the strategos, Basil Apocapes, is trustworthy. Give him my compliments and watch his back."

Leo told his troops on parade later that morning. "We are going to Armenia," he said simply, and could have heard a pin drop. With the certainty of orders, the pace of the regiment's deployment preparations increased.

That evening Leo arrived home—a modest brick dwelling with a courtyard, garden and stable. After his squire and a servant took his horse, Leo entered the quiet house. His wife, Agatha, a beautiful patrician woman of independent means, heard his footsteps on the tiles and hurried downstairs, greeting him with her friendly matter-of-fact manner. "You didn't make it back last night? Where are they sending …?" She halted mid-step when she saw him.

Everything now was so simple, but the simplest thing very difficult. He removed his helmet and placed it on the entrance table. "I'm taking the Sixth to Vaspurakan. We leave in a week."

Agatha turned to hide a tear. "A week. Armenia? The Seljuks! Oh, Leo!" A moment's composure, then she faced him. "For how long? Years?"

"I don't know. The summer. It's nothing. More raids I expect."

"Raids? Like Artsn and Kars, you mean?"

" We've beaten them before." Leo shrugged off his hauberk and sword then stepped forward and placed his arms around her. He felt her brush her hair back from her face and knew the movement hid the wiping away of tears. She would show no emotion now, but later she would cry, alone, or on her sister's shoulder.

She withdrew and poured goblets of wine. "What should I do? What about Smyrna?"

Leo had not forgotten the planned holiday that summer at her family's provincial estate. "You should go ahead. I'll join you if I can take leave and detour by there on the way back," he said.

Near Manzikert
Dawn, 20th April 1054

Irene Curticius trotted south from the triple walls of Manzikert through the first streaks of dawn as though visiting her brother, Damian, in the lakeside city of Artzké. Once satisfied that any prying eyes were lost behind her, she turned the black stallion west into the undulating steppe, keeping the landmark of snow-capped Mount Sippane before her. Instinctively checking that her bow and sword were secure and frequently looking over her shoulder, she cantered to the low ground seeking to conceal her journey.

Content she was out of sight, Irene slowed the horse to a swift walk and was conscious of a thrill of anticipation for the assignation she was to keep with her suitor, Theodore Ankhialou. She had been busy for days preparing for her ride: telling of her intention to go to Artzké, readying her horse and gear for the journey, while hiding her true intention from her father. Now she felt a sense of freedom.

A dark hatred for him had troubled her for as many of her twenty-one years as she could remember. She could not recall any one event that sparked her inner tumult. In her recollection, John Curticius' treatment of her had been stiffly distant and formal, aside from his occasional drunken outbursts of anger. Hers was a confused hatred, an almost physical revulsion at his presence, accompanied by shame at her failures as a dutiful daughter. She wished to love him and partly did, but she felt confined by him, as though she was dying within and wilting without.

Theodore Ankhialou, the only son of a Roman family that had acquired estates in Armenia after the Byzantine takeover, had been posted from Ani a year ago to command Manzikert's irregular cavalry. All that a rebellious young woman might desire, attentive, dashing and rich with estates in the north, he had openly courted her at the fair. Irene turned to the handsome young man as if to the sun.

Her father had condemned the association and used his rank to have Theodore posted sixty miles away to Archēsh, but they had communicated through letters borne by trusted hands. Occasionally they met at a deserted hut concealed in a shallow valley mid-way between the two cities. It was not so derelict as to be objectionable and there was grass and water for their horses. The few trees around the yard provided pleasant shade and a supply of dry firewood that would give off little smoke in contrast to the dung cakes that warmed the citizens of barren Vaspurakan during the snowbound winters.

Hours later as she rode over a crest, Irene saw the hut, half dug into a slope. Theodore's grey horse was already there and whinnied at her approach. She wanted to look her best and was annoyed that the warm spring day had made her perspire in the effort of riding thirty miles for a kiss. Black hair bound under a dark *keffiyeh*[19] and her grandmother's silver chain at the neck of her favourite green riding outfit, she moistened her lips with her tongue, touched her hair and smoothed her loose trousers over her black boots.

Theodore Ankhialou appeared in his blue tunic, smiled disarmingly and assisted her to dismount. With eyes only for each others' eyes, they embraced.

"Hello Beauty," he said.

"How is Archēsh?" she asked, stepping back to admire him.

"The poorer without you. When will you come?"

"When I can escape my father, and after you've made sure the Saracens[20] never do." She smiled with mock severity.

"The Saracens?" he laughed, taking the reins of her stallion to unsaddle the horse and release it into a yard where he had already placed a pail of water and cut grass.

She embraced him again, feeling the warmth of his arms around her. "It's said their Sultan is at Tabriz?"

"Don't worry. That's far from here. If they come to Archēsh, I'll deal with them."

Theodore lay asleep. Irene, propped on her elbow beside him, gently caressed his hair. She felt a growing sadness at the lengthening shadows outside, for they must soon part. Her thoughts wandered. Reflecting on what he had said about joining him in Archēsh, an attractive picture came to her, of the city by the lakeshore with its trees and cool summer breezes. She imagined a life with him, liberated by his strength and independent wealth. He stirred and she smoothed a lock of his dark hair away from his ear. Theodore murmured and she leaned forward and lightly kissed the nape of his neck.

---

19 *Keffiyeh*—flowing fabric headdress of the Arabs.
20 Generic term for the peoples of the Middle East and North Africa.

With a sigh, she lay back and stared at the beams supporting the roof, the fine house-dust in the shafts of sunlight slanting through cracks and the threads of cobwebs in the corners. Contrary to the rumours and regardless of Theodore's ardour—this day more than ever—she ensured their passions remained unconsummated. Despite the intensity of her feelings, part of her still felt lost, with a hint of annoyance that his sleeping was robbery from their precious time together.

She rose softly and looked without seeing through the window. Theodore's plea for her to live with him in Archēsh had not come with a marriage proposal. That lack of propriety piqued her. In her mind's eye she saw again the Manzikert matrons spitting "actress" behind their hands. They may as well have said "whore."

Looking at Theodore's sleeping form, Irene felt snared. Was her suitor as he seemed, rich and unbecomingly ardent, or a trap from which she may not be able to escape? What did he want? All people played games and enacted mating rituals. She knew that much from watching the pecking order from farmyard chickens to, she sighed, the city fathers and their wives. Biting her bottom lip in thought, she only then noticed distant figures approaching the hut. "Theodore. Wake, my love. There are riders coming."

He sprang up and peered through the window. "They're ours, Beauty. But we're caught this time. It looks like your father."

Bracing themselves for the scene, they gathered their few things, straightened the hut and went outside.

The half-dozen Roman cavalrymen halted a bow shot away. One rode forward alone.

Cold inside, Irene watched her father, in a mail corselet and boots, walk his horse up to them. He did not dismount. She saw only grey dullness in him and did not discern the pleasant demeanour that others remarked upon.

John Curticius stared coldly at Theodore Ankhialou. "You are not at your post?" There was a hint of helplessness and concern for the social and military consequences of the encounter. .

Theodore took a moment to finish saddling. "On leave, Princeps.[21] I have my turmarch's signature. I was …"

"That's something then," Curticius snapped. "Be kind enough to accede to a father's rightful demands and never ever meet, speak, nor communicate in any way, with my daughter again. Is there anything about that you do not understand?"

Theodore was insolently silent.

"Do not let me detain you from your obviously important duties at Archēsh."

Theodore turned from Curticius and swung to his saddle. On the grey, he was a striking figure and knew it. After a tender look at Irene, he limply saluted Curticius and cantered away.

Irene flamed at her father, "How dare you spy on me?"

---

21 A Byzanine Army appointment title for chief of staff.

"I've more to do than check your flights of foolish fancy. Mount up." He watched her stallion tense as it sensed her outrage. "As it happens, I was out here anyway, moving a few drifting nomad families back from whence they came, before the Seljuk trickle becomes a flood. Thank your stars I found you before they did."

The group turned their horses for the journey home, Curticius looking straight ahead at the horizon. "And we've had reports of unknown riders using that hut." He looked sideways at his daughter and continued pointedly, "I should have known, when I saw you in that green outfit this morning."

"Perhaps you did, Father." She threw one more barbed look at him then concentrated on trying to make her horse outwalk his.

Constantinople,
Late morning, 20th April 1054

Charles Bertrum turned from his inspection of the cell. "You've done it this time, Guy d'Agiles! No way out of here."

"Where are we, anyway?" Jacques watched Charles complete his inspection. "At least we can see something now it's daylight."

Guy returned their looks. What would have happened if he had chosen another inn, or not gone out to check their horses? "I don't know—couldn't see a thing through the blindfold. Still in Constantinople. Somewhere in the palace, probably in the cells of their barracks."

Charles leapt up, seized the bars of the high window and with a grunt, hauled himself up to peer out.

"At least," Jacques said, glancing up, "we're not dead and they've fed us, even if heiresses are not in abundance here."

Charles chuckled. "They're in abundance out here though. Hullo, my sweet!" he waved and called in appalling Greek to a scandalised chorus from beyond the bars. "This is the palace all right. I can see the Hippodrome."

Sitting in the straw covering the stone floor with his back against the wall, Guy recalled the previous evening's events. Clearly they had blundered into an ambush of some sort, which had not gone according to plan. "The thugs," he thought aloud, "were in the pay of the three mounted fellows, one of whom looked like an eastern barbarian, I think. Then I went out and they panicked. That Swordleader said it was a trap, they were the wrong ones and that one of the couriers was a girl."

"Woman," Charles dropped from the window and turned to face his friend. "The last three times you've told the story, he said one of the couriers was a woman. And he wanted us dead, especially you. You're too forlorn, Guy. They'll work out we had nothing to do with it and we'll be out of here."

"Then the troops arrived," Guy continued irritably, knuckles pressed against closed eyes.

Charles, restless, heaved himself up again to the view from the high window.

"Their count wanted to know if I would recognise their leader."

"We could always join the palace guard when we get out of here." Charles lowered himself to the floor again.

"More than that," Guy continued as if he had not heard. "Their count said, exactly—the one that got away will know you." He looked vacantly at Jacques. "The one that got away will know you."

Jacques looked from one to the other. "Keep your voices down."

"It was a trap within a trap. Both went wrong and we were in the middle of it."

"Still are," croaked Jacques. "We should take that old woman's advice and head for home as soon as we can. It mightn't be great, but it's safer."

"I think you're right," said Guy.

They fell silent and stood as approaching footsteps halted at their cell door, then there was a metallic clang of bolts slid open. The heavy door swung out to reveal a young officer of the Scholae and ten men in civilian clothes, swords under their cloaks. "I am Tribune Balsamon, Sixth Schola." He motioned to Jacques. "You, come with us."

"Where're you taking him?" remonstrated Charles.

"I'll go too!" Guy stepped forward.

"Stay here," Balsamon ordered.

Guy and Charles banged impotently on the door as Jacques was marched away. Their situation had seemed bad enough when they were together. Now the sense of helplessness was oppressive. Guy paced the cell, wondering where and for what purpose Jacques was taken as Charles sat brooding.

Some hours later, the door opened again and four armed cataphracts in mail shirts entered the cell.

"Where's my man?" Guy asked, trying to sound calm.

The soldiers ignored the question and handed them light brown military cloaks. "Put these on and come with us." They watched as Guy and Charles pulled the quality waterproof garments around their shoulders. A cavalryman stepped forward and arranged the hoods over their heads. "Let's go."

Thus disguised and unbound, they followed uneasily as their escort led them from the barracks and departed through the main palace gate with its quarter-guard of Khazars from the Third Hetaeria,[22] then crossed a wide street with its idling crowd and entered the bulk of the Hippodrome through a small side entrance. Guy thought of making a bolt for it, but because of the hoods, could not catch Charles' eye. They passed through empty stables of the chariot teams—Greens, Blues, Reds and Whites—and onto the track with its tiered stands. Guy had been an occasional spectator at the races; one of the things visitors did. He had been amazed at the reckless violence of the drivers from the Blue and Green factions and did not doubt the tales of their sanguinary past.

---

22 The Emperor's bodyguards.

They approached four men discussing a grey horse, lame in the near foreleg. One was an officer of the Scholae in undress uniform, the second appeared to be his squire, while the other two wore the picturesque costumes of the eastern frontiers. Guy recognised the barbarian in the threadbare blue coat from the fight at the inn. The man's eyes flickered back.

The officer had the lithe appearance of a professional cavalryman: a straight fellow of middle height in his early thirties with a touch of humour in his hazel eyes. He looked up as they approached. "Ah! Good. There are secret passages, but sometimes it's as easy to hide in the open." He spoke Latin. "Guy d'Agiles?"

"Yes."

"I am Centarch[23] Bessas Phocas, Sixth Schola."

"The one who arrested us?"

"Yes. Regrettable but necessary."

"Who ordered you?"

Bessas Phocas paused. "Count Bryennius."

"Bryennius." Guy repeated.

"Charles Bertrum." Guy's friend stepped forward.

Bessas nodded.

"Where has my man been taken?" Guy asked.

"To collect your belongings, settle your affairs in Constantinople and send, via one of my men, the personal items you will need for the next few days. You will meet him again in due course."

"Settle our affairs?" Guy said doubtfully.

"Yes. I hope the three of you don't owe too much—it'll come out of your pay. You need to lie low, after last night."

"Pay?"

"Yes." Bessas was not about to elaborate.

Guy relaxed a little and glanced at Charles. If they were to be paid, imminent death or imprisonment seemed unlikely. "It's a fine horse. Yours?" he asked in an attempt to make the conversation less strained. Guy noticed the light in Bessas' eyes, for the Greeks were notoriously humourless, especially when dealing with Latins.

"Thank you," Bessas replied though his brown beard.

Some deep instinct in Guy told him to check the horse's hoof for the cause of the lameness. He bent down by the leg. "May I?"

"Of course. He's been unsound for days. No one is able to determine the cause."

Guy lifted the hoof. "A knife?" he asked, feeling the exchange of glances behind his back.

An exquisite blade was dropped to the sand at his foot.

"That is Togol, our Cuman scout and an excellent fellow. You met last night."

---

23 A commander of a squadron, about 100 men.

"I remember." Guy found an object driven into the underside of the hoof. "Looks like a stake lodged in deep." The grey flinched as he prodded at the deep commissure beside the frog. "I can't move it. Do you have pincers?"

The squire hurried away and returned with a pair, which he passed to Guy.

With some effort, Guy drew forth a short stake smeared with pus and blood, then gently put down the leg. The horse shifted its weight normally and turned its muzzle to him.

"The wound will need cleaning."

The scouts murmured approvingly as the squire led the horse away.

"I'm in your debt," admitted Bessas. "And embarrassed. I should have seen it."

"Yes, you should!" said Charles.

"Sometimes things are overlooked when one is busy." Guy glanced angrily at Charles. They were not in any position to antagonise their captors.

"Have you been here long?" Bessas switched the conversation back to its purpose. "You speak some Greek?"

"Several weeks. A little."

"Had you found a position?"

"Not yet," Guy replied, being careful not to appear too desperate. "We were looking when we were arrested."

"Then you won't be missed." Bessas remained silent for a moment. "You and your comrades have been overtaken by events. You two will leave by boat tonight, with Centarch Lascaris and Togol here. Your man and animals will follow, initially by sea. As soon as we reach the port of Trebizond, David here," he indicated the Georgian scout standing nearby, "will guide your man to a hideout near the city of Karin where you will be reunited."

"We've never heard of these places." Guy said.

"Quite so." Bessas dropped to one knee and drew a rough map.

Guy knelt also, trying to orient the rough lines in the sand. "Where are Cae … um, Caesaria and … "

Charles leaned on his shoulder. "Melitene?"

Bessas pointed to places half way along the intended journey.

"Far to the east," Guy murmured.

With prudence born of habit, Bessas stood and obscured the sand map with the toe of his boot. "Yes. Far. The three of you …" He stopped speaking as an orderly approached. "Excuse me," he said and left the two friends standing alone.

Charles spoke under his breath while seeming to stare at some point in the Hippodrome. "We're hardly guarded. We could slip away. Jacques would be thinking the same. He would know to look for us near the last safe place we were together. Near the inn."

"They're cunning, Charles, and ruthless, and they have us in check—except that we're pawns, not kings. Jacques will be too closely guarded and they have your horse and all our gear. Let them unite us. Then let's see what can be done."

"Jacques is your man, Guy. I'm with you, whatever you choose."

Bessas returned. "As I was saying. After you meet up, you will proceed to Karin, locate the attackers from the inn and capture or kill them. If that's done, you're free to go. If not, you'll volunteer to join a band of Frankish mercenaries in Karin—that is preparing to march to Vaspurakan—so you can continue the hunt. Only after that will you have anything to do with us, as we'll probably share the road from then on. The only contact with us is to be discreet, through David and Togol. When we meet at Karin, that will be the first time we have met. Of course you're volunteering, you understand."

"Volunteering?" Charles grinned.

"The count doesn't want anyone along who will hamper us." Bessas looked straight into Guy's eyes. "Your word on it?"

Guy and Charles exchanged glances. "Our word."

"Good," Bessas said brightly. "Tonight you begin a long journey and you should rest. As you've given your word, you will not be escorted."

"Why Vaspurakan?" Guy asked. "What's so important?"

"The shepherd king," Bessas answered as he walked away with the scouts.

Guy watched them go. "We're doing the very thing that woman at the inn warned us not to do."

Chapter Two

How Frail The Time Of Man

Near Karin,
Late afternoon, 3rd May 1054

That night Guy and Charles accompanied by Centarch Lascaris, Togol and a farrier of the Scholae, had crossed the Bosphorus by boat to Chalcedon. They each took their armour, weapons and a small bundle with a spare shirt, comb and toothsticks. Togol and the soldiers carried their personal saddles and accoutrements. The farrier also carried a handful of essential tools and a selection of horseshoe nails in a small pouch, all rolled in his leather apron and strapped to the saddle. On the Asian shore a detachment of cavalry provided them with seven horses: saddled mounts for Guy and Charles, with military cloaks over the cantles, saddlebags containing hardtack and a goatskin of water. With rolled mail shirts strapped over their pommels, the five departed on their six hundred and fifty mile ride leading two relief horses between them.

Lascaris was a spare man of few words, the farrier fewer and Togol even less. Guy soon understood why, for Lascaris set a hard pace: sixty miles a day, stopping only to eat and change horses at military exchange posts every twenty miles or so. They snatched sleep when they could. Sometimes they walked and led their horses to rest them and ease their own stiffness.

Mostly at a steady trot they passed through mountains and rolling fields dotted by the estates, villages and cities of the Byzantine Empire's Anatolian heartland. Here armies had traditionally been recruited, warhorses bred and the staple grains grown. Guy saw the tell-tale signs of ceaseless wars and oppressive taxation. Many maimed men eked out a bare living on the charity of others, while people spoke of fickle seasons, near empty granaries and high taxes.

The mere hint of Cecaumenus' authority brooked neither questions nor stinting support from the garrisons. At Nicopemedia and Ancyra they had bathed quickly, salved their saddle sores, ate lightly and pressed on. Five days into their journey, a full moon enabled them to travel easily for several nights and rest away from the road by day, observing who else travelled the route. During a half-day rest at Sebasteia, Guy noticed the number of Frankish soldiers and the paucity of native Greek troops. The senior officer there had confided that an Armenian man and Greek woman had passed through the previous day and changed unbranded horses, but their opponents from the fight at the inn had vanished in the vastness of Asia Minor, if they had entered it at all. They encountered some Greeks who might, by their mannerisms, have been Swordleader, but none seemed familiar or travelled with a barbarian bowman. The five had pressed on through Koloneia into western Armenia with its craggy brown-grey mountains framing sparse valleys of light green grass interspersed by patches of melting snow.

On the eleventh day, they halted at a wayside inn two hours ride west of Karin. Guy, fighting to remain awake, barely noticed a more relaxed air in Togol or the knowing glances from the elderly couple that ran the house. Togol led them from the rutted dirt main-road some miles north into a picturesque hidden valley, where nestled an abandoned farmlet with a cave behind, high in the rugged northern slope. After securing one horse for immediate use in an enclosure near the hut, they released the others to graze, sank to the ground and slept. Lascaris took first watch.

Now they roused in the late afternoon as the woman from the inn arrived leading a laden donkey. "Togol, if you've returned, there's trouble afoot. Who're these men and why are you all so tired?"

"Riding is hard work, and you ask too many questions, woman." Togol turned to his companions. "This lady and her husband, I trust with my life."

"Hush, you'll still ride easily if you live to ninety," she smiled kindly. "Lads, sit down. You have the look of huntsmen pursued, but you can relax. No one comes this way."

Except our tracks, thought Guy as he helped the farrier unload the donkey.

The two friends and the farrier sat on the ground, Guy on his saddlecloth with its acrid odour of dried horse sweat on wool. His short shoes were falling apart and his trousers frayed from riding.

Lascaris, tall in scuffed boots with the slight breeze ruffling his fair hair, introduced them by first names only. Then the officer too reclined on his saddle blanket. "How do you know Togol?"

The grey woman busied herself preparing a meal of bread, wine, greens and cold mutton. "There is little enough to tell. Togol left the lands of the Cumans—further away than the Kurds[24] and Seljuks—beyond even the Caspian Gates. His

---

24 Kurds—an ethnic group in various dynastic emirates bordering Armenia to the east, south-east and south-west.

wanderings led him to the Shaddadid[25] city of Gandja, which was soon besieged for a year and a half by that brute, Kutlumush. While Gandja suffered, other Kurds joined Ibrahim Inal and Kutlumush on the raid against Artsn, despite their ruler in Dvin's sworn fealty to the Emperor after Cecaumenus had devastated his lands. Togol, insulted at such perfidy, carried warning of this to Cecaumenus."

Guy listened closely, noted Togol's concept of honour and was surprised that a nomad from beyond the Christian frontiers would have one. The Cuman, sword and bow case around his hips and a hint of fair colouring in his long hair, stood gazing at the distant mountains as though scarcely listening. Guy had given his word to Bessas: he would not want Togol on his trail if he broke it.

"But," continued the woman, "he was caught at Kapetrou by some of his former associates and only saved by Michael Bryennius."

"Count Leo Bryennius' father?" Lascaris asked.

"Yes, the father," she said. "In those days my husband and I lived near the battlefield. Togol was one of the wounded we treated. He left for Constantinople with Michael Bryennius." She fell silent, as if thinking of those terrible times. "It all seems so long ago. Will Michael return?"

"No," said Togol. "He was nearly killed by the Patzinaks and was saved by one of them. He lives, but will soldier no more."

The woman blew through her teeth and clucked. "Where were you, Togol?"

"Scouting with his son."

There was silence for a time, then Lascaris remarked, "It seems a small world out here, where everyone knows everyone else?"

The woman regarded him keenly. "You're only partly right. It is a very big world as well, but large as it is, there is not room for everyone."

Lascaris nodded. "Has anyone interesting been through?"

"As you see, a trickle on the road. Those who suspect trouble from the Seljuks and wish to flee. Kelts at Karin waiting to march into Vaspurakan. The usual army comings and goings."

"No courtiers or thugs from the capital?"

She chuckled. "Is there any other sort from the capital? No. Not that we have seen. We can go into Karin and look, if you like?"

"That might be very helpful." Lascaris seemed pleased to have his small army reinforced.

They ate greedily as though nothing could assuage the exertions of that ride. After the woman left, Lascaris reviewed their situation. "We'll stick to the plan. There's no evidence of the group from the inn near the Golden Gate being in front of us—that would be difficult for them, for we left soon after and have travelled fast. Togol and I will ride separately into Karin each day and see what we can find. If there's anything suspicious, I'll get a message to the old couple and they will relay my orders. For now, rest here and wait until your man arrives, then proceed as planned."

---

25 A Kurdish dynasty.

"All armies are the same," grumbled Charles. "Hurry up and wait."

"I ate too much," groaned Guy.

"In the meantime," Lascaris continued without heed, "my good farrier friend here will cut your hair quite short, Guy D'Agiles. The man we seek threatened a long-haired Kelt, did he not?"

Guy and Charles waited impatiently for four days. They explored the valley and hills from where they could see the road back towards Constantinople and eastward to the ancient battlements of Karin. Together they slept, ate, stood watch, tended their Roman horses and awaited the summons that would end their quest and their confinement.

On their fourth night in the valley, the two friends and the farrier were lazing around a small fire as Lascaris reconnoitred Karin. A low hiss from Togol on watch signalled the approach of shod horses. They rolled with their weapons into the darkness.

Guy strained his senses, then heard Togol call softly.

"It is I, Togol. I have the Kelt called Jacques, David, and Centarch Lascaris' squire with me."

Guy leapt to his feet, unexpectedly reassured by the presence and calm voice of the groom. "I have your mule, Charles Bertrum's horse, our gear and the horse I rode here. But, I can tell you, seasickness is to be avoided." Jacques, grinning broadly, approached them then muttered to the ground at their feet. "We're united again. Now—to get out of here ..." His face fell at their silence.

Guy hesitated. "Jacques, we cannot, for I gave my word."

"You what?"

The fortress of Baberd,
Evening, 6th May 1054

Leo Bryennius sat comfortably on the Baberd castle battlements allowing his thoughts to roam as he watched the sunset colours in the light cloud and the shadows lengthen in the valley below.

His wife had retired early that last evening in Constantinople as he finished his preparations and slept fitfully before rising in the dark. With his squire, Taticus Phocas, he had left his home leading two spare horses and a pack mule, along the dark streets to the Prosforian Harbour on the Golden Horn. Agatha had not risen to wave him off. Leo had not looked back.

At the waterfront, the three hundred men of the regiment waited together with their hundred squires, a handful of Cuman and Patzinak scouts and two dozen Frankish mercenaries. Leo had been pleased to see his special charge, the mercenary, Jacques, blend into the crowd without attracting attention. An imperial courier, Bardas Cydones, with his servant had joined them bearing palace orders for escort to Vaspurakan. Leo was suspicious of the coincidence, given the speed and secrecy of their preparations, but imperial couriers seeking military escort were common. Nonetheless Leo had sent Centarch Sebēos to the Domestic to verify the courier's credentials as their animals were loaded through the side-doors of the transports and secured in stalls. Sebēos returned and confirmed Cydones' orders. Leo had directed Cydones to stay close to the standard-bearers, who with Sebēos, had orders to watch him closely. Constantinople with its sumptuous comforts, delights, intrigues and memories then slipped from view behind the sleek stern and dipping oars of an imperial trireme.

Despite the turbulent waters and execrable reputation of the Black Sea—ships simply disappearing or carried off by hostile Vikings—the voyage to Trebizond had been uneventful. While it was a hundred years since the last major Norse invasion fleet was destroyed by flame-spewing Roman ships, imperial flotillas remained vigilant, especially since the last Rus seaborne expedition against the Empire only eleven years earlier.

The force sailed past the lights and battlements of historic Sinope and after four days at sea, disembarked at the walled harbour-city of Trebizond. Bessas had discreetly despatched Jacques to rendezvous with Lascaris' party. The scout, David, and a squire, both mounted, accompanied them leading Charles' mare and Guy's mule. Leo's regiment had then spent some days at Trebizond, resting horses and acquiring information and provisions.

Trebizond, a key Byzantine trading post and bastion on the Black Sea coast, was protected from the great strategic crossroads of the Anatolian plateau by pine-forested mountains that plunged in folds down to the coast. The citadel and circuit walls—sited between the precipitous eastern and western ravines—protected the northern battlements overlooking the walled harbour. The city was a place of rich variety. Serene sea views from the stone cathedrals contrasted vividly with the tortuous streets, where Alan and Georgian traders from the Caucasus rubbed shoulders in the heat with Norse mercenaries and the rich gowns of veiled Byzantine daughters brushed the dresses of Rus whores.

In Trebizond, Leo had an encounter, unlooked for, unexpected. There had been kind words and lingering looks from the beauty. They walked at sunset along the sea wall, chatting of the classics and horses with other thoughts unspoken. Her striking form and graceful carriage turned the heads of passers-by. "You're interesting," she sighed with a lingering look, taking his arm and encouraging another outing. Instead, her servant came to Leo's tent and demurred that her lady was betrothed and would not see him again. Nothing should interfere with the gravity of money and marriage—a soldier bound for the Muslim frontier had little to offer.

The regiment had marched from Trebizond, four days uphill along the rough, winding road which was flanked by forested defiles and surrounded by grey crags, bare and menacing as though tossed up by the underworld. They came at last into the stony mountains and bare hills surrounding Baberd, with its triple-walled fortress overlooking the town nestled below in the narrow valley of the Chorokh River. A brigade of three-thousand bearded Varangian[26] and Rus mercenaries held the stronghold that guarded the intersecting roads: from the interior to Trebizond and laterally along the river valley.

Earlier this evening of their arrival, the garrison had entertained the Sixth Schola with drinking and dancing. The highlight was a friendly contest between a number of Varangians and a wayfaring Armenian, Tatoul Vanantzi. They laughed and brawled, upsetting tables and overturning benches before collapsing in a heap, to roars of approval from the onlookers.

Now Leo swilled the last of the red wine in the goblet and drained it as the shadows lengthened over the toy trees and fields below. The imperial courier, Cydones, strolled alone further along the battlements. Leo was momentarily irritated that he was not escorted. Still, it was difficult to be with someone all the time and remain discreet, while Cydones seemed only to be similarly taking in the pleasant evening air. Who was he? Who knew the regiment was leaving Constantinople and arranged orders for him to join them? What was he up to? And for whom?

"Melancholy?" The mighty Tatoul approaching with two goblets of red wine, interrupted Leo's thoughts.

He accepted one. "Never, Tatoul, merely reflection. I was thinking these battlements have a different feel to the sea wall at Trebizond."

"We both know it's some journey you make, for you look a hunter. May I join you? And what was it about Trebizond?"

"I hope it was not that obvious? The sea was serene, and very beautiful."

"No. It's not that obvious. And isn't this pastoral scene one of peace and beauty?"

They talked for a time, reticently at first, both seeking trust in allies during dangerous times.

Tatoul was returning to Kars after visiting friends in Trebizond. "What do you know of our new Seljuk neighbours?"

"Little enough, I confess, for I have not soldiered in these parts before. I'm told they are ever more numerous and aggressive—the tribes unlikely to give up their raiding and migrating. It seems their Sultan, despite some problems maintaining central control, has a renewed hunger for conquest after consolidating on the Iranian plateau." Leo paused. "Were you at Kars in January?"

"No, at my estate. I hastened there with my men as soon as I heard. Kutlumush gained complete surprise. It was as though there was no organised resistance at all. My God, Leo, after they got such a bloody nose at Kapetrou, and after Aaron and Cecaumenus killed Prince Hasan and many of his followers at Stragna, we thought they would stop. But Kars has changed that. But if a lone regiment of Scholae are marching to Armenia, someone knows something. Why do they send you, if you have not soldiered here before? And why so few?"

---

26 Varangian—(often) mounted infantry of Scandanavian origin. See glossary.

"Only horse in the stable at the time, I suppose." Leo smiled. "If the threat is real, an army will come, but they need time to organise and train."

"And you're the time!"

Leo grimaced good-humouredly and sipped some wine. "One can win battles and still lose the war. The Sultan can lose a few and it will make no difference to him. I don't think we can afford to lose a single battle. What worries me most are rumours Tughrul now has a siege train. That would mean he is serious this time, and it will not do to just hide behind city walls, hoping he gets tired of it."

"This time?"

"It is almost certain."

"Well, Leo, many Armenians hate you for your Roman annexations, but our little Kingdom of Kars cannot stand alone. I for one welcome your legions as allies, as long as you keep your damned tax-collectors away."

"I would feel as you, but know that they are not my tax-collectors. They're a heavy burden on our own people as well."

Uninvited, the imperial courier joined them and commented pleasantly on the evening colours. Leo and Tatoul returned his greeting then steered their conversation to the more inclusive and agreeable subjects of horses and the voyage. Throughout, Leo wondered how much Cydones had heard. He could not consciously fault him, but remained wary of the courier. "Will you be long in Manzikert, Bardas?" He asked while maintaining the appearance of a vague gaze over the valley.

"I don't know, really. I am to meet an official there who should arrive from Baghdad and Isfahan. It much depends on him."

"Isfahan, Tughrul's capital, eh? One of ours or one of theirs?" Leo joked.

Cydones looked condescendingly at him. "Ours. No one you would know, I suspect. The Magistros, Modestos Kamyates—a most important man, he won his title for his penultimate role in the delegation that secured the freedom of Liparit from Sultan Tughrul Bey."

Leo's heart sank. He knew of Kamyates and suppressed a desire to ask if Cydones was sure Kamyates was one of ours. "I've heard that," he replied slowly as if lost in inconsequential whimsy. "Oh, well. Good for him," he said, as though approvingly before changing the subject. "I must say, Bardas, I do admire your saddle."

"Speaking of which," Cydones rejoined, "I'll go on earlier tomorrow with my servant."

"Very good. I'll furnish an escort for you."

"Don't bother," Cydones said, rather too quickly. "In any event, it's only two days ride and my groom is a handy fellow. I've no fear."

"No bother," insisted Leo. "Indeed, those are my orders as you showed me at the dock."

"Very well." The imperial courier snapped, before recovering his usual charm. "That's kind. We leave at sunrise."

"They'll meet you at the main gate."

Cydones, seemingly aware he would hear nothing of any value to him, moved on.

Tatoul followed Cydones with his eyes. "You know the fellow he is to meet?"

"I know him. It will be an interesting summer I daresay."

"Then God be with you. Sounds like I'd better get an early start tomorrow. I'll be at Kars, or my estate near there."

"Manzikert."

"Then Count Leo of the Scholae, God go with you, and may the ramparts of Manzikert be as serene for you as the sea wall of Trebizond." He clapped Leo on the shoulder and was gone.

Leo felt he would have cause to remember Tatoul Vanantzi. Lingering silently on the darkening battlements, he studied the waxing crescent moon rise over the silent mountains and wondered if some Turk from the far-off Oxus mused on it as well.

Near Baberd,
7th May 1054

Bardas Cydones evaded Count Bryennius' escort, leaving Baberd an hour before the appointed time with his servant, Petros Doukitzes, a swarthy citizen from Melitene. Once a Roman cavalryman, Doukitzes had participated in the Byzantine occupation of Armenian Ani in 1046 and the failed attack on Kurdish Dvin the year before that. Skilled with knife and bow, an excellent rider but cruel horseman, Doukitzes had been recommended to Cydones by the one who arranged the thugs at the inn. The imperial courier was assured that Doukitzes, a deadly killer, was a "cleanskin"—no one of consequence would know his name or face. Much of the time he grunted acknowledgements rather than spoke and Cydones had never met anyone less interested in the affairs of the world. Nevertheless the man had been a hard-working, discreet and useful travelling companion. His mischievous audacity, when it came to the fore, gave him a touch with common people that enabled him to enlist their sympathy and assistance.

Cydones had not told him much. He simply alluded to a secret task from the palace that could incur some danger but paid well. For the time being, Doukitzes was useful. If he became troublesome, Cydones would kill him without conscience. Thus the imperial courier noticed everything, strength and weakness, about Petros Doukitzes.

Anxious to evade any patrol Bryennius might send after them, Cydones kept up a steady pace, intending to reach Karin in a day. The two trotted through mountain-fringed steppe, stopping briefly at noon at a pleasant rivulet to eat bread and water their horses. Entering Karin long after dark, they lodged at an inn. The exertion of the day caused Cydones to readily fall asleep. The next morning he arose stiff but refreshed and reckoned he had at least a day before Bryennius would arrive in the city and seek him out.

Despite Cydones' ingrained contempt for the army, prudence dictated that he needed to be careful of Bryennius. The officer must have been sent for some purpose and insisted on providing an escort when Cydones had made it plain he wished to travel alone.

Before he left Constantinople, Cydones had made discreet inquiries about the long-haired Kelt with an indifferent horse that he had encountered at the inn. He had learned that imperial troops had arrested and imprisoned some Latins and none knew their fate. Not recognising anyone among the Franks with Bryennius' column, his assailant at the inn had faded from Cydones' conscious thoughts.

The sun had barely risen when Cydones rose and walked a turn of the drab stone city looking and listening for any sign of his quarry. He roused his snoring companion and they breakfasted at the inn before checking their horses. Then Cydones reluctantly—because it betrayed his interest—inquired whether a travelling couple had yet passed through Karin. He tried a direct approach to the officers in the citadel, counting on the authority of his office to bluff an answer from them. All professed ignorance, though he doubted the honesty of two. Disappointed, Cydones and Doukitzes searched the town for any trace of the couriers, whose despatches warning of the impending Seljuk attack, he must prevent from reaching Manzikert.

Manzikert! The imperial courier had never given the fortress-city at the limits of empire any thought before this. Now it loomed large in his consciousness. He wondered and asked too much about the place. As was his custom, he sought solace in red wine, dragging Doukitzes to a tavern where he discovered to his immense satisfaction that he could still function when his companion had collapsed in stupor.

Cydones dragged him upstairs to their simple room and threw the barely coherent thug onto a bed. Then, his head still dull from the wine, he cloaked himself in someone's nondescript travelling cape from a peg near the entrance. With a sense of freedom, he set out for the caravanserai outside the circuit walls where he had been told that merchants, cameleers and others from the Muslim lands might be found. This pleasant distraction would allow him to practice his language, see the sights and learn what he might.

He studied the construction of the brick caravanserai with its eastern influence: a double storied building surrounding a courtyard where camels, donkeys and mules were tied or hobbled, as their masters rested in the upstairs rooms. The animals boasted by their trappings of the vast exotic worlds of the Silk Roads.

In the market next to the caravanserai, Cydones lost himself amongst the rows of produce and goods. Wheat, oats and barley from local fields were stacked in burlap sacks beside loads of goods from across the chimera of the Muslim frontier: cloth and carpets from Bukhara, copperware, leather and paper from

Samarqand, saddles and quivers from Tashkent, silks and wool from Zeravshan, metalware and weapons from Ferghana.

While bartering over a pair of colourful woven camel-bags, Cydones found himself in conversation with a Kurd from Tabriz whose interests seemed far wider than the price of the bags. "But it is not a very good caravanserai," remarked the Kurd. "It is not like that built by the great Mahmud the Ghaznavid near Nishapur."

"Indeed?" returned Cydones affably, wooed by the stranger's warmth. "I've not seen it."

"It's your loss. You're from Constantinople? You have that manner. From the palace?" The Kurd spoke passable Greek and looked Cydones straight in the eye as if trying to gauge his reaction to such a leading question.

"Really?" Cydones replied in Arabic, finding the multi-lingual Kurd interesting and somehow intimidating.

"I see much," the Kurd returned, also in Arabic. "It amuses people in Tabriz who are interested in such things. It can be … profitable. Each must make his own way in the world, y'know?"

"Exactly!" said Cydones, concealing his shock that a stranger could pick him as one who might trade secrets. Was he so obvious? His heart beat wildly and his mouth was so dry he could not refrain from licking his lips. "D'you work for such people?"

"No. No!" the other protested with a gesture. "That would be bad for business." He paused. "But messages can be … passed. You see?"

"I understand," Cydones mused aloud, shocked at the blunt approach and his own reaction to it. Something must be afoot in the Seljuk court for their questions to be so blatant, as if the answers were needed urgently. "It'd not do for such people to learn that a regiment of imperial Scholae from Constantinople have left Baberd, marching for Vaspurakan."

"No, it would never do. How many? Who leads?"

"The Sixth Schola. Three hundred, four, counting their squires. Count Bryennius commands."

"Not many squires?"

Cydones was surprised a wandering Kurd would know such detail of Byzantine military tactical organisation. "No. Money is short."

"Do others come?" the Kurd asked.

"No."

"Not so!" said the Kurd in Greek, loudly enough for the closest people in the crowd to hear and dismiss it as mere bartering. "Feel the quality of these bags," he continued as he slipped in a few golden *nomisma*[27], the byzants referred to by Franks. "You should take these bags, they'll suit your purpose very well."

With a furtive look around, Cydones passed some copper coins and made to leave, the bags over his shoulder. Close by, a hooded figure knelt examining the front shoe of a fine chestnut horse with a red leather saddle. Cydones worried

---

27 Nomisma—standard gold coin of Byzantium.

whether someone watched him, but the hooded figure, evidently satisfied, straightened and resumed a conversation with a cameleer.

"Perhaps one day, here will be built a proper caravanserai?" the Kurd said under a public smile. Then he finished, his voice slightly raised for the benefit of those around, "Please come again and bring your friends."

Cydones walked away, uneasily conscious of how simple and profitable another betrayal had been. At the hairs rising on the back of his neck, he glanced furtively around the crowd but could see no one familiar.

The following day, Petros Doukitzes had more success with the grooms than Cydones had with officials. One remembered a reserved woman and said that the couple had changed horses days before and would certainly be at Manzikert by now. Cydones was crestfallen. He had failed and now faced a prolonged stay in Armenia and the dangers of a besieged city. Bitter as he was, Cydones was not idle. Using his rank and position, he learned all that he could about the defences of Karin in particular and the Byzantine-Armenian frontier provinces in general. Once in the business of peddling information, every piece of a puzzle could be useful—and rewarding. Cydones decided to stay ahead of Count Bryennius and press on to Manzikert.

Karin,
10th May 1054

"Five days in Karin, and I have not seen anyone who looks like Swordleader, damn it," said Guy. "He must've gone on already." Wearing sidearms but no armour, he and Charles sat at a table in a secluded little tavern, one of their meeting places with the scouts. Jacques remained close to the cramped room they had rented, watching over their gear and animals in the stable behind.

On their first day in Karin, Guy had secured an interview with Robert Balazun, the leader of the Frankish mercenaries bound for Manzikert. The black-clothed Norman was a tall, powerful figure with a hooked nose and ready laugh. Like many of his kind, Balazun had left Normandy in search of land and wealth: either through conquest, or the seduction of an heiress. He bought Guy and Charles a jug of wine and accepted their services, but said he would not pay wages until the band started their march eastwards. Guy had not liked him—the Norman was too loud and arrogant.

"Karin!" Charles looked around at the mixed crowd. "A craphole between worlds. And the women are more coy and more covered than in Constantinople. I didn't think it was possible."

Guy laughed. "It's not so bad."

David Varaz, the scout, approached them and sat at their table.

Guy greeted him, "We've walked around so many times the beggars know us by sight."

"Sometimes when hunting it is best to lay in wait," said the borderer and horse thief. "I've come to take one of you to the market to spend your handful of silver coins on—what is it? Trousers, shoes, bow and, ah yes, a horse."

"Not all at once," grimaced Guy. "Centarch Lascaris is not very generous."

"No. But he's a smart one. It wouldn't do to splash money around and draw attention to yourself. Put this on." David handed Guy a strip of yellow and tan patterned silk to wear turban fashion. "Not so tight, loose. Now you'll look like just about everybody else. Anyway," he grinned, standing, "only a fool would buy a horse, by God."

"How else does one get a horse?" Guy also rose.

"Thieve one, of course," David laughed, leading the way with a self-assured strut as he farewelled Charles. "Your turn tomorrow."

They walked uphill past the citadel and turned east along a main thoroughfare leading to the Kars gate. "This isn't the most direct way to the market."

"No. We need to visit someone."

They passed beyond the recently repaired and strengthened circuit walls to where Guy found himself in a shantytown of makeshift houses and lean-tos arranged into little streets. David—left hand resting on his sword hilt with the little finger caressing his cased bow, right fist on the hinged leather lid of his quiver—singled out a man lounging against a rail and spoke to him in Armenian.

When finished, he turned to Guy. "I am looking for a priest—one who knows many and much."

"What's this place?"

"A squat. Or refugee camp if you like. People who escaped from Artsn fled here. Most haven't been able to find the money to start again, or leave—lost everything."

They picked their way through the poverty, coming at last to a small wooden dwelling. Guy followed him through a dark entrance and saw David enter a tiny room bathed with sunlight where an oilcloth cover was drawn aside. Six people sat on cushions around the walls eating a sparse meal from a low central table. They looked up quickly and their expressions brightened as they recognised the tough little Georgian.

Guy followed him, both surprised and ashamed, as they gasped and shrank back from him—an armed stranger. They recovered and a middle-aged man with a dark beard rose to welcome him. This was the priest and he introduced the family: an old man with the red weal of a sword scar across his face, his daughter in her thirties and a beautiful granddaughter in her late teens who forced a smile and quickly averted her eyes. A nephew and the orphaned boy of a neighbour looked at the foreigner with the open curiosity of children.

Guy sat in the place they made for him and courteously accepted a small cup of wine and piece of bread.

David stepped outside with the priest.

The woman watched Guy glance around the room, saw him gauge their cleanliness and paucity. "Do you speak Armenian or Greek?"

"A little Greek."

"I am sorry we can't offer more."

"I understand."

"You are of the Kelts in the city who will march to Vaspurakan to fight the Turk? A friend of David's?"

"Fellow traveller."

"You must be a friend, or he would not have brought you here." She paused. "You know what comes? What confronts you?"

"Perhaps a little. I have heard something of Artsn. Of the massacre."

"Then you do not know?"

Guy was aware of the way in which traumatised people cannot stop talking about what was done to them. He did not know whether it was best for them to blurt it out, or bottle it up within, relying on God and time to heal invisible wounds. "I am reluctant to pry."

"I see. But you should know what faces you and why David is so … driven." She looked away, surrendering to the flood of toxic memories. "We were too proud or foolish to follow Cecaumenus' advice and seek shelter in Karin, so were forsaken by God, some say because of our wicked ways. We had no city wall and only a few troops. Ibrahim Inal surprised the town and the citizens refused his demand for surrender. Inal became so frustrated with the resistance that he fired the city and put the populace to the sword. Those who could get away fled— at least the battle enabled some to escape. Children were led in bondage from the city, babies hurled mercilessly against rocks, young people blackened by fire, respectable elderly folk killed and maimed, maidens outraged and herded into slavery."

The woman was silent for a time. "The Greeks excuse their failed diplomacy and wasted battles by saying the Seljuk columns are huge. They aren't. But they are fast moving and daring. And their arrows are terrible, like the rain. That day the raiders set fire to houses, churches and public buildings where people tried to shelter. A severe wind came up and fanned the flames so the smoke billowed in a great cloud. The infidels stripped the place of all our gold and valuables. Forty camels were needed to carry the plunder from the bishop's treasury alone and a hundred and fifty priests were killed during the sack."

"Your family survived?"

"There are the remnants of three families in this room. Some fled in panic and with God's grace escaped. Others feigned death." The woman lowered her voice. "Our poor little Tamar was …" She motioned to the silent young woman who sat rocking on her knees, looking at the floor. "Still more hid in cellars that were not discovered. If the murdered and maimed and those enslaved were here, we would be fifty."

Guy lowered his gaze.

"Has David told you anything? Of himself?"

"I know he was at Kapetrou."

She smiled sadly. "He has not, has he? David was a landowning borderer and one of Liparit's officers. He loved our eldest—a beautiful girl. She was taken at Artsn but our soldiers were unable to rescue the captives, so she was taken to the Muslim lands. David followed in disguise, to the slave markets of Tabriz and Baghdad but could not get near her. A thousand dinars she fetched in Baghdad. A cavalryman of the gulams gets forty a month, a Daylami foot soldier, six. Most slave girls cost perhaps twenty, less when many are taken. A thousand dinars! David did not have it, of course, and after the auction he could not find her. A different man returned home."

"What do you mean?"

"Something in him has died. He hates the infidels and … Hush! Here they come."

Guy left with David soon after and they walked together to the market by the caravanserai. Guy wondered why the scout had taken him to the family. "They are good people," he ventured.

"Yes," replied David solemnly. "I wanted you to meet them. For by God, you three Kelts have made little secret of your desire to return to the safety of your own lands—though so far, you've kept your word to Centarch Bessas Phocas. Why do you want to return to where there is no place for you? If there was, you would not be here! This is the end of the Christian lands. Beyond here are pagans and Muslims. You came as a soldier of fortune. Now you know the price, if you're prepared to pay it, stay and welcome. If not, go now and be damned, by God. That is all I have to say."

Thereupon they reached the market where Guy, suddenly with much to think about, paid increased attention to searching the faces for any who might be the Swordleader.

David Varaz immediately changed the subject as though the previous conversation had not occurred. "Riding pants you need now," he observed with his familiar good-humoured grin at Guy's worn linens. "The best stall for them is over there. Get boots in Manzikert. They'll be cheaper there and if you buy them here, you'll be tempted to wear them on the march and get sore feet."

Guy purchased some tan coloured linen trousers and then they strolled around taking in the sights and wares for sale. It grew late and as they turned to go, Guy accidentally brushed against a tall man walking distractedly by with a pair of camel bags over his shoulder. Guy felt a sudden, overwhelming tension and turned almost involuntarily, to stare at the retreating figure. The stranger in his travelling garb was walking away in no particular rush. Nothing seemed remarkable about him.

Guy turned to follow David, scanning the faces of the crowd and fighting the deepening sense of unease.

Karin,
Mid-morning, 11th May 1054

The Sixth Schola rode the cobbled streets of Karin, the jostling crowd parting before the cavalcade of burnished mail, helmets low over shadow eyes, drab campaign cloaks rolled across the bunched muscle of blue blood horses. Leo was proud of his cataphracts, men drawn from the military elite, the sons of the estate-owning families of Anatolia and Macedonia, born to horses and arms. Bureaucratic attacks on the soldier-farmer class and the losses in ceaseless wars against the Normans, Arabs, Kurds, Seljuks and Patzinaks had made such men rare enough. From the head of the column, he surveyed the Armenian throng with its sprinkling of Kelt and Varangian mercenaries. The hand and donkey carts of tradesmen and pedlars crowded the side streets while shutters opened in the little stone houses and shops. Leo could not see Cydones or his servant.

The princeps of the Karin garrison, riding on Leo's left, had met them at the city gates to guide them in and organise their reception. "If you halt your column here in the square, the guides can show the men to their billets and stables. I'll take you to the governor."

"Very good." Leo threw up his arm to signal a halt, a few paces before turning his prized Kuhaylan gelding, Zarrar, out of the column. Behind him the tribunes and decarchs repeated his signal and the column came to an orderly halt. "Centarch Phocas, with me. Centarch Sebēos, with the guides—see the regiment into billets then report to me."

The princeps led Leo, his squire and Bessas up to the fifth century Roman citadel. They rode through the barbican guarding the citadel gates, ducking under the low arch. Inside the gate-yard Leo dismounted, handed the reins to his squire and walked under the raised portcullis of the main gate and up the stone ramp into the citadel. On the ramparts Leo met George Drosus, the strategos of Iberia and Ani, and the Norman knight, Robert Balazun, with whom he was to proceed to Manzikert. There was no warmth between them, merely formal courtesies and military acceptance: a perception by the Frank of privilege and arrogance matched the Romans' veiled suspicion of the mercenary's motives and loyalty. Balazun led sixty-two knights and four-hundred spear and bowmen, mostly Norman mercenaries and took his leave after arrangements were made for the journey to Manzikert.

From the battlements, looking north westward beyond the lower town, Leo could see the circuit-walls standing sentinel over the wide, light green valley of the uppermost reaches of the Western Euphrates[28] and beyond that, the grey stone and blue haze of the Pontic Mountains. To the east, a bald rise two miles distant blocked any view of the other strategically important invasion route: the valley of the Araxes River[29], which drained eastward through the Plain of Basen

---

28 Now the Kara Su which has its source near Erzurum (Karin) in Turkey.
29 Now the Aras River which flows eastward, joining the Kura which drains into the Caspaian Sea.

with its Kapetrou battlefield, to Armenian Kars and Ani and beyond them, the once Armenian now Shaddadid capital of Dvin and thence the Muslim world.

"It is quite a view," said Leo.

"Yes," agreed Drosus. "We're pretty much on the watershed between the river systems here. It is no wonder Karin has been so strongly fortified and contested for so long—since the ancients."

Drosus, as straight as he stood, then led Leo to his chambers where Drosus' undersecretary joined them. The men sat down to refreshments and work. Drosus detailed the military economies imposed on him, mentioning that none of his troops had yet returned from the Patzinak front. "We're down to the bare bones, Bryennius. Talking soldiers, professionals and mostly mercenaries at that, we have two thousand in the city garrison here and another eight thousand scattered throughout Iberia and Ani. Theodore Vladislav in Taron has three thousand. The catepano at Van has five thousand for the defence of Vaspurakan—and he is very much on the front line. These can be augmented by militia and armed locals, but it's not much of an army for you. Scattered all over and many of them infantry— fine for defending walls, but inadequate to fight the Turk in the open."

Drosus knew what he was talking about. He was Aaron's deputy during the campaign of 1048 and led the embassy to ransom Liparit from Tughrul Bey. "Got a message by carrier pigeon from Apocapes at Manzikert. Couriers arrived. D'you know him?"

"Strategos Apocapes? Only by reputation. I look forward to meeting him. People speak well of man and soldier. Also, speaking of Manzikert, I am looking for two others, an imperial courier named Bardas Cydones and his servant. They left my column against orders at Baberd, hell-bent on getting to Manzikert ahead of us."

"Hmm! Cydones called in asking after the couriers. My spies tell me he sniffed all over town and left in a hurry this morning. I had no grounds to keep him here."

"Did he mention that an associate of yours, Modestos Kamyates, will meet him at Manzikert?"

Drosus leapt to his feet. "Associate! Kamyates! That pissant! What's he doing there?"

"He's been on an embassy to the Seljuk capital apparently." Leo was heartened by the reaction.

"What?" Drosus stormed. "Embassy! I'll tell you something. When we went to get Liparit back a couple of years ago, Kamyates kept pushing the line that the Georgian pretender would need to agree to a peace pact with the Sultan. And he got it. So there'll be no Christian Georgian allies in the next campaign."

"No. It seems not."

Drosus went quiet, steeped in thought.

"Well," said Leo. "I've no need to sniff around town. I'll be on my way tomorrow and will send a detachment after Cydones immediately, to intercept him before he meets Kamyates at Manzikert."

"Perhaps he was just in a hurry," mused Drosus sardonically, staring out of an arrow slit. He turned to Leo. "And what would they do should they catch him? Arrest him? Tip him off and give grounds for a grudge? No. I counsel that you outwardly do nothing, and when you see Cydones next, apologise that the escort missed the appointment and you chastised the decarch in charge."

Leo smiled at the wisdom, covering his embarrassment at the mistake he might have made.

"No need to wear out your horses and men. Balazun's Kelts won't be ready to march for days in any case. Take the chance to replenish your supplies and rest up a bit. Look around. Learn about the place. Can't give you horses though, except for local use. Don't have enough myself. I see David Varaz has returned with you. He's a useful man. Keep him for the time being."

Drosus walked Leo to the door. "For the future, visit Kars and Ani if you can—good to know the lay of the land. I'm glad you've come, but I have to tell you, the Empire's strategy is flawed. Just holding a few key cities is too flat-footed and allows the enemy too much freedom of action. We need a decent field army to crush them when they're caught in our web of fortresses. Kamyates in the area means trouble, but his presence alone is not evidence of anything. It'll take an actual invasion by the infidels to move the powers that be. As soon as I have proof they have crossed the border in force, I will call—and damn loudly too, mark my words—for an army to be assembled further back, Caesarea perhaps, to destroy the Seljuks so thoroughly this time that they don't return. Look around and dine with me two nights hence, and I warn you, my chessmen have been lonely."

Few visited the ruins of Artsn, but as his men rested at Karin, Leo with Cecaumenus' scout, Maniakh, rode on borrowed hacks to the devastated city. He was struck by the stillness in the abandoned streets of other people's memories. Their horses snorted at the grotesque black shapes of burnt-out houses, silent in their overgrown gardens near the gutted tenements. A pack of dogs skulked away as they rode by, bows ready, alert to the possibility of bandits.

Leo wondered what it was about a ruin that was so touching. He tried to imagine the refugees around Karin in their former homes: hopeful maidens in rich gowns, urgent fathers, disappointing sons, stoic mothers greying with the years. Often in his travels, he had noticed a tiny timber farmhouse, dilapidated but alive with the family in it, a hundred years past its expected ruin. Over the next hill might be a stone villa, built to last for generations, which had collapsed soon after abandonment, as though the structure's soul left with its people.

A sacked city, Leo saw, was this and more. Charred, smashed walls were everywhere with tiled roofs caved-in by the fires. Broken pottery and glass, like shards of human lives, littered the ground and crackled under their horseshoes. There were frescos with the likenesses of those who once lived there. Faded writing described where there had been shops: Emma Fine Wines, or Constantine Kapsomenos Blacksmith. In places a rough, unfamiliar script marked the walls—impress of the raiders' contempt. The smell of blood and burning had passed with time, but evidence of fire was everywhere. Most of all, there was an eerie silence, even when the lonesome breeze rustled the weeds in the streets.

"It has ghosts, this place," said Maniakh. "Only six years and already the wilderness returns—how frail the time of man." Maniakh fell silent, embarrassed, as Leo looked at him.

They withdrew from the ruins and dismounted under cover, leading their horses to a place on a rise where scrubby bushes provided concealment but allowed good views all around. Over a lunch of bread and cheese from their saddlebags, Leo wondered what the scene would have been like before the attack. There were trees and gardens, no doubt, but no defensive walls. Oak, birch and beech still grew along the riverbank. He imagined the Seljuk hordes pouring over the distant crest in the early light.

Maniakh tore off another crust, took a draught from his goatskin, noticed Leo's watchfulness and took his ease, closing his eyes and letting the tension flow from his body. "Horse-archer, what happened here?"

Leo told what he knew, including facts from an eyewitness account given by a priest in Karin. "It wasn't just the city, Maniakh. The Seljuks pillaged twenty-four districts."

Maniakh, a hint of red in his brown beard, hair worn long over his shoulders and reins in his hand, took in what Leo said. "Is it true the Muslims placed dead pigs in the arms of the slain, as a sign of disrespect?"

"It is said, but I do not know."

"Waste of a good pig! What happened after they destroyed the city?" Maniakh sought the details of both heroic and horrible deeds.

"It's said that after Artsn, Ibrahim Inal's raid was repulsed from Karin and almost trapped at Kapetrou. But he escaped with a hundred thousand captives, ten thousand camels loaded with booty and many thousand coats-of-mail. The country around is now said to be inhabitable only by snakes and scorpions—as you see. The Emperor, to his credit I have to say, then sent troops to restore the frontier. Thereafter many fortresses were built to shelter the population."

Maniakh was silent for a time. "Did their God punish the people for their wickedness?" He sat up as though refreshed and unbidden, took up Leo's surveillance.

"Some speak thus but I cannot say. I doubt God punishes people for wickedness, not in this life anyway, for many do great evil and appear to suffer no admonishment for it." In the resting awareness of soldiers and perceiving Maniakh's vigilance, Leo eased his back against a rock and stared into the blue reaches of the heavens. They were like horses: one standing watch as its mate rested, an unconscious, primal instinct. Leo's eyes closed occasionally, but he remained alert to any sound beyond them and their mounts. "I think they were just ordinary people trying to get through life and thought they were safe enough this far back from the frontier."

Maniakh chewed on a twig. "And no one came to help them?"

"No. No one came."

"Of course, the steppe people hate walls. I've heard that old Tughrul's collecting miners and engineers." Maniakh stared off into the haze. "What would he want such people for d'you suppose?"

"Where did you hear this, Maniakh?"

"People talk, in the markets." Maniakh answered with disarming evasion.

"Do you believe them?"

"Yes." The scout gazed squarely at Leo. "Horse-archer, you should choose carefully which pile of stones you hide behind."

"I should give you more pay." Something in the ground caught Leo's attention and he rose and picked up a half-buried and tarnished silver spoon. He rubbed the loose dirt from it and slid the handle into his bootleg. "A good campaign spoon is hard to find."

"That's the truth of it. The Seljuks sack the richest town in the land and they leave you a spoon! This Sultan is a most unthinking man, Horse-archer." Maniakh rolled to his feet. "You'll have the best of him yet."

Leo gathered his reins and mounted lightly, catlike in his country horseman's way. "Let's hope you're right, Maniakh. For there'll be no pay for you if we do not," he joked.

They arrived back at Karin in the brilliant colours of sunset and returned their horses to the garrison stable-master. Leo drank little enough, but that night he sought out Bessas and they stayed late at an inn outside the military quarter.

Togol found them. He was dressed comfortably in a knee-length tunic, more like a Roman countryman than a barbarian. "We've found the imperial courier and his man. At least we found where they stayed."

"What have they been doing?" Leo, leaning on his elbows at their table took in the Cuman's unfamiliar appearance, feet pale in the sandals and the hair worn from the insides of his legs from riding.

"Nothing much. Resting. Buying things for their journey. Asking a lot of questions. They left in a hurry."

"Nothing, eh? Perhaps that explains their desire to get here so soon," said Bessas.

Leo grinned. "Cydones gave us the slip for something and I'll warrant it wasn't resting."

Togol pulled up a stool and leaned close to Leo. "Want us to kill them, Horse-archer?"

"No! We cannot go around killing people on suspicion. Besides, they might yet lead us to something."

Togol grumbled indecipherably into his beard.

"Anyway," Leo said over his goblet, "if it must be so, you get them to play polo and I'll do it—and make it look like their fault."

The fortress of Manzikert,
Afternoon, 13th May 1054

Basil Apocapes, patrician, deputy commander of Vaspurakan and commander of the fortress city of Manzikert with its surrounding districts, rode up the cobbled ramp and into the cool shadow of the citadel gate-tower. Lean from the constant exercise of arms and riding, he was thirty-six years old with flecks of grey in his light brown beard and riding-clothes soiled from weeks in the saddle. Accompanied by a small escort, Basil had just ridden a wide circuit of the vast lake, called by locals the Sea of Bznunik. It was an annual tour after the snow melted to tie-in the defences with his superior at Van. He had to plan how he could, with overstretched resources, defend the people, their customs and commerce, against the expected summer raiding by the Seljuks and their Kurdish allies.

The lake made defence difficult, because the Muslim Marwanids[30] controlled the western shore from Khlat' to beyond Baghesh, so Roman troops could not move freely to respond to any threat on the southern side. With much of the *theme* strength at Manzikert, the Muslims could raid on the south around the cities of Van and Agthamar. If he stripped the garrisons on the north side to campaign in the south, the natural northern invasion route from Tabriz and the city of Her, through Berkri and Archēsh, would be exposed. The province did not have enough cavalry and most of the troops had been dispersed to garrison the fortified cities. Kelt and Varangian troops were adept enough at defending walls, but could not match the Seljuks in swarming cavalry fights in the open. After years of misrule from Constantinople, the remaining local Armenian troops were indifferently armed and despondent. He sighed.

"Something wrong?" Count Daniel Branas, who had ridden with Basil, spoke from behind him. Branas was a tall, muscular professional Roman soldier of Armenian descent. He was the same age as Basil and the two men were firm friends.

"We need more mounted archers, Daniel." Basil removed his sword belt with its bow-case and quiver and looped them it over his left shoulder. "And I need a bath!"

"We need more of everything!" Branas, the Adonis of Manzikert, swept a crumpled felt hat from his shock of unruly dark curls. "And so do I."

Grooms led their horses away to the citadel stables. "Go to your family," said Basil. "We'll dine on the roof at sunset. Bring them."

Basil and his wife were the first to arrive at the highest tower of the citadel, his favourite place of solitude and reflection. From here he could look down on the citadel battlements, the cathedral, circuit walls and ditch that protected the city. From here, Basil could observe far in almost every direction, except to the northeast where a low crest inhibited the view of the road from Archēsh.

---

30 Kurdish (sometimes mentioned as Arab) dynasty centred on Amida (now Diyarbakir in Turkey).

A wooden table held a light meal of roast lamb, spiced vegetables, bread and cheese. Basil poured red wine into two silver goblets, passed one to his wife and sat back in one of the timber chairs. The servants withdrew discreetly. Through the late afternoon, the couple discussed what to do. Basil wanted her to take their children to safety with her relatives in Georgia. His wife refused. "If I go, the people will lose faith in you and then you would lose the city."

Branas arrived on time, bathed and with his beard trimmed. He greeted the couple and Basil waved him to the table. After a glance around the scenery, Branas poured himself a drink, took some food and sat. "My wife thanks you for bringing me back—finally. She'll join us after the servants have put the children to bed."

Basil chuckled. Mariam Branas was a fiery, dark-eyed Georgian woman with four small children who used the citadel as a playground. "I'd better stay out of her way for a while."

"I wouldn't say it's that bad," Branas said quietly. He paused and smoothed his robe. "She mentioned we have a visitor, some courtier from Constantinople who has been to Baghdad as an emissary. And Isfahan, evidently."

"Isfahan! I've heard." Basil wondered why Branas was raising the matter so delicately.

"I have to say," Branas started, "Mariam doesn't like him. Too charming by far and asks too many questions. And she is not often wrong."

"The princeps informed me after I got back," Basil said with a faintly bemused air, recalling the exasperated expression on Curticius' face as he relayed the news. "He is going to bring Modestos Kamyates here to join us, that we might afford him such hospitality as Manzikert can offer."

"Who knows he is here, apart from John Curticius and my wife?"

"Therein's the rub. Kamyates has busily acquainted himself with some of our officials and many of the Normans. He's already sent despatches to Constantinople informing his friends of his safe arrival here and his intention to remain as our guest for the summer. With one of my damned couriers, too!"

There was a long pause while they listened to the sounds of the city: the hum of ten thousand conversations, a dog barking, horseshoes and wagon wheels on cobblestones and somewhere beyond the staccato commands of the changing guard, the ringing of a hammer on an anvil—the musical five-tap of a blacksmith shaping hot metal.

"Prudent fellow isn't he?" Branas remarked into his goblet.

Basil grinned humourlessly. "Of interest and before he gets here, there are reports of reinforcements."

"Oh? The Kelts of Karin, finally?"

"Yes and not quite. John Curticius mentioned that he received a separate message from Karin saying there are Scholae and Kelts there, preparing to march here. Couriers brought despatches in our absence, warning of an impending Seljuk invasion. There are no further details and the two couriers could provide none, though they did say they were despatched by Cecaumanus himself in great secrecy—and haste."

"Scholae?" Branas murmured with obvious surprise. "Unusual. How many? The couriers specified invasion, not raid?"

"Yes, invasion. Only one regiment, the Sixth, a Count Bryennius commanding. But why the ..." Basil's voice trailed off. He had the uncomfortable sense of a high-stakes game being played on the chessboard of his command: high-level military despatches conveying vague warnings, imperial troops in token numbers and the sudden appearance of a senior diplomat returning from the empire of the shepherd king. Who could he trust and what would be the consequences of a wrong move, for the people of the district and himself? "Of course, I've sent a courier to inform the catepano at Van, of how much I know. But Daniel, I believe I'm going to need you now more than ever. I will keep news of these reinforcements quiet for the moment. Let's see what it's all about!"

"Whatever you ask." Branas reflected for some moments. "I wonder if someone knows something we don't. Perhaps this Bryennius has some answers."

"He was to leave Karin with a few hundred Kelt foot and horse[31] as well as a handful of citizens. So they will be awhile getting here."

"Hundreds more Kelts?" whistled Branas lowly. "We should be grateful, but we haven't been given the money to pay the disgruntled bunch we already have."

"As long as they fight the Seljuks," Basil said, not commenting on the common concern that many of the Frankish mercenaries were more interested in carving out their own fiefdoms rather than serving a Greek-speaking empire they despised. "I've quietly sent the couriers, Yūryak and Martina, back to the castle of Arknik, to cut their path and report back. At least then we can get barracks and billets ready for them."

With a warning cough, Curticius appeared with Modestos Kamyates who trailed him with the insolence of one accustomed to being in front. During the exchange of greetings, Basil took stock of the two.

Curticius, the chief-of-staff of Manzikert, was responsible to Basil for the military administration of the city and district. It was a demanding appointment involving: the arming of troops, repair and provisioning of fortresses, the production of plans of attack and defence and the conveying of clear orders so that all knew what they were supposed to do. Reserved to greyness, Curticius was likable and industrious, but could be moody at times. Ambitious in the normal sense, Curticius possessed no great tactical or strategic flair. Rather he was steady, prone to occasional oversights amongst the press of his duties and the imperfections of a military system now starved of adequate resources. Curticius had a dominant wife, Anna, and two grown children: a son, Damian, who commanded a troop of Armenian horse at Artzké, and their rebellious daughter, Irene. From his vantage point in the citadel, Basil had often in the past seen her ride out to meet the devil-may-care officer, Centarch Theodore Ankhialou.

---

31 Collective nouns for infantry and cavalry.

Mindful of the family's reputation, Basil had not intervened when Curticius had used his position to have the presumptuous officer transferred to Archēsh. Basil knew that neither Curticius nor his wife enjoyed Manzikert and dreamed of an easier life closer to the heart of the Empire. Curticius' Achilles heel was an over-indulgence in wine. Basil had cautioned him more than once over the habit.

Basil gauged Kamyates as the newcomer accepted a goblet of wine from Curticius. The courtier, richly attired in long silk robes acquired in the East, spoke court Greek with a lisp he tried to suppress and cultivated an air of learning. Kamyates flourished letters of introduction bearing the Emperor's seal, and safe conducts from a high official of the Abbasid Caliphate, and Nasr ad-Daulah, the Marwanid ruler of Amida. "I have been away eight months," he said.

"You must be keen to return to Constantinople," replied Basil.

"Certainly. I will have missed much of importance during my absence."

"Then you have chosen a roundabout way to get there." Branas said from the side. "Surely it would have been quicker to travel straight up the Euphrates to Melitene? And you could have sampled some of Nasr's three hundred concubines at Amida on the way back!"

Basil noticed Kamyates flash a momentary glare at Branas and gave his friend a cautioning glance.

"To administer the Empire, one must know all its rustic, dark corners." Kamyates made an insult of explanation.

"Oh, come, come," interjected Curticius. "Manzikert is not that bad. See! We've tasty food and passable wine. Certainly you cannot dine with a view of the Bosphorus meeting the Sea of Marmara, but a snow-topped mountain, healthy crops and grazing stock are no bad thing. After all, agriculture underpins all civilisations. What is a city without food?"

"What indeed?" Kamyates resumed his charm and nodded to the princeps.

Basil also smiled socially as he handed Kamyates a plate. It might have passed as relief that the momentary tension had subsided, but inwardly he was pleased. Branas had asked the obvious question in an off-handed manner that had provoked a revealing response. Curticius had smoothed over the tension.

Something else troubled Basil. Some weeks before, he had sent a scout on a secret mission to Seljuk-dominated Tabriz to ascertain whether the rumours of larger than usual military preparations were true. He had hoped the man would have returned by now, or sent word. The lack of news and concern for the man's safety gnawed at him. Kamyates had not mentioned it. Basil was not going to ask. "What's this Sultan like?"

"A truly amazing man," Kamyates answered, perhaps too quickly. "He claims to be of Hunnic royal stock, the son of Michael, the son of Seljuk. His early life was one of danger and privation. His father was killed in battle when Tughrul was quite young. He has been wandering nomad, mercenary for the Qarakhanids of Bukhara[32], defeated prisoner of the great Mahmud the Ghaznavid and exiled

---

32 A Turkic tribal confederation in Central Asia.

refugee in Khwārezm on the Oxus. But the Seljuks had their revenge on the Ghaznavid's son by luring his army into a drought stricken region and defeating it at Dandanqan, near Merv.[33] It was a pivotal battle of the Muslims, after which the Seljuks became an empire. Tughrul is now in his fifties, very pious and hardy. At the height of his strength and power, I would say."

Kamyates warmed to his description, seeming to enjoy his show of knowledge. "Aside from his view that we are unbelievers, he has no particular grudge against we Romans. Tughrul sees himself as saviour of the Abbasid Caliphate of Baghdad, and his main aim is its superiority over the Shi'ite Fatimids of Cairo. The Abbasid Caliph, Al-Ka'im, has appointed him a lawful king of much of Persia and bestowed on him the title, Asylum of the Muslims."

Basil attempted to measure Kamyates' reliability as an observer. "Do you know him well?"

The courtier smiled thinly. "Of course not. He's surrounded by a cloud of courtiers."

"Rather like us, eh!" Branas said, deadpan.

"Quite," Kamyates retorted with a sharp look at him.

"What's he like as a man?" asked Basil.

"A contradiction. Religious reformer ..." Kamyates paused in thought

"Not a zealot?" Branas asked seriously.

The courier ignored the question, "... a man of ambition, jealousies and great forgiveness—as he forgave his foster-brother, Ibrahim Inal, after his revolt three years ago."

"How did he become Sultan?" Basil was becoming uneasily aware of how little he knew of this tempestuous new neighbour.

"It is said that after their victory at Dandanqan, the Seljuks elected a king by drawing lots—arrows marked with the favoured candidate from the tribes and placed in a bundle, from which a child withdrew one."

"So we're about to be done over by child's play," Branas appeared as if he was intent on the food.

"Of course not," Kamyates snapped. "The Sultan has no intention of invading. He is only concerned with the Muslim world."

Basil beamed. "Modestos, it is fascinating. Tell us more of your travels."

Manzikert,
Evening, 13th May 1054

Modestos Kamyates returned to his apartment after meeting Basil Apocapes and his two key officers. His servant had lit the lamp and arranged the room with his master's clothes hung on pegs with personal and official papers secured in a trunk. Through his wine-induced weariness Kamyates felt a vague disquiet. It

---

33 The ruins of Merv are near Mary in Turkmenistan. See map p. iv.

should have been easier at Manzikert. Decorum demanded far more deferential behaviour from Apocapes towards a magistros. Instead, the soldier had been merely polite. Kamyates' unease sprang from the curiosity they had displayed about his travels and Apocapes' obvious interest that he was staying at Manzikert rather than the provincial capital at Van. It was subtle, but when he dwelt on it now, it seemed too well informed and their interest too keen. In particular, he wondered if his denials of seeing any evidence of the Sultan's rumoured siege equipment had been convincing. It was essential that Apocapes was kept ignorant of the fury about to envelop him.

Kamyates disrobed and lay on the bed, staring at the stone walls and vaulted ceiling, wondering how he could tolerate the coming weeks and conscious of a growing awareness of just how much he hated those who were not sufficiently deferential to him. His rise through the bureaucracy had led him to expect it. How did it come to this, to Manzikert? He sighed deeply.

Well born, he had risen quickly through the imperial bureaucracy by identifying rising stars and fawning for their approval and support. Also, he had made it a practice to bully and slight those of lesser rank to get his own way and learn the secrets of others. Talented competitors had been easily sidelined by the simple expedients of faint praise and malicious rumour.

With a gift for languages he studied first Arabic, then Persian and finally mastered the Seljuk tongue with its Kunic script. His Seljuk tutor had befriended him and then enlisted him in the service of Tughrul Bey. The Seljuks rewarded liberally and all Kamyates had to do in return was to explain their point of view sympathetically at the Emperor's court, as though philosophically and conscientiously examining all aspects of a problem. Thus he had played a key role in the under-estimation of the Seljuk threat, pruning of the native Byzantine and Armenian armies as well as making constant calls for troops to be redeployed from the east to the west in order to face the closer Patzinaks.

Several years ago his tutor had instructed him to seek an appointment with the Roman embassy of George Drosus to the court of Tughrul Bey, to negotiate the ransom of the Georgian pretender, Lipirat. That had been Kamyates' real entrance to the fascinating east—Tughrul Bey himself, the Kurdish emir of Amida who acted as intermediary, the Seljuk vizier and their spymaster, Bughra Dumrul—all now flitted across his memory.

For his most recent journey, Kamyates had taken the desert route from Melitene and Amida thence Baghdad, even though he hated horses and loathed camels. His stay in the Abbasid capital had been interesting and agreeable, especially since his hosts had found him pleasing young companions of smooth complexion and submissive demeanour. Kamyates was instructed by his hosts to exceed his imperial orders and travel to the Seljuk capital at Isfahan, for a secret audience with Tughrul Bey's spymaster.

The Emir Bughra Dumrul had demanded to know all Kamyates knew of Roman plans and capabilities for the defence of their Armenian provinces. His first attempt at holding back prompted such a stinging rebuke that he had then told them everything. The Seljuks directed him to return to the Roman court by way of Armenia, being careful to deny any warlike preparations he observed on its borders. On return to the Emperor, he was to emphasise the unruly, provocative behaviour of the Roman frontier troops and assure the Emperor that the Sultan's only intention was to safeguard the Sunni Abbasid Caliphate from the Fatimids. If some Roman frontier fortresses were to fall, that was due to the incompetence and provocations of their garrisons—that they could not defend themselves, even from the migratory tribesmen over whom the Sultan regrettably had no control.

Kamyates' servant, trusting innately in the greater goodness and wisdom of high office, tended to his master's horses and administrative needs, knowing and caring little of his comings and goings. Kamyates wished it that way, so his servant, if ever questioned, would portray the impression of open and trusting ignorance. He could tell any interrogators little and nothing that could not be easily explained.

Kamyates sighed again. The bed was soft after the hard wooden chairs of Apocapes' tower. Despite a few days rest in Manzikert, he remained stiff from the weeks of riding and unhealed sores remained on his legs from where his inexpertly chosen saddle had chaffed him.

There were dangers yet, he reflected. Apocapes was obviously not as stupid as he had thought a provincial soldier might be and Branas had a habit of asking trick questions. There was the complexity of remaining at the fortress on some pretext while the Seljuks subjugated Vaspurakan and Armenia. Nor might a Seljuk victory be as easy as they had foreseen. Kamyates had been tasked by the Seljuks to assist them by bribing a guard to leave a sally-port open, or to convince the Manzikert officers to surrender the town. Within the city, duty officers were never alone, keys stringently controlled, sentries constantly supervised and their watches changed at irregular intervals. Couriers maintained contact with the other major garrisons and Basil himself had just returned from a tour of the defences. Kamyates thought Basil was unlikely to simply surrender Manzikert or the district. There were difficulties ahead.

Not all was bad news. He had already achieved something. When Basil had mentioned the existence of a massive stone-thrower at Baghesh, left there thirty-two years before by The Bulgarslayer in his war against the Kurds of Her, Kamyates had scoffed at the engine's age and unimportance. Basil had pressed the desirability of secretly sending a party to burn the machine. That had been Kamyates' chance to attack Basil. "How dare you? Nasr ad-Daulah is our friend and you would insult him." Kamyates smiled at his own brilliance, for Apocapes had acquiesced. The strategos would have been a fool to ignore the advice of such an important official. It was a significant moment in the business of establishing his influence over Manzikert and Kamyates savoured it.

While he already had his instructions, he considered it desirable to open some form of communication with the Sultan's spymaster. It would enable him to both pass information and know what was happening. After all, he had to remain alert for the unexpected. Already he had recognised Oleg, the beefy commander of Manzikert's Rus and Viking mercenaries, from the blonde soldier's days with the Varangians in Constantinople, ten years before. If the Viking had recognised Kamyates, he had betrayed no sign of it, but the bureaucrat was troubled by the thought.

There was another intangible. Before Kamyates left Constantinople, he had arranged that a confederate, Bardas Cydones, travelling as an imperial courier with despatches for the commanders of Karin and Manzikert, should meet him in Vaspurakan. Cydones would pass on the latest news from Constantinople, but his more important role, when they returned to the Court, was to verify Kamyates' account of the Seljuk campaign of 1054. So far, Cydones had not arrived.

Kamyates sighed and rose, going to the window to watch a detachment of Kelts pass by in their distinctive mail and sectioned, riveted helmets. They reminded him that only one man in Manzikert had shown him appropriate respect. That was Reynaldus, a stocky Norman mercenary in his early forties, to whom Kamyates had responded with flattering acknowledgement. He still hoped he could win over John Curticius, the princeps. Curticius had already betrayed an appetite for wine, as had his wife, for her preference for a finer life in the large cities. It would all take time.

Chapter Three

A Skirmish

*Tabriz,
Evening, 19th May 1054*

The Arab soldier and poet, Derar al-Adin, sighed and reclined comfortably beside a fountain in the shaded, walled garden of the house of Emren Dirse's aunt in Tabriz, capital of the Seljuk dominated emirate of the Ravvadid Kurds. The city lay one hundred and twenty miles southeast of the Byzantine frontier—two days' steady ride on fresh horses.

Derar was undecided about Tabriz. Often it seemed just another featureless provincial city trying to mitigate the heat and dust with shade trees and practical architecture. Damage from the earthquake thirteen years before was still visible, reflecting the lack of will and wealth to undertake the repairs. For the discerning visitor, Tabriz had pleasant if expensive distractions. The bazaar was famous for its carpets and textiles. There were thermal springs in the area which could be enjoyed when out riding or hunting. A sprinkling of Christian Armenians amongst the majority Muslim population added variety to the local culture while the influx of professional soldiers and the Seljuk hordes brought the energy and social abandonment of men about to go to war. The town thrived, with the court of Tughrul Bey dispensing fear and largesse in unequal portions to local rulers, holy men, merchants and troops.

In his thirty-fifth year, Derar had left his estates near Aleppo months before and ridden to Baghdad accompanied by a Roman slave, Farisa, who reclined reading, on cushions nearby. Derar idly watching her was suddenly aware that she was no longer a scrawny and frightened but rebellious child. He had bought her at Amida six years earlier, after the Taghlibi Arabs had taken so many that beautiful captives came very cheaply. She had become a gifted linguist, speaking Greek, Arabic, Kurdish and some of the Turkic language. Faced with the possibility that their journey would carry them close to Roman lands, Derar extracted her word that she would not attempt to escape, in return for freedom when his quest was over.

He reminded himself that a slave girl should not be foremost in his deliberations, for he was on the cold trail of his older brother and a nephew who had left home months before with the avowed intention of joining the rising military power of the Seljuks. The brother concerned himself with the fight against the heretical Fatimid caliphate.[34] The nephew, Zobeir al-Adin, was attracted to the unreasonable notions of honour and glory. Derar had been moved by his sister-in-law's entreaties to find them and having tender feelings for the woman, agreed to undertake the search. He left his younger brother in charge of the family estates and brought little, in the belief less risked least lost and more incentive to return home.

Losing their way in a sandstorm, Derar and Farisa were aided by a Bedouin tribe whose hospitality, in the unwritten lore of the desert, warranted recompense. Thus they had arrived at Baghdad with three horses, two camels, and somewhat less gold coinage than he had started with. The city had cost him dearly while weeks of enquiry had revealed only that many adventurers had gone north to join or profit from the expected Seljuk move into the Roman eastern provinces.

In Baghdad, Derar hired a second servant; a Seljuk named Zaibullah, once an armoured cavalryman of the Abbasid Caliphate, who claimed to know the way to Tabriz and something of the country surrounding it. Reaching that city at the end of its bitter winter, Zaibullah soon learned the Seljuk spymaster had hired Derar's brother and nephew as interpreters. Derar was dismayed to learn that the two men had recently departed on a scout across the Christian frontier and he could only await their return, or go after them. They could have been anywhere, so Derar decided to wait at Tabriz, a known point to which they should return.

In Tabriz and running out of money, he had shamefully taken his black Mu'niqi mare to the markets to sell. A manly Seljuk had demanded to know what hidden fault the mare had for he could find none. Derar had bristled so the nomad asked what ill fortune forced the sale. Derar explained a little and the emir, Emren Dirse, seeing the Arab's love of his mare, offered to ask about employment as a scout or interpreter. Derar had skills to sell, for he could read and write in Arabic and Persian as well as speak the Greek tongue of the Romans. The two men became friends and when Derar had later quizzed Emren Dirse about his access to the Seljuk spymaster, Emren had replied that he had cut short a hunting trip to find his father. The old nomad was now missing, evidently on the same mission as Derar's relatives. Derar and his companions were pressed to stay at the spacious house of Emren Dirse's aunt.

---

34 Largely North Africa based Shi'ite Muslim caliphate with its capital in Cairo.

In this way Derar kept his mare and was duly employed by the Sultan's spymaster, thus gaining entry to the court, which he studied with the intensity of a man aware that his fate now lay in the hands of these powerful and tempestuous princes. While he performed his duties assiduously, Derar noticed the tensions between Kurds and Seljuks and learned of their recent past of bloodshed and reprisals.

White robed Tughrul Bey had arrived in Tabriz escorted by four hundred youths of the *Gulâmân-I sura*, the palace guards, bearing the Sultan's seven horsetail standards at their head. Tughrul Bey: The Falcon; Sultan of the Seljuk Turks; Client of the Commander of the Faithful; conqueror of Khurasan with mud-bricked Nishapur and Merv; and of Persia with the cities of Rai, Hamadan, and Isfahan. In his wide dominions, the shepherd king was father of his soldiers and people and the guardian of justice and peace. It was fourteen years of painstaking consolidation since he was acclaimed lord of the Seljuk hordes after they vanquished the lion banners of the Ghaznavids in the three-day battle of Dandanqan. Now destiny beckoned.

The Sultan's family came also. His father-in-law, Osketsam, a younger man than Tughrul by years, was charged with the siege operations. The famed Ibrahim Inal, governor of Azerbaijan and scourge of Artsn, also visited, ostensibly to coordinate the planned movements of the invading columns. Ibrahim Inal and his colleague, Kutlumush, were of the old roaming culture of raiding and plunder who conquered new areas for subsequent Seljuk administration under Tughrul. Inal was a soldier of fable. He had revolted once and been forgiven, but the watchful scrutiny of Derar saw the fleeting envy that crossed Inal's sunbaked countenance as he regarded his half-brother, the Sultan.

Thus, Tughrul Bey, iron-haired and bearded, over fifty with his time running out and knowing it, sited his invasion mounting-base at Tabriz and demanded the loyalty of the emir of the city, Wahsudan ibn Mamlan, taking his son as hostage. He would subdue the troublesome Roman frontier and open the lands beyond, before turning his attention to the stricken Caliphate that awaited his clemency in Madinat al-Salam, the City of Peace, once a village called Baghdad. Tughrul Bey rose each day to pray, ride and exercise under arms, fasting on the second and fifth days of the week. Beyond his personal devotions, the affairs of state swallowed his days, during which he never forgot his fate to rule the Muslim world. He held court toying with two arrows, symbolic of the power churning from the steppes of Central Asia.

Derar al-Adin knew that armies held few secrets. Tughrul Bey had collected the largest force in years, complete with a siege train of specialist troops and engines for attacking city walls. Many wives and children accompanied the expedition in the common knowledge that the newly won territory would be colonised. The valiant could win the hands of Seljuk maids by deeds of honour. Those who desired could take brides from amongst the scented women of the captured cities.

Few were told of Tughrul's specific plans to capture two key Roman fortresses that guarded their frontier, Manzikert on the Arsanias River[35] and Karin by the Araxes. Even fewer knew of the Roman traitor who would betray Manzikert to the Sultan; those who did understood a terrible death was the penalty for disclosure. In a blow, the Sultan would secure and occupy his northwestern flank before taking Baghdad the following year, after which he would turn on the Fatimids in Cairo. The re-direction of the energetic Seljuk hordes into Roman territory would keep the tribesmen from preying on his new Islamic subjects in Khurasan, Mesopotamia and soon, Baghdad. Choosing battlegrounds favouring the swarming tactics of his horse-archers, Tughrul despised sieges. Derar had seen him scowl disdainfully at the battlements of Tabriz and boast, "Only the weak need walls."

Tughrul's closest advisors controlled the other advantages he had in the coming offensive: the circle of deceit sowed by his representative in Constantinople. Paid and guided by the Seljuk ambassador, Byzantine traitors soothed away their countrymen's fears and prevented any warning reaching the puny garrisons on the frontier. Despite Islamic soldiers from far and wide flocking to his standards for the impending jihad, it seemed the Romans suspected nothing: so much so that Tughrul doubted his good fortune and feared a trap. He had sent more spies and scouts to assuage his fears.

Tughrul Bey needed to win the Armenian campaign, in order to blood his new professional army and so sate the tribesmen with Christian blood and plunder that they would not provoke trouble for him. The tribes had to assemble and be disciplined; they were his very strength and his greatest weakness. He could scarcely control the stormy migrations of those whose numbers, loyalty and arrows underpinned his military power. Many of their horses needed to gain condition on the lush spring grass of Azerbaijan and their bare hooves harden. Tughrul willed the melting snows of Vaspurakan to stream away and the terrain dry so his army could move its baggage and engines over the tracks that passed for roads and so unshod hooves would not wear away as if by whetstones. He wanted the Armenian harvest gathered, so food and fodder were conveniently stored for the taking. Importantly, the Sultan awaited the return of his scouting parties so he could confirm the dispositions and temper of the Roman armies.

While he too waited, Derar reflected on the Sultan's life—from rustic steppe prince to suzerainty over a vast empire that encompassed snow-capped mountains, frost-bound steppes and hot deserts, from the sumptuous cities of the conquered to the black tents of his tribes. What drove this shepherd king who controlled so many destinies as if by whim? The question intrigued Derar. It would all be for nothing if Tughrul's empire of legend and dream of a secure Sunni world died with him. The question of succession also troubled the heirless Sultan's advisors. "Perhaps a Roman girl from one of the cities to be captured," one had sniggered to a colleague. "They're favoured in Arab harems. Some have

---

35 Now the Murat River or Eastern Euphrates which flows by Malazgird (Manzikert) in eastern Turkey.

given birth to sons that became caliphs, so they ….." The whispered conversation had moved on from Derar's hearing.

Weeks passed as Derar proved increasingly useful to the court. He heard nothing of his relatives, as if they had vanished into a void. At length, he secured approval to accompany a planned exploratory raid into Vaspurakan. Never forgetting his purpose, Derar readied his weapons and emotions for the journey, surveyed the surrounding mountains and wondered what lay beyond. He selected the horse he would ride and chaffed under a mask of serenity for the raid to get under way.

Farisa bit her lip and remained silent as the apocalypse of horsemen made their preparations.

East of Karin,
Morning, 20th April 1054

Guy looked from his saddle at Count Bryennius' column marching in its own dust eastwards from Karin. Alone with their thoughts, each toiled forward, people and animals sweating to the accompaniment of horseshoes on stones, the lurch of cartwheels and calloused leather tread of Norman infantry. For some this was a higher purpose of duty, destiny or both. For others it was another passage in the business of life, carting goods to sell where paucity promoted profit. One rode with ambition, another with greed. Some sought adventure, others to escape whatever was now behind the western horizon—lover, creditor, poverty or pestilence.

Karin was the last city on the journey, the final chance to slink away. None had, despite their fears. All seemed caught in a destiny beyond their control, seduced by the simple habit of taking their place in the ranks. Horses and troops had been fed and rested in Karin, but two hot days on the march had quietened even the most boisterous as they sweated under the weight of leather and iron. Men's legs and shoulders ached from the tramp under their loads as blisters beset the negligent and inexperienced.

The blue sky, streaked with high white cloud, reached endlessly over rolling steppe. The grasslands, broken by lines of rugged mountains and stony hills, still bore patches of unmelted snow on the green tinge of sward and a spring breeze was yet to become the summer's furnace breath from the southern deserts.

In Karin, Guy and his companions had not found Swordleader or Bowman from the fight at the inn. The night before leaving Karin they had debated the courses open to them. Charles had argued for return to Constantinople, reminding them of the Armenian woman's warning about not travelling east of Caesarea and pointing out that adequate pay would not make them wealthy.

Guy struggled to answer Charles' caution. As if drawn to the frontier world they were entering with its rich fabric of new names, places, sight and smells, he recalled the refugees from Artsn and David's grief for lost love. "We've been there, Charles, and found nothing. We now have pay and people with us. And protecting Christians from the infidel is a worthy calling."

Jacques reluctantly sided with his master. "True, it is further to go back than forward and we do have pay for the first time in months."

Charles had simply thrown up his arms.

There were few secrets in the markets and inns of Karin. When the column had formed under the walls two days before, a disparate score of citizens had joined it, seeking protection from whatever fears the steppe might hold. At this first meeting of ranks, Roman and Frank had eyed each other suspiciously, separated by language, religion, dress and custom. The armed men had looked with mixed feelings on the merchants and other travellers: scorn for soft usury and self-seeking indulgence, envy for the fine clothes and horses. The soldiers stared at a merchant's beautiful wife on her matching grey horse. None of the poorer women, walking with their babies or small children next to the creaking baggage carts, failed to notice the yearning stares at beauty and privilege.

By this morning of the third day, the column marched in a subdued silence broken by occasional low conversations or the chivvying of the Norman sergeants and Byzantine decarchs, the veteran commanders of ten. As they progressed from Karin, the walled estates and clustered villages became ever further apart.

Guy rode in the rear guard with the Frankish knights and mounted sergeants-at-arms. Most wore swords over mail hauberks reaching to their knees and carried spears and shields. He lifted his gaze from the column to two distant raptors circling high in the blue sky. Were they a pair matched by human hand, or a couple that had mated by chance in the wild? They ranged with seeming purpose over the valleys and hills. The specks drew inexorably closer and he imagined crafty Saracens, warned by the falcons of approaching strangers, lying in wait. The arrows of the infidels come like rain, the woman at the inn near the Golden Gate had warned. He shuddered inwardly at the thought of lying on the steppe, arrowheads frothing blood-wet in the lungs or bile-soaked in the stomach. Like a shadow, doubt crossed him again.

Riding next to him, Charles sat straight in his deep wooden Frankish saddle. He had rolled the mail coif[36] back off his head so it curled in folds around the shoulders of his hauberk. Green linen trousers, tight around the lower legs and a dusty pair of ankle length shoes protected his lower limbs. Shield on his back, Charles suspended his helmet by its throat-lash from his sword hilt and carried his spear in his right hand as his left held the reins. Jacques strode with the soldiers escorting the baggage. The groom's brown hair hung from beneath a shapeless felt cap to frame his stubbled double chin and cling in damp licks around the nape of his neck. He carried his crossbow over one shoulder while his sword swung from his left hip. Charles and Jacques betrayed in their countenances and movement an unconcerned interest in their surroundings. Their evident calm

---

36 Armoured hood for the head and shoulders.

in contrast to his own unease perplexed Guy, for neither had been keen to come forward of Karin.

The thought caused him to recall with some fondness the interlude in Constantinople. Certainly, they had been poor as he fretted over a horse, but they rented a reasonable apartment—beyond their means—with a rooftop vantage point and stabling behind. They enjoyed easy evening meals in the glow of the sun setting over the Bosphorus, or the Golden Horn gleaming silent and silver in the moonlight, the dark shapes of scores of ships and hundreds of boats swaying gently to the sounds of the great city at night. In his mind's eye floated a vision of the gaily-clad young ladies with jewelled hair rebelliously uncovered at market, or the black habits and veils of older women, pre-occupied clergy, obsequious officials and richly caparisoned palace guards. His thoughts drifted back to veiled eyes taking in his strange Frankish dress and shoulder length red hair, to meet his own gaze and then look away, sometimes quickly, often not. Markets were well-stocked with wine, spices, foodstuffs, textiles, and perfumes. In other quarters, there were horses of numbers and types he viewed with envy. Blacksmiths and armourers were all busy. Constantinople teemed with people, bartering and haggling, while an endless crowd of workmen carried urns, boxes and bundles in that timeless commerce of the crossroads between east and west. Lamp-lit inns and eating-houses bespoke half a million tastes and as many opinions. Looking back it seemed dreamlike, false, a waiting.

Guy's reflections returned to the present as Balazun drawled, "Those damned Greeks are up to something." Taller even than Charles, Balazun's every fibre bespoke strength and confidence. He wore his brown hair cropped short and shaven-behind in the manner some Normans found fashionable. Guy envied him, for his might, fine arms and the black Castilian stallion he rode.

Guy looked to the head of the column where Count Bryennius dismounted to join Togol who was kneeling, studying the ground. Bryennius remounted and casually circled chestnut Ruksh on his haunches, sweeping the horizon with a searching gaze. Centarch Bessas Phocas was with him and the three conversed for a short time.

"They've found something," Balazun said.

So Guy had seen. Easing his seat in the saddle, he noticed that the circling birds of prey had vanished. A subtle movement in the centre of the column caught his eye and his gaze fell on the woman wearing the bright blue cape so fine its fabric caught the breeze. The garment protected her blond hair and fair skin from the sun and dust while concealing her beauty from the lewd stares of the soldiers. She was Serena Cephala, a young woman from Constantinople. Accompanied by two servants, she had joined the column at Karin. Guy had earlier noticed Serena's merry blue eyes and now saw the hood move slightly towards Centarch Bessas Phocas.

Guy and Charles caught each other's glances. "Beautiful, but not rich enough," joked Charles.

True to their role as Frankish mercenaries, they had kept their distance from the Roman officers. Guy observed Bryennius with interest.

Unusual for a Byzantine, Bryennius was close-cropped and clean-shaven. He sat easily on his horse in the working dress of a Roman cavalryman in patrol order. Under a tan linen surcoat, he wore a well-made mail coat below which his drab fitted trousers were tucked into buff coloured, knee-high riding boots. The count was well armed: a dagger and quiver of thirty arrows at the right hip, on his left a straight broadsword of excellent Syrian steel and an ornate leather bow-case. A strip of faded green cloth wound loosely around his helmet kept the sun off the metal. Strapped to his saddle were: a light brown military cloak; mace in its pouch suspended from the pommel; saddlebag for hard rations and other essentials behind his right thigh; balanced by a goatskin of water on the near side. At a little distance, he seemed to merge imperceptibly into the red ochre country around Karin.

The horsemen of the Sixth Schola were similarly, though less expensively equipped and mounted. They carried spears with a leather thong allowing the weapon to be slung from an arm when the bow was in use, and almond-shaped shields that were smaller and lighter than Guy's. The white cloaks had been packed away and each man had strapped to his saddle a drab greyish-brown cape the Greeks favoured for their "shadow warfare".

Bryennius rode up to Balazun and addressed him in passable Latin. "Robert, it's time to raise our guard. I'm taking some of my men to follow-up the tracks of two shod horses that crossed our line of march. Would you care to join us?" It was an attempt to bring the Romans and Franks together. "That man, on the mule, perhaps?" Bryennius continued, gesturing indifferently towards Guy. "Also others not riding stallions. Mares or gelding will be more …" He paused, searching for the word, "… subtle than your entires." The war stallions preferred by the Franks were not particularly well suited to the stealth needed for patrolling.

Robert Balazun did not move in his saddle. "We hide from no man. Guy, go with them. Take Charles and the men I placed under him."

With mixed exhilaration and apprehension, Guy kneed the mule awkwardly to where the patrol was forming up.

Bryennius addressed the group. "Suspicious tracks. Two horses shod in the Persian manner. Enemy scouts perhaps. We will capture or kill them. Move out into extended arrowhead. On contact, form skirmish line with a ten-man reserve under Centarch Lascaris at centre rear. Line of march, toward those two snow-capped peaks in the distance. I command. Centarch Lascaris is deputy. David, Maniakh, Togol, screen me a visual distance ahead and forward flanks. Engage only on my order or if the enemy surprise us. Remember, we're after prisoners and dead men cannot talk. We rejoin the column at the castle of Arknik tonight or tomorrow. Questions?"

The men remained silent, some shaking their heads.

"Good. Move out."

Thirty riders left the road and commenced a wide, dispersed sweep to the north. The main column, under the command of Bessas Phocas, continued its slow progress to the east.

Bryennius' patrol rode for several hours, keeping to the low folds in the ground as the sky clouded over and the air grew heavy. They alternated trotting and walking to the smell of horse sweat, the creak of leather and soft tinkle of mail. Quivers rattled and sword scabbards swung against hard, booted legs. They detoured to the occasional village to ask for local information, but no one had seen the strangers.

In the late afternoon, David Varaz's warning gesture towards a thicket on a low rise ahead was the first sign of their quarry. Bryennius hand-signalled imminent action and there was an expectant thrill as bows were drawn and arrows nocked.

Togol walked his horse back to the count and they conversed.

Bryennius signalled again: hostiles ahead, form skirmish line, flanks forward, advance-spears, march-canter. The Franks couched their spears as the flanks loped forward.

Guy could see a horse on the rise ahead grow restless on its picket rope. A man appeared and saw the patrol. He uttered a warning cry, flung himself to saddle and sought escape from the encircling horsemen.

"Charge!" signalled Bryennius. Then he shouted at the quarry in Greek, "Stand fast! Stand fast!" A soldier at his side repeated the cry in Arabic and the Seljuk language.

"Three! There are three!" one of the flankers yelled.

The arching arrows of the left flank missed the escaping rider and a decarch of the Scholae motioned two cataphracts with him in pursuit.

Guy, his heart beating and mouth dry, hoisted his shield higher, gripped his spear and spurred his mule clumsily forward into his first real skirmish as he saw two strangely clothed men and richly furnished horses in front of him.

The second hostile, stranded by his saddled horse galloping off after the escapee, reached for his long lance but was struck in the side by a Frankish spear. The third of the surprised men, long grey hair flowing under a tattered skin cap, deftly mounted a beautiful chestnut mare. Guy saw his booted left foot in the stirrup, knee to the shoulder and the tight inner rein, guiding the already cantering horse in a circle around him, the momentum hoisting him to the saddle. The mare turned on her hocks, head and tail up, eyes wild with excitement, sensing urgency of her rider who drew his bow and nocked an arrow while looking for the weakest part of the closing circle.

With a sickening certainty, Guy saw the warrior glare straight at him. Guy took the first arrow into his raised shield. The second, unloosed in less time than the telling, grazed his mule on the rump. The plunging beast would have unseated a lesser rider, but Guy drove his pain-maddened mount to head off the escaping rider.

The cornered Seljuk tried to check his horse and pass behind the mule. Guy dropped his spear and grasped the chestnut's bridle, dragging the horse down with him as the mule fell. Amongst the tumult and shouting, there was a moment of silence as the longhaired rider was thrown to an involuntary gasp from the onlookers.

Dazed, Guy struggled to his feet, sliding his sword from its scabbard. In the background, he could hear Bryennius shouting, "Rally on me. Rally on me."

The nomad lay still in the dry grass at his feet. His chestnut heaved itself up on its forelegs, dodged Guy's attempt to seize the reins and trotted off a few paces, frightened, but reluctant to leave her fallen master. The count rode up, ordered pickets posted and looked at the still figure stretched on the ground, "Broke his neck, I would say."

"What manner of man is he?" a Norman asked.

"Saracen," whispered a cataphract.

"Persian," said another.

Bryennius looked at the fallen stranger and distressed horse with its red leather saddle equipped for a journey. "Looks Seljuk."

George Varaz nodded. "He is, by God. Damn him."

A spear cast away, the second stranger writhed silently on the ground, biting his wrist to stop crying out. In his eyes, there was hate and behind that, acceptance. The cataphracts looked at the wounded man, then at Bryennius.

"Arab. He would not talk, even if he could," Bryennius said. "He does not have long."

"Muslim?" David asked, kneeling. At a groan of assent, the scout and Bryennius turned the stranger to face Mecca.

The mortally wounded man looked into Bryennius' eyes and wheezed a word, "Az … Az … a … z." There was silence but for the mournful breeze in the coarse grass. The Arab slumped.

"What did he say?" David asked, looking at Bryennius.

"Az?" Bryennius said doubtfully as he stood. "Aziz? Perhaps Azaz, a battle near Aleppo—the Arabs whipped one of our less distinguished Emperors twenty-five years ago. He may have been there and recalled his greatest moment in his last." Bryennius looked pensively at the dead men, then said rhetorically to Lascaris, "We followed the tracks of two who seem to have met the third here. How many others are there and what are they up to?"

They all looked in silence at these, their first enemies of this campaign, seeming so small and crumpled on the steppe.

Bryennius squinted after the pursuit. "And who and what is the one that got away? It looks like he's caught that loose horse for his flight—must be a handy sort of fellow."

Guy, still shaken from the sudden action and his fall, watched as the dead were searched. The pouch at the Seljuk's belt contained: blank parchment, writing materials, a silver trinket and six pounds of gold *nomismas*—two years pay for a count of the Scholae. His sword and dagger scabbards and quiver held nothing significant. A wider sweep of the area revealed a marked goatskin map thrown into the bushes.

Bryennius ordered the loose chestnut caught and the saddlebags emptied. Several attempts to catch her failed. Guy studied her with growing recognition, certain he had seen the horse and saddle at the market outside Karin.

Not even Togol of the steppes could place a loop over either her head or leg, so artfully did the chestnut mare duck and weave. "Seen a rope or two in her time!" he grunted in frustration, recoiling the lasso after the fourth attempt. The mare would not be caught by strangers nor abandon her master.

Centarch Lascaris called out to kill her with arrows.

Guy saw his heart's desire and most pressing need, a riding horse, trotting ownerless in circles before his eyes. Despite the dried sweat, hollowed flanks and the mud caked on her legs, he could see she was a quality mare of the desert breed. Sooner than the archers could draw, he ran forward and pulled at them. "No! Stop! Don't kill her! Don't kill her!"

The archers looked uncertainly at Bryennius. "Lower your bows, men."

Guy strode to the count. "I'm certain I saw her and that saddle near the market in Karin. And she's too good a horse to just kill."

"We could discuss that, but some other time. In Karin, you say? I want the contents of the saddlebag and very quickly. And we cannot wait here all day. My orders are to get to Manzikert as soon as practicable and it is inadvisable to leave the command fragmented. I must balance those known facts against delaying here."

"You shall have it."

"Indeed?" Bryennius dismounted. "You want the horse."

"Yes. I want the horse."

"What's your plan?"

"I'll lash the body of her master over my mule and lead it back to the road until I find an enclosure. I'll lead the mule straight in. The mare might follow."

"On your own?" Bryennius studied the youthful stubble and keen blue eyes behind the pitted metal of Guy's burnished nasal. No one knew whether there were other hostiles in the area. If the escapee did circle back to link up with friends, or to learn the fate of his companions, the prospect of a lone figure leading a mule across the steppe might make a tempting target. "You're bold. But good enough. You get the horse, saddle, weapons, armour and accoutrements. The empire keeps any documents, maps or money." Bryennius gave his horse a rub under the sweated brow band. "You know the way to the road?"

Guy pointed. "By nightfall."

"Agreed."

Guy watched Bryennius lead his horse towards Togol and David Varaz and confer with them. Saddles were exchanged as the best mounts for the pursuit were readied for their journey. Togol mounted a heavier gelding of the type used for pulling artisan's light carts. Pursuit until capture—with such scant instructions to guide their destiny and so little time to prepare, the two scouts mounted and started after the fugitive and the three soldiers already chasing him.

After securing the dead Seljuk on Guy's mule, the patrol mounted. Bryennius summoned a cataphract and ordered the man to ride to the last village passed and request the locals bury the dead—the patrol had no digging tools that would penetrate the hard ground. The count then circled his forearm and pointed the way back. They departed at a brisk walk, deploying into arrowhead on the move.

Charles drew rein by Guy. "I'll stay with you."

"Thanks, Charles. But no. You must lead your men and we don't need to cross Balazun. Bryennius would not allow it anyway."

"See you at tonight's camp then, a castle called Arknik. I'll tell Jacques."

"Don't bother." Guy did not want Jacques wandering the steppe looking for him. "Thanks, but tell him not to worry."

Charles shot him a glance and rode on. "Good luck," he called over his shoulder.

Guy restrained the mule as it suddenly tried to dart after the riders, then began his journey. He was inwardly jubilant when the mare started to follow, for it gave him hope that his plan might work and by nightfall he would own a horse he could not have dreamed of. He watched the patrol draw out of sight, the last sign of it a horseman looking back silhouetted on a rise.

Soon he was alone on the empty steppe. At first he followed the patrol's tracks, but these were spread out and criss-crossed by others, perhaps of local peasants searching for stock. To keep his bearings, he fixed on the sun as it broke weakly through the cloud, and steered a course to the right of it.

He walked as quickly as he could, carrying his spear in his right hand with the reins and his shield on his left arm. The mail byrnie[37] weighed down on his shoulders and chest and on the sword belt around his waist. Perspiration prickled his hair under the helmet and his feet started to hurt in his cheap leather shoes. After a time he felt the first blisters on his heels.

He strode onward with the sun lower and the afternoon grey and bleak. Fear gripped once when he turned around and thought he saw a rider in the distance and realised his vulnerability to mounted archers. He looked again but could discern nothing in the uncertain light.

Later, fatigue overcame self-discipline and he hooked the leather strap of his shield over the pommel of his saddle. It grew darker. Increasingly uncertain as his progress did not reveal the road, Guy scanned the barren landscape around him but it all appeared depressingly unfamiliar, though when on higher ground he was relieved to see the sharp outlines of two snow-covered mountains close together far to the north.

He led the mule on, the corpse draped awkwardly over its saddle. Guy hated the sight of it and tried not to look. Every time he did, some part of him ached with deep guilt. The chestnut mare stopped to crop grass and Guy inwardly

---

37 A short sleeved mail shirt reaching and covering the hips.

cursed risking his life to capture her. She kept grazing, snatching at the low grass and lifting her head occasionally to watch the retreating mule. His hopes started to sink. She made to follow, but stood on a dragging rein and stopped. Seeing a chance he turned and approached her, but she took a practiced step back off the rein and trotted away. Guy turned and continued his journey. The mare picked more grass then finally, to his relief, followed once more.

The clouds cleared for a time to lighten the west in a gilded sunset that cast soft rays on his cheek. Guy watched as fine bands of pastel pink and grey clouds streaked the pale blue of the sky. It was still and silent. Despite everything, the discomfort, danger, loneliness and burden of guilt, he felt a strange quietude under the infinite sky.

The matter of the universe perplexed him and thinking on it kept unease at bay. He had heard that the world was round and noticed the vehemence of those that ridiculed the idea. Thus lacking certainty, he imagined it as a gigantic chest, with the land and seas in the bottom, the sides and lid formed by the heavens, the sun, moon and stars caste by the divine hand in their courses. He could not fathom any notions of heaven, hell or beyond. "Better to leave such thinking to the priests and beggars," he mumbled to the mule. His thoughts thus turned to religion, and the incessant conversation of the citizens of Constantinople, about God and Church, the hatreds between Catholic Rome and Orthodox Constantinople. How they could talk! For a time his mind was distracted from the pain of his blistered feet and doubts to wonder on the forces that shaped the world and the affairs of people.

In the last of the light he found old wheel ruts indicating an oft travelled road. Feeling the dirt with his fingers he discerned the tracks of many shod horses and men. Elated, he turned into the darkness encroaching from the east. With the sense of sight reduced by the night, Guy removed his helmet to improve his hearing. Occasionally he halted, to listen and be reassured by silence and the nearness of the following horse. Once she nickered softly. After some time he sat by the roadside to rest, chewing on a crust of dry bread from his saddlebag and sipping from the goatskin.

The mule nuzzled close, begging for crumbs. He stroked its muzzle. "When I ride this Saracen horse, a day's leave for you." He rested for a while, his mind wandering to the dark and what it might contain. Seeking solace in movement he rose and trudged on. Within a half a league, a human form loomed ghostlike on the road. Guy sighed with relief when Jacques challenged quietly, "You've caught the horse?"

"Not yet." Guy tried to banish any emotion from his voice. "But I will." He felt reassured by the presence of this loyal peasant who fell-in and walked beside him. "Good to see you. You took some risk, though"

Jacques shrugged. "No more than you. I'd have none blame me if you didn't return home."

Home, so far away and long ago. "Is it home if you must leave?"

Jacques was silent for a few strides. "Must leave? Does it matter? We're here now and need to reach the castle tonight, or spend the night on this plain. That's all."

They walked some time in silence. "I took a life, Jacques."

"I heard. It can happen when you take a sword on the road. There was a fight and it was him or you. From what I heard he took a chance and broke his own neck. Don't dwell on it. Seek penance when you can and forget it."

"Still, it was I that wanted to continue this journey, and I fear there will be a cost."

"Charles Bertrum and I would not be here if we didn't want to be. Destiny or choice, we are not your burden."

The discussion ended, they walked on in the rising breeze which brought scudding clouds in the darkness above. It sighed through stunted bushes at the roadside as they crested a rise and started down the other side, realising they had followed the track where it passed into a thicket. Hearing voices, they froze, senses strained. The mule stepped close and rubbed its head on Guy's back. The sounds came again, faintly in the distance. Jacques pointed to a dim glow through the trees. Then a close voice quietly challenged, "Who's on the road?"

"Say nothing," hissed Jacques, as a figure appeared in the dimness beside them. They sensed rather than saw the spear point.

"Who goes there?" Guy retorted instinctively with more authority than he felt. He thought the challenge had come with an Armenian accent, but was unsure. It was too late to ready his spear without immediately starting a fight.

"A local—a friend," came from the dark.

Guy spoke with the innate authority of the mounted warrior. "Soldiers of the Emperor!"

"Should we be impressed?" someone else said to returned laughter.

"A group," muttered Jacques.

Other armed figures approached. Guy and Jacques were beckoned from the road into a small circle of flickering firelight where they found two others squatting on the ground. Guy's eye was drawn to a slight, balding man wearing a leather jerkin over a homespun tunic. A saddled and knee-hobbled horse was tied to a bush behind him.

"You don't sound Greek?" this man queried fluently with a slight accent Guy could not identify. He inspected with practiced eyes the two Franks and the mule with its burden. Guy saw his interrogator had already noticed the chestnut mare waiting uncertainly at the edge of the firelight.

Guy hesitated before answering, reluctant to give away too much. He knew there was little to gain by revealing they were alone. "A riderless horse we have yet to catch. We're with a larger party."

The bald man mused on this a moment, but said nothing of it. "Where are you making for?" he asked with the guarded familiarity of the traveller.

"We're seeking the next castle where our column will have halted," Guy said.

"That's Arknik. We saw the column on the road and a smaller group, a patrol or something, hastening to catch up. You two aren't Normans then? Kelts though? Do you know where it is?"

Guy and Jacques exchanged glances. "Arknik? Further along the road I expect." Guy spoke with a show of confidence. "We'll find it."

The stranger studied them for a short time. "It isn't quite that easy. The fort is off the main track a distance, on higher ground for observation and defence. You could miss it in the night."

Remembering his relief at finding the line of the road at dusk, Guy had no desire to blunder around in the dark hoping to stumble on a single point such as a castle. He was already late and he did not look forward to a rebuke from the count. "You've got a suggestion?"

"You could stay with us. There are four of us armed, but extra swords are no debt with the Seljuks around."

"Thank you, but that cannot be. We must press on." Guy added an afterthought, "You've seen them too?"

"The Seljuks? Not apart from the one I see you have there. There are signs, though. Interesting tracks in out of the way places. Odd people all of a sudden have a little gold. More Kelts for the frontier forts. Rumours." The bald man rose and looked at the chestnut mare as she grazed closer with her reins dragging.

Guy took in his short stature and slight build. "What do you know of spymasters' gold?"

The bald man turned abruptly, looking at Guy. "I said nothing of spymaster's gold. I could ask you the same question?" He switched his gaze to the mule and its burden. "One learns to smell the stench of it."

"How do you know so much?" Jacques demanded. "Some book-learned presbyter? Or other dark business?"

"You ask a lot of questions, stranger. But I've nothing to hide. I am a horse trader, a calling that takes me far. Who killed the Seljuk? And who now owns the horse?"

"His death was my misfortune and penance." Guy touched the cross of his sword hilt and made a silent prayer. "And I will own the horse."

The horse trader studied Guy for long seconds, as though gauging the worth of this wandering Frank. "She's flighty, sure enough, but you seem to know what you are about. That horse will be your fortune. Keep the saddle. And out here," he paused, "a wise man would learn the skill of the horse-archer. Since it's a Seljuk weapon, you might use the thumb ring, the better to draw the bowstring."

Guy chose to hide his ignorance of this obviously desirable art. "Good advice. Who're you?"

The horse trader looked long at them, as though considering whether to answer. "I am Simon Vardaheri. This is Leon Magistros and his sister, Joaninna. I met them while they were visiting their parents in Karin. The mother is ailing and Joaninna is a healer. The others are shepherds from Arknik. We were making for the fort when overtaken by darkness. The rest of the party was afoot, so

I've walked with them. We've finished our dinner and were going to stop here overnight."

"Everyone out here seems to have a reason to be abroad at night on foot?" Jacques muttered.

"On foot is how the poor normally travel," the woman said from behind her shawl. She did not move from her place near the fire, but even in the dim light Guy could see her take in the worn shoes of the two Franks. She would have noticed his painful, shortened step. "Or those who like walking."

Jacques allowed himself a smile.

"Simon Vardaheri is a gentle man, and such a man would not ride while his companions walk." Joaninna rose and looked over Jacques. She motioned to the embers. "There is a little bread left, if you will have it."

Jacques needed no second invitation. He stooped, and grasped the portion of flat bread, breaking off half and handing it to Guy.

Deciding to remain silent and avoid further slights, Guy looked at Leon. Tall and lean in his shirt and cap, the young man appeared to be a peasant, but the easy manner in which he carried his spear indicated some training. Guy judged him a simple fellow, but robust and good-hearted. The two other men were of similar stamp. Joaninna in her dark dress and stout shoes seemed more complex and resourceful than her brother.

"If you're moving on, we'll go with you," Vardaheri offered.

As they set off, Jacques moved close to Leon and asked quietly, "Why did you halt and not keep travelling through the dark?"

Leon looked keenly at the sweeping clouds and bushes swaying in the breeze. "For fear of demons and goblins." He repeated with such conviction the common fears held by many ordinary folk, that Guy and Jacques exchanged a quick glance. "They live hereabouts," he went on, "and enter the bodies of unwary people. It's said that by night any stray boar, wolf or serpent could be the devil incarnate or one of his companions or evil spirits."

Guy fought off his own childhood fears as around him the windblown bushes heaved wildly. "Have you encountered such beings?"

"Not I," Leon answered through his thin brown beard. "But I've spoken with many who have, and others who have seen them come from their victim's mouths while they sleep."

"Your sister? Does she know of potions and spells?"

The horse trader broke into their conversation. "Wise people don't talk of such things. Joaninna Magistros heals the sick. It's only the feeble minded or wicked who accuse the innocent of sorcery."

Guy and Jacques looked at the woman striding steadily in the dim light, bundle over her shoulder. Not much reassured, Guy muttered a precautionary prayer. Beside him, the horse trader walked on in silence. Guy noticed he carried no weapons, except a cheap butcher's knife such as a farmer might use.

Vardaheri, seemingly prompted by the previous exchange, explained. "Hereabouts, I mean the empire not just Armenia, not all women are high born and gifted with suitors. Their lives are set when they are still girls, the marriageable ones matched off early to husbands who keep them with child. Large numbers of children make up for the many deaths of the young from disease, war or other misfortunes. So, lucky women are early bound to a life of breeding, managing their husbands' household and sometimes, his business affairs. That is the life of choice for a well-born lady. Others may marry artisans or peasants and live an acceptable life—though they may also toil at the forge, field or shop bench while still spinning, weaving and breeding. Many men die in battle, so widows are common—a disaster for all. Not all … most, for it usually brings poverty. A few widows continue to run their husband's affairs. Some might remarry, though it's rare. Many turn to God and become nuns, which provides sanctuary and a type of family. But an independent woman, without the benefit of a rich upbringing or providing husband, must either sink to what people call low occupations—actresses and the like—or find some other means of making a living. Joaninna Magistros has become a trusted midwife, a skilled healer of people and horses. In your life you must guard against those who speak of sorcery and the devil to explain everyday affairs. Mankind is a strange bit of furniture and does not need other help to be capable of great evil. Or great good."

Guy nodded understanding and resolved to think more carefully before he spoke in haste before Simon Vardaheri. "How far to Arknik?" he asked, changing the subject.

Simon led the small group towards the fort where a single lantern, almost indistinguishable from the stars on the horizon, flickered in the watchtower. They were challenged by two of Bryennius' mounted cataphracts, who directed them to a track leading from the road. Guy sensed the yard wings and heard the chestnut mare snort suspiciously. Mounted cataphracts closed behind and the gate swung shut on the trapped mare.

Soldiers lifted the burden from the mule. Guy was unsaddling it as Bryennius appeared with two of the regiment's farriers bearing torches, the light from which played on their features in the breeze. Bryennius studied Guy with his prize and burden. "Good. Say nothing to anyone."

Guy looked on as they ran his skittish mare into a smaller yard where Bryennius lassoed and unsaddled her. The count tied a loose thong around her neck so she would be easier to catch the following morning. "Your new horse has a loose shoe," he mentioned casually to Guy as he picked up the saddle and carried it outside the yard. "My men have some water and hay for your animals."

Guy realised he had not noticed the sound of the loose shoe amongst the press of other distractions. "Thank you," he said, inwardly cursing Bryennius for his fault-finding.

The torchbearers came close as Bryennius emptied the saddlebag. "You'd better re-shoe her in the morning. " Kneeling in the flickering light of the torches, Bryennius rifled through the saddlebags. "We'll stop here tomorrow to attend the feast. It will be a chance to show the locals that we are here to protect them. You can find a blacksmith then. It will probably be the last chance before Manzikert."

He passed the money and the annotated goatskin maps he retrieved to the centarch. "Bessas, see what you make of these. Get that body buried, deep, in the enclosure, so the grave is obscured by hoof prints before morning. Keep the men quiet about it. Hold the citizens who came in with the two Kelts and make sure they talk to no one until Lascaris or you have a chance to speak with them."

Bessas scanned the documents. "Looks like they knew about us."

The two officers exchanged glances, then Bryennius turned to Guy. "Karin? Near the market you said? The horse?"

"Yes. There were two hawks out in the steppe today. And no sign of them at the camp we attacked."

"So there might have been someone else," Bessas concluded. "I'll take these and go over them."

"Thank you," said Bryennius as he waited for Guy to feed and water his horse and mule. At the count's request, Guy related what had befallen him since the skirmish.

"Did you see anyone out there?" Bryennius asked.

"I thought so, a horseman, for a moment. Did you drop someone off behind me?"

"I did, as it happens."

"If the information on the horse was that important, you could have just killed it, or caught it some way—you had enough men."

Bryennius was silent for a time. "Enough men? There were thirty out there today—good men. But you were the only one who thought differently. Reason enough to give a man his head and see what he's made of. But I was short of time and not going to take chances."

They sat together for some time, backs resting against the rails, savouring the stillness as people do in that end-of-day weariness.

Guy broke the silence. "Will your scouts catch the one that got away?"

"We must wait and see, but I would not like to be running from them. Togol can track like a wolf, David knows this country backwards and there are good soldiers with them. And Togol is riding Speedy."

"Speedy?"

"Yes," said Bryennius warmly. "Interesting, restless old horse. Once a chariot horse, he has been in this regiment longer than any other mount or most of the men. All he wants to do is go. Who could know what spirit drives him?"

Bryennius asked Guy about his past: how he came to Byzantium and what had prompted his risky actions during the day.

Guy told him the facts about his travels from Provence to the inn near the Golden Gate, but for his actions this day, he was lost for an answer. "I needed a horse."

"Makes sense."

The breeze had dropped and the clouds cleared to the west in a towering white bank lit by a waxing three-quarter moon. They watched it, clear and very beautiful.

"Well, congratulations. You have yourself a very fine horse." Bryennius glanced sympathetically at Guy. "Everyone's been told to keep quiet about what happened after the skirmish today. That includes you. Now, you had better get some sleep." Then the count rose and walked into the night.

Guy reflected on how exhausted he felt. It was a month since the fight at the inn. So much had happened, and yet it was only the beginning of whatever would be. He took his cloak from his saddle and lay down near where Jacques was already snoring quietly. He arranged his weapons and other equipment and made a deliberate mental note of where he was, the sentry posts and layout of the defences. If attacked through the night, there would be no time to casually roll over and come to one's senses, as a mercantile fellow safely ensconced in Constantinople might do.

The castle of Arknik,
Late evening, 20th May 1054

Leo left Guy d'Agiles and returned to his vigil by the yard wings where he waited for Maniakh and the troopers whom he had tasked to shadow Guy through the afternoon. It had been an eventful day with the consequences not yet played out. He looked at the sky, knew the night for a hunter's moon and wondered about the pursuit on which he had sent Togol, David and three cataphracts—the effect of orders on peoples' lives. Leo was sceptical of prayer, but in the darkness he regretted that day's dead. Nonetheless he wanted to account for all in the Seljuk group, silence them, know their business and find their contacts to turn them to his advantage. He wished for a prisoner and needed any information carried on the two horses that escaped the contact. The Romans were too few so must inflict a bloody penalty on the enemy in every fight. The nomads must not win the scouting war.

Leo was surprised at his determination to apprehend the authors of the strange tracks earlier that day. Splitting the command had been risky but right. He could not be everywhere and do everything so he had to depend on others. Now he waited impatiently for the different threads, or consequences, of his decisions to come together. The ever-dependable Bessas had brought the column to Arknik before darkness. Leo had arrived with his patrol shortly after with the trooper detached to organise the burial getting in before sundown.

Now Guy d'Agiles was in. Leo wondered what chance had led this wandering Kelt across his path. He had blundered into the affair at the inn, caught a glimpse of his assailant, healed a lame horse, completed a feat of endurance in the ride to Karin, foiled the escape of an experienced steppe warrior and won his horse. The young man was quite unlike most other mercenaries that came to Byzantium seeking their fortune.

Restless, Leo walked to the yard where Zarrar and Ruksh came close and stood beside him, their sweet breath warm on his cheek. "Hello boys," Leo whispered gently as he caressed them around the ears where the bridle headpiece rested on the long marches, the horses lowering and moving their heads to the touch. Suddenly they raised their heads, ears pricked, staring into the night.

Leo followed the direction of their gaze and presently made out the white-blazed face of Maniakh's mare in the moonlight. The horsemen reined to a halt before him, reporting all was well and that the patrol had simply shadowed Guy d'Agiles at a distance.

"The Kelt caught his horse?" Maniakh asked.

"In the yards here, as he planned. He did well."

"Good. Did he say anything?" Maniakh asked.

"He thought he saw a rider. It crossed his mind I had dropped men off behind him. He knows now."

"Good. Smart young fellow. Good judge of a horse. All has turned out well for us!"

"Yes, Maniakh. It's a start."

"I'm glad we didn't have to kill the mare. She's too good for that."

"Yes. Nothing of Togol?"

The Patzinak shook his head in the moonlight. "He'll be right. You'll see."

"Let's hope so." Leo turned to the soldiers. "Have your squires put your horses away, men. There's a hot meal for you inside the fort." He spoke quietly as they gathered around him. "One thing, no one is to speak of where you have been, nor what you have done or seen."

With murmurs of assent, the soldiers left for their meal, but Maniakh lingered, in the indirect manner of someone who does not wish to raise an awkward subject. "Are we in Vaspurakan yet?"

"Yes, Maniakh. Soon after we left last night's camp."

"What's the rest of it like?"

Perplexed by the question, Leo searched for Maniakh's deeper purpose. "You have never travelled here before? I have not seen it either, though my father spoke of it and I have read some. It's quite large, perhaps one hundred and fifty miles north to south and almost two hundred east to west. Much of it is barren and mountainous, with fertile valleys and steppe between, like the terrain here. The province has a very large salty lake in the middle of it, ten cities, about seventy castles like Arknik or better, and over three thousand villages."

Maniakh was silent. At length he said, "I must learn to read like a Roman, Horse-archer, who lives here?"

"Armenians—though many left twenty years ago, because of increasing pressure from Kurdish emirates and migratory Seljuks, some of whom also live here apparently. Many of those Armenians now live around the Western Euphrates. I'm told there're still quite a few Arabs and some Kurds in the south-western parts of Vaspurakan."

"Arabs?"

"Yes. A legacy of their conquest three hundred years ago."

Maniakh was silent for a moment. "The Frank will need to be careful, lest someone recognises his new horse."

"That is true," replied Leo, looking at the man with growing comprehension. "Fear not. We will be vigilant and watch for who seeks the Kelt."

His concern and curiosity evidently now more satisfied than his hunger, the Patzinak grunted approval and left.

Leo watched Maniakh disappear past the sentinels, then toured his command to ensure, once more, that all was in order. Suddenly he saw a figure furtively move into the shadow of a tree and observe the burial. They crept forward to the rails, close enough to see the Seljuk's corpse in the moonlight and the grave being dug. A young Macedonian sentry saw the newcomer and ran forward with a challenge, "Halt! Who goes there?"

Bryennius stepped up to the pair facing each other, "Very good, Aspieties," he said.

"Count?"

"Well done. Carry on. We don't want to run-through the landlord of Arknik when he has been so hospitable, do we?" Leo turned to the landlord. "Hello Tigran."

"Bryennius," Zakarian said, startled at Leo's unexpected appearance. "I was taking my evening stroll to make sure all is well for the night."

"All's well."

"As I see. Trouble?"

"Not at all." Leo saw Zakarian still studying the burial party. "He fell off."

Zakarian nodded, understanding that his interest was unwelcome and turned to leave, taking a look into the enclosure at Guy's chestnut mare.

Leo watched the landlord draw out of earshot. "Damn!" he said under his breath.

"Something wrong, Count?" the sentry asked.

"No, Aspieties. And certainly not your fault. It just never fails to impress me how the circle of knowledge of a secret, or the consequence of a deed, just keep getting wider."

Chapter Four
A Red Dress

*Arknik,
Morning, 21st May 1054*

Awakening suddenly in daylight, Guy was conscious that he was at Arknik and had slept past stand-to. Embarrassed that his hard-bitten comrades had allowed him this luxury, he struggled to rise and instantly felt the effects of yesterday's exertions. His feet were tender with swollen blisters, his legs felt painful and stiff and one shoulder ached from the fall. The fact of taking a life burdened his conscience, forcing him to his knees to pray for forgiveness. He felt nauseating shame for what had occurred and what might lie ahead. Murmuring prayers, Guy wondered whether sincere regret over the taken life might reflect an absence of deliberate sin. Others walked by but paid him little attention, devotion being common.

Guy stood, breathed in deeply and stretched painfully while taking stock of his surroundings. The fort was of uncut stone on a knoll overlooking the track to Manzikert. Animal enclosures nestled close outside the walls. Shepherds and herders were already moving horses, sheep, cattle, sheep and goats to graze in the surrounding steppe and hills. Smoke from cooking fires scented the air with the smell of baking bread as the bustle of a manor farmyard mixed with the metal murmur of troops, enhanced the carnival atmosphere of the day's market before the evening's feast. .

"You're awake!" Jacques was up already.

"Hardly," mumbled Guy as he tugged off the byrnie that he had not removed since the start of the previous day's march.

"Go get some breakfast. Then we'll go over your spoils—work out what to keep and what to sell."

Guy nodded. First, he visited his new mare, which recognised him but snorted suspiciously. She had eaten the hay and drunk from the wooden trough, so he threw her some more hay and stood still as she came close and sniffed it.

Guy limped into the stone confines of Arknik. Inside the wall were stables, warehouse, barn and living quarters, as well as enclosures for valuable and subsistence livestock in the event of a raid. During an emergency, the stronghold might be capable of holding five hundred souls: the family of the local lord, the wealthier landowners of the rural military caste, and some of the peasants. Those who could not shelter in the castle would have to take their chances in the hills.

Guy had seen similar outposts on the road over the past few days. They served as wayside inns and local administrative centres, little different from his father's *fief de hauberk*[38] though more sophisticated. The central residence, of local stone weathered to an uneven brown, was three storeys high, surmounted by a castellated tower. With its raised entrance and arrow-slit lower windows, it served as a castle keep. Guy ventured into the inn, a low stone building with a tiled roof. Sitting at a bench he ordered breakfast. Through an open unglazed window—the heavy timber shutters, with their arrow-slits, propped open—he watched Bryennius confer with Bessas. The centarch in turn addressed twenty assembled Normans and Romans standing to horse—a patrol to scout ahead. He wondered what they would find.

He devoured bread, cold roast lamb and sliced oranges from a board brought to him then washed it down with milk from a bronze goblet. His hunger assuaged, Guy was again struck by the exertions of the previous day, a day that had begun as uneventfully as many other days. Despite his soreness he felt a quiet pride. A few months ago he could not have imagined how a day might change him. He had acquired a splendid horse, Jacques treated him with a new respect and he looked forward to riding beside Charles again, rather than trailing him on the mule.

He finished his meal and made to pay but the winsome, dark-eyed local woman who served informed him the column's quartermaster was paying for the troops. Nonplussed at her inquiring look over him, Guy rose and limped to the enclosure where Charles and Jacques awaited, sitting side by side on a top rail and looking out over the wide valley. They were enthusiastic about Guy's newly won wealth. Jacques had already examined the weapons and pronounced their excellent quality and worth. Guy, fond of his father's broadsword, gave the superior straight-bladed eastern weapon to Jacques who immediately attached it to his belt, putting aside the cheap one he had carried from Provence. Guy decided to keep the long sabre attached to the saddle. It was light and flexible, ideal for mounted use.

Of particular interest to Guy was the horseman's short composite bow with its carved leather case and matching quiver of arrows with different heads, for

---

38 In Western Europe, a military fief or landholding, held by a knight in return for armed service to an overlord.

mail, lamellar[39], hide or flesh. Sewn into the outer surface of the bow case was a small pouch containing wax and spare bowstrings. Guy took up the weapon and examined its glued, layered curves of sinew, wood and horn.

"A master craftsman made that," Jacques said.

Guy agreed, putting aside the bow and examining a slender, curved dagger and its silver sheath. "Jacques, I have my old byrnie that fits well, and the Seljuk's will be too small for you. If you can trade it for another your size, do so. If not, simply sell it and anything else of value."

Passing by the mule and giving it an affectionate pat, Guy made a more detailed inspection of the chestnut mare. She had bright eyes and an alert carriage, but as he moved towards her she leapt away, turning her hindquarters towards him.

"Ride her now, Guy," Charles suggested mischievously.

"There's no dirt in her at least!" Jacques observed from outside the yard. "She could have kicked your head off then."

Another moment and Guy had his hand through the thong Bryennius had placed around her neck and the mare acquiesced. He slipped on the halter that was handed to him and stood back to observe the animal. Despite the hollowed-out look from her exertions and the dried sweat and mud caked on her legs, she was obviously of a superior Arabian strain. A quick look at her teeth revealed she was a six-year-old. Guy could now see she needed reshoeing. He knew the Arabians by reputation and suspected that Balazun's rough Norman farrier was not the man to shoe this horse. He looked at Jacques who seemed to read his thoughts.

"I can do it, but not that well," the groom said. "I'll seek a suitable blacksmith."

No farrier was available that day and early afternoon found Guy and Jacques by the mare's yard despondently staring at her worn shoes and rough hooves.

Bryennius appeared at the rails wearing a split leather apron over old clothes and carrying a heavy leather bag. "Nice mare," he said.

Guy was surprised by his appearance, but felt pride in the count's approval of his horse and evident respect for the manner of her capture.

"Found someone to shoe her?"

"No," they shuffled in unison. "But," Jacques explained, "we've found a set of barely worn shoes that should fit."

Bryennius examined the shoes and looked at the mare's hooves. "These would easily get her to Manzikert, it's only three or four days march. I must shoe Zarrar," he said as if it was a task of no consequence. "I'll help you shoe her afterwards, if you like."

Bryennius cold-shod Zarrar, shaping and fitting a set of shoes one of the regiment's farriers had made for him. The shadows moved two handbreadths, the time passing in the feel and smell of horses in yards. Nearby, hooves scraped and there were fights over hay. From inside the hamlet, hammers sounded on anvils against the breath of bellows and whine of grindstones. Outside the

---

39 Body armour comprising overlapping plates of iron, horn or hardened leather, held together by leather or silk lacing.

stronghold's wall, the distant farm sounds of fowls, goats and cattle bespoke another peaceful day.

Every so often Guy observed Bryennius straighten and survey the land and sky, then look back at his men. Guy would follow his gaze, finding himself looking for smoke, dust, and the movement of horsemen or startled animals.

Leaning with his chin on the top rail, the picturesque streaks of white cloud led him to reflect. By day without the canopy of stars, the limits of the world he had imagined seemed undeniable. While contemplating the nature of God, the sin of a death revisited him like a recurring shadow and he looked for any sign of the unknown Seljuk's grave, but hoofprints had obscured any trace. Guy noticed this compulsive guilt grew as he dwelt on it, and any distraction was welcome. No wonder soldiers drink so, he found himself thinking.

Bryennius started Zarrar's last hoof, the near hind, bending up the old nail-ends with precise hammer taps on the buffer and carefully removing the worn shoe with pincers. Zarrar, obviously bored by the familiar process, stood perfectly still but amused himself with snorting, wild-horse noises. "Put the fear of God into you if you didn't know him," Bryennius said without looking up as Guy grinned.

Domnos and Maria Taronites, a merchant and his wife who joined them at Karin strolled up. Taronites, heavily built and bearded, trod carefully in his fine shoes. His wife's beauty, when not concealed by a veil, had attracted the interest and gossip of the soldiers.

"Good afternoon," Taronites said in a show of friendliness not mirrored in his eyes.

Guy answered politely.

Bryennius grunted an acknowledgment with barely a sideways glance. Zarrar moved his head slightly to regard the strangers with the insolent curiosity of military horses towards citizens—knowing their own and who be strangers. "Whoa there, Zarrar," said Bryennius conversationally, as the horse's weight moved.

Domnos Taronites stared at Leo with unconcealed disdain.

Maria looked at Guy's chestnut, away to the horizon, then at Bryennius' bent back. She wore her long brown hair out, and a breeze caught it. The shimmer of yellow silk and scent of Persian perfume captivated Guy. She stared directly into his thoughts, then modestly away again, brown eyes under the waves of hair. Her roving glance swept back to him. "She's beautiful, and well-earned."

Guy blushed, pleased.

She flashed a bright smile and brushed hair away from her face. Then, with a dismissive nod from the merchant, they were away. With a half-turn, slim under the rich robes, Maria looked back once and met Guy's eyes. Then her glance dropped to Bryennius and quickly away, as she turned to follow her husband.

Bryennius stood, perspiration glistening on his tanned skin. "You're done," he said to the horse as he looked in silence after the departing couple. He motioned to Guy. "Stand by your mare's head and hold her loosely. Stroke her softly so she thinks about you and not about me. Stay on the same side as me, and don't let her kick. Cover her eye with your hand if need be. And keep feeding her a handful of grain every once in a while if she gets restless."

The two men worked quietly in the afternoon heat, tools blistering hot to the touch and the sweat now running off Bryennius. Between them, they gave every chance to the nervous mare, easing the shoes on, soft hammer-tap at a time, nail by nail, the mare biting nervously at Guy's hand when he offered the grain to her. At the end, they had seduced a set of Roman shoes onto the Seljuk mare and set a horseman's bond between them.

In the lengthening shadows, Bryennius and Guy walked back up the rise to the fort. "She'll be a different horse now," Leo remarked. "With shoes on you can give her some work and nothing is as amenable to suggestion as a tired horse."

As they neared the gate-tower, two strangers rode by. The closest was a dark-bearded man on a liver chestnut mare with white socks behind. Wearing rough travelling clothes and carrying a bow and sword, eyes masked by the shadow of a jaunty grey felt cap, defiance of the world was present in every movement and gesture. A hooded falcon secured by its light chain rested on his right arm. The second rider, swarthy and middle-aged, appeared to be the servant of the first. Similarly outfitted and also carrying a hawk, he was mounted on a gelding of indifferent type and conformation. They dismounted at the inn where the master entered boldly while the servant held their horses and slyly looked around at the unexpected soldiers.

Guy sensed the count's interest in the pair. Bryennius looked like a blacksmith as he loitered at the well with Guy. They watched, satisfied that the travellers had not noticed the rough-clad Roman officer amongst the common people. Guy drew a lesson from the count's ability to merge into a crowd. A closer look would reveal the hardness and calculating eyes of a soldier, but in a hunter's first perusal of a crowd, Guy thought Bryennius would have the advantage.

A warning from the tower heralded the return of Bessas' patrol. The mounted men rode through the gates in column-of-two with the brown smell of hide and grey smell of iron. Guy saw the dark silhouettes of spears and helmets, manes nodding to the walk. He read the horses' tired ears betraying equus thoughts of rest and fodder and the water trough, of joining their special mate and standing, heads down in rest, gaining comfort just from the nearness.

Guy felt an unfamiliar tingling thrill, a powerful notion that he was now part of some grander story. The world grew around him in the sounds of shod horses, murmur of armed men and a jaded whinny answered. Bessas dismissed his patrol while the last picket was withdrawn to the night sentry posts.

The stranger came out of the inn.

"Y'know," said Bryennius. "Falcons have a different use from supplementing the table. They are quite excellent for plucking messenger doves from the air."

Guy shuddered, remembering the circling hawks of the previous day.

The count approached the stranger's horse. "A fine horse, sir," he opened in hesitant tones. "White socks on a liver chestnut—not a common colour. Where's she from?"

The stranger, gathering his hawk from the other man, looked at Bryennius and evidently took him for what he appeared to be. "I bought her in Salamast. She's for sale if you're interested."

"Beyond my price, I'm afraid. Always like to look at a fine animal though. Salamast is far away. What brings you here?"

The stranger, looked more intently at Bryennius, then mounted and rode off, calling over his shoulder, "People asked too many questions in Salamast."

With a wry grin, Bryennius returned to Guy. "He certainly gets around," was all the count said.

Manzikert,
Afternoon, 21st May 1054

Within his rooms in Manzikert, Modestos Kamyates wrestled with his anger. He knew when his temper got the better of his carefully cultivated court reserve, the muscles in his jaw tensed under his beard and his faint lisp was accentuated. He had never forgotten the chagrin when someone years before dismissed his "sulks" and walked away in contempt. Kamyates had a deep longing to be taken earnestly, for he knew he was a deadly serious person.

The imperial courier, Bardas Cydones arrived at Manzikert shortly after the noon changing of the guard and had immediately sought him out. This lack of discretion was dangerous and indicative of Cydones' facile approach to security. The imperial courier was too used to the palace where the bureaucrats held the power and paid most of the informants. Worse, Cydones had blabbered almost incoherently about imperial military couriers getting through and a regiment of Scholae, commanded by a particularly boorish and obdurate count, on its way to the city.

"Don't do that again," Kamyates snapped at the fatigued Cydones. "I do not give a tinker's curse if you were ill on the road vomiting your heart out, as you say, in some woe begotten village." He paced the room, working up a show of fury to impress upon the newcomer just who was in charge. "A bit of discretion would have been nice—a casual bumping into me. How nice to see you! What a surprise finding you here! Instead you blunder in here with your show of knowledge and puffed-up self-importance. If Basil Apocapes has the place as laced with spies as I would, they will know already we are quite in league."

Still exhausted from a quick trip along the length of the empire and wrung-out from a stomach complaint suffered on the road, Cydones wilted under the abusive scorn of the senior official.

"I am most sorry," the imperial courier blurted, trying to allay the onslaught. "You're right, of course. In any event I'll be more careful in future."

Having established his positional superiority, Kamyates now moved to get what he wanted from the meeting. He had to know what was going on, establish who knew what, then further subordinate Cydones as a useful helper and if necessary, convenient scapegoat. Such usurious exploitation of his position of trust and other people was second nature to Kamyates—self-interest was how he lived and all he stood for. He vented a deep breath and spoke in a quiet, conciliatory tone. "Anyway, we shall put that behind us. In our own company, we know we are amongst friends. I am sorry you became unwell on the road—it happens in these backward parts. Your wife and children are well?"

"Yes, thank you." Cydones hesitated. "Though I'm worried because my Seljuk, um, friend, in the capital said they would be 'looked after' during my absence. I believe it was a threat."

Kamyates felt a flush of sympathy as he involuntarily recalled the occasion when Bughra Dumrul had menaced him. "That's just part of it," he sighed. "It means you must do as they say. They pay well for it, do they not?"

Cydones brightened as he managed to change the dismal subject. "I've a letter from your wife."

"Is she well?" Kamyates tucked the letter into his robe.

"As beautiful as ever. Your boys also. You must miss them, being away so long."

The cold eyes of Michael Kamyates turned once more to Cydones, but he smiled a social smile. Before leaving Constantinople, he had ordered his youngest son castrated, so that the youngster could rise with other eunuchs to the highest offices, close to the Emperor. That would assure the continuation of Kamyates' influence into old age and the flow of information and riches into his household and extended family. That Cydones had not mentioned it, or unwittingly passed a coded message from his wife, meant the operation had probably been successful. "Of course. Shall we get down to business—I think we're safe to talk here in my rooms."

Cydones breathed a little easier.

"You say," Kamyates said, "the pair you intercepted at the inn were decoys for a trap and this Bryennius commanded the ambush party. You are also sure that you and the Seljuk ambassador's man escaped without trace."

"The Seljuk stayed in Constantinople."

"As he ought, since he works for Abu 'Ali ibn Kabir, their ambassador. Before I left I arranged with my colleague in the administration, who shall remain nameless, to use his friendship with the Domestic of the Scholae to assist any arrangements for your passage here, including if needs be, with the very people hunting you. Very good! I like that! However you slipped up antagonising this Bryennius by absenting yourself from the column during the journey."

"In any event, I wanted to catch the couriers and take care of them before they arrived," said Cydones.

"I applaud your commitment to instructions," Kamyates snapped, "but you are too late. The couriers had already arrived here and delivered their, albeit vague, warnings before you even reached Baberd. Consequently it has taken me quite some time and effort to assuage Apocapes' concerns. Put revenge from your mind. They left on the Karin road days ago."

"Have you seen them? Do you know what they look like?"

"A couple, I hear. They're now immaterial. This ... Bryennius ... we may have to take care of him, I think. The Kelts who blundered into the ambush were arrested and imprisoned, you say?"

"In Constantinople!" Cydones seemingly willed himself to believe that this loose end was tied-up. "One attacked me, but I heard a number were arrested at the inn. I don't know if they were part of the same group. I suspect not, since the one I fought was on his own outside."

"A servant watching their horses, perhaps?"

"Perhaps. He wore no armour but carried a sword. I hasten to say that a number of Kelts accompanied the flotilla to Trebizond and there were others already waiting at Karin. I've looked carefully for the one from the inn—after all my life depends on it—but I've seen none that make me suspicious above the normal caution that befits men such as us."

"Quite," Kamyates replied icily, pupils pinpricks in his brown eyes at Cydones' comparison with him. "Anything else I should know?"

"No." If Cydones had not been on his guard when he entered Manzikert, he was now.

Kamyates let the silence linger while the other man looked down, as though he already knew what Cydones might withhold. Finally he continued. "Now then. The Sultan wishes to capture much of the eastern frontier, roughly to the Euphrates. Of course, we don't want quite that—it would be too much. But Vaspurakan, Manzikert, Ani and a few thousand Armenians are of no importance to us. In any case their loss would negate the need to waste more troops out here. What do you make of its defences?"

"Karin? Very sound, I should think. It was untouched when the nomads pillaged Artsn."

"Good. We don't want the nomads going too far. Now, you and I have a job to do. We need to give Manzikert to the Sultan when he comes. This is best and most safely achieved by persuading Basil Apocapes to surrender the city and avoid a sack. We have people in neighbouring Archēsh who have been persuaded to do just that. Self-interest is a wonderful thing. But if that is to no avail, then we need to arrange for a gate to be left unguarded or a sally-port open one night."

"Shouldn't be too hard," agreed Cydones, "but how do we ensure our own survival in the event that the Seljuks break in? The slaughter would be prodigious."

"I admit that is a risk, but if it comes to that we have no choice." Kamyates enunciated the plans he had been formulating, under Seljuk direction, for months. "We simply do our best to make sure the city is unprepared for defence and dispel any rumours about the Sultan's siege train. Apocapes should only expect the usual lightly armed raiders and have no inkling of what is about to befall his city. That fractured belief will do much to persuade him that resistance is futile. If the Sultan has to breach the walls, you and I will hide in the cathedral in our very best robes so that we look like we're worth saving because we know where all the gold is. Tughrul will have a squadron of his palace guard make straight for the cathedral to rescue us. It's quite simple and there is little to fear."

Cydones seemed to stop breathing.

Kamyates thought the imperial courier was considering his options: to cut and run at any time, find some corner of the empire where he was unknown, or openly go over to the Seljuks to administer their new provinces. "Now that you know the plan I have confided—trusted—in you. What do you think is the biggest threat to it, do you think?"

Cydones paused. "Bryennius. He's suspicious and unpredictable with no concept of diplomacy or how things ought to be. A cloud of scouts and trusted officers surround him and his troops are loyal."

"Then we must find a little job for him to do, somewhere where he will be less ... umm ... less amongst his friends."

"And undermine his influence with Apocapes."

"You're learning, Cydones. Well done!"

"And cause some of his officers to see things ... more clearly."

"Quite," said Kamyates smiling. "Now, we mustn't be seen to be too close."

"Do we have any help? My servant is trustworthy to a point."

"A local landowner is also active on our part," Kamyates smirked, "He wants to see the last of us."

Arknik,
Early evening, 21st May 1054

Back from his patrol, Bessas reported an open road ahead and discussed with Count Bryennius the arrangements for the next day's march. Time passed quickly while he checked the change to night-routine and listened to Lascaris pass orders for the continuation of their journey. His dark grey gelding, Hector, walked loose-reined next to him; occasionally rubbing his head on Bessas' mailed shoulder. He would return the affection, and caress the horse's head as he talked to the men.

A few oil lamps lit the stone, timber and straw of the stables as a handful of grooms and sweepers moved around. Bessas' squire indicated an empty stall and brought fodder and a pail of clear water. Bessas removed his helmet then unsaddled, sponged and dried Hector with clean rags left for the purpose. With horseman's hands he massaged the horse, caressing, reassuring, and feeling down a lifted leg for injury or a loose shoe. Hector looked back affectionately throughout, ears moving and the hard hide leaning firmly back against the grooming strokes. Throwing a blanket over him, Bessas fed boiled barley with finely chopped hay his squire had prepared and stood companionably by his mount. He turned to a slippered step behind him and recognised Serena of the column and the blue cloak.

"You're kind to your horse," she said softly as she leaned over a stable half-door to give her own mare an apple. Instead of her riding habit she wore an embroidered light grey silk gown.

"As are you," replied Bessas. "And we have not been properly introduced."

"Serena Cephala," she said, "though we are hardly strangers, since we have already been riding together, in a way, on the march …" thus dispensing with the formality of a formal introduction "… and you have been busy with your duties."

"Bessas Phocas. I am with Count Bryennius."

"Yes, of the Scholae. And you are being modest. You are also a centarch and the count's deputy, a position carrying much responsibility, but no additional rank or pay."

Bessas blushed, surprised at how much she was prepared to betray her interest at their first meeting.

"It is comforting to have an escort of the Scholae so far from home," she said, before correcting herself. "So far from Constantinople."

"You are far from the city," he agreed, attempting to change the subject from himself and trying not to stare. "Where are you going?" Bessas, with his man-smell of iron and leather, was leaning on the loosebox door, his gaze straying to her from the water pail and the fresh straw covering the floor.

Hector chewed contentedly, one ear on them, moving his head around occasionally to better see them.

"Manzikert."

"Oh! Manzikert? I thought Ani. Or Kars, at least." He fell silent, realising it would have been better not to mention Kars, sacked four months before.

"Yes. I know. Manzikert!" She laughed a little at his discomfort before explaining. "It's awful. Rustic! But rather exciting. My parents live in Manzikert. Father is a civil official." She glanced down. "I don't know what Kars would be like, now. Presumably there are people there, but it takes a very prosperous place to recover from being pillaged."

Bessas changed the subject from the destruction of Armenian cities. "Why were you in Constantinople?"

"I've been staying with my aunt," Serena laughed. "My parents trusted her to make a proper lady of me, kind soul that she is. I learned the things a well-educated young woman should know, reading, The Bible, the classics, numbers, spinning and weaving." She made a face of mock horror. "Forever spinning and weaving. And the household arts." Flickering shadows from the lamps played on her refined features and loose blonde hair. "They rather thought I should get married."

"Married?"

"Yes, married," she smiled at him. "That's what women do."

"Yes," he replied after a pause. "I suppose so." There was a reasoning side of Bessas that thought this young woman would have been better advised to stay in Constantinople, married to a rich merchant or bureaucrat. But there was a passionate turn to him that was captivated by her. "Are you married?" he asked, embarrassed at his own boldness.

"No," she laughed. "My chaperones were far too earnest in their duties and their choices were altogether too ghastly. Since the most ardent of my suitors didn't much care to visit Manzikert …"

"Oh, they have no idea what they'll miss," he laughed.

"No they won't," Serena said with a far away look.

Then her eyes met Bessas' and suddenly neither knew what to say.

Serena glanced away at Hector chewing his grain. "You ride well," she murmured. After that, they spoke for a time of horses, the journey and the need to join the others at the feast, but they dallied instead. Hector turned to her and the lovely girl stroked his grey face, running a soft hand gently over his big black eyes. "Aren't you beautiful?" she whispered into his muzzle. Hector accepted the caresses, sniffed the scent of apple and another horse on her hand and gazed happily at Bessas who returned the look with envy.

Suddenly, Serena stared past Bessas towards the unmistakable slight scraping sound of a horse's hooves being lifted in turn from a stone floor. "What kind of horseshoe is that?" she whispered.

Bessas stole a glance around, caught a glimpse of a Persian shoe and wondered about the owner of the horse.

Serena tugged his sleeve. "Don't stare."

To allay any alarm by the owner of the Persian shoe, Bessas said in a conversational tone, "Shall we join the others?"

Serena nodded and turned to go.

Bessas gave Hector one more pat and thinking of Serena's display of affection towards his horse, whispered good-naturedly, "Groveller!" Then, picking up his saddle and accoutrements, he followed her into the courtyard where people drifted in the flickering torchlight towards the great hall of the landlord's main residence.

Bessas was impressed by Serena noticing the unfamiliar shoe. "You are very observant. That type of horseshoe is found throughout the Muslim lands and that man rode in with a companion ahead of us this evening. There's something about him."

Passers-by gave them odd looks, as though struck by their shy intimacy.

"We had better go," Bessas said, concerned for her reputation. They parted. He carried his gear to where his squadron was camped, washed from a pail and dressed in the clean clothes that his squire had laid out. Then, Serena very much on his mind, he headed for the feast.

Inside the hall Bessas observed the crowd clustered loosely into social groups. The landlord and his richly-robed family mingled with the Roman officers, some of whom had donned formal robes rather than the clean riding clothes worn by most of the soldiers. A handful of the wealthier Norman knights, having picked up a smattering of Greek, joined this group that was attended by the lord's slaves.

Cataphracts mixed confidently with small-landholders and artisans, while the peasants, hereditary renters of small plots who might own a few goats and sheep, perhaps a single cow, kept to themselves in the reserved manner of their class.

The wealthier Arknik women wore flowing gowns of vibrant, richly embroidered silk; the poorer imitating them with shirts or tunics over long skirts. Young ladies and girls appeared carefree in their rich colours, contrasting with the darker dress of married women. Their hair gleamed and the occasional jewel sparkled. How different they now seemed from the sombrely clad, reticent figures he had seen through the day. The women, under the watchful gaze of their men, served spicy food. Some responded with blushes of offended modesty to the licentious stares and furtive remarks from a few of the wine-emboldened soldiery before the decarchs stopped it.

Living as they did on this military road, if the track could be thus described, the locals were accustomed to bands of marching troops. They knew Tagmata[40] troops this far east was unusual, and for that reason both interesting and alarming. Byzantine troops tended to be much the same, some good, others bad. They marched into Arknik, wanting food served, horses tended and women if they could be had. Then they swung into the saddle or shuffled into dusty-footed files, shouldered their shields and weapons and neither mourned nor mourning, moved on to their destiny in the vastness of mountains and steppe. This contingent was better disciplined than most—certainly more so than the unruly Patzinak and Uze mercenaries who passed through during the earlier Armenian wars. Being direct from Constantinople, these Scholae had interesting tales of the wider world.

Bessas noticed Bryennius engaged in a conversation with the horse-trader, Simon Vardaheri: the count deeply interested in the exchange and asking much, to which the horse trader readily responded.

Through the crowd, his gaze met Serena's. They each circled the room socially, meeting close to where Guy d'Agiles was making his way through the crowd as though looking for someone.

Guy looked interrogatively at him

"I have not seen your companions yet," said Bessas. "People are still coming. Will you ride your horse tomorrow?"

Guy smiled. "If God wills it."

"Your God, or that horse's infidel God?" Bessas grinned. While admiring the young Kelt's feat the day before, Bessas recognized that a different toss in fortune's game could have seen Guy sprawled on the steppe with two or three arrow shafts letting his lifeblood into the dust.

"Don't tease," Serena admonished. "He captured the horse and will ride it as well." Then she smiled at Guy. "I saw her, a beautiful mare. She'll surely serve you well." She turned to Bessas again, saying with a trace of humour, "It's the same God anyway."

---

40 The Byzantine central, professional field army of about 30,000, predominantly cavalry, based in or near Constantinople.

"That's true," Bessas said, still grinning, watching Guy as the young Frank gazed at Serena. He wondered where this Frank's loyalty would be: to the Romans who kidnapped him, a rebellious Kelt warlord staking out his own personal fiefdom in Armenia, or to some lithesome girl he fancies in Vaspurakan. "Drink up!" Bessas encouraged mischievously, "It's a celebration."

Guy recovered and thanked her, but laughed at Bessas' joke.

"What do you think of Arknik?" Serena asked Guy. She was one of those infallibly polite women who converse with strangers at a gathering, more so if they were on their own.

Guy glanced around the room before answering. "I expected something different out here. I don't know what. This is the same as gatherings in all the lands I have travelled. There is the local lord in his grand house with its wall of stakes or stone. There are artisans who live nearby, peasants and those who contribute in some other practical way. Then there are the others, priests and the like—local variations, but the same, everywhere." Guy's voice trailed off as he saw the landlord of Arknik, Zakarian, engage in a quick word as he brushed past the falconer who had ridden into Arknik that afternoon.

Bessas and Serena subtly followed his look and exchanged glances. "We used to have a tradition of small, independent landholders," Bessas continued as if nothing had happened. "Everywhere the same. Yet everywhere different." He clapped an arm good-naturedly on Guy's shoulder. "And well spotted."

"Where's your home?" Serena moved the conversation forward.

Guy hesitated. "Provence, in the Frankish lands, although the Burgundian kingdom now rules much of it."

"What's it like?" Her fingers played with the base of a silver goblet as her eyes held his.

"Provence?" Guy answered with mixed feelings as though uncomfortable with the subject of home. "Golden in the summer. Like parts of Thrace, I suppose. It has mountains and forested meadow. It's not like here, where it looks green and fertile at a distance, but up close the grass is thin and the ground hard."

"Yes," Serena agreed. "Armenia is certainly stony and largely treeless, though it has beautiful places. Have you come to learn the art of war so you can go home and achieve some purpose? Or will you stay?" It was as though Serena looked through him. She glanced downward, "One shouldn't ask."

Their host, the landlord of Arknik rose to speak. Serena smiled at Guy and turned politely to listen.

Arknik,
Early evening, 21st May 1054

Martina touched the red dress into place, stepped into her slippers and opened the door to admit Yūryak. Bathed and a little rested, she delighted in the caress of silk and hint of scent. The dangers and privations of their long ride had salved her soul a little and she enjoyed feeling feminine. "How do I look?"

Yūryak stared before entering the small room they rented in Arknik's inn. "It's the first time I've seen you in a dress."

"I wore one today," she countered, determined not to allow a friendship to become something more.

On Basil Apocapes' order, they had back-tracked to Arknik, by-passed on their original journey to Manzikert, before Count Bryennius' column had arrived from Karin. The strategos wanted confirmation reinforcements were on the way and an assessment of their battle readiness.

Martina had earlier donned a commoner's coarse workaday dress to learn what she could as people mingled at the market outside the walls and visited the camping troops. The talk amongst many citizens was of the clash with a Seljuk scouting party on the previous day and versions of a young Kelt's capture of a Seljuk warhorse. She had also seen strangers ride in with hawks on their gauntlets and learned their names.

Yūryak paused. "Not like that dress. Did you buy it today? Anyway, you asked."

"I did, at the market, and the slippers. It's not too much?"

"No. Everyone is dressed in their finest for tonight. We'll fit in well enough."

"Not too well, that would be careless. And you look rather dashing yourself!"

"Well, we are dashing to the feast," he said, stepping across the small room to flop face-up across the single bed.

"You will surely win some local lady's heart tonight."

"I wouldn't know what to do with one. I'm still tired from the ride out here. I was expecting a rest at Manzikert, not be sent here within a couple of days to see if the rumour of reinforcements was true. At least we arrived before the troops and got a room."

"Fortunately true."

"What is?" Yūryak put his arms behind his head, closed his eyes and sighed.

"A room. And troops! Three hundred Scholae, with only a hundred squires instead of three. Sixty-two Kelt horse and four hundred foot. A Norman named Balazun leads the Kelts and Count Bryennius commands the Scholae." She turned to look at Yūryak with wry sympathy, snatched a silk scarf from the bed and threw it at him. "And, yes, it's been hard on the seat bones." Arching her back, she stretched a half-turn in the dress, tugging at the waist to improve the fit. Reflected by lamplight in a hand mirror, Martina thought her hair and face passed muster enough for Arknik. "Have you heard anything about him?"

"You have been busy. I was going to ask a few drunk soldiers tonight. Heard about who?"

"Count Bryennius?"

There was a silence, as though Yūryak was searching his recollections. "Nothing in particular. He must know something if he's been sent out here so soon. I think he was in charge of getting us away."

"All those men, marching away again, so soon after the Patzinak wars. His wife must be upset."

Hearing nothing, Martina turned on her heel in time to see Yūryak close his eyes. She silently chided herself, knowing she had been caught. "Wake up, sleepyhead, it's time to go."

He raised an arm lazily and she hauled him to his feet.

"Anyway, he can certainly shoe a horse!"

"Who can?" Yūryak opened the door for her.

"Count Bryennius."

"He shod a horse?"

"Two. Come on!"

They entered the hall and felt the disquiet of strangers looked-over, before the locals returned to their doings. Martina saw Bryennius in a corner conversing with a countryman as the patrician-looking Centarch Bessas Phocas, talked with a beautiful woman in a light grey gown. A red-headed young Kelt conversed with them.

Yūryak touched her back lightly. "We'd better blend in. Let's find the food."

Before long cries for silence announced the landlord, Tigran Zakarian, standing upon a bench seat to welcome his guests. Stocky and powerful under his formal robes, Zakarian brushed the dark hair from his eyes, took a sip of wine and cleared his throat. There was a hush—courtesy from the visitors, discernible unease from his people.

"Welcome, soldiers and travellers, to the hospitality of Arknik," he began with a smile which twisted to a smirk. "We seem to have had rather a few visitors from Constantinople lately." Some in the crowd managed crooked grins, while there was a momentary murmur from amongst the Roman soldiery.

Martina noticed but could not attach any particular significance to it. Instead she felt a warmth, of belonging to that place of spiced food, scrubbed women, the earth-equus smell of off duty cavalry mingling with people who won their living from the land. Turning to listen she saw in sudden sharp clarity the rough stone walls festooned with weapons and hangings. Colourful carpets from beyond the Muslim frontier covered the flagstone floor on which long trestle tables were laden with food and wine. Flickering oil lamps cast an orange light and dancing shadows across the crowd.

"Many …" Zakarian went on with a lighter tone, "… many of them bearing arms? Why? Are the infidels about to fall upon us again? We all know the fate of walled Kars, a mere two days ride away, on the Day of Epiphany this very year. It does no good to dwell grievously on it, but we must look to our futures. So we shall pray, bring in the harvest and see to the defence, if needs be, of our poor walls of Arknik. And now, of all times, we must be grateful to those who place themselves in harm's way for the common good."

"Common what? Common good!" The falconer who rode in that afternoon stood defiantly, cloaked and capped, dagger at his belt. All could hear the rage in him. "What would that effeminate race, the Greeks, contribute to any common good?"

Martina gauged the crowd's reactions before leaning close to Yūryak. "It's Bardanes Gurgen."

"Digging his grave deeper."

"Yes," Gurgen continued, his face afire. "We'd scarcely seen off the Arabs, who occupied Mantzkert—its proper Armenian name—and much of our land, before you corrupt and perfidious Greeks tricked and bribed your way in, taking our blessed city, Ani, nine years ago. Then you stole estates, persecuted our church, castrated and dispossessed our noblest soldiers and dismantled our army of fifty thousand. You ravaged the countryside with your landlords and tax collectors until there was nothing. There were once seventy well-guarded castles in Vaspurakan. Now? Helpless!" Gurgen glared around at the silent faces. "Helpless! With the infidels on the doorstep. The sooner you tax collecting Greeks with your land-stealing mercenaries are gone, the better."

He had spoken treason in the presence of the Emperor's soldiers and the intensity of the silence stopped his outburst.

Martina saw the Centarch Phocas exchange glances with the blonde woman and the Kelt, then move towards Gurgen, but a slight shake of the head from Bryennius stayed him. Tigran Zakarian hovered unhappily in the background as a glowering silence from the Romans provoked sympathetic murmurs from the Armenians. Normans looked on in amused silence at this trouble between allies.

Bryennius rose and strode across the hall to stand beside the landlord and confront Gurgen.

Count Bryennius! This was who the Augusta said she might trust. With the hardness of a professional soldier and the arrogance of the Tagmata, his gaze swept the room over her, then back again. Their eyes met for a moment before the rhythm of his address obliged his attentions away. Then she sensed someone had seen through her and looking around suddenly, saw the red-headed Kelt quickly avert his gaze. Unease touched her—she could not afford an uncovered moment.

"Hardly helpless!" the count replied evenly to Gurgen.

"Ah! The nosey blacksmith!"

"I … we", Bryennius waved his arm inclusively of Romans and Franks, "neither know nor endured the history of this land as you who were born here. Nor is any person here the author of it, thus none should be faulted. But I must set you right on some matters. First, people here may wish to check the facts for themselves, but my recollection is that a Roman army under John Curcuas, himself Armenian I think, recaptured Manzikert and Khlat' from the Arabs over a hundred years ago. I do not believe it was you, or the Armenian state."

"Second," Bryennius continued. "When your king, John Senekerim, thirty years ago ceded his realm in return for extensive lands in the west, it was because he knew that he did not have the power to resist the increasing Kurdish and Seljuk incursions."

Some of the older locals nodded slightly. They were listening.

"Third. We soldiers here this night are sent so the fate of Artsn is not repeated. The Emperor orders and we obey."

There was a murmur of assent from troops and citizens alike.

"Last," Bryennius paused to make the point. "All are now confronted by a terrible common foe. Bitterness between us no matter how provoked by past injustice, will do nothing but harm. From such harm will come mistakes, and from mistakes, catastrophe."

There was a grim silence as his words hung in the air.

"Bah!" Bardanes Gurgen blustered. "Catastrophe for whom? And what will you accomplish with your legions—a lone regiment of Scholae with a few hundred more Kelts on foot. The nomad king quakes in his tent at your approach."

"I doubt Tughrul Bey is sleeping rough this night. I rather fancy he has finer quarters in some city. In any case, we are here and I intend to smite Seljuks, not Armenians."

The stranger glared defiantly across the circle at Bryennius and made to leave.

"Do not turn your back on me," snapped Bryennius. "Who are you?"

"I am an Armenian, wronged, my father carried off in chains, my mother dispossessed, their estates stolen by barbarian mercenaries for one of your Emperor's friends. I've wandered homeless since. What use would I have for a name?" He turned to leave but cataphracts blocked his way.

"I asked you a question."

Gurgen made to push through the soldiers.

"Arrest him," Bryennius ordered quietly. Then he murmured instructions to Centarch Bessas Phocas who departed with the prisoner and escort.

Martina noticed Bryennius waited a decent interval before departing with Tigran Zakarian and his wife. That was the signal for many of the troops, mindful of the march on the following day, to retire also. A few revellers stayed as the local musicians and dancers threw aside the inhibitions caused by so many strangers. She wanted to remain, but Yūryak insisted, "We must be on our way before too many are up."

Arknik,
Late evening, 21st May 1054

As Guy and Serena turned to listen to the landlord, he mused on her questions about the purpose of his journey: whether he would stay or return home to Provence, matters he had not considered. Home? Guy knew at that instant he could only return if he had no need. To ride a fine horse back and thunder on the gates of his father's fiefdom was one thing. To slink back defeated by the world was another.

As Guy's consciousness turned to the drama between the rebellious falconer and Bryennius, he noticed a woman in red; fair-haired in the lamplight, she wore the festival day dress of a commoner and was striking in a way that caused his look to linger. Languid eyed, lips parted, she studied Bryennius closely. She turned her head suddenly as if by sixth sense. Guy averted his gaze back to the exchange between the count and the falconer. When he looked again, the woman was lost to his sight as the crowd moved to make way for the troopers escorting the hapless Gurgen from the hall.

Recalling their conversation, Guy turned to Serena. "I came to see the world and find I know little enough of it. Which one was right, the count or the falconer?"

"That is the pity of it, she said. "Both, in their own ways and fate has set them against each other."

"I feel sorry for him, that man with the hawks." Guy reflected on his own dispossession by birthright. "What will they do with him?"

"I shouldn't worry. He is very lucky, for he was intemperate before two just men, Bessas, that is Centarch Phocas, and Count Bryennius. I doubt they will do more than lock him up overnight until he cools down, then send him on his way. With others he may not have been so fortunate." She looked around. "People are leaving—it is the proper hour, so I must also leave. Farewell, we will meet again on the road."

Charles came up and thrust a spilling goblet into Guy's hands. "Did y'see that. One more, then I'm off to my blankets."

"Thank you. I might do the same, Charles. Have you seen Jacques?"

"Turned in already. Long day tomorrow, he said."

Not saying much, they stood and watched the mood of the gathering revive until an engaging local woman smiled at Charles and grabbed his arm as she whirled past.

Guy leaned against a stone pillar. He took in the sparkling eyes of the young men and women dancing and the smiles of the older folk. Some of the men approached him, telling in broken Greek of the local history and events celebrated in this feast. A matron of the district seized him for a dance, the crowd smiling good-naturedly at his ungainly attempt. He saw the girl who served breakfast at the inn in the arms of an artisan and Leon Magistros clapping in tune to the dancers, a goblet of wine on the table beside him. His sister, Joaninna was close by, drinking wine, swaying her hips to the music, watching the rhythmic pumping of the life of that small community as it came together.

Time passed and the crowd thinned. Guy left and made his way through the night to where Charles and Jacques were already asleep. Rolling into the folds of his cloak he stared for a time at the canopy of stars and felt the night breeze brush his face.

Sometime later he woke abruptly, conscious he was at some outpost beyond the Euphrates, lying still so any would-be assailant would be unaware of his watchfulness. Somewhere, a woman screamed; and again. No one stirred, so Guy leapt up, pulled on shoes, seized his sword-belt and made for the sound, passing through the dark space between the stables and the row of shops. There he saw two figures struggling in a shaft of moonlight: the merchant, Taronites, dragging his wife by the hair.

Guy dropped his military belt and stepped from the shadows. "Lady, are you all right?" he asked, glaring at the merchant.

Taronites looked around, a pitiless wildness in his eyes. The sobbing woman slumped to the ground as her husband growled through bared teeth, "Mind your own business!"

"You have just made it my business. Lady?" Guy asked as though Taronites was not there.

Maria hurriedly wiped away her tears. "No. It's all right. Thank you. A misunderstanding." She smiled weakly in the moonlight. "My fault."

There was an awkward moment when no one moved.

"I'm all right," Maria reassured him.

Guy still glared at the merchant. "Very good," he said slowly, then retreated into the shadows, retrieved his military belt and retraced his steps.

Reaching his tossed-aside cloak he sat, looking around at the sleeping forms. Unsettling images of the encounter with the merchant and his wife came to mind. Recalling the man's hate-filled countenance, Guy knew he had made another enemy.

Charles, without stirring, drawled from beneath his blanket, "Fire breathing dragon, or some peasant's goblin?"

"Both and neither!" Guy removed his shoes and lay down.

"Well, I hope she's worth it." Charles grinned to the stars.

Guy looked crossly at him but said nothing. His gaze was drawn once more to the night sky, his thoughts to its majesty. He reflected on how much untellable experience was crammed into each day of this life. For all his fears and uncertainties, he was suddenly glad he had not stayed at his ancestral home: better to journey far and perhaps return—one day when there was no need—to the wonder of those who had not ventured.

When not busy with some important or trivial physical task or mental challenge, Guy allowed his thoughts to roam of their own volition to what really perplexed or preoccupied him. He wondered why a glance from the woman in blue, Serena Cephala, and a couple of brief encounters with the merchant's wife had lingered in his thoughts. This troubled Guy, offending his piety. He wondered if he were trivial in affairs of the heart and contrasted his own inner turmoil to Charles' complete lack of concern with such matters. Yet he did not consider Charles a bad person. No one did, for the blonde knight was universally popular.

He lay there thinking for what seemed a short time, until a rough voice shook him. "D'Agiles—your turn to mount guard."

Guy sat up with a start. Looking around, he realised where he was, and that he had slept. Pulling on his byrnie, he rose and taking up his weapons, drowsily followed the nameless Norman to his post.

Guy stood his watch in the main-tower during the two coldest, darkest hours of the night, just before dawn. These posts were double-staggered: two men on for two hours, one changing on the hour. It ensured sentries were alert and there was no treachery, but meant few knew the luxury of adequate sleep.

Leaning against the stonework, Guy peered into the gloom. He had stood guard enough to know how the mind played tricks: if one stared too long at something in the dark, it could seem to assume human form and appear to move. Better to force the stare move on and look back suddenly at any shadow of doubt. For the moment it seemed quiet. With a sigh, he let his head rest for only a moment against the stone merlon.[41]

"Don't go to sleep!" hissed Bessas, from beside him.

Guy felt ashamed. "Do you never sleep?" he whispered.

"Of course. But something woke me." Bessas spoke quietly without looking at him.

Guy felt alarm almost burst through his chest and his fist tighten on the spear. "What?" whispered the other sentry, a local boy who stood close, listening also.

"Don't know," Bessas whispered, helmet under an arm and head cocked to one side. "It went quiet of a sudden, I think. The night does that sometimes."

Bessas was right. It was still: no bird or beast stirred. Even the spaced snoring from some sleeping figures seemed part of a deeper silence.

The accumulated fears of civilization welled almost unbearably in Guy. He swallowed. "Do you hear anything?" His voice felt small and far away.

Bessas listened for a time. "No." There was a pause before he spoke again in a hush. "Nothing, and no dog has barked. If it's men, you will hear a distinct sound, a scabbard or shield against a stone, or a stick breaking on the ground. If it is a horse, a shoe will strike something, they'll crop grass or snort softly to each other. Cattle will get up and rush if disturbed. These are the things to listen for."

Below them the guardroom door opened and a pale shaft of yellow light splashed across the inner courtyard. The commander of the watch would have noted the flame on his time-candle burn down to a marked ring and was now doing his rounds, telling the sentries to change.

Guy's Armenian companion acknowledged the watch commander's head appear at the top of the ladder. He checked that Guy had observed and understood, then left to wake his relief. This turned out to be a local peasant, a pleasant, unshaven boy with a sure knowledge of the valley. The lad spoke a little Latin, his speech laced with unknowing oaths acquired from passing soldiers. He whispered the features of the landscape as the light slowly improved.

Already the decarchs were stirring the sleeping forms with that quiet insistence that bespoke a day's march. As soon as it was light enough to discern trees and the village outside the walls, the mounted picket trotted out to occupy observation posts in the distance. Charles appeared on the ladder, hurriedly offering leftovers for breakfast. Then he left as quickly as he had come to help

---

41 Merlon—the raised part of a battlement between two embrasures or crenelles.

Jacques saddle their mounts. Guy gulped down the cold lamb, fruit, bread and milk, knowing how fast he would need to move when released from his post.

From his stone vantage point, Guy could see the preparations for the march. Byzantine decarchs and Norman sergeants supervised loading the baggage. Heavier horses were backed up to the carts and harnessed by the teamsters, contracted citizens from Karin. There was an ordered bustle, the angry clatter of hooves on cobbles as one of the Sixth Schola's pack mules objected to its lot, the clang of dropped weapon or dull thud as a shield bumped another while the men formed up. At a signal from Bessas, the column moved off in its composite groups. With less to do than the mounted troops, most of the foot were soon tramping off with the lead carts down the slope and wheeling left onto the Manzikert track. Dust rose in thin curls, hanging heavily in the morning air. Guy noticed Serena and her maid cantering in bursts of silken colour to the van to avoid it.

Domnos Taronites was already mounted and waiting with obvious impatience for Maria to saddle up. Guy thought it unusual that no servant had been assigned to prepare her mare. Was it her personal choice, or public slight for private rancour? Guy wondered if her veil was drawn so tightly to hide a bruised face. A cataphract moved to help her as she struggled with her saddle. The trooper then legged her up and as she settled on the horse she leaned forward and briefly touched his bare arm in gratitude while Taronites glowered. With a nod the soldier led his roan off to join his section. Smoothing her light travelling robe, she glanced around as if to see whether her husband had observed the innocent exchange of kindness. Maria's roving gaze noticed Guy watching. She looked at him then bowed her head slightly as she kneed the horse on behind her husband.

With an abrasive yell, Balazun waved Guy down from the tower. Guy needed no urging to skim down the ladder and jog through the gate to where Jacques had already saddled the mule. Impatient and ungainly, the animal pulled against the reins while Guy slung the strap of his water skin over the high pommel, stuffed the cloth-wrapped breakfast leftovers in his saddlebag and tied his cloak behind the cantle.[42] Then with part thrill, part trepidation, he entered the enclosure and caught the snorting Seljuk mare.

Guy arranged the unfamiliar bridle in his hand. It was a simple strap affair with a jointed iron snaffle with long cheek bars to stop the bit pulling sideways through the mouth. Narrow leather reins were joined at the ends with a thin leather lace. He saw the reins had often been knotted about half way along their length and suspected the reason had something to do with the techniques of mounted archery. Slipping the reins around her neck, Guy bridled her as gently as he could. The mare, excited by the activity around her, put her head up and rolled her eyes at his unfamiliar manner. She backed up a couple of steps until her rump touched the rails, took a step forward, then with snorts and suspicion, allowed him to bridle her.

---

42 Cantle—the raised rear of a saddle seat behind the rider.

Holding the reins in one hand, Guy took the Seljuk saddle from a rail. It smelled as old saddles do, of other riders, of the dogs and goats of the black tents and of man-sweat dried on horse-sweat. A simple, robust design it comprised two felt-padded and shaped parallel boards with pommel and cantles of the same timber screwed and glued into place. Rawhide straps from pommel to cantle covered with a thick leather seat, provided support and comfort for the rider. Breastplate and breeching were attached to the wooden frame by sturdy leather thongs laced through holes in the frame. Delicately etched bronze stirrups were attached well forward on the tree by leathers buckled at the bottom, so the rider could simply lean down and alter their length. Guy hesitated before the unfamiliar equipment.

Maniakh, handing his own reins to Jacques, climbed into the enclosure.

Guy watched as the mercenary ran leathery hands over the horse and felt saddle pad, checking for burrs and grass seeds. He then placed the blue felt saddle blanket and saddle on the mare's back. Using a stick to reach under the horse, the scout hooked the end of the braided girth and gently tightened it. He led her around the enclosure once and then tightened the girth a hole. Next, a shaped sheepskin, dusted by banging it firmly against the rails, was laced into place over the seat.

"Good saddle," Maniakh pronounced. "Long sword under leg here," he explained, strapping in place the long sabre the nomads used against people on the ground. "Second quiver here. Cloak here. Food here," he grunted, indicating the saddlebag. Maniakh untied the lace Bryennius had placed around the mare's neck and buckled her light, decorative leather collar in place, slipping it through a keeper attached to the bridle headpiece so the collar would not slip down and impede breathing. The collar had a small bronze plate riveted to it and from that hung a henna-stained tassel in a bronze holder. Smaller bronze plates with etched pastoral scenes decorated the collar. The nomad slipped his hand through the strap and looked at Guy as he tried to explain something obviously important in his accented Greek.

His words were beyond Guy's limited but growing knowledge of the language.

"He says," Simon Vardaheri explained as he approached, "it identifies the owner when horses are grazing in large herds on the steppe. The collar is left on so they can be easily caught. He says to be careful lest strangers ask how you acquired the horse and tassel."

Struck by the kindness, Guy smiled at Maniakh.

"Let's put the collar and tassel on the mule," Jacques said. "That'll fool 'em."

"Leave it where it is." Bessas rode up behind them, taking in the situation at a glance.

Guy shot the centarch an irritated glance for reminding them they were still tantamount to captives, bait in some Roman plan.

"You ride now?" Maniakh asked in halting Greek as he handed the reins to Guy.

Guy took the reins, looking doubtfully as the mare bunched under the saddle.

"She looks rather fiery," Jacques said. "New shoes, a couple of good feeds and a day's rest. She's ready for anything."

"Yeeessss, she is!"

"You might want to lead her for half a day, until she gets used to the new arrangement," Bessas suggested. "There's a long, steady hill a few hours ahead. Mount the mare at the bottom. A tired horse is less inclined to buck, rear, bolt, throw itself down, kick, grab your foot in its teeth or plain refuse to go forward." With the self-assurance that comes from being well mounted, Bessas had cheerfully listed a fraction of the things that could go wrong when mounting a strange horse. "Then again, she may very well just walk quietly away."

"Perhaps I'll lead her awhile," Guy decided, at which Maniakh stepped forward to loop the Seljuk's weapons belt around the cantle, securing it in place with a leather lace.

Guy, mounting the mule, nodded in agreement with Bessas and with thanks to Maniakh. Jacques handed the mare's reins to Guy and they joined the column. He saw the vanguard moving ahead and the screen cantering out beyond them as the Frankish horsemen deployed as flank and rear guards. Two squadrons of the Roman regiment remained standing to horse beneath the castle walls while their squires herded the spare mounts, some four hundred of them, into the rear of the column. Blocked by the carts and marching foot, the herd soon settled into a relaxed, grazing walk, pausing to snatch mouthfuls of the softer valley grass.

Looking back as Arknik receded in the distance, Guy asked Charles, "What are the Greeks doing?"

His companion simply shrugged. Like many Franks, he would ride down a nightmare if one should present itself, but saw fighting as a simple affair. He had little patience for the wisdom of the Byzantine military manuals, even if he could have read them.

Robert Balazun rode by and looked at Guy's horse with interest but without comment. Looking down from his big black warhorse, he answered Guy's question. "The Scholae are going to remain a little behind as rear guard, but will keep us in sight. If we're attacked, we are to circle the carts and hold our ground, stay alive and keep the enemy distracted. Then the Greeks will charge them unexpectedly—surprise!"

Guy did not like the man with his small blue eyes and loud, aggressive manner. He wore his helmet and heavy mail hauberk and his long kite-shaped shield was looped by its shoulder strap over the pommel, so it rested on his left knee to be raised quickly. Balazun gazed around at the steppe and let out a breath. "I need a fight. I haven't had one since I left Rome."

Charles and Guy glanced at each other. They had heard of Balazun's earlier wars: suppressing peasants or fleeing the cataphracts of George Maniakhes after the lost battle of Monopoli where the Byzantine general defeated a Norman invasion of southern Italy. Balazun would have been a young knight of barely twenty-one years and the disaster could scarcely be attributed to him. Nonetheless, his martial prowess was not the stuff of legend.

"Oh well," Charles replied breezily, "you might get your wish yet."

Balazun stared back at Charles, not sure whether he was being insulted. "Anyway, keep a sharp lookout," he ordered, "and don't break from the column unless I command it." With that, he rode to the lead.

"Keen for blood!" said Guy with some distaste as Balazun rode away.

"Hmmm," Charles mused.

"Though he does seem to be trying to learn from the Greeks." Guy's chestnut mare walked on a loose lead at his right knee as he occasionally caressed her forehead and neck He talked to her and fed her titbits to win her confidence.

"As though they have anything to teach!"

Guy did not agree with his friend. This was no sleepy mob plodding along in its own stupor. Both bands moved in self-protected groups, each able to detect and fend off an attack and support the other. The slow-moving carts, colourful civilians and braying pack mules might even invite attack by appearing relatively helpless, but the attackers would then be easily surprised by Bryennius' regiment. There was always attack and defence, pin and hook, hammer and anvil, left and right hands, security and surprise. This wily way of war was different from the Frankish heroic tradition with its legend of Roland and Oliver.

Guy wondered about the chase from which none had yet returned. He remembered Bryennius' emphatic instructions as Togol and David had filled water skins, stuffed dried food into saddlebags and glanced hurriedly at the map. Then the two had galloped into the dead-grass landscape. Where were they now?

The cool air of morning gave way to a light breeze and finally the heat of the midday march when the column halted. Knights dismounted, drank from skins of water and conversed in groups, leaning on their spears, here and there sitting or lying to ease legs stiff from riding. The footmen simply rested their shields on the ground and lay down with their weapons, removed helmets and ran rough fingers through hair damp with perspiration. Salt crystals had formed on shoes where the sweat had soaked through the leather. Teamsters walked the lines of their charges, keeping animals in line, checking the pins and greasing the spoked hubs. Most snatched a morsel from shoulder bags, washed down with water they carried in skins or small jugs. Some of the soldiers joked of sore feet or heavy spears and of what they would be doing now had they married that girl and stayed in the village—as though that mattered anymore. Those few who had wives went to where they had been walking as a group near the rear of the line of carts. Soldiers' women, that hardy and philosophical breed, undertook the little rituals of care and support.

Taronites and his wife dismounted wordlessly near their servants. Maria sat on a bundle taken from one of the carts and sipped water from a goblet handed to her by her maid. Guy saw the maid look in his direction several times and wondered what she knew. Serena Cephala, with her servants, also dismounted and silently joined the quarrelling couple, as if to distract their anger.

Guy and Charles dismounted where Jacques sat uncomplainingly beside his crossbow at the edge of a circle of resting infantrymen. Jacques took the reins of the mule while Guy stroked the muzzle of the chestnut horse. Together they ate their bread and cheese and sipped water in silence.

Bessas approached them leading Diomed and accompanied by his squire. "Well, your new horse seems quiet enough! You could probably ride her when we move on. If not, we start to climb that hill in a league or so."

After an hour, Bessas, signalled "Saddle up!" The column rose to its feet and into order.

Guy decided to ride his mare. Instructing Jacques to mount the mule and carry his sword, byrnie and the bow, Guy removed his spurs and prepared to mount. As he did so, she backed away nervously. Gathering the reins around her neck, he tried again to place his left foot in the stirrup. The unfamiliar Seljuk saddle with its lower pommel felt strange, even before he sat in it. The mare backed away quickly, pulling Guy on his tender feet after her. Half a dozen paces they went thus, until Guy soothed her to a halt. Then, impatient, young and inexperienced, he vaulted to her back as he had done on other horses.

It was a mistake. As soon as Guy hit the saddle, the mare, with that deep ancestral fear of a predator's claws in her back, exploded into the first buck. He did not have time to find his stirrups or shorten the reins. With a grunt she launched into the air, bounding forward, her head between her front legs, back arched like a cat. Then she thudded to the ground with a bone-jarring shock. The wooden pommel hit Guy's groin and he winced in pain, conscious of the great strength of the horse.

In a few moments a circle of onlookers formed. Some cheered, others laughed.

"She thought you were going to kill her," Charles shouted, grinning.

"Stick your spurs int'er, d'Agiles," shouted a knight, doubled over with laughter.

The wiser looked on in concern, for the grave of a horseman is always open. Simon and Joaninna moved quickly to join the circle around this acrobatic display by those ancient companions, man and horse. The chestnut mare, head down and mane flying, spun half a turn and gathered herself for the third buck. Frightened by the people yelling and gesturing, she wheeled again and bounded forward through the third and then two more bucks in rapid succession.

"Hang on, miles[43], a teamster called out, using the Frankish term for a mounted warrior he may have learned from passing bands of mercenaries. "They've only got seven good bucks in them."

Guy felt like he had taken hellfire by the tail. Deep pain seared his groin, his back jarred with every thudding impact and the world spun dizzyingly without focus. He leaned back and pulled as hard as he could on the reins, trying to shorten them and so get the mare's head up. In his blurred vision he could see nothing of her in front of the saddle. Then she sprang forward again and galloped a few paces, glancing off the back of a cart as though intent on scraping off the rider. He felt a searing pain in his right leg. With a squeal of mixed fear and rage,

---

43 Miles—a Frankish term for an armed horseman or knight.

the chestnut half fell away from the cart, regained her balance and ripped into another buck.

As she thudded to the ground this time, Guy came off, slamming into the hard earth, grazing knees and palms and knocking the breath from him. Deeply shamed, he rose as fast as he could and limped after her, as she galloped around looking for a way out of the circle of peculiar-smelling, strange-sounding people.

Michael Taronites was loud in his ridicule. "Some cataphract the nosy Kelt is," he laughed without humour. "Can't even ride his stolen horse."

"Be still. Don't move," Simon Vardaheri said with such authority that the crowd stilled. They held out their arms to make a fence and the mare slowed to a trot, blowing hard, snorting and looking around her with pricked ears and white, staring eyes. Then she stood still, watching suspiciously, as Vardaheri walked to her. The mare sensed something in the man and allowed him take the reins.

"Oh she just got a fright," Simon explained to no-one in particular, but loud enough for everyone to hear. Then to Guy he murmured, "It's sometimes best to mount a strange horse very gently so they get used to the idea. Are you alright to get back on?"

Bessas motioned the crowd away. "Move off. Move off." Taken aback by his unwitting role in the drama, he rode close to them. "Perhaps not that quiet after all, I see. Mount up on that mule there, Jacques, and we'll see if she'll come quietly along with us."

Guy nodded gratefully, appreciative of Simon's intervention and balm to his pride. Overcoming his reluctance for a repeat performance, he took the reins as Simon held the chestnut's head, speaking soothingly to her in a language Guy did not recognise. He mounted quietly and found the off-side stirrup with the toe of his shoe. Simon looked at him. Guy nodded, reins gripped short to prevent them being pulled through his hands again, feet forward to guard against inadvertently goading her flanks or being pitched over her head. Jacques started forward on the mule. Bessas stepped Diomed forward and Simon led the mare by the bridle for her important first few steps with her new rider.

"Just relax," Vardaheri advised.

Guy nodded, concentrating on every bunched, explosive muscle beneath him. Simon let go of the bridle and to Guy's relief, the mare walked nervously but steadily alongside the mule. He felt like he was on a much taller horse, such was her strength and the spring in her step. Guy guided her between Jacques and Bessas. The mare cocked an ear at quiet Diomed, who for a moment turned his head to her in friendly greeting.

"She's right. She has her tail out and is walking along quite well," Bessas encouraged. "Have you named her?"

"I hadn't thought."

"May I suggest Sira?" Bessas said.

"What is Sira?" Guy was beginning to relax as the mare calmed and moved gracefully forward into her swift walk.

"A Persian queen of long ago."

"Si-ra." Guy liked the idea and in his mind's eye imagined a beautiful woman against a backdrop of columns and gardens. "If she hasn't turfed me again by this night, Sira it is."

They rode to a flank of the column as it began to ascend the escarpment Bessas had described. Men leaned into the climb and draught animals shouldered their breastplates and collars. Infantrymen, in unspoken sympathy with the beasts, put shoulders to the sides of the carts to help them.

Guy guided the mare through the long grass at the steepest side of the hill. She lowered her head a little and he could hear her breathing sharpen. As they went up and her breaths became more laboured, he waved his arms, flapped clothing and made strange noises, teaching her not to be startled by sudden events. Half way up the hill he dismounted and mounted again. Two thirds of the way up the slope, he dismounted and girded on his byrnie and sword. He donned his felt hat, mounted from the off-side and trotted the mare up the last gentle grade near the crest.

Jacques beamed. "You're like a knight again, except for that ridiculous hat!"

Guy smiled with renewed confidence. "With fair skin, I'll bear the hat. You're olive complexioned, so you don't have to worry. Anyway, out here, nothing is ridiculous!"

"You're right. Nothing's ridiculous out here."

At the crest, Guy urged the mare into a canter. Her perfect motion bespoke long leagues[44] ridden over steppe and mountain. He liked the Seljuk saddle and worked out how he would tie his cloak at the cantle and how the goatskin of water might be hung from the pommel and fixed with a thong. He realized how much the count and Bessas had become role models with the workmanlike cut of their weapons, accoutrements and tack. More than that, there was in their warlike preparations a studied calmness and knowledge, very different from the quarrelsome Normans.

Above Guy, the blue sky stretched over the low green hills, rolling on to browned-off higher ridges with their drifts of snow in the gullies. Occasional thickets and small groves of birch, oak and poplars dotted the shallow streams and valleys. The tan-grey crags of rugged foothills dipped in places to reveal distant snow-capped blue mountains.

Guy allowed himself a moment of satisfaction. He now was superbly mounted and a mare held the promise of offspring. Young and strong, he could run a mile in armour and swim half that bare. Rare for his class, he could read and write in Latin and had gathered a smattering of Greek. He had no ties aside from his companions and was favoured by a little Byzantine gold in a leather pouch under his byrnie. Being thrown from Sira—for that was her name now—had not noticeably degraded his reputation with the people of the column: indeed if anything human failing and perseverance had enhanced it. He was conscious that he had been drawn so far into his adventure that the deep fears and doubts

---

44 League—old unit of distance of three miles, about the space covered in one hour by a person walking.

seemed to dissipate with each day. Now his world was centred on the column: its armed men, toiling animals, equestriennes on their well-groomed ladies' hacks and knights on their warhorses.

There was another short halt as the rear gained the top of the escarpment and a reconnaissance party trotted off to identify the coming night's campsite. The guides spoke of a temporary camp ahead often used by Roman troops and hence already partly fortified with a ditch and berm.[45] Commanded by a Roman centarch, the reconnaissance would select, mark out and picket the camp, then guide the various elements of the column to their assigned places.

Guy looked back for any sign of the count's regiment, scanning the landscape to no avail. Then he saw them on a distant slope, spaced irregularly like grazing cattle. If he had not known they were there, he might not have seen them. A closer scrutiny betrayed the occasional glint from an uncovered helmet or spear point. Sombrely, Guy reflected on what he might miss, in war or life, because he did not already know something was there. He had gained a valuable horse cheaply, perhaps, but what would be the true cost?

---

45 Berm—embankment of soil excavated from the ditch.

Chapter Five

The Fountains Of Manzikert

Near Count Bryennius' camp,
Late afternoon, 22nd May 1054

Leo Bryennius watched from a rise as the first elements of the column occupied the campsite laid out by the guides. Sited on a low hill close to a running stream with a few trees inside the perimeter providing shade and some concealment, the place had obviously been occupied by previous marching columns and chosen so no nearby grove or thicket could conceal enemies. Norman horsemen screened to the east as carts and wagons were guided into a rough square where the teams were unhitched and teams of men started repairing the protective surrounding ditch and berm inside it. Others filled water containers or grazed and watered the animals. There were too many spare horses to allow loose inside the small camp so most were hobbled and sidelined, then grazed under a strong guard nearby. When the semblance of a defendable camp was made, the screen was withdrawn and replaced by a closer mounted picket. As they withdrew past the sentries, the knights tossed the reins to their servants and retired to their baggage. In the mild weather, only Robert Balazun and the wealthier citizens had their servants pitch their tents.

In the soft light of early evening, Leo led his regiment into the camp through one of the four entrances. They off-saddled in the centre, where their squires had already hobbled the spare horses along picket lines. The squires took the late arrivals out to be similarly fed and watered and saw to the unloading of pack mules. Before dark, the mounted picket was withdrawn and sentries posted on foot around the perimeter. One troop of cataphracts saddled and knee-hobbled their mounts in case of emergency, the men eating and sleeping with the reins in their hands.

The camp stood-to just before dark and Leo did his rounds with Bessas and Balazun. First they toured the perimeter, ensuring the sergeants of foot had properly prepared their fronts and were ready to receive an attack: sentries posted, spearmen in the foremost rank to form a shield-wall on the berm, with archers behind them. The knights and cataphracts in the centre were to support any part of the perimeter. Leo hid his impatience. Unlike a practiced army on the march with its engineers and baggage train, this column was too slow and noisy as raw troops and accompanying citizens searched for their kit and sought a place to sit and eat their cold evening meal.

It grew dark and the word was passed to stand-down into night-routine. All were tired and most slept who were not detailed as sentries or to work-parties. A few lounged in small groups and talked quietly. Leo permitted one small fire, such as a group of travelling citizens might have, to enable his missing scouts to locate them in the dark. The camp quietened as the moon rose.

Bessas approached and stood by the fire next to Leo, scorch marks of campfires past marking their bootlegs. "Count, have you ever been in a camp attacked by barbarians at night?"

"Yes. And I was once in a camp that thought it had been, and that was bad enough." They were silent for a moment, each after their fashion taking in the night, the stillness of the firelit camp and the soft breeze. "I'd hoped David and Togol would be back by now."

"They may've stopped for the dark part of the night."

"Perhaps. Bessas, you told me this morning you were suspicious of that outspoken Armenian at the feast last night, yet let him go."

"Gurgen? He was drunk."

"Which might explain his passion, but not his presence at Arknik?"

"He claims to be from Archēsh and that he travelled to Karin to visit his sister …" Bessas seemed less certain.

"Which puts him within reach of where we contacted the Seljuk patrol."

"True! He said he was told that she—his sister—was ill. The horseshoes that aroused my suspicions are the work of a blacksmith from the city of Her, who now has a shop in Archēsh. So he says."

"How convenient!" Leo snorted. "Kurdish Her is now under Seljuk suzerainty. And it's not far from the border town of Salamast, half a day's ride I'm told. Did Gurgen see Guy's new horse?"

"Not that I've seen, or heard. But he did speak, very briefly with Zakharian at the festival."

"Yes, so I saw. It isn't surprising that they'd know each other. Zakharian watched us bury the Seljuk scout in his yards. I do not know how much he saw or if he knows who it was, but he linked the corpse with d'Agiles' horse."

"Lucky d'Agiles," Bessas said grimly.

"The falcons?" Leo asked.

"Sport and game for the journey. Gurgen also said he sells a few pairs," Bessas answered. "Y'know, I watched them, Gurgen and his man, exercise the birds this morning. Quite interesting. They walked down past the cattle enclosures with the birds in hand. One cast off one, then the other. The first bird rose very quickly, the other circling underneath it. They flew far away until they were specks, then returned and swept in low around the handlers. Gurgen's bird came to rest on his glove where he replaced its hood. The other must have been a younger bird, more wilful, or less confident in its handler, for it alighted on the ground a spear's length from them and waited for the glove to be offered."

"What of his man?" Leo asked.

"Ananias? Just that, Gurgen says," said Bessas. "I've heard no different from anyone."

"Gurgen decided not to accompany us?"

"He thought it unwise after his outburst. And he thought he would travel more rapidly cross country by paths he knows."

"That wouldn't be hard," said Leo.

"We couldn't kill him," Bessas joked. "That would be un-Christian, and if we chained up every Armenian yokel who damned our empire, the fleet would want for anchor cables."

"I know enough Christians who are quick to kill, but you're right. At least we're aware of him. We should be at Manzikert in a day's march, so any Seljuk raiders he was reporting to would need to move quickly to catch us in the open. We could've left him in a dungeon at Arknik for a couple days, but it would've made a poor impression on the locals, and him if he's innocent. And we didn't really know much about that landlord. That's the problem when you are strangers in the land."

"Speaking of strangers," Bessas said. "There were two others at Arknik that the locals did not know—an Armenian, a soldier by his look, accompanied by a handy sort of woman with him, perhaps his wife for she wore a ring. Some thought they were just a travelling couple. They left well before us this morning."

"Which way did they go?"

"The sentries reported they rode off towards Karin, but they could have circled back."

"True," Leo observed. Thinking back on events at Arknik, he remembered a woman in a red dress listening intently and watching him closely during his intercession between Zakarian and Gurgen. There had been some presence about her and despite the immediacy of the disturbance with Gurgen, she found a niche in his reflections. "People come and go I suppose."

"Perhaps," Bessas replied before falling silent.

"Speaking of secrets and handy women," Leo said with a glance at his companion. "You seemed to be getting along with Mistress Cephalus last night."

"Yes," replied Bessas with a glance back. "We have hardly met, but I rather like her."

"Good," Leo said after a thoughtful silence. "Seems a very fine young woman and rides well. Light hands on the bridle rein can tell you something of a person."

"Yes," Bessas mused.

"I am going to turn in," Leo said. "You might do the same."

"Should I wake you if the scouts return?"

"Yes. Do, please."

"If they haven't by daybreak?"

"Then we will wait here a day and give them a chance to catch up."

"What will we tell the worthy citizens who are keen to get behind stone walls?"

"Tell them the truth—that we remain here on good grazing in a secure camp while we wait for one of our detachments to catch up."

The following day the animals filled their bellies as Leo paced the camp and rode the surrounds, between reading snatches of Dictys' Diary of the Trojan War while reclining against his saddle. Reflecting on the book's treatment of the effect of war on the character and fortunes of people, he read aloud, "When we were sated with Trojan blood, and the city was burned to the ground, we divided the booty, in payment of our military service, beginning with the captive women and children."

"I beg your pardon?" asked his squire, looking up.

"I said, what price Manzikert," murmured Leo, at which he rose and scanned the horizon, chafing at the delay, worried for his missing men and longing for certainty in this journey.

The lost patrol did not return that day so the column passed a second night under arms on the steppe.

Just after sunrise, six horsemen entered the camp amidst the preparations for the day's march. Togol rode Speedy a long bowshot in advance. David Varaz led a saddled but riderless dun Turkman gelding. With them were the three cataphracts who had pursued the escapee from the skirmish. One led a seventh horse bearing a bound and blindfolded stranger.

Leo walked over and looked up at the Togol's gaunt face. "Well done, my friend!"

The Cuman swung gracefully from the saddle as the first elements of the column stepped off on the Manzikert track. "Mighty old horse, Speedy!" Togol dropped his belt of weapons to the ground and stretched. "I've got a damned stiff neck from turning round waiting for t'others all the time!"

Stroking Speedy's forehead, Leo greeted the horse. "Hello, Old Man. You didn't let them get away, did you?" Speedy stood in his acrid smell, saddle hot and saddlecloth plastered with sweat and hair. They had walked since first light so the bay horse had cooled, but caked-sweat and dried grey rivulets plastered down his legs told the temper of the pursuit. Leo noticed the shoes had been all but worn off on the hard ground but Speedy seemed not the least distressed. He looked around in his calm, head-down manner, ears half-pricked at his familiar fellows in the lines and waited patiently to be unsaddled.

Togol with a sweep of long fair hair eased his saddle from the horse's back and threw the empty water skin to Leo's squire to fill.

David Varez, stiff-kneed, joined the little group around the dying fire.

The cataphracts drew up and unsaddled their tired mounts as their squires came running. Two horses were trembling with exhaustion and wet with a heat-sweat that had not dried with the hours of walking they had done. A cataphract's roan mare sank with a groan and made to lie down. Her rider and nearby squires rushed to stop her, get her to her feet, to be led around, properly cooled, groomed, watered and fed a little.

The soldiers stood like chessmen of iron and leather and watched: practiced eyes taking in the unspoken language of horses and the evidence of the chase. Leo turned to his squire. "Taticus, please organise breakfast for these men and care for their horse. As soon as you can, commensurate with other attention to them, have them stand up to their knees in that cold stream—will do them good. And have a change of mounts brought up. Thank you."

The Arab was pulled from his horse and pushed to his knees at Leo's feet. "Give him a little water," he ordered.

Maniakh walked over to them and good-naturedly chided the Georgian "Took you long enough!"

"You forgot to tell the Arab's horse to wait for us, by God." David answered in the Turkic tongue. "Otherwise we would've been back days ago, without chasing him all over the country." David looked at Leo and changed to fluent, if uncultured, Greek. "He had a real good horse, but nothing on Speedy. Togol and bay Speedy just rode him down over a day, a night and into the next morning. The Arab stood no chance. He had no bow, only a spear—so Togol lassoed him out of the saddle."

As the column's baggage train with its guard of mounted Normans moved off, the cataphracts dispersed in small groups outside the ditch waiting for the word to move. Leo listened to the scouts as in their manly ways they tried to be matter-of-fact about their experience. As the tale progressed over breakfast, the difficulties they overcame emerged: lost tracks and fear of ambush in the night, the Arab in desperation jumping his horse off a high cliff into a river and Togol, not daring the leap, plunging down a nearby slope to cut the Arab's tracks where they left the water. A cataphract related the exhilaration of the capture, the terrified Arab wrenched from his horse, Togol towering above him, spear aloft, demanding submission.

David told how the prisoner had been unable to take his eyes from Togol and Speedy, until they had blindfolded him with his own black turban. His worn boots scraping on the gravel, David stood before the kneeling captive who shrank back, his mouth clenched in a grimace of resolve. "He's the handsomest boy in all of Arabia though."

"Togol gets the black mare," Leo said. "How did you catch the dun, David?"

"It is the horse that galloped free from the contact."

"I know."

"She baulked at the cliff," David explained. "Had nowhere to run so we lassoed her. Good horse—I've been riding it to rest mine."

"So it belongs to the dead Arab? Keep it."

David nodded. "Thank you, Count," he said, removing his cap and running dirty nails through his hair. "Saves me stealing one!"

"Has the prisoner seen it?" asked Leo.

"No," said Togol.

"What else have you got?"

"A marked goatskin map," David answered. "Some gold, parchment, quills and ink in the saddlebag. Nothing written except a name stamped onto the saddle, the same etched into the sword."

Leo studied the map and nodded to Bessas who instructed some nearby troopers to hold their shields around the captive so he would be unable to see around when the blindfold was removed. Bessas stood with his back to the morning sun. Togol removed the blindfold and the Arab winced and squinted in the light. Togol dropped the turban: the Arab's gaze lingering on it for just a moment.

"You are a prisoner of the Roman Army. What is your name?" Bessas demanded in crisp, unsympathetic Arabic.

The prisoner was silent, insolent, barely bearded and as handsome as his mother must have been beautiful.

"You've been caught spying," Bessas stated flatly, "inside the Roman Empire. There is no help for you."

The Arab looked back in silence, attempting by some mistake on the part of his interrogator, to determine the fate of his companions and chances of his own survival or rescue.

Togol moved menacingly to Bessas' side and glared down. The Arab's eyes widened.

Bessas took in his clothing and well-made boots: the dress of the frontier, which might equally have been worn by Christian or Muslim countrymen. He continued conversationally, "You are going to the dungeons. You're obviously rich and someone will wish to ransom you. But we must know your name to spread the word, so your mother …"

The Arab's eyes flickered, then he looked down.

"… knows where to find you."

The prisoner was silent.

Bessas let it drag out. "It is mothers who provide the ransoms you know. Their love is unconditional. But the nomads who sent you here have no such care."

The prisoner continued to stare at the ground.

"It would be useful—and in your own best interests—to know your name," Bessas said, as if it was of no real consequence to him, "so we can spread the word you are alive. Otherwise, your relatives will believe you dead and leave you to your fate." He paused. "A man can be a long time in a dungeon, his life seeping away while he scratches on the stone walls with his fingernails." Bessas waited through the long silence.

"I am Zobeir al-Adin."

"What were you doing, Zobeir al-Adin, sneaking around on Roman lands?"

"Not Roman lands! Arab lands until we drew back and they became Armenian borderlands. Then you Romans invaded."

"Hardly Arab lands! Armenian. Christian lands. The Armenians and Romans have always been close."

"Arab lands of the faithful. We built the fortress of Manzikert ..."

"Manzikert? I doubt that. Word is, it has been a settled place for a very long time."

Zobeir al-Adin fell silent. At length he asked, "Where're my companions?"

There was a long pause before Bessas said, "I ask the questions."

The Arab was silent and looked at the ground again.

"I'll tell you this much," Bessas said, staring hard at him. "By sundown you'll be thrown in the dungeon of an impregnable fortress. The word might be spread that you have deserted to us, for it is known we pay very well. If you ever got out, you would be an outcast with a price on your head. On the other hand, should you prove, shall we say, co-operative, we'll see what can be done. We've no fight with the caliphates, provided they stay on their side of the frontiers. Think hard on it—this is no friendly polo match."

Taticus Phocas brought some food and water for the prisoner, placing it in front of the kneeling youth. Zobeir al-Adin looked hungrily but doubtfully at it.

"Why bother poisoning you if we simply wished to kill you?" Bessas shrugged.

Leo, who had been standing back a little, walked over and picked Zobeir's black turban from the ground, the Arab furtively following his every move. Motioning Taticus Phocas to pour water over it until the material was soaked, Leo turned and held the turban at arm's length to the sun. As he suspected, the procedure revealed Arabic script, black lettering on black cloth and only visible when wet—secret writing.

Leo glared at the visibly wilting Zobeir, "He has a shy hand, it seems. Translate it."

Bessas held the turban to the light. "Scouting notes, by the look: garrison strengths and locations, roads, bridges, mood of the people, conditions in the land. Not the sort of thing the average incidental traveller or merchant would secretly record."

"As I thought," said Bryennius. "Translate it in full later. We seem to have three horses and three men out of that lot. I wonder if that was all of them, and whether any will come looking for them?"

Zobeir was staring at the ground in front of him.

"He was interested in Manzikert," said Bessas.

Togol spoke through a mouthful of food. "He'll be even more interested now."

Leo grinned without humour. "Bessas, as soon as the Arab's had a little to eat and drink, get him mounted on a mule and up to the column. Chain him on a cart and contrive to have d'Agiles ride by on the chestnut mare he captured to see if Zobeir recognises it. After he starts, let him go for a while, then get Togol to lead the other Arab's horse past. See if that elicits a response. Did you notice the reaction when you mentioned his mother?"

Bessas glanced at Leo. "I did."

North-west of Manzikert,
24th May 1054

It was the mid-morning of a lovely day. A pleasant breeze played with manes and tails, bearing the dust away from the line of march. Guy and Charles rode on the flank of the column, Jacques accompanying them on the mule.

Jacques had changed since they left Constantinople and it struck Guy how little he really knew about his companion. Some fire, hitherto unobserved by Guy, seemed to have come to life within the servant. The weight had fallen off him and he had developed a ruddy, tanned complexion together with an easy confidence and commanding presence. Guy suspected that his years missing from the village had not been spent cloistered in a monastery.

Guy removed his felt hat and could feel the coolness in his hair. He ran his fingers through the unfamiliar scrub and felt the itchy sensation of sweat and body oil.

Charles did the same in unconscious imitation. "I'm looking forward to a bath. I got used to it in Phanar—a bath and clean clothes. I rather miss Cons ..." His voice trailed off.

Guy rubbed his stubbled jaw. "We look like pigs, brigands or such."

"Where will we live in Manzikert, d'you suppose?" Charles wondered aloud as he urged his horse to keep up with Guy's mare.

"Billeted with some hapless family who can't understand our language. The stables? A storehouse? Tents even? The troops already there will have the best accommodation. And horses the same." Guy had been wondering himself about these small but consequential aspects of their future home. Thus they passed the time.

Guy had observed as they broke camp that morning, a group trot up from the rear with a blindfolded, bound figure who was pulled from his horse rather roughly, briefly questioned fed a little then blindfolded again and chained on one of the carts. Guy wondered about this little drama. Rumour had it Togol and George had captured the fugitive from the skirmish. Later, Guy watched with interest as David rode to the captive's side and leaning over, pulled down the blindfold.

Togol, leading horses captured from the Seljuk party, appeared from behind him. "Guy, you come," Togol motioned with his broken Greek. "We liven up Arab.

See what he makes of us riding his damn Saracen horses." The scout seemed bemused by what he was about to do.

Togol and Guy drew closer to the track and urged their horses into a faster walk to overtake the cart. As they drew abreast of the captive Guy watched the Arab look closely at the captured horses, angry comprehension in his eyes. The Arab's stare rose to meet Guy's. Then he spoke in a language Guy did not understand. He looked inquisitively at Togol.

"He wants to know where the owners are? Don't tell."

Guy favoured Zobeir with a superior shrug. "Does it matter?" he asked in Latin, thinking the other would be unlikely to understand.

Zobeir returned a hateful stare, speaking angrily in Arabic. Guy did not comprehend the language, but discerned the intent of the look well enough.

Togol laughed dismissively and interpreted. "He said, enjoy the mare while you can, Frank. You won't for much longer."

The Cuman laughed but the Arab had spoken with such vehemence that Guy wondered at the truth of it.

Zobeir lapsed into a sullen silence. Nothing more was to be gained, so David slipped languidly from his horse onto the cart behind the Arab and retied the blindfold as Guy rode off to report the exchange to Bessas.

In the mid-afternoon the column halted on high ground. Sitting on a grassy verge with Charles and Jacques, Guy saw Bryennius, riding Zarrar, approach from the rear at a slow trot. Some way behind him the regiment halted in low ground. Bryennius joined Balazun with Bessas and the scouts at the head of the column. They dismounted and led their horses to the highest part of the crest, where they conferred. Bryennius then glanced at the prisoner, looked over the column and rode back, nodding to Guy as he passed.

Real leaders are different from the others, Guy thought. When ordinary people rest, they are constantly moving, checking, thinking. He wondered what force drove them: higher duty or maniacal ambition. Watching Bessas, still on the crest and looking beyond it with evident concentration, Guy asked Charles, "What wells sustain them?"

Charles looked up blankly. "What are you talking about, Guy?"

He clambered to his feet. "I'm going to have a look around." Leading Sira, he made his way to the crest. Jacques rose and pulled the mule with them.

It was warm now and a blue haze shimmered in the distance. The ground, Guy observed, was quite open and fell away gradually to a distant shallow valley where sunlight gleamed on a river or stream. Some twenty miles beyond and dominating the scene, was the massive snow-crested bulk of Mount Sippane. Far to the northeast, other snow-covered peaks could be seen on the horizon. Becoming aware that his gaze was darting all over the scene, Guy recalled Togol's advice: take in everything, closest first because that holds the nearest danger, then the middle ground and finally the distance. Study the ground from right to left, the opposite way from which you read, that way the habitual stare in straight lines of literate people will be less likely to miss things.

Guy looked more deliberately at the scene. "Jacques, shepherds," he nudged, pointing a short distance to their left where a rudimentary hut stood in a hollow with men, dogs and a flock of sheep nearby. He followed the track with his gaze, taking in more houses, sheep and goats. Some were substantial dwellings with stone walls—the houses of the wealthier landholders of the district.

In the middle distance was the river valley, which wound from Guy's left or northeast, to his right, the southwest. He could make out the green of trees following its course and the patchwork of cultivation along the valley. "It looks rather cool and peaceful," he said to Jacques.

"It has the look of prosperity," the other agreed. "Inviting and easy. I daresay that is how the Saracens would perceive it. Another valley seems to split off from the main one and go ..."

Guy looked at the sun and their shadows. "South?"

"I see the walls," Jacques cried. "We've arrived. The fortress! Manzikert. See! Beyond the village, in the trees."

Guy looked and could only make out the dim outlines of tiny dark shapes amongst the foliage in the distant valley floor, before picking out the dark outline of the citadel and forward of that, the circuit walls. "I see it," Guy said, a hush in his voice as they stared in silence at the place they had both longed and feared to reach.

"Well," said Jacques, "It looks peaceful at least."

"How'd you know?"

"No smoke plumes. The blue haze of peace is different from the black plumes of war," Jacques mused distantly as Guy looked sharply at him.

They returned to the column as Guy reflected that, through the morning's ride he had missed the evidence of their approach to a city. The road had been better marked by use, and had secondary tracks leading from it to other towns or villages. There had been dwellings, wells, and copses of tended trees with domestic animals and shepherds looking on from distant hillsides. Now he watched carefully as a party of horsemen assembled around Bessas. He recognised the column's quartermaster and reasoned they were an advance liaison party that would ride ahead to inform the garrison of their approach.

The main body of the column consolidated under Count Bryennius and people became excited with the expectation of their journey's end. Soldiers and citizens craned their necks to see if they knew any of the advance party. Their expressions betrayed envy in which they imagined their companions soaking up the luxuries of Manzikert while they still toiled along the last miles of the track.

Balazun rode up. "D'Agiles. Bertrum. Go with those Greeks. Make sure they don't rob us or end up lodging us with the hogs. And make sure I get the best quarters in the citadel—and the best looking whore." He laughed amicably into his stubble.

Charles chuckled and grinned at Guy as they rode to Bessas who departed with forty men including Roman and Frankish officers, a dozen cataphracts, as many mounted Normans and the servants of the wealthy. They entered the wide, shallow valley of the Arsanias River, crossing the stream by an arched stone bridge. The water beneath, clear and swift-flowing with spring's flushing by melting snow, looked to be between knee and girth deep where the bridge stood: perhaps a horse's wither in depth either side of it. The valley floor was densely cultivated and the little wooden and stone houses were closer together. The road was better formed here and small herds of horses, cattle, sheep and goats grazed in rudely fenced fields, or under the care of shepherds outside the enclosed areas. Birch, oak, maple and poplar trees grew more thickly ahead and as they approached the main village, Guy could now see the stone walls of the fortress with the imperial standard flying above the highest tower of the citadel.

Guy was exhilarated. As Sira walked well he had no need to continually push her on, as many others had to with their horses. The mare's energy and confidence were infectious and he was conscious of being richer in many ways for catching her. Breathing in deeply, he beheld the valley and its sights and scents with a young man's romance and enthusiasm.

David had visited Manzikert several times. "There's a town outside the fortress, but the main part of the city is enclosed within the circuit walls. That's where the rich live, though there are the lesser houses of merchants and a poor quarter as well. Many of the landowners have town-houses as well as their estates, while the poor generally live in the villages outside the walls. In dangerous times, by God, they take shelter inside as they can, or flee to the hills."

"How often does that happen?" Charles broke in.

"Not often," David continued. "Though Manzikert has been attacked before, it's a powerful fortress and difficult for nomads to capture unless carried by surprise. That is how the Seljuks …"

The Georgian scout, Guy noticed, correctly described the Seljuks rather than using the generic "Saracens" as many did.

David paused and looked at him with a raised eyebrow.

Guy recovered. He would not want to cross David. "My horse made me smile," he lied. "Please go on. I am interested," he said truthfully.

David regarded him for a moment through dark, expressionless eyes before continuing. "That's how they captured Kars—three day's ride north of here—last January. With stout walls and a citadel on a steep prominence, it was untroubled for many years and grew rich with trade from land and sea. During the Festival of the Revelation of Our Lord, the priests and people were celebrating mass in the cathedrals when the infidels attacked. The city was without a night watch, so they just rode in and put swords to work."

The power of a Seljuk surprise attack struck Guy as a point to remember.

David was silent for a moment, his gaze lost in his horse's mane. "The bloodshed was terrible. Some citizens escaped to the citadel before the gates were barred. The old, most of the men and babes were killed out of hand and the beautiful women raped then borne away over the saddlebows of the conquerors. For the remainder of that night and the day that followed, they ransacked Kars, then taking their captives and plunder they set fire to the city and left for their own lands."

"What happens to Christian soldiers if they are captured?" asked Guy, his gaze on the walls where destiny had carried him. As he drew nearer to the weathered black stone, Guy felt a sense of reassurance, of entering a place of refuge and comfort—the end of the journey and the beginning of something else.

"Ask Vardaheri. He was captured by the Arabs at the disaster by Azaz fortress, near Aleppo, twenty-four years ago. The Roman army was defeated and ran—that Emperor's fault. Vardaheri was one of the lucky ones, if you call it that, being captured and enslaved. Some are beheaded—those they consider dangerous or wish to make an example of. A few might be ransomed. Most become slaves. You aren't a leader, nor have rich relatives who would ransom you—your fates, by God, would be death or enslavement."

'Don't try and cheer us up,' Charles laughed.

Guy pondered David's words and a deep fear of infidels boiling out of the dark played at the edges of his consciousness. He recalled Bessas' restless checking of the pickets at Arknik and Bryennius, that early morning, already awake in the pre-dawn cold. Recalling this, he resolved to be like them and never taken by surprise.

"How did Simon Vardaheri escape?"

"Saved his life by seeming to adopt Islam, joined the Abbasid cavalry in Baghdad and was then caught by the nomads on the caliphate's eastern frontier. He escaped from the Seljuks in Samarqand and ran away, some say with a slave woman, some rich fellow's concubine, far to the east where her home was in an empire behind great walls. Their pursuers tracked them and caught them when they were almost safe—seized her and thought they killed him—bound him helpless on the bare back of an unbroken horse and set him loose on the steppe. God alone knows how Vardaheri lived. Savage nomads found him, cared for him and gave him the horse. He eventually followed his tormentors back to Samakand, killed his love's master and burned down his house, but couldn't find the woman. He returned to the Christian lands eventually."

"Vardaheri," Guy wondered aloud, thinking with renewed respect of the unassuming horse-trader. "Isn't that wall a fable?"

"He said there were many intersecting walls. Ask him yourself, but you will need to get him to drink a lot of red wine first."

"Did he renounce Islam?" Charles asked.

"You can ask him that as well," David laughed.

The advance party from the column passed through the town with its little houses and shops. People, mostly in the working dress of peasants, stopped in their everyday affairs to watch the cavalcade. A crowd of noisy children followed, some riding hobbyhorses and playing at soldiers. Local people called out, asking where they were from and what news they had.

Guy searched the crowd for familiar faces, but saw none. "No sign of Swordleader," he said to Charles.

"I never got a glimpse of him. He could be anywhere. I never knew the world was so big."

The party reached the main western gate of the fortress and were granted admission to the gate courtyard where Bessas spoke to the guard commander, a Norman sergeant-at-arms. Frankish foot lounged on stone benches by a small fountain in the shade of a plane tree. Some of these, recognising their countrymen in the mounted party, walked over to exchange news and greetings. From them it was learned that the surrounding area had been quiet although there had been rumours of Seljuk scouting parties and many of the local people were uneasy.

The advance party dismounted and Guy led Sira to a water trough where the mare drank before the sergeant-at-arms led them into the fortress. The fortress city was more spacious than Guy had imagined, with gardens and fountains interspersed amongst areas of dense housing and fields, where troops drilled and livestock would be held during an emergency. The fields were mostly empty now to save the grass.

Leading Sira, Guy overheard Bessas and the sergeant discussing the important minutiae of military life: who would be housed where, how many troops, who commanded the fortress. The sergeant did not know all the answers, but was happy to pass on his own observations. They loitered with their bored horses outside the stone building that housed the garrison quartermaster, while Byzantine officials finalised the details of where troops and animals would stay. The flies found them. Bessas emerged occasionally to inform them of what was happening while officials and soldiers came and went. Passing locals stared briefly at the newcomers as they went about their business. Guy noticed there were more veiled women here than in Constantinople and grinned to himself as he recalled the many occasions when Greeks had counselled him that cities were fonts of evil. The Manzikert citizens, he could tell, were accustomed to seeing the soldiers of the Roman Empire and a few more Frankish troops were not unusual.

Eventually an Armenian minor official came and led Guy and Charles to where several long stone buildings were arranged around a courtyard. The newly arrived Frankish knights were to crowd into one building. Guy noted the route there from the main gate in case he had to lead the column in. They tied their horses to hitching rails and entered their quarters. He asked the guide who occupied the nearest stone barracks.

"More Kelts. And Norsemen, Varangians," the man explained.

"Varangians?" Guy blurted. "What are Varangians doing out here?" He remembered the Varangians of Baberd and made a mental note to avoid their drinking places. "They're a long way from the sea?"

"They're not the palace guard unit," the guide explained, "but men from the Varangian lands. Wine bags, some call them—war bands brigaded together to fit into the Roman Army. These came out with the imperial forces after Artsn. Some stayed. Others came after them. Many went back last year to fight the Patzinaks."

Guy and Charles roped off rooms for the knights and occupied a small room at the end of a barrack block for themselves, marking it by stowing their saddles and other gear there. They claimed another room for Balazun, making sure it was some distance from their own. In the mid-afternoon they led their horses to the stables and secured covered stalls so their mounts could move around rather than be tied up for long periods. Guy noticed Taticus Phocas, roping off similar stalls and some enclosures outside the buildings, undoubtedly for Count Bryennius' horses and pack mule.

Moving in occupied some hours: searching for water pails, feed bins, fodder and wells required time and information. Children arrived as the advance party set up for their comrades and themselves. At first the youngsters watched shyly from a distance but as they understood the Greek of the soldiers, or the Frankish attempt at it, they came closer and for a copper *nummi*[46] would industriously tend horses or haul feed and water. All the while, they quizzed the soldiers about their far-away lands and boasted how they would one day travel there.

As afternoon turned to a perfect evening, Guy and Charles bet on the toss of a coin. Guy lost. Charles headed for a bath while Guy set off through the unfamiliar environs of the city to meet the column. His blisters were healing so he enjoyed the stroll. He turned into the tree-lined, paved avenue and noticed a bridle path alongside it, part of a larger track system inside the walls.

It was then he saw, in the light slanting through the trees, a woman cantering a proud black horse gracefully towards him. Breath-taken, Guy was suddenly ashamed of his cheap, travel-stained clothes, unfashionable hat and worn shoes, while the city and its comings and goings seemed far away and hushed. As she drew closer he discerned the loveliness of the rider and the high breeding of her Arabian stallion in his trapping and tassels. Unveiled, an ornately patterned silk *keffiyeh* trailing down her back, she rode astride wearing a rich blue riding tunic visible beneath a light red and gold patterned mantle through which the sunset gleamed golden. With polished tips of leg-fitting black boots neatly placed in bronze stirrups from the steppes and fine gloved hands light on the bridle reins, the beauty passed as if a dream to the sounds of equus breath and hoof beats on the tanbark. Neither horse nor rider so much as glanced at Guy as they passed.

He forced himself not to look back for a long while. She seemed out of place, too perfect for this frontier place, as though it would have been more proper to see such a vision in a Constantinople park, or fabled Babylon. At length he turned and saw the mantle rising and falling with the horse's gait. He let out a breath and watched until they disappeared along the trees on the incline towards the citadel.

---

46 *Nummi*—a Byzantine coin of minor value.

A hand clapped him on the shoulder. Startled, he turned to see the watery eyes and wine-breath of an unkempt local drunk staring into him. "The princeps' daughter, Irene. She's not for the likes of us, lad. Forget her. Buy's a drink with mercenary's gold."

"Be gone!" Guy backed away in alarm.

In pensive silence he reached the main-gate of the western wall and waited there with the other guides for Bryennius and the column to arrive. As they drew up, the marching men smiled a weary, journey's-end greeting and regarded the soldiers of the garrison with curiosity. They asked a thousand questions about the place, mainly concerning their lodgings and where they would eat. Jacques appeared. The peasant had loaded their possessions onto the mule at the last halt, the better to disengage from the inevitable confusion of unpacking the carts in the torchlight and shadows of their first night amongst the fountains and gardens of Manzikert.

The valley of the Arsanias near Manzikert,
Late afternoon, 24th May 1054

As Leo led the column into the bend of the valley of the Arsanias River, he studied the surrounding lava stone country by the softening light. This road was the logical way out if something went wrong. The valley leading to the south, towards the lakeside fortress-city of Khlat' ruled by the Marwanid Kurds, was one of the possible Seljuk approach routes. The bridge and nearby ford across the southward flowing Arsanias River were marked by a copse of trees and mill-house. Downstream the river turned west, followed on the south by the Mush road towards the Marwanid heartland around far-off Amida, and beyond that Roman Melitene. He estimated the likely camping ground of a besieging army would be along the river flats, close to water and grazing. Peasants were hauling in grain and hay and he wondered if the city was taking precautions in the event of a siege or whether this was the routine seasonal harvest.

After crossing the stone bridge, Leo reckoned it a mile and a quarter eastward across the valley floor to the town outside the fortress walls. Half way the road climbed a steep embankment, the height of a mounted man and marked by lava outcrops signifying the furthest extent of the river in full flood. He thought to himself any enemy would have trouble tunnelling through that much rock, unless they find crevices in it. The fortress itself stood further back on a slight rise.

Entering the township at last light, Leo noticed in the midst of his military observations, a candle burning inside one of the crude timber huts. The earthen floor had been swept clean and the tiny flame danced above a silver candlestick on a spotless white tablecloth bespeaking the pride of the poor.

No stone structures stood within ballistae range of the circuit walls and the timber buildings were close enough to be set alight by the defenders, thereby offering neither shelter nor fuel to any attacker. A bridle path for exercising horses seemed to encircle the walls at extreme archery range. This would also enable the garrison to debouch small units in most directions by the many secondary tracks that converged on the city. Leo suppressed a desire to leave the column and canter a lap, to see this place and its approaches from every angle.

On Manzikert's walls depended his mission. On them he might die. They mirrored Constantinople's triple-walls and were designed to extend the range at which the garrison's engines and archers could engage the enemy, keeping their siege engines so far from the walls that they would be ineffective. The first obstacle to an attacker was the ditch, or fosse. Painstakingly cleaned out to a depth of a mounted man and twenty paces broad, it was crossed by a timber bridge. Its moist bottom was cultivated with vegetable gardens where timber dam walls at irregular distances meant the ditch could quickly be flooded to form a moat. Immediately above the steep scarp[47] of the fosse, a breast-high castellated stone wall would protect archers and spearmen who would strive to prevent the enemy either crossing or filling the gap. Next, another twenty paces behind the scarp breastworks, a castellated fore-wall and twin gate-towers loomed in the twilight. He estimated the fore-wall at twenty-five feet high and could discern the shadows of the soldiers thrown by oil lamps or candles, moving behind the loopholes of their shaped stone caverns. The towers, a mix of round and pentagonal-prow type, all jutted forward to allow enfilade engagement along the front of the wall. Guards saluted and allowed the column through the heavy iron gates and under the portcullis.

Surveying these forward western defences as he rode from the outer-gate to the gateway in the main wall, Leo saw with satisfaction that most of the fore-wall towers were of the Roman open-gorge type: without a back to them, so there was no protection against missiles from the main wall, if the attacker should capture the fore-wall. The fore-wall itself was a solid gallery wall—stone-arched and loopholed chambers in the upper levels to protect archers and ballistae-men from incoming darts and arrows—surmounted by a castellated battlement. From these cramped galleries, the defenders could still shoot from under the protection of the stone walkway above them. Spear and bowmen manning the battlement above would have to rely on the merlons[48] for protection from incoming missiles. The largest two towers of the fore-wall, containing the gates and portcullis system, were fully enclosed: a vulnerability, the enemy could defend them if they were captured. These towers contained bolt-shooting ballistae at the loopholes and a stone throwing mangonel on the highest level.

The levelled space between the fore-wall and main wall was some twenty paces wide. Larger, more powerful stone throwers on wooden wheels were positioned here so they could shoot over the fore-wall. Given time and planning, they could be hauled back through the gates or hoisted by chains and levers over the main wall. If not, they could be denied to the enemy by simply burning them. Leo was reassured by the forty foot main wall with six-foot merlons rising above

---

47 Scarp—the inner side of the ditch around a fortification. See diagram p.vii.
48 The higher parts of castellated battlements. See glossary.

that. There were towers, ten feet higher again, staggered so that they covered the intervals between the towers of the fore-wall. The main wall was substantially thicker than the seven feet thick fore-wall. Its iron outer gates opened inwards under the arch of twin towers to reveal a raised portcullis and a gate courtyard with two rear towers, all connected by a high curtain wall to control entry, foil surprise and strengthen the defence.

The column's guides were waiting in the cramped gate-yard with its shade tree, water trough, hitching rails and stone benches around the walls. As Leo rode up, Bessas, standing with two strangers, saluted. Leo wondered if the taller of them was Basil Apocapes, for the man had the habit of command about him. Whoever it was, they had come to meet him.

Bessas undertook the introductions.

One stepped forward. "Count Bryennius? I'm Count Daniel Branas, the strategos' military secretary. We await his return from Khlat' where he's been talking to our Kurdish neighbours. On his behalf, I bid you welcome to Manzikert."

Leo gripped the stranger's hand as Zarrar's stepped forward to sniff him.

Branas rubbed the horse's head. "Oh! You're nice, and very forward too! How d'you do?" While Branas' manner appeared to conform to Byzantine dicta against too much public laughter, his eyes twinkled with humour. He did not wear armour but a sword swung by his leg. "And I introduce Reynaldus, one of our senior Normans."

A stocky, brown-haired and angry-looking knight grimaced a greeting.

"We've been expecting you," Branas continued, "though I do confess we were hoping for more cavalry. We'll not press upon your time tonight. Get your men settled and we can discuss the final arrangements for your quarters and duties in the morning when you meet with the strategos. There is no immediate threat, so your men will be excused military duties allocated by us for seven days. Do you need medical or veterinary support?"

"No, thank you. We are in good shape. Except, we have a prisoner who seeks the hospitality of your dungeon. And we—I—misplaced an imperial courier, Bardas Cydones, who seemingly tired of our company at Baberd. He was to meet a fellow named Kamyates here. Also, two … ahh … others should have arrived some time ago."

Leo noted Reynaldus' sudden interest and the way he moved closer to overhear.

Branas observed the glance at the mercenary and he smiled secretly to Leo. "All's well. A prisoner? One of your own or someone else?"

"A wandering Arab."

Guards opened the inner gates and through them Leo observed the final stronghold, the citadel, on the eastern side of the city.

Branas looked intently at Leo for a second then summoned the sergeant of the guard. "Unlucky for him! Trouble on the road?"

"A Seljuk scouting party," Leo replied. "We killed two and captured a third. I think that was all of them, but cannot be sure. The prisoner has not been properly interrogated yet."

"So it has started." A sombre look crossed Branas' features.

"Yes. I suspect it has. The Arab is technically your prisoner now. But no torture, please. And we need a plan to properly exploit him first."

"A man after my own heart." Branas watched as Zobeir al-Adin was marched to the citadel. "I look forward to his story."

"As one can't keep secrets forever," Leo said, "subject to the strategos' approval, it is probably now safe to let the word out that we have the Arab as prisoner. And three of their horses: one captured alone by a red-headed Kelt who prevented its rider's escape."

"All of Manzikert and beyond will know the secret by tomorrow!"

"I'm grateful, Daniel. You realise I do not command the Kelts now the journey from Karin is over. The strategos there placed them under my command only for the march here. This is Robert Balazun, their leader." Leo beckoned the hook-nosed Norman forward.

Balazun stepped up and gripped Branas' hand. Leo, watching closely, thought the two got along to a good start.

"Robert Balazun. We've heard well of you and regret you were kept so long at Karin. Welcome to Manzikert. I trust it will be a comfortable and enjoyable home for you and your people."

Leo watched Branas look straight at Balazun's eyes as he spoke. Balazun beamed.

"We have some Kelt horse here already," Branas continued, "and we'll link you and your men with them. The foot will be placed under the command of the Count of the City, as defending the walls is the most likely action for them."

As the men discussed the immediate arrangements for the first night, restive horses looked with pricked ears at the unfamiliar sights as they moved to better view these new affairs and surroundings of the world of humans. Balazun's stallion lashed out viciously at a local's donkey which skidded out of the way, as though being kicked at by horses was nothing unusual.

"Missed!" some wag of the guard laughed.

Balazun, pulled off balance, irritably gave the horse a whack with the reins. Sharing the joke, he turned to the man. "He aims better at people!"

There was returned laughter which Branas observed with amused detachment. "Best we get out of here. Go now to your quarters and good night to you. Two of my runners will be with you for the night and will fetch me if needed." Using the pretext business was concluded, he moved aside with Leo. "My billets officer tells me your regiment arrived without orders."

"That is right," admitted Leo, hoping the breach of military procedure was not going to present problems. "I marched here at the, ah, personal suggestion of Cecaumenus. But he gave me no written orders."

Branas whistled under his breath. "It's a long ride without orders. We shall sort it out with the stratego in the morning." Then, fishing, he remarked, "I'll say this, your arrival is interesting! Our little district seems to have become quite popular amongst travellers—unauthorised Scholae, Arab spies, returning diplomats, couriers civil and military, the list goes on."

Leo grinned. "As you say, we shall sort it out in the morning."

The newcomers to Manzikert followed the guides to their quarters. Horses and mules were unsaddled or taken from harness, groomed, watered, fed, watered again and put away for the night. Personal kit from carts was dumped in piles on the ground while men with oil lamps searched the shadows for their own belongings. A late meal had been prepared in the soldiers' mess and men filed though with their spoons, cheap goblets and wooden bowls to take the soup from cauldrons. Servants moved among them, passing out water, wine and more bread. The soldiers felt safe now, behind stout walls and housed in adequate quarters. They drank, talked, wrestled and fell over in boisterous release. Franks and Norsemen from the other barracks wandered in to greet the newcomers and trade news.

Leo, Bessas, Lascaris and the lean, bearded Sebēos, after moving into their quarters and discarding their armour, dined together. Leo gave directions on the administration of the regiment for the following morning. Relieved of responsibility for the Kelts, he could now concentrate on his own men, learn the nature of the fortress and surrounding terrain and solve the riddle of the threat from the Seljuks. Would it be nothing at all this summer, another severe raid, or a far more serious penetration?

Bidding them goodnight, Leo wandered alone through the town, coming at last to the main wall. He climbed the stone steps to the battlements and looked across the silvery valley of the Arsanias. Far above the full moon reflected brilliantly on a bank of high, white cloud: beyond it the star-filled midnight-blue of forever. A hint of warm breeze caressed the oilcloth covers of the engines crowded on the cool stone. He touched a ballista—the working parts slick, silent and deadly on their oiled mountings. Heavy iron bolts were stacked against the embrasure and Leo was reassured by the careful preparations of this far-flung fortress.

He wondered idly what fortune had led him to this place, and what lay in store now. Would the Seljuks come? Would there be fighting? He felt no particular fear. There had been gnawing tension before leaving Constantinople—held in check by the pace of preparations and weight of responsibility. A moment's private nerves on the fourth day of the voyage had been fleeting and all but forgotten. Was the gnawing fear there still? Would it return: sudden and overwhelming like a death stroke, or like disease, putrefying from the inside? He was committed now. All that mattered was doing the job, one foot in front of the other.

He indulged himself in melancholy thoughts of Agatha and the fair woman in Trebizond, wondering if he would hear from the beauty, a note perhaps, if she safe in the comfort of the fortress-harbour, either heard or heeded about what passed in the light brown craggy hills of Vaspurakan.

A soldier has to think someone cares when they ride away.

The distant hum of the late-stayers in the mess carried through the still air. Throughout the rest of the city, there was silence. Here and there, a soft yellow light glowed through a curtained window or open doorway. One showed from an upper level window in the citadel. Leo wondered whether someone was bent at a candle writing, or being romanced by wine and poetry. Perhaps they enacted the rituals of marriage: the ablutions and desultory phrases before retiring.

Leo heard a sound that seemed out of place. A cloaked figure moved along the ramparts towards him. At first he thought it was a sentry and made to greet the man, but the cloaked figure carried no spear and did not pause to look out over the wall or at the city as a sentinel should. Instead, they continued methodically, as though searching for cracks in the stonework where water had weakened the works, or counting the engines and their stocks of stones and darts. Despite the hood covering their head, Leo thought something about the figure seemed familiar. Instinctively, he lowered himself into the shadow behind an engine and held his breath as the cloaked figure passed, sword scabbard scraping on the cover of the ballista.

Leo stepped out behind him, "Halt! Who goes there?"

The figure exclaimed in surprise and turned. "It is only I, Tigran Zakarian."

"What are you doing here?" Leo was equally surprised.

"I come to Manzikert often—have a town house here. Now? Taking the night air, like you. It's a beautiful evening."

"Very good. So it is, but I was just on my way back to get some sleep, so I bid you goodnight."

"Goodnight, Count Bryennius. We must break bread again before long?" Zakarian hurried on his way.

Leo remained in place and looked long at the moon. Did Zakarian's presence mean something or nothing? There was so much to learn of this place and its people.

Manzikert,
Evening, 24th May 1054

Irene Curticius rolled onto an elbow and watched moonbeams flitting with the curtains playing in the breeze through the open window. She had ridden her black stallion, Shahryād, for two hours that afternoon, enjoyed an unhurried massage and bathed luxuriously before dining with friends who nonchalantly discussed the arrival of more troops. Normally, she would have drifted off to sleep and was irritated she could not. Perplexed and vaguely thirsty she sighed, rose and slipping on a robe, took an oil lamp and went downstairs. Entering the pantry she was startled by the gnarled face of the family's Bulgar servant.

"Cook! I didn't expect to see you. What are you doing?"

The woman waved a poker. "It's not that late, dear, and I'm after a mouse that has left little messages."

"It would be a male mouse then." Irene grimaced to her confidant, nurse, lookout and often spy of many years.

The servant grinned. "No doubt. And why're you up? Can I get you something?"

"I came down for some milk. I'm thirsty. I can get it."

The woman took a goblet from the shelf and turned to a timber lined bronze box of packed snow in which a jar of milk was stored.

Irene drank, her roving glance taking in the substantial earthenware urns and jars that contained much of the household's store of foodstuffs. They reminded her how close to the land they all were. "Father has stored enough for years. We could survive the flood."

"The princeps is a prudent man."

Irene looked at the old woman who had been with the family since before she was born. The daughter of a Bulgar prisoner of war, she had been drawn into servitude as well. "It's not fair, Cook."

"What isn't?"

"Well. You a slave and your father before you! When Aaron, a hero of Kapetrou, was the son of a defeated Bulgar king. And the grandson, Theodore Vladislav, now is strategos of Taron, our neighbour."

"Child, you'll learn that life is about wealth and power, opportunity and convenience. Besides, if I were freed, which I've been offered I have to say, where would I go? What would I do for food and a roof?"

Deflated, Irene sat on a bag of barley and lifted her bare feet from the scrubbed stone floor. "But it's still not fair."

"More?"

Irene held out the goblet.

"Why so thirsty?"

"I don't know. I couldn't sleep—even after I went riding today."

"Your first day out in a while?" The old woman knew the answer.

"In five weeks! I've been a prisoner. No wonder he keeps so much food! It was so good to get out of the house. But in a way I felt like a bird when the cage door is opened—reluctant to leave, to go too far." How different the scene at the hut could have been if Theodore Ankhialou had asked for her hand within the hearing of the soldiers. Instead there was just the memory of his parting glance soliciting her to come to Archêsh.

"Your father's worried about you, and about his household's reputation. And it has taken the abbess this long to still the tongues of the city's matrons."

Irene blushed as the cook continued.

"The household is the most important thing in your culture. John Curticius is the head of this household. It all seems to run smoothly enough, but think of the decisions he must make, the sacrifices to keep his career and thus the money coming in."

Irene looked down and pouted. "Everyone sees things differently."

"He's not the only husband who discourages friends from visiting their wives while they're away and locks up his daughter. Perhaps your parents think Theodore Ankhialou isn't the right match for you."

"But we get along. And he's dashing and handsome and … rich."

"So it's said. But rich in what? The cook paused. "If I were you, I'd look for a husband not quite so close to the frontier."

"Why should I? Irene sulked with the vanity of a young woman who knows she does not lack for suitors.

"These're troubled times."

"The Saracens? Theo said he would deal with them if they come as far as Archēsh."

"Bold words, easier to say than do. You were in Constantinople with your mother and her family during their last raids. Here we heard of the terror of Artsn and saw the men leave, and return after Kapetrou, some dead, many wounded. And the time before that when Aaron and Cecaumenus trapped Hasan at Stragna. My friends here remember when Kutlumush defeated Stephen Lichoudes of Archēsh and either—we don't really know—tortured him to death at Her, or sold him as a slave at Tabriz. Is it any wonder your poor mother wants to get you all out of here?"

"She's never said."

"No. She is too good a wife to make a public row of it. Even in the house."

"Is that why father drinks? Is that why he had me learn the bow and took me hunting?" She thought back on the lost days of childhood.

"Only he can answer that."

"Will there be trouble?" Irene wanted the world to be wonderful, to find a mate who would satisfy the empty reaches of her yearning. The last thing she needed were the hoof prints of apocalyptic nomads coursing across her life.

"I don't know, dear. But more soldiers came today. Kelts and Scholae."

Her friends had not mentioned the Tagmata troops. "Scholae. From Constantinople?"

"Only three hundred," the servant said with a twinkle in her eye. "Perhaps you may find a nice young tribune amongst them. Twice that many Kelts."

"Pshtosh! I saw one of your Kelts this evening when I was riding. He did not look very impressive with his worn out shoes and dirty clothes."

"Well one of them, a redhead my friends in the market tell me, killed a Saracen armed with a bow, then captured his horse and brought it in alone across the steppe. And the same Kelt defended a lady being attacked at Arknik."

"Well. It wouldn't have been the Kelt I saw today! What kind of horse?"

"They say a chestnut, an Arabian mare. And if your Kelt today was that feeble you wouldn't have noticed him!"

"I don't like chestnuts—too temperamental. Anyway …" Irene's voice trailed off as she thought back, "He wore a crumpled old hat, like an engineer's."

"No," the servant smiled to herself. "You wouldn't want temperamental."

Chapter Six

Irene

*Manzikert,
Evening, 24th May 1054*

Michael Kamyates led Bardas Cydones through the moonlight to the civilian stables where they kept their horses. "It's an innocuous enough place to meet," he explained. "At this hour there will be few here and people have a reason to come. Meeting here, the sound of running water in the fountain outside masks conversation from anyone not standing close to you."

Wineskins slung over their shoulders, they gave their horses a cursory check and exchanged simple courtesies with the attendant. Kamyates was careful to pay heed to those whom he really regarded as menials. Many people made the mistake of neglecting or being rude to those they considered unimportant, for the seemingly invisible people in life were often observant of their surroundings and could form a like or dislike of people; something that could come back to bite the unwary in the chess game of life.

They moved outside to the fountain, where Kamyates remarked, "In the open is often the best place to hide. See, there are a few others hanging around simply because it's a fairly pleasant place in itself, for Manzikert." The two dallied, playing with the water, swigging wine and talking of old times and faces in the capital.

"Have we come for any particular reason?" Cydones asked after a time.
"There'll be an early start for the strategos' council in the morning."
"I've arranged to loiter here occasionally in case one of my Armenian contacts wants to talk. It's a natural meeting place, for they use the stable—they're from

out of town. That inn over there is another." Kamyates watched as a tall local entered the single storied stone building.

Time passed and they made small talk, Kamyates noticing that Cydones was bored and too lacking in self-discipline to hide it. The tall figure emerged from the inn and made for the stables, deviating towards Kamyates as he neared.

"Pleasant evening for a social wine." Tigran Zakarian greeted the pair.

"Tigran, what a surprise!" said Kamyates. "Let me introduce you. Bardas, the landlord of Arknik, Tigran Zakarian. Bardas Cydones is our most trusted courier from the palace. He's borne despatches for the strategos and me. You're both former soldiers of a sort and have an eye for a horse, so you should have much to talk about."

Zakarian listened impatiently to the preliminaries, but his frequent, furtive looks around betrayed tension. He looked at Kamyates with a fleeting sideways glance at Cydones.

"He's one of us." Kamyates answered, his look to Zakarian hinting that he had reservations about the imperial courier.

Zakarian hesitated, looked at Cydones and smiled guardedly.

Cydones smiled too, seemingly unaware of the exchange.

"Sorry to be so blunt about this, but my estate has been quite busy lately. Seljuk, er, travellers. Kelts, Bryennius' regiment. Two more travellers, Yūryak and Martina …"

Kamyates saw Cydones grimace in the moonlight.

" … and they returned three days ago."

"Interesting! What's this Bryennius like?" Kamyates asked. "I don't know him—too far below me in the pecking order."

"I've never met anyone more ruthless," Zakarian said, staring into the water of the fountain as though hoping to see someone's soul reflected there.

"Really?" Kamyates smiled indulgently. "We've already decided to do something about him."

"Well, be careful. You wouldn't credit it—there were a few skiffs of rain the day before he and his troops arrived at Arknik. From what I can gather, some Seljuk travellers crossed the road and left imprints of their Persian horseshoes. Someone noticed them and Bryennius was onto it—gave chase himself with thirty men. I was doing my rounds when this Kelt from Karin shows up with a chestnut mare the Seljuk emir rode. Then I see them, the Scholae, burying a body in my stockyard. They obviously hoped the grave would be obscured by morning …"

Kamyates blanched. "Did you retrieve it? Were …"

"I didn't bother. I'm certain it was the emir and they would have searched him thoroughly anyway."

"But he might have had secret writing on him …"

"In which case, it's still secret or buried in my yard."

Kamyates muttered an expletive. "What of the others in the party? Bryennius and his men only got here this evening and there are already rumours of a prisoner, a handsome young Arab."

"I don't know about any others." Zakarian answered. "I'm sure they buried the emir. I think the chestnut horse was his. The young Arab might be a prisoner. The older Arab, his uncle I think, I can't account for. Bryennius was very guarded about it when he stopped over at my place. Come to think of it, he was in no hurry to get here. He stayed a day at Arknik—to attend the festival he said—and …"

"Camped a night on the steppe I'm told," Kamyates added, "as though waiting for someone to catch up—like a patrol."

"Hence," Cydones ventured, anxious to join the conversation, "a prisoner or two? As you said, the town is flush with rumours of an Arab spy caught by someone, Bryennius' men, I think."

"Who might know altogether too much," grumbled Kamyates. "Now, to take care of Bryennius? It seems he is here without orders."

"What?" It was incomprehensible to Cydones that someone would act without orders, the cover of superiors and the cocoon of the protected.

Kamyates smiled. "I'll make sure this puts Apocapes in a bind."

"One of his, Bryennius', officers," Zakarian offered, "a Joshua Balsamon, seems ambitious and, er, open minded. That is, he will listen to other views."

"If we can learn where Bryennius is and what he's up to, that will be helpful," Kamyates said.

"I buttered him, Balsamon, up at Arknik. I'll keep the association going."

"Good, Tigran. At the appropriate time, let him know I'm not without contacts in the Sacred Palace and could arrange a promotion for him in one of the other tagmata formations, the Excubitores, perhaps. Better still, introduce us when the time presents itself."

Zakarian nodded. "That would be a useful lure. If we can't convince Apocapes to surrender the city and it comes to an assault, there are a couple of places on the north and west walls where there is water damage that has been superficially repaired but not properly fixed—lack of money, I suppose."

"Excellent work." Kamyates was concerned lest they be noticed, their familiarity being too evident for a chance meeting. "We should move on before we're noticed."

"One other thing," Zakarian lingered as if staring into the fountain. "Bryennius had a disagreement with one of our hotheads, a dispossessed Armenian nobleman called Bardanes Gurgen. He shot his mouth off at Arknik and Bryennius arrested him after he called him a blacksmith."

"Who did?"

"Gurgen. Bryennius shod his own horse at Arknik. Gurgen must have seen"

"Bryennius arrested him for calling him a blacksmith?" Cydones made a show of being affronted.

"No! For speaking treason. Bryennius had no choice." Zakarian favoured Cydones with a superior stare. "Let him, Gurgen, go the next morning though.

Bryennius doesn't have the killer in him. But an idea would be to steer clear of Gurgen. He's attracting attention, proving the perfect diversion and may well be a useful scapegoat."

"A blacksmith!" Kamyates wondered aloud.

Manzikert,
Early morning, 25th May 1054

Leo rose at daybreak and mounting Ruksh, toured the city. The chestnut gelding would arch his neck and prick his ears at new sights as though to say, "Just you look at that now!" Leo loved the sound of the iron shoes on cobbles or tanbark, and the quick rhythm of a swift walker. The western gate was already open, and despite the early hour a trickle of people went about their work. Leo left by the gate and cantered a lap of the bridle track around the walls. He paused at a substantial stream-fed lagoon outside the south-eastern corner. It had been included into the defensive scheme and could be used to flood part of the ditch. In addition to the township by the western wall, a village could be seen a quarter mile from the north wall.

Re-entering by the north gate and riding down one of the main avenues lined with oak, beech and plane trees, he noticed the market quarter was quiet, but saw that men toiled at warehouses and granaries. Bundles of cut hay were already being unloaded from carts into neat stacks. Some shops were open and riding past a forge, he saw men stripped to the waist toiling in leather aprons over the firestones. Close by, there was a small, fenced field with a few horses grazing. They were well-bred and Leo wondered who owned them. Wherever there was space, away from the fences so the animals could not reach them, were vegetable gardens and orchards of apricots, quince, pomegranate and other fruits.

With the villas of the wealthy higher up the rise, the blocks of little stone apartments were crowded close together in the residential quarter. Looking back down from the town to the lower parts of the market and military areas, Leo calculated the fortress was a lop-sided oval shape with the north and south walls each a thousand yards long, the others perhaps seven hundred. It was no crowded place as Karin or Trebizond, but was clearly an important cultural, administrative and military centre with a sizable population, perhaps thirty thousand, that in times of trouble would be swelled by those from outside the walls, unless the gates were barred against them. Leo had observed four main gates at the compass points in the circuit walls.

He rode back to his quarters in the military district, which had now come to life as men tended horses, exercised in arms and occupied themselves with the rituals of garrison life. Leo had given most of the regiment a day's local leave to explore the fortress and town outside, after which there would be a program of reconnaissance and training, as well as whatever tasks the strategos might give him. The men could already be seen in pairs or small groups, exploring their new environs.

Count Branas arrived to escort Leo to Basil Apocapes' rooms. Leo wore armour, helmet and sword for the occasion. Together they stepped up the gentle gradient to the citadel, Branas passing on all he could in the time they had. "Apocapes is truly sorry he couldn't see you yesterday. He went to Baghesh, by way of Khlat', to talk with the local representative of Abu Nasr Ahmad Nasr ad-Daulah, the Marwanid Kurdish ruler of Amida. Abu Nasr is friendly—enough—and we try to keep him that way. Indeed, six years ago he used, at the Emperor's bidding, the Arab Banu Numair tribe to capture the notorious raider, al-Asfar al-Taghlibi."

"I heard of that," Leo recalled. "The Taghlib's captured so many of our people that a slave could be bought for a pittance. I'm glad Abu Nasr is friendly, but it gives him a tight rope to walk with Tughrul Bey, doesn't it?"

"It surely does, and he knows it." Branas nodded to a sentry as they passed into the citadel. "This Sultan holds sway over many lives."

Inside they entered a courtyard that branched off to stables, armoury, dungeons, commissary, infirmary and the other functions necessary to a last bastion. The smaller area, solid walls and commanding towers meant the citadel could hold out longer if the city fell.

The two men stepped through another smaller iron gate into the donjon[49], well-covered by positions for archers and cauldrons of boiling liquid. A forced-entry there, Leo reflected, would not be pretty. A clerk with ink-stained fingers met them and led them up several flights of stone stairs and along a passageway. While waiting in the outer chamber Leo observed, through an arrow slit, the city and bend of the river and was struck by what a commanding position and excellent view the citadel afforded. The Arab influence showed in the light and airy interior design. There was something more to the feel of the place than one would expect from the starkly functional Byzantine military architecture, although the Roman strengthening of thirty years had made its mark.

A guard admitted them into the room. In the corner close to a cold fireplace was a crowded writing desk with a stand of arms and armour nearby. A panel on the wall behind the desk displayed maps of the area and plans of the fortress. On the other side of the large room, a dozen men and a woman were seated around a long table. As Leo and Branas entered the room, a well-built man in his late thirties walked towards them.

"It is the strategos of Manzikert, the patrician, Basil Apocapes," Branas whispered.

Leo saluted and advanced.

"Welcome, Count Bryennius." Basil extended his hand.

They clasped palms.

---

49 Donjon—a tower keep, the last bastion within the citadel.

Leo removed his helmet and placed it under his arm. This was not the first time he had walked into a gathering of men with whom he was to campaign.

Apocapes wore ordinary riding clothes rather than the robes favoured by high officials. Leo noticed his boots with their wrinkles at the ankle, washed-over marks of old saddle grease and grey stains of dried horse sweat in the worn leather. Half-Georgian, half-Armenian, whose family held extensive estates in Georgia, Basil was the son of the frontier legend, Michael Apocapes, a tent guard of the once Georgian ruler, David of Taiq. Simon Vardaheri had already told Leo of the commendable role of Apocapes' father in the ill-starred Syrian campaign of Emperor Romanus III that had culminated in the disaster at Azaz near Aleppo. The stamp of the father was on the son. Apocapes spoke deeply in deliberate Greek with the confident air of command, backed with experience of war. His demeanour bespoke a keen intellect and willingness to listen. Instinctively Leo liked him.

"We've been expecting you," Basil continued, "but were hoping there would be more soldiers with you. I am sorry I was unable to meet you last night, but Daniel has no doubt seen to your immediate needs. I hope you have been made as comfortable as possible." Basil lowered his tone as he stood close to Leo, "Daniel tells me you brought a prisoner, an Arab?"

"Yes, Sir. I would like to talk to you about it privately, if I may?"

"Of course. After this."

"Also, you know I am here without written orders?"

"Daniel did mention it. Don't worry about that." Basil turned and raised his voice slightly. "Now you must meet your brother officers." To the wider group Basil continued, "Gentlemen, let me introduce to you, Count Leo Bryennius of the Sixth Schola. He will remember all your names, of course!"

There was a ripple of laughter. Basil then steered Leo by the people who were now significant in his life. "First our Princeps, John Curticius. John does the hard work of coordinating the overall military affairs of the city and wider district."

Curticius had a red nose with small broken blood vessels near the eyes and smelled faintly of stale wine. Curticius in turn scrutinised Leo and formally greeted him.

Leo recognised the next face.

"Oleg, commander of our Varangians and Rus[50]."

Mutual and pleasant recognition flickered between the Viking and Leo, for they had known each other in Constantinople years before. Large framed and ruddy, Oleg grinned cheerfully, "What price this? What fool errand brings you?"

"A fool's errand."

"It's good to see you, my friend," Oleg boomed through his blonde beard. In his rich scarlet tunic, the Viking was not seeking to hide.

"We're fortunate," Basil continued, "to have two regiments of Varangians, mixed Norsemen and Rus. A turma of Varangians were amongst the troops

---

50 People from around Kiev and other Viking trading posts on the Russian rivers.

sent out after Artsn. Most have since returned to Caesarea, but we are lucky to have retained Oleg and his men. Thus we have in our company Oleg's wife, the beautiful Olga. Invite yourself for dinner!"

They moved on.

"Raymond de Gaillon, Leader of the Kelts. There are a handful at Artzké and more at Archēsh." Basil said. "You know of course, that two of the five frontier corps are Kelts. Raymond spent some time at their main garrison at Melitene, but now has the fortune to see the Christian frontier beyond the Euphrates. And blessed are we for it. He has, with the addition of the Kelts who came with you, five hundred horse and a thousand foot."

Raymond, swarthy and dark haired, greeted Leo in halting, accented Greek. Leo detected only professional courtesy from him.

"Theophanes Doukas!" Basil's trust in the man was evident. Stocky, olive complexioned, brown bearded with the serious expression of things on his mind, the Greek-Armenian nodded a welcome to Leo.

"Theo is a sort of Count of the City, as we call him, for he is charged with its tactical defence. For this he controls most of the troops in the fortress, including Varangians, Kelts, the theme infantry and armed townspeople. It's the worst job in Manzikert. He has to be diplomat, soldier, builder, fire fighter and many other things as well."

Leo liked and sympathised with Doukas.

Basil took a step to halt before a man in his late thirties of middle build with straight, brown hair worn shorter than the usual Roman fashion. "Our chief engineer, Karas Selth." The engineer, with his clean shaven smile and sparking blue eyes, seemed at first impression, to be likeable and cooperative. "If you have a problem," Basil smiled, turning to Leo, "with fortifications, siege engines, miners, tunnels, Greek Fire[51], or plumbing, Karas is your man. But steer clear of him when he's in his experimental frame of mind."

There was a good natured chuckle from the others in the room.

Moving on and glancing back at them, Leo felt he could trust Selth and Doukas. "The Bishop of Manzikert."

A tall, austere, grey-bearded figure rose from his seat at the table.

"His practical role in the defence is to oversee the distribution of food and shelter to the populace and refugees." Basil was known as a kind and pious man and the public respect he accorded the bishop appeared heartfelt, but ever the practical soldier, he would also have respected the deference of ordinary people to organised religion.

"Ah! Abbess!" Apocapes' regard was apparent for the charming woman in her middle years who smiled warmly at Leo. "No doubt you're surprised to see

---

51 Greek Fire—a weaponised, napalm-like liquid or semi-solid (possibly naphtha-based) that could be projected through pumps and tubes (effectively medieval flame-throwers) or as pottery grenades by both sides during sieges. Although naphtha was widely used by fire-troops throughout the Middle East, this and its associated technology was refined by Byzantium, thus its name.

a woman in this council. The monastery will provide additional hospital space when … if needed, and as a refuge for the homeless. The abbess, along with the bishop of course, is my window to the fears and aspirations of the ordinary people of the area. She knows everybody and everything. Out here the people place great store in faith. They trust and confide in the men and women of God, especially those of their own Armenian Church."

Basil and Leo paused before a stout man richly dressed in silks of the east, with a thin social smile and cold eyes above his brown beard.

"D'you know Modestos Kamyates, from the Court?" Basil asked as Leo locked eyes with Kamyates.

The courtier rose, "I am most surprised to see you here, Count Bryennius. No! I do not believe we have met."

Leo could tell Kamyates was both furious and uneasy at his arrival. "No. I would remember if we had."

Basil looked intently from Kamyates to Leo.

"You have despatches from the Emperor?" Kamyates stared rudely in a failed attempt to intimidate. He had an air of aggressive confidence: the mark of a man accustomed to being feared by others and for good reason.

Though unsurprised, Leo was glad he had entrusted the despatches he carried to Branas' safekeeping the previous evening. "There are despatches for the strategos."

The courtier's smile did not change, but his eyes flickered narrower for a moment. "Perhaps I can have them, given my post at court."

Leo had not expected this test to come so soon or so openly. "Perhaps not. They're already with the strategos' staff."

"That's me," said Basil. "I'll take care of them."

Kamyates was prepared. "If we cannot see your despatches, perhaps we can see your orders. Show us what you're doing here and on whose authority."

"Orders, also, are for the strategos!" Leo caught Kamyates' stare and glared back until the courtier looked away.

"He's right," said Basil.

Kamyates conceded darkly and resumed his seat.

"Daniel," Basil ordered. "Fetch these despatches, please. Let's hear the wisdom of the palace."

Branas, who had been standing as of stone in a corner, left to get them.

Curticius attempted to smooth over the tension. "What news from Constantinople, Count Bryennius?" I seek to know especially of the disagreement between the churches of the Patriarch in Constantinople and the Pope in Rome."

Leo began. "I don't, of course, know the last news you've had. The capital is quiet. The thirty year truce, concluded with the Patzinaks last year, seems to be holding, though many troops are kept on that front in case the treaty and bribes we paid fail." In the mixed company, Leo chose to ignore the Norman defeat of the Pope at Civitate in Italy, Byzantine troops avoiding battle and contributing to the defeat. "The Seljuk emissaries in Constantinople hear blessing called for their Sultan in Friday's prayers in the mosque, such is their influence now. Their embassy has access to the court but has failed to achieve the Sultan's demands that the Emperor offer tribute."

Basil's jaw hardened. There was a collective grunt of disapproval from the table. "How dare the barbarian," uttered one.

Kamyates remained aloof.

Leo continued. "As we left by sea in the early spring, the schism between the western and eastern Churches had become much worse. There was talk of ..."

"What has happened?" asked the bishop as the abbess gasped.

"The Frankish Pope Leo IX died in April, but the Patriarch in Constantinople, Michael Cerularius, and the visiting envoys of Pope Leo seem likely to excommunicate each other."

There was an angry murmur.

Gently spoke Basil, but with iron in him. "There will be no such schism in this command. We're all Christians here. One God! And by God, there will be a united front to the infidel from this place. I ask unity of no man based on ignorance. Count Leo, if you please, what do the presbyters quarrel about?"

Such trust was a compliment Leo could have done without as he sensed Basil's purpose. Looking at the expectant faces turned towards him, he took a breath. The grasp for power—who would control the souls and purse strings of which people—was the key issue, as was the celibacy of Rome's priests in contrast to the Orthodox approval to wed. But there was more, including the Greek philosophical underpinning of the Orthodox Church and the ancient Latin legal basis of the other, in their relation to state and society. It had to be simplified and diffused in this room.

"Thanks, so much, Sir," Leo smiled, getting a laugh from Basil and a nervous titter from the gathering which helped reduce the tension. "I'm no expert on church doctrine, but I understand there are four main unresolved differences. First, the theological issue of the Procession of the Holy Ghost. The Latin Creed states the Holy Ghost proceeds from the Father and the Son, our Orthodox Creed states, solely from the Father."

The bishop stared ahead, his eyes unfocused.

"Second, is the issue of the use of leavened bread by we Romans or unleavened bread by the Latins during the sacrament. Third, there is disagreement over our Roman prayer invoking the Holy Ghost at the consecration of the Host, a prayer omitted by the Latins. Finally, there is no agreement over the Latin desire for primacy of the pope of Rome over the patriarch in Constantinople."

"There! Nothing for us to worry about. Right Bishop?" Basil did not wait for an answer. "Greater minds than ours can fix this. We can just concentrate on our duty to the people of the district and their safety."

No one disputed his point, but there was a heavy silence as each considered the gravity of the religious split and the implications for their higher loyalties.

Branas returned and paused as he entered the room, conscious of the change of mood.

"Read them, Daniel. A summary will do," Basil said, trusting his military secretary to omit any contentious points.

Branas opened the parchment and gave the gist. "No immediate threat to the capital." He skipped the aggressive moves by the Normans against Byzantium's increasingly tenuous hold on Italy. "Truce with Patzinaks holding. Black Sea quiet. So on. Harvests good. So on. Southern frontier with the Fatimid Caliphate, quiet—famine persists in Cairo. The Emperor is sending grain. Possibility of light summer raiding by Saracens into Armenia." Branas paused after the reference to Armenia.

Leo noticed that the imperial despatch referred generically and misleadingly to Saracen rather than Seljuk raiding.

None wished to question the conventional wisdom from the capital in public, particularly with Kamyates present.

"Light summer raiding, eh? That seems positive." Basil glanced at Leo, as if inquiring whether he agreed with the assessment.

Leo remained silent, seeking a more discreet time.

Basil sensed it. "Very well, Abbess, gentlemen. We're almost done. As you know, I travelled to Baghesh and received assurances from Marwanid emissaries that we'll have no trouble from the emir's subjects at Baghesh or Khlat'. If there are no questions, let me release you to your duties. Count Bryennius, remain."

"I will stay also," Kamyates insisted.

Basil blinked quickly out the window to conceal his irritation, then looked back into the room with a smile. "Of course, Modestos."

Oleg punched Leo playfully in the shoulder on his way out, but he whispered a warning. "Watch your back, for you have made an enemy." The Viking took a step back. "See you around," he said loudly enough for the others to hear.

Basil, Kamyates and Leo were soon alone.

"May I see," Kamyates demanded.

Basil handed the document over. "Do you agree with the assessment in the despatches, Count Bryennius?"

"No. It was an adequate description of the overall situation, but I believe they are wrong in their interpretation of the main threat and have underestimated the danger from the Seljuks."

"How dare you question the wisdom of the court?" Kamyates flamed.

Basil silenced him with a gesture and looked to Leo.

"It is true, the Patzinaks are the more immediate threat from the perspective of Constantinople, but they are not the most dangerous to the empire. Truce aside, the Patzinaks have long lines of communication from north of the Black Sea and around into the old Bulgar lands. Also, the Rus harass their flank and rear to some degree. Moreover, should they penetrate to Constantinople, they will come to nothing against the walls, as has happened before. They have no state power to speak of, no siege capability, nor can they gain any since they have no alliance with the Kelts or the Arabs. Even if they besiege Constantinople, they cannot isolate it from resupply by sea. The Patzinaks have no navy, so they cannot cross the Bosphorus in sufficient force to conquer the vital heart of the Empire—Anatolia and Cappadocia, our heartland and grain basket, where we breed remounts and from where we raise our armies—are beyond their strategic reach."

"So?" Basil enquired.

Leo continued, "There are credible reports indicating Tughrul Bey is planning something much greater than summer raids this time—more a permanent shift in the balance of power on the frontier. The reports indicate that the Sultan is assembling a powerful army, including a siege train …"

"I never saw it," interrupted Kamyates.

"… to move against our frontier fortresses. Moreover they now appear to have virtual control in Baghdad, giving them access to the state power of the Abbasids. The Seljuks are a formidable new force …"

"We have beaten them before," Basil said.

"True. But now they combine their own strength—and confidence—with the administrative wealth of the Abbasids, as well as the obedience of the different Kurdish emirates around Armenia. And the Sultan is angry that his embassy has been unsuccessful."

"Hearsay," interjected Kamyates. "How can Bryennius know what the Sultan thinks?"

Basil shot a look at Kamyates, "You have made a fair point, Michael." He looked back to Leo. "But, if what Count Bryennius says is correct, even partly, it alters things here completely. We have not prepared for a siege by a professional army. Nor has a major invasion been foreseen, though I have concerns about it—which my superiors at Van do not seem to share." He walked to the window, stared out for a time, then turned to look at them. "Even if their intentions are short term, it will make little difference to those who are slain, robbed and enslaved."

"The count is wrong," Kamyates sneered. "He has been here not a day and thinks he knows everything."

Basil looked long at Leo. "I had one of my s…" He stared out of the window for a long time, then turned once more to the others. "Anyway, enough! I will take your views under advisement. Count Bryennius! I am told you have a swift chestnut. I have a grey that is unbeaten in a five mile gallop and it is my sin—one of my sins—to love an occasional wager. I will meet you at the military stables after lunch and we shall try them."

Kamyates glared at Leo as they left.

Manzikert,
Morning, 25th May 1054

A shaft of morning sunlight woke Guy as he lay with a blanket drawn loosely over him. He had slept late like many others weary from the journey. Across the cramped room Charles was curled under a blanket.

Jacques saw him awake. "Rest up. I've fed our animals. It'll be a warm day, even if last night was cool."

Embarrassed, Guy thanked him. He had never quite overcome his shyness at having a servant. Partly it was an independent streak, but the natural human dignity of Jacques did not sit well with subservience. Guy thought of Balazun and his expectation that someone would feed him, clean his equipment and wash his clothes. In return, his servants would receive no recognition or gratitude, simply a beating for their own meagre needs for rest, food or shelter. Yet Balazun never seemed to care nor be penalised for it.

That thought led Guy to again ponder the notion of good and evil and the nature of God, a mental journey that took him almost immediately to the dead Seljuk. Again there was that cold, empty feeling of guilt and loneliness in an enormity of time and space he could barely imagine. He rose and prayed, kneeling on the folds of his cloak, seeking the peace of mind that did not come easily.

Charles awoke, looking more refreshed than Guy felt and glanced disinterestedly at his act of penance. "Why worry? He'd have killed you without a thought." Charles rolled over and looked at their companion. "Where's breakfast, Jacques?"

"The cooks have a late breakfast on in the mess. It's good! A rich beef stew. Also bread, milk and fruit aplenty. The water is good and they even have some of that boiled coffee berry drink Simon Vardaheri has spoken of."

"Excellent. I am hungry," said Charles as he sat up, ran his hands through his hair and rubbed the sleep from his eyes. He pulled on his shoes, leaned his shield and spear over his saddle, which rested in the corner, rolled up his hauberk and drew his folded cloak over it. "Will our things be safe here?" he asked doubtfully, looking at Jacques. The theft of expensive armour and accoutrements would be an economic and martial catastrophe for a warrior.

Guy rose to his feet and looked with the same question at Jacques.

"Robert Balazun has arranged a picket, to keep an eye on our band's belongings," Jacques informed them. "There are no certainties but it will be safe enough, I believe. Otherwise we must guard it ourselves."

After a shave and other ablutions, Charles and Guy breakfasted leisurely. Jacques accompanied them, having developed a taste for coffee. Other small groups also enjoyed the unhurried meal. The stone buildings seemed less imposing by day: cracks in the flagstones were visible and years of passing feet had worn the thresholds. Guy could see where generations of soldiers—Armenian, Roman, Arab, Rus, Norse and Norman—had scratched their marks in the walls and on the wooden tables.

Charles drew his dagger. Guy noticed the look on Charles' smooth, shaven face. It struck him how, despite the rough company and precedence of the scratched tables, Charles made some effort to conceal his minor vandalism. The knight had quite small, white hands. Guy watched, fascinated that the same hands, so skilful and strong under arms, should mark the surface so delicately.

"Guy, no sign of Swordleader or Bowman?" asked Charles.

"No, though I have looked twice at many people."

Charles looked up and saw Guy staring, smiled and bent down again to his task. "D'you think anyone will remember we were here?"

Guy was distracted, looking through the open doors at the battlements as he reflected on the whereabouts of his assailant from the inn by the Golden Gate.

"Guy?" Charles was looking in earnest at him. "Will anyone remember we were here?"

"If you keep scratching that table they will." Guy looked back at his friend, surprised at Charles' sudden despondency. "I don't know. I suppose it depends on what deeds we do."

"Deeds?" Jacques spluttered coffee over the table. "Speak no more of deeds. Deeds are for fools."

Guy, surprised and a little vexed, looked at Jacques for a moment, then turned his attention back to Charles. "Does it matter?"

"I've a feeling this is going to be different from seeing-off an untrained rabble from the next landholding, or wooing maidens in some dell." He spoke with an air of such gloom that Guy and Jacques looked at each other.

"Enough. Enough! I go to sell your Tusk's corselet[52]," Jacques laughed.

"Mail is expensive. Ask four *nomisma*," Guy stood as well. "If you cannot get a good price, try swapping it for a set for yourself." He was aware he was being generous and that Charles had noticed.

Jacques nodded and left.

"Come, Charles." Guy said. "Let's inspect our horses. Vaspurakan must be filled with rich damsels in distress, but to save them you'll need a sound horse."

Guy was struck by the order of the stables. They were designed to keep a cavalry force of some hundreds in a state of order and health for weeks, if not months. The main stable was a two-storied stone building that could be made defensible for a short period. Designed along a cobbled central lane with the floor sloping inward to a shallow drain, the stable had thirty comfortable stalls on either side, the end spaces occupied by rooms for veterinarians and blacksmiths. Access to the ground floor could be barred by closing massive doors at either end. The upper stories comprised rooms for grooms, tack and a large loft for fodder. There was also an interior well. The building was dry, light and airy, well ventilated but without draughts.

Behind the main building were several compounds, each comprising three long rows of loose-boxes faced inwards to enclose a square. The main compound contained hitching rails, some shade trees, a well, a few wooden bench-seats and wash-points for horses. This provided a natural meeting point for warriors, squires, farriers, veterinarians, grooms, healers, traders, saddlers and armourers. An enterprising local had set up a small shop selling food and drink. The square was a place of enthusiasm and knowledge, humour, gossip, ready assistance on all

---

52 Corselet—sleeveless, hoodless body armour reaching the hips or just below.

matters equine and dogged opinion on most other subjects. A number of cats and small dogs were encouraged to live around the stables as defence against pests.

Beyond this were yards for breaking in and exercising horses, an obstacle course for advanced mounted weapons training, an open riding area leading out to the track around the inside of the circuit walls and small spelling-fields with their shelters. There were birch and plane trees in the area to shield the animals against the summer sun. The wealthier warriors had rented some of the small fields for their own horses; Balazun's black Castilian stallion ran in such a field which had been double-fenced for the purpose.

An efficient Byzantine official, an old soldier, ran the military stables. Guy had already observed that considerable effort had been made to conserve the natural grazing inside the fortress by keeping much of the horse herd outside the walls under a strong mounted guard. He had heard of a similar but much smaller stable for wealthy citizens, on the other side of the fortress and he wondered if the beautiful rider from the previous evening kept her mount there.

Labourers were mucking-out stalls and sweeping the cobbled lanes with stiff-bristled yard brooms, carrying the manure in hessian sheets to a central pile from where it was carted away by the wagonload to fertilize the valley's gardens. As the two Franks walked past such a wagon, the locals on top of the load of straw and half-dried manure nodded respectfully. Nearby a trickle of wagons and carts unloaded hay, barley, millet, oats and wheat into sheds and silos near the yards and other storage areas near the commissary. Still more carts rumbled on their spoked wheels towards the citadel. Groups of men sweated with pitchforks or bag hooks to drag fodder from the wagons into neat stacks, some under hard cover, others secured off the ground on low platforms, to be covered against the elements by heavy oilcloth.

Guy watched a group of women bring lunch to the men: bread, cheese, cold meat, fruit, water and milk. Horses or oxen were quickly unyoked and tied up while the workers rested in the shade of nearby fruit trees. Against the background of everyday conversation, children took apples from the baskets and skipped to some favoured horse and offered the fruit to the grateful dipped heads and kind brown eyes. Guy saw a young couple seated together watching their child take a slice of apple and approach a restive young carthorse. The father cautioned, "Be careful of that horse. He's only young and doesn't know he could hurt you." The child paused, looked back, smiled a happy, confident smile and went on to the young horse, which gently took the fruit and sniffed the youngster as the child in turn stroked its forelock. Guy wondered if the conversation of the parents followed the danger that approached from afar, or wished it away? How could they ignore the nomads if the unthinking actions of a carthorse would concern them? Did they discuss the child's abilities, hopes or happiness? Or live for the moment; watch that the child was not trampled and concern themselves only with the everyday affairs of food, work and shelter? Did they consider spiritual things? Guy found himself contrasting the imagined simplicity of the family to the reticent calculation of Bryennius.

The two friends moved on to Sira's yard where the mare walked over to them. She sniffed his gift of a quartered apple, her black eye on him all the while. Guy could see the dried bran on the long whiskers of her fine muzzle. Sira's upper lip and tip of her muzzle puckered, reaching out, testing.

"I wouldn't trust you either," said Charles.

Sira took the apple quarter with such delicacy that she did not touch his hand. Drops of apple juice fell on the ground and a few stray chickens ran to them. The mare, ignoring the fowls, nodded her head in enjoyment. The horse in the next yard put its head over the rail, wanting some apple also. Sira turned viciously at the other horse, her ears flat against her head. She returned to Guy, looking for more.

"Hmm," observed Charles with false gravity. "She doesn't seem very Christian, but at least you won't have to worry about another horse ever stealing her food. Come. Let's look around the town."

As they walked from Sira's yard, a lithe, smooth-faced youth led a saddled dun gelding by them. The youth wore a loose, mid-thigh length, long-sleeved tunic bunched over a belt, to which were attached bow case, quiver and dagger. The gelding, fourteen and a half handbreadths tall, looked exceptionally tough with its black points; dark brown mane and tail joined by the black dorsal stripe. The youth nodded and continued, their eyes hidden by the shadow of a shapeless felt hat. Something in their manner made Guy think their paths had crossed. He paused and looked after them, but could not place either horse or rider.

Near Manzikert,
Afternoon, 25th May 1054

Basil and Leo laughingly slowed their excited, blowing horses to a trot and swerved south from the worn path. The knee-to-knee gallop had basked both in the bonding glow of sporting exhilaration. As Leo patted the arched neck and tossing chestnut mane before him, Basil grumbled good-naturedly, "Don't think I want to race any more. Should've listened to Oleg. He warned me not to challenge any horse of yours. And don't think I didn't notice you holding Ruksh back as I urged mine on!"

"He does love a gallop."

Both men wore felt jerkins, swords and cased bows.

"You wear a Turkish thumb ring?" Basil remarked as they reined back to a walk.

"I find it easier to draw the bowstring."

"You must be skilled. That's why your scouts call you Horse-archer?"

"They've taken enough pains to try and teach me."

"They would not use the term if it wasn't a compliment. You seem to have their trust." Basil got straight to the point. "Now we're alone, I can tell you that I sent one of my own spies to Tabriz three weeks ago. He was only supposed to have a quick look and should have returned by now. Do you have anyone in your regiment whom you could trust to go to Tabriz?"

"Yes."

Basil appeared to consider this response for a few moments, as though calculating whether such a rapid answer might have bespoken vanity, stupidity or forethought. "I'd like you to send them. Simple instructions. Go there. See what's going on. Verify the location and if possible the intentions of the Sultan, then report back. If they can learn the fate of my man, so much the better, but not at risk to the mission. Make sure it's all done quietly. There are too many keen eyes and wagging tongues around Manzikert." The two men rode on a way before Basil continued, "How long would your man need to make the journey and return? Two weeks, say?"

Leo thought before answering. "About that, perhaps three. I'd want to send a team, two or three men."

They rode towards the higher ground on the other side of the valley from the fortress where Basil resumed the conversation. "There's more. Your prisoner?"

"Zobeir al-Adin?"

"Modestos Kamyates wants a private audience with him. It will be hard to deny him, given his rank and influence. Speaking of whom, you've not got off to a good start with him and you need to fix it, because I can't afford to antagonise him."

"I understand, Sir, and will do my best. Since you have raised the subject of Kamyates, I need to get a couple of things off my chest."

Basil's moustache twitched once. "I'm listening."

"The imperial courier, Cydones, dropped Kamyates' name before he did the bolt on us at Baberd. They obviously know each other—quite well I would say. We do not really know where Kamyates has been or who he's met. He makes much of his part in the much-vaunted embassy to free Liparit, the result of which is that the Georgians are now neutral and will be no help to us. Then he shows up here, straight from the Seljuk heartland. And he knew I was here without written orders. Cydones must have told him—and how did he know?"

"I suppose you have a point there."

"And," Leo paused wondering how to convey it. "Before I left, Cecaumenus told me to watch your back."

Basil's moustache twitched twice and an eyebrow arched. "From whom?"

"He did not say. But if I'm to do it, you need to tell me what's going on."

"I will remember that." Basil rode for some distance in silence. "How much does your prisoner know?"

"I'm certain he was on a scouting or spying mission. He'll start to feel lonely soon and will talk, but I doubt that he knows that much. He betrayed an interest in Manzikert, which is logical—it would be a key objective for the Sultan. The documents with him show detail about our dispositions and the military aspects of the local geography. What we do not know for certain is what level of command sent them, either the Sultan intent on invasion, or a local emir planning a slaving and looting raid?"

"There were rumours of a Seljuk group being around here. Praise God, if you have caught them."

"I am betting it's the Sultan," Leo continued. "Thus far, the prisoner has spoken only his own name. We now have their marked maps—his turban had secret writing on it. They do not show much, but indicate a Seljuk mounting base at Tabriz and scouting through Archēsh and Manzikert to Karin, which of course does not rule out other parties scouting other routes."

They were silent again. Manes nodded and nostrils flared to the pink as their horses drew in deeply of the warm air as they climbed the higher ground. The smell of horse sweat rose as the two rode on, wild oats caressing their boot tips.

"I suggest," Leo mused aloud, "showing the captured horses around a bit to see who knows them, or who they react to."

Basil looked at Leo. "Good idea." They rode on in silence for a few moments. "Your unit seems to be in good shape."

"Thank you. There is always room for improvement. I need to familiarise my men, and myself, with the local area and conditions."

"Your officers are reliable?"

"I believe so. Antony Lascaris and Bessas Phocas in particular are good, thoughtful men. Sebēos, too is very competent." Leo knew something was coming, but could not yet determine its nature. "The younger officers are, like all young officers, enthusiastic and willing enough, but need proper instruction and control. Also, like many young men, they are apt to be gullible when faced with slick-tongued senior officials. Of them, Balsamon is wilful, but I cannot otherwise fault him."

"You trust your scouts?"

"We've three and I trust them all. David Varaz, is a Georgian. He is moody, but tough and effective, speaking the Seljuk tongue to a degree, having travelled in their lands. If he has a fault, it is that he hates them too much. I am told he lost one he loved to them ... as a slave ... from Artsn. He fought with Liparit at Kapetrou and entered Roman pay thereafter."

Basil looked sharply at Leo. "Kapetrou! Your scout was there, you say?"

"So he's told me."

Basil looked long at his pommel, as though recalling the battle where Liparit was betrayed: the Romans and their Armenian troops near the fortress of Kapetrou, their Georgian allies approaching from the north-east, all dispersed to forage and to seek contact with the elusive Seljuks. Then came that endless, tumultuous night: the long approach march and the couriers coming and going on jaded horses as commanders tried to co-ordinate their widespread columns. In the ferocious running engagements, the Seljuks although badly mauled, had surprised Liparit, captured him and escaped the trap.

Leo sensed Basil's pre-occupation and was silent.

"Kapetrou!" Basil muttered. "Hard to say who won. We owned the field after, but failed to destroy them or free any prisoners." Then, sharply to Leo, "He must tell me about it some time."

"Very well, I will arrange it." Leo paused. "Our Cuman, Togol, left his tribe after an indiscretion—with a chieftain's mistress, apparently. He is unlikely to return. Indeed he's learning to speak Greek. He tried to warn Cecaumenus before Artsn and my father saved his life at Kapetrou. He is with us. Togol is an animist, and rumoured to be a sorcerer. He might become Roman in time, but we'll never make a Christian of him."

"A sorcerer, eh!" Basil laughed. "He and the bishop can get together!"

"Maniakh is a Patzinak. He is one of the men who saved Cecaumenus and my father at Diacene …"

"Your father has been in the thick of it. How is he?"

"He has made a reasonable recovery from the wounds suffered at Diacene, but is not fit for military service."

"I am sorry to hear that. He lives a good life?"

"Good enough he tells me. As I was saying, Maniakh was detached to me for this mission by Cecaumenus himself. He is well paid and would settle on military land if it were allocated to him. Maniakh is a quiet and deep man who knows much of the oral tradition of the steppe peoples."

"That's good. Knowledge is no burden."

"And then there is Vardaheri, not exactly one of my scouts."

"The mysterious horse trader! I know him. And trust him—that is enough!"

Drawing rein at a large, flat rock that overlooked the valley, they dismounted and sat, taking care to keep the horses apart.

"Count Bryennius, I like your style. I have my own scouts, but I want you to take control of the scouting and the cavalry. Branas has been trying to cover it but has too many other duties. It will take a little while to take over and you will need to keep him informed. The local scouts and guides are a close-knit lot—I've assigned Cecaumenus' two couriers, Martina and Yūryak, to them until they return to the capital with despatches. There's a rambling house with a walled garden in Manzikert we use for the purpose—our own little Office of Barbarians—which is more discreet for people to approach than the citadel and is quite near where your troops are quartered. Also I will set aside a room in the citadel. But for the moment, the city house is more appropriate."

"And …" Basil looked at Leo, "it will give you some space away from Kamyates. He wants to know and influence too much of what goes on for my liking. If he is right, our preparations will harm few. If you are right, we will be fighting for our very lives before long. Find out what the Sultan is doing. The key is whether their main effort will be in the south against Manzikert, or the northern route into Armenia proper, from Dvin along the Araxes. The most direct and likely Seljuk approach into Vaspurakan is from their base at Tabriz, bypassing Van, coming through Her and Archēsh and then here—so we need to screen in that direction. Archēsh has a reasonably powerful garrison—they should impose quite some delay and provide us some warning. I do not entirely discount the Seljuks coming from the south by the Kurdish cities of Baghesh and Khlat' either. We need to check on your theory of a siege train as well. That worries me."

Basil stood. "Your Scholae are the best body of cavalry we have, so I would suggest you get them out to assist training the local theme horse and to learn the lay of the land. One of your officers can see to that."

They rode by a circuitous route back to the fortress, ambling under the portcullis to the salutes of the Norman sentries. They parted at the tree-lined avenue from where Leo returned to the military area. He handed Ruksh's reins to Taticus Phocas and sent for Bessas, Maniakh, David and Vardaheri.

Near Manzikert,
Mid-morning, 28th May 1054

Guy felt good. Well rested, he had explored the fortress, walked through the town outside the walls and ridden in the valley. Under Maniakh's tuition, he began to practice with his bow on the target range in the fortress. He had cleaned his newly won saddle and had a saddler in the city replace the worn girth and stirrup leathers. In the next shop Guy spent a significant part of his limited coinage on a new pair of buff-coloured cavalry boots of the type fashionable amongst the Romans and their frontier troops. Many stained them black, but he preferred the raw leather look. Despite the private expense, most preferred them to the white, protective leggings of layered and glued linen issued to many imperial troops.

Now, on his fourth morning at Manzikert, Guy found a secluded area of flat ground along the valley and was trotting and cantering circles and figure-of-eights in the warm air. For mounted archery training, he had brought an old sack stuffed with dried grass, which he tied to a young tree and shot at from various angles, distances and gaits. Having expended his limited supply of ten practise-arrows, Guy cased the bow and was preparing to dismount and reclaim them when Sira almost unseated him by spinning around to face a noise behind them.

He recovered from the start and saw a woman on a well-groomed black horse emerge from a copse of trees and shrubs. She rode astride as most people did. "Hello," he greeted, feeling foolish at being caught unaware, but trying to appear nonchalant as he dismounted.

She drew up near him. "Hello," she replied in polished Greek, also dismounting. "Can I help?"

Guy felt it was the same horse and rider he had seen cantering the tan track during his first evening in the fortress. "Thank you," he replied.

She led her horse around, searching the ground for Guy's arrows. She approached and handed him four shafts.

He thanked her and wiping dirt from the iron heads, fed them into the quiver at his right hip. "I am more accustomed to sword and spear."

Removing her *keffiyeh* and tossing back her long black hair, she watched him in silence, her green eyes roving over his actions and the chestnut mare.

Seeing the light in her eyes, the sheen of her tresses and the slightest hint of perspiration above her soft upper lip, Guy was certain she was the good rider on the splendid black.

"So it is you," she said softly.

He looked blankly at her.

"People speak of a Kelt, who ventured alone across the wilderness to acquire a chestnut Arabian mare. A Kelt who prevented the escape of a nomad spy and defended a lady at Arknik."

"People talk too much," he said.

"So it seems," she smiled. "Come! Ride with me awhile."

They rode, talking, for some miles along a circuit of the bridle tracks that fringed the valley, her smile flashing sympathetically when he stumbled on the new language. As if by unspoken agreement, they kept the conversation light-hearted, tales of horses and the exigencies of rural life. In the same vein they did not introduce themselves; Guy fearing it was symbolic of the fleeting nature of their ride, as though names did not matter, because the future held no promise. Their horses walked easily together, the riders knee to knee. Guy felt a thrill every time their legs brushed as their mounts came together at a narrowing of the track.

Too soon, they halted on a rise, the fortress and town in sight. Guy could feel the gentle breeze in the trees and long dry grass and hear the distant calls of cattle, the mill working and a church bell. Both looked down, knowing they had missed the service. Their stirrups touched and Guy glanced at his lovely companion, a question in his eyes.

"It would cause a scandal if we returned together!" she said. "But it would be nice to ride again."

"It would. We can meet here—when you are able."

"I'll send a message." With a bewitching smile, she rode on, turning in her saddle to wave.

Sira made to follow, but Guy reined-in the mare as she looked with pricked ears and impatience after the black stallion. "That's a magnificent horse," Guy called. "What's his name?"

She halted and half-turned. "Shahryād. Named after a warrior who fought the Arabs, three hundred years ago. Tāryūn, daughter of the Lord of Khlat', went to his aid with four thousand horsemen."

"A fine name, then. And yours?"

"Irene. Irene Curticius."

"I am Guy d'Agiles."

"I know!" With her brilliant smile and a wave, she cantered away.

Guy lingered on the rise with his thick-headed thoughts, when Bryennius ambled up on Ruskh, nodded a greeting and glanced at the hoof prints but said nothing. For some reason, Guy knew that he never would.

Bryennius looked at Guy's bow case and quiver. "How is the archery going?"

"Slowly. You've been out?"

Bryennius nodded.

Guy had seen him, constantly walking the defences and riding the area for miles around the fortress, checking every rivulet, fold in the ground and crack in the old walls. Guy had asked Maniakh what the count was doing, to which the Patzinak replied that when the time came, the count would know the battlefield better from the Sultan's view than the shepherd king himself.

Maniakh! Guy had not seen him for two days. Now he remembered Joaninna Magistros had asked him that morning whether he had seen Simon Vardaheri. The Patzinak scout and much-travelled horse trader had vanished. "Do you know where Maniakh and Simon are?"

Bryennius again studied the tracks on the ground. "No."

Guy looked back, realising the count might not know where they were now, but he had sent them somewhere. He begrudgingly respected the count for not telling him; there was too much talk in Manzikert.

"Shall we head back?" Bryennius said. "Ruksh here has enjoyed about as much of this view as he can stand."

Guy glanced at Ruksh, unconcernedly making with Sira the muzzle-touching, smelling talk of horses, and smiled as he turned Sira towards the fortress.

"Your mysterious Swordleader does not seem to have appeared?" Bryennius remarked.

"No. I've looked closely at a dozen men, but, no."

"Is there one who makes you uneasy?"

"I had that feeling in the market at Karin, and looked around but could see no-one."

"Yes. The market. You told me. Interesting that incident made an impression on you. Oh well, keep your wits about you." With that Bryennius lapsed into thoughtful silence. They were soon riding their swift walkers back though the village when Guy noticed a man looking closely at them. "Isn't that the landlord of Arknik? What's he doing here, and so soon after our arrival?"

"Yes," Bryennius answered quietly. "Tigran Zakarian. Say nothing."

They drew abreast of the Armenian, who had occupied a position before them in the main street. "Bryennius?"

"Tigran."

"Riding, Count Leo?"

"Riding."

"Pleasure or purpose?"

"Riding is always a pleasure, Tigran."

"On such fine horses, I'm not surprised," observed Zakarian, walking around their mounts to study them.

"That was a most pleasant evening at your stronghold, Tigran. What keeps you so far from home?" Bryennius asked.

"Pleasant if you enjoy burying people under my stockyards," the Armenian countered, before answering the question. "Oh! You know! Supplies. Gossip. Different company. To be honest I like town life—I have a good head man at

Arknik, so it runs itself really. And, I wish to make sure I have lodgings in the town in the event of another raid—supposing I get warning enough."

Zakarian walked to Sira and stroked her forehead. Guy expected the mare to be more nervous with a stranger.

"Where'd you come by the chestnut, young fella?" Zakarian asked with the natural authority of his class.

"I've had her for some time," Guy answered warily.

"Indeed?" Zakarian returned, unused to being challenged by one so young.

"Indeed."

"If you need a horse, Simon Vardaheri always has a few for sale," Bryennius suggested, outwardly helpful and apparently distracted by a graceful woman walking along the street.

"Vardaheri isn't in town," Zakarian snapped.

There was a long pause. "I wouldn't know."

Guy saw Bryennius still apparently watching the woman, but he could sense that the count had just tripped Zakarian.

Zakarian knew it. He tensed involuntarily then with an effort, relaxed. He forced a smile, "Well. If you ever want to sell this mare, think of me first."

"I will. I'll think of you, that is," Guy responded.

Zakarian nodded and stood back.

They moved on.

"Well done," Bryennius said to Guy as they rode under the portcullis. "Report to Robert Balazun. He has orders for you."

Balazun's instructions were to meet Bryennius at the stone Barbarian House for unspecified duties. Before releasing him to his new task, the big Norman admonished Guy to tell all he learned. By noon Guy had washed, fed and watered his mare and identified the house. Allowed through the gate, he entered the large house and found Bryennius, Branas and Bessas studying a large map attached to the wall. Within a few minutes, it was apparent that he was now part of the strategos' scouting organization. Guy had no doubt that his capture of Sira and his attempt to learn the language had something to do with his selection and was excited by the prospect of more interesting work and potentially, more pay.

"We'll get you into harness straight away," said Branas, ushering him into a large back room where a pretty young woman sat at a table. "Martina, can you get this fellow settled-in please? Isaac knows about it."

The woman watched Branas leave. "Welcome, Guy d'Agiles?" she said, speaking fluent Greek with what Guy thought was a provincial accent. Her table was crowded with parchments and sketch maps where it appeared she had been transcribing rough field notes into more formal copies.

"Yes," he said, noticing her men's riding dress and the military belt on the peg behind her.

"I'm Martina. Isaac will see you presently. Don't worry, you'll soon learn the ropes, but until you do, if you need help, ask and anyone will try to assist you, especially Isaac, the chief clerk, who knows all and everyone."

Guy looked across to see a young dark haired man bent at a desk covered with papers. Isaac glanced at him. "Don't depend on her for advice! She's never here. Count Branas has her riding all over the country looking around."

"Not alone, I hope?" Guy said, his attention returning to the woman. He noted the dagger on the belt and was surprised to recognise her as the youth leading the dun horse at the stables on the first morning.

"Usually with someone, often Yūryak," she smiled.

Then Guy remembered where he had seen her before—the festival at Arknik, where she had worn a red dress in the crowd. "You must get around a bit!" The notion of a woman doing such work was a shock, although he was not wholly unprepared. He was suddenly thankful he had heard from Irene of Tāryūn and from Bessas, on the journey from Karin, about the tale of Gregory's daughter during the Muslim capture of Tripoli centuries before. The stories had seemed remote until this moment. "What do I do, exactly?" he asked.

"Exactly? The same as the rest of us," Martina laughed. "Find out what old Tughrul is up to. Can you read?"

"And his tens of thousands of followers," Isaac chipped in without looking up.

"Latin? Yes. Greek? A little."

"Start with these," she said. "You can sit at that table there, by the narrow window."

Guy took the sheaf of papers and sat. So much reading was not something he had counted on.

"I am sorry if I seem brusque," she said, "but we are rather busy just now. We can talk more in a while."

"Of course. I understand," Guy replied. Exhaling a long breath, he looked out the window and saw the citadel with its imperial flag and theme pennant trailing lazily in the air. Knowing Irene's father was princeps, Guy wondered if she looked from a window upon Manzikert and whether she thought of him. Constantinople seemed so far away and Provence but a dream.

Chapter Seven

The Fight At The Wadi

Manzikert,
Morning, 26th June 1054

As the pleasant spring turned to a hot summer, Guy's attachment to the scouts altered his life in small but significant ways. He soon noticed he was no longer part of the companionship of the Franks: while they were familiar, they knew little of what he did and he did not share their daily duties, gripes, jealousies and brawls. He was conscious of appearing different from them. His old, handed-down mail byrnie lacked the weight, length and coif of the hauberks most of the Latin knights wore and he had adopted the practice of winding a scarf around his helmet to mitigate the heat. With Roman boots, Seljuk bow and horse-equipment, he had assumed a frontier-like appearance. For scouting Guy carried his spear, but he dispensed with the heavy kite shaped shield, or carried a much smaller almond-shaped type Jacques had acquired from the sale of the Seljuk's corselet—the identity of the buyer being the groom's secret.

"You look like a damned barbarian," Balazun snorted one day.

Count Branas had attached three trusted Armenian frontiersmen to Bryennius for scouting. They were Arshak, Ruben, and the courier, Yūryak. They were men who could ride fast along the little known mountain tracks and use the bow as well as any nomad; horse and cattle thieves whose skills and shadowy networks were suddenly useful. They were also of conflicting loyalties; to Christendom even under Byzantine suzerainty, to their own people and land, Byzantine gold, personally to Basil Apocapes and not least to each other

Interesting callers came and went from the Barbarian House: priests from the outer districts brought information, peasants seeking safety told of horsemen passing in the night, travellers reported dead bodies on the byways. All of this, and the unanswered questions—brigands or the enemy—were recorded by the clerks in their journals and as annotations on the maps covering the wood panelled walls. Patrols came and went.

Guy had heard nothing of Maniac or Simon Vardaheri since his first ride with Irene and imagined them in heroic exploits, dramatic confrontations and daring escapes, but did not mention the men.

Nor did Bryennius.

With her old cook as go-between, Guy had secretive rides with Irene. Every third morning Guy rose earlier than usual, left the fortress by the main gate and cantered northward to loiter near the trees where they had first spoken. These were chaste rides, if touch alone be the measure of such things. She would talk of horses or the frontier with perception and depth, or ask him about his past and of other lands. That was his ration: a ride and a smile, parting always as before.

Who art thou to steal my heart away, he would ask silently and chafe inwardly when, in a hunting party, she laughingly cantered next to Balazun, or when men mentioned her—Irene the unattainable.

Every fibre of his being said run, ride away, but he did not.

His languor was deepened by Charles' and Jacques' apparent contentment. "There's time yet to get away," Jacques had said when Guy half-heartedly broached the subject. Within the sheltering walls, paid, fed and distracted, Guy's companions contributed to his hopeful wait-and-see ennui.

At length he determined to confess his feelings to Irene at their next outing, but circumstance intervened.

Manzikert,
Morning, 26th June 1054

John Curticius burst into the Barbarian House and past Guy d'Agiles to where Leo was pondering a map. "My God, Bryennius. You must help me. My daughter has gone. Anna's in such a state—giving me the devil for it! The scandal! Her black horse, Shahryād is missing as well. I've been out half the night, even to the hut she and that blackguard used from time to time. Bryennius, you've got to find her. Irene's out there somewhere."

Leo turned from the map, glanced at Guy d'Agiles and saw the young Frank blanch. "Gone? Can you think where, Sir?" the young Frank whispered.

Curticius glanced uncomprehendingly at Guy, then back to Leo.

"A moment, please, Sir. Guy, get the princeps a chair. Then leave us please and have someone see to his horse." It was done. The door closed a little too loudly, Leo thought.

"She has a … suitor I suppose you'd call him—that Ankhialou fellow—in Archēsh, damn him. She may've gone there. Or to her brother at Artzké."

"At either place she will be safe."

"If she makes it. You know what happens in these times," Curticius choked. "All manner of cutthroats about, infidels, refugees becoming brigands on the roads."

"She has a good horse and knows her way." Leo passed the princeps a goblet of water and watched him drink deeply.

There was another long pause before John Curticius answered. "Yes. My God, Bryennius. The scandal. A daughter's reputation. And mine. What did we do wrong?"

Leo believed himself the last man on earth to be advising a distressed parent. Who knew what passed between fathers and daughters? He did not have the time or resources to search for a wilful young woman probably already with a suitor. "We'll do what we can, Princeps." Reluctantly, he added, "Would you have me send out a search party?"

Curticius looked at the count who now controlled most of Manzikert's cavalry. "Would to God you could. You cannot … but if you hear something …"

"Of course. We have scheduled patrols going out south, east and between in the next day or so. I will ask them to keep an eye out."

"Oh, thank you. Thank you." One hand on the back of his neck, Curticius turned to the map, eyes roving it.

"Would you like to rest a while and join us later for the midday meal?" Leo took Curticius by the shoulder and steered him towards a back room which held refreshments and three comfortable lounges for the people on the long night duty, or scouts waiting for tasking.

Leo did not need the additional drama. Since his arrival at Manzikert he had been busy training his men and running the Barbarian House—the comings and goings of the net of mounted pickets, patrols and spies Basil, Branas and he had woven around the fortress. The demands were continual and draining; training, a quarrel in the ranks, financing the scouting, constant reconnaissance and participating in daily meetings.

The meetings had been taxing enough when the strategos' council was a small circle, but this had grown to include chattering officials, each of whom had some self-proclaimed critical role to play in the defence of Manzikert. Decorum and prudence dictated that they—the senior warriors, veterinarians, quartermasters, doctors, billet masters, clerks and priests—were all present and had a voice in the deliberations. Leo had to bite his lip and endure their long orations on any subject near to their hearts, influence and careers. Certainly the matters were important, but they might have learned the virtue of brevity. His confidantes in this were Branas, Selth, Doukas, Oleg and the abbess.

All the while, Kamyates and Cydones sniffed around spreading their slurs.

While others had taken their ease, Leo was taxed for time. Whenever he attempted to rest, there would be a message for his attendance with Basil or

Curticius. Zarrar and Ruksh, with their worn shoes and sweated backs attested to the hours he had spent familiarising himself with the walls and terrain outside. He explored the little gully where a tunnel could be cunningly started, noted the dryness of the pasture and dallied in the little hamlet of K'arglukh. With its stone house, well and animal enclosures on higher ground, the settlement might serve as a headquarters for the Sultan.

Days spent walking Manzikert's defences revealed the tricks of ground and architecture that would influence the battle. The deep, poplar-lined gully to the south, with its rushing creek, would act as an obstacle in the camp of the besiegers. Iron-barred drains under the walls must be guarded. A ragged line of solid stone buildings in Manzikert should be fortified to form an inner wall in case the circuit walls were breached. A forgotten track that dropped from an almost invisible sally-port through the ditch and into the country beyond, could be used to steal into the enemy camp. He listened to the town's inhabitants with their unspoken fear, but was heartened by their quiet determination not to yield to the fate of Kars or Artsn.

Everyone wanted something; certainty about the Seljuks, the replacement of a lame horse or worn saddle, time off, money, his opinion on this matter or that, or his blessing of some scheme. Even his squire, willing as Taticus Phocas was, needed instruction and oversight in the ways of warriors and war. What weighed most heavily was that Vardaheri and Maniakh had not yet retuned from their scout to Tabriz.

Curticius emerged after a time looking a little more refreshed. He declined lunch and left the Barbarian House to resume his duties despite the turmoil of his private life.

After a late morning parade in the heat to inspect the fitness and preparedness of the men and horses of the Scholae and the other cavalry, Leo decided on some much-needed rest. Bessas agreed to assume his duties for the afternoon and Leo returned to his quarters where he donned a comfortable linen tunic and sandals. Satisfied few people were around to disturb him or he them, he threw his cloak down outside his room in the shade of the stone veranda. Lying down, he closed his eyes—his sword half under him so he would waken if anyone tried to take it. In the quietness he could hear the footsteps and rummaging of odd individual comings and goings, the distant sounds of the military quarter and town, the sounds of peace and all's well. Opening his eyes lazily, Leo could see beyond the buildings to the clear blue sky decorated by high white tufts of cloud. He felt a gentle breeze take the edge off the heat and was aware of a sense of restfulness. Then he fell into an exhausted sleep.

Awakening in the late afternoon and feeling thirsty, he rose and drank from a clay jar suspended from a beam and washed his face in the bowl of water on the bench in his quarters. Lethargically, he sat on the veranda step and began the familiar mind-clearing task of cleaning and checking his weapons and turned his thoughts again to the matters of Manzikert.

Leo looked up as Martina approached, wearing riding clothes and her careless felt hat. One of the Barbarian House group working mostly to Isaac and Branas, she eased her weapons belt slung over her shoulder and smiled at him. "It's about time you rested," she said.

He was surprised by her candour and the sudden realisation she noticed his movements. In their daily world of reticence, occasional formal pleasantries and plenty of other things to concern him, their fleeting encounter in a dark passage of the imperial palace was not in his foremost thoughts. "You've just finished?"

"Yes. I was going to change into something cooler." She hesitated. "I just saw Modestos Kamyates watching you. He seemed … intense."

"Indeed. Where was he?"

"Hiding in the bushes at that corner behind me," she said without looking back. "He left when I passed by."

"Thank you," he murmured, suppressing the urge to seek out the courtier and provoke a violent confrontation. "That is useful to know." Leo read the concern on her face and tried to make light of the incident. "Doesn't pay to close your eyes around here, does it?"

She smiled. "No. It doesn't."

"You do not get much time off either, so make sure you also get some rest."

Instead she dallied and they talked of horses. In response to his question she described growing up in Syria and learning Arabic from neighbours. A groping stepfather had led her to run away to herd cattle in Anatolia.

"In my youth, I too drove cattle and broke-in horses in Anatolia," he said.

Their eyes met suddenly in the knowledge of a shared other experience: horse sweat and the open sky, long days in the saddle, swift galloping musters and slow droving trips to markets. Each knew the other had been through it and understood.

At length she excused herself. "Anyway, I must change my clothes," and went her way.

To Leo's surprise, she reappeared after an interval, looking feminine in a cool robe with her brown hair back in a gay bow. "I thought you might enjoy this book—Kasia."

"Thank you. Ah! The poetess. That is very thoughtful of you and I will be delighted."

"You know of her?"

He opened the volume and made room for her to sit. "If I'm not mistaken, her independent, some say impudent, answer to the Emperor Theophilus in the bridal line-up meant she was not favoured with the golden apple. She later founded a monastery. That is her, isn't it?"

Martina had freshly bathed and wore the faintest hint of an alluring scent. "Yes," she breathed, edging closer to see the pages as he turned them.

"Appreciating poetry probably isn't how you learned to use the bow. We were distracted by the worthy subject of horses before, and you did not tell me what journey brought you to Manzikert."

"No, we were distracted," she mused and told him of her being drawn to Constantinople, of her employment by a remount dealer where she was noticed by a tribune of the Excubitores. Soon she was translating documents for the Office of Barbarians and enjoying more money and a wider social circle.

Leo noticed her wedding ring. "That is still far from Manzikert?"

Martina she saw his glance. "I married, not by the usual arrangement as a teenager," she grimaced at the convention, "but later, for love of a cataphract of the Excubitores."

"Did he teach you how to use the bow?"

"No." She paused, glanced down and then into the distance. "Another." She looked down again, long, then up into his eyes. "They needed someone who would not be noticed to bring a message, so I came with Yūryak bearing despatches for the strategos. We have been employed by him since—until it's time to take despatches back to Constantinople. And that's how I came to Manzikert."

Leo now placed her as the woman in the red dress in the dimly lit festival hall where he had confronted Gurgen. "You seemed so knowledgeable and at ease I thought you had been out here for some time. You were at Arknik when we came through?"

"Yes. The strategos sent us to check the reports of troops on the way."

"Doesn't give much away, does he?"

"No, he doesn't. Everything's so secret. Only Count Branas, the strategos, princeps and a couple of others know we are the couriers. We arrived by night with a pass that got us direct access."

"Perhaps too secret. Were you told you were pursued?"

"We weren't told exactly by whom. There was a plan to get us away. That was you, wasn't it?"

"If you can call such a hasty, scatter-brained thing a plan."

They looked at each other with silent questions about the roles they played in the affairs of Vaspurakan. Leo closed the book and put it down by his side. She shifted away in the smallest concession to society's conventions.

"Anyway, it didn't seem too dangerous. Who'd notice another woman with a provincial accent like mine travelling the roads? The money's good." She paused, thinking to herself. "Did you ever find anyone after us?"

"No proof, Martina. But between us I would be careful of Cydones and anyone close to him."

She looked down for a time. "It's all so melancholy. Who to trust? Theodora told ..."

Leo watched her for a moment, realising she was sworn to some confidence. "Well, at least horses do not lie," he said.

She looked up and smiled.

Two hours passed as they conversed freely. With a little crowd of his men now socialising further along the veranda, Leo was acutely aware of their being together for so long, risking the gossip of impropriety. Watching her speak, with her clear eyes and expressive lips, he was suddenly conscious of being grateful to her for the company, at risk of her own reputation.

With darkness gathering, she looked around and seemed to also sense the little audience that looked their way from time to time. "I'd better go." There was a long moment before she looked into his eyes. "I must."

Leo stood as she did. "Thank you. It was delightful. I enjoyed our talk. Very much!"

"It was my pleasure," she smiled, hesitating a moment as though she would say something. Then she was gone.

Leo felt a loss as she left. Despite his constant dealings with people, he had little real intimacy with anyone—the monk-like solitude of the professional warrior. He loved the charm of the conversation with her, but chafed at how the social and military concerns about others' perceptions of propriety had intruded into his consciousness, stealing the simple pleasure from him.

As Leo dined that evening a dusty courier from Artzké rode to the citadel bearing despatches of a rumoured Seljuk raiding party some two-hundred strong, moving westward south of the Sea of Bznunik. Leo was summoned and accompanied by old Arshak, entered Basil Apocapes' rooms to find Bessas, Curticius, Branas and Doukas already there.

By flickering lamplight, Basil pounded the map on the wall. "Leo, I was going to send you on a cattle raid along the river valley anyway, but things have changed. I want you to take your regiment down here, to the west, first thing tomorrow. See if you can intercept any Seljuk raid and inflict maximum casualties. Arshak knows the country. The best places to intercept them are here, or here in the theme of Taron." Basil pointed to two small settlements marked east of the border city of Mush. "I'll send a galloper to Theodore Vladislav and alert him if your presence in his theme and the possibility of a Seljuk raid."

"If there's no sign of them there …" Basil studied the map in silence. "… then you may push patrols further south toward Baghesh to determine whether they're exploring the route to Melitene. Bear in mind you may cross into Marwanid Kurdish territory there. Avoid the Kurds. Don't get decisively engaged with the Seljuks if they are in greater strength than you are certain you can handle. Be back in no more than three days. Your main task is to bring the cattle. We need the hides and meat, both of which we can dry and store. It is more important to secure them than get involved in a private war. Any questions?"

Leo looked at the map and ordered his thoughts before answering, "First, the cattle and intelligence, second, to inflict casualties if I can. I propose not to take the squires or a pack train, but leave them here to fill the gaps. We can leave at first light. How close to Baghesh am I to go? Visit the town itself?"

"No need. The Kurds would be neutral in any contest and I have visited the place several times. Save yourself a detour! And we do not wish to provoke them."

Leo looked at Bessas. The centarch nodded.

"We're as one," said Basil. "Tagmata troops on the prowl and a bloody nose might unsettle and dissuade the nomads. But I do need those cattle, both for us and to deprive the nomad of them. Remember the Seljuk raid is a rumour as yet—the cattle are real enough. I want you out before sun-up and back inside three days."

Leo saluted and with Bessas and Arshak, turned to leave. On opening the heavy timber door of Basil's study, he was irritated to find Modestos Kamyates standing in the torch-lit stone passageway. "Kamyates?"

"Bryennius! I thought you had the day off?" Kamyates said superciliously.

"As I do."

"I heard there was a courier," Kamyates looked past Leo. "Where're you off to in such haste?"

"Indeed!" Leo gave a non-answer and turned to Basil with a raised eyebrow.

Curticius caught Leo's eye with a pleading look. Leo nodded sympathetically.

"Please bid Modestos enter," Basil said resignedly. As the courtier entered the room, the strategos gave his beaming, inclusive smile. "Modestos! Just the man. I've opened wine which I think you'll like. Yes, we've had some droll rumour from an outpost, but it'll come to nothing."

Leo did not hear the rest as he and Bessas dashed from the citadel with Arshak struggling to keep up. As they left, three files of burly Varangians jogged down the roadway from the citadel, boots crashing in cadence on the flagstones, mail tinkering and the occasional thud of a sword scabbard or spear against a shield. The leaders and rear carried torches and there were the darting shadows of double-headed battle-axes against stone walls as they reached the foot of the slope, breathing heavily under their helmets and beards, settling into the jog to the gates.

Leo recognised one of Doukas' tribunes with them. The man slowed to a walk to inform Leo the sentries were being doubled and none, except official messengers, would be allowed to leave or enter the fortress until noon the following day. The regiment could deploy with some security as to their intentions.

Runners fetched the tribunes while the decarchs collected their men and supervised the preparations: light marching order, no arrow-proof bards[53] for the horses, but an extra blanket under the saddle. Hard rations for three days were distributed with grain bags for the mounts. The squires also gave the horses an extra feed in the dark, checking all the while that they had water to drink. Then the regiment slept except for the occasional restless or disorganised soul still packing until after the end of the second night watch. In the lamp-lit rooms of the Barbarian House, clerks laboriously copied the available maps, providing enough for each tribune.

Leo awoke after a three hours of restless sleep.

---

53 Bard—horse armour, like a horsrug, made with either: mail, lamellar, glued felt, or silk padded with cotton wadding.

Troopers rose in the dark, some alert with vigour and the thrill of an imminent fight, others still stupefied from interrupted slumber. Someone coughed. Sparing of words, they tugged on boots and mail shirts. Men breakfasted quickly in the mess, the torchlight reflecting weakly from interlocked polished iron rings so the mess looked like countless distant stars. In murmuring groups, carrying saddles and weapons, they made their way to the stables and walked the laneways of the yards, seeking their squires and horses. There was movement of hide and the sudden smell of fresh manure and urine, as the tension of the troops transmitted itself to their mounts.

Bluish in the weak moonlight, the regiment assembled, men leading their horses to the forming-up-place for each troop and easing them into line. A small, silent group of women watched. One of them, on seeing a familiar face in the ranks, darted forward to give a trooper a linen bag, food perhaps or some other small comfort, and a kiss, then backed away, still looking at the shadowed features under the helmet rim.

Leo mounted Zarrar. "A clear morning, Antony? Are scouts and interpreters attached as discussed last night?"

"Yes, Count, mostly." Lascaris swung to horse. "I've told-off the three Armenians. Yūryak with Bessas, since Bessas also speaks Arabic. Arshak is with you and as he does not read the tongue, I've told the woman to ride with you as she does. Ruben's with me."

"What woman?"

"From the Barbarian House. Martina Cinnamus. There was no choice. I couldn't find another interpreter at short notice. And she was keen to come."

Suddenly faced with his feelings, Leo was reluctant to expose her to danger. "There is no one else?"

"No, Sir."

"Very well. What of D'Agiles and his man?"

"At the head of the column with Togol and David Varaz," Lascaris said. "D'Agiles is riding his chestnut mare. I found a spare horse for his man"

The centarchs formed like ghosts around Leo who now reinforced the gist of the previous evening's orders. "My command group is first out the gate. Then the Third Squadron under Sebeos—straight west to the river line, on the south side. Bessas, you're next, with the First Squadron. When through the village, swing south. When well out of sight of Manzikert, cut northwest and pick up my track, close up as left flank-guard. Screen to the south. Antony," he said, turning to Lascaris. "Last out with the Second. Follow the road west, but do not cross north of the river. Close up as rear guard. Questions?"

The officers shook their heads so Leo trotted to the head of the column and greeted Togol and David on their captured mounts. Martina, wearing a felt, arrow-proof jerkin, smiled shyly.

"Ready?" Leo hoped his grin to her appeared encouraging.

"Ready!"

Guy d'Agiles still looked downcast and Leo was glad he knew the reason. The young Frank needed to get over the Curticius woman.

The regiment moved off in column of fours at the walk. They started in the eerie touch of horseshoes, soft creak of leather, and muffled iron sounds of armour and weapons. A horse blew somewhere, clearing its nostrils and several others followed. Riders spoke softly to quiet restive animals as Leo led the column into the shadows of the tree-lined main thoroughfare. The gate towers loomed and Leo reined in as Basil stepped from the shadows.

"Zarrar looks good, real good. What've you been feeding him?"

"Your barley, I believe."

Basil laughed. "It is good grain! Remind me to arrest your squire!" Then he became serious. "There's nothing more than we knew last night, unless you have any last questions?"

"No questions."

"Good luck," said Basil as Leo saluted and trotted to the lead.

Two squadrons, each a hundred strong, peeled off as arranged. It grew light as the fortress disappeared behind them and they extended into open patrolling formation. Leo rode in the centre behind Sebēos and his standard-bearer while Martina, David, Guy and Jacques were close by. He noticed the woman had rolled up her sleeves above the elbow, the measure of comfort in disregard of society's convention of women covering their arms above the wrist. One troop was spread out around them, the other dispersed forward in arrowhead as screen with the Armenian scouts still further ahead. Leo kept the pace to a quick walk, looking disapprovingly at any man who had to jog his horse to keep up. He varied who he rode with—Sebēos, David and Togol, then amongst the cataphracts, speaking of the raid, horses or answering their questions about the history of which some had a notion they were now a part.

The sun rose and the day grew warm. Gallopers trotted in from Lascaris and Bessas, reporting them in position. Leo lagged behind, looking to the rear left flank for the distant shapes of men and horses. They were there, faintly, if one knew what to look for.

Leo noticed cattle here and there, small groups of up to a dozen grazing peacefully and paying the dispersed horsemen little mind. Left for now, they could be collected on the way home. He was enjoying the ride and being outside the walls, for emotions inside the fortress became oppressive as the unpredictable future teased at people's nerves.

Pausing on another slight rise in the ground that would be unnoticed by a casual traveller, Leo could watch Sebēos' squadron move out of sight over a similar rise ahead. How the ground could play tricks: friend to the wise and foe to the unwary.

Scanning the hills to the south he noticed a subtle hue in the haze but could not fathom the source. Dust? Smoke? His own thoughts jumping at shadows, perhaps? He waited.

Bessas rode up with Yūryak on a dun mare at his side. The Armenian, a brown-eyed young man affecting long brown hair with drooping mustachios, looked workmanlike in a faded brown tunic under his horn-lamellar cuirass, bow and sword at his hips. He owned a small landholding near Manzikert.

"You've seen it too?" Bessas gestured to the distant smudge in the sky.

The three of them looked at it. "There is a track that way, leading from Baghesh to Sasun," Yūryak said.

Bessas eased in his saddle. "It's dust more than smoke I think."

"You might be right." Leo squinted under his helmet, peering over his forearm held level below the eyes to cut the reflected glare from the ground. "It could be Roman troops from Taron. We've probably passed into their area by now. Or it could be hostile. I'll tell you what I'm thinking. We will camp overnight in the village of Sashesh, ahead. I am told it is on a low knoll, has stone buildings and yards with two good wells, so it is quite defensible. We can conceal our strength there. Tomorrow, we'll collect the cattle and set a trap for the hostiles, if that is what the mystery proves to be. The dust of a big herd of cattle will surely attract their greed or curiosity. I will take the mustering party. You, Bessas, will be to the south-east as the hammer, Sebēos near the village as the anvil and Antony Lascaris somewhere east of there on some defensible higher ground as reserve. Any cattle you come across, hunt them back up river, we can collect them on our return march." He looked inquisitively at Bessas as he completed his outline. "You have linked up with Antony?"

"Yes, Count."

"Pass on my intentions to him. Think on it. We will discuss it tonight."

Bessas smiled. In Leo's parlance that had entailed some robust debates in the past, with rank having no privilege.

Leo turned Zarrar. "I'll tell Sebēos." He cantered forward in Zarrar's matchless, rocking stride until he reined in alongside Martina. Their horses swung their heads together for a step in equine greeting.

"Do you feel like some cattle-lifting tomorrow, Martina?"

She turned her face to him and laughed, teeth gleaming and her eyes alight beneath her hat. "It's a while since I've heard that."

Leo smiled. That is why he had used it, referring to the virtual cattle theft practiced by many of the Empire's irregular troops to supplement their paltry incomes. The crime had been so widespread that many of the irregular troops were called by the derogatory term, cattle-lifters. "Yours is a fine horse. Did you get him out here or ride him here?"

"I rode another out here but it needed to spell after the journey, so Count Branas found him for me. He reminds me of a horse I rode years ago, so I named him Little Zarrar."

"Zarrar is this horse's name," Leo said.

Zarrar's ears flicked back.

Martina looked at Leo's horse and their stirrups touched as they drew together. "Why did you name him after an Arab champion of the Yarmuk[54]?"

Leo looked at her, surprised by her knowledge of history. She was close to him, in sharp outline against the sweep of steppe and sky, bridle hand easy with loose reins, her tanned forearm resting lightly on the bow case. Their stirrups touched again. He smiled into her eyes. "Well! When he was a youngster, Zarrar here was none too pretty and no friend of the Romans."

She laughed, the corners of her mouth alive with vibrant humanity. "He is now a fine horse and friendly to one Roman at least."

Leo blushed under his helmet and glanced at her again before looking once more at the southern horizon. He turned to her. "You obviously love horses rather than use them merely for duty—perhaps we should go for a ride when there is some free time?"

"That would be lovely. There are some quite beautiful tracks out of Manzikert. I could show you," she offered.

"Splendid. I'm planning to buy another horse, a brown mare—she'll need some quiet work. In the meantime we should enjoy this ride." He was aware of having spoken beyond decorum again and the familiar feeling of impropriety encroached. Making an excuse, he motioned on Zarrar. The horse did not respond, as if reading Leo's real wishes. He touched Zarrar with his heels and the bay leapt forward, ears back in momentary irritation, as though thinking, Make up your mind!

It was always the same when soldiers approached a village. Such was the recurrence of conquest, civil war and outright banditry; the poor lived in a continual state of apprehension. It was no surprise to Leo that after he sent in the van and enveloping flankers, there was a familiar pattern of dogs barking, mothers calling, pale-faced children looking out from half closed doors while the men, surprised in the open fields, looked on helplessly.

"Clear, no hostiles," Sebēos called before seeking out the headman in the fading light to explain that the regiment would stay overnight.

"Look," the elder pleaded, "we all know the game is up out here. Either Basil Apocapes gets the cattle or the Persians do." The man looked Leo in the eyes. "But leave us something."

Leo thought before speaking. "We muster in the morning but will not take your horses, sheep, goats or grain. I'll sign a requisition for the cattle. Take it to the strategos. He will pay you if he can. Mount some men and I will allow you to draft out two hundred head of your best breeding stock and an ample number of killers. We will pay for the food and fodder consumed tonight and your women are safe. Then you should conceal your stock somewhere in the hills and hide the money when we leave. Now, come, share a jug of wine and tell me of this place."

---

54 This battle (August 636CE), near the Golan Heights, was fought between Byzantines and Muslim Arabs. The Byzantines lost control of Syria, paving the way for the early Islamic invasions of the Near East and North Africa.

The headman showed his relief and accepted the offer.

Lascaris deployed mounted pickets from his squadron and posted sentinels on foot around the perimeter as horses were kept saddled with girths loosened. Men removed the bridles for feeding and watering, then knee-hobbled the mounts for the night, with spare blankets and cloaks thrown over them for some protection against arrows. The village men spit-roasted a number of sheep and pigs, while the women brought platters of bread and clay urns of soup. As this was underway, the decarchs supervised the drawing of water from the well.

Leo called the officers over. They talked long with the Armenian scouts from Manzikert and local peasants who described the terrain to them; the locals sketching a rough map on a piece of parchment. By their drawing, a shallow, dry wadi cut the plain, east to west. "It is easily crossed," the peasants concurred.

The regiment breakfasted, Leo noticing, in the way of such trifles, Martina's interest in the silver spoon he had picked up at Artsn. The unit mounted and moved off when it was light enough to ensure they were not riding into an ambush prepared through the night.

Leo led half a dozen mounted peasants and as many cataphracts to muster, accompanied by Guy, Togol, David and Martina. Alternately walking and trotting in a wide sweep to the southwest of Sashesh, they started the smaller herds back towards the river to be collected later. All knew they were the thinking bait and controlling mind in the trap. After crossing the wadi, Leo estimated they were at the furthest limit of a useful sweep for cattle, so he swung eastward.

Riding dispersed, a spear-cast between riders, they soon had a herd of some three thousand, the cattle bunched in the bellowing of separated cows and calves, or mournful lament of bullocks dimly recalling other days of fear and pain at the hands of men. After the first couple of herd-like rushes forward, or away from the breeze, the cattle forsook escape and settled down to a stolid walk in the face of the shouting, whistling riders.

Leo had more than cattle on his mind. Often he drew away from the dust to look around at the lay of the land and for any sign of the raiders whilst enjoying a gentle breeze from the south.

Mid-morning, he motioned Guy and Togol to him and indicated a low, gentle sided ridge spotted with scrub-oak about two miles distant. "Guy, take a slow trot to that high ground to the south. Ride its length a mile or so. Let yourself be sky-lined on it. Then come and tell me what you see. If there are hostiles there, circle your horse twice, then come quick. Hold your spear high up parallel to the ground if you think they know there are more than just a few cows and drovers here. If you get chased, ride like a fiend and look for me, then do as I direct. Togol, Jacques—if Guy gets chased back, we will make a fight of it. One of the pursuers will be out front, faster, prouder and hungrier than the rest. I want to capture him. Then will come one or two, perhaps three others on better horses. Jacques, I want you to take the second, as far out as you can, with your crossbow.

And the third if you are able. That should give the others pause. Then we hope Bessas comes quickly."

They all looked grim as Guy trotted off on Sira, jamming his floppy hat on more securely.

"Where's his helmet?" Leo asked.

"He didn't think he would need it chasing cows," Togol replied.

Leo looked at Togol who shrugged. They watched until Guy was a speck on the ridge.

The morning turned hot under a cloudless sky. They rode on until the watchful silence was broken by Togol. "It's damned far to see, but something is happening with Guy. He's circling his horse. Now he is leaving the ridge. Pretty damn fast too!"

Leo could make out the dust of many riders crossing the ridge in pursuit. He snapped into action. "Get the herd moving, north," he ordered, flinging an arm out, "that way!" Then he put Zarrar to the gallop, drawing alongside Martina.

From her expression she had guessed something serious was afoot as their horses grabbed the bits in excitement.

"Martina, message for Centarch Phocas! Probable hostiles to our south. Small band. Twenty or thirty. Could be others. They are in pursuit of Guy d'Agiles and probably do not know the regiment is here. Ride to Bessas and tell him to come quickly from the west. His object is to relieve us and to inflict maximum casualties. No pursuit. Make sure you tell him no pursuit. Stay with him and report to me after he engages."

Martina's face clouded with concentration and she glanced past him through the dust. Little Zarrar was already bunched in anticipation under her as she calmly repeated the message.

"Good. Like the wind, Martina." Leo reined in Zarrar after the bay made to dart after Martina's mount. Leo watched her gallop away, reproaching himself for endangering her by allowing her to accompany the raid.

Then he turned Zarrar on his hocks and galloped to Togol and Jacques. Togol was mounting, having just set fire to the grass. The drovers were shouting on cantering horses amidst the leaping flames, smoke, dust and confusion. The herd took on a startled rushing momentum of its own, with the peasants of Sashesh driving it in flight across the dry watercourse.

"Into the wadi," Leo roared.

Togol, David, Jacques, Arshak and five cataphracts rode plunging horses into the wadi which was just deep enough to shelter a mounted man from sight.

"Dismount, men. Spread out. Take post. Give d'Agiles room."

Two cataphracts grasped the reins. The rest drew bows and scrambled up the sides to crouch below the lip of the wadi. Jacques lay panting on the ground at the edge of the channel straining the crossbow arms against his feet while hauling with all his might on the string. He nocked a dart, placed another between his teeth, gulped two breaths of the smoky, dusty air, then waited behind a concealing tuft of rough grass.

Leo, straight and stern, sat the excited but obedient Zarrar above the wadi. He needed Guy to see him. Below him, David and Togol shook out lassos.

Guy closed at full gallop, head bent beside Sira's neck, but he was not holding his spear up to indicate that the pursuers knew of the presence of Roman troops. Leo saw him look up and wipe his eyes. Leo waved his spear and shouted. Guy changed direction toward them with the first galloping pursuers two bowshots behind him. Leo rode into the wadi, dismounted and threw the reins to a cataphract. He turned just in time to see Sira pause in a half rear at the lip.

"Keep going! Keep going!" he shouted and gestured urgently at Guy to ride through the wadi and on, to give the appearance of continued flight.

Guy, white-faced with his hat gone, leapt his mare into the channel and scrambled up the other side into the lifting dust made by the disappearing herd.

Drumming hoof beats signalled the arrival of the first pursuer close behind. Too late he saw the wadi, held horses and crouching Romans. The rider, an Arab by his dress and equipment, jerked the black horse to a halt and tried to turn. Lassos snaked out from both sides and the Arab, still mounted on his black horse, was snared and dragged screaming into the dry watercourse. The horse, unbalanced by the turn, fell in with him. Leo glanced back at a confusion of plunging horses and struggling men. Togol jumped on the Arab and dealt him a hefty whack. The black horse lay struggling in a tangled lasso.

Leo heard one of their horses nicker.

Quickly he looked at the approaching riders, then back into the dry watercourse and saw Togol's black mare peering over her shoulder, with pricked ears and nostrils distended in recognition of the Arab's horse. The black was struggling to rise and a cataphract made to grab it. They were about to fight for their lives so there were more concerns than a loose horse. "Leave it," shouted Leo. "Watch your front."

David knelt beside him, uncasing his bow. "Seljuks, alright."

"Hostile Seljuks, men. Cataphracts—take the second. Jacques—the third." There was a seemingly long pause, with the men crouching dry-mouthed in the heat and dust. Leo settled his troopers for the shock of contact. "Hearts up. Make ready. Shoot!"

A big Seljuk on a grey mare crashed to the ground a spear's length from the wadi, two arrows buried deep in her chest. Her dazed rider crawled behind her for cover. Leo heard the jolt of Jacques' crossbow and saw the third horseman grasp uselessly at his breast. His bay mare galloped on, the rider slumped forward, fingers entwined in the bloodied mane. A spear-cast from the wadi he collapsed down the near side, dragging the horse into the fall with him.

The other pursuers reined up and retreated a little.

Jacques sprinted forward, flung himself on the fallen bay horse's neck and seized a front leg, preventing the animal from rising.

"That fool is going to try and have the horse," Togol exclaimed, half in astonishment, half in admiration.

Jacques, lying awkwardly, struggled to hold the terrified horse down while reloading his crossbow.

Togol uttered something unintelligible and he too rose and walked almost casually, mace in hand, to the downed grey where he dealt a fatal blow to the bowman hiding behind it and another to the wounded horse. With an almost disdainful glance at the milling riders two furlongs[55] away, the Cuman walked to where Jacques lay. Togol slid the mace into his belt, from which he took a length of rope, slipping it around the horse's front legs. Jacques rose and together they dragged the struggling animal by the rope and bridle to the wadi. Despite its trying to rear away, the ropes around its legs always brought it down closer to safety. They pulled the struggling beast bodily into the hole after them.

Leo thought about calling them for fools, but decided that no harm had been done. Indeed their coolness might indicate to the enemy that the wadi was held in greater strength.

"Kelt! You are surely the prince of horse thieves." David declared.

Guy cantered back from the dust cloud and joined them. The colour had returned to his face, which was red with effort and excitement.

"Aspieties," ordered Leo. "Take a man and a handful of spears each and make it look like a hundred men are here. And do a lot of shouting."

He peeped over the lip of the wadi. The Seljuks were still milling in confusion two furlongs distant. He could see no sign of Bessas through the dust of the distant cattle, but took some comfort from the fact that it would obscure Bessas' presence from the Seljuks.

Togol crouched next to Leo. "Horse-archer, we must have got the leader."

Guy crawled up, breathlessly. "You captured the first one? He seemed to know my horse for he kept calling out. He would trot toward me, and I would trot away. He would walk, so would I. When he cantered. So did I. When he stopped. So did I. When he galloped in pursuit, I galloped in flight."

Togol, his brow knitted at Guy's broken Greek, discerned the meaning and roared laughing. "No wonder he was browned-off by the time he got here."

"He knew your horse, you say," asked Leo. "Togol's mare definitely thinks she knows the black horse that he was riding."

Guy allowed a foolish-looking grin of triumph mixed with relief. Then his face grew serious. "As long as they don't get him back now."

"That is right." Leo looked across the plain. There was no sign of Bessas, but despite it seeming like ages, little time had elapsed. "C'mon, Bessas, damn you," he muttered to himself. "It all depends on you now."

A few bolder nomads were drawing near, still mounted, trying to discern what was ahead of them.

---

55 Furlong—literally "furrow's length"; a measure of distance equivalent to 220 yards or 201 metres.

"Jacques, see if you can get that fellow in black," Leo said. He now examined the wadi more closely and found by happy chance, that should the Seljuks enter it further along, his patrol had taken cover in a slight bend that gave them some protection from enfilading missiles.

Jacques, his crossbow charged and shield slung over his back, settled at the lip for the shot.

Leo reckoned he had a few minutes to take stock for fight or flight. Hoping Martina was safe and with Bessas, he slid to the bottom of the wadi and approached the dazed prisoner who was looking around in confusion. The captive's glance lingered on the horses captured during the taking of Zobeir al-Adin: Guy's chestnut, Togol's black and David's dun. Guy's mare whinnied. The Arab, dust from the fall over his clothing and in his beard, glanced at the mare, then looked silently at Leo. Leo tried to converse in Greek and his few words of Latin. The prisoner did not respond, except with a flicker of the eyes at the Greek question about his name.

Arshak tried the local Armenian dialect but the Arab gestured that he did not understand.

"Togol, try the language of the steppes on him. And blindfold him, please. He's seen enough."

Togol scrambled down from where he had been kneeling and glaring at the prisoner, roughly blindfolded him with the Arab's own black turban.

Leo made a mental note to check the turban for secret writing later. He returned to the lip to face the enemy.

Jacques shot. There was a yelp of pain and the black horseman's mount reared uncontrollably and threw its rider as Jacques readied another bolt.

"Well done, Jacques. I'd say you hit his leg and fixed him to horse and saddle both." Leo observed the milling, shouting riders draw off. "That gives us a bit more time."

He turned to the men in the wadi. They looked at him and he was surprised to see the pale, frightened face of one cataphract crouched in the dirt, clutching his bow, an arrow nocked to it. Leo was suddenly conscious that he felt no particular fear and supposed in a reflective moment that he had been too busy. "Well done, men! First chukka[56] to us. We'll make a fight of this, now. They look like tribal horse-archers so it will take a while for a leader to organise them. Swallow some water while you have the chance." He looked at the fearful cataphract and knew he had to give him something to do. "Quieten those horses if you can," Leo ordered gently, clasping the man by the shoulder. "And get that black one up on its feet."

Leo glanced at Zarrar. The gelding was looking at him, head up and ears pricked with excitement, as though he found it all thrilling. "Whoa there, Zarrar. Good boy," he said.

---

56 Chukka—a time division in the games of polo and polocrosse

The frightened cataphract loosened the rope and leapt back as the Arab's black horse flailed to its feet in a cloud of dust and rattling accoutrements. It nickered gently as an answer came again from Togol's black mare.

Leo observed this and saw David Varaz walking forward to pick up the lasso and re-coil it, without conscious thought, just long, prudent practice. He saw the prisoner cock his head at the whinnies. "David, these captured horses know each other—interesting!"

Turning again to the group he rattled off more steadying orders. "Lay some cloaks over the horses, and get under your shields, men. The next thing we can expect is a few arrows."

"At least we will have plenty to shoot back," Togol announced happily.

They all laughed, the black humour settling their nerves a little.

"After that they might charge," Leo thought aloud. "But I think there'll be a lot of crawling around and trying to take us with arrows first. Our main purpose is to keep them distracted so Bessas can take them unaware." He made his way to Zarrar, giving the horse a hug around the neck. He pulled greedily from the water skin and unstrapping his cloak, dragged it in loose folds over the saddled horse.

There was a shout of triumph from Jacques, "Count! Another down."

"Very good. Keep down! What are they doing now?"

"Dragging the last one I hit out of range."

"Horse-archer," Togol said. "I can converse some with the prisoner. He says his name is Derar al-Adin. He wants to know if we are brigands." Togol was looking at Leo across the ordered confusion in the wadi bottom.

"Brigands, eh? I guess after a morning of cattle lifting that's debatable. Tell him, yes. Why?"

Togol spoke with the prisoner. "Ransom," Togol called back. "His friends out there are carrying gold."

"Say nothing!" Leo wished to prolong the captive's agony of uncertainty.

There was a period of tense inactivity while the men in the wadi waited, fidgeting with weapons or calming horses. Some prayed. Leo noticed the rough line of stunted bushes growing on both lips of the wadi or just below it and thought to put them to use. "David," he said. "Grab your lasso, and Togol's."

The Georgian scout sensed his intention and together they hurriedly strung the twisted greenhide ropes along the edge of the wadi, making them fast to the bushes a foot above the ground. "Well," grunted David. "That'll be a nasty surprise for them if they charge us."

"Look out!" cried Jacques. "Arrows!"

A dozen shafts buried themselves in the rear wall of the wadi. There was a pause and more arrows, fired at a higher trajectory, plunged down. Like everyone else, Leo cowered under his shield. Another arrow shower came. Then another, the shafts rattling like armfuls of dropped sticks. Leo felt two thuds into his shield, saw one plunge into Togol's saddle and heard the Cuman swear. A cataphract screamed as he took a shaft in the thigh. Arshak's gelding had a bloody weal on its neck and Zarrar half-reared and lashed out dangerously as an arrow grazed his rump.

Men were looking uncertainly at Leo and he knew they had to hit back. "Aspieties," Leo ordered. "You and two others—up there with Jacques. The four of you, pick any exposed target and concentrate your arrows against it until it is killed, wounded or driven off. Then move onto the next. I do not want them shooting at us with impunity."

"Togol. We can't depend entirely on Bessas, he may have trouble we do not know about. We must be ready to make a run for it. If so, we'll try and induce the enemy to give chase. If they do, and get foiled on these ropes, all, except you Togol, will double back at my command and slip it into them—close range archery. Be ready to get the Arab mounted."

Dragging his shield and spear to the edge, Leo set them down, propping the shield against his knee in front of himself. He drew his bow from its case and while studying the Seljuks on the plain, selected an arrow from his quiver.

"Count! That small thicket, half a furlong in front," Aspieties indicated calmly, "There are two of them hiding in it."

Guy and David had joined them on the lip. A desultory scatter of arrows clattered around them, many of the feathered shafts lodging into the wadi well down from the area occupied by his group. "On my command," Leo ordered, "give the thicket two arrows each. Jacques, you and me—we shall take them when they move. You take the right one. Make ready! Now!"

Five arrows sped to the thicket. Another flight followed closely, slicing through the thin branches. Two figures rose and started to run. "There they go," someone shouted.

Leo breathed in deeply, quickly drawing back the bowstring to his cheek. He sighted along the shaft and over the protective bracer strapped to his left forearm. He felt the tension in the bow, the strain in the tendons of his right arm and the thumb-ring biting into the flesh and pressuring the knuckle. Relaxing the tension a little he let out a slight breath, then in again and marked the running figure. Squinting along the shaft, he let out a little air, held his breath, marked the man and released the arrow. At that moment he heard the jolt of Jacques' crossbow. The figure threw up its arms and collapsed. Jacques shouted in triumph. They all loosed at the other running figure which fell and lay still.

"Same again," Aspieties called, warming to the tactic. "A hand's span to the left and another half-furlong further distant. Behind that dark bush—two more there."

They all looked. Leo saw many of the Seljuks were now moving uncertainly towards their led-horses. Would they withdraw or charge? "Give them a few arrows and be ready to mount quickly and withdraw," he called, catching Togol's eye.

"Horse-archer," David spoke calmly. "Half-left. Spear points beyond the rise. It's Centarch Phocas, by the pennants."

A hundred mailed horsemen topped the low rise: as skirmishers at the gallop, levelled spears in the first rank, busy bows in the second. With shouts and exhortations, the armoured cataphracts crashed into the surprised nomads, scattering their led-horses, piercing the tribesmen with arrows or spitting them on spears. A handful of their quarry managed to mount and flee. The remainder fought without hope.

Martina peeled off and galloped towards Leo.

He remembered the strung out lassos and walked towards her, waving her to pull up. "David," he called over his shoulder, take down the ropes."

Martina checked her lathered horse, took in Leo at a glance, looked into the wadi and back at Leo. "You're still alive—I was …"

Leo heard Bessas in the distance roaring, "Rally on me! No pursuit, damn your eyes! Demetrius, control your men." The plain was filled with dust as cataphracts reined in wild-eyed, reefing horses—despatching the remaining nomads who did not surrender while the decarchs yelled for their own men in the confusion.

"Martina, thank you. You did well."

She stepped from the saddle and looked at him. They did not speak until Leo asked hoarsely, "We have a prisoner. Can you talk to him?"

Glancing at his party to ensure all were still living or being attended to, Leo watched while Bessas re-organised his men. Pickets were posted and a troop told-off to screen to the south, the most likely direction of approach by hostiles. Decarchs accounted for their men, and ordered the dead, wounded and all prisoners searched, weapons collected and any loose horses caught with one badly maimed animal destroyed.

Bessas cantered slowly in a wide circle, alert to any new threat and ensuring actions were completed to his satisfaction. Something caught his attention, for he dismounted, picked it up from the ground and dashed it against his leg to remove the dust. He then led Hector over. Leo could see the black skin under the horse's grey coat, the foam around the leather breastplate and the pink inside the distended nostrils as Hector sucked in air after the gallop and rubbed his head against Bessas in the shared exhilaration of the charge. Bessas pulled off his helmet and ran a dirty hand through his handsome hair.

Leo suddenly became aware of how hot and uncomfortable his own head was. A great weariness came over him and he felt unsteady. He moved quickly to keep his balance, blinking the feeling away. Undoing the throat lash of his helmet, he eased it off and ran his own grimy fingers though the iron-grey scrub, feeling the cooling breeze. "Report?"

"Two dead," Bessas reported. "Four wounded. Some horses hurt, none seriously. I saw a dozen or so enemy get away, a few loose horses with them. We hold eight prisoners, five of them wounded."

"Who is down?" Leo asked.

Bessas replied without hesitation. "Sergios and Niketas. The cousins, Stoudites."

"Damn! Good men. We will take them with us. Well done, Bessas. Perfect timing. Detach a section to help the peasants gather up the herd, but keep your men and prisoners away from my group. I also have a prisoner I wish to keep quiet about for the moment. Screen me to the south, please."

"Martina did very well," Bessas said. "We saw the sudden dust and were moving towards you anyway, but she found us and brought us around your flank by the best route. You had their attention and that allowed us to surprise them." The centarch paused as he looked past Leo. "Hey, d'Agiles!"

Guy peered over the lip of the wadi as Bessas spun his dropped hat through the air. "Don't be so casual with your gear," he ordered with mock fierceness.

Guy caught the hat and after a brief examination, looked up and smiled broadly.

"Don't know what's been on his mind," Bessas remarked sympathetically, "but I will warrant he has not been giving it much thought in the last little while."

"Had their attention, eh," Leo mused as he turned back to the wadi. "Let me tell you, being the bait does not have much to recommend it. Whatever was on his mind, Guy did well."

The prisoner in the bed of the wadi was as silent as death. He had heard the tumult of the charge and the Greek cries of the rally. Around him, he felt the exhilaration of those so recently threatened with extinction. He awaited fate with trepidation.

Leo, together with Togol and Martina stood over the prisoner. "Let's have a look at him." The blindfolding turban was removed and checked to reveal no writing.

The Arab blinked up into the sun at Leo, comprehension growing in the Arab's eyes. "You are no brigand. A Roman! The one giving the orders."

"Arabic," said Martina. "I can interpret."

"Your horse survived its fall," Leo spoke in Greek, Martina interpreting.

"Allah, the merciful, the compassionate, be praised."

"What do I say?" Martina glanced at Leo.

The Arab looked from the captured horses to Leo and spoke first. "Who are you?"

Leo ignored the question, asking his own. "Who are you and why do you ride with the Seljuks?" Leo observed the Arab closely as Martina distracted him by interpreting. "Mercenary?"

"I am Derar al-Adin," the Arab flamed insolently. "I ride for no other man's gold. I have fine estates. I am a patron of poets and painters. I hunt and write poetry. A famous stable I have, and a sumptuous harem." He stared at Martina, standing in the dust, reins in her hand.

Martina glanced down, then at Leo.

It needed no translation. Leo glared at Derar and roared, feeling oddly cold inside, but acting the role of a man genuinely outraged and capable of violence. "Look at me! And I have you."

Martina took it up.

"And someone else probably has your harem," he sneered. "It seems a common enough practice in your lands."

Derar was downcast. The truth spoken had touched a raw nerve. He rattled off more Arabic.

They both looked to Leo. "He asked again who you are?"

"I am a Roman soldier and my name does not matter, not now, not forever more. I ask the questions and, Derar al-Adin, I want straight answers from you, or I will leave you stretched out in the dust with your friends, for the carrion eaters."

"I ride with the Turkoman because I seek one who has travelled far away," Derar finally admitted.

Leo remained silent.

"My sister-in-law's son, and his father."

Leo looked on unsympathetically, wondering why Derar would refer to a sister-in-law rather than brother and nephew.

"Her son's mare," Derar continued, "the black one, you have there. The father was riding a dun. They accompanied a Seljuk emir on a chestnut mare from the city of Her."

"Why did they do that?"

"The Seljuk is a trader."

"Spy!"

Derar remained silent.

"And you have come for a horse?" Leo asked as though puzzled.

Derar turned his eyes to Leo's and discerned no misunderstanding in them. "No. Not for a horse. For my nephew."

Leo and Togol exchanged meaningful glances, then sat comfortably on the side of the wadi facing the kneeling prisoner. "And what will you do when you find this far-riding son of your sister-in-law's?" Leo asked in a very relaxed, conversational tone of voice.

Martina noticed the change in Leo and Togol and matched her manner as she also sat.

"I will return him to his home," Derar murmured.

"Are you of the Abbasids or Fatimids?"

"I owe my allegiance to the Commander of the Faithful in Madinat al-Salam."

"Sunni?"

The Arab showed some surprise, for the unbelievers were notoriously ignorant. "I am Sunni, although hailing from close to Fatimid lands."

"The Seljuks are Sunnis also."

"They are nomads."

"Who have exploited their considerable military prowess and the corruption of the Abbasid Caliphate to their own ends." Leo continued, searching for Derar's feelings and allegiances.

"That is true," returned Derar, evidently seeking to fathom Leo's game, to both engage him in conversation and make some room in which to negotiate; men were less likely to kill out of hand those with whom they had conversed. "The Seljuks are now the pre-eminent military power in the Muslim world."

To Leo's satisfaction, it seemed Derar considered him to be a difficult and prickly Roman whom he did not wish to antagonise. "You risk much for this duty you have assumed?" he asked pointedly, seemingly returning to the matter of Derar's missing relative.

Martina, noticing the slightest edge returning to Leo's tone, kept her tone neutral, allowing Leo to convey the emotion, or lack of it.

"Against a sister-in-law's wishes and the entreaties of the boy's grandmother, what can be done?" Derar spoke with an air of resignation.

"What exactly was this group you were with?" Leo asked, seeking to prolong the conversation until he found a way to better exploit it.

"A Seljuk raiding party," Derar admitted, now evidently a little more comfortable that he would not be executed on the spot. "Two hundred, perhaps more, scouting the road to Sasun to test the Roman defences. This group had peeled off to forage. As I was searching for the boy, I came with them. The survivors will soon bring relief."

"Good. Let them," Leo retorted with a display of aggressive confidence. "What position do you have with the Sultan?" He turned the interrogation back to the question of Derar's access to the Seljuk court and his allegiances.

Derar hesitated, sensing the danger. "None."

"None?" Leo knew the Seljuks used Arabs and Persians to administer their growing empire. He glared in disbelief at the prisoner.

Derar grew afraid he would be killed on the spot and his nerve faltered. "I have some access … to his court."

"More than access, I think," Leo accused in that misleading conversational tone he slipped back into. "Were you not here to spy out the Roman lands, under cover of searching for the missing boy?"

There was a long pause, after which Derar drew a breath. "No! Though some might accuse it."

"And is it not true that the Abbasid caliphate would wish to know the mind of the Sultan and would not be distraught at his misfortune against the Romans?"

Derar remained silent, unmoving.

Leo, letting the question linger, studied him. "Which way will they come, Derar?" he asked quietly.

The questioning was becoming more conversational again; the Roman relaxed because he clearly had the upper hand, while the Arab became accommodating because he sensed the hint of achieving both freedom and the object of his journey. Derar would look at Leo as he spoke to determine the mood, then at Martina as she interpreted.

The young woman sat to one side, watching Leo as he spoke in Greek, then at Derar as she interpreted into Arabic. She might stumble over a word occasionally, traces of perspiration on her upper lip, booted feet in front of her, bow case at her hip. If Derar did not understand, he would look to the others and then back to her. Togol might intercede in Turkic from time to time. Leo was struck by how quickly they adapted to this form of communication, having all done it before in other circumstances.

"Their army assembles at Tabriz," offered Derar, beginning to provide details, "with the advance guard already forming at the city of Her. The Sultan …"

Leo held up his hand to signify a pause. "Togol, you may release our guest's bonds, please."

It was done and Derar placed his hands in his lap. "Thank you."

Leo gestured as if it was nothing more than courtesy warranted. "The Sultan?"

"Yes. The Sultan and his main force will come through Berkri and Archēsh into Vaspurakan—isolating Van and keeping the Seljuk strength to the north side of the Sea of Bznunik." There may be secondary incursions, along the valley of the Araxes, for example. The Sultan will lead in person."

"So it is Manzikert? The Sultan commanding?"

"Yes. At least Archēsh, and I would suggest Manzikert, with the Sultan there."

"What strength?"

Derar shrugged. "The bulk of it is a mix of Seljuk regular troops and irregular tribesmen. Also Kurds. He brings a siege train, with mostly Persian engineers—troops from every quarter, Daylami infantry from the northern provinces and Prince Alkan with the men of Chorasmia. Counting all, perhaps thirty-five thousand. The Sultan Tughrul Bey has such influence over the Abbasid lands now."

Martina interpreted in hushed tones and looked to Leo.

He showed no emotion. It was more or less what he expected. "When?"

"It would have been already, but there was a fire in the engineer's camp in Tabriz," said Derar.

Neither Togol nor Leo batted an eyelid. "Fire is an unruly servant!" Leo said while wondering whether Simon Vardaheri and Maniakh had a hand in it.

Martina conveyed his deadpan observation.

"So it seems," Derar agreed without showing emotion.

"When, Derar?" Leo asked again, sounding almost disinterested, as though he knew anyway.

"Another moon, perhaps sooner!"

"You will be with them? With the Sultan?"

Martina glanced at Leo before she interpreted, as though she guessed what was coming.

"If I live past this day and return."

There was a long silence as Leo looked at the ground between his sweat-streaked, dusty boots. Then he stared straight into Derar's dark eyes. "I know the rider of the black mare is in a Roman dungeon. A handsome boy. Uninjured. Zobeir al-Adin is the one you seek."

Derar's eyes flickered. "The father?"

"Dead on Roman ground where he spied."

Derar clenched his jaw, but with effort recovered his composure. "My brother was at the battle at Azaz, where you Romans were defeated. You've done for him at last. Was it proper?"

"He died facing Mecca," Leo said gently.

"Thank you. The son is in health?"

"For the moment." Leo wondered whether Derar would be determined on revenge, which could be consuming and come in many forms.

"For his return? What do you ask?"

"There is no ask about it. You will be my spy in the Sultan's tent and you will give me Manzikert."

Derar suddenly made to leap up but slumped instead. "You don't know what you ask," he spluttered. "It's impossible!" Then in a voice so low, so pleading that Martina could hardly hear, "You don't know the Sultan."

"You have no choice, Derar. I have Zobeir and Manzikert is my price. If the city falls he dies. If you lie to me, he dies. If you die, he dies. Regardless of whether Tughrul Bey is dead or alive, only when his army retires defeated from the walls of Manzikert and beyond Vaspurakan, will I deliver Zobeir al-Adin to you." He read the comprehension in Derar's eyes as Martina interpreted. "Think well on it. If I am safe, you are safe. Who are the Sultan's spies in the Roman lands? I presume he has some. It would be unthinkable that he did not. If the Sultan's spies hear about Zobeir and our link with you, and it gets back to the Sultan … you need only imagine."

As Martina finished interpreting, Leo thought Derar now wore the countenance of a man deeply distressed.

"I do not know who the spies are," Derar protested. "Or if there are any. A once minor emir by the name of Bughra Dumrul is the Sultan's spymaster, and he keeps all such things to himself or one or two trusted subordinates."

"Bughra Dumrul?" Leo repeated the name after Martina had interpreted.

"Yes! That is the name of your opposite!" Derar ventured, exploring Leo's true role with the baited question

Leo said nothing as both Martina and Derar looked at him. Not taking the lure, he gazed at Derar. "Seljuk spymaster, eh? What's he like?"

Derar collected his thoughts. "Dumrul is hardy and cunning. He's made a deliberate attempt to refine himself, affecting Persian robes and learning spoken and written Arabic. It shows the direction of their interest and attentions, I think, towards the caliphates in Baghdad and Cairo." Derar looked down for a time to mask his discomfort with the treachery. "A magnificent horseman and famous with weapons, he has taken on a preference for the softer, perfumed women of the settled areas. They in turn have encouraged him to bathe and learn something of the arts—the barbarian masquerading as a civilised man. He works closely with the Sultan's vizier. Don't underestimate Bughra Dumrul. He's ruthless. He caught one of your own men in Tabriz."

It was another baited hook from Derar, seeking to determine Leo's position in the Byzantine hierarchy and ascertain what scouting resources had been deployed into the Sultan's lands.

Martina gave Leo a warning glance.

He did not react to the Arab's searching comment about spies in Tabriz, merely remarking, "In times of strife, any innocent man can be persecuted. How long ago did this occur?"

"Six weeks, perhaps," Derar shrugged. "Before the last full moon."

Inwardly, Leo was relieved that it was unlikely that the man caught was one of his, but Basil Apocapes would no doubt be troubled when told. He shrugged, suggesting the subject was of little concern to him. To show further interest would only confirm the Arab's obvious suspicions. "What of the Sultan?"

"He was born of the steppes," Derar answered, obviously thinking himself on safe ground, "and ..."

"I know all that shit! What goads the murdering bastard? What is in his heart?"

Derar paused, surprised at the anger and penetrating question, searching himself for the answer. "What drives him? I have never considered. Religion, perhaps ..." He paused again, brows knotted. "He has no children—children, especially male children are very important to the Turks. His brother, Chagri Bey, pushes the Seljukian Empire to the east, to Ghazna and Hind, with his sons, especially Alp Arslan, at his side. Tughrul has followed with his administration the forays of Ibrahim Inal and Kutlumush, both of whom have sons and heirs. Tughrul doesn't. Envy perhaps ... might explain ..."

"Wives?"

"Several, apparently. He is known to dance the Turkish dance at his wedding. It is said he will take a bride from amongst the captive women this summer, and that he plans to marry the daughter of the caliph, al-Ka'im, and give his own sister in return to cement control of Baghdad."

"So the Sultan fancies a bride, does he? And empire? Derar, what of this pious, unquenchable thirst for conquest? Where does that spring from?"

Derar paused again. "Heartfelt, perhaps. He may believe he is the salvation of his people. Or more. A Seljuk prince I have some trust in has told me the Sultan spoke of the need to unite the Seljuks—if world dominion is to ..."

"World dominion?" Leo's glare bored into Derar.

"... be achieved. So one said, the Sultan said." Derar paused. "Who can know? Perhaps he desires the winning of fame, admiration and status amongst the Muslims—to prove manliness in ways that the meanest tribesman feels no need."

Leo was silent, listening, staring at the ground between his feet. At length, he looked up. "Derar, it is always a pleasure to converse with one interested in the arts. One can learn many things."

Derar bowed his head slightly in acknowledgment of the compliment that was perhaps mocking.

Leo looked on in silence.

The Arab broke it. "How am I supposed to get messages to you?"

Although Derar al-Adin's last statement might signal a collapse of his resolve, Leo was still cautious. "When at the fortress of Manzikert after the Seljuks come, attach them to an arrow and shoot it by night during the third watch—if not then any time you are able—against the interior side of the second tower, north of the main gate, on the western wall."

"Western wall, second tower north of main gate. And word from you?" Derar asked.

"There is a prominent, charred tree stump, a furlong from that tower. When I desire to contact you, I will attach a message to an arrow and shoot it into that stump or the ground very near. You can retrieve it by night."

"Do not use my name!"

"Of course not. I will address it to Prince."

"What do you want to know?" Derar asked, undermined by his own lack of power in the unfolding events.

"You must tell everything, especially the Sultan's personal movements and their plans of attack, at least one day ahead. I want to know about engineers, engines, fire, mines and miners. Tell me also their wider campaigns and the identities and discords of their leaders. And I particularly want to know about their damned spies, Derar."

Derar nodded sombrely. "If good sense prevails and there is no war, how do I secure the release of Zobeir al-Adin from Manzikert?"

"I never said he was at Manzikert. However, you can simply ride there with a ransom, after the campaigning season but before the snow comes. I will then arrange for his return to you."

"I must know where he is."

"When I choose to tell you."

"If I have something to give before?"

"Come, or send a messenger to the Barbarian House in Manzikert," Leo answered.

"Barbarian House?"

"Yes." Leo replied nonchalantly. "They will pass the word. Your messenger should state they seek a blind man on a pale horse. That way my men will know the message is from you."

"Barbarian House," Derar repeated. Then he looked at Togol and David in their flamboyant dress, and comprehension came to his eyes. "A blind man on a pale horse," he repeated. "It is done, then?"

"One more thing," Leo countered, before agreeing any bargain had been struck. "Do you know anything of a dark-haired woman on a black stallion—a Roman-Armenian woman, a beauty, who may have gone to Archēsh?"

Derar looked blankly. "No. Is she important to you?"

Martina scrutinised Leo as she interpreted.

Leo smiled inwardly at Derar's attempt to find any lever he might use at some future time. "No," he replied blandly. "It is done. You are free to go."

"My horse?"

"Take him."

"He's a dog, not worth stealing anyway," Togol interrupted with an obvious mistruth, to a look of fury from Derar. "Broken down ... sickle hocked ..."

Derar, realising he had only been taunted, calmed himself. "The boy's horse?"

Leo smiled at the insolence and shook his head. "It now belongs, fairly won, to another."

Derar shrugged.

They all rose gravely and leading their horses, scrambled from the wadi before mounting. Derar looked sombrely at the evidence of the fight as Togol peeled off and rode over the ground, reading the signs of the skirmish.

Derar turned to Leo. "One never gets used to it. I hope the murdering bastards, as you say, that set these ill-fated stars in their courses think it worth it!"

"On that we can agree, Derar. Farewell."

"Roman, I ask once more, who are you?"

Leo shook his head and motioned Derar into his journey.

Derar spoke over his shoulder to Martina as he rode by.

Leo looked to her.

She hesitated. "The Arab said one could buy all your feelings for the lowest coin of the Romans. His last words were, until next time, Horse-archer, and bay horse."

Martina passaged her mount sideways that her knee brushed Leo's. She leaned forward and caressed the bay horse's neck. "Be careful, Zarrar," she whispered. "The Saracens know you now."

The Arsanias Valley, East of Sasesh,
Late afternoon, 28th June 1054

Those who fought were buoyed for a while by exhilaration, then they carried on by will alone, moving their emotion-drained selves mechanically. They slumped in their saddles under the brazen sky, covered by the dust of the slow moving herd: two slain troopers lashed over their own saddles; four others held hunched in theirs only by the efforts of their friends and the regiment's mounted stretcher-bearers.

The relieved citizens of Sashesh had collected a thousand head of the best cattle, the Seljuk weapons and horses as well as the little gold found on the slain. Leo had them send messengers to Mush with warning of the presence and intentions of the Seljuks as he sent two pairs of gallopers by different routes to Basil.

Leo had watched Jacques mount his newly won horse and noticed the quiet pride Guy had shown in assisting him. Like Guy before him, Jacques had souvenired the bow and quiver of his fallen foe. Leo wondered whether some woman from beyond the Oxus would feel something in the wind this night—that her love would return no more, his horse and weapons now the trophies of a stubble-faced Kelt from beyond the Bosphorus.

In the late afternoon, Togol rode near. "Horse-archer. How come Sunni and Shi'ite amongst the Muslims?"

Leo looked at Togol and wondered why the question.

Togol saw his look. "Your people argue with the Latins about God, the Saracens argue amongst themselves about God. I am confused."

"A reasonable question, Togol. Long ago, some four hundred years past, Mohammad, the Muslim Prophet, had a few key deputies, the four caliphs—Abu Bekr, Omar, Othman and Ali. The last married Fatima, the Prophet's daughter. After the death of Mohammad, it's said Ali claimed a dynastic succession based on kinship by marriage, but was opposed by the others. Ali acquiesced, ensuring a Muslim unity that conquered an empire stretching from the Oxus River to the Pillars of Hercules and the Frankish lands."

"That's where Jacques fought the Muslims then," mused Togol. "You must draw me a map when we halt. For the Kelt, Jacques, he has spoken of the wars between the Christians of …" he fumbled for the words, "… León and … Castile who fought the Muslims."[57]

Leo looked full at Togol, the question in his mind about Jacques' horsemanship perhaps partly answered.

"The difference?" Togol prompted.

"Ah, yes. United, the Arabs conquered vast lands, but the intellectual split between the followers of Ali and those of the other three dogged them. Now the Abbasid caliphate of Baghdad is the centre of Sunni power where they honour the memory of all four caliphs, giving last place to Ali. The Fatimid caliphate in Cairo is the centre of power for the Shi'ite, who remain true to the memory of Ali. The two branches of Islam are mutually antagonistic, something that has worked in our favour."

"And the Allah of both is the same as your Christian God?"

"In general, yes, except the Muslims believe there is one God. Christians have complicated the matter with the Father, Son and Holy Ghost. At worst, the Muslims think us unbelieving polytheists," Leo said with a wry smile. "At best, they probably think us confused and ignorant."

"So why this endless fuss and conflict?"

"Because they can agree on nothing, even though the major religions of our world have three things in common," said Leo.

Togol looked at him, brows furrowed.

"First, they are all led by old men who tell everyone else how to live, and live very well off the proceeds themselves. Second, they all have a history of the conquest of other peoples' lands, of sacked cities and massacred victims."

"Third?" pressed Togol.

---

57 These Spanish wars were part of the slow, faction-riven Christian re-conquest of Spain from the Muslims. The period of Jacques participation was during the childhood of the famous El Cid, (c1043–1099), who campaigned from about 1060 until his death.

"I'll think of something."

"Horse-archer," Togol chuckled, "you know too much. How do you rest your head or your heart?" He mused on his own question for a while and was then drawn into a discussion on his own beliefs that lasted long into the ride.

Leo found himself having some sympathy with Togol's animism, the notion that animals have their own spirits and that other things making up the natural world, have their own aura. Leo had noticed the morbid fascination of cattle with their fallen kind and the way trees wilt when their neighbours are cut down. He drank from the tepid water of his goatskin. "Tell me of sorcery, Togol."

Togol looked guardedly at Leo. "There is little to tell. If all—the sorcerer, and their victim or patient, and the wider clan—believe in the sorcerer's magic, the sorcerer will have power over his fellows. If any do not believe in the sorcerer's magic and can sway the others, or enough of them, the sorcerer will have no power." After a time he said, "Perhaps we should cast a spell on the Sultan?"

"Perhaps you're right."

In the late afternoon the regiment halted for the night. After bedding the cattle down and posting pickets, the men ate a cold supper of double-baked bread—hardtack—in small groups while holding the reins of knee-hobbled horses. It rained a cold drizzle and the force spent a miserable night on the steppe sheltering under their cloaks beside shivering horses. First light crept slowly, then dawn, followed by the red sunrise gleaming on the high clouds as the light rain lifted. Breakfast was a double handful of boiled barley, a little grass and a drink from a rivulet for the horses while the men had last of the hardtack and a sip from the water-skins.

They pushed wearily forward during the morning, leading their mounts much of the time and halting occasionally to graze them. Late in the afternoon, John Curticius, with an escort of cavalry, met them on a rise within sight of Manzikert. "Well done, Leo!" he said, eyeing the cattle.

Leo turned his head slightly, once.

Curticius bowed his own. "Thank you. I didn't expect ... wrong direction. But, thank you." The princeps straightened in his saddle. "There has been no further word of hostiles, save from your gallopers. You have wounded, I understand." He turned in his saddle and bellowed for the medical orderlies. "Marcus," Curticius continued, indicating the quartermaster at his side, "and his assistants will look after the herd. Take your men to barracks, Leo. I'll ride with you. The strategos will want to speak with you on your return."

The Sixth Schola, in column-of-four, halted a mile from Manzikert. There they dismounted, loosened girths and led their horses into the fortress. Leo noticed a small group of soldiers' women waiting inside the gates, searching for faces in the ranks. They watched him pass by, recognising him and knowing his role in the fate of their men. Leo hoped beyond mere wishing that none of the fallen were special to any of these women. He had seen it before, the tearful rushing to the friend leading the burdened horse; the comforting arm around—then later, a soldier seeking a companion, the woman a new ally in life.

All things were fleeting. He slipped an arm over Zarrar's neck and the horse turned his head to him as they walked along together. "So many soldiers and widows in this Empire of the Romans, Zarrar." Something made him look back, to see Kamyates and Reynaldus glaring from behind the little crowd. Slowing, he enabled Bessas to catch up. "Don't look around. Kamyates and Reynaldus just watched us come in. Remind everyone again that no one is to speak of what happened over these past three days. No one."

Taticus Phocas, with his adoration of Zarrar took the horse's reins and fussed over the graze on his rump. Leo passed by the Barbarian House where Bessas was already going through the despatches. There was nothing urgent.

"Come!" Basil led Leo up the stone stairs to the citadel's highest tower where there was nothing above them except the red afterglow of the sun and the floating double-headed eagle of Byzantium. Leo thought fleetingly of Constantinople and Trebizond, deciding they did not matter anymore.

A servant brought water, wine, bread and cheese. After she left, Basil waved Leo to a chair. "Now we can talk."

Leo relayed the events of the last days and noted the growing interest in Basil's face.

The strategos rose and paced. "Imagine that! A prisoner who gives us hold over one in the Sultan's court! Imagine Tughrul Bey's army down there on the flat. And him giving orders every day and us knowing what is said." He slapped a merlon and stared into the distance for a long moment. "By God. Imagine that. Who else knows?"

"Bessas, Togol, David. And Martina—she interpreted the interrogation."

They exchanged glances. "Very useful young woman," Basil said.

Leo continued. "Guy d'Agiles and his man. Six of my cataphracts. All sworn to secrecy."

"Will they be discreet, or should I lock them up?"

"They can be trusted. If I have the slightest hint to the contrary, you will not need to lock them up. I will."

"Keep it that way," Basil said. "Tell no one else for the moment. I'll speak with the princeps, Oleg and Daniel to ensure the prisoner is kept safe and that his fate is as you've promised."

They were silent for a time, then spoke of other things while darkness crept across the sky. Basil finished with a reluctant request for Leo to reconnoitre—to Artzké, certainly, and Archēsh, preferably—as soon as practicable to inspect the defences.

Leo left the citadel and made for his quarters. He would have passed by the Barbarian House but a candle burned inside. Intrigued by who would be working late, he entered and found Martina scanning a sheaf of papers on the table that served as her desk. "You should get some rest," he suggested gently.

She looked up. "I was making sure there was nothing important that had to be done. It seems not," she said, replacing the paperweight, a worn horseshoe from her journey to Manzikert. "You've seen the strategos?"

"Yes. He's pleased by our good fortune and intends to keep quiet about it. He wishes me to go to Artzké, and Archēsh if I see fit. I leave tomorrow."

"Tomorrow! But you've just got back. And you will miss the fair. And a market! The day after tomorrow—it is Sunday and everyone goes. You need rest, like everyone else."

"It should not be too arduous, just another horse ride, but it is a pity about the fair." He paused, imagining. "It would have been very pleasant. Make sure you go. Do not let Centarch Phocas keep you here. He would work an ant to death."

Martina smiled and rose slowly, still looking at the papers on her table. "Can I get you anything at the fair?"

Leo was touched, perplexed by how to show his feelings without betraying them. "That would be nice. Perhaps a tan shirt, cotton or linen. As you can see, this one has had better days. And," he smiled, "I like surprises." He made to leave. "I'll give you some money before I depart."

"When you return will be fine, I don't think you'll rob me," she smiled, blowing out the candle. "There's no one else here. I checked."

With the door locked behind them and a word to the sentry, they strolled down the narrow, cobbled street to the military quarter, the shadows of the stone houses cut by shafts of silver moonlight. At the corner where their ways parted, they dallied, speaking of pleasant things far removed from the troubles of Manzikert.

Chapter Eight

A Gift

The Artzké Road,
Morning, 30th June 1054

Leo left money for Martina and departed the city early the following morning. Riding Ruksh, he was accompanied by Togol and an escort of a decarch, Loukas Gabras, and four cataphracts leading spare horses. They wore mail shirts but left their helmets behind; opting for the practicality of shapeless felt hats or headscarves.

The detachment covered the southward first eight miles of undulating steppe in an hour of alternate trotting, cantering and walking. Staying on the rough track, they began climbing the low foothills with snow-capped Mount Sippane always to the east. The hills were a tangle of bare knolls cut by small streams and gullies. Reining in, Leo looked back over the plain and saw the tactical advantage conferred on any force holding this high ground against an approach from Manzikert. The party dismounted, studying and memorising the terrain for future reference. Leo marked his salient observations on the rolled goatskin map he carried. "Good cavalry country," he remarked to Gabras as they ascended the hills of ancient volcanic rock, sparsely covered with stunted shrubs and yellow grass.

The party proceeded south-east until with audible gasps the riders beheld the Sea of Bznunik, which stretched southward in its blue depths to distant brown mountains and sparkled out of sight to the east. Descending from the high ground, they rode through blooming yellow wildflowers at the fringe of the flatlands of tilled fields and hamlets towards Artzké. The city was built on a knoll overlooking the lake with the landward sides protected by formidable fortifications, the other by the waters.

Leo's clipped Greek was persuasive and the unexpected visitors were soon speaking to the garrison commander, an effete, world-weary turmarch from Cappadocia. He complained of the unpredictability of local Kurds, the insolence of his Norman garrison, his unreliable handful of Patzinak horse and the understandable resentment of the Armenian citizens.

Leo's party borrowed horses for a tour of the area while their own were groomed, fed and watered in the citadel stables. "I have little choice but to defend the city," the turmarch said defensively, irritated at what he perceived as Leo meddling in Apocapes' name. "There's enough manoeuvre room on the plain for the Seljuks to bypass me here and go on, either southwest through Baghesh and on to Melitene, or north to Manzikert. Incidentally, I do not share Basil Apocapes' sanguine view of the good intentions of Abu Nasr ad-Daulah of the Marwanids, I have it he is too accommodating to the Sultan."

As they paused on a spur which allowed a good perspective of the local area, Leo asked the officer's opinion of the unfolding situation. "Is Baghesh militarily significant for us?"

The turmarch, looked in the direction of the closest Muslim fortress, out of sight to the west along the northern shore of the lake. "Khlat' is much closer—a reasonable but lightly garrisoned frontier fortress ensuring Amida's control of their local Kurds, and to keep an eye on us of course. Baghesh is further along, at the western end of the Sea. That is the Marwanid's regional bastion, but I believe it is primarily defensive, against us, and the Seljuks for that matter, if Abu Nasr realises how much a threat to him they really are. The key to the defence of this district is our city of Archēsh, farther to the east along the lake shore. Or Manzikert itself—if they come by there. Either way, Archēsh is the cork in the bottle. Its neck for me is the road by the lakeshore. I do not have enough troops to fight in the open or try to block the road. I'm very confident I can hold out behind my walls and the water until the nomads return home."

"Horse-archer," Togol hung back and whispered fiercely to Leo, "Their land walls appear strong—but how can they be so sure of the water?"

Leo silently agreed with the scout. He knew they now had to visit Archēsh and scout the ground between there and Manzikert before he completely understood the broader battlefield.

Leo asked after Irene's brother, Damian Curticius. A fine young officer, he was told, but out patrolling with his men. His sister, a beautiful girl indeed, had not visited, nor been in the town as far as the turmarch knew.

Leo's group dined at Baghesh and pressed on, taking advantage of the cool, dimly lit night to ride to Archēsh, the lake shimmering in the ghostly light on their right and the mountain a silver sentinel on the left.

Manzikert,
Early morning, 1st July 1054

Serena Cephalus dressed and crept through the dark house, taking care not to wake her watchful maid, Eirene. Taking an apple, she closed the door behind her and with a sigh of relief that no light or cry followed her, made her way through the pre-dawn streets of Manzikert to the citizen's stables.

It had only been days since one of those periodic, moralizing sermons in the cathedral about the sinful consequences of having so many soldiers around and the need for the city worthies to guard their daughters. Of her feelings for Centarch Bessas Phocas, Serena did not know what vexed her most: the cautionary sighs of her parents or the icy silences of Eirene.

Bessas was already there. They embraced in the depths of the stable until she broke free for a moment, to give her mare the apple. Serena feared for her mount—should the Seljuks come—that the mare would be pressed into service as a remount or killed to feed a starving city.

Bessas took her hand and they felt their way up the wooden steps to the loft where he spread his cloak on some stacked bags of barley. They kissed. "There was no need to meet this way," Bessas whispered. "We could meet at the market, or I could visit."

"People gossip," Serena sighed. "I couldn't stand all the knowing smiles. Or Eirene's huffing."

"She only cares for you." Bessas lay beside her, his head propped on an elbow, and ran his hand through her hair.

They were silent for a time in their little nook. A stable cat found them and settled in, purring.

"What will become of us, Bessas?"

"We shall get through the summer and both return to Constantinople. Once there I will take my father's advice, become a merchant, grow old and fat with you at my side. He will love you."

Serena smiled in the dark and poked him in the ribs. "Don't you dare get fat!" Then she nestled closer to him.

They heard approaching footsteps and saw the uncertain flickering light of a lamp being brought into the stable beneath them. He placed a finger over her lips as they heard the voices of the snobbish courtier, Modestos Kamyates, with the imperial courier, Bardas Cydones. The two officials fed their horses hurriedly, speaking indecipherable murmurs all the while. There was a pause after which Kamyates said audibly, "I can hear a cat." There was a further muted conversation and the men departed, with the courtier saying, "Anyway there's no hurry."

Serena and Bessas breathed easier but said nothing. After a time, Serena whispered, "They came to check their horses but said not their names—not the actions of horsemen caring for their mounts. Their exchange was far more furtive and urgent. They were using it as a cover to …"

"Plot," agreed Bessas. "I think I made out a reference to Count Bryennius and Archēsh. I suspect the comment about there being no hurry was meant to be overheard—a precaution."

"You should tell him."

"I will. But what?"

"We should go," Serena said.

"We must wait, Serena. They noticed a cat purring, so may know someone was in here. They could be waiting outside."

Manzikert,
Early morning, 1st July 1054

Kamyates stepped from the stables and glanced at Cydones in the first grey light touching the city. "There were too many shadows in there, and I have never heard a cat purr without people around."

"A stable boy perhaps," replied Cydones, perplexed at the urgency of the summons to a meeting.

"Stable boy be damned! It could have been anything from an illicit couple, to someone following us. Is there nowhere in this disgusting remote village to have a private conversation?"

"I quite agree," Cydones said. "That's something that has worked in our favour so far."

"Yeess." Kamyates exhaled slowly. "That is why you're here. There's been an important development." He was satisfied with the growing unease on Cydones' face that he would be confronted with some accusation; he enjoyed keeping his subordinate in a constant state of subtle anxiety. His cultivation of the Norman mercenary, Reynaldus, meant that he did not depend on Cydones as much anymore. "It seems Bryennius has not been open with us, nor Apocapes for that matter."

"Really?"

"One of the Roman officers listens too much and talks more."

"Which?"

"That is of no consequence," purred Kamyates. He enjoyed the put-downs he could inflict on Cydones.

"I am told that Bryennius, on his cattle patrol a few days ago, had a little fight."

"I've heard," interjected Cydones, anxious to display his knowledge.

"And?" retorted Kamyates.

Cydones stared blankly.

"Did you know," Kamyates said with a faint air of triumph, "that Bryennius caught a prisoner. And then, our rustic count of the Scholae let him go again?"

Cydones grappled with this new intelligence. "Why?" he asked incredulously. "Is he working for the Sultan?"

"I doubt it, but that's a good rumour to spread, especially back in the capital. Only three people know what transpired between the count and his prisoner—Bryennius himself, his scout Togol and that girl, Martina."

Cydones let out a short, sharp breath through his nose at the mention of the courier who had evaded him. "Of the three, she is the softest target and I have a score to settle."

"Leave her to me," Kamyates snapped. "Bryennius and Togol left with an escort and spare horses this morning. They took the track south, to …"

"Khlat'!"

"No. Artzké, I'll warrant. Bryennius hasn't been there yet. Nor Archēsh. If I'm right about Bryennius, he won't be able to resist going on to the latter. He will be tired and off his guard. No one will be expecting him, so that is the ideal place to arrange a tragic mishap. You go directly there today—you'll easily get there ahead of him and be much fresher. Arrange a brawl or something."

"I'll get Petros Doukitzes to do the work. But I should have an excuse to go there myself, in case I'm seen."

Kamyates drew himself up. "Of course you don't. You're a senior official, expecting promotion. As well you know, the dullards that never leave the capital bow—however petulantly—to those with greater knowledge. It is naturally in your—and the empire's interests—for you to see all you can."

Cydones was reassured. "I'll leave as soon as I've found Doukitzes."

"Make sure he does not mess it up. If he does, kill him, he knows too much anyway."

Archēsh,
Early afternoon, 2nd July 1054

Arriving at Archēsh after noon, Leo found the turmarch, a brown-bearded Armenian, was more forthcoming than his counterpart at Artzké. As before, they rested their horses and most of the party while Leo, Togol and Loukas Gabras, on borrowed mounts, accompanied the turmarch on an area tour during which Leo told him something of what he had gleaned the day before.

"My colleague at Artzké who briefed you yesterday is correct, though I would add that our betters at Van are not much help. Archēsh is the cork in the bottle. Basil Apocapes has a choice. He can conduct his main defence forward here, or back at Manzikert. There are risks both ways."

Leo thought on that for a moment. "Room for manoeuvre around Archēsh, at first glance, seems very limited. I am told if the army was to concentrate here the Turk could easily outflank us by going around beyond the high ground to your north. A main defence at Manzikert would seem to provide better possibilities for manoeuvre and keep the Turk ensnared and vulnerable to one of our relief forces."

"Perhaps you're right, but it's a gamble. And personally, I wouldn't rely too much on relief columns! They take troops, money, time and preparation. And there are none. Everything has been sent west to the Patzinak front or, in the case of the old Armenian regiments, disbanded so they can be more efficient taxpayers."

Leo knew the man was right. "Can you hold here?"

"I think we can defend the city, Bryennius, but only for a short time."

While the town seemed better prepared than Artzké, in Leo's quick estimate it fell far short of the preparations Selth and Doukas had been making at Manzikert.

Completing their tour, the turmarch led them to his official suite and waved them to divans.

Leo said nothing of Simon Vardaheri and Maniakh, though they were never far from his thoughts. The other matter, he had to raise at some point. "I seek also to speak with Irene Curticius, the princeps' daughter from Manzikert."

"Ah! She is here. I sent Curticius a message, y'know." The turmarch rose and called into the void beyond the drapes. Boots sounded in a stone passageway, and a well-cut, handsome fellow with long black hair and mustachios soon emerged. "This is Centarch Theodore Ankhialou."

Although without armour, Ankhialou was instantly recognisable as a soldier with his sword and knee-high black boots. A white scarf wrapped loosely around his head, in the manner of many on the frontier, was worn almost as a turban. The young man managed a social smile at the saddle weary trio in front of him. "You ask of Irene Curticius. She is quite safe and does not wish to be disturbed."

Leo remained seated and let the silence hang, breaking it in that quiet, do-your-duty tone he had for presumptuous or incompetent people. "I will see her nonetheless. Now go do as you're told."

The young man's eyes blazed at Leo, then at his commander who assented with a flick of his head. Ankhialou left.

"Curticius is an old friend," the turmarch said as he looked out the arrow slit at the crowded marketplace below. "Bad business."

Servants brought food and drink as they spoke of the military and commercial affairs of the district. Reluctantly but dutifully, Leo raised the weaknesses—unrepaired walls, poorly maintained engines and slovenly soldiers—he had observed in the city's defences.

"We do what we can," his host exhaled. "Most of the few troops are concentrated in Manzikert and Van. I need more men and the money to pay them. But thank you for your advice. I'll look to it."

Suddenly Leo sensed they were being watched.

Irene appeared in a shimmer of crimson silk from behind the drapes with Ankhialou behind her. "Count Bryennius," she greeted graciously.

The men rose and stood, silent.

"As you can see," Ankhialou sneered. "She's ..."

Leo interrupted. "I am sure Mistress Curticius can speak for herself."

With a fleeting glace of irritation at Ankhialou, she met Leo's eyes. "It is very kind of you to come this far enquiring of my safety. As you can see, I am well."

Ankhialou moved a step closer to her and placed an arm possessively around her.

"Are my family well?" Irene asked.

"Well enough. We did not see your brother at Artzké, but believe he's also fine." Leo responded as though it was an everyday social call in Constantinople.

"Thank you."

No one knew what to say, until Irene smiled. "You have all ridden very far and must be tired—your horses also. Are you resting here the night?"

Leo wondered if she was searching for an opportunity for a more discreet meeting.

A darkness crossed Ankhialou's face as he realised too much information was being passed.

"They will stay in the citadel stables. I offered the count accommodation here, but he wished to get away early," the turmarch said, missing the black look from Ankhialou.

Togol, neither fooled nor intimidated by the polite exchange before Irene's suitor, stepped forward. "Mistress, none of us have ridden the direct road to Manzikert, by which we must return. A guide would be useful, if you should ride with us?"

Ankhialou took a step before Irene could answer. "The road's easily followed, even by stupid people, but I'll furnish a guide." He paused in the room's heavy silence. "Was there something else?"

Their business finished and welcome worn, Leo turned to the turmarch, "With your approval, we shall retire to your stables and leave at first light." This gave Irene a few hours to re-consider and confirmed where to find them. Leo was not particularly prudish, but he recognised Ankhialou's manipulative control over Irene and it offended him.

"If you have some time before your journey, the market in Archēsh has many fine wares," she suggested.

Leo thanked her before she was ushered out by Ankhialou.

"Let me know if there is more I can do, but it looks like rest is your main need," the turmarch offered after the pair had gone.

Leaving the citadel they found an inn with cheap but worthy refreshments. Fatigued from the exertions of the cattle raid and a day and night's riding since, they returned to the stables and rested on clean straw in an empty stall. Propped against his saddle, Leo watched Ruksh lay down with a contented groan and the horse's ear move to the sounds outside. Lazily, unguided, his thoughts turned to Martina. He remembered the fair and her offering to get him anything—a kindness he should return. He sat up. "Togol, I'm going for a walk, for I cannot sleep."

"You want me to come too, Horse-archer?" said Togol, though the scout did not stir.

Leo grinned. "No. I will not be long and it's merely a stroll."

"You damned Romans and your walking!"

Unarmoured in grimy riding clothes, Leo strode to the bustling market beneath the citadel walls. Irene had been right, the market was well stocked—saddles and carpets from Persia, silver, copper and tin from Armenia, gold, iron, paper and silk from Bukhara, sugar and spices from Baghdad and the wine of Shiraz.

For no apparent reason, his hackles rose. He turned a corner and waited but no one suspicious seemed to be following. Still alert, he turned into another crowded aisle where half a dozen tongues competed as one. There he found a few stalls selling perfumes and other gifts.

"For a lady?" one handsome, dark-eyed stall-keeper asked in her accented Greek.

"Yes! A lady."

"A lover?" She plied him with samples.

"No. More a…"

"Something more subtle?"

"Yes, subtle."

"You're far from home?" she ventured, turning to him with another vial.

"As are you. What accent do you have?" Leo asked her as Vardaheri unexpectedly caught his eye from the crowd.

The woman had not noticed. She smiled, intent on Leo. "I'm Arab from Baghdad, but Christian and have lived here many years."

Vardaheri sidled up. "Is it good perfume, stranger?"

Leo hid his pleasure at seeing the horse trader. "I'm no judge, friend, as this good woman now knows," he replied with the air of someone wishing a meddlesome stranger to move on. He saw Maniakh mingling in the crowd.

"See you at the end of the next row of stalls," whispered Vardaheri, stepping away.

From the corner of his eye, Leo followed the direction they took. The woman presented him with another vial to sample, dabbing some on her own wrist and holding it out for him. "Yes, this one," Leo decided.

"Nine *follis*. One *solidis* from you, thank you," she said, taking his Roman gold coin. "Your change." She handed over the perfume and a few unfamiliar silver and bronze coins. The woman saw him examine them doubtfully. "Kurdish coins," she explained. "They're common around here. People will accept them."

Leo thanked the woman and left. Surprised at the scant change, he realised that Byzantine currency was in decline throughout the Empire's easternmost cities, another reason why it would be so hard to defend Vaspurakan.

He found Vardaheri. "You've ridden hard, Simon?"

"There was a most deplorable fire in Tabriz and we had to lay low for a while," Simon grinned and they both laughed. "We left two days ago and ended up being chased much of the way. Praise the hosts that we were well mounted."

"I heard of the fire and wondered if it was you." Leo did not have to embarrass them with gushing praise.

"How did you hear?" the horse-trader gasped.

"A story for another time."

"It wasn't as destructive as we hoped," Vardaheri volunteered with satisfaction, "but it'll slow them down a little. We got into Archēsh and thought someone familiar would show up eventually. Then we saw you and one who seemed to be watching you. He ducked out of sight and left when you turned around unexpectedly. I don't think he saw us, but I swear I have seen him in Manzikert."

Leo was perplexed and wondered who it would be. He doubted their interest was benign, or they would have shown themselves. "Simon, this town seems to be full of eyes and ears. We leave tomorrow with a guide provided by Irene Curticius' suitor. At dawn we take the direct route back, the right hand fork, away from the lake. So be on our trail by sunup and follow just like other travellers until a few miles away from this place."

Leo had to complete one more task at Archēsh. With the falconer, Bardanes Gurgen, and a farrier from Her on his mind, Leo returned to the citadel stable and told his men of his meeting with Vardaheri. Then he inspected the horses' shoes. Setting down the leg of a light bay mare, Leo remarked, "Manuel, your mare could use shoeing and I need an excuse to visit a blacksmith."

"I can take the horse, Count. Or do you wish me to accompany you?"

Togol opened an eye and then stood. "I feel like a walk."

Leo and Togol, leaving their armour and keeping only a commoner's knife at their belts, took the horse by a simple halter with no Roman military trappings to draw attention to it and asked directions of locals.

"Kavadh, Farrier and Blacksmith," Leo read the sign. "Hello. Anyone there?" he called.

A strongly built man with dark eyes, a shock of curly black hair and greying beard entered through a doorway in the rear. "Yes, sirs?"

Leo's glance took in the man's leather overlapping-split apron. "Will you shoe a horse, please?"

"Of course. Of course." Kavadh approached their mare and picked up a front leg. "Passing through? Yes. She needs it—been ridden a way. Nice little mare. You can't do it yourselves? You have the stamp of fellows who could."

"Normally, yes," Leo returned in a countryman's casual tones. "But we don't have tools with us. She is about due for a proper shoeing anyway."

"She's been properly enough shod. Army farrier, Roman!" Kavadh looked them over. "Do you want to leave her here awhile? Lots of people are getting horses done in case they want to leave in haste!"

"We'll wait," replied Leo.

"Is she quiet?"

"A pleasure to shoe, ordinarily," answered Togol with a comical sideways grimace to Leo.

Hoping Togol was right, Leo shot an irritated glance at him. The Cuman held the mare while Kavadh got to work.

The farrier was sociable and forthcoming, discussing the town, Normans and his journey from Her because of the disruption caused by the weakening caliphate. They let the blacksmith carry on with his work, getting to know the horse, pulling off the first shoe and selecting one he had pre-forged to shape and fit. Time went by, horse and blacksmith both at ease and the task progressing quickly while three hooves were done.

Leo looked casually around the shop, as any visitor might. Amongst a pile of rusted used shoes in the corner were a few solid horseshoes with round holes in the sole. "Interesting shoes," he observed.

Kavadh, sweating in the rhythm of his trade and looking to Leo, replied between breaths in the staccato manner of workmen. "You're new around here then? Persian we call them. Take a bit of work to fit and put on. Can cause contracted heels if overused. Good for a soft footed horse in stony country though."

"Do any use them hereabouts?" Leo asked.

"That is why I keep a few." The blacksmith, holding a coal-red iron shoe by tongs, belted it into shape over an anvil by the forge. "Bardanes Gurgen gets me to do one of his horses that way." He plunged the hot shoe into a tub of water, placed it on the anvil, put down the tongs while taking up a pritchel and forced the point into a nail hole with a heavy hammer. He moved to the horse, lifted the foot being shod and lightly tested the still hot shoe for fit. Acrid smoke came off the foot as Kavadh continued speaking, "Sometimes Bardanes journeys far—to Karin I think he said—sick sister or something. I suggested he try them when he brought the mare here stone-bruised one day."

Interested, Leo stooped and picked up one of the Persian shoes to examine it more closely. "Seems I've heard the name. What's he do?"

"You ask a lot of questions, and Gurgen is a good customer," said Kavadh without looking up. "He's nothing to hide from honest folk. Buys and sells livestock, I think. Sells a few falcons for good prices—he has a knack with them." The blacksmith was quiet for a moment, concentrating on rasping the underside of a hoof flat. "Word is, his family used to be well-to-do, but some Roman stole their land."

That seemed to confirm Gurgen's own story as told at Arknik, Leo thought, noticing a sheepskin-covered saddle over a rail. It looked familiar and lifting the skin, he saw it was a fine Roman military saddle, worn but well cared for. "Is the saddle yours?"

"No. Though I wouldn't mind if it were!" Kavadh said, dropping the rasp and the near hind leg. "It's a good'n. Too good for the arse who brought it in this morning. Wanted his horse shod on the spot and wouldn't take no for an answer. I had a few to do and she was a bitch—must have learned it from him. I told him to leave her and come back later. She's out behind learning some manners."

Leo looked out of the back door to the shop and saw an unfamiliar horse tied in the shade of a tree. Leo lifted the saddle flap and made out a name carved faintly into the worn leather. "Bardas Cydones," he read aloud. "The imperial courier," he said under his breath to Togol. They exchanged glances. "Have you seen the owner of the saddle with Bardanes Gurgen?"

Ready for the nailing, Kavadh picked up the foot again and glanced at Leo as he reached into an old felt hat for a nail. "I have—with a few people—this morning—having their breakfast," Kavadh went on, his friendly, conversational tone concealing his curiosity. "You interested?" He continued with his work, carefully driving nails through the shoe and both quarters, before picking up the cadence after the shoe was set on the foot.

Almost subconsciously, Leo listened to the rhythm of Kavadh's hammer work: three spaced tentative taps to start the nail on the correct course until the nail head showed through, three confident double-taps to drive it home and finally two hard hits to force weld the nail head into the grove of the shoe. Then the dangerous nail-tip was twisted off with the hammer claws. "Not really," Leo lied. "Always on the lookout for a good horse or saddle though."

The blacksmith tapped over the nail points and rasped the hoof wall and clenches to acceptable smoothness. His work done, Kavadh stood. "As your quiet friend said, a good mare to shoe." Togol gave Leo an exaggerated look of relief behind the blacksmith's back. They paid Kavadh and led the mare away down side lanes.

"I think the blacksmith of Her is as he seems, Togol," Leo said. "But I did not know our imperial courier, the constant companion of Modestos Kamyates, had business in Archēsh."

Back at the stables, they settled down to sleep. A cataphract soon roused Leo with the news that a lady was asking for him. He rose, tugged on his boots and went to her.

At the main door, Irene Curticius passed him a basket of food for the journey and expressed gratitude for his concerns, with assurances of love for her parents and disquiet at their distress. "Guy d'Agiles, is well?"

"Well enough, considering you left so suddenly."

Irene was silent for a moment biting her bottom lip. She looked at him briefly and then dropped her gaze to the flagstones with their dusting of dried manure and windblown straws. "The fair was coming around again." She raised her gaze to meet his. "That's where I met Theodore, last year. I hadn't heard from him for some time so I came to Archēsh. To know how he felt. I'm reassured."

"Reassured?"

She looked at him, saying nothing.

Leo nodded impassively. It was not his business and he had no wish to become involved. Reluctantly, he hinted at his doubts about the defensive preparations of the fortress and relayed her father's concerns.

She looked down throughout and bit her lip softly.

"Any messages?"

Tears almost came as she glanced down again, then shook her head and looked at him. "I'm in a good place. I don't want to mess it up."

Leo noticed she said nothing of love. Too tired for excess etiquette, he took his leave and thanked her again for the food. He did not know what or how he would tell Guy.

Early the next morning Leo and his party left Archēsh, followed the track westward across the steppe and after a few miles entered a patch of brush. The bold cataphract, Tzetzes, had allowed his swift-walking bay horse to draw ahead. Riding just forward of Ankhialou's guide, Tzetzes gave a strangled cry and slumped in the saddle. A dozen armed men burst from the undergrowth and the little party was hotly engaged with spear and sword for several moments until the sudden, violent intervention of Maniakh and Vardaheri surprised the ambushers. After a brief, bloody skirmish, the remaining assailants fled back into the thicket. Four of the others writhed wounded on the ground. Of Leo's party, Tzetzes was badly wounded, one cataphract nursed a slashed forearm and another a stab wound to the thigh.

Not until they turned Tzetzes over did they find the dart caught in the folds of his mail where it had caused a deep puncture wound close to the neck opening. Maniakh examined the dart. "Majra!" he exclaimed, referring to a grooved piece of wood held in the hand, so an archer could shoot short darts from an ordinary horseman's bow. "See the long thin iron head of the dart—for piercing mail. The work of a hired killer, made to look like brigandage."

Togol knelt close to Leo and whispered harshly. "The attacker aimed at a well-equipped Roman, riding a bay horse near the head of the group. They were after you. The dart may have been poisoned. Don't tell Tzetzes—to know might kill him."

As they tended the wounded and mustered the stray horses, a rider galloped towards them from the direction of Manzikert. It was Bessas' squire, Cosmas Mouzalon, who slowed his mount on seeing them and trotted in to dismount before Leo. "The centarch's compliments, Count," the young man said quietly to Leo while brushing straight black hair from his eyes. "He heard part of a conversation between Modestos Kamyates and Bardas Cydones and feared you were at risk. I see he was right and I am too late."

Leo and Togol glanced at each other, then at the stricken Tzetzes.

"I have just ridden past a hamlet," Mouzalon said. "They might be able to aid him there."

Leo considered the idea. "That is the best we can do. Togol, Simon, two men and you with me. We're going after them. Cosmas, guide these men to the village then return to Manzikert and inform the strategos." He turned to the decarch, Gabras. "Loukas, remain with Tzetzes in the village until we return. Take the wounded brigands as well. Tend them and see what you can learn. If we have not retuned by sunset tomorrow, return to Manzikert and brief the strategos."

Leo conferred with Togol and Simon Vardaheri. "What price Ankhialou's guide?" he asked.

"He's with us, I believe, Horse-archer," Togol answered. "I saw him turn and strike down him in the blue tunic."

"And I noticed him wound that youth wearing brown," said Vardaheri.

"He can come with us. Let's get after their friends," suggested Leo, giving Ruksh a quick check-over before mounting.

Manzikert,
Afternoon, 2nd July 1054

Already deeply upset by the news of Irene's leaving, Guy felt drained from the emotional and physical exertions of the cattle raid and was grateful for the two days' rest awarded to the regiment by Bessas. The men tended their horses, checked their weapons and equipment, rested, ate and then scattered in groups of friends to whatever took their fancy in Manzikert and its immediate environs.

Much as he wished to see Irene, Guy had been glad not to have to leave with Bryennius for Artzké. It would have piqued him, had they continued to Archēsh, to see Irene with Ankhialou. He had never felt like this before, as if a blade had sliced into the heart of him. That night after he had learned of her going—that blackness before the cattle raid—had been long and empty, ending with the pre-dawn saddling up, girth straps clammy-cool to the touch. The first day's ride had passed as a blur, but his sudden flight from the Seljuk scouting party and the fight at the wadi had brought his existence sharply back into focus—riding and fighting for his very life, crouched in the dust, skulking from the arrows of the infidels with fear clenched in his chest.

Irene Curticius! Now she dominated his thoughts again as he waited impatiently for Count Bryennius to return from his reconnaissance with news of her.

He reflected on what had brought him to Manzikert; of the hunt for the traitors who had attempted to stop the couriers, the latter rumoured to be Martina and Yūryak. As for their pursuers, Guy had seen none that he could swear was Swordleader who had escaped him near the Golden Gate. In Karin, he had once felt the hairs on the back of his neck rise, but had recognised no one around him. Of the new faces that filled his life, most were good fellows, some were boors, others bullies and braggarts. Only the seemingly friendly attentions of the imperial courier, Bardas Cydones, made him uneasy; there was something slyly manipulative about that man. Despite all the faces he should have studied more closely, he had been captured by Irene's. His melancholy returned, accompanied now by self-reproach.

Guy sought solace in the company of friends and a score of distracting little tasks. The three Franks had idled at the fair earlier this day, but Jacques was impatient to check his newly won mare. Guy had not seen anyone who might have been their quarry and he was too introspective to enjoy the outing, so they returned to the fortress.

They looked over Jacques' captured bay mare, her new master petting and brushing, speaking softly and giving her occasional treats. They had been perplexed for a name for her, Jacques adding the complication that she should also be named after a Persian queen, to uphold the newest if widely unknown tradition of their native district. They apprehended Bessas who passed by to visit his own horses. Joined now by David and Arshak, they all peered through the rails at the bay that looked back at them.

"Nice mare. A Persian queen, eh?" Bessas pursed his lips in concentration. "Arzema!"

Jacques glanced at Guy, then at Bessas. "Arzema," he echoed doubtfully.

"I'm running out of Persian Queens," said Bessas.

There was another flicker of glances. "Arzema, it is then!" announced Jacques happily.

"She's in season," Bessas observed, "and would leave a good foal by Balazun's black Castilian stallion." He then left, waving away their gratitude.

"Very in-season I would say, and she would, by God," said David, with Arshak mumbling agreement through his grey beard.

They all looked at Guy and Jacques, then at Balazun's horse in his enclosure at the end of the lane. Their steady stares then turned to Guy.

"Robert Balazun would never agree," he protested. "And we could never pay the service fee."

"Balazun doesn't need to know," quipped David. "It would be a well-bred foal, out of the field by moonlight!"

That night, they—with the willing if noisy assistance of Balazun's stallion and the distraction of his groom—potentially doubled Jacques' herd. He returned Arzema to her yard and the four conspirators assembled in their triumph. Smug at stealing a march on the arrogant Norman and grinning to each other, they set out for their barracks by a longer, less obvious route. On the way, they tarried at a crowded inn, stuffy with the smell of stale wine and ale.

"Balazun's horse is just like his owner, by God," David grinned. "I thought he was going to wake the whole city." Roaring with laughter they drank more wine. Sometime later, they emerged into the darkened street to see Martina and Yūryak passing by. The couple nodded a greeting and went on their way.

"She's nice," Guy remarked.

Jacques said nothing so Guy turned to look, as though the groom had not heard him.

"I have eyes," Jacques muttered.

Guy could not fathom his meaning, but meant to ask later when they were alone. "Then keep them sharp, for look who comes." Guy switched to his rustic Greek as Bardanes Gurgen approached with his servant and the scowling Reynaldus. "Bardanes?"

"How now, P'rang?" the Armenian replied, a hooded falcon perched on his arm. The raptor turned its head towards Guy as he spoke. Gurgen's man, Ananias, shorter, swarthy, stubbled and silent, stood behind him.

"Guy d'Agiles, it is."

"D'Agiles," Gurgen corrected himself.

The knight made a dismissive greeting, but Guy thought his expression more definitive. It was little wonder his Normans referred to Reynaldus as Poo Face.

"Buying or selling?" Guy asked, looking at the bird.

"Bought. A Peregrine falcon," Gurgen answered socially with obvious pride and expertise. "You're interested in hawking?"

"I know little of it," Guy said, taking in the Armenian's tall, well-proportioned frame that was accentuated by his belted tunic and long boots. Guy found he grudgingly admired the physical presence of the man and his courage in speaking his mind that night at Arknik. "You must come out with us some time, Guy d'Agiles?"

"Thank you, Bardanes. That would be interesting and a quiet ride for Jacques' new mare," Guy replied, wondering if it was mere coincidence these three had been so close to Martina and Yūryak.

Reynaldus and Ananias sniggered. The hint of a smile played around Gurgen's lips as he exchanged glances with his servant. Guy was unsure whether it was evidence of malice, a practical joke or their simple amusement at his inexperience.

"When are you planning to go?" Jacques stepped in.

"Tomorrow," Gurgen smiled. "To the east—there's a marsh there and we might land a waterbird. There will be a hunting party, leaving early and it will be a long day, so bring lunch."

Guy hesitated. The Armenian seemed well intentioned and friendly relations with the locals and a better knowledge of the terrain were both desirable. "So soon? It sounds interesting, but I must seek the approval of Centarch Phocas."

"Does he really need to know?" said Gurgen. "A man cannot move for meddling Greeks."

"Bah!" Reynaldus sprayed. "Why does Balazun let you mess around with the Greeks and their damned scouts anyway? What good is it?"

To the Armenian, Guy replied, "He'll notice I'm gone and want to know where. To blindside him would be discourteous and would draw more attention." Then turning to Reynaldus he reasoned, "We, that is all of us, must know what the Seljuks are doing. How many there are and if and when they will attack."

Reynaldus regarded Guy condescendingly for some moments, then asked with genuine wonder, "Why? We just kill them when they get here."

Guy was stunned by his wilful ignorance and opened his mouth to reply, but he recalled Bessas' satirical advice: never argue with an idiot or they will reduce one to their level. "Perhaps."

Gurgen waved a hand in acquiescence.

That night before the hunt seemed airless. Guy lay awake next to his cast-off blanket for much of it, thoughts drifting from Irene to the fight in the wadi and the wounded cataphracts from the skirmish there. He flinched at their suffering, recalling the agony of their journeys back to Manzikert. Most of all he wondered whether the forthcoming hunt would take them to Archēsh; if he would see Irene, or be able to bear doing so.

He rose early, grateful a breeze had cooled the night and a few hours rest had finally been possible. His melancholy returned and he was anxious to escape the confines of Manzikert, even for a day.

Guy and Jacques breakfasted and while the latter saddled the horses, Guy walked to the Barbarian House to collect the map Isaac had promised and to fill his goatskin from the sweet water of the well there. Isaac was his own age and wore, beneath his dark curls, the grin of irrepressible optimism. He was known for fiendish practical jokes, particularly on Oleg, who would shrug them off with a laugh and the promise of awful retribution. Isaac handed Guy the map and he sat at his table to study it. He noticed Isaac working on something else and asked what it was.

"Tell no one," Isaac started uncertainly, as though debating whether to share his secret. "I am writing the story of these times—of Manzikert and deeds done, of you capturing a horse, Togol apprehending Zobeir al-Adin and of the fight at the wadi."

Guy was grateful but embarrassed that his desire for a horse threatened to become a steppe epic. He rose and clapped his hand on Isaac's shoulder. "Your secret is safe with me, Isaac, but don't leave out Kamyates and make sure you tell your own part as well. That would only be fair."

"But I haven't done anything."

Guy waved Isaac's self-doubts away. "It's not over yet. I once heard Bessas say, we are heirs to all that has gone before—that were it not for Homer and Dictys there would be no Trojan War, no Helen or Hector, Achilles nor Agamemnon. This just seems life for us, but only a fool would not feel something in the wind. Perhaps someone, one day, might learn something of value from how well, or badly, we here now face our ordinary lives. That can only be if it is known, and for that someone must tell the story."

The hunting party, fifteen strong, assembled two hours after dawn and started along the dirt track to Archēsh. It was a capable looking party of men who were irked by life behind the walls, or were drawn to the hunt by the promise of something new.

"We're going to the swamp that lies to the north west of Mount Sippane to look for waterbird," Gurgen explained from his saddle "It is about twenty miles to the swamp. A third of the way to Archēsh, but well south off the road."

In addition to the two falconers and Reynaldus, the hunt comprised a mixed group of Normans, Varangians and Armenians. Guy was surprised to see Bessas, his squire and Count Branas there.

"The strategos ordered us out," Bessas explained in answer to Guy's look. Branas can check his outposts and I am to learn the lay of the land, and …"

Guy knew he meant to keep an eye on Gurgen.

They rode from Manzikert with its fountains, trees and many gardens, crossed the lava strewn crest a mile east of the town and jogged through cultivated land, much of which was now being harvested by peasants wielding scythes and sickles. A few, tunics sweat soaked and beards matted, stopped to look at the horsemen riding by.

Guy had spent days on his father's holding and knew a little of how the days passed for the harvesters: the sky and aching shoulders, back and legs, the constant swishing of the crop as it wavered and collapsed in windrows[58] behind the blade. Water and a crust for lunch, blistered hands and aching back had been his memory of it. He waved to a peasant but the man ignored the gesture and continued working.

"I'd lay the whip on him!" snarled Reynaldus as he made to ride at the man.

"Leave it," snapped Oleg. "A peasant has his pride, and his work. We'll need both if the Seljuks come."

Reynaldus glared at the formidable Viking but said nothing.

The hunting party left the Manzikert-Archēsh track and followed a bridle path. Further from the fortress and its environs, stock grazed in the harvested fields and on the lower slopes. They too lifted their heads at the horsemen. Then through the warm air came the pungent, unmistakeable smell of an abattoir. Here were carts laden with freshly flayed hides. Salted meat, covered over with linen to keep it clean, was laid out on racks to dry in the warm breeze. Oleg, observing Guy's interest, rode close on a brown gelding. "Part of the herd you brought in, slaughtered to provision the garrison. The hides can be used to pad the walls against rocks. When soaked with vinegar, they are proof against fire, or can strengthen a wooden palisade, God forbid, if we need to repair a breach in the walls."

After some discussion of siege techniques, Guy asked after Oleg's plain horse.

"It is just a garrison horse," the Viking explained. "The Romans provide them to us to use. Unlike them, we don't have much of a cavalry tradition— we're sailors, preferring to fight on foot. Have you ever tried to use a battle-axe from the saddle? Impossible? Not impossible," he grinned. "Nothing with an axe is impossible, just damned hard. Yet," the Viking continued amiably, "horses or mules enable one to reach the fight more quickly. If one can't sail to battle, riding is next best. Walking is undignified and after a while your feet hurt."

"Oleg, where do you come from?" asked Guy.

The Viking laughed. "Everywhere and nowhere. From cold lands far to the north west. Viking lands. My people travelled down the rivers and made our way to Kiev on the Dnieper, Novograd and other settled places where we established

---

58 Windrows—rows or lines of hay exposed to the wind to dry.

trading posts. They intermarried with the locals and eventually converted to Orthodox Christianity. A new culture has formed, Kievan Rus. Viking, Varangian and Rus, all mixed up."

Gurgen led the hunting party at a ground-covering walk. A broad, yellow-green plain stretched in undulating folds before them. In the distance were hills with mountains behind. The watercourse to their north, a tributary of the Arsanias, was hidden in a thin smudge of distant green to their left. Beyond the stream was a prominent range of bare, brown hills with patches of thicket and a few hardy trees. Towering in its conical bulk to the southeast stood snow-capped Mount Sippane.

"It's a good landmark," Oleg explained. "It dominates all and you can't mistake it. Immediately beyond it, to the south, is the Sea of Bznunik."

For future reference Guy noticed how the bare ground to the south sloped gradually away in a tangle of steep gullies and washaways before rising to the lower slopes of the mountain. He also saw also how the Manzikert-Archēsh track swept to the north in a wide bend around the broken terrain.

A whoop from the front heralded a chase, two of the Normans galloping south towards the rough country in pursuit of a deer. Sira bunched and snatched the bit, wanting to race away, but with her ears back the mare steadied and listened for Guy's word.

"We're off," Oleg beamed as his horse leapt away. "I hope we find one of these famed Asian lions," he called back over his shoulder.

"That's the way," Bessas said, watching Guy keep his mare to a measured pace. "But we'll need to keep up with them—without letting our horses learn bad habits of rushing along fighting the bit." Picking his moment, Bessas waved his squire back towards the Archēsh track with a message for Bryennius.

The hunting party galloped for miles after the darting deer: strung out, thoughtless, spears ready and with reefing, racing horses crashing over the loose stones in the foothills. Gurgen galloped with them, his subtle hunt lost from his control, the startled, hooded falcon with its talons deep into the padded leather of his gauntlet. He laughingly cursed them for indiscreet, barbarian hunters, but Guy could see he too was caught in the exhilaration of the chase. The deer, fleet, terrified but on her own ground, escaped by plunging down an impossible ravine.

Bessas spoke for all when he said, "She deserved to run free."

The group walked their horses for a time, then lunched under some trees before pressing on as the sultry afternoon became overcast. The long ride and rest in the shade had calmed the most unruly horses and tired the men. Beyond their own perspiration they breathed the salt-sting of horse sweat and the thick dark odour of lathered woollen saddlecloths and braided hair girths. They were moving northward off the mountain's slopes when light brown clouds reflecting the summer-scape crept around them in the still afternoon, the sun searing through the opaque cover, making the day overcast-bright without casting shadow. Guy realised they were now down off the stony higher ground and skirting the edge of the marsh.

"We can cross here where this rivulet enters the swamp," Gurgen said as he kicked his horse into the water.

Five riders plunged in before Guy urged Sira into the muddy water. Another nine followed. The afternoon stillness was replaced by the sound of horses splashing up to their girths. Guy knew he would never forget the sight of grey-brown water reflecting the overcast sky merged together in a close, horizonless world. On this natural canvas, the sharp dark outlines of the mounted figures loomed large. Hard men they looked, straight in the saddle, sombrely dressed, mostly bearded and their rakish caps or wrapped scarves low over searching eyes. Bow cases and swords nestling against booted legs. They rode in good saddles, craftsmen made and well-used, each with its rolled cloak behind the high cantle and saddlebags splashed with muddy water. The horses were alert, tough and confident, enjoying the cool water churning around their legs.

They crossed near the edge of the swamp to emerge, girths dripping, on the other side. Gurgen dismounted to check his horse for any injury caused by an unseen snag in the water. Most followed his example. All the while, the dispossessed Armenian nobleman stroked and whispered to the falcon on his arm. A breeze sprang up through the rocks and yellow grass, sighing through the leaves of the scattered pines. The men paused, checking girths and shoes, taking a swig of water or whatever else might be concealed in a skin. A gust of wind crossed their cheeks and clear sky showed through the dispersing cloud to reveal a solitary heron lifting from the water, suddenly blue in the clear light. As she rose, the heron was sharply outlined against the backdrop of brown hills becoming visible through the shifting vapour.

Only Bessas had yet seen the bird and he caught Guy's eye with a silencing glance. Standing next to Diomed and looking across his saddle, Bessas was watching Gurgen while keeping an eye on the heron.

"Ananias," exclaimed Gurgen. "Look, a waterbird. Let's go."

The two falconers mounted awkwardly, birds balanced on their gloved arms, lures of dead hares swinging by their mounts' shoulders. Quickly they kneed their horses along the bank in the same direction as the slowly ascending heron; the white bird remaining over the seeming safety of the water. Guy quickly mounted and trotted after them, Bessas and the others following. He could see Gurgen and Ananias peel off the leather hoods and cast their birds. The female climbed higher and faster, winging into a wide, searching circle. Guy watched her mark the heron and change direction, striving to rise above and behind the fleeing water bird. The male tiercel rose steadily to shadow behind and beneath the quarry—in the heron's blind spot.

The men rode swiftly, boots home in stirrups, all eyes on the deadly contest above while the horses plunged through washouts and leapt the stunted bushes. Already the birds were far ahead, the heron flying hard in panic now. The raised faces of the galloping riders were flushed with the excitement and lust of the chase and Guy wondered if his expression mirrored theirs.

The falcons attacked, the female dropping like a stone to assail the unprotected back of the heron, the rush of talons and beak forcing the waterbird down towards the gliding tiercel, which in turn struck from underneath and behind. So calculated and skilful was the assault, it was quickly over. The maimed waterbird fluttering to earth with the raptors winging close overhead.

The falconers galloped up to the vanquished heron, lying grey-white on the ground, flecks of blood on the neck and wings. Gurgen remained mounted, looking to his hawks, both of which remained intent on their quarry. With a speed that belied his stout build, Ananias dismounted and roughly grabbed the heron, breaking its wings to prevent escape, pinning it to the ground by driving its own beak though a wing. He then ushered the crowd of mounted spectators away from it. Foaming horses sucked in air as riders ducked in their saddles away from the circling raptors. Ananias soothingly called to the hawks which glided, wings outstretched to the ground very near the weakly quivering waterbird. Folding deliberately, the hawks stalked towards their quarry, to tear on it before the hushed riders.

Guy turned away and saw Bessas, wooden faced, masking his distaste. The remainder were watching silently. Guy sidled up beside the centarch. "Gruesome effective are they not?" Guy said, surprised at the croak in his own voice. "I've never seen it before."

"Me neither." Bessas looked at Guy. "And thus they call Tughrul Bey, The Falcon." It was the warrior in Bessas, Roman soldier in every fibre, which finished the hunt by observing in his clipped tones, "You had better gather up your birds, Bardanes. It seems we have company."

Following the direction of Bessas' gaze, Guy could see no one. He searched the distant low rise with the brush-covered ridge behind it. Then there it was, a slightly darker shape—the head of a man. As Guy watched, a stranger who had been observing them using the ground to shield himself and his mount from their view, rode to the skyline.

"He's not much concerned about being seen now," Branas said to Bessas as the two quickly mounted, looking around.

"So I see." Bessas replied.

Branas signalled the men to shake out in arrowhead and ready their weapons. "Reynaldus. Send two of your men after him. We'll follow at a distance."

Resenting the Armenian's authority but powerless to refuse, the Norman motioned two knights forward at the walk. The distant horseman waited until they approached within bowshot, then calmly turned his horse and walked away.

Bessas swore resignedly. "Here we go."

"Follow him—at a trot," Branas hailed in accented Latin to the two Normans in the lead of the hunting party, which had now changed significantly in character to become a fighting patrol. The two knights broke into a trot. The stranger did the same. Soon all were holding their horses back in a quick hand-gallop. After a couple of winding miles through open country, the galloping lone horseman attempted to induce them over a rise.

Bessas urged Diomed forward and caught the two Normans in the lead before they started to descend the other side. "Pull up. Pull up." Ahead lay a long, narrow valley, open in the middle with thickets and stunted trees lining the walls which were steep sided enough to make riding difficult: a perfect place for ambush. "Halt!" commanded Bessas. They all paused on the crest and observed the retreating figure stop teasingly. Bessas stood in his stirrups and cupping his hands to his bearded jaw, yelled abusively in lurid, gutter Greek, punctuated with similar Armenian phrases.

The lone horseman hesitated, then waved them on. Bessas motioned on the two Normans. It made little difference that the stranger now allowed them to approach, for he had lured them within range of his patrol's concealed bowmen.

'Well done, you rogue!" Bessas laughed when he joined them.

He proved to be an irregular cavalryman from Manzikert, one of the screen, who spoke with Bessas and Branas before the three of them retuned to the ridge for a better view of the surrounding terrain. Guy watched them, three centaurs on the wide harsh earth, conversing, turning to look this way or that, the stranger pointing eastward in what Guy reckoned to be the general direction of Archēsh. He looked but could see no sign of the city.

At length, the hunting party was led some miles to one of the screen's hidden camps in a high valley. Hobbled horses grazed near a few stunted trees where other mounts were tied and crude bowers provided shelter. Riding and pack saddles were hidden in the shadows where an almost smokeless fire smouldered near blackened utensils. Men took up their weapons as the unexpected group rode in.

The newcomers unsaddled, leaving their horses to graze under guard while they were entertained with a meal of braised pork and vegetables. Glad of the food and rest after the hard ride, they accepted an invitation to stay the night. Most retired early to their cloaks, but with the inquisitive nature and energy of youth, Guy used his standing with Bessas to sit in on the conversation, taking place a discreet distance from the camp, between Branas and the leader of the irregulars. Centarch Seranush Donjoian had been a cavalryman when Armenia was its own country. The years since working his small holding had kept him fit with the unmistakable stamp of a warrior.

Bessas listened from a nearby stump.

Branas was reinforcing the screen's role in the defence of Vaspurakan. "When you and your four hundred men get a hint of the arrival of the Seljuk screen, or their vanguard, send us word by galloper, immediately. Then get out of their way. Your main task is to provide early warning, stay alive and then to harass the nomads' rear without being decisively engaged. Fall on small detachments. Kill their couriers. Run off their herds. Burn every blade of grass, so there is no feed to sustain their animals, especially in the lowlands and valleys where the Turcoman main columns will move. Kill anything that looks like a siege engineer or engine.

They will hunt you with a ferocity we can hardly imagine. If pursued, split up so they have no firm target, but forever themselves run the risk of ambush—as you did to us this day."

All the while the tap of a riding whip on Donjoian's bootleg betrayed the moral pain and physical tension the man felt.

"Do you have any questions of the centarch or me?" Branas asked, glancing at Bessas.

Bessas, still seated on the stump, asked, "How are your men?"

"They are good men," Seranush Donjoian said with quiet confidence. "The armies of the Armenians are not as we once were, as abundant and colourful as wildflowers in spring." It was a rebuke for the two Romans. "But these men know what is at stake. The people of the outlying districts will flee to the hills if they have time. Am I to protect them?"

"Only as you can without prejudice to your orders," Branas said. "If we try and defend everything, we'll end up saving nothing."

Bessas then spoke up. "Aggressive offence is the only real defence, Seranush. As the main fortress of Manzikert draws them like honey, that will give you some freedom of action and you must use it to strike them hard. If you can hit the Seljuks, as they seek out those hiding in the hills, that's good. But no heroic last stands, that is what they want you to do. Every action of yours must be directly aimed to trouble the personal thoughts of the Sultan."

"If they withdraw?"

"First get word to us. Mindful of your inadequate strength," Bessas suggested, "try to slow and worry them while we, together with any field forces that come to our support, harass their flanks and rear. That's much to ask, I know."

Donjoian nodded, pursing his bearded lips. Branas asked him how he was deployed and planned to fight. The man spoke with conviction and clarity for some minutes, describing an outpost line thinly spread across the Archēsh-Manzikert approach, with the main strength of his squadron, about two hundred cavalry, held back in secluded places, ready for use. Finally Donjoian asked, "How long will we need to be here?"

Branas shrugged. "Three months, four, perhaps. Until they're defeated or they leave. That is, if they do come."

"Can you hold Manzikert?"

Branas was silent with doubt.

Bessas rose, sensing something was at stake. "The Turk will bleed to death before the walls of Manzikert. My word on it."

"Pray God you are right, Phocas," Donjoian replied. "For my wife and child are in Manzikert."

"As is my love."

Guy saw a bond form between these two, but turned quickly so they did not see the look he knew crossed his own countenance as he thought of Irene.

The hunting party stayed the night in that place of overhanging branches lit softly by the coals, the restless breeze amongst the trees and the stars winking through the cloaking foliage.

Guy awoke in the dim light of a crescent moon, to an awed gathering around the low fire. Men knelt in prayer, one of them having observed a bright new reddish-white star in the constellation Taurus[59]. Some thought it was a good omen; others voiced their terror of things to come. There were doubters who thought the constellation looked no different, and still more who did not bother with such things as the night sky. Guy thought it looked different but was not sure. He too fell to his knees and with the great mystery of the depths above him said a prayer.

Later he wrapped himself in his cloak. His mind wandered restlessly across Irene, the raw mating of Jacques' mare with Balazun's stallion, hawks tearing on the dying heron and the strange new star. It seemed as though nature itself had taken a darker turn and Irene was lost to him. Sometime not long before dawn he fell asleep, to be woken a short time afterward to return to Manzikert.

A hamlet west of Archēsh,
Late afternoon, 4th July 1054

Leo cursed under his breath after abandoning the fruitless pursuit of the attackers who, having wounded Tzetzes and the others, had escaped the skirmish. He led his five weary companions on their jaded horses into the hamlet where his men tended the wounded. As they approached, Loukas Gabras was already directing those in the village to provide food and drink for the returning horsemen and their mounts.

"Tzetzes lives?" asked Leo, dismounting.

"Yes, Count. But he's poorly," Gabras replied. "A woman has given him opium to ease the pain, but the infection is spreading. We need to move him back to proper care as soon as we can."

"Alright, Loukas, we're empty handed and have lost a day. Our horses were too tired—have them cared for, will you please—and the miscreants knew the country too well. Did you learn anything from the captives?"

Gabras motioned nearby villagers to look after the horses just ridden in and gestured to the wounded attackers who sat bound in a group with bandages covering their wounds. "They're merely hired thugs from Archēsh and know nothing."

"Very good," said Leo. "Detail some of the villagers to assist Ankhialou's guide to escort them back to Archēsh for handover to the turmarch."

Grabnas waved two nearby cataphracts to the task then turned to Leo. "For moving Tzetzes, we have made a horse-drawn litter from two poles. The village smith has given us a pair of small, iron bound wheels and an axle padded with

---

59 This was the supernova, the Crab Nebula, observed in North Asia and the Middle East.

leather to keep the rear off the ground. We've prepared food and water for the horses you have ridden in. We can move any time you say."

"Good man. I'm sure Tzetzes will be grateful for your forethought. We will move as soon as men and horses have had something to eat and drink and we have changed saddles to the spare mounts."

Day turned to a long night. It was the cataphract, Aspieties, who drew their attention to the unfamiliar light in the heavens. None had seen it before and the sight of it prompted fear and doubt. "A new star?" one wondered aloud. In the dark, lonely expanse of Vaspurakan, with their dry-sweated horses and wounded comrades, most prayed. So busy was each man then with his private fears, only Vardaheri noticed Leo, unmoving in the saddle, studying the blemished sky, his thoughts his own.

Tzetzes was incoherent and writhing in pain when the group reached Manzikert, where they carried the wounded man to the hospital and roused the nuns. Leo gave Ruksh to his squire and rode a duty horse, one of a small number kept saddled for official use, to the citadel. Basil questioned him about the ambush and they agreed that conjecture did not amount to proof against Kamyates and Cydones. Before they parted, Basil asked if Leo had seen the celestial display. He admitted to seeing it after it occurred and simply shook his head when asked if he had a view on its significance.

Then Leo sought out Curticius to relay the news of his daughter, pleading fatigue to avoid a long drinking session. He paused at the Barbarian House to leave the wrapped bottle of scent on Martina's desk.

There remained Guy. The young Frank was not at the Barbarian House, nor his quarters. Near the end of his endurance, perplexed by the new star, depressed by the wounding of Tzetzes with its implications, and the melancholy duty of his last call, Leo went to the stables to visit his horses and perhaps find Guy. None of the few at the stables had seen the young Frank. Leo still did not know what or how to tell him.

Leo finally retired to his quarters where he lit a taper from the oil lamp outside and touched it to the wick of a candle in his room. The fragile flame threw shadows on the whitewashed wall and Leo noticed his. It struck him what an ageless thing it must be, a soldier returning to a room far from home, candlelight and the sound of arms laid to rest. Dropping his hat on the bed, he pulled the mail shirt over his head.

He noticed his squire had wiped his saddle then saw the neat little pile left on the chair: a tan shirt as he had asked for and another of similar pattern, but in rich blue cotton, both tied in a neat parcel with string. On top of them was a small leather bag. Leo emptied into his hand a set of flints, such as Togol had used to light the grassfire on the cattle raid, and some coins. By his reckoning, too much had been returned.

Leo cut the string with his dagger and unfolded the shirts to examine them. Two sheets of parchment floated free. His brow furrowed in bewilderment at the neat lines of meaningless Greek characters in Martina's hand: a coded message. As to the keyword that would unlock it, he had no clue. In frustration he replayed in his mind's eye every conversation, every look he had shared with Martina trying to recall a word that would have significance for none but them. He stared at the candle flame for long minutes. Finally he took up a sheet and wrote down a coded alphabet using the keyword "Kasia". That failed and he tried again with "cattlelifter". The messages came forth.

> *Count Bryennius,*
>
> *I had to leave with Count Doukas before your return, but something has happened and I do not know who else to tell.*
>
> *At the fair I was followed by Modestos Kamyates who pinned me against a stall and caught my arm until it hurt. He was very menacing and demanded to know what took place between you and Derar al-Adin at the wadi. He did not use his name, only referring to him as the Arab. He also wanted to know why you let him go.*
>
> *Kamyates only stopped when he saw Yūryak approaching, looking threatening as only Yūryak can. Kamyates threatened to kill me if I told anyone.*
>
> *I told him nothing.*
>
> *How did he know? So few do. Someone must be talking.*

Leo, working by candlelight, bent to the second sheet where Martina's message was continued in a more personal vein.

> *Leo,*
>
> *I dreamed last night that Kamyates was chasing us down a long dark street in Constantinople. We ran around a corner and there was a blue mosque where the barracks of the Scholae should have been.*
>
> *Isn't it silly?*
>
> *But be careful.*
>
> *M*

He straightened thoughtfully and burned the decoded pages, folding the originals and tucking them into the leather pouch at his belt.

Chapter Nine

From Archēsh

Manzikert,
Afternoon, 6th July 1054

Guy walked slowly towards the Barbarian House, his last conversation with Count Bryennius a raw scar across his soul. It had not been the count's fault. He had found Guy the previous evening at the stables grooming Sira. Bryennius, bareheaded, wearing a blue tunic, approached and leaned against the rails. Guy had climbed out of the yard. "You're back?"

"I looked for you last night."

"I went out with a hunting party and we didn't return until late. I searched for you then. I suppose we've been moving in circles. Did you see the new star? It's there yet!"

Bryennius was silent: both knew he had not come seeking Guy's opinion on a star. They had leaned against the rails, looking through them at Sira.

"I spoke to Irene in Archēsh," Bryennius had started after a long pause. "Twice. The first time she was with Theodore Ankhialou. It was evident to me that he maintains a close control over her and she was not free to speak freely. He at first tried to prevent us from seeing her …"

"Us?"

"Togol and Gabras were with me. It was in the turmarch's chambers."

Guy had tried to imagine the meeting: Irene with her formal face on, standing beside an indistinct Ankhialou with the count staring him down and Togol glaring from the side.

The count had lifted a booted foot to the lowest rail, sword swinging from his hip. "Irene assured me she was well and asked after her family. Togol in his style asked her to return with us, but Ankhialou was having none of it."

Guy listened, staring at a wisp of hay in Sira's yard.

"Later she came," Bryennius had continued, "and spoke to me, alone, at the stables. She asked after you and I think regrets her conduct towards you."

Guy had looked at the count. "Was there any message?" his words as though his mouth was full of sand.

"I asked. No message."

It had cut like a knife.

Another long pause. "She merely said she's in a good place and doesn't want to mess it up."

"A good place? Not mess it up?" There was another silence. "What does that mean?"

"I don't know, Guy. Who can say?" Bryennius had let out a long breath. "You should be happy she's at least physically safe and not being led off to a slave market somewhere. I can tell you though, she—I thought—was not glowing with happiness and her visit to the stables was apologetic. She seemed … diminished … in a way. But, Irene has made her choice—wealth and status—and being under his power." The count had stood back from the rails and looked at him. "I know it's not what you wished to hear. If you and your companions want to leave and never give her another thought, I will release you. You've all got some pay coming and have done as much as we asked—more. Take some time, and let me know."

Walking with his recollections, Guy drew near the Barbarian House, with its well and apple tree in the stone-walled yard, to revise the map Isaac had given him for the hunt. He was surprised when Kamyates and Cydones shouldered wordlessly by him on their way out.

Isaac looked up as Guy entered. "The wandering Kelt returns! How was it? I've wanted to get out that way, towards Archēsh. Did you get that far? Was the map all right?"

"What did they want?" asked Guy. "I didn't think they were allowed in here."

"Hello to you too! They're not. They bluffed the sentry. They're after maps and any information a lowly clerk might inadvertently divulge," Isaac mimicked the superior courtly tones of Kamyates. "Arseholes," he huffed in barrack room Greek. "Eyes everywhere. I gave them an old, rather inaccurate map I keep here—just in case—to keep them happy and ignorant."

"I am sorry. I had something on my mind." Guy grinned and spread the map Isaac had given him before the hunt. He explained the approximate position and extent of the swamp, noting that when riding the terrain, it seemed further away from the road than how it was represented on the skin. "Anything happening here?" he asked.

"No. It's been quiet," mumbled Isaac without looking up.

"Are Martina and Yūryak here?"

"Yūryak's around," Isaac mumbled again, still studying the marked map Guy had brought. "Martina left this morning with the count and some scouts on a ride around the south and west. They'll be gone days I suspect. The strategos sent them with orders for the garrisons and men in the hills."

"Count Bryennius?" In Guy's mind, Bryennius was "the Count". "He sure gets around!"

"No," Isaac said, looking up and staring unseeingly at Guy for long moments. "Not Bryennius, Doukas. But, now that you mention it, I noticed something yesterday morning." He paused, his brow furrowed as he recalled in a new light the meeting he had witnessed. "Martina came in before she left and found a small package on her table. She opened it, read a note inside and then examined a small bottle, smiled a little to herself and seemed suddenly more alive. I sensed she was going to look at me, so I quickly stared down at my work."

Isaac looked away as though recalling the scene. "Then, after a while, Count Bryennius came downstairs, he must have been working up there—we hadn't recognised his new horse, Dido—and he gave us an offhand wave on his way out. Martina ran after him. I could see them outside." Isaac looked through the open window as though reflecting on the past event. "He was about to mount when Martina approached him. She was smiling and there was lightness, a fire in her. Count Leo, also, was smiling. They must have spoken for a while because it was some time before I heard him ride away. Martina said nothing when she came in, just got her things and left with Count Doukas and the others."

Guy and Isaac looked silently at each other. Guy pictured Bryennius with Martina, and thought back to her familiarity with Yūryak outside the inn four nights past and Jacques cryptic remark at the time. Irene—all that passed between them, yet she had left without word to join Theodore Ankhialou.

"Are you all right? You look very sad."

Ashamed he was so easily read, Guy made an effort to brighten. "I'm fine, just hung-over. Two people talking means nothing." He was silent for a moment and then changed the subject. "What sort of name is Dido, anyway? Another queen I'spose?"

"Don't worry," Isaac laughed. "Centarch Bessas Phocas says Carthaginian, not Persian! Now, about your spider's scrawl on this map?"

Manzikert,
Afternoon, 12th July 1054

Apart from Bryennius' departure on a visit to Ani, Guy noticed nothing significant after the hunt. There were more travellers' tales, training at-arms, work parties, guard duty and further drilling of the local levies and townspeople. Then on the eighth day, a stranger rode to the western gate and asked for someone from the Barbarian House. A runner was sent and soon Bessas, Guy, Togol and a cataphract trotted down on the duty horses.

Togol looked at the newcomer. "Seljuk, I'll wager."

They dismounted before the stranger who, they noticed, was furnished with an excellent highbred steed and weapons to match.

The Seljuk spoke first in Turkic. Togol interpreted. "I seek a blind man on a pale horse."

They took care not to exchange glances. Bessas turned to Cosmas Mouzalen and said audibly, "Water and feed his horse, please."

Togol interpreted courteously for the stranger who relaxed a little.

Guy knew the squire would lead it by the other captured horses, to see if any recognised another.

The group walked out the gate and conversed, sitting on the low rail of the bridge over the ditch.

"I must talk with the Horse-archer, a count who rides a bay horse," the Seljuk demanded.

"Alas, he is not here. He has tasked me to assist you in his absence," Bessas answered.

What a time for Bryennius to be away, thought Guy. He was staggered at the leagues the count had ridden since his arrival at Manzikert. Guy once asked him how he managed it. Bryennius had merely smiled something about a good saddle and said it was better to get the riding done early. A person could take one's ease on the walls later.

"I can speak only to the count with the bay horse," the newcomer insisted.

"He is not here," maintained Bessas.

Togol broke in to a fleeting look of annoyance from Bessas. "Who sent you?" The Cuman glared at the Seljuk.

The stranger considered Togol's blunt approach, his eyes dark in the shadow of his round felt cap, taking in the ditch and the walls, the little wooden town, the houses and rich gardens of the valley. "One who was his guest."

"You've already been told he is not here for several days more." Togol interpreted what had been said for Bessas. "But he has entrusted us."

The Seljuk looked at them for some time and then broke his silence. "I am Zaibullah and I cannot wait several days. I have instructions to see one held here to determine his condition and offer ransom. You understand?" he replied.

"We understand, Zaibullah." Togol replied, telling Bessas in Greek, "He wants to see the prisoner. They offer ransom. Derar al-Adin wants to make sure he isn't being tricked."

"Very well," Bessas said. "But he must submit to the blindfold when inside the fortress."

Togol made a sign and Zaibullah acceded to the blindfold.

The dungeons of Manzikert instilled a sense of foreboding. Poorly ventilated and shielded by their depth from the intense summer heat and deadly winter cold—despite scrubbings and changed straw—they retained the smell of unwashed people and fear. Most of the few prisoners now held were members of the garrison, confined for minor offences, drunkenness or fighting. Guy had heard that a couple of Armenian rebels and a priest—blasphemous by the doctrine of Constantinople—were also detained and he hoped that the strategos' reputation for piety and justice were warranted.

"Wait there," the fair-bearded Varangian commanded, pointing to a cell illuminated by a distant shaft of sunlight. An empty latrine bucket and earthenware water jar comprised the only furniture in the cell. Guy could see where hundreds of names were scratched into the walls with last messages or drawings, some quite elaborate, of the Virgin or a saint.

A Norseman disappeared, scratching his head, boots scraping the flagstones, to fetch Zobeir from his more comfortable detention.

Guy could see Zaibullah straining his senses through the blindfold to ascertain the whereabouts and condition of the dungeons. "You keep here the one I seek?" he asked, sniffing the dank atmosphere.

Some part of Guy, not far beneath the surface, was glad the Turk felt a similar discomfort. He longed to be out of the place, away from the confines of its dark, ringing silence. For the first time in his life, he understood what it meant to disappear into a fortress dungeon.

Bessas gave the lie. "Tell him, of course. It's the dungeon. Where else would we keep a prisoner?" The centarch motioned to Guy and said quietly in Latin. "Go to the strategos. Tell him, and no other, what happens here now."

It was Guy's first time inside the citadel. He was awed by its size, the sophistication of defences and luxury of construction. Nor had he appreciated until now just how many Varangians were concealed inside its massive walls. The cunning of the garrison dispositions dawned on him. Reliable Varangians were posted inside the citadel, where imperial power would be held to the last. The less trustworthy Franks were quartered in the city outside with still more Varangians. The Latins could defend the circuit walls, but were for the moment subtly denied access to the citadel in large numbers, lest the ever land hungry and opportunistic Franks attempt its capture. Bryennius' Sixth Schola was quartered in the town to show that the imperial troops would fight for the people. Theme militia and armed townspeople were also located inside the city. The garrison was thus subtly and finely balanced under the firm hand of Basil Apocapes.

"D'Agiles?" Basil greeted him. "This is unusual?"

"Yes, Strategos. Centarch Phocas' compliments." He lowered his voice before continuing. "We've a Turk, who came looking for the Arab prisoner, Zobeir, with the avowed intention of determining that he is alive and to offer ransom—five hundred dinars."

Basil leaned back in his great chair and sucked in a breath. "Zobeir is a fine chess player and interesting conversationalist. It would be a shame to lose him."

Guy smiled. "He, the Turk, is at the dungeon with Centarch Phocas now."

Basil looked out for a moment through the open window—latticed, glazed casements opening inwards, the shutters thrown open—then back at Guy. "You don't say?" From below came the sound of a sentry pacing the citadel ramparts—the rhythm of slow steps and the spaced tap of a spear haft on stone. Basil waited until the footsteps retreated. "Does Centarch Phocas request or require my presence?" The strategos' blue eyes bored into Guy; not critically Guy thought, but inquiring.

"Centarch Phocas knows what he's doing—fishing—showing the emissary from the prisoner's uncle that Zobeir al-Adin is alive and wriggling. And confusing the Turk about the Arab's exact location within the fortress."

"So, no? What sort of Turk?"

"Togol thinks a Seljuk. He says his name is Zaibullah."

Basil shrugged. "A Turk working for an Arab who has access to the Seljuk Sultan's tent?" the strategos said slowly, looking Guy up and down.

Guy wondered about himself: a Frank, nominally paid by a Norman, working for a Greek who called himself a Roman, both of them commanded by a half-Armenian, half-Georgian loyal to the Greeks. Then he thought of Togol, a Turkic Cuman, working for a Roman, commanded in turn by a half-Armenian-half-Georgian who fought for the Greeks against the Seljuk Turks.

Their eyes met, as though they had read each other's thoughts. "Interesting, eh?" Basil laughed. "Give my compliments to Centarch Phocas and tell him all is good and to carry on. Five hundred dinars is barely enough. It would be nice if we got some token of good faith from the Turk."

Guy made to leave.

"Before you go."

He halted and turned.

"You haven't been up here before?"

"No, Strategos."

"It's quite a view. Come. Look out the window."

Beneath them the city nestled inside the circuit walls and beyond them, the town, village and gardens.

"Your mare goes well and is sound?"

"She is made of fire, Strategos."

Basil was looking out of the window with a far away expression.

Guy's gaze followed, drifting out to the low spur beyond which he had first spoken to Irene. On that point it lingered.

"Your fair riding partner is in Archēsh, it seems."

There was silence but for the unseen sentry's returning steps.

Guy was speechless. Then he understood. His trysts with Irene had not gone unnoticed by Basil who even at that far distance would have recognised the horses and patterns and timings of their rides. He looked in embarrassment at Basil who smiled sympathetically.

"I need a messenger," Basil confided abruptly, "to carry a despatch to Archēsh. It may be dangerous and can only be entrusted to ... a man of some daring with a good horse. It will be a lonely ride. If word comes that Seljuks are on the move, the turmarch at Archēsh must be informed. When most would want to flee the advancing Seljuks, you would be riding toward them. Are you interested? No private heroics. Just go there, deliver the despatches and return."

"Of course."

"Tell no one except Count Bryennius and Centarch Phocas. Take two days to prepare yourself and your horse, then be ready to leave at a moment's notice."

When Guy returned to the dungeons, Zobeir and the stranger were face-to-face with the blindfolds off. The young prisoner was joyful that he had not been forsaken. His relief was replaced by cries and lamentations when he realised that he was not being released. Both were blindfolded again and the men parted.

They rode with Zaibullah some miles from Manzikert. Guy could see them look each other over, in case of a more fateful meeting in the future. Zaibullah stared hard at Togol, then made to ride away.

Bessas did not let go of Zaibullah's reins. "A word from your master?" he asked.

"The Sultan will move by the next full moon," the Seljuk said defiantly. "The southern route, Berkri, then Archēsh."

"That's no secret," snapped Togol, handing him a linen bag of food for his journey and another of grain for his horse.

Zaibullah slipped the drawstrings over his shoulder and nodded in gratitude.

"You'll be unaware—though 'tis no secret—the Sultan has gone to Gandja to impress his suzerainty upon the Shaddadid emir, Abu'-Aswar Shawur. All the Kurds are with the Sultan and the Georgians are sworn to neutrality. You're alone." Zaibullah smiled coldly. "Until we meet on the battlefield." He turned his horse and cantered away.

Togol followed the Seljuk with a long stare. "Told us nothing we didn't know or couldn't work out," he remarked, spitting into the dust. "Well. The shepherd king is on his way."

Guy looked after the retreating figure and realised his mouth was very dry. An aching loneliness touched his heart. Provence suddenly seemed very far away.

Manzikert,
Afternoon, 14th July 1054

Leo's interest overcame his weariness during the hard seven day round trip to Ani, during which he detoured to reconnoitre the northern bypass around Archēsh. For this trip he rode Speedy and swift-walking Dido while Zarrar and Ruskh rested at Manzikert. Each man of his small escort led a spare horse to enable a faster journey

Evidence of past Seljuk and Kurdish raids was everywhere with the damage done to agriculture and commerce already incalculable. Further north in Armenia proper, where the open persecution of the Armenian Church by that of Constantinople was a running sore, the populace was even more resentful of Roman rule.

At double-walled Ani, protected on two sides by deep defiles, Leo had delivered Basil's descriptive letters of the situation around Manzikert to the local commander, with a request to pass them on to the strategos, George Drosus at his headquarters in Karin. The officers at Ani thanked Leo for the warning, saying the same level of Seljuk activity was not evident in Iberia and Ani. He thought they were over confident and probably missing something. The news supported his theory that the main enemy blow would fall on Manzikert, but he could not persuade Ani to spare troops to assist with the defence of Vaspurakan.

Hastening back by way of fire-scarred Kars, Leo and his escort travelled rapidly, snatching a few hours' sleep on the ground occasionally and eating quickly in wayside inns or in villages. During the ride north Leo had noticed the group chatted happily about the unseen lands and new sights. They were quiet during the return journey, partly from fatigue, mostly because every man's thoughts played on the maelstrom into which they felt they were riding.

Leo talked of military affairs and horsemanship with his companions but kept his lonesome thoughts to himself. He was relieved when he saw Manzikert at peace. Alerted by the sentries, Isaac, breathless from running, met him at the main gate. The clerk informed Leo of a meeting with Apocapes that evening. In the meantime, Isaac continued, the strategos desired Leo to bring himself up to date with the scouting reports and get some rest. Isaac did not offer any advice on how Leo might do both.

He threw Speedy's reins to Isaac and rode Dido to the Barbarian House, meaning to go over the reports first. He was taking the almost empty water skin from his saddle to fill it from the well when Martina rode in on Little Zarrar. She dismounted with a friendly smile.

Circumstance had thrown them together.

"Just back?" they asked in unison, and laughed while they tied their horses to the hitching rail.

"This is the best water in Manzikert, isn't it?" she exclaimed, leaning over the well as he dropped the pail on its rope, to a splash below.

"It certainly is that, and the coolest." He pulled the pail to the surface and filled their waterskins. Each took a mouthful and slung the bags over their pommels before untying their mounts and leading them to a nearby trough. They stood holding the reins and watching the horses drink: sucking the water through their teeth, then pausing, heads down with dripping muzzles companionably close, to drink again.

Saddle weary herself, Martina had come to the Barbarian House to see if there were urgent duties, before looking to her horse and lastly to her own needs. It was that quality in her that had led them to relate to each other, about matters apart from the city and the Seljuks.

"Good trip?" he asked.

"Interesting. Hot! But I wanted another ride around the district, so got my wish."

Leo looked at her, his expression a question.

"I'm to take despatches to Karin and Constantinople."

Circumstance was pulling them apart.

"Good for you," Leo heard himself say. "When do you leave?"

"Tomorrow night." Martina revealed, looking into his eyes.

"We must have some wine before you go," he ventured, seeing at once her dark hair tied back, bewitching eyes and the smile dancing at the corners of her mouth. Leo felt uncomfortably like he was staring, studying, needing to etch every detail of her onto his memory in case their paths never crossed again. Finally, fearing she could see through him, he glanced away into the distant blue of the valley.

If Martina noticed, she did not betray it. "That would be nice. Tonight at the inn near the stables, some of us are getting together. That will be the last chance, I think." She looked away, then back to him. "When you get back to Constantinople, you must visit … us."

Watching her smiling and chatting with him, his own replies seemed far away. Suddenly the real world and its cares were distant, as though he was this moment in a fairy tale. Never before had Leo felt quite like this, pausing, smiling, speaking of horses and books and other unwarlike things. They dallied in the shade of the apple tree and raided its bounty; Leo reaching up with his bow while Martina held out her hat to catch the falling fruit. It felt like they were two children in an orchard, laughing as a few apples fell to ground while they scooped them up for their grateful horses. For a brief, enchanted interlude, it seemed as though they were far from Manzikert and not bearing arms.

Little Zarrar nipped at Dido and Martina's hand was brushed accidentally against Leo's. She turned suddenly as if she would say something but both remained silent as their eyes met.

Something inside said—say nothing. "We never did get to have that ride," he murmured.

"No. Time went too fast."

A horn sounded from the citadel. He glanced towards it. "That's for me."

"The story of your life! There are rides around Constantinople—with even more prying eyes," Martina smiled. "When you return?"

"When I return."

They tied their horses to the hitching rail and buoyed by her closeness, Leo followed her through the back door of the Barbarian House to collect his notes.

Martina greeted Isaac and walked to her table.

Isaac proffered Leo a sheaf of maps and papers. "There are more on your desk, Count."

"Thank you, Isaac. Will you send a runner to my squire and ask him to care for Dido, please. I do not know how long I will be."

Tucking the bundle under his arm and with a parting glance at Martina, Leo started upstairs, pausing a moment at the third step as Isaac's look struck him.

Later that afternoon, the key members of the council gathered: officials in their robes, soldiers in shirtsleeves and boots around the large table in Basil's big room, an almost orderly line of weapons and mail shirts on the floor near the door. Leo told them briefly of his journey and gave his best advice. "A major Seljuk offensive along the approach, Tabriz—Her—Berkri—Archēsh—Manzikert, is likely in the near future. It will be the full moon in a week."

"Surely if the Sultan has been recently in Gandja, then that would indicate the northern route to Ani and Karin," Kamyates proposed. "If at all, I hasten to point out, in the midst of all this conjecture."

Leo foiled Kamyates' attempt to lull the council into a false security. "Indeed the Sultan may have been in Gandja to shore up his alliances. But as far as we know, his main force has remained at Tabriz, with some elements deploying forward to Her. The Sultan has to move now, or he will run out of time before autumn."

"They have moved in the snow before," Kamyates interrupted scornfully.

"Not with an army like this," Leo countered. "Not with Daylami infantry and Abbasid siege engines. Not with heavy cavalry, and carts, and women to populate the areas they intend to make vacant."

Kamyates glowered. "You would know. You who have been here but weeks and you who release Seljuk prisoners and …"

"Enough!" roared Basil. "I believe Tughrul Bey is moving already. A host advances at the speed of the slowest machine. The screen and advance guard will ride far ahead, searching for the weak places. Thus we could be subjected to immediate assaults for up to a week before the siege train arrives and the real fun starts."

"Are you sure they are coming?" Doukas asked gloomily.

"Yes, Theophanes," Leo said gently. "They are coming—later than we might think, because this is no cavalry raid as in previous years. Tughrul Bey means to make a major change to the balance of power on the frontier and to this end is assembling a serious invasion force. The roads have dried after the spring thaw so they can now move their baggage and heavy equipment and their tribes' horses unshod hooves will have hardened. We have gathered most of the harvest for their taking and have no significant field army within striking distance of the frontier. It is perfect for them."

"And we've heard nothing from Van?" Doukas asked.

"Nothing," said Basil. "In the absence of intelligence to the contrary, I must agree with Count Bryennius. We'd better make our final preparations and I need to do a ride-around of the forward defences, especially Berkri and Archēsh. Daniel, prepare an escort and two pack-mules for me please. Princeps, get the last of those who intend coming inside the city ready to move. Identify some place for them to stay and useful work to do. See to it that those who want to take their chances in mountain, cave and forest are also ready soon."

"The men in the hills know what they have to do," Branas said. "I told them not to fire the grass until they know the enemy is upon us, otherwise our own stock will perish next winter for no reason."

Leo added his thoughts. "We need to warn Archēsh and send despatches to Karin, so they know to press for a field army to come to our aid, or move against the Seljuk main host. If troops from Karin, Kars and Ani can screen away the Sultan's light horse and we can all combine to hit the main body of Tughrul's army while it is encamped around Manzikert, we may really hurt them."

"You're right," said Basil. "Though I doubt we have enough cavalry to accomplish that. And …"

Reynaldus and Bardas Cydones pushed past the sentry and entered the room. The knight, through ingratiating himself with the Norman leaders, had risen to a position of considerable power in the Frankish ranks, second only to de Gaillon himself.

Reynaldus, Leo thought, would lose an army out of his own vainglory and ambition. Cydones whispered to Kamyates.

"Messengers? To where? With what news?" Kamyates demanded.

Kamyates, Leo thought, would do the same to an empire.

"The official despatches have gone already," Basil said. "I sent couriers to Karin two days ago. They left at the same time as the party taking our messenger doves there."

"You did not tell me." Kamyates' voice unconsciously pitched a level higher than usual.

"I could not find you." Basil said before continuing to issue orders. "I wish preparations to be made so I can address the garrison and the townspeople, all at once in the square, so that I can convey to them the importance of this battle and how we will fight it. Princeps, arrange it and let me know the where and when. Make sure interpreters are placed throughout the crowd."

Curticius nodded and wrote a note.

Basil looked around the gathering. "Remember, friends—we have met them in open field before and beaten them, outsmarted them, outfought them. Hearts up! If there are no questions, that is all. Thank you."

They rose to go. Basil motioned Leo to remain. Reynaldus stared with hatred at him as he left.

"Wine, Count Bryennius?" Basil offered.

Leo accepted.

Basil poured one for each, then sat with a sigh. "It'll be soon?"

"I think so." Leo replied, taking a seat.

"Get as much rest as you can. I need you to keep working as you have been. Centarch Phocas has briefed you on the visitor we had who was asking about the Arab prisoner?"

"He has, Strategos."

Basil seemed about to speak. Instead his head slumped forward to rest on a hand, elbow propped on the chair-arm. He massaged his temples for long moments, goblet balanced in his free hand. With a sigh he looked across at Leo. "Apart from you and a few others, I have never felt more alone. Before this, it had never really occurred to me that we would need to face the enemy without completely trusting some of those around us. Sometimes the burden weighs heavy."

Branas entered by another door, poured himself a drink and pulled up a chair.

Basil, having thought through what he wished to discuss, began. "Leo, I asked Daniel to join us. We're in for a real fight and I fear we cannot do it, if it's just a case of slugging it out with them. We have to have an edge somewhere, and your spy in the Sultan's camp is our best crack at out-thinking them. But, and speak plain, do you think they have a similar advantage—a spy in our midst? Close to me, even?"

Leo had never seen Basil this tired or morbid. The evening light streamed through the arched window, the shadows of the latticework falling as an uneven pattern across Basil's features. Leo considered his reply—treachery was a sensitive topic. "I think they probably do. More than one, possibly, and working at different levels."

Basil looked sharply at him, eyebrows raised. The brown moustache twitched slightly, but he said nothing.

"We would be rash to assume they do not," Leo continued, "and foolish to sow discord amongst the citizens by over-reacting. At the lowest level, a number of people might earn a little gold and safe passage by leaving open a sally-port, a tower unguarded or some such thing. These we have already covered, by placing the most reliable troops on the vulnerable places, and never singly. There is also close supervision by junior officers."

Branas nodded. "It's done."

"Make sure of it, I beg you," murmured Basil. "It might be low level treason and difficult to police, but it is potentially catastrophic."

Leo continued. "For the most part, the lower ranks do not have enough grasp of our order of battle and plans to be able to pass that to the enemy in sufficient detail or accuracy for it to be of use to them. The world of ordinary soldiers is the world of their immediate comrades and work. They are mostly loyal to their standards and what they represent. There is little to fear from them, I think. Above them, though, are a range of officers, clerks, merchants, priests and the like who have education, ambition and the knowledge to pass on, for favours, gold or simply to save their own skins. That is based on opportunity—the risk of treachery increasing with their doubts about our success. It decreases with reduced opportunity and confidence in their leaders and situation."

Basil thought on this a moment. "Do you have any hard evidence of the Seljuks recruiting such people?"

"No," said Leo slowly. "Not since we killed that scouting party on the march out here. The Seljuks may not know of their fate. Nor would it be in Derar al-Adin's interests to enlighten them. Zobeir has not been able to cast much light either. He was horseholder and lookout—not a very good one at that. The most dangerous category of spy ..."

Basil fidgeted in his seat.

Leo paused.

"Go on."

"... are those near the top, the ones who can pass on detailed information and identify our greatest weaknesses. Or they may seek to have us adopt plans which would actually aid the enemy. They may have been enlisted as spies by the Seljuks or their allies long ago and far away. Their commitment may be blackmailed, philosophical or financial, but whatever it is, there will be cunning and self-interest involved."

Basil grinned. "I've had a couple of people tell me you must be a Saracen spy because you named one of your horses after an Arab champion. You're also not deferential enough towards the bureaucracy and you are slipshod in your prayers. Grievous faults all, y'know."

"Hmm," Branas broke in. "Perhaps Leo should have given Zarrar a good Greek name like—Epialtes."

Basil laughed. "Tell that to that fop, Kamyates. Zarrar is too good a horse to name after the traitor of Thermopylae anyway. How's his wound from the wadi fight? I saw him the other day—his usual self. Low self-esteem is not one of his problems. Your danger is that your squire will kill him with love."

Leo, with a sense of relief he kept to himself, took Basil's words as an order not to tell Kamyates anything. "Zarrar is well," he replied in a lighter vein. "The wound has almost healed. Simon Vardaheri …"

"Our mysterious horse trading friend?" Basil interrupted.

"The one," confirmed Leo. "Vardaheri gave me a potion he learned in the Arab lands, the contents of which are his secret. But it's very effective. The hair is growing back over Zarrar's wound already."

"Arab potions! Vardaheri!" mused Basil. "Another I've been warned about. Who's on your list of people not to be trusted, Leo?"

"I have no proof, only suspicions. But I do not trust Kamyates, Cydones, Reynaldus, Zakarian or Gurgen."

"Trust? Or like?"

"Trust, Sir."

"Quite a list for a small place like Manzikert!" Basil mused. "Cydones was in Archēsh when you, um, when you … when your group was attacked."

"He was seen there, with Gurgen."

"Speaking of Archēsh," remembered Branas. "We've had no word from there."

"No we have not, now that you mention it." Basil looked at Branas, alarm flashing across his features. "Thank you for bringing it to my attention. I'll send someone with despatches, probably Guy d'Agiles, if you can spare him. And I need to get there myself as soon as I have made final arrangements here."

"Good man for the job," agreed Leo. "He has an independent mind though, so give him clear orders."

"Be assured of it," said Basil with a secret smile between them. "The cataphract, Tzetes, is it? He lives?" Basil had an enviable talent for remembering names. "Gurgen is in the city, isn't he?"

"Gurgen is. Tzetes lives and is grateful for it," Leo reported. "Joaninna Magistros is a skilled healer and has been of great assistance."

"Been warned about her too," Basil said with a twinkle in his eye. "Sorceress evidently!" He thought for a while. "Word is, Cydones is diplomatically friendly with the Seljuk ambassador at court, as is Kamyates. And rumour has it Reynaldus is in communication by letter with Hervé, whom one hears it is best to have in front, of rather than behind you."

Leo knew of the Frankish mercenary—everyone did—and thought he was at Kars or Ani, but was not sure.

"Kamyates is the centre of quite a social swirl. He's seen with Zakarian, Cydones, Reynaldus—quite a network when you extend it. Leo, Zakarian is cultivating a friendship with your young officer, Balsamon. Cydones also pays a great deal of attention to the princeps and his wife. Watch your backs, both of you. It'd be well if we were a united band on our side of the walls. But I fear we are not."

Leo left the citadel and walked alone to the inn where Martina was farewelling her friends and admirers. She looked happy and in the press of the crowd proffered her wrist. Leo breathed in the scent he had brought her from Archēsh. Threading his way to the bar, he bought two drinks and they stood amidst the loud bustle of a soldiers' inn. No private word could be had and others wished her attention, so after an interval, Leo drained the goblet of wine and made to go, saying, "Martina, if I do not see you before, I will see you off tomorrow night."

The next day began for Leo as most days did at Manzikert. He rose early, dropped in at the Barbarian House and visited his horses. This morning he checked Little Zarrar. Martina's horse looked well and seemed content. A half-full pail of water, empty feed bin and leftover hay from the previous night indicated Martina had prepared him well. Recently shod, the dun looked fit for the journey.

After a solitary breakfast, Leo spent most of the morning with Basil in the citadel, writing the despatches that Martina and Yūryak would carry that night. These outlined the situation as it appeared to them, noting that the enemy host had not yet been reported before Archēsh or even near Berkri. They discussed it and decided to refrain from any written mention of their spy in the Turkish camp—leaving it to Martina to tell Cecaumenus in person—although a description of Kamyates' actions was included.

A detailed tour of the city's defences with Doukas and the engineer, Karas Selth, occupied the remainder of the day. Leo knew how drained he felt at the end of it and could tell his companions were similarly affected, for they bore the burden of their appointments heavily. Beyond his weariness, he was glad of the exertions, for they kept his mind from that night's farewell.

The goodbye came soon enough.

Manzikert was dark and quiet when Leo, wearing his sword but no armour, collected the despatch pouch from Basil's clerks. Tucking the package into the folds of his tunic, he walked down to where Martina and Yūryak were saddling their horses by torchlight.

She looked up and smiled. "It's a good night for it," she said, continuing her preparations. "Not too bright but enough light to get by."

"It is a little cooler as well," Leo replied. He did not mention it, but had noticed that there was just enough breeze to carry away sound, an advantage if trying to remain discreet when out at night. It was a double-edged advantage though, for it could mask pursuers as well.

"Yes." She ran the surcingle through and felt that her saddlebag, water skin and cloak were securely strapped to the saddle.

Leo passed her the despatches. Without a word she belted them around her waist underneath a felt jerkin.

Yūryak talked softly with Ruben as he finished saddling. The latter held a blazing oil torch, its light flickering over Little Zarrar's saddled back.

Martina turned to Leo who stepped closer so he could better see her face. Hesitating a moment, he passed a package wrapped in a silk scarf. "I'd like you to have this for your journey."

"Will I open it now?"

"It's for your journey, so, yes," he said.

In the torchlight Martina undid the bow and held up the silver spoon she had seen Leo use at Sashesh and had admired several times since. "But this is yours!"

"I have another. It's a handy spoon for a journey." Leo spoke quietly, self-consciously, a voice somewhere inside him warning—say nothing, say nothing.

"Thank you. It's lovely. I will take care of it."

"Make sure you look after yourself, and keep a spurt in your horse." In his mind all the while—say nothing, say nothing.

"You have our address in Constantinople?"

"Yes," he said evenly, as the deliberate whisper continued inside his mind—say nothing, say nothing. "You had better make a start," he said.

Side by side, Little Zarrar at her shoulder, reins slack, they followed the two Armenians to a tower in the main wall. Cataphracts of Leo's Sixth Schola saluted and allowed them through the sally-port, which was locked behind them. Passing through vegetable plots, they made their way to a nearby fore-wall tower where more of Leo's troopers waited. There was a softly spoken exchange of passwords: the challenge and whispered countersign. No torches were exposed, though an oil lamp gleamed dully through the crack of a partly open door into the tower. The decarch of the guard unlocked the iron sally-port door and swung it silently inward on its greased hinges.

Leo nodded. Yūryak bent and passed through into the starlight, his horse ducking its head and following. The cloak strapped over the pommel scraped against the low stone arch. Ruben stood off to one side with the soldiers.

Leo followed and waited outside the wall as Yūryak mounted and turned his horse onto the narrow, steep path down the scarp into the ditch. Leo heard them clamber out the other side. A low hiss signified that all was clear.

Say nothing, say nothing—repeated silently over and over in Leo's mind as he quietly called Martina.

Leading Little Zarrar, she appeared in the night-gloom outside the wall and mounted neatly, leaning down from the saddle toward him. "Farewell, Leo," she whispered.

Leo clasped her proffered hand and was surprised at her strength. In his mind all the while, the commanding thought—say nothing, say nothing. "Keep well, Martina," he whispered.

They shook hands, the gesture more eloquent in its reserve than any embrace might have been. With a last look back, she motioned her horse down the scarp.

Peering intently into the gloom, Leo could just see her climb Little Zarrar from the ditch and glide like a fairy tale into the dark. There was the touch of a horseshoe on a stone, then nothing but the night and the whisper of the breeze. Like a statue, Leo stood and listened for a long time, ears straining until the night was deafening. How much he had wanted to say. He waited for a time, but no distant sound signalled anything but a stealthy getaway by the pair. He sighed long.

Slowly, Leo returned through the sally-port and paused while the guard locked it. He led Ruben to the minor gate in the main wall through which they had passed earlier. A low whistle, challenge and countersign and they re-entered the fortress. Ruben asked if he was needed further. Leo shook his head and thanked him.

Then, alone in the dark he deliberately picked his way across the empty, littered space towards his quarters. He was aware of a deep sense of relief that Martina was leaving before the fortress was engulfed in its destiny, but something else … His steps slowed and stopped. He sighed deeply and sank to the stones in an unguarded moment of deep missing, the dim night moon washing blue over him. Suddenly, he felt like crying. He remained motionless, head bowed on his sword hilt, eyes open, staring yet unseeing, not knowing how long passed, until the warrior inside stirred, to rise and go on because there was nothing else to do.

Manzikert,
Midday, 6th August 1054

Three weeks after that stormy meeting of Basil Apocapes' council, Kamyates chanced upon Cydones on the north wall. Few moved in the midday heat, the nearby battlements being deserted but for a bored Rus sentry watching over the valley's village, hamlets and gardens. The two lingered over trivialities, taking in the scenery for some minutes.

Kamyates sighed, lost in his melancholy thoughts. He missed the luxury and stimulation of big cities, Constantinople or the Muslim capitals, and wondered how much longer he could endure this drab garrison town. Expecting Tughrul Bey's invasion in early summer, he had hurried along the barren journey from Isfahan in late May. All should have been concluded by now. Dejection turned to anger when he recalled Zakarian telling him that Apocapes had despatched two more couriers without telling him. There was nothing to be gained by raising it with Apocapes, other than a face-saving show of knowledge. The evidence was in itself useful; Apocapes had, either wittingly or not, demonstrated that he did not trust him. Since the last formal council meeting, the stratēgos had completed another inspection of the theme's forward defences. To Kamyates' satisfaction, Apocapes had been unable, due to lack of military and financial resources, to do more than exhort his commanders to more strenuous efforts and vigilance.

"That's unusual!" Bardas Cydones exclaimed.

Kamyates disinterestedly followed his gaze to the point where the track to Archēsh wound out of sight over a low crest a mile east of the fortress.

"A rider!"

"I see that," Kamyates sniffed. Their relationship had become tense. Cydones' henchmen had failed in their attempt to kill Bryennius as he returned from Archēsh and Petros Doukitzes, who led the attack, had not been heard from since he obviously feared being murdered for his failure. Kamyates had similarly been foiled when he tried to elicit information from Martina about the prisoner taken and released after the skirmish at the wadi. He wondered whether she had told anyone. Cydones had, in that infuriating manner of subordinates volunteering to make up the shortfalls of a superior, offered to seize her and make her talk. Kamyates had assented, but she was never alone and vulnerable, as though someone had seen to it. Neither of them had seen her for days before it dawned that she had left Manzikert and had too much of a head start to bother pursuing.

Cydones glanced in irritation at his companion. "See, he's flogging his horse and it can scarcely trot. He's ridden far and fast."

Kamyates' heart leapt. Cydones was right. Someone had ridden in great haste from the direction the Sultan's army would come. "Who guards the north gate," he asked, motioning to the gate towers near them.

"Rus and Varangians." Cydones was observant and having once served in the army, had an eye for military affairs that were a mystery to Kamyates. Suddenly they heard a warning shout from a sentry.

"Let's get down there." Kamyates moved with an urgency that had Cydones trot down the steps after him. The two silken-gowned officials arrived at the gate as the rider stumbled from his horse.

"What's going on?" Kamyates demanded in patrician tones of the lone Varangian who had come from the guard room.

"A messenger," the soldier said, wiping flecks of chicken and breadcrumbs from his red beard and wiping greasy fingers on his striped trousers. "Sire."

"Messenger from where?"

"I don't know."

Kamyates glanced at the wiry, sparsely bearded youth who had ridden in with his boots, riding pants and loose tunic all sweat-soaked. Having sacrificed weight for a speedy ride, he was protected by a felt jerkin and carried only a sword.

Incoherent with fatigue and excitement, he was uncertain as to whom he should convey his despatches. His lathered horse sank to its knees with a groan and lay down.

Perfect, thought Kamyates and seized his chance. "We've been expecting you," he said with a show of authority. "Come! We'll take you to the citadel."

The Varangian stepped forward uncertainly. His orders were to escort all messengers immediately to the strategos or princeps.

"Do not interrupt your lunch, my friend. We have the authority to take him to Basil Apocapes—the strategos—but do have your men take care of that poor horse." Turning away, Kamyates motioned the youth and Cydones to follow. He quickly reconsidered, realising the presence of an unexplained horse might raise unwanted questions. "On second thoughts, you've enough to do with your duties—we'll return and take care of the horse. Look after it in the meantime."

The Varangian hesitated and gave in.

As they walked along the thoroughfare, Kamyates flicked a meaningful glance at Cydones. He wanted the imperial courier to gain the youth's confidence and lead him to a quiet place—the narrow lane they had identified as the site where troublesome people could be accosted or killed with little chance of being seen.

"Trouble?" Cydones asked.

The youth nodded, overawed by their rich garments and brusque official manner. "Berkri has been stormed and the populous massacred," he sputtered. "The turmarch at Archēsh sent me to warn …"

It had begun. "It's well he chose such a plucky fellow," Kamyates said to the despatch rider. "But you look done in. To be truthful, you look a sight. Get a grip of yourself. Apocapes hates garbling messengers. He chews them up, I've seen it. There's a little inn down this lane. You might like to have some food and drink and order your thoughts. It'll only take a minute, a few steps, just to get your breath. One gets few chances in life to make an impression with a strategos. It'll be worth it. Then we'll take you straight to him. And take off that hot, sweaty jerkin, it stinks. You'll not be allowed to wear it in the presence of the strategos anyway."

The youth, relieved at such kind assurances, removed his soft armour and followed Kamyates into the lane where Cydones struck him many times from behind with a slender dagger. Together, hearts racing, they pushed the limp corpse into a cellar. They checked their clothes for blood stains and the imperial courier dashed a pail of water over the spots on the cobbles.

"Good work." Kamyates spoke partly in truth, mostly as a gesture of comradeship and shared peril. "That's one warning Apocapes won't get. Get rid of the horse and the corpse as soon as you can."

*The Archēsh Track,
Morning, 16th August 1054*

In the early morning light of a new day, Guy cheerfully rode alone from Manzikert along the Archēsh track, the despatch belt under his drab linen surcoat. He whistled softly to himself, glad to be free of the unease in the fortress. Carrying his spear and shield, Guy wore helmet and byrnie, boots, sword and bow. On his saddle he carried a cloak, water and food enough for two days. He planned to travel steadily to save a burst of speed in the mare and intended a stop at the camp of Seranush Donjoian, which might furnish some intelligence of the road ahead and would provide a convenient respite, ensuring grain for his mare and a measure of security while they rested.

Basil Apocapes had summoned him in the first dark watch of this new day. Guy had entered the strategos' chambers to find the princeps, Bryennius and Branas already there. Basil had looked grave in the lamplight. "You know why you're here, D'Agiles. The counts have been pointing out to me that we've not heard from Archēsh for some time—the routine courier is overdue two days. Worse, the gate sentries report hearing rumours of Saracens in eastern Vaspurakan. We'll send a mounted patrol out after sunup to establish contact with the screen and learn something of events at Archēsh. I will leave tomorrow or the day after to again reconnoitre as far as Berkri, but I want you gone well before first light. Take the despatches—being written now—to the commander at Archēsh, ascertain the situation there and report back to me or these men. Be quick and be careful, you may encounter Seljuk patrols. Any questions?"

"No questions." Guy had made to leave when Curticius grabbed his arm, his face a vacant, pleading hollow. Guy had given the princep's hand a squeeze—a promise.

"John, that's enough!" Basil said. "D'Agiles, I told you—no heroics."

Guy had left in the dark. At a smart walk until first light, later broken by short spells of trotting and cantering, horse and rider passed sights at once familiar yet changed. The harvest and much grass hay had been gathered and peasants no longer toiled at this work. Cattle, sheep and goats grazed under the care of bored shepherds. With the morning sun still low in his face, Guy turned off the road to be a less obvious traveller. He knew if he stayed south of the road, he would be between it and the Sea of Bznunik and therefore could not become lost. Although Mount Sippane was an excellent landmark, even by night, if there was any doubt, Guy would find Archēsh where the Manzikert track met the lake.

He thought of Irene and wondered what he would find in Archēsh, his fanciful expectations alternating between hope and doubt. Guy rode with his shield on his back, the surcoat hiding his mail and a dark blue scarf wrapped around his helmet to both keep the hot sun from the metal and cover the shine so that he now blended into the landscape. He was surprised at how he had changed in a few months. It was second nature to him now that when coming to a fold of ground or a rise, he would halt below the crest, able to see over it, unseen, surveying the bounds ahead in case danger lurked. Once he would have merely ridden on in confident ignorance.

The sun was up a hand's breadth when he first dismounted in a low depression with a line of sheltering timber. There he offered the mare a drink at a small stream. She sniffed it and drank a few mouthfuls, impatiently lifting her head to look around, ears pricked, water dripping from her muzzle and the iron bit. "Drink more, Sira! You never know when the next one will be." At the sound of his voice she gave him a sudden rub of acknowledgement over his face with her muzzle. Guy spluttered, wiping off the water. "I deserved it—starting to sound like Togol."

Conscious of a state of freedom and calm, he took a swallow of water and surveyed the enormity of the empty landscape around him. Not so long ago it would have frightened him, both the place and being alone in it. Now he felt confident enough to deal with its exigencies, for he was splendidly mounted, well-armed, capable in his sense of direction with a folded map tucked down the leg of his boot and possessing enough understanding of the local languages to get by.

Hours later, leading the mare up a rise and halting below the crest, Guy looked around to recognise landmarks from the hunt and memorise more. He decided to mount and in that very moment with his foot in the stirrup, he was suddenly aware how hot it had become, how brittle the yellow grass was and how the sky had burned a brilliant blue. The mare made to turn for home as he stepped into the saddle. Guy kneed her gently back to the east with a sympathetic chide as a sudden uneasiness touched him. With the sun high, he recognised the low feature that dominated the valley where the camp of the irregulars had been and rode closer, expecting to be challenged. The mare stopped and snorted; ears pricked, flicking back to him, then forward again. "Steady girl." Guy breathed softly, experiencing a sudden fear. Quickly he slipped the haft of the spear under his left thigh and drew his bow, making ready an arrow. Then he urged the tense mare on towards the sound of flies.

Only the naked dead sprawled in the looted dell. Sixteen of them, most eviscerated, purplish intestines stuffed in the blood-blackened and screaming mouths of the severed heads. Guy fought down the bile rising in his throat and looked around for any evidence of nearby Seljuks, but he seemed to be alone with the dead cavalrymen and flies in the midst of the gagging smell of death. Two men, stouter than the others, had been forced down on their knees, their hands pinned wide by stakes, the skin flayed off along the arms and shoulders and the sinews taken. Guy in his shock had heard that the Seljuks did this to make bowstrings. Close by, a horse with a Roman saddle lay with its legs stiff and belly swollen. Guy did not dare dismount in case he had trouble regaining the saddle quickly if attacked.

With nausea welling inside and the animal instinct to flee almost overwhelming, Guy turned from the scene and trotted away, controlling the tense, rushing mare, seeking the cover of the sparse trees and thickets where he could. He reasoned the camp had been surprised while most were away, that the Armenian screen might be damaged, but intact along its outpost line. Uneasy, he wondered why they had not alerted the fortress. Pausing in some concealing low ground, he marshalled his thoughts. To return to Manzikert, even to warn them, seemed pointless, since he had little to report but the deaths of sixteen irregular troops. He had not delivered his despatches nor ascertained conditions at Archēsh. Above all was his own moral code to save Irene if he could.

Dry-mouthed and with an empty feeling inside, he rode east, keeping to the higher ground away from the road. He walked Sira, aware he would need to husband her strength more than ever now. As darkness approached he sought a thicket in which to hide for the night and found one, dense and extensive on an insignificant looking knoll with a clear view of the distant Archēsh-Manzikert road. Guy dismounted and led the mare into it where he cleared a space and sat with his back braced against a trunk, the reins of the saddled mare wrapped twice around his hand. Thus he prayed; for Irene, his salvation, for the souls of the slain and the survival of the people. He saw again the strange new star and prayed the more because of it. As darkness gathered, he saw two pinpricks of light on distant hills and wondered if it were the Armenian irregulars. Surely they would not be so careless now.

All that Bryennius, Bessas and the scouts had told him of the Seljuks and soldiering began to play in his mind. He was now in the area where the Seljuk screen would be searching out Christian posts and guarding against any prowling Roman troops. Guy realised the Seljuk main body might be besieging Archēsh already. If their screen was composed of tribesmen under their own emirs, then their discipline may be more lax and the temptations to looting and rape the stronger. Hence they might be less interested in a single rider, especially one moving eastward. Sira sniffed his ear with her soft muzzle as though wishing to know his troubled thoughts. Guy reached up and stroked it, glad of her company.

It grew dark and the waxing moon rose. Guy thought about food and almost gagged at the thought, but knew he should force some down. Groping to his saddlebag, he offered a bruised apple to the mare. She disdained it, so he threw it deeper into the thicket. Dry mouthed, more than water could slake, he chewed on overcooked roast beef and stale bread. Swallowing a sip of water, he considered remaining awake, lest the Seljuks creep upon him. A cloud crossed the moon as a breeze sprung up through the thicket. Guy prayed again to keep Leon Magistros' demons and goblins from his overplayed imagination. Through it all, Irene's face came to mind, again and again. Later, reasoning he would need all his strength in the morning, he allowed himself to doze, reins in one hand, dagger in the other.

He awoke with a start in the darkness and sat listening. The silence seemed deafening with its breeze and the sounds of small creatures about their nocturnal toil. He felt his courage draining from him and ruefully recalled his confidence of the previous morning in comparison with his present fear of being alone in this great emptiness with the Seljuks about. He shook violently for a time until, by sucking in air and whispering an almost forgotten prayer, he regained some semblance of self-control.

It was at this lonesome, wavering point that Guy determined to complete his mission. If he stayed away from the high ground and imitated the same cunning tactics he had used before the wadi fight and that the irregulars had employed against the hunting party, he might get close enough to Archēsh to at least determine whether the town had fallen or was besieged. If he happened to stumble on Irene in his quest and was able to offer assistance, then … "Worry about that bridge when we get to it!" Guy quoted Togol's frequently stated philosophy. He rose stiffly and gently stroked Sira. "Let's go."

Guy led the mare for hours, watering her in streams where he could and allowing her to pick at the grass as they progressed, until the first grey steel touched the eastern sky. Then he mounted and they walked on, now keeping to the lower, darker places. Finally they approached a low black crest. Sira stopped suddenly, ears pricked, as a strange tongue came faintly to them. It was answered from somewhere close by. His heart pounding, Guy, hunched in the saddle, leaned down by the mare's neck and peering into the dimness, whispered for Sira to be silent. On the rise before them, there were figures silhouetted against the glowing dawn. He backtracked and circled around, finally finding a vantage point where he could look towards Archēsh without appearing obvious. Dismounting and kneeling, he urinated. His stomach a knot, a short while later he urinated again, annoyed in the knowledge that it was from nerves.

As it grew lighter Guy noticed an odd, distant whine, but was too concerned about his immediate surrounds to pay further attention to it. He could see Seljuk outposts on the hills around and wondered if he had been observed. It occurred to him that, with the scarf around his helmet and the Islamic origin of his horse and equipment, they might mistake him for one of their own from a distance. He worried the distinctive outline of the almond-shaped shield would betray him so he abandoned it under a stunted bush.

Looking across the valley, he could see the city walls, the sea of felt tents before them, horse herds grazing in the distance and the siege train with its wagons and engines in line-of-march. He was too late: Archēsh was already surrounded by the enemy. Guy wondered why the machines were not deployed, until he followed the outline of the walls and saw the gates open. He realised the equipment was no longer needed. The town had fallen and the noise Guy had been hearing without recognition was the sound of the sack, a distant screaming.

He watched helplessly, his mind numb with horror and fear for Irene. A Seljuk patrol rode past, looking straight at him. Caught out, heart in his boots, Guy brazenly looked back, unable to breathe. They rode on and he gulped air in relief. The hours passed and with them, his indecisions; he could offer help to no one, had observed all he could and must warn Basil as soon as possible. Reluctantly he decided to ride away.

Then amongst the enormity of the scene stretched out before him, Guy noticed a disturbance ripple through the tents. A rider on a swift horse galloped away from the city along the Manzikert track. Instinctively, Guy rose and watched. It was too far to be certain, but something in the horse's stride reminded him of Irene's stallion. A ragged pursuit was being organised in the camp. Two mounted Seljuks gave chase but were already several bowshots behind the fleeing rider. Others would have been saddling up. The route the fugitive must take curved around the spur-line below Guy. Already the Seljuk picket further down the spur was mounting to intercept the flying black horse.

In a trice, Guy checked his saddlecloth for scalding folds and tightened the girth a hole. He snatched the cloak from the saddle and tied it loosely around his neck, so the flapping folds might foil arrows which would otherwise stick in his back or Sira's rump or flanks. With a thumb, he plucked the string of his cased bow to ensure tautness and flung himself to the saddle, with Sira already plunging down the stony length of the spur in pursuit of the cantering picket on their rangy Turkmene horses. With a feeling of detached calm, Guy closed on the five Seljuks as they made to intercept the fugitive. Two of the tribesmen were shaking out lassos.

Guy was certain it was Irene now. She had lost her headdress and he could see her dark hair tied behind, the set of her face and the glimpse of a mail corselet under her green tunic. She also had donned a cloak which flew behind her. Guy could see the familiar black boots and forward set of her legs in the fine saddle she used, bow case and quiver rattling at her hips. Irene saw the gap closing and was riding for life, urging the black horse on and screaming his name, "Get-up! Shahryād. Shahryād. Shahryād." The valiant stallion strove with nostrils flaring pink after the mile long sprint through the Turkish camp.

As he closed, Guy had a detached feeling that, with the greatness of her horse and her own skill, Irene might have outmanoeuvred the Seljuk picket. He hit them from the rear at the gallop just as they bunched before Irene on the track. The first he took in the neck, wrenching the spear free with a flick of the wrist as he passed. Whirling the spear over his head, Sira on her haunches as he jerked her around, Guy slashed another across the eyes with the point and smashed the front legs of a white mare from under her rider as he turned Sira onto the Manzikert track. He had a fleeting image of Irene as she passed, staring at him first with astonishment, then recognition. Guy broke free of the melee and settled in the saddle, Sira giving her determined little snatch at the bit as she lifted into the gallop.

Irene checked the black horse and looked past him. "C'mon, Guy. C'mon. On my left. On my left!" She gestured urgently.

He remembered then that she was left handed and would be able to cover their right rear with a Parthian shot from the saddle, as he could attempt to cover their left. A look passed between them as Guy drew abreast of her and she pushed Shahryād back into the gallop again. Knee to knee they raced away, their gallant mounts seeming to know their peril. Quickly they settled into a bounding unison of pounding hooves and honest hearts, lungs heaving like bellows. He turned in the saddle and saw a shouting, strung-out group of about fifty in pursuit, all waving spears or bows.

Irene also turned and looked again, then at Guy. She wiped tears from her eyes so that he wondered at the emotion of the close escape and whatever else had happened at Archēsh. For all that, she had not lost her senses, for it was Irene who shouted, "We have to rein in these horses to save a sprint in them." She looked over her shoulder again. "Even if it means they get closer."

So they eased back on the foaming bits and Guy knew he had never been more alive; with the highest joy and the most putrid fear, senses naked like a wild thing.

Gradually in that long race for life, the lead Seljuks drew closer. Arrows whizzed by and Guy saw one strike Irene's flapping cloak. Then he noticed several lodged awkwardly in his own. One grazed his bridle hand, drawing blood and another seared his right leg below the knee. A big Seljuk on a chestnut horse drew near, making ready a lasso. His actions made Guy think they were after their horses, especially Irene's stallion. This would have made little difference to their fate if the Seljuks had caught them, but it changed the rules of the hunt a little. The Turk was racing neck and neck with them now. Guy glanced at Irene.

She looked across at the Turk and then behind. "He's the only one close," she shouted.

The Turk's rope snaked out as he stared fiercely at Guy and shouted something that was lost in the rush of that wild ride. He was big and handsome, his cap gone; long hair and moustache flying back over the shoulders of his lamellar cuirass. Guy noticed the Seljuk's horse gasping in air as it had been flogged to catch them. He saw the quiver, the loose red trouser leg and boot with the toe curled up. In practiced hands the rope was coiled and again snaked out. Guy foiled it with his spear a second time.

"Kill him, Guy! He knows your horse!" Irene cried.

Guy, standing in his stirrups as they raced over the hard ground, was not sure of the spear cast at the rider. As the rawhide lasso was coiled a third time, he raised his spear overgrasp, as though to foil the rope again. Instead, he drew back and hurled it deep into the racing chestnut's shoulder. Horse and rider fell heavily and lay still.

Rise after rise passed as Irene and Guy on their reeking steeds splashed through the shallow streams and past the deserted wayside hamlets. Sira and Shahryād galloped in unison now, rejoicing in their strength as they drank the wind in foam tossed draughts, their crouched riders stirrup to stirrup in the flight from Archēsh.

Slowly, another rider gained on them, whipping his gasping mount, guiding the magnificent beast into a position in their right rear, where normally it would be impossible for the intended victim to strike back. Wielding his light war axe, the Seljuk had not counted on a left-handed archer. Irene, twisting gracefully in the saddle, reins loose, goose-feather drawn to her cheek, sent the slim reed shaft driving into the folds of his armour, dangerously close to his exposed throat. Taken aback by the sudden threat from beneath the cloak of the woman whom he had already thought his prize, the Seljuk drew back, screaming his outrage.

As the country through which they galloped altered, Guy recalled how the road made a broad northern sweep around a range of low but rugged hills interspersed with stony creeks and gullies. As they entered this stage, they rode over a low crest. Looking back, they discovered their pursuers were gone.

Comprehension gripped him. "They've taken a shortcut and will try to get ahead us," he explained above the rush of their ride. "The country is too open to hide, and the screen are scattered and may not be alive, even if we could find them. Nor is there any sign of a patrol Basil was going to send." He thought desperately for another way out of danger, but could think of none. "We must ride for it," he said, surprised at how calmly the words came out.

Irene looked back at the deserted track behind them and nodded.

They clapped heels into the heaving flanks and drove their knuckles into the pumping shoulders until their fingers were brown with stinging salt sweat and the animal oil of horsehide. They flew for mile after mile. Guy's mind raced with the rhythm of the ride as he looked around for sight of the pursuers; seeing Sira's chestnut ears moving forward and back, an ear cocked on Shahryād, as though to match her stride to his.

He saw Irene crouched in the saddle, going with her black horse and giving him everything. She looked back at Guy for long seconds.

Nothing was said. There was nothing to say.

In a burst of gravel, they rounded another bend hugging a low hill and suddenly saw their pursuers close on the road a bowshot behind them. Yells of abuse and outrage bespoke the Seljuks' heedlessness now, about harming their prized horses. Guy reasoned, and thought Irene would know too, they had at least another twenty miles to gallop before reaching Manzikert. Whereas they had to husband the strength of their horses and keep ahead for the whole distance, their Seljuk pursuers held no such thoughts. The tribesmen would have been prepared to goad everything out of their horses, confident in their ability to recover after the capture.

Something struck Guy's helmet. Raising his hand he felt an arrow caught in the blue cloth he had wound around it. He pulled at the scarf, tossing it aside and reproached himself for not saving to buy a mail coif before this. The Turks were coming dangerously close and their archery more accurate.

Guy drew his bow and nocked an arrow, concealing the motion under the billowing cloak. He glanced back and marked a Turk riding closer. Dropping the reins on Sira's neck, Guy turned far to his left, brushing aside the cloak with his bow arm. Drawing the arrow in a fleeting sight picture, he discharged at the chest of the closest horse and thinking he had missed, cursed himself. Another look back revealed his target faltering, the foam from her mouth turning pink. As they rode away, he watched that grey mare die, the blood welling on her still galloping chest. Even at that distance, he could see the light going from her eyes when she went down in front, only to try and rise and continue the mad chase.

It was desperate now, Guy and Irene both shooting backwards from their saddles and the Turks drawing ever nearer. Guy saw Irene look back more often and was perplexed to notice her glances seemed less in fear than calculation. With a swift, precise movement she thrust her bow into its case and reached for her belt. Then Guy understood, for she opened a leather pouch with her free hand and brought forth gold coins which she scattered behind them. Already the main body of their tormentors were reining up, dismounting to claim the treasure. Guy saw the leaders hesitating, each man debating with himself whether to continue the pursuit to its unpredictable conclusion, or make certain of part of the spoils in the dust merely for the picking up. Irene dispersed two more handfuls, throwing them wide of the track so more time would be consumed in the search.

Guy cased his own bow as they galloped away. As the squabbling Seljuks fell behind to specks in their dust, Irene and Guy slowly eased their sweating, flying horses back to a steady hand-gallop.

Thus, Guy and Irene escaped to Manzikert, peering into the setting sun to make sure all was well at the fortress. In the dusk there were the disbelieving faces of the guard as Guy shouted to hell with the password and to close the damn gate. "Take post. Take post. The Seljuks are up. Berkri and Archēsh have fallen," he commanded in tones that brooked no argument. Behind them as they cantered from the northern main gate towards the citadel, they could hear the sergeant's Frankish shouts and the trumpets and horns sounding the alarm. They dismounted in the citadel courtyard and asked the guards to lead their steaming horses, to loosen the girths a little after a while and take out the bits, but not remove the hot saddles. Varangians assisted them to the strategos' quarters.

Basil Apocapes took one look. "Archēsh gone up?"

"Yes." Guy replied. "And Berkri before it."

"Before you were able to deliver my message?"

"Yes."

"Alright. Relax as you can—you're amongst friends. I, and the key officers, need to hear what you have to say, but I must get things moving for the defence." Basil motioned a servant to bring food and water for them.

Branas and Theophanes Doukas, already in the citadel and brought running by the clamour from the main gate, appeared on the scene. Basil rattled off orders for a score of immediate actions for the defence of the city. "And Daniel, assemble the council here in an hour for briefings. They'll need that long to get the final preparations underway." Basil turned to Guy and Irene, his expression grave. "Irene, I'm glad you escaped. Sit down, please, both of you. You look done in. The message?"

Guy passed the despatch case, still sealed, to Basil who glanced at it and placed it on the table. "Thank you for trying, D'Agiles. It was a damn fool errand I sent you on; I am grateful to God and your own skill that you have returned to us and brought with you the princeps' daughter."

"It was not my doing alone," Guy said.

Count Branas re-entered. "The fore-wall is manned and the gates guarded as the locals seeking refuge come in. The Kelts are getting the townspeople to their places now." Guy was struck by how calm Branas was.

The strategos, also measured more than ever, looked through his window at the last redness in the west. Then he turned to them. "When the others are here, we'll hear your report. Take your ease and think on what you will say. And, well done, both of you. Guy, now that battle is joined, you will need to revert to Robert Balazun's command, he will have need of your skill."

"Very well," said Guy, having enjoyed the interest and excitement of the scouting role and hoping his tone did not betray reluctance.

Refreshments were placed between Guy and Irene, but both remained too keyed-up to do more than slake their thirst a little. He took the time he now had to collect his thoughts as the council members came and assumed their places; a report they wanted, not a story. A glance sideways at Irene revealed she was thinking the same. Guy noticed Bryennius arrive and give him a wink. He smiled back weakly; aware of how clean they all were in their light robes, though Bryennius and Doukas in their rough dress looked like they had been working.

The abbess entered and made straight for Irene, kneeling by her and looking into the younger woman's eyes. Irene smiled a weary smile and touched the abbess' arm. Reassured the abbess rose to her feet, saying to Guy, "God love you, gentle knight."

Guy noticed that Reynaldus, Kamyates and Cydones were in the room and wondered why it had been Martina and not the latter who had carried the latest despatches from Manzikert. The obsequious bonhomie and flattery of Reynaldus towards his superiors were as obvious as the glares he cast at Guy.

Curticius walked towards his daughter with tears of relief streaked across his face. He squeezed her shoulder and Irene responded with a hug. As she stepped back her tunic fell away at the collar to reveal the light mail she wore underneath. With a jolt, Guy noticed the leather craftsmanship around the collar and learned the identity of the mysterious buyer of the mail shirt taken from Sira's former master.

Irene saw the look. "Our cook swore Jacques to secrecy because I didn't want you to think … to get the wrong impression."

Guy stammered out, "Why …" before Basil quietened the background hum by rising to speak.

"Gentleman, Abbess. I regret to confirm very disastrous news. Archēsh has fallen to the Sultan after an eight-day siege about which we evidently knew nothing. Before that, Berkri was massacred and we did not know about that. I do not need to tell you it makes a bad beginning. I will find out why we began this campaign in ignorance. But before that, we'll have each relate how their preparations stand."

It took some time: what had been minor tasks days ago had suddenly become major obstacles. Finally Basil signalled to Guy and the rest hushed.

Guy related his finding of the overrun camp.

Reynaldus broke in. "You didn't think to return here and tell us?" The Norman's eyes blazed with accusation and self-importance, seeking any chance to belittle another in the presence of their comrades.

Guy noticed Bryennius lean forward, but spoke first, not wanting the count's defence of him to lead to further friction between Frank and Greek. "Those were not my orders."

Reynaldus fumed.

Guy described his arrival at Archēsh and observations of the Seljuk army, finishing by simply stating he had met up with Irene and they had ridden back together.

"What happened at Archēsh?" Karas Selth looked to Guy, wanting to know the details of the Seljuk's siege techniques.

"Perhaps I can describe that," Irene offered calmly, continuing after the murmurs of assent. "In Archēsh, we heard of Berkri's moat and walls being carried by assault, the city taken by storm and devastated by massacre ... the important citizens taken away ..."

"Berkri," Kamyates interrupted rudely with the certainty of one who had travelled through there, "has changed hands several times in past decades, always with prodigious slaughter. It is important to the Caliph, al-Ka'im, but unimportant to us. Forget Berkri."

"Do not forget Berkri!" rasped Basil. All eyes switched from Kamyates to him, still standing. "They were our people massacred, remember." Basil's glare bore down on Kamyates. "Nicetas Pegonites retook it twenty years ago and we've held it since. Its loss represents a major rent in the defensive fabric of the province, not to mention the morale of the remaining population. No more interruptions. Go on, Irene."

"Thank you, Strategos." She had been looking at Kamyates with undisguised revulsion. "Some people not trapped in Berkri escaped," she continued in hushed tones, "and brought the news. A courier was sent to Manzikert. It seems he did not arrive? The fate ..."

"A courier? You're sure?" broke in Basil. He looked around the gathering. No one spoke. Bryennius, Branas and Doukas, shook their heads imperceptibly, brows knotted, perplexed. Basil looked back to Irene.

"I am certain. I was there when he, a youth, a good rider on a fair horse, was despatched."

"When?" Basil demanded, his expression betraying rising alarm and anger.

Irene maintained her patrician mask, but beneath was the turmoil and fear of the last days. Every eye was on her. "Tuesday last week."

Branas spoke up. "Nothing has been either reported or recorded, Strategos. But I'll make inquiries."

Basil looked as though suppressing a boundless fury. "Go on, please, Irene."

"The fate of Berkri made the townspeople of Archēsh so fearful that many had no taste for battle. Within a day we were surrounded by the Seljuk light troops and none could escape. The walls were subjected to violent assaults for eight days. They had endless numbers to hurl at us and soon people wearied of the fight. After a week, their siege engines arrived and at the sight of them, any remaining courage deserted the garrison. A deputation from the town went in submission offering gold and silver, horses and mules. They surrendered the fortress city of Archēsh to Tughrul Bey himself with the words, 'O conquering Sultan, go and take the town of Manzikert, and then we and all Armenia will submit to you.' After the gates were opened, there was no general massacre, but their troops sacked the town anyway and many citizens were killed or outraged, our soldiers enslaved or killed."

"The lesson is clear," Kamyates said. "Resist and die, or submit to the Sultan and be spared." Everyone looked at him. Sensing advantage in the shocked silence, the courtier was about to continue his argument for capitulation.

"There'll be no surrender here," said Basil.

"I urge you to reconsider," Kamyates enunciated, deliberately undermining Basil's authority. "Many lives are at stake and the lesson is clear. Submit and survive, or resist ..."

Basil silenced him with a glowering stare, but a look around the room showed the courtier's words had struck a chord with some.

Cydones, with a sideways glance at Kamyates spoke up so all could hear. "If I might be so bold, there is a third way."

All looked at Cydones.

Basil glared at Cydones. He had been manoeuvred into hearing out the proposal, thus giving some credence to whatever it proved to be.

Guy noticed Kamyates staring uneasily at the imperial courier.

"Flight, or more correctly, withdrawal." Cydones looked around the room. "Get out while we still can—it's no disgrace. Live to fight another day."

Kamyates visibly relaxed.

"We have a head start and can make for Taron, or Karin." Cydones sensed some support and smiled confidently. "Save the people. The sooner ..." His voice trailed off at the look of fury that crossed Basil's face.

"You forget, perhaps, two important factors," Basil reasoned in the measured tones of command. "First, it is the oldest lesson in tactics, that it is much easier to destroy a fleeing enemy in the open, whose sole thought is of escape, than it is to attack them in a strong defensive position where they are prepared and able to sell their lives dearly. Second, my orders say nothing about surrendering the district in general and Manzikert in particular to the enemy. On the contrary, I have been ordered to hold them. That brings me to the third point. For any of the city's leaders, indeed anyone wealthy enough to own a horse, to flee now would precipitate a collapse of morale and induce panic. Except for necessary patrols, on their way out as we speak, I have ordered the gates barred and walls patrolled. Any questions?" He stared at each face in turn, saving Kamyates and Cydones for last. "Is there anything about that you do not understand?"

Curticius broke the silence and returned the discourse to a less contentious thread. "Daughter, what became of the turmarch of Archēsh?"

"I don't know."

Basil sat, still glaring at the two bureaucrats from the capital.

"How did you escape?" Kamyates demanded.

Bryennius leaned forward suddenly, the movement catching Irene's eye. Guy noticed Bryennius shake his head imperceptibly as all turned to Irene.

"I was lucky," she said. "When I was outside the walls and in danger of being captured near the enemy encampment, Guy D'Agiles most gallantly came to my assistance."

All eyes flickered to Guy. Reynaldus and Kamyates glared blackly.

"Strategos," she asked. "If that's all, will you excuse us, we must tend to our horses, for without them …"

"Of course! Thank you very much. Your reports have been most useful and I will speak with both of you later." Basil rose.

Guy and Irene stood and moved, stiff-kneed and saddle-sore, to the door. As Guy opened it, one of Basil's clerks ushered in Isaac from the Barbarian House who made straight for Bryennius, whispering in the count's ear. Guy turned to hear what followed.

Basil regarded Bryennius with a raised eyebrow.

"Sir," said the count. "Reports are starting to come in. Smoke plumes in the far distance and credible descriptions of strong Seljuk groups—north, south and east of us."

"What are you saying?" Cydones smirked.

Bryennius hesitated, seemingly to gauge Cydones expression and the purpose of the question.

"He is saying," said Basil, "that the net has been cast around us and will soon be drawn tighter. So, any who planned to run from here have left it too late." With a wave, he sent Irene and Guy to their rest.

As the Varangian sentry closed the door on the sudden babble of voices behind them, Irene turned to Guy and gave him a hug. "Did you see Reynaldus? He went purple when I told them what you did! I thought he was going to explode. He's such a small man in his heart and hates others being praised or recognised."

Jacques, Charles and Vardaheri, had taken their mounts from the sentries and were massaging the animals all over. Horses and men looked up as Guy and Irene approached.

Jacques stood. "Welcome home, Mistress. We feared never to see either of you again. But if anyone could get you away from the Turks, it would be this man."

Irene smiled at him, then at Guy.

"The Mistress got herself away, actually," said Guy as the group headed for the stables in the yard of Curticius' walled house.

They unsaddled and rubbed the horses down firmly with clean straw. Sira, knowing she was being cared for, nickered softly to Guy as he removed his weapons and armour. Under Vardaheri's direction, they then washed both horses all over with vinegar and tepid water, again rubbing them dry. Jacques removed their shoes and Vardaheri allowed them a small drink of lukewarm water. They then swathed both horses entirely in blankets and gave them, at intervals, a small damp mash of finely chopped hay followed by meadow hay with more water. From time to time they led them around a little and massaged their legs. The care took most of the night. Shahryād and Sira were then released into adjoining loose-boxes as the first grey steel tempered the eastern sky.

"We'll watch over them," Jacques stated. "These horses will be worth a fortune when news of their journey gets out. You two—go and rest."

Irene, carrying her mail shirt and cloak, walked the score of paces to the back door of the villa and slumped onto the stone step, her head on her drawn up knees.

Guy, feeling as if he was swaying on his feet, lingered next to Jacques and Charles. They pretended to look over Sira. "Charles, Jacques, we've stayed longer and further-out than we meant. We're all mounted and there's still a chance to get away. You should go, now. You have good horses and could evade their patrols. Bryennius would release you—I know it. "

"And you?"

"I'm staying."

"For her?"

"Yes." Guy whispered looking towards Sira without seeing. "There're a few reasons, but in the end, for Irene." His gaze returned to Jacques. "I'll see you both off and give you a letter for my father."

"We're not going."

"Not going? But why?"

Jacques stared at the ground for a moment and then looked back at Guy. "It's too late. Charles Bertrum wanted to return as soon as we got here—and certainly as soon as I had a horse as well. But we didn't. We came as wanderers. Now all have reasons to stay."

"What?" Guy stammered.

Jacques threw up his hands.

Guy feigned manly understanding, but realised shamefully that he had been so absorbed in his own world that he had little noticed what had befallen his companions. He recalled Jacques' tenderness to Joanina and a young Rus-Armenian woman, Flora Asadian, with her arm around Charles. "That's true," Guy admitted. He searched their faces for long moments. "Is there hope here?"

Jacques looked down at the ground and with the toe of his shoe, toyed as if absently minded, with a pebble. "The towers of Manzikert are strong and there are good people here to defend them." He brought his heel down on a stone, as of to crush it. "And this is where destiny and our choices have brought us."

Guy knew then, through the journey man and master had become comrades. His eyes lit to Jacques.

Jacques suggested, "You'd better go to her. We'll talk when you've had some sleep."

Guy hobbled across to Irene, sitting down next to her and placing his armour and weapons on the step beside him. They were tired and filthy. Now they had stopped moving, the weariness was crushing. Both averted their eyes, staring at the flagstones before them. In the silence Guy felt he had to speak. "Praise God you escaped."

She was quiet for a time, collecting her thoughts. "Someone hid me in the town and helped me through the Seljuk lines. Do you know, for all his dash, Theodore's was the first and loudest voice for surrender." Her tears started. "He was going to give me up to save himself." She convulsed for long minutes, the tension and terror of the last weeks bursting forth then draining away in exhaustion. She did not look at him. "The turmarch, knowing his duty and his wife their fate, gave me their savings of gold before … The blacksmith, Kavadh, hid me in his loft for the first day while claiming my stallion belonged to a Turkish emir and he alone was charged with its care. He shod the conquerors' horses and engaged in banter and religious debate with them. In the midday heat of the second day of the sack, Kavadh, pretending to the role of a Turk's slave acting on his master's orders, led me from the town. A ghazi sentry at the gate doubted his story and was about to detain us, so I did as Kavadh had told me. I lashed his face with my whip as though he was my oppressor and jumped Shahryād through the closing gate. I pray he got away in the furore."

Irene looked him full in the face. "Then you were there, on the track, fighting single-handed. You came for me?"

"The stratetos asked me …"

"I know … despatches." She smiled wearily. "Basil picked his man. No one else would have accepted such a mission. You did and you stayed. Why?"

He searched for words, but they all seemed trite.

She waited.

"When I was riding towards Archēsh … into the unknown, all the while my reason was telling me to watch for the enemy, to be prepared for flight, yet in my heart … I could only see your face."

They turned to each other and it seemed to Guy there was no gulf between them now.

"Not this face, I think."

He took in her wry smile and the tear tracks in the dust beneath the tossed hair matted with dried perspiration. Taking a cloth from the purse at his sword-belt, he heaved himself up and rinsed it under a nearby water pump before returning to her side. "Let's look at you."

Eyes closed, chin up, she allowed him to sponge her face. "Guy, were you making plans with Charles and Jacques to leave?"

"No. We just found each of us was planning to stay, whatever the others decided." He dropped the cloth by his helmet.

She reached out for his hand and held it in silence for a time. "If the city falls, don't let the nomads have me."

"I will not desert you."

Chilled in the morning air, they shared an intimacy hitherto unknown, neither wanting to move from the step, as though it would shatter the moment of completeness with another.

At length, Irene wiped her eyes with a grimy tunic sleeve. "I'm sorry." She looked at him and then at the horizon, saying in a distant tone, "You can't help who you fall in love with."

"No. You can't help who you fall in love with."

They remained side by side until the last star faded, the last but the new star in Taurus, which shone on into the new day.

END OF BOOK ONE

~ BOOK TWO ~

THE TOWERS OF MANZIKERT

The story so far, from Book I: The Past is a Small Place

In 1054CE, concerned by reports of a looming Seljuk invasion of the Armenian provinces of Byzantium, the Empress Elector despatches a courier, Martina, to warn a frontier commander, Basil Apocapes. A Roman officer, Count Leo Bryennius, is directed to protect her getaway and arrest the as yet unidentified Byzantine traitor and Seljuk spy, Cydones, in Constantinople. A wandering Frankish mercenary, Guy d'Agiles and his two companions, Charles and Jacques, unwittingly spring the ambush. They are arrested by Bryennius who presses the three into accompanying his regiment to Armenia, where he has been ordered as a forlorn hope to strengthen the neglected defences. Guy d'Agiles, Martina, Cydones and Bryennius' regiment are then swallowed in the vastness of Asia Minor.

During a patrol clash on the march to the east, Bryennius captures a Seljuk spy, Zobeir al-Adin, an Arab. On reaching Manzikert, Cydones teams up with a senior Byzantine diplomat, Kamyates, also spying for the Seljuks. Their mission is to ensure the Byzantine-Armenian province of Vaspurakan and Manzikert fortress fall to the Sultan that summer.

Guy, Bryennius and the frontier commander, Basil Apocapes in the midst of their preparations for war, are faced with the dilemma of moral men—are suspicions alone grounds for convenient arrest or murder?

At first sight, Guy is drawn to Irene, the daughter of a senior Byzantine officer but his hopes are dashed when she runs away, in defiance of her parents and society's values, to join a suitor, Theodore Ankhialou, in the nearby city of Archēsh.

Across the Muslim frontier, the Arab soldier Derar al-Adin, searching for his missing nephew, joins the Sultan's army. In his quest for Zobeir, Derar crosses into Byzantine territory but is captured by Bryennius in a skirmish. Realising his advantage, the wily Roman releases Derar on parole to spy on the Seljuk army.

Basil, frustrated by lack of intelligence from the garrisons closer to the frontier and wishing to convey his concerns to them, orders Guy to Archēsh with despatches. On arriving, Guy discovers Tughrul Bey's invasion was underway and the city has fallen. Irene and he are thrown together in a terrifying escape during which they reach Manzikert and warn the city.

Guy, Charles and Jacques know they can flee before the Seljuk army surrounds the city, but Guy vows not to desert Irene. His companions have their own reasons for staying. Each eschews safety to face the fury encroaching from the east.

After the fall of two cities in as many weeks, the Seljuk horde coils around Manzikert and the citizens are given a stark choice: death, or surrender, handing over their fairest daughter as a bride for the Sultan.

Chapter Ten

I Will Take As Wife The Most Beautiful Girl

*Manzikert,
Early morning, 21st August 1054*

By moonless night they stole, black-clad horsemen, ghazis[60] all, dismounting in a shallow wadi a mile from Manzikert. The first bold souls stole by foot to the dry ditch and into it, then slithered up between the merlons of the scarp breastworks. Ropes snaked out in the night, catching on the battlements of the western fore-wall. Men climbed them with their soft-booted feet braced against the facing stones until they could cautiously squeeze through the narrow crenelles.[61] Ten, twenty, gathered in the shadows on the battlements; the wall sentry slain before he could raise the alarm.

By the same means they scaled the highest platform of the gate towers. The noisy death of a relief sentry as he tried to gain the observation platform, alerted the guard. Now the town dogs started to bark, but too late. Surprised, the tower's defenders responded with shouts, the brave attempting to recapture the upper chamber, the craven shrinking from the clamour. Christians died in the fight, hacking and hewing, stabbing and cursing, the shame of their watch surprised threatening the safety of all within.

At the clash of arms and the shouting, the forward detachment of the Seljuk army, five hundred picked raiders of the *gaziyân*, rose like a shadow and galloped for the western gate. They had plunged like a spear down the Archēsh track

---

60 Ghazi—an Islamic cross-border raider.
61 Crenelle—on battlements, a space between two high merlons for the defenders to shoot through.

that night, brushing aside the screen, forcing it broken and fragmented into the foothills. In the confused night battle, Seranush Donjoian, the Armenian centarch commanding—a slash across the forehead and blood in his eyes—despatched warning couriers. Two lost their way in the foothills while another pair were overtaken and killed on the track.

Now the ghazi raiders surged their horses quietly into the ditch at a weak point, collapsing the soil wall. More ropes snaked out and black riders scrambled up the walls of Manzikert.

Inside the fortress all were awakened by the tumult and the cries, "To arms! To arms. The infidels have taken the western gate." Men grabbed armour and rushed to their posts on the walls or saddled horses in readiness for action. Women hurried after them carrying water or wick-burning oil lamps of pottery or metal. Others who had previously been touched by the wrath of the nomads felt again the paralysis of terror.

Guy d'Agiles, woken by the clamour, pulled on boots and byrnie and belted on his weapons. Barely recovered from the ride from Archēsh four days before, he set his helmet upon his head, took up his spear and an old shield Jacques had obtained for him. Taking a deep breath, he followed his man and Charles Bertrum into the night as the horsemen of the Scholae swung to saddle. From out of the gloom, Basil Apocapes rode up bareback on his grey horse. He wore a sword over his short tunic and carried a shield and spear. An orderly rode behind carrying the Byzantine commander's helmet and mail coat.

"Quickly," said Charles. "To Balazun."

"Wait," counselled Guy. "See what the strategos says."

Apocapes was angry and apprehensive at the surprise won by the Seljuks at the beginning of the fight. Nevertheless he spoke calmly. "Count Bryennius! The city is in deadly peril. The Seljuks have overpowered the guard and captured the western gate towers of the fore-wall. More of their horse are arriving. They mean to defend the towers until the main body of their army comes up. We still hold the flanking towers but we must isolate the enemy in the gate towers and recapture them." Basil calmed his horse as a detachment of Armenian irregulars, leading saddled mounts, ran past him to form for battle. "Ride from the north gate, Leo. Screen to the northeast along the Archēsh track with one regiment of the irregulars. Take your Scholae, wheel around to the western wall, assault any enemy outside in the flank—kill them or drive them off, to stop them reinforcing while we recapture the towers." Basil took a moment to quieten his horse, half rearing in its excitement. "Leo, don't get caught out there, but buy me some time. Return by the south gate if under pressure. Any questions?"

"No questions." Bryennius saluted and turned Ruksh to shout orders over the noise. After a short delay, the orders relayed by the bawling tribunes, six hundred horsemen trotted out of the north gate.

As he turned to go, Guy saw the concentrated features of Bessas Phocas under his helmet and Serena Cephala rush to his warhorse's side. She took the Roman officer's hand for a moment before the equine rush of the column bore him away.

Guy, Charles and Jacques found Robert Balazun at the section of western wall facing the main gate, forming his mostly Norman troops for whatever task Basil gave him. "You Provencals," Balzun said. "Wait by me in case I have special jobs for you."

It was now first cock-crow. Guy noticed the fullish moon low in the western sky and wondered briefly what ill fortune should bring it on through the day, when that night they would surely need its light. The dawn was shrouded in a blue haze caused by the many grass fires started throughout the district to deny the Seljuks feed for their animals. In the lost towers, there was no discernible movement, though some said they could see dark faces peering at them from the arrow slits and crenelles.

The city's leaders clustered on the battlements engaging in a lot of urgent, emotional discussion. Reynaldus, the surly Norman mercenary, was berating no one in particular about the negligence of the watch, adding nothing to the solution of the crisis but ensuring that his voice be heard and his presence remembered. Outside the walls, the fierce cavalry fight had ended with many ghazis killed and the remainder driven off. The watchers saw Bryennius signal with his spear that the area outside the gates was secure.

Theophanes Doukas, the count of the city, spoke. "Both towers have three floors, each with two ballistae inside. They could fit up to twenty fighting men on each floor, that's a hundred and twenty. If they still hold the towers when their main body gets here, then we're damned. The Sultan can start peeling back the defenders on the fore-wall like an orange skin. Then get engines close enough to start assaulting the main wall here."

"There's no question that the immediate re-capture of the towers is vital." Basil spoke deliberately in his gravelly voice, his squire nearby him with the armour and accoutrements the strategos had yet to pull on. "Who'll take it on?"

Guy felt his guts tighten as the Frankish leader, Raymond de Gaillon, stepped forward. "They were Norman held towers. It is a matter of honour that their brother Franks regain them. We'll need support from this wall, and from Selth's engineers."

"Thank you, Raymond," said Basil. "If direct assault does not work, burn them out and quickly. We'll clean up the mess later."

Under the direction of Doukas, a heavy and continuous concentration of darts and arrows was started against the ghazis in the towers, clattering and clanging against the loopholes like sudden gusts of rain. In the growing light, before following Balazun from the wall, Guy overheard the strategos say to Count Doukas, "I've seen it." Following their gaze, he saw the immense dust cloud to the northeast with the thin line of Armenian irregular horse, specks on the Vaspurakan steppe, riding hopelessly towards it.

Burdened by armour, weapons and foreboding, Guy, Charles and Jacques, followed Balazun out of the main gate to form up on rampart of the fore-wall. Ninety Franks were with them. Guy knew a similar number were approaching, along the fore-wall on the other side of the captured towers. De Gaillon led the third storming party on the ground level. The plan was brutally simple—to assault simultaneously, smash down the doors and enter fighting.

Crouched around the heavy battering ram, a long, iron-shod beam with ropes looped around it as carry-points, they had a moment's grace, just time enough for a private prayer. It had all happened too quickly for much contemplation before this. Balazun faced them, his back to the hostile tower. He had laced up the protective flap of his mail coif to cover his face below the eyes. Like a feather he held the kite-shaped shield in his left hand while wielding a short handled battle-axe in his powerful right. Behind the helmet's rim and nasal, there was fire in his eyes as he exhorted his storming party to courage. "Even you, D'Agiles," Robert Balazun roared happily. "Let the heathen see your face this day!"

Guy managed a self-conscious smile as the others laughed nervously at the good-natured joke, crafted from his two wild rides from pursuing Seljuks.

In those brief seconds, Guy saw in sharp clarity the archers on the main wall, with de Gaillon's group forming up below them covering the battering party with their shields. From the hostile bowmen in the tower ahead, arrows sped towards them, sticking in shields with a gut-wrenching thud. Through the crenelle at his left shoulder, Guy observed Bryennius' horsemen maintain a desultory archery against the towers. Six cataphracts cantered up, a ladder suspended by ropes between them. A dozen troopers with two more ladders followed them, so the Turks in the tower now had to guard against a threat of assault from that quarter as well. Balazun turned and faced the tower. Guy closed his eyes and sucked in a deep breath, mouthing a short prayer for Irene and the city if they should fail.

Then to a shout from Balazun accompanied by a ragged cheer from the Normans, Guy, Charles and Jacques were lurching forward behind the footmen struggling with the battering ram on the narrow rampart. A dozen arrows fell amongst them. Turkoman faces, dark under their helmets, rose to shoot at them from the observation platform. The Seljuk bowmen were now spared the arrows off the main wall, as archery from there ceased for fear of hitting the Normans and Bryennius' men. Another dozen Seljuk arrows thudded into shields or foiled in armour. One of the footmen, struck through his unprotected face, fell with a cry. Jacques leapt forward and took his place, seizing the rope handle and yelling like one possessed, his stare fixed on the wooden door.

A heavy ballista bolt tore away four men in a shrieking crimson ribbon. Seeing the confusion on the beam, the Seljuks rained arrows on the men around the foiled ram. Hunched against the missiles, Norman footmen pushed past Guy to disentangle their wounded comrades from the carry-ropes and take up the heavy timber.

"Quick," roared Balazun excitedly. "Quickly, before the infidels reload." They started forward again, arrows plunging amongst them. The iron ram-head hit the door, with a loud thud and the sound of splintering wood, but still it held firm. "Again," roared Balazun, "and again."

Holding his shield over his head, Guy plunged his spear through a loophole. Through the slit he could see forms struggling to reload the ballista, the inside of the tower filled with shouting, jostling men. An archer aimed at him. Guy drew back hurriedly and hurled his spear.

"Get back," a Norman footman shouted from behind him. The man, stubble faced under his iron helmet, sweating and excited, thrust folds of heavy felt into the slit, forcing it deeper and holding it in place with his spear. He grimaced at Guy, "Let them try to shoot through that while we knock on their door."

There was a searing pain in Guy's arm as a stone dropped from above, landed heavily on his shield and fell at his feet. Not daring to look up, he drew his sword and noticed Norman archers at the rear of the storming party, shooting up at the crenelles above to suppress the defences. With a groan the door gave way, hanging crazily from its hinges while the ghazis thrust out with their spears or discharged arrows through the gaps. Normans fell.

Balazun was the first man in, screaming prayers and oaths, buffeting with his shield and swinging the battleaxe against the sea of moustached, bearded faces in front of him. Charles drove straight in after him, undergrasp spear first, forcing the heavy head through a round shield into the softness behind it, then drawing his mace to batter into the gap, sword swinging at his side. Two more Norman knights stormed in, Guy and Jacques after them. More followed into the dimness, the stone room taken up by the two ballistae swinging wildly on their frames as the fight surged around them. The floor was slippery with blood and thick with torn, spitted corpses, Christian and Turk.

Before Guy struck a serious blow the fight was over; the last four Turks tripping in panic back up the stairs. Balazun, wild eyed, glanced around and shouted, "Geoffrey, Charles, downstairs! Guy, with me!" All around men gasped for air, like so many horses at the end of a race.

Guy was aware of his friend plunging downstairs, knights and footmen after him, tripping and slipping in the stained, dark space. Guy turned and followed Balazun into the fray. He would never forget the image of Balazun's coif beneath the iron helmet; the expanse of his mail back, linked iron-ring skirts of the hauberk swinging wildly over cross-gartered trousers, as step by step Balazun lifted the Seljuks upstairs on his shield in a struggling, stabbing mass. There was a deafening roaring and shouting, clanging of sparking steel on steel in the confined space. A Seljuk, cloven through the skull, threw his arms out awkwardly and gurgled horribly as he collapsed. A black arm reached out and grabbed at Balazun's battleaxe arm. Guy, loosening his grasp on the leather handgrip inside his shield, seized the Seljuk's wrist and jerked the ghazi forward off balance, so the Seljuk cavalryman sprawled down the stairs. Guy slashed at his exposed forearm and cried out to one behind him, "Seize him, seize him!"

Balazun, Guy, Jacques and others boiled up the stairs, forcing open the trapdoor against the men above trying to close it on them. Squinting into the sunlight, they fought, their demonic inner selves drawing on some wellspring of strength and power until the observation platform was theirs.

Charles appeared from below, stating that all floors had been cleared. Thus ended the fight for the southern tower. Balazun, heaving under his mail coif as he gulped in air, his face, arms and armour basted with blood, signalled Doukas on the main wall that the tower was secure. Jacques, tore off his helmet, peeled back the sweat-soaked leather coif from his neck and looked over the side of the wall. "Open the gates!" he shouted. "Let the Greeks in. Clear this tower. Strip the infidels of their weapons."

As the mayhem in the northern tower also died away with the violent deaths or capture of the ghazis, Bryennius' horsemen entered through the gates and gallopers were despatched to recall the Armenian screen.

Doukas ran up and supervised the reorganisation. The dead were cleared from the tower and walls, with trotting cataphracts dragging the slain ghazis away from the fortress. The Christian dead were carried inside the city for later burial, the priests uttering prayers over their shrouded figures, while women and friends wept over a few. As the concentrated carnage of the towers was cleared, someone called for water to wash away the bloodstains. Half a dozen traumatised and rightly fearful prisoners were bound and blindfolded, then marched off to the citadel for questioning. Guy could read the shock in their blank faces and tried to imagine their thoughts, for they were powerless, not knowing whether they would live for minutes more. Balazun sent him to report to Apocapes.

With the sun now well up, Guy found the strategos on the main wall with his military secretary, Count Branas; the two looking at each other with mixed relief and concern, as the clamour beneath them fell into order, signalling that Manzikert had survived its first test in the coming battle. "That was too close, Daniel," Basil whispered as he donned his armour.

"I fear God is not with us," Branas replied. "All were at their posts. Doukas and I were walking the walls, neither of us at the threatened place at the right time."

Manzikert,
Morning, 21st August 1054

Shaken by the ease with which the Seljuks had surprised and almost penetrated the defences, the strategos ordered more townspeople, stiffened by Normans and Varangians, to the fore-wall. What people had dreaded for so long had come to pass and ordinary citizens moved forward with their own fears to repel an assault now only hours away.

Balazun placed Guy in command of sixty men to defend a section of the fore-wall half a furlong north of the western gate towers. Normans manned the tower on Guy's left, one section of wall removed from the western gate. Varangians held the tower on his northern flank to his right. Many of the men under his command were townsmen, young and old, Armenians mostly, with two Kurds and a handful of Arabs, their culture lingering in the south-western parts of Vaspurakan and Taron. Some wore the characteristic Byzantine-Armenian armour of irregular troops, predominately lamellar cuirasses with plain pot helmets and round shields. Others wore the standard raw silk coats padded with cotton wadding, their heads protected by long strips of linen or cotton, wound turban-like around felt caps. They were armed with swords and spears and the occasional mace, but a few also carried more familiar instruments, such as sickles and axes. Guy's little command included ballistae-men in their galleries beneath the banquette, with Frankish and local archers. Stones, arrows, and darts were stacked against the parapet, along with the water skins or jugs and small personal bundles brought by the men. Braziers glowed under blackened pots of scalding water or oil, ready for pouring over the wall.

Behind Guy, the main wall was crowded with bowmen, slingers and ballistae-men, ready to shoot over the heads of their comrades on the fore-wall. Looking to the plain, Guy could see to his half-left, the road from the western gate and the yellow-grassed fields beyond. To his front and extending to his right was the southern edge of the nestling village of timber dwellings.

Along the wall faces were turned towards him and Guy suddenly felt very young and inexperienced. The men were silently judging him, waiting for orders. Amongst them, Guy noticed a wan-looking Leon Magistros.

"Get a grip of them, now," Jacques urged quietly while seeming to point to something in the distance. "You fought already this day and they will follow you. Tell them what to do."

Guy stepped forward and removed his blood-spattered helmet. "Soldiers," he called clearly in his rudimentary Armenian, trying to portray confidence without arrogance.

"Good start," Jacques whispered. "Keep going."

"I am Guy d'Agiles. Can you hear me? Do you understand what I am saying? We are here to defend this wall, between these two towers."

Charles, by Guy's side, interpreted the gist of his words for the Franks amongst them. Understanding, the men nodded.

"We have been brought together by circumstance and God's will. There will be no withdrawal from this place except by my command, for the lives of all in the city depend on us holding it. Stay with me at all times. I will get to know your names by and by, but for now, let me see you and your weapons."

"Inspect arms!" called Jacques. The men stood with their backs to the battlements and held forth their weapons.

Guy went down the line in imitation of Bryennius, inspecting their arms, exchanging a word with each, seeking to know their expertise, asking after their story or loved ones. Thus Guy learned he led few professional soldiers; five Frankish knights and a dozen Frankish archers and spearmen. A number of the Armenians had previous military experience in the Roman or Armenian armies and others had trades such as cobbler or blacksmith. There were several minor merchants, shop-keepers and local peasants. Guy was surprised to learn he also commanded a Kurd who had travelled with the caravans far into the Saracen lands and a couple of Arabs. With some pride he noticed they addressed him as "centarchos" or "centarch".

Guy appointed as his deputy, Aram Gasparian, once a free landholder and officer of Armenian cavalry before the regiments were disbanded and his lands stolen by Romans with connections at court. Gasparian's fluency in Greek and Armenian together with his grasp of their plight and physical presence made him an obvious choice.

Gasparian, Jacques, Charles and Guy gathered in a knot.

"Aram," Jacques began, "you know these men. May I suggest," he turned to Guy, "that Aram trains the men to fight and supervises their guards, rest and other work. Aram can teach them what to do. You must know what to do and lead them in action." The brown-bearded Armenian agreed.

"You," Jacques went on, addressing Guy, "must know Apocapes' plans and how the battle is to be fought. The men must know how and why they fight, and trust that if the fore-wall is breached and there is no way to recapture it," he paused meaningfully, "they will not be abandoned—that they have a good chance of getting back inside the city to fight again. Hope! They do not ask certainty of you, but they must have hope."

"All right," said Guy. "We're agreed on how to do this. The other matter is that we have a handful of infidels amongst us. Keep an eye on them until we are certain of their loyalty."

As they talked, it occurred to Guy where Jacques might have been for all those silent years. The peasant knew too much of war for him to have been sequestered in a monastery. Guy waited until they were alone, as they sat on the warm flagstones, their backs to the parapet. "Jacques?"

The groom gave a vague grunt of acknowledgment, as though his thoughts were far away.

"Where did you go when you left my parents' estate?" Guy asked. "The first time—years ago?"

Jacques hesitated for a time, as though remembering, or trying not to. "Does it matter?"

"Perhaps not, though now we are here, I'd like to know. There is no reason beyond that. I would not compel a comrade to talk, but you seem to know about this work and I must know how skilful you are. I heard that ... you fought against infidel people called the Moors."

Jacques looked sideways at Guy. "I was in Castile, with Ferdinand the First—the one they call The Great. I learned some hard lessons there, fighting Christian and Moor alike."

They were silent for a time after that, though Guy was now even more curious about the other man's experiences, but refrained from further questions and turned his attention to washing the dried blood from his helmet, face and hands.

In the late morning, the observers on the ramparts could discern many groups of horsemen approaching from the northeast, the dust behind them betraying the presence of a large army. Word was passed along the walls for every second leader of the troops to attend the main square of the city to hear the strategos speak. Balazun sent Guy as he was the most likely of the Franks to understand what was being said. Hoping to see Irene, Guy strode to the square and shouldered his way amongst the citizens and soldiery. The Sixth Schola were drawn up afoot in precise ranks as local Armenian troops, Varangians and Franks mingled with the citizens.

There was great tension in the air as the thoughts of all were drawn to their fate. For many, the unexplained creation of a disorderly new star, coupled with the coming of the Seljuks, seemed like the Creator's punishment for some unknown sin. A few looked at their neighbours in fear and condemnation. Others, consciences pricked by some small but shameful transgression, concealed their thoughts. Even the wasted illumination of the moon in daylight seemed against them. Thus they waited, many praying silently, to hear the strategos speak to them, looking in their fear towards a strong leader.

In this the people of Manzikert were well served. Basil Apocapes, wearing the armour of a common theme cavalryman, mounted the steps leading to the main cathedral in Manzikert. The crowd occupied every vantage point around him.

Guy looked for Irene but could not see her in the host of long garbed, mostly veiled women. He had not seen her since they parted after the ride, both being busy in different ways with the last minute preparations for the coming battle. Then, with a hint of perfume, she was standing next to him, lifting her veil and smiling. Guy saw her look quickly at his rumpled, grimy attire under the mail with its brown stain on the shoulder. Her smile faded when she saw the fatigue and strain evident in his countenance.

Her mother, Anna, an attractive Armenian woman in her late forties—patrician, reserved, her eyes looking like the touched up aftermath of tears above an aquiline nose—smiled at Guy. He read it as reserved approval, the sort that parents show a favoured, if not entirely longed-for suitor. "How now, Guy d'Agiles?" Anna Curticius greeted warmly enough. "You've been hotly engaged already. Praise God you're all right. Let us pray you do not need to ride from this place with my daughter."

"Let us pray, indeed," Guy agreed. It had not occurred to him what might be done if the fortress fell. He had no wealth to buy their freedom, nor could he imagine in the chaos of the city being carried and sacked, being able to find Irene and get her away though swarms of Seljuks. Those considerations were all secondary to the mere matter of surviving the fury of any assault that breached the walls.

Irene moved closer to him, quickly took his hand, gave it a squeeze none could see and stepped apart a little. She was scrubbed and perfumed, her clothes smelling of the dried wildflowers placed in the cupboard. In her green eyes, he read pleasure and trust. "You're well?" she asked.

"Quite. And you?" He was embarrassingly aware of the people around whispering and staring. They were not ill-intentioned but news of the couple's escape had become widespread in the city, so when together they attracted attention. "Our horses are well also, I believe."

"Yes. I was worried about them." Irene was careful to keep her apparent orientation away from him. "Charles and Jacques have been diligent in their care."

Doing the same thing, he tried to speak on what lay between them. "I wanted to come and talk to you, but the first attack was this morning …"

"I heard they captured a tower, but were driven out by the Kelts, you amongst them." "I'm now posted to the fore-wall …" He paused as he heard Irene catch her breath, "…very near that place, so we've had no chance to talk before …" Unsure how to finish, he fell silent.

"I know … the battle. It might be prudent if we delay any talk beyond … pleasantries … until after it is done. Until we know what will become of us."

"Perhaps. But know if I can be of service to you, you have only to ask."

Irene glanced down at the flagstones, her long lashes blinking once, twice, thrice. "I know," she murmured. Then she looked directly at him, a determined expression in her green eyes. "I will pray for you. Have no fear."

As they spoke the high sun glared down on the stillness, the air haze-blue with smoke. Guy could see Reynaldus, Kamyates and Cydones lurking in the group that flanked Basil. A less contrived but more forceful presence by the commander's side were Branas, Selth, Oleg and Doukas, all in subdued discussion over a chart. They put it away when a hush descended on the crowd as Basil stepped forward.

Irene moved imperceptibly closer so her robes brushed against Guy. "The strategos is about to speak." He could see her biting her lower lip softly in concentration.

"Soldiers, men, women and children of Manzikert," Basil began in his great, clear voice. Speaking Armenian, he paused between the phrases so interpreters standing on crates and shouting to the different contingents could relay his words in their various languages. "I know not whether it is necessary to impel you to be of good courage, for enthusiasm is upheld by circumstance, I think."

There was a nervous titter from the crowd, but it was an improvement on the deep gloom that had prevailed minutes before.

"We know why the Seljukian come—women, slaves, death and theft. No one in the whole world gives way to those who are seeking by violence to rob them of life, or virtue, or possessions. And you are not ignorant that nothing but valour and strength stops the Seljuks when they bring war to their neighbours. The struggle with them is not a hard one, my friends. We've grappled with them before and prevailed over them in open fight and a familiar task entails no difficulty whatever. Consequently, we shall be obliged to despise the enemy as having been defeated in previous combats and having no such grounds for courage as ourselves. All perceive the necessity in which we are involved. All know their duty. Remember that, where safety is despaired of, the safest thing to do is to not court it, for an over-fondness of life may bring on destruction."

Basil paused and swallowed to ease his throat, already hoarse from the shouting of the fight that morning. The crowd was as still as death.

"Let us be resolute against the enemy, calling to our aid assistance from above, for God is wont to save above others, those who find hope of safety in themselves.

Take heart, my comrades and brothers, take heart and fear not, for this is a simple matter for God. As they come upon us with their carts and horses, oxen and elephants, let us recall the name of our Lord, be proud of God eternally, and confess His name that He gives strength and steadiness to His people is blessed for all time. Hearts up. Hearts up!"

The strategos knelt in prayer, "Lord, I fear no evil, for thou art with me. I fear not the myriads of their soldiers which surround me."

At that, the crowd, citizens and soldiers all, knelt and prayed as the tonsured priests moved among them, carrying crosses and dispensing blessings. Guy knelt in the silence of the smoke hazed air, broken only by the chanting of the religious men. The strategos then walked among the crowd. As often happened, orphans for whom he was a benevolent father figure followed him in adoration. Widows reached out to touch his clothes, so did he also care for them. The ordinary people of Manzikert, their ranks swelled threefold by the refugees from the surrounding district, knew their greatest test yet was upon them. None hoped for a more able or inspirational leader. As the solemn prayers died away the applause started, beginning within the ranks of the Scholae who stamped their spear hafts on the flagstones and roared as one voice, "Manzikert! Manzikert! Manzikert!"

The strategos waved to them with a smile as the rest of the crowd took up the great shout, clashing weapons on shields and stamping their feet. Echoing through the square and the alleys, streets and public buildings, the low-pitched roar sounded across the walls so the sentries there looked inward in wonder. Across the plain the great shout rolled, "Manzikert. Manzikert. Manzikert."

In his life, Guy had never seen such a release of emotion.

The gathering in the square ended as Basil departed with his staff. Guy turned to the two women and said, "I must return to my post."

"Come and sup with us when you get the chance, young man," Anna Curticius invited. .

"Yes do, Guy," Irene whispered. Then stepping closer to him, she gave his hand a momentary squeeze. "Do." The women moved off amongst the crowd.

Guy was left standing alone, an empty feeling creeping upon him as he watched Irene move away. After their meeting and the crushing despair of her sudden departure to Archēsh, there had been the emotional intimacy of the ride and the hours afterwards. Now she seemed distant, her messages as mixed as before. All Ankhialou had needed to do was simply summon her, and she had gone in defiance of convention and her family. What did it take? What did he have to do? He was vaguely aware of the thinning crowd moving by, some staring at him.

Suddenly Bessas was standing next to him. "Thank God for short speeches. The courtier, Kamyates, would have just been getting warmed up by now!" The centarch looked at him with concern. "Are you all right?" Bessas followed the direction of Guy's gaze. "Ah. Not all right, eh?" He gave Guy a soft punch on the arm. "She's been through a lot and will need some time."

"I suppose so," Guy said, appreciating Bessas' concern and feeling hope rekindled.

The Walls of Manzikert,
Late Morning, 21st August 1054

An hour later, Count Bryennius, Bessas and the scouts joined Guy on the wall.

The Seljuk army filed into the valley, clan standards dancing on the spear-tipped staffs, the drooping horse tails variously dyed in green, red, yellow or black. Dusty riders expecting imminent plunder, looked over the nodding manes of their mostly buckskin Turkmene horses, mocking the townspeople by the mass of their host and deliberate preparations

First came the clan groups of tribal Turkoman on unshod horses, the Seljuks and some of the twenty-four tribes of their Oghuz cousins, each under their own woollen or cotton banners, blue and red being common. The main tribal flags were surmounted by a horsetail to display their status. Of the Oghuz tribes, the Kiniks rode in pride of place, their black-maned Kazilik mounts, like the others, having a knot tied in the horse's tail. Predominantly men with some taut, long-haired women riding astride and armed with them, the clans rode in loosely ordered files behind the leaders of their war bands.

There were roughly clothed people, little washed and mostly unarmoured archers on the Shihry and Nesaean breeds of Khorasan. Tribes from around Khiva and Ferghana, the Seljuk's eastern cousins from the Jaxartes River, were also in the van with their scant beards and skull caps close on shorn heads. Men of the defeated Ghaznavid Empire followed, vassals now of the Seljuks. Kurds, mounted swordsmen mounted on heavier Persian horses, made common cause against the Christians. Large men, from Bukhara and Samakand, were there, with their dark faces and beards impassive above the brilliance of their horse furniture.

In their tens of thousands, the Seljuk army swarmed into the plain between Manzikert and the river bend and along the Arsanias, some fording the stream looking for better grazing on the northern side. Herd boys drove spare horses and baggage-laden camels. Dust rose thickly to engulf the blue smoke haze, so that the sun shone dully as a tarnished bronze orb though the opaque air, giving an eerie half-light in the middle of the day.

On the walls of Manzikert, the watchers were quiet but for muted comments or infrequent staccato orders to the troops. Most observed the Seljuk army in awe, others in fright. Many prayed, kneading in their hands the beads and charms, icons and talismans of luck or hope. Guy overheard the former soldier in Vardaheri speaking quietly and deliberately, "In the advance guard are the tribal Turkoman, fanning out now to select their camping grounds according to steppe precedence and the power of their emirs. See the lines of saddled horses, heads down, drinking at the rivulets that feed the river. They've finished their ride and will soon pitch their tents."

"Ghulams[62]," Count Bryennius observed. "There, in black. Black banners, black turbans, black equipment. They ride the horses of Syria and Arabia. How many do you think? Five hundred? A thousand?" he estimated roughly as the host in their widespread columns arrived. "Two, five, ten thousand. By God, Vardaheri, Tughrul must have stripped the caliphate to assemble such a force."

"That's them, all right," said Vardaheri, dispassionately. "The Hassa Ordusa, the Imperial Guards."

Guy could see the disciplined columns of ghazis riding on the Seljuk flank and he shuddered at the difficulty a few hundred had caused that very morning. They rode insolently, studiously ignoring the fortress, as though it were beneath their contempt. Under the direction of the guides, they formed a camp on the plain near a knoll, the place Count Bryennius had identified as a likely location for the Sultan's household. Squadrons of ghulams peeled off, halting in a phalanx facing the fortress. These guarded against a foray by the garrison, for the Seljuk army could have been vulnerable when preoccupied with its administrative tasks. The calm order of it all conveyed deep menace.

Bryennius called Guy close, saying, "Keep an eye open for our friend, Derar al-Adin."

"Horse-archer," Maniakh said. "A rider comes."

Togol looked offhandedly at the approaching rider. "It's not him."

Guy peered between the merlons to see a solitary Seljuk riding along the edge of the ditch, calling out to the men on the ramparts. None answered.

As the horseman drew abreast of them, Maniakh challenged in the language of the steppes, "You're bold, stranger. State your business before I prick your worthless carcass with a goose-feathered shaft."

The Seljuk replied in kind. "You rogue! You couldn't with your own piss hit the ground at your feet." Maniakh grinned as he interpreted the insult. The Seljuk explained his business.

Maniakh turned and interpreted for the others, "He seeks a horse—a chestnut mare ridden days ago in flight from Archēsh." Maniakh turned to look once more at the rider. "I might know a man who knows someone who has heard of such a horse." To mock the gravity of the Seljuk's request he added, "And I seek a dancer from Tabriz."

The rider looked back in silence for a time and then asked with an air of indifference, "What's her name? I presume it's a woman?"

"She danced as Hurr in the bazaar," Maniakh said ignoring the slight and with such obvious interest, that the horse trader, seated with his back to the parapet, let out a low moan, which caused the count to look down sharply at him.

"She's here, or soon will be," the steppe rider relayed, as though it was of no consequence. "What were you doing in the bazaar at Tabriz anyway?"

---

62 Ghulam—a (usually Turkic) professional cavalryman of the Seljuk state and Abbasid Caliphate: something equivalent to the troopers of Byzantium's tagmata.

At that moment Guy recognised, with a start, the Seljuk sitting his horse at the edge of the ditch, as the one whose horse he had killed with his spear during the ride from Archēsh. "I thought I despatched him on the road." He had been certain that no man could have survived such a heavy fall. If all those now entering the valley were as difficult to fell, it did not bode well for the defence.

On learning Hurr was with the Seljuk host, Maniakh moved sideways to better see the emir through a crenelle. Simon Vardaheri stood, looking embarrassed. "I didn't tell you about that, did I, Horse-archer?" he asked.

"No, I don't think you did," Bryennius replied with a trace of irritation as he strove to understand the relationships being revealed.

"Maniakh became infatuated with a dancer in Tabriz," Vardaheri started awkwardly. He wasn't alone, the whole town was bewitched."

"Infatuated?"

"Must be quite a dancer," Guy quipped and immediately wished he had remained silent, as deep eyed Maniakh, the quiet nomad who knew the languages and traditions of a host of peoples, shot him a scornful look.

"I've seen none like Hurr," Vardaheri said. "When she entered the circle of light, you could have heard the sun rise. She finished her dance by dropping to the floor, on her stomach, head up, back arched and the graceful leg of an acrobat high behind her. At that moment, she looked up into Maniakh's eyes. It was fate."

Maniakh was looking wistfully at Vardaheri, remembering.

"Anyway, they got to know each other." Vardaheri explained. "And she didn't betray us when we were hunted by the city guard after we burned their siege engines."

"And you didn't think to relate this?" Bryennius asked in a surprisingly conversational tone, seemingly more moved than angry. Sometimes it was hard to tell what his deeper feelings were.

Vardaheri spluttered. "How could I know she was going to show up here?"

Bryennius gave Guy an exasperated glance and said to Vardaheri, "Simon, ask the Turkoman what he wants with Guy's chestnut mare, should anyone know of it."

"She's of the bloodlines held by my family and precious to us," was the reply.

Vardaheri turned to interpret, adding, "I think he's as he appears to be." The horse trader looked through the crenelle again. "What's she worth to you? Should we know of her."

The horseman looked for a moment at the ground, then at the figures on the wall. "Exchange for another mare, a good one."

Vardaheri remained silent.

"And safe conduct for the thief, if he throws himself on my mercy before the city falls."

Bryennius took a longer look at the horseman at the ditch. "He seems pretty damned sure."

Vardaheri relayed, "You seem sure, nomad?"

"Oh we are sure. We know a very great deal about your city. You should surrender now while the Sultan can control his troops. You don't have long to think about it, Count Bryennius."

Vardaheri and Bryennius exchanged glances. "Thanks for the advice," the horse trader replied courteously. "Who should we ask for, if we should happen upon someone who knows of this chestnut mare?"

"The Emir Emren Dirse," said the rider.

"Is that you?"

"I am Emren Dirse." The rider turned his horse towards the Seljuk host as if to return there, then swung her on her haunches back again. "And you can tell your friend that Hurr sleeps in the tent of my cousin." So saying, he cantered off.

"Who would've tol…?" Vardaheri began.

Bryennius shook his head. "The enemy could have had a score of people in and out of Manzikert in the last weeks, or a spy here yet. Or both."

They all looked gloomily at the Seljuk army fanning out in its own dust over the river valley.

The Arsanias Valley near Manzikert,
Morning, 21st August 1054

Within sight of the fortress, Derar al-Adin sat his chestnut gelding, Qurmul, named after a fabled steed of Islamic legend that had enabled a daring escape. Escape! The notion led his thoughts to the patrol clash with Roman cavalry at some nameless wadi where he had been captured and briefly detained. It has been no escape. At every moment he was conscious of remaining a prisoner.

Derar was hot and longed to take his ease, to pull off the long leather boots, arrow-proof quilted cotton tunic and the short-sleeved mail shirt over it. A light, round shield was strapped to his bridle arm and in his right hand he carried a long spear held crossways over his horse's wither at an acute angle so not to accidentally touch another. He had become accustomed to the constant feel of his straight sword of excellent Syrian steel that swung in its wooden, leather-covered scabbard by his left leg.

Unlike many Arabs who were primarily spear and swordsmen, Derar was handy with the composite bow and wore a bow case and quiver at his waist belt. These were a gift from his friend, Emren Dirse, these two men drawn to each other by an interest in the Bedouin horses. When the luxury of time permitted, the two discussed and debated the Arabian strains endlessly over wine and games of chess, amongst other subjects that interested them: poetry, philosophy, religion and women.

Derar's man, Zaibullah, rode on his left. He noticed, in the idleness of the moment, Zaibullah's long hair with its plaited side braids hanging down past the rim of his iron pot helmet. The Seljuk had placed his spear against his saddle under his near side thigh and wore his shield on his back, over his cuirass of oiled and polished horn lamellar. The Turk fondled the ornate handle of his curved sabre occasionally, a subconscious check that it was still there, and drummed his strong fingers on the leather quiver that hung from his right hip. The visual effect, Derar mused, was of practiced skill, the look of a warrior. He wondered about this complex wanderer who had become attached to his own household. Did someone spy on the spy?

Derar, his nose and throat irritated by the smoky air, sniffed and spat distastefully onto the dry ground. He had entreated the Sultan's spymaster, Bughra Dumral, to allow them to accompany the vanguard of the Seljuk army. Thus they had thus ridden in easy stages for two days and the previous night, the mounted figures moving like ghouls through the smoke haze and dust in the starlight. With the wellbeing of his nephew and his promise to the boy's mother foremost in his mind, he had chosen to ride with the van to ensure he entered Manzikert early. Being in the lead of the army had other practical advantages. One avoided much of the dust entailed by moving with the main body and a comfortable campsite was more likely to be gained.

For a day and a night they had ridden over a deserted landscape where the burnt grass scrunched to black powder under the hooves. The Romans had cut and hauled in as hay, much of the useful grass and burnt off what they could not. Derar knew the garrison had deliberately reserved some pasture near the fortress, for if the city survived, they would need it for their own animals. The besieging Seljuk army would reduce it to dust in days.

Derar had reached the environs of Manzikert just as the Armenian irregular horse had withdrawn safely behind the circuit walls. He hoped the forward detachment had captured and controlled some vital part of the defences so the city would quickly fall by storm or surrender. It took only a glance to see they had failed and paid dearly in the attempt. The bodies of men and horses lay scattered on the plain before the fortress. Saddled mounts moved aimlessly or sniffed the corpses, manes draping over the unseeing faces of their masters. Others, unnerved by the trauma of battle and having galloped to exhaustion in aimless circles, simply stood still, heads downcast, reins dragging, saddles twisted where a rider had clutched it in his fall. They waited with the patience of their kind, for someone to come and feed them and show a gesture of kindness. Many stood near where they had sought to drink from a brook. Some good horses there, Derar observed with his practiced eye and exacting standards, but none worth the wrath of a clan if taken.

As Derar sat in his warm saddle, the late morning sun beating down through the oppressive haze, he heard a roar, accompanied by the rhythmic clash of weapons, issue over and over from the fortress, "Man-zi-kert! Man-zi-kert! Man-zi-kert!"

Zaibullah and he looked at each other.

"They wouldn't be so cocky if they'd seen what happened at Berkri and Archēsh," Zaibullah said.

Derar grunted agreement and turned to more practical matters. "We'll pitch our tent there, by that poplar lined stream which runs from south of the fortress into the river. Camp on the far side, for the stream with its rocky bottom and sharp gully will be an obstacle to the Romans. There, where the ground rises," he pointed, "enough to drain away the water if it rains and from where we should get a look at our own encampment and the fortress at the same time. Some grass remains along the stream and we can take our ease under the trees. We should be here no more than a week. I think the Sultan will camp on that knoll, where the stone house is. From there he'll have a good view as events unfold."

The pair dismounted to wait and lounged on the close-cropped green river bottom with the battlements visible beyond the lava step. They watched the tribesmen continue to arrive. The clans of the van and flank guards, stiffened by regiments of border-raiding *gaziyân*, filled the bottoms of the river valley around them, moving loosely to the Sultan's grand design. Guides would mark out and supervise the occupation of the huge encampment, to circumvent any disputes between the quarrelsome bands. Ten miles behind were the main-guard, the first disciplined columns of the black clad ghulams of the *Hassa Ordusa* and landed knights of the *sipahiyan* with their followers. Behind them marched the main body of the army: endless streams of cavalry and infantry, and then the baggage train, herded into the places designated by the mounted guides. Derar watched the screen and flank guards move out to protect the army as it made camp and wondered at the forces that had led him to be trapped of his own volition in such momentous events.

Bughra Dumrul, arrived early to observe the temper of the defences. One of Tughrul's senior generals, Isma'il, rode with Dumrul. Commanding the advance-guard, Isma'il's main task had been to fight, immediately from the line-of-march, any mobile battle the Romans might offer in the open, or exploit any effective penetration of the defences by the forward detachment. Isma'il had already been twice robbed of easy blows when the captured towers could not be held, and when his disorderly, dust-shrouded flanks had failed to trap the Armenian irregular horse. Despite hearing several descriptions of Manzikert's fortifications over the preceding months, Isma'il blew loudly through his bearded cheeks in exasperation at the evident strength of the fortress.

Derar admired Isma'il's horse and envied him for the lithe, long limbed, combative dancer who shared his tent. For some reason, the thought caused him to ponder on the Horse-archer's fair interpreter of the wadi fight. His glance flickered to the distant walls and he wondered if she were behind them. He mused on what he might do to save the young woman if the nomads took the city. The thought led his mind's eye to the Sultan's instructions to Isma'il for the terms of surrender to be delivered to Manzikert, "And tell them this, tell them I, the Sultan, will take as wife the most beautiful girl among you." Derar recalled with distaste the torn gowns and tears at Berkri and Archêsh.

The arrogant Roman soldier, he cared less about. Dumrul's spies had learned the officer's identity, Bryennius, the commander of only three hundred. Derar mused on what he might do with the Roman after he had rescued his nephew. With both Dumrul and Derar after him, the Roman would get his just desserts. Derar had learned to live uneasily with the fear that Seljuk spies in the city would come to know of him. For the moment, Derar had to trust that the Horse-archer knew his work and would safeguard his identity as a Roman spy in the Sultan's court.

Derar removed his iron helmet of the pointed Iranian type, richly inlaid with silver and having a slender nasal and light mail aventail. Running artistic fingers through the sweat damp locks of his wavy hair, he watched Zaibullah lead his horse to where Farisa, veiled against the dust on her black mare, was tending his two baggage camels. The woman looked at him and then at the city. She was even slimmer from the journey, eyes as dark and bright as the desert night sky, at once alive with interest and dull with unspoken concerns. When she smiled, which was often, her full lips parted over strong white teeth. No humour played in her eyes now, as she observed the army moving into place about the fortress from where the last shouts were dying away to leave a brooding silence.

Did she think, now, of her Greek origins, Derar wondered. From her circle of acquaintances in the bazaars where she bought their needs, or from hearing the gossip of the grooms, farriers, armourers, healers and other followers of the army, she was an invaluable source of information. But would she run if she got the chance? Derar had no reservations about slavery. In the culture, it was as old as history, but in this particular instance he was beginning to have doubts.

Derar watched furtively as Zaibullah assisted Farisa with unloading the baggage and setting up camp. The Turk had once been a ghazi for the caliphate, where his courage and intelligence had come to notice. Derar's well-placed friends had told him Zaibullah had done some spying for the Caliphate when he had visited his tribal relatives. The friend of a friend had recommended him for this journey, and thus far, Zaibullah had not been found wanting. Despite his preference for the finer things of the agricultural lands over steppe and desert, Zaibullah had easily re-adopted the dress and ways of the nomads and played his part well as a hired companion. Cheap he was not: the promise of more gold and further employment at the completion of this journey together with decent treatment seemed to hold his loyalty for the moment.

Derar observed the easy way Zaibullah and Farisa co-operated to establish their black tent and camp, knowing a bond was developing between them: friendship from the woman, more from the man. He would need to be watchful, lest Zaibullah's feelings for the woman overcame his mercenary loyalty. Farisa took the lead in caring for their stock, drawing water and starting the fire, for they had not eaten since noon the day before.

Seeming to feel his gaze Farisa glanced up and Derar sensed she felt more than servitude towards him. He smiled with genuine warmth to her, and then looked away to the unfolding scene and sighed. Yes, his gold coins had saved her from an uncertain future, and there had been no end of jealousies and petty demonstrations in his extended household when he had brought her home, but his heart had been touched elsewhere.

To hide his thoughts, Derar turned on his heel, as if to check the tightness of his girth, and looked over his saddle westward along the river valley. He had planned simply to track down his brother and nephew and talk them into returning. The whole task had become more complex with the death of the former and imprisonment of the other.

Personal consequences loomed large. Somehow, Derar confronted himself, he had to either prevent the capture of the city, or rescue his nephew before or during the sack, a seemingly impossible task. In the meantime he must blend usefully into Tughrul Bey's army, maintain access to the Sultan's inner circle and appear useful at least and indispensable at best to those he betrayed. All this, remain undiscovered and pass his intelligence to the Horse-archer.

Somehow a plan would come to him, and he would yet escape down the Arsanias with his nephew and companions, hiding out amongst the pockets of Arabs in Mesopotamia. Down the river they would travel away from the Romans, perhaps to Marwanid-Kurdish Amida on the Tigris, then west to the Euphrates, to the white tents of the Arabs of Syria—people careful of horses' pedigrees and hospitable to strangers. There, Derar reasoned, they could make their way peacefully away from Roman and Seljuk alike, shunning the black tents of the brigand tribes of the desert's edge. In his mind's eye he appeared at the home of his brother, with his nephew at his elbow and the eyes of his brother's widow accepting the mixed news.

Derar turned back to his tent. He had chosen a black one in Tabriz both for its campaign utility and to blend in with the army. Neither of his companions knew his full design. The agony of deceit he withheld from them. Derar trusted Farisa. Zaibullah had already unwittingly passed one message, disguised as a boastful threat, when he had ridden to the fortress weeks ago to ascertain the whereabouts of Zobeir. Derar did not know how Zaibullah would react to his double game if he found out.

In the late afternoon, with the Seljuk army still moving into place, Derar saddled his black mare, Zanab, and rode with Bughra Dumrul and his escort to parley with the garrison. Horsetail standards and kettledrums announced their intention. Quieting his restive horse, Derar scanned the battlements but could not recognise a familiar face among the helmet shadows looking down. While they waited Derar furtively marked the tower against which he had been instructed to shoot his message arrows. This would be difficult on a dark night.

They waited, motionless except for the nod and toss of horses' heads and the breeze playing with the standards, their shadows long on the ground before them. Derar took the opportunity to examine the formidable defences.

To a blare of trumpets, the city gates swung open. A high-ranking officer, accompanied by a standard-bearer, rode out. Derar looked with keen, professional interest at the good horses, the mail and the fine weapons. The officer, an impressive, bearded man, rode boldly up to them and halted silently without ceremony, the standard-bearer to his left. It was not Bryennius.

The silence was oppressive.

Dumrul's interpreter initiated a formal greeting. "In the name of God, the merciful, the compassionate, our Sultan Tughrul Bey, Client of the Commander of the Faithful, Lawful King and Asylum of the Muslims, commands you to surrender the city."

The Roman, the low sun golden on his face and armour, made no reply. Derar admired his nerve and show of absolute confidence.

Dumrul tried again. "Berkri resisted and was shown no mercy. Archēsh surrendered and was spared the worst. Surrender now, and when our Sultan occupies Manzikert, he will take the most beautiful girl among you as his bride, but the city will be spared the excesses of an unregulated sack. The terms will not grow more generous, Roman. Nor will they be repeated."

Derar saw in a clear image the Roman horsemen and walls, the line of horses' heads and horsetail banners in the barest breeze. He had come looking for his nephew, but now found himself in a cruel war where even the horses were terrible, with their ears and manes and eyes. Derar swallowed.

The Roman allowed a long pause, then spoke, his voice ringing clearly in the Persian tongue. "Go tell the Sultan, return to his own lands. There is nothing to discuss." With that the two watchful Christians backed their horses a dozen steps away from the danger of close quarters and swinging them on their haunches, galloped for the gates.

Isma'il watched them go and uttered an oath. "Then take this for your supper, Dogs." He heaved his chestnut stallion around in a half-rear and galloped to the lines of waiting men. "Attack!" he screamed. "Attack! Attack!"

Chapter Eleven

Comes The Shepherd King

The Walls of Manzikert,
Evening, 21st August 1054

Guy watched from the battlements as Count Daniel Branas parleyed with the Seljuk officers, amongst whom he was almost certain he could make out Derar al-Adin on his black mare slyly scanning the battlements, but the light was deceptive, the low sun sending an orange glare against his eyes.

As Branas withdrew, Guy knew his dismal expectations had been met. "Here they come, men. Make ready! Remember, shoot only two-thirds the range." Guy walked along his stretch of wall, repeating the firm orders that had been passed through Balazun from Count Doukas. "Mind our men at the scarp breastworks behind the ditch."

He heard the iron gates slam shut behind Branas and the roar as the waiting nomads gave a great shout and hurled themselves forward in a dismounted, thickly massed crescent. The Seljuks carried their personal weapons and scaling ladders, their dancing standards held aloft by the boldest as their drums, fifes and trumpets screamed a deafening cacophony. Guy, shading his eyes with his hand, saw the leaders pass the furthest ballistae range sticks, then rush by the two furlong markers. Archers posted along the scarp breastworks were already engaging with disciplined arrow showers. Seljuks were falling.

Guy heard men near him utter the soldier's prayer, "Lord Jesus Christ, our God, have mercy on us, Amen."

"Ballistae!" he yelled hoarsely over the tumult. Men manning the bolt-shooting engines hunkered down in their protective galleries and peered out through the arrow slits searching for targets. "When you have a knot of them, shoot at will."

Charles, Jacques and Aram Gasparian were moving calmly up and down the wall directing and encouraging the men.

Guy watched the enemy come within easy range. "Archers!" The bowmen gave their weapons a last check and fitted arrows. "Make ready." Judging the closing distance, he knew the longer infantry bows on the wall outranged the weapons of the Seljuk horsemen, but as soon as these came into range, the defenders themselves would be showered with incoming arrows.

"At the enemy to your front, two furlongs—shoot!" sounded repeatedly from the commanders along the ramparts. With an ominous swish, hundreds of arrows leapt in a great arc from the walls. Then hundreds more in a second torrent, after which the discharge became an irregular hail as the attackers came within range of the engines and archers on the main wall.

The infantry supports on the concourse between the walls, sheltered against the fore-wall under their mantelets[63] of interwoven light branches. They were tasked to guard the sally-ports as the archers from the scarp-breastworks retired through them, and relieve any threatened point.

The hellish scene burned into some part of Guy's soul like a glimpse of the underworld. The sky was darkening and smoke was everywhere. Squinting into the setting sun, the men on the walls could only make out in the dimmest, fear-filled abstract, the multitude of their attackers. The main wall behind them glowed orange in the sunset while the battlements cast skirmishing shadows over the men. These, sweating and cursing, heaved on the screaming sinews of the ballistae, their sun-gilded helmets bobbing forward again as they placed the heavy bolts in the grooves. Archers nocked arrows and drew their bows, peering quickly through the crenelles into the darkness that rose from the river, seeking a mark for their missiles. Spearmen crouched against the stones, waiting for the moment when they would have to expose themselves to Turkish arrows, to push away a ladder or spit the men on it. Engines on platforms built into the gallery walls and atop the towers lobbed rocks or clay pots of Greek Fire into the attackers, the liquid from the bursting containers being set alight by fire-arrows.

The noise was deafening; the screaming of the wounded and fearful, the hoarse, bellowed commands of the leaders ever more urgent. Mangonels groaned as soldiers swung back on the ropes to launch another rock or fire-pot. Ballistae cracked ferociously, speeding the lethal darts on their way as Seljuk arrowheads sparked on the stone and clattered around the defenders. Every man, senses sundered, wore the look of earthly concentration as they subjected their mortal selves to this now their work.

A red glow in the west bid farewell to the sun, though the fierce day was far from over. It struck Guy how much time had passed. Several of the men under his charge had been maimed by arrows and crawled down the steps from the

---

63 Mantelet—a portable shield or protective screen to shelter a number of soldiers from enemy weapons.

wall. Four lay dead and he was ashamed that he could not name them. Glancing at the main wall, he was relieved that his own men would now be invisible to the Seljuks below them.

"They're in the ditch. Our archers are retiring from the scarp breastworks," Charles yelled, directing their men to cover the city's soldiers as they withdrew behind the fore-wall.

"We lost too many men trying to defend the scarp," Guy muttered to Jacques as the defenders of the breastworks fell back under their shields fifty feet to scramble through the sally-ports to safety.

"The infidels lost a great many more," Jacques replied. 'Nor have we finished using the ditch and breastwork to torment them."

From below and behind them the sally-port guard parties reported all was well. "Number One sally-port secure. Number Two sally-port secure." Those from the scarp breastworks sank to the ground gasping for breath. Some wept. Others cursed the heathen and looked for a place on the crowded fore-wall until the decarchs ordered them back into line. The shout went up for medical orderlies while some of the wounded in their distress cried for their mothers.

The Varangians in the right flanking tower pumped a jet of Greek Fire along the front of Guy's section of wall. He heard howls and shrieks below and braved a quick look. The very ground was afire and immolated men ran crazily, screaming and beating at the inextinguishable burning. Noting a huddled group of fifty or so in the firelight who were forcing a ladder up the fortress wall, Guy motioned four men to grab the handles of the cauldron of boiling water. They staggered under the weight of it as he guided them the few paces to where to tip it. They made ready with the unwieldy cauldron as Guy prayed none would be hit or lose their footing, spilling the scalding liquid amongst their comrades. "Now," he wheezed. The torrent sprayed with a hiss, through the purpose-designed sluice in the stonework, forward of the wall to the accompaniment of screams and oaths from below. Several bags—made of paper or other flimsy material—containing quicklime were thrown down after the boiling water, in order to cause burns and noxious vapours.

"Here!" Guy indicated a crenelle. "You and you. Here," he ordered in his basic Armenian. "Keep them away from the base of the wall, men, so they can't start knocking out the facing stones to undermine it."

A ladder searched upwards. An Armenian fisherman tried to push it away with a pitchfork, but in an instant the weight of nomads on the ladder pinned it to the wall. Encouraged, the Seljuks threw up more ladders. Tribesmen in loose trousers and horn lamellar armour stepped up, holding their silk-bound, spiral cane shields over them. A Seljuk appeared in the crenelle next to Guy where a blacksmith spitted him with a pitchfork, toppling the man backwards off the wall. From the dark a javelin transfixed the blacksmith, who with a cry collapsed onto the rampart. A Seljuk berserker entered the gap and slashed at Guy who parried with his shield and thrust with his spear but could not penetrate the man's defence, as the attacker could not strike him. A second Turk appeared on the other side of the merlon, then a third. Guy was terrified of being overwhelmed in the din and flickering firelight. Suddenly, all was black as the flames died down. The darkness was full of stabbing, screaming shadows, the clash of weapons, showers of sparks as steel struck stone and the dull thuds as shields took the impact of blows.

Guy heard the strategos' great voice above the clash of arms when a Turk facing him went down, cloven to the chin as another sheet of flame lit the scene for a moment. "Well done, d'Agiles. Carry on!" Basil Apocapes roared as he went, exalting his god and exhorting his soldiers.

"Step aside left," Jacques shouted and discharged his crossbow full into the chest of Guy's immediate antagonist.

A knot of heavily armed and armoured cataphracts loomed in the blue starlight and the few Seljuks that had gained the battlements were banished from it.

"Good. Good, men. Well done," Guy heard Jacques shout as he glanced over the wall. "But it's no use trying to push the ladders straight out with that much weight on them." The groom took a grappling hook on a rope and leaned out through a crenelle while another held the back of his belt. Jacques swung the rope and let fly the hook so it caught across a ladder, then hauled back quickly before the Turks could unfix it. "Heave! Heave!" he grunted as he pulled the flesh-laden ladder sideways. Others grasped the rope and with a whoop the defenders felt the ladder topple sideways. Jacques moved forward to shake the hook free and retrieve it before the Turks recovered. "The damned thing's snagged. Pull! Wait. Pull now!" They heaved away and were rewarded by the empty ladder appearing. Hands reached out and seized it as it fouled on the merlons.

"This is one they won't use again," a townsman exclaimed in triumph.

"You've the hang of it now. Good fellow." Jacques slapped the man on the back and moved on.

Suddenly, the attackers melted into the night. There was momentary jubilation on the wall, the leaders looking over the side, urging caution that the hasty attack had been beaten off, but the battle was far from over. Men waited at their posts, staring into the ink before them. The groans and cries from the littered space between the ditch and fore-wall covered any possibility of hearing a silent attack. Tense, exhausted, the smell of naphtha[64] and burnt flesh in their nostrils, the defenders waited. After what seemed like an eternity, the word came from Balazun and was whispered man to man through the dark along the wall, "Half stand-to."

Guy groped quietly along the rampart, immersed in the whispered, unshaven, rank-breathed, green-sweat smell that had become them in only a day. "Every second man, rest in place."

A shadowy figure approached, "D'Agiles?"

"Count Bryennius?"

---

64 Naphtha—a volatile, highly inflammable, limpid, strong-smelling, bituminous liquid, likened to or comprising petroleum or paraffin oil: used for lighting, in solvents and weaponised as an anti-personnel or anti-materiel incendiary.

"Yes. You and your men did well. They hit you hardest."

Jacques, coming from the other direction and unaware of the count's presence, interrupted. "Guy, you'd better get some rest. This night's barely started."

Guy clapped Jacques on the shoulder in acknowledgement. "I have to sit down," he said to Bryennius. With his back to a merlon, he felt for the ballista frame in the gallery-space to his left, drew forth his water skin and took a long draught. In a soft ripple of mail coat, Bryennius sat beside him. Guy could tell he had been in the fighting: there was that unspoken knowing.

"I think I saw Derar out there," Guy said, offering Bryennius the goatskin.

"I saw him." Bryennius passed back the skin without taking a drink. "I have some, thank you. That tower on your right flank is the one he should shoot his messages against. I have men posted there to retrieve them, but keep an eye out anyway."

Guy was utterly spent from two desperate fights in a day. Mind, body and emotions had all raced: now he was drained. "Is that the best they can do?"

Bryennius thought before answering. "That was a heavy rush, but it was only like a fit of rage. In a deliberate attack, they will use fire and stone-throwing engines to soften us up. First they will use waves of second grade troops, tribesmen most likely, to tire us out and exhaust our supply of arrows and other weapons. Finally they will assault with professional heavy infantry, into a breach if they can make one."

Guy pictured the depressing images and sighed. "Will they come again tonight?"

"Probably. Just before dawn most likely, out of the dark while you are silhouetted against the first light."

Guy accepted the warning. "Are you posted on the wall?"

"No. With Basil, mostly. At any one time I have fifty men under orders to reinforce any threatened part of the wall. And I have to keep a reserve of another hundred with saddled horses, ready to defeat any penetration. So, with some resting, others under arms and the remainder doing whatever needs doing, it is quite busy. I'm still supervising the scouting, but Isaac has taken over much of the day-to-day running of it. You're here for a while?"

"I suppose so," Guy replied. "I don't know when we'll be relieved or by whom. It isn't as though Basil has endless numbers of troops."

Guy fought off sleep. It was quite dark and he remembered the moon rising that morning. He now missed it and would have been comforted by it. How far he had come, and with such hopes, for this—trapped in a besieged fortress with a fine horse and love unspoken. In a day the wall had become his world and he could imagine no end to it, as though he were in the grip of some vast design from which there was no escape. The whispered conversations along the wall seemed small in the immensity of the world. His thoughts strayed to the night sky and the diminutive nature of his reality under it. That reminded him he had never seen Bryennius at prayer. Overturning the desire to look sideways at the Roman, Guy asked, "Do you believe in God?"

There was a long pause before Bryennius answered. "The proof is all around," he gestured with a sweep of his arm. Then, to the softest scrape of a nailed boot on the stones, the count rose, saying, "I have duties to attend to. Keep well, Guy." In a moment, he was gone.

They slept in snatches, the men rousing those to take watch with tired taps on the shoulders, or a shake of the leg. During the third watch, word was passed from the right that large numbers of enemy had entered the town with the probable intent of looting it.

Guy was summoned to orders, on the wall overlooking the village. Taking Aram Gasparian with him, Guy followed the short, helmeted, lamellar-armoured guide along the starlit rampart, through the heavy walkway doors of the dark, candlelit cavern of the tower and onto the next section. There, half a dozen armoured figures were grouped around the stocky frame of Count Doukas. He, coif loose around his neck and conical helmet pushed back from his brown bearded face, acknowledged Guy's arrival with a nod. Antony Lascaris and Oleg were part of the whispered discussion on the walls. Guy assumed they would be part of whatever was to occur.

Doukas outlined the plan. "The enemy are in the village," he started in low, deliberate tones, "and somewhat distracted, it seems, by the ample stocks of wine we so negligently left there." There were grim smirks in the night.

"Our object is to teach the Sultan's hordes that Manzikert will be no easy prey for the Seljuk hawk. We will do this by causing mass casualties and burning the town so it provides them no cover, no shelter and no firewood. The assault group is assembling on the concourse between the walls now. As soon as we're ready, archers will send flaming arrows into the far side of the town so the timber structures catch fire." Doukas paused, looking around to make sure all knew their parts. Sensing no hesitation or uncertainty, he continued. "When the flames are sufficiently advanced, the assault group, a hundred each of Varangians, Normans, Romans and townsmen led by me, will leave by two sally-ports, form up in the ditch, then attack in two waves close together. The third wave will remain behind the scarp merlons to cover our withdrawal."

Guy glanced behind them and sensed the heavily armoured troops forming up in the space between the walls. Priests moved amongst them, crosses high, softly chanting prayers accompanied by the kneeling soldiers. "Lord Jesus Christ, our God, have mercy on us, Amen."

Before the walls were the close-packed, sun-bleached little wooden houses of the poor. Beyond them in a huge, irregular crescent in the plain of the river valley, the campfires of the Seljuks winked in the night. From the village came the noise of shouting and breakage.

The details were covered in Doukas' orders: how archers and ballistae on the walls would support the attack; when musicians on the walls would sound horns to warn of Seljuk reinforcements; how engineers would carry clay pots of naphtha into the burning village to ensure the destruction by fire; and the sequence of withdrawal.

Doukas laced up his coif and strapped his helmet down over it, signalling an end to discussion. As flaming arrows streaked away by the dozen, the men commanding the assault party descended by the stairs to the concourse between the walls. Led by Doukas and at an unspoken sign from their commanders, the ranks turned and groped their way to the respective sally-ports, the starlight glinting softly on helmets and shields, spears and battle axes. Two at a time, they left the small, strongly guarded doors that were kept open to enable their return.

Asking Aram to inform their men of what was happening and have them stand-to, Guy turned to watch the unfolding drama below him.

A line of fires had started in the far side of the town, a full bowshot from the walls. The flames took hold quickly in the dry wood and spread rapidly, the smoke rising straight up in a blue plume. Against yellow-red flames, he could discern milling nomads, intent on looting. Dark shapes deployed in the ditch, here and there stumbling over the slain. Ladders, each the height of a mounted man, were thrown against the side of the ditch, then the assault troops paused, awaiting the signal.

At a wave of Doukas' spear arm, the first wave rose from the ditch and quickly formed a double line, axemen and spearmen to the fore, bowmen and torchbearers at their elbows. Guy watched the refused-centre form as the flanks of the line went forward more quickly in order to draw the enemy into the centre. "So that's what Doukas was training them for that day," he mused with grim admiration.

The phalanx of the second wave waited, then they too went over, a spear cast behind the first. The third remained impatiently behind the scarp breastworks, to cover the withdrawal of those who had gone into the town.

Guy saw the bobbing torches start forward amongst the houses and clearly heard the shouts and clash of weapons. There were screams of anguish from the dying—those who did not fall silently from the spear points, or topple cloven and soundless to the paths where a day earlier children had played and washing waved in the breeze. On the walls, the watchers saw the iron tide, raw with rage and determination, surge into the surprised, wine-wasted tribesmen and *haşer*[65]. Firelight showed through a window as the doors were burst open and mailed figures entered with flailing steel.

The Seljuks in the village stood little chance. Constant raids had conditioned the invaders to despise their Roman and Armenian enemies, who would shut themselves up behind walls like pigs in sties, only the easier to be terrified, herded and slaughtered like swine. The nomads caught in the village, drunk and distracted by looting any small treasure that might add to the few comforts of their rough camp, had not expected such a violent sortie from the fortress. Trapped against the flames through which they could only escape by dashing in

---

65 *Haşer*- ordinary citizens drafted to their Sultan's army and paid a wage.

twos and threes, most turned to the fight. Wherever knots of them tried to form a defensive front, clay pots of naphtha were hurled against them from behind the assaulting Christians, spattering them with the terrifying mixture that would ignite at the slightest spark.

The tide of Christians seemed to rise from the shadows and engulf them, the reflection of the flames making it appear as if their very helmets and shields were afire. Bearded Vikings, with great shouts calling on pagan and Christian gods alike to protect them, swung their long-handled, double-handed axes, smashing through the flimsy cane shields and brushing aside the light Iranian swords. Heavily armoured Normans, clean-shaven and screaming the strange tongue of the Latins, drove in with undergrasp spears, the arrows of the tribesmen useless against the iron bosses of their long shields. With these mercenaries were the townsmen and peasants of the area, fighting with fear, desperation and pride.

All were urged on by the indomitable Theophanes Doukas, ploughing into the nomads like a one-man torrent, screaming all the while, "Give it to them, Manzikert. Give it to the sons of bitches. You there, archers, don't just gape at the heathen, pour in't them. We're on show here. Don't just poke at 'em like kids looking for tadpoles. Stick the bastards." Interpreters struggled to bawl over the tumult, Doukas' orders in the different languages of the soldiers.

Many nomads died there, until the survivors fled and the hot flames rose higher in the night. As the fight petered out, Guy could hear Doukas' roar, "Good! Very good, men! Make about. Reform. No running there. Make about. You there, there, with the fire, make sure everything is well alight after us. Close up. Close up! Retire. Retire. Spears to the enemy, men. No running!"

A horn sounding from the wall warned that the main enemy encampment was responding to the sudden eruption in the night. Guy heard approaching hoof beats and could sense small knots of horsemen drawing closer, but all the Seljuks could do was maintain a desultory harassment of Doukas's sally, the engines on the wall keeping them at bay. Guy hurried to his own men, in case the skirmish in the village drew on another general assault by the Turks.

He could hear the din as the defenders on the fore-wall started shooting, covering Doukas's assault force as the men dropped down into the ditch with their relatively few dead and wounded and filed back through the protecting third wave. Inside the fore-wall, the sergeants and decarchs pushed the assault party back into rough ranks, where nerve-strained men overjoyed with their own survival in the inferno they had created, sank to the ground. Youths carried water buckets along the ranks, ladling out the cool liquid. Medical orderlies of the garrison and nuns from the monastery that had been converted into a makeshift hospital, bent over the wounded. Mounted medical orderlies, their quiet, patient horses saddled with extra stirrups, gently lifted the maimed and bore them inside the main wall to the hospitals. Priests in their sombre mantles moved amongst the men and murmured prayers and forgiveness for the souls of those who had sinned in the death of their fellow man, infidels that they were. "Lord Jesus Christ, have mercy on us."

"Lord Jesus Christ," Guy repeated, "have mercy on us."

Three nuns and some women of the city appeared as black forms in the dim blue light. Mounting the ramparts, they brought food and drink to the famished, thirsty soldiers. More than one nun, Guy supposed, took the vows because war had widowed them or stolen their betrothed. Who could know what thoughts they kept to themselves as they offered succour to strangers. Gently they spoke, softly they moved, with the muffled sounds of urns and baskets and the scent of cold roast meat, cheese, fresh baked bread and watered wine.

A feminine form came close and held out a damp cloth with which Guy gratefully wiped his tired eyes and grubby, unshaven face. It was Joaninna Magistros, he could tell, her abundant dark hair tied in a light scarf. She had a shawl around her shoulders, for the air this night seemed suddenly cool. He finished by rubbing the rough cloth firmly over his filthy hands. Guy was amazed at how calm and commanding Joaninna appeared, the younger women moving quickly and efficiently by her suggestions to share out their meals. He could not see Irene amongst the shifting, murmuring crowd on the ramparts.

Joaninna noticed. "She's on the southern wall where they fear the next attack."

"How is she? Please tell her I'm well."

"You had no need to ask," she said, handing him another crust of bread. "Irene is well enough, given all." Then she moved on.

Before dawn, they stood-to again as a heavy assault was mounted on the southern wall, the Seljuks searching for a weak spot as they endeavoured to wear down the physical and moral strength of the defenders.

With daylight the hot sun rose like a brazen shield over the walls of Manzikert to reveal the ditch and plain beyond littered with corpses, the air tinged with dust and smoke and thick with the stench of burnt flesh and naphtha. The stones of the walls grew hot while men wilted in the rays. Guy watched Jacques approach along the wall, and was surprised at how dirty, dishevelled and utterly weary his man looked.

Jacques similarly regarded Guy and said, "You look done in. You should try and get some rest."

It struck Guy now, that they had endured only the first night and day of whatever might come. Everything before in his life now seemed remote. Even the ride from Archēsh had the distant air of long ago and insignificance in its consequences. "It is only the second day, Jacques," he replied wearily. "You have worked wonders and you also must rest."

Some hours later, Balazun, with Bryennius, Doukas and Selth, inspected the section of the defences under the Norman knight's command. The soldiers were instructed to clear their personal belongings from the walls as the bundles impeded manoeuvre along the fighting platform. Workmen from the town arrived, hauling rolls of felt from warehouses and placed them along the inside of the wall as sheltering awnings. Made of heavy felt, these served a double purpose, for soaked with vinegar, they could be used to suppress fire and if suspended an arms' length in front of the walls, they would soften the impact of rocks hurled by besieging mangonels.

More workmen and soldiers hauled rocks, bundles of arrows, ballista bolts, javelins, stones and urns of drinking water, waste-oil and Greek Fire to the walls. Parties of the boldest youths passed through the sally-ports to retrieve bundles of used arrows and darts from outside as well as any Christian dead. By mid-afternoon, all was still as those who had defended the walls that night, rested in preparation for what next befell them as sentries watched over the smoke-shrouded Seljuk camp.

The Seljuk Camp at Manzikert,
Sunset, 22nd August 1054

Tughrul Bey had brought his army to Manzikert: this vexatious fortress he would subdue before turning his attention to the stricken caliphate that awaited his clemency in Madinat al-Salam. Escorted by squadrons of palace guards on bay horses, the shepherd king arrived the morning after the night skirmish in the burning town. Dressed in plain white robes, he rode a sumptuously caparisoned Arabian, gifted several years before by Nasr ad-Daulah of Amida. Irritated by the repeated failures, he ordered another attack late that afternoon of the second day and watched impatiently as the tribes with their scaling ladders had again flung themselves at the battlements. Grimly, the Seljuk ruler watched his subjects fall back once more from the walls, where the Romans, in daylight, had re-occupied the scarp breastwork to increase the range of their missiles. Having seen enough, Tughrul Bey and his entourage rode a lap of the fortress, studying the ground and the walls before retiring to the comforts of his pavilion, from where he could hear the reports of the emirs.

Derar had ridden with them, noting that at one point the track bypassed a small rocky outcrop and veered sharply inside ballistae range. He noticed a scattering of arrow shafts sticking in the ground well short of the track. It occurred to him then that no arrows had struck near the bridle track, which he had thought was within range. It seemed odd to him and he made a mental note to avoid that place.

Late that night, Derar pulled off his armour and boots and laid his weapons by his side. He slid gratefully under the cover with Farisa. Laying there he listened to the sound of her breathing and the murmur of the camp.

She listened to him listening to her. "Are you all right?"

"Yes," he replied before his thoughts turned inward. A deliberate attack against the eastern wall was planned for the following night, the tribesmen taking much of the day to get into position by a long and circuitous march out of sight of the defenders. He had to warn the Romans.

The Seljuk preoccupation with the other side of the fortress enabled Derar to steal away when the moon was low. Heart thumping in his chest, he sped the arrow warning of the imminent attack. He heard with satisfaction the iron tip strike the side of the tower, the strange oath of the Armenian sentry and the scuff of booted feet on the ramparts.

The attack, launched the following night, was easily beaten off. Derar watched as the wounded and maimed streamed back into the camp. Standing there, his mind dealt with the calamitous choices with which he was faced. The Seljuks had welcomed him and afforded him every courtesy. They were aware of his quest to find his nephew and having respect for family affairs, did not press too heavily about the matter. Derar had told no one, apart from Farisa and Zaibullah, of the whereabouts of Zobeir al-Adin. Zaibullah knew of the imprisonment of his nephew but despite the Turk's previous visit to Manzikert, nothing of Derar's continuing contract with the Romans. Derar knew the moral pressures were already difficult and would get worse. The penalty for failure to maintain the pretence did not bear thinking of. Already he felt in the glances of the beaten men filing into the fire lit camp, accusations that logic told him were not there. With an uneasy feeling in the pit of his stomach, he retired to his small campaign tent and allowed Farisa to undress him and start to work the tight muscles of his neck and back.

The Seljuk Camp, Manzikert,
Morning, 24th August 1054

Derar had just finished a meagre breakfast of bread and strong coffee when uproar broke out in the camp near the Sultan's pavilion. Word soon spread that the Sultan, some advisors and a detachment of *gulâmân-I suray* had been taking a morning ride on the bridle track around the circuit walls, when a storm of arrows and darts from the fortress walls had engulfed them. There had been three rapid volleys, enough to transfix and wound men and maim many of their horses. The Sultan's mount, not the gift horse but another, fell mortally pierced with darts, the guards slipping from their horses to cover Tughrul with their shields as they withdrew. People in the camp cited it as proof of the cowardly, perfidious ways of the Romans, as they shook their weapons and roared abuse at the walls.

Derar instinctively knew where the ambush had occurred, the rocky place where the track deviated towards the fortress, the outcrop making a perfect aiming mark. He reasoned it was a deliberately planned event, not a random opportunity by soldiers on the walls. This he mulled over in his mind as he walked through the strung out camp to the tent on the knoll where the Sultan conducted his councils. He entered and mingled with the group of about fifty crowded in the tent while another two hundred or so lesser chiefs waited outside. Those inside sat cross-legged on the ground, reclined on cushions or sat on overturned pails. Or like him, they stood.

There were the colourful tribal emirs, a few more ornately dressed in silk brocade coats than their rough-clad followers. Some were independent and troublesome enough to consistently test the Sultan's patience and leadership. The black clad emirs Samuk, Kāfūr and Kijaziz, conversed easily together. Their followers numbered in the thousands of tents. Mighty Dinar kept his own counsel, glaring dourly, his hard eyes catching Derar's so the Arab looked away. The paunchy, shifty-eyed Seljuk quartermaster, Erdal, with his weak smile kept close to the influential Samuk.

Many of the Sultan's relatives were present. Ibrahim Inal was there, probably so the Sultan could keep an eye on his tempestuous half-brother and draw on the chieftain's experience from the raid on Artsn. Tughrul Bey's father in law, Osketsam, stood close by keeping a crafty ear on any conversation of Ibrahim Inal's. No one seemed to know where Kutlumush was: still estranged Derar was told.

Close to those two close relatives of the Sultan, was the Emir Arsuban, who while attentive to them, maintained a paternal eye on his own son, a beautiful young man in his elegant armour, assigned to ride with the foolhardy religious zealot, Koupagan. Another minor prince of the royal line, who had participated in the raids of 1047 and 1048, gave unwanted advice to Isma'il, still smarting from his failure to capture Manzikert four days before. Isma'il could scarcely conceal his annoyance: for the Romans had destroyed, through the ruse of an apparently undefended camp, the earlier raid at Stragna River, killing Crown Prince Hasan in the process; and punished the subsequent raid at Kapetrou. Standing beside Isma'il, Hurr held, if her bemused expression was any guide, a similarly disdainful view of the vain young nobleman. She wore no sensuous silks now, her pleasing countenance made handsome by the armour and weapons she wore.

These people would tear him apart if they knew of Derar's double game. He did not particularly consider it treachery, that being the province of those who would assist the nomads in their impending conquest of the caliphate. These Seljuks with their almond eyes and Asian complexions, stood strong as the rising power of the Muslim world from the Oxus to Aleppo. They knew it. All knew it.

Persian courtiers, Arab mercenaries and others who dealt with the planning and administration of the army, gathered near the Sultan's chair. The Persian scribe, Ames, busied himself self-importantly over papers while Prince Alkan, the commander of the Sultan's troops from Chorasmia, carried on a self-consciously earnest conversation with the prince of the Daylami infantry. Both were resplendent in expensive armour as if they knew history would remember them, Derar found himself thinking.

Looking on were the senior officers of the Sultan's professional army: youthful palace guards, *Gulâmân-I sunray*; lavishly equipped imperial guards, *Hassa ordusa*; landed knights, *Sipahiyan*, and *Gaziyân* raiders. Others commanded specialist siege engineers and fire troops as well as the myriad of others pressed into service or hired to equip, feed and doctor the army in the field. Many were

Turks recruited as child soldiers by the Abbasids who rose through merit. Now, reading the wind, they had thrown in their lot with Tughrul Bey.

To Derar's surprise, a small number of Franks, already far from home when serving the Romans, had travelled ideologically and geographically still further, by allying themselves with the nomads. They were universally despised and mistrusted as opportunistic land-grabbers, but temporarily useful ones.

Less surprising, a handful of Georgian and Armenian renegades had joined with the Seljuks and largely adopted the dress of the nomads who crowded on the borders of their ancient lands. With these was the Roman officer who had turned traitor to his kind at Archēsh.

This man Derar approached. "Theodore Ankhialou," he greeted in Greek. "The hospitality of the army is to your liking?"

Ankhialou merely looked at him, the hint of sly insolence still in him.

Despite neither liking nor trusting Ankhialou, Derar sympathised with him: seemingly trapped by closing doors, he had taken the only one that appeared open to him. It was widely known that the Roman-Armenian woman, who had escaped from Archēsh with an unknown Frank on a stolen mare, had been Ankhialou's special interest. Both were generally supposed to be now in Manzikert.

Derar thought back to the fight at the wadi, the Kelt on a captured Seljuk mare and Bryennius' questions about a missing beauty. The tale of a knight riding into the jaws of death to rescue a maiden from a doomed city appealed to his romanticism, and Farisa's, for she had commented on what love it must be.

Ankhialou's special interest or not, it was also commonly held, especially by those who had a vested interest in the Sultan siring a male heir, that the woman retained her virtue and was thus a suitable bride for a caliph. Others argued that, between Ankhialou and the Frank, chastity was impossible, especially amongst unbelievers. How anyone could claim certainty was beyond Derar, but it crossed his mind that Ankhialou would want to preclude any interest from other claimants to the woman, by hinting at his carnal prowess.

Ankhialou grunted that the hospitality was as one would expect.

"How long will the city hold out?" Derar asked.

"Not long. They're divided and the governor doesn't have many soldiers."

Derar regarded Ankhialou keenly. His knowledge of the city's layout and Roman habits was potentially useful. "You want it done quickly?"

"It should've happened this morning. I told Isma'il what to do," Ankhialou snapped as he looked more closely at Derar. "I'll take her back. And I will kill the Kelt."

Derar was surprised at the emotion displayed. "A commendable intent, but you mistake my interest. I am no voyeur and have my own reasons for wanting Manzikert to fall." Secretly, he was happy for the gossip about Ankhialou and the woman to continue, for it distracted any idle curiosity away from Zobeir al-Adin in Manzikert's dungeons. He concluded Ankhialou was too emotionally unreliable and sought a way to finish the conversation, "It is jihad and must be finished qui ..."

All fell silent as the Sultan entered. Tughrul Bey made light of the attempt on his life that morning, but Derar was judge enough of men to know the Sultan was livid at the simple cunning of the plan and how narrow had been his escape. After sitting, with a show of calm openness towards ideas, Tughrul invited comment on the best means of reducing Manzikert.

The debates ranged to and fro. Some pressed for the city to be invested by a stay-behind force while the main army ravaged wider Armenia. The second group countered, equally eloquently, that the fortress was too powerful and the garrison too aggressive to be left intact, threatening the lines of the invading columns. The latter voices argued that the Romans were fully capable of giving battle to the withdrawing Seljuks when they were most vulnerable, laden with booty and prisoners. "Remember," one said, "the raid by Ibrahim Inal and Kutlumush wasn't the ride-around they would have us all believe. They, we, were lucky. Artsn was rich and unwalled, but we barely escaped entrapment and destruction at Kapetrou." Angry murmurs of agreement and dissent followed.

Tughrul saw his chance. "Which is why I am here!"

A hush came down like a mist. Derar watched as Ibrahim Inal's features remained unmoved, but he guessed the emir was piqued at this public slight.

Samuk had been silent during this quarrelling but now he stood. The Sultan gestured him to speak and all listened. "Remember we overpowered Berkri and Archēsh in days," he began, pacing the tent, eyes flashing, white teeth gleaming in his beard, a straight sword in its fine scabbard swinging against his booted leg. "But the Romans here have gathered or fired the grass for leagues around. Thus there is little fodder and we cannot all stay indefinitely. The fortress is so powerful, and the garrison too warlike, we now see, to leave only a small force. The siege train with the infantry and more supplies will arrive within days. We here might annoy the Romans, for a few more days until our siege engines and infantry arrive. Then we could leave the infantry here, with some cavalry support, and engineers of course, to reduce the walls."

Derar al-Adin saw the knowing glances between Tughrul Bey, Bughra Dumrul and Isma'il.

"As they do that," Samuk continued, looking around at the intent faces, "we despatch the light troops to ravage the countryside. There're rich pickings to be had. Strike terror into their hearts, destroy their will to resist, provoke their armies into the open so we can confuse them with our speed and destroy them with our numbers at the right time and place. We'll exploit the weak and vulnerable places, then return and deal with Manzikert at leisure. Above all, we must capture the key frontier fortresses and empty these lands so our people and their herds can settle here."

Emren Dirse sidled up alongside Derar, muttering under his breath in the Persian tongue, just loud enough for the Arab to hear, "Samuk feels the call of lovelies and loot, and wants to be free of old Tughrul's iron hand while he pillages and kills, but he speaks a cruel logic."

Derar tried not to show his astonishment at the direct criticism, of what they were about to do, from this high-born Seljuk warrior.

The Sultan stifled further debate. "Leave us. I will pronounce what is to be done."

Derar made to go but Tughrul motioned him to stay. It was soon clear that the Sultan had determined on the plan already: Tughrul wished to spy out frontier country himself, drive off any Roman relief force and conquer a sizeable slice of the Byzantine Empire's territory, thus earning for himself the renown Ibrahim Inal and Kutlumush boasted. Samuk had simply acted out the part of informed general consent to lull the emirs into thinking they had a voice in decisions. Another method for this, Derar was learning, was for the Sultan to commit the tribes to assaulting the walls. In the bloody repulses they learned a harsh lesson: that without Tughrul Bey's genius for organisation and collecting the materiel resources for war, the tribes were incapable of defeating the Romans.

The following morning, marauders were despatched in their tens of thousands across the land to destroy, rob and kill as many of the unbelievers—those unworthy of enslavement—as could be found.

Koupagan led the northern, right-flank column. With that group, Arsuban's son led his father's tents, while the father remained with the Sultan's council. The huge raid, comprising many thousands of Seljuk and Kurdish light horse, rode north. Detachments of these widespread right-flank columns would feel their way north-eastward to destroy the Christian settlements towards the Caucasus. Koupagan Bey's main raid would move north of Kars and ravage the country from Vanard westward to Baberd, finding a way to the fabled Roman cities of Caesarea and Trebizond.

Dinar led the left-flank column along the Arsanias to the west, seeking to awe the Marwanid Kurds, pillage Taron Theme and sack Mush, then explore the route through to the rich Byzantine city of Melitene. Throughout they would fan out and pillage.

The long-haired horsemen of the left flank raid rode south, seeking the places the Armenian captives called Sim Mountain. Tughrul, in the centre, would leave troops to invest Manzikert, then advance on the key Roman fortress-city of Karin and attempt to capture it with the main body of the army.

The silent watchers on the walls of Manzikert would understand from the breadth and movement of the dust clouds that the entire land was being subjected to awful depredations and know their own fate when the columns returned.

That night the church bells started to toll. Sound and shadow covered the stealthy figure of Derar, as he stole to the fortress wall and released another message-bearing shaft into the fortress. At first light a messenger dove rose from the ramparts of the citadel and winged northwest towards Karin.

The Seljuk Camp near Manzikert,
Morning, 26th August 1054

Derar awoke before his fifth dawn outside the walls of Manzikert and quickly pulled on his unwashed shirt and dusty boots. He had voiced a preference to stay with the besieging troops at Manzikert, but the Sultan had ordered him to accompany his own centre-column. Thus Farisa and he rose and saddled their horses, leaving Zaibullah to guard their camp and attempt, should the fortress fall, to rescue Zobeir al-Adin. The church bells still tolled in the fortress as Derar and Farisa prepared themselves for the ride.

They overheard the Sultan ride by with Dumrul and Isma'il. "What is that unceasing, frightful clamour?" the Sultan asked.

The Seljuk spymaster looked dismissively towards the fortress. "The unbelievers at their prayers. It shows how terrified they are."

Tughrul glanced contemptuously at Dumrul. "So terrified that they've driven us off, several times!" He turned to Isma'il. "Get this place into order while I'm away. Clear away the bodies lest we all die of the foul vapours and pestilence that comes with them. Prepare for mining and an all-out assault, soon, within days, of my return. Be quick. I'll not be gone long."

Derar al-Adin chose his black mare, Zanab, while Farisa rode her mare and led chestnut Qurmul as their spare. With their cloaks, water skins and rations firmly strapped on and their weapons about them, they mounted and rode with Emren Dirse, a bowshot behind the Sultan's standards.

Derar and Emren Dirse had been brought closer together by the fate of their relatives. Trotting northwest out of the valley, they paused on the high ground and looked back towards Manzikert to see the blackened hills around, the plain turning to brown dust by the hooves and the fortress defiant amongst a sea of black tents.

"Look," exclaimed Emren, pointing to the eastern steppe leading to Archēsh, "the siege train and infantry are starting to arrive. That'll finish the unbelievers." He turned in his saddle and flashed a smile at Derar. "I hope they don't break in before we return. For the Romans of Manzikert will be weaker by then, and I want my father's horse and the head of the man who stole her—after he tells me how he came by her and where the old man is."

They cantered forward to the lead of Emren's two hundred tents. Derar could see the Sultan and his party ahead: seven horsetail standards amongst them, a camel with the Sultan's tall personal banner as a rallying point and kettledrummers mounted on mules to relay battle orders. Far beyond the Sultan was the screen, well-spaced out on a broad front, killing, raping and plundering as they went. Derar could see the smoke from the fired peasants' huts and the cultivated fields trampled beneath the hooves. Their horses shying at the grotesque forms, they rode over the outraged bodies of people who had thought themselves out of the way of the warring armies,

Late in the afternoon, they descended from the higher ground with its craggy places, to the streamside settlement of Dvaradzo-Daph. From the smoke and screaming as they rode into the outlying areas, Derar knew how ghastly it would be. "Stay close," he warned Farisa.

They camped that night, amid the spitted old people and children cut down amongst their burnt houses, sheds and enclosures. With the air thick from the smoke, the nomads gathered around fires, roasting sheep and goats and drinking the wine they found for the taking. For firewood, they laid beams across the doorways of the little houses and hitching teams of oxen or horses to the heavy timber, simply pulled the dwellings apart to loud cries of applause. The gold and silver found was started back to Tabriz on baggage camels and captured horses. Hacks, saddles and what little arms and armour were found, were claimed by those who happened on them. Then the brutalised survivors were herded together. Through that long night of tears and anguish, the women were raped in front of their men, who except for a few kept as slaves, were then killed with swords.

Sick at heart, Derar stumbled from the fire-lit, hellish scene with its cries and lamentations. In the three-quarter moonlight he tripped on something in the darkness and found Emren Dirse similarly indisposed, sitting on a rock. He recognised the emir by the set of his felt cap, brooding shoulders and the warhorse grazing nearby. "What ails, friend?"

There was a long silence before Emren responded. "Dandanqan was not like this, Derar. Battle is one thing—but I have no heart for this."

Derar heaved a long sigh and joined him on the rock. "Why did you come?"

"To solve the fate of my father and find his chestnut mare." Emren looked at the moon and continued. "Borne along on the folly of my father and the avarice of his people. I am nought but a prince of thieves."

They let silence reign between them until Derar heard a sound behind him. He did not turn. So complete was the devastation and so strong their host, he felt no fear but, sensed it was Farisa with their horses. She had taken the bits from their mouths and had been holding them while they grazed greedily on the green grass of the valley floor. There was a little food and water on his saddle. Not feeling hungry, but with the soldier within warning him to take some nourishment, Derar ate and drank a little. Finding a flat place close to Emren Dirse, he wrapped himself in his cloak, and lay down beside Farisa, their horses knee-hobbled, the reins held in their hands. The whole time she had said nothing and avoided his eyes.

Derar stirred in the dawn and found Emren Dirse, still sitting, dozing.

Then Derar saw the two skinny figures, a teenage girl and her younger brother, at the foot of the emir's rock.

Emren awoke. "If they'd tried to run away during the night, I would not have stopped them," Emren said. "But they couldn't understand my language." With that he rose and turned, bellowing for an old man of his tribe, whom he ordered to take the two captives with the column of prisoners and booty that would be chivvied away in the long walk to Tabriz, thence to the slave markets of Baghdad, Bukhara and Samarqand. "Take them safely to the house of my aunt in Tabriz."

Derar walked off and bought a small urn of pungent coffee from a Seljuk boiling a kettle of water into which he had dropped a handful of the berries. Returning to where Farisa was caring for their horses, he poured cups for the woman, Emren Dirse and himself. They squatted on their booted heels, sipping the black liquid, watching the scene of rough horsemen saddling up. The dead looked pale in the morning light. Their blood had dried black or soaked into brown splotches in the grass while the air reeked of smoke from still smouldering dwellings. Bawling emirs were organising baggage camels and carts, supervising the whipping of the prisoners onto their feet.

Wretched women and children shuffled past. Some maintained a look of defiance that the mounted guards would soon beat or rape out of them. The more enterprising had thought to snatch whatever they could from the ruins of their lives, anything that might serve as a moral or physical support during the march into captivity, which they could scarcely imagine and only dread. Derar dropped his gaze, stared at the ground in front of him and finished his coffee.

Farisa and Derar mounted and rode in the van, behind Emren's two horsetail standards as the Seljuk host trotted northward along the stream that flowed from Dvaradzo-Daph to the plain of Basen. Emren rode silently on his dun mare, ruling with heavy hand, forbidding any distraction after plunder. Such a pace did he set his well-mounted men, that a messenger from Tughrul galloped forward to tell the van to slow down so the rear might keep up.

In the early afternoon, Derar and Emren Dirse spearheaded ten thousand horse—tribal Seljuks, Turkic ghulams, Kurds and a sprinkling of renegade Christians—down into the fertile plain of Basen, decorated as it was with little hamlets and by fields of cattle with other domestic animals.

North of the stream the impregnable fortress of Kapetrou on its precipitous rock had stout triple-walls with many towers, all crowded with soldiers and engines. Forward of the walls, forbidding earthworks comprising a palisaded mound guarded by a thick bed of stakes and other obstacles behind a broad, deep ditch, enclosed fields containing the town's livestock and gardens. Many soldiers and their horses manned these works, sunlight on their spear points. They clashed their weapons and roared loudly for the Seljuks to come and fight.

An emir, with the insolence of success against Berkri and Archēsh, led his men forward to be met by such a storm of darts that many were killed and the remainder driven off.

The Sultan saw it. "We'll not bother with this place. Ride on and fire the villages."

This was done as the Seljuk host jogged west to where the plain narrowed to its head near the village named Du. While this hamlet was massacred pitilessly, Tughrul Bey rode with a small group of his advisors to the crest of a promontory from where they could see in the distance a mighty fortress, stronger than any yet encountered. There was debate whether it was the famous citadel of Theodosiopolis, or Karin, or Artsn of the Romans—rebuilt.

At length, the Sultan silenced the babble and summoned Theodore Ankhialou, who informed them the fortress city was Karin of the Armenians, called Theodosiopolis by Romans. During their conquest and occupation, the Arabs had called it Kālīkalā. The ruins of Artsn, he explained, lay a short ride beyond by the Western Euphrates.

Derar considered the battlements of Karin and the ground around it. It looked impregnable to the forces the Sultan had with him. Moreover, if they had attempted to storm it, they would have been vulnerable to an attack against their rear from the Roman troops at Kapetrou.

"Leave me," commanded Tughrul Bey, sitting on a rock and staring into the west. The sun sank behind a bank of clouds, turning them golden and sending gilded shafts of light into the eyes of the watchers from the promontory.

Derar al-Adin, dismounted and holding Qurmul, waited listlessly, slapping the ends of the reins softly against his boots in physical boredom and spiritual desolation. In the lower ground of the Plain of Basen, he saw the raiders fan out, looting and pillaging. His mind turned to the intricacies of the shepherd king's strategy and tactics. The Sultan's object was to secure the major frontier fortresses and stabilise the border with the Christian lands before preparing to move on Baghdad. As the Horse-archer had correctly discerned after the fight at the wadi, the Sunnis of Baghdad would not be too disheartened should Tughrul Bey fail in Vaspurakan, despite their hope the Seljuks would protect them from Iranian Shi'ite Būyids and the Shi'ite Fatimids of Cairo.

The fortresses of Karin and Kapetrou obviously could not be carried with the means the Sultan had with him. Moreover they were too far inside Roman territory to pose a serious threat to the Seljuk rear around Tabriz, when Tughrul moved on Baghdad. More importantly, protracted Seljuk siege operations against either would uncover the Sultan's army to a stroke from the Roman armies now mustering, according to Tughrul's spies, at Caesarea. As it was the far-flung Turkish bands, with the indiscipline inherent in pillaging, were vulnerable to Roman counter-attack.

But Manzikert? Manzikert, isolated and defiant, remained a burr under the Seljuk saddlecloth. Guarding the south-eastern approaches to Vaspurakan, Armenia, Taron and Mesopotamia, as well as providing a mounting base for Roman attacks on Her or Tabriz, the fortress posed a definite threat to the Seljuk rear.

Derar mulled over this as if he were the Sultan. He concluded that Tughrul would return to Manzikert to force the capture of the city, thus wresting Vaspurakan from the Christians. Concentrating his main force on Manzikert would allow the flanking columns to withdraw to it if they were menaced by the Romans. Tughrul had already stunned all by the precipitous capture of disputed Berkri, the loss of which over twenty years before had so piqued the Commander of the Faithful in Baghdad. The surrender of Archēsh had greatly enhanced his prestige. Overwhelming Manzikert would crown the success of his campaign, paving the way for permanent settlement.

At the thought of soon returning to the besieged fortress, Derar's mind turned to the problem of rescuing Zobeir and keeping his designs from the Seljuks.

At length, Tughrul rose and walked thoughtfully to them. "Tonight we camp here. Tomorrow, we return to Manzikert."

Chapter Twelve

The Landscape of Fear

The Seljuk Camp at Manzikert,
Evening, 29th August 1054

Derar al-Adin had camped impatiently with the Sultan's entourage that cool night outside Karin. He wanted done with the sanguinary pillage and hoped the summons to the royal tent would furnish a pretext to get away. Although uninvited, Emren Dirse had accompanied him to the dismay of the Sultan's functionaries. Derar transcribed Tughrul Bey's dictated orders, reminding Isma'il to commence undermining the Manzikert circuit walls as soon as possible, with the object of mounting an overwhelming deliberate attack within two days of the Sultan's return.

For similar reasons, Emren Dirse had begged leave to accompany Derar, stating that he was anxious to return because his father's invaluable mare was thought to still be in the city.

The Sultan did not need a reluctant emir with the horde. He smiled. "Anxious for the unbeliever not to escape once more? You should've got him first time. Who'll lead your people?"

"My younger brother Beyreh with Burla's guidance."

Tughrul, seated on a camp stool, had thought on it awhile, tapping his boot as if absent-mindedly with an arrow. Suddenly, he looked up. "Beyreh will do well enough with your sister's advice—it will do him good. Go. It'll be as well to have you looking over Isma'il's shoulder."

With a spare horse for each and another for Farisa, captured by Emren Dirse's men, the three had ridden rapidly back the way they had come. Losing their way just as darkness descended across the plundered countryside, they took a wrong turn and happened upon a castle and village. Intrigued, they had ridden closer and found the fort intact, guarded by a detachment of ghulams. It had been ransacked but not destroyed, nor had the peasants been killed or enslaved, though many had been bashed and violated. A ghulam told them they were ordered by Bughra Dumrul to protect the place and its people.

Derar and Emren Dirse looked at each other. "Our spymaster must have his reasons," Emren remarked.

Derar kept his own counsel, but his mind was racing: could the holding belong to someone of use to, or allied with, the Seljuk spymaster? But who, and where were they? Or Dumrul could simply have been staking out a claim for subsequent ownership?

Farisa asked, seemingly innocently, "What is this place called, for we have lost our way?"

"It is called by the unbelievers, Arknik," the soldier replied.

"The girl has confessed our embarrassment," Derar said, shooting her an appreciative look. "Which way is it to Manzikert?"

In answer, the ghulam escorted them to the track and pointed the way as Derar inquired after the master of these lands.

"His name is Zakarian. I'm told he's in Malazgird," said the soldier, using the Turkish name for the besieged city.

The three resumed their journey, reaching the army camped around Manzikert late the following afternoon. Emren Dirse conveyed the Sultan's authority, Derar his word.

Isma'il, in order to please the Sultan's messengers with the progress of the tunnel, took Derar and Emren to the engineer's camp. The forward edge of this was marked by the position of two mangonels and four of the heavier ballistae. The spoil was carried away in baskets and used with other materials to gradually fill crossing places in the ditch, most of which was still dry. Only some sections on the north east corner, and the south east corner near the lagoon, had been flooded to form a moat. Osketsam, the Sultan's father-in-law, accompanied them, proclaiming his role in command of the tunnellers and boasting that he would be in the mine when they had dug far enough to hollow out a cavern under the walls. Isma'il, eager to impress, showed them the timber reinforced entrance and complained about the lack of useful beams. The engineers and the Daylami prince wanted to build moveable siege towers, but no heavy timber was available. "It's disappeared in the smoke of ten thousand campfires," Isma'il moaned. He explained that the other two mangonels and remaining four heavy ballistae were positioned to cover the north wall, threatening two separate breaches in the walls, thus splitting the defence since the Christians would have to plan to fight simultaneous penetrations.

Isma'il suggested that all would be ready for the main assault a week hence. "That will be the seventeenth day of the siege—a reasonable effort considering the distance over which we've had to operate from Tabriz."

Emren Dirse whistled despondently through his teeth when Isma'il told him of the garrison's recent daring sorties, over two days, to collect food. "Ayeee!" Emren exclaimed. "Who will tell the Sultan? I'm glad I was with him at the time. You tell him!"

In the early evening, Derar sat in the lamp-lit guard tent by the Sultan's dark pavilion and used the excuse of writing a despatch to the shepherd king to scratch a note to the Horse-archer. No one had tasked him to write the Sultan an account of the siege operations, but he hoped that having begun the process of writing his reports, the Sultan would be tempted to confide further instructions. Osketsam came and went, taking his ease in the far corner of the tent when not immediately occupied with his duties.

To the Romans, Derar wrote a quick account of the manoeuvres of the three columns and the devastation of the rural districts. He noted the little castle Arknik had, unlike other places, been spared and was under guard with the owner believed to be in Manzikert. Derar outlined the interest in the woman who escaped from Archēsh, as well as Ankhialou's presence with the Seljuk army. Finally, he warned of the tunnel, describing its location and direction in detail. He was careful to highlight the estimated date of completion and date planned for the main assault.

With the note to the Horse-archer tucked in the small leather pouch at his belt, Derar handed his official despatch to Osketsam. The emir studied it, his mask-like visage framed by the light beard under the black felt cap, betraying no sign of cognition or anything else regarding Derar's neat Arabic script. Derar started to worry that he could actually read, or was suspicious enough to summon another. Osketsam looked directly with his hard eyes at Derar. "Show me the other thing you wrote," he demanded.

With his worst fears rising in his throat, Derar passed him the note intended for Bryennius, while his heart beat so hard that he was certain Osketsam would surely see his chest thump in time.

"What is this one?" Osketsam unfolded it unhurriedly. "Why did you not show me and why does it not go to the Sultan?" His eyes bored into Derar's.

"Alas, I'm ashamed," Derar said softly. "It is a poem, for one far away."

"What's wrong with the girl you have with you?" Osketsam, still holding the paper, asked in the sort of conversational tone that Derar had learned to mistrust in many people. "She's comely and serves you well? Or am I wrong?"

Derar realised he was still on dangerous ground, talking about the vagaries of love and marriage with the father of a Sultan's bride. He watched the parchment move close to the candle flame.

Just then Ames entered the tent. The Seljuks used the thin, richly-gowned Persian as a court scribe. He wrote well and had a reputation in the camp as a poet of note, the wealthier soldiers entreating him to write lines they might use to court women. Derar had heard that Isma'il paid Ames to write romantic poems for Hurr on his behalf.

"Ames!" Osketsam called across the tent.

Ames paused, turned and made to join them.

Derar reached out and slowly took a corner of the note in Osketsam's hand, saying, "Bother not Ames with this poor effort, for he is a famous poet and it would shame me to have him read it."

"What is it?" Ames asked.

Osketsam did not let go. "A love poem," he spluttered with amusement. "The Arab has written a love poem."

"Oh, as they do," Ames sniffed.

Osketsam laughed openly at the snobbery. Unlettered in Arabic himself, he released the incriminating correspondence and ushered Derar sympathetically out of the tent, bellowing for a courier as he did.

Derar walked a furlong from the dim light of the guard tent, his heart still thumping as if it would explode. Almost sobbing at the reprieve, he paused in a dark place, wrapped his despatch to Bryennius tightly around an arrow shaft and replaced it in his quiver.

In the small hours when he thought Farisa was fast asleep, Derar rolled on his elbow and crept from their tent. He walked quietly to where he thought the outpost line would be, then sank to his belly and paused, listening, wondering if a silent sentinel in a dark shadow had seen him. With the moon a crescent low in the sky, Derar remained long, uncomfortable hours on the hard ground. He stilled his desire to move, knowing that he must outstay any who chanced seeing him. With the infinite patience of a hunter, he waited so that the lack of movement would cause any observer to think they had imagined it, or, for their curiosity to overcome them so they would investigate. Derar gripped his dagger and laid low, the silence of the still night heavy on him.

After a long interval with the night breeze blowing across his lightly clad back and making him surprisingly cold, Derar saw the sentries change and betray the location of their post. They did not point or look in his direction so he crept forward until he reached the stump. Searching with his fingers, Derar felt several arrows but none bore a message. In his mind he considered the possibilities: the Romans were being careful not to leave evidence to betray him, or one of their messages had been found and even at this moment a trap was now being sprung by Dumrul's men. Suddenly uneasy, he shot quickly at the tower and then crawled back by another way.

Not long before first cock-crow, Derar entered their tent hoping to find Farisa asleep. Stealthily, he crept under the cover, propping himself on an elbow to see her more clearly as his eyes became accustomed to the blackness. She was lying awake but said nothing, just putting her arm around him as he moved closer to her.

With the arrival of the famous Abbasid military engineer, Abramas, from Archêsh where he had been enjoying the fruits of his labours, the conduct of the siege took on a more deliberate design. Abramas was once an architect and builder but found war more profitable. His presence re-energised the assault on the city. The wild attacks of the tribesmen over the previous nine days had served to distract and wear down the defenders. The noise of drums, trumpets and horns played intermittently during the nights, with occasional fierce nocturnal attacks, deprived the defenders of Manzikert any respite. Now the Sultan's engineers, supported by Daylami heavy infantry and ever more slaves herded in from around the countryside, pushed forward the tunnelling in earnest and laboured to fill parts of the ditch, despite the casualties. The army was split into three teams: one working as the other two rested. Thus the stranglehold tightened around the city.

This, Derar al-Adin relayed to the Romans.

Manzikert,
Afternoon, 30th August 1054

From the arrival of the Seljuk Army, Guy spent eleven exhausting days on the fore-wall during which there were many probing attacks and two heavy assaults on his section. All had been beaten off. Several men under his command had been killed and many more bore minor wounds. He had seen the irregular troops of the enemy ride off to devastate the countryside and watched the fanfare as the Sultan himself departed to the north.

The day after the Seljuk columns had deployed from the besieged city, the strategos had acted in response to the bishop's warnings about the dire food supply in Manzikert. While the over-confident Seljuks investing the city were pre-occupied with plundering and laying out their huge encampment, hundreds of citizens in small parties with pack animals had crept from the city under cover of darkness. Necessity overcoming fear, they dispersed to gather fruit and vegetables, goats and sheep, carts and draught animals from the many secluded gardens and meadows that dotted the area. David Varaz led horsemen to where the remnants of the cattle herd that Bryennius had brought from Sashesh grazed unheeded along rivulets in the steppe. That night and for the following day, these citizens gathered what food they could find. The next night as Count Theophanes Doukas diverted the Seljuks' attention to the west by leading a noisy sortie from the walls, the citizens brought the vital supplies in by the eastern gate, protected by a screen of irregular horse commanded by Apocapes himself. Scores had died in the food raids, but they ensured the city would not soon succumb to starvation.

Cydones, in one of his strolls along the wall, had paused by Guy to ask how his study of the Greek language was going. In the ensuing conversation, Cydones commented on the raids. "Many praised God's infinite wisdom for making the Sultan so stupid," Cydones related, "but in truth Apocapes cursed his own lack of forethought and thanked his luck that the success and daring of common folk had rewarded him."

Guy had mixed thoughts about the imperial courier. He did not trust the man, so he remained silent when Cydones asked a rhetorical question about how Apocapes knew to chance the raids. Still, when he was in the mood, Cydones could be amiable and informative, passing on the benefit of his languages and travels.

On that occasion, Cydones, given his past army experience, expressed interest in weapons and fortifications and had a lengthy discussion with Jacques about his "Frankish bow", which Jacques allowed him to try at a discarded shield beyond the walls. Cydones had hit the target and Jacques, in the enthusiasm of a shared interest, complimented him. In that flush of accomplishment, the citizen of Constantinople glanced up at Guy's eyes, as though to ensure his skill with the unfamiliar crossbow had been noted, then blushed and looked away.

The look had not escaped Jacques' notice. "He fancies you," the groom later stated bluntly. "Be careful—men can be more dangerous than women when their feelings aren't returned."

Guy thought no more of it; he had enough problems.

Derar al-Adin had fallen silent after his second message, which informed the Roman defenders of Manzikert that most of the Seljuk army was departing to ravage the land. Those in the small circle that knew of him hoped despondently that he was with the Sultan and had not been killed in one of the assaults.

On the fifth day of the siege Guy watched, with detached trepidation, the lead Daylami units of mounted infantry ride their camels into view and the poorer foot begin to tramp into the Seljuk encampment. The first engines of the siege train arrived soon after. Sentries on the walls marked the arrival of regular caravans of camels and mules carrying hay and grain from the direction of Archēsh. With the mass of Seljuk irregular horse gone and those outside the walls now comprising mostly professional cavalry, infantry and engineers, the camp took on a more ordered appearance. Tents were neatly laid out in ordered streets and a row of shops under goat hair awnings also sprang up. Most of the Seljuk animals were herded away for the scant grazing that remained. By night, the defenders could hear the music in the Seljuk camp as dancers, singers, storytellers and poets entertained the host. Within a day of the siege train arriving, the investment of the fortress took on a different feel. The sporadic, costly attacks by unsupported troops ceased. The engines, eight powerful ballistae and four mangonels, were positioned forward of the Seljuk encampment opposite the west and north-west sections of the wall. Engineers gradually pushed them forward until the rocks they heaved could batter away at the walls with repeated, mortar cracking thuds. These reverberated sickeningly through the stonework, causing pockmarks on the surface as the facing stones fell away exposing the mortared rubble beneath and lashing the defenders with vicious flying chips. Lines of slaves bore heavy stones to the machines while others laboured with the baskets of soil, or cotton bales they found in a warehouse, to build protective works around the Seljuk engines. The relentless toil went on day and night.

The swirling, unpredictable assaults assumed a more frightening order, being preceded and supported by a heavy rain of rocks, darts and arrows. With the Daylamis came a special corps of *naffatin*, fire troops, armed with bronze flame projectors and pottery grenades for the naphtha. The sticky, inflammable liquid was set alight by fire arrows, though Guy saw instances of the clay pots being ignited by a wick on bursting. Although the defenders retained the advantage of height and stone defences, the *naffatin* brought a frightening new threat. Barrels of vinegar soaked earth and buckets of sand in which men urinated, were used to smother the foul smelling flames. When they ran out of urine, the pungent runoff from the stables was collected by townspeople and carried in pails to the walls.

The soldiers defending Manzikert hung the heavy felt awnings they had hitherto used for shelter over the front of the walls to protect the stonework. Suspended a pace from the walls by heavy beams, the felt dulled the impact of the rocks. Ballistae-men and archers harassed the Persian engineers, keeping them at the greatest range possible, forcing them to protect the siege works with mantelets. By day archers moved forward, occupying the castellated stone scarp breastworks above the ditch, to better harass the Seljuk siege engineers. At night, they withdrew behind the security of the fore-wall. Workmen daubed with white paint the interior outline of the fore-wall merlons so the defenders on the main wall could better see at night the line of battlements over which they had to shoot. Thus the heavy, heartbreaking work of war continued, accompanied by sudden death or maiming. Some were driven mad by the unbearable tension from which there was no escape, except in the constant, mind-numbing fatigues or recourse to faith.

Bryennius, with Doukas, Branas and some of the scouts, came often to look out over the hostile encampment, to observe the changes to the layout and activity, or sense any variation in the temper of the besiegers. Then they would move on in their ceaseless vigil. The strategos, usually accompanied by Count Branas, also visited the western wall twice a day, for it faced the greatest concentration of the Seljuk encampment. Basil Apocapes always encouraged the men and women on the walls and offered prayers for the salvation of the city.

Irene had come with other women to the wall. When not bearing baskets of rocks or bundles of bolts, the women brought water and wine, bread, cold meats, vegetables, fruit while it lasted and in the evenings, urns of gruel. When she came with a group, Irene would favour Guy with a smile and some personal delicacy. Guy savoured those occasional moments when she visited, wearing a Frankish helmet over her scarf-bound hair and with her weapons belted on over a mail corselet. How clean and fresh she seemed, like a playful spirit with the sun or moon behind her, while he, unwashed and unshaven, might be checking every detail of his duties, or taking a moment's respite, sitting with his back to the parapet.

Guy had twice been to check on his mare, relying on Taticus Phocas and the scouts of the Sixth Schola for her everyday care. He enjoyed Sira's welcoming whinny, her sniffing the strange smells on him and licking his hand after the treat he gave her. She remained sound in wind and legs after the flight from Archēsh and he allowed himself the sin of pride, for Sira's great gallop had been run in the shoes he had tacked onto her. On his second visit, he reshod her, chiding himself for not finding time earlier.

Guarding the precious warhorses was a constant task. Desperate refugees and black marketeers tried to steal the animals for meat, or so they would be mounted and perhaps able to flee should the defences be breached. Several unwanted visitors to the stables had been severely beaten; one almost to death.

There was something consoling about the military stables. David, Togol and many of the cataphracts, knights and irregulars came and went, caring for their own and their friends' horses. It was from them Guy learned of the many killed and their burial in pits. It seemed incomprehensible that people he had known would never more laugh, drink or seek love.

Fear pervaded the city. The bells tolled often and a constant stream of people visited the churches, begging not to be forgotten and their sins forgiven. Often the anxiety was unspoken: a haunted look in the eyes, eating each frugal meal as if it were the last, fretting at the noise of an attack or a sudden ringing silence. The bright new star, sometimes still visible during the day, was much discussed. Most feared it as ill-omened, its arrival coinciding with that of the nomads. Others tried to portray the star as a benevolent sign, proof that the city was forewarned of the attack and had not fallen while it shone above. Under Basil's direction and example, most townspeople threw themselves into their work with commendable fortitude.

By the eighth day of the siege, the stench of bodies decaying in the hot sun, and the increasing numbers of rats, had become unbearable. Daniel Branas rode alone from the city to parley. Guy watched him ride out, unarmoured except for a shield. He felt ashamed at the sting of his envy for the courage and ability of the man. Riveted to the parapet, scarcely able to breathe, Guy saw a knot of richly dressed and mounted Seljuks gather around the messenger. With his knuckles pressed to his mouth, Guy wondered if Branas would be struck down or taken. He returned, however, a Seljuk officer accompanying him to the wooden bridge over the ditch. They had paused, gesturing left and right as though discussing the conditions under which the grisly work might be done.

The truce lasted a day, with soldiers and workmen from the town clearing the many dead from the ditch, under cover of the task affecting a few repairs to the scarp as well. Grieving Seljuks buried their nobles—those not carted home by rich relatives—in funeral mounds. They burned the unnamed poor in great pyres. Guy knew he would never forget that peculiar stench of Manzikert, the combination of roasting flesh and naphtha. He prayed for the fires to burn out and a clean breeze to blow from the snow-capped mountains far to the north.

Now, at mid-morning on the tenth day of the siege, Guy and his men were relieved on the walls. He was sure of the days because he had scratched a mark for each. The relief—Varangians, peasants and townsmen—filed onto the ramparts and placed down their weapons and personal bundles, looking from the red-bearded Rus from Kiev who commanded them, towards Guy and his men.

The newcomers eyed those who had been on the fore-wall with awe. To those who had come from inside the safety of the main wall, Guy's men seemed like immortals: gaunt, red-eyed, bandaged, unshaven in their reeking clothes and unburnished armour. As their physical selves had shrunk from the strain, a presence had grown in them. Guy thought back to when these men had trembled at the approach of the nomad host. Now there was an indefinable quality about them, a quiet self-knowledge that they had withstood that test of courage and could do so again. Guy understood with sudden insight that his group had passed a rite of passage in life, bearing him along with them. He knew the newcomers could see it and envied it, impatient for their own test as they feared its coming.

After the introductions, Guy explained the layout of the defences and the procedures for taking up arms, repelling attacks and resting and feeding the men. He indicated the salient features of the Seljuk camp: where the Sultan's pavilion stood empty for the moment, the lines of the ghulams around it, the shops and stalls and the great ring of tribal camps, that were now quiet. The Rus asked after the siege engines and Guy indicated their positions. Finally, he pointed to the horse lines and adjacent area where the Seljuks were stockpiling fodder hauled in from afar.

"Quite a cosy little city they've built," the Rus observed before asking about the party of cataphracts posted around the tower to their right and the Roman centarch who had just arrived and was looking over the plain.

Guy, seeing Bessas and knowing these men were placed to collect any message from Derar in the Seljuk camp, lied that he did not know, but supposed it had to do with the sally-port next to the tower. He showed the Rus the scratch marks where he had been keeping count of the days and asked him to continue the practice, to which the fellow readily agreed.

Last off the ramparts, Guy followed his men back through the western gate of the main wall. A small group of wives, lovers, children and friends gasped when they saw the shadows of people they had known. Gasparian lined up the little band for orders. Suddenly shy in front of the spectators, Guy stiffly thanked them for their efforts and dismissed them for a day, telling them to assemble with their arms at the small chapel near the soldiers' quarters at the same time the following day, or immediately if there was a general alarm.

Priests and nuns stepped forward to care for the souls and wounds of those who had no one with whom to walk away. The gate-guard silently witnessed the scene and returned to their routine duties. The crowd cleared and Guy, Jacques and Charles were left there.

Joaninna Magistros threw her arms around Jacques while Charles embraced his attractive, auburn-haired Flora Asadian. Guy thought she was one of the Rus camp followers, perhaps the daughter of some passing Varangian, for she spoke fluent Armenian and Rus, communicating with Charles in the smattering of Greek and Armenian he had picked up. Flora smiled at Guy.

Joaninna had become a legend on the walls. She was one of those who, unnoticed in ordinary life, rise above others in a crisis. She was always where the fighting was thickest, carrying supplies to the walls, tending the wounded and comforting the dying. Through all this, she had worn the felt jerkin of an archer over her brown dress and set a cooking pot on her head, until Jacques found her a helmet. Everyone knew and loved her as much as the abbess, who was equally engaged in the defence of the city and the welfare of the casualties. Guy was surprised at the affection for each other that Joaninna and Jacques displayed. The groom stood with his arms around the woman while she nestled her cheek into the crook of his neck. Neither spoke.

Guy felt suddenly alone, more so when Joaninna noticed him glance around.

"Irene may have been called away," she said. "There were many injured on the northern wall again last night."

"Do you wish to sup with us?" Flora Asadian asked.

Charles added his own entreaties.

"Thank you, but I've things I must do." So saying, Guy heaved his load higher on his shoulder and walked, weary in body and soul, to his quarters.

Bryennius found him there before Guy had time to remove his armour. The Roman was several days unshaven and looked as tired as Guy felt.

"Guy, I have something to tell you. I wondered whether to, and it doesn't change anything, but you should know."

Why would Bryennius seek him out? Guy felt a vague sense of alarm. Suddenly he was glad of the way fatigue dulled the senses.

"You know the Sultan demanded a bride?" said Bryennius.

"Irene?"

"In a way. I received a message from ... our friend ... last night. It seems some in the Seljuk court are keen to see old Tughrul sire an heir and they have an interest in the woman who escaped from Archēsh and the one who rode with her."

Guy sat and removed his helmet and belt. "You're right, I'd want to know. And it doesn't change anything." He started to tug the mail byrnie over his head.

"There's another thing. Ankhialou's with the Sultan."

Guy finished pulling off the byrnie and slumped. "I'm in the way of both of them, aren't I?"

"Yes. And Irene would be aware of it too."

"Does she know?"

"No. Perhaps. I do not know. You should tell her," said Bryennius.

"Me! She hardly speaks to me." A thousand irrational fears and schemes were coming to mind: going over the wall one night with Togol to guide them through the enemy camp, a fight to the death with Ankhialou, or a confrontation with the Sultan.

Bryennius looked at Guy as though he could read his thoughts. "Nothing has changed, Guy. By defending the city, you defend Irene, and all the people.

Just keep your head down doing it." Bryennius looked closely at Guy. "Just do as you've been doing." Then the count of the Scholae left.

Guy lay down with a great sigh. "What to do?" Images of Irene during their flight from Archēsh came to mind, but no plan suggested itself to him before he fell into a restless, dream-laced sleep.

Manzikert,
Morning, 30th August 1054

Centarch Bessas Phocas had noticed Bryennius' relief when cataphracts found Derar al-Adin's second message arrow. Bessas had shot the answering arrow into the stump at first cock-crow that morning, instructing Derar to report whether there was only one Seljuk tunnel and verify when it was timed for completion. He then ensured the cataphracts intercepting the message arrows were not disturbed by the changes on the wall as Guy d'Agiles' men were being relieved.

Bessas then joined Bryennius at the strategos' council in the citadel. By his reckoning it was the eleventh day of the siege. Basil Apocapes no longer tolerated any self-important posturing in council. After hearing brief reports, he dismissed all but Branas, Doukas, Selth, Bryennius, the clerk Isaac and Bessas. They poured over a chart of the fortress and its environs.

The engineer, Selth marked where the Seljuk tunnel would be. "We've done some preparatory work but didn't know exactly where to dig, until this morning. The little church, here, close to where the Seljuks mean to breach, has a garden wall around, providing a good base to start counter-mining. We can get the tunnelling well advanced before it becomes too widely known."

The last statement, they all knew, was a reference to the possibility of a Seljuk spy in the city.

With a booted foot on a chair, Basil said, "Karas, pick your men and do it quietly. Start counter-mining immediately. The priest there is a good man. He once was an engineer himself, but left the army to seek a quieter life."

There was subdued laughter at the unintended humour.

The meeting broke up in the late morning. Bessas and Bryennius walked, unconsciously in step, towards their quarters. They had been up all night and intended to rest through the day while large-scale activity in the Seljuk encampment would be visible. They did not talk much. It was hot, more so under the weight of armour and weapons they now wore routinely. From the foot of the citadel, Bessas could see hills in the distance, the sweep of the river through the dust haze and campfire smoke. "It is a wonder there is anything left to burn," he reflected.

"Dung, mostly, by now," Bryennius said. "And they have plenty of that."

Bessas remembered how green the valley had been when he first saw it, rich with trees, gardens, grazing stock and the picturesque town outside the walls with hamlets up and down the valley.

He thought of Serena Cephala and the inner ease he felt when with her. Before the siege, Bessas had been invited to visit her parents' villa in the upper part of the city. He had stayed late that night, and felt a remarkable sense of wellbeing in her household. There had been something about the easy conversation and the ambience of the house: aromatic food, the rich carpets and exotic objects collected in the family's travels. Bessas had spent long hours that night, unchaperoned even after the house went dark, talking in the moonlight flooding Serena's upper floor chamber. The clean, refreshing breeze had played with the silk curtains as they held hands and planned their future.

Bessas now looked sideways at Leo. The older man, his head bowed in thought, was carrying his helmet by its throat lash. Most of the regiment were now usually clean-shaven and close-cropped in imitation of him. The count now wore several days' stubble and grey bags underscored his sleepless eyes. Bessas was glad the man was here, for he thought the count the thinker of the fortress.

It was Bryennius who had the idea of ambushing the Sultan as he followed the bridle path around the walls on the second day of the siege. Bessas had been on the walls with Bryennius and Doukas, waiting for the group of Seljuk nobles to pass by the rocky outcrop. After the first flight of arrows and bolts were released with obvious effect, Doukas punched a merlon in excitement so hard that he grazed his knuckle and did not notice the blood. Bardas Cydones had been there with a face like thunder. The crack of ballistae and twang of bowstrings had scarcely fallen silent before the imperial courier had hurried away.

Within an hour of the attempt to despatch Tughrul Bey, Isaac had told Bessas that Modestos Kamyates had berated Apocapes about the perfidy of Bryennius, accusing him of reckless disregard for diplomatic propriety in attempting to take the life of a foreign sovereign whose name was cited in the *khutba*[66] at Constantinople. Kamyates had also alleged Bryennius was a Saracen spy because of the Arab name of his warhorse and a host of other transgressions, real and imagined, against the Byzantine church and bureaucracy. As Isaac had reported the tone of their conversation, Apocapes could not afford to upset Kamyates' powerful friends if he wished to reach high office. "Very well, Modestos," Basil Apocapes had replied wearily, "I'll speak to the Count." Whether he ever did or not, only the strategos and Bryennius knew.

There was something odd about Cydones, Bessas thought: always too friendly, too eager to engage in conversation and find out what was occurring. With his flat denial that he had been in Archēsh, despite the fact that Bardanes Gurgen had confirmed it, Cydones had simply deepened suspicion of the dispossessed Armenian falconer's loyalty. Despite his charm, Cydones' outrage over the

---

66 Friday prayers in mosques.

attempt to kill the Sultan and end his campaign had seemed indicative of his true sympathies.

Bessas was intensely suspicious of the courtier, Kamyates, from the first time they had met. It was common knowledge that Kamyates had been an emissary to the Abbasid and Seljuk capitals and had remained in Vaspurakan, awaiting he said, instructions from the court. Yet, when Cydones had arrived, the imperial courier bore no written orders for Kamyates, not that anyone had seen anyway. Kamyates simply dismissed the discrepancy by saying, "When it's between conspiracy and confusion, I'll wager on confusion every time." Who knew what was said between them? And what of the strange meeting in the stables that Serena and he had witnessed?

His thoughts returned to Serena, her powers of observation, blue eyes, tumbled hair and the rise and fall of her breast as she breathed. He looked around and wondered what would become of them. A sick, empty feeling came over him and he turned his mind once more to the work.

Arknik! Bessas turned to Bryennius as they walked and said, "The note from Derar said Arknik was not destroyed and had a picket of ghulams on the orders of Dumrul himself? And Tigran Zakarian is still in the city. I saw him yesterday."

"What was he doing?" Bryennius glanced at Bessas as he spoke.

"Talking to that merchant who came out from Karin with us."

"The fat one? Or the one with the wife that's too good for him?"

Bessas was surprised that Bryennius had noticed the woman. He looked quizzically at the count. "The latter, Taronites."

"He's black marketeer. She's working in the hospital. Tzetzes is doing well, by the way."

Bessas wondered what the count thought about Zakarian. He asked.

Bryennius looked at him. "I don't know. It's interesting that his castle hasn't been plundered. Could mean that he's dealt with the Seljuks for protection. But by the same token, there have been plenty of occasions when we have, when raiding the Muslim lands, left untouched the estates of the very ones we wished them to be suspicious of."

"Bardanes Gurgen, our falconer, is also in the city," Bryennius continued. "David has been keeping track of him. I've asked Derar whether we have a rotten apple inside the walls."

They walked past the Barbarian House. Although the scouts still lived in it, the place now served an additional purpose. The strategos, Branas, Doukas and Selth used it as the temporary headquarters for conducting the battle for the city. As he walked past, Bessas saw Bryennius glance at the familiar wall and untended garden with its well and trees. He thought the count might have been about to speak, but Bryennius said nothing.

They reached their quarters and parted.

Chapter Thirteen

LACED WITH INTIMACY THAT GESTURE

Manzikert,
Midday, 1st September 1054

At noon of the second day after their relief from duty, Guy led his men onto the main wall. After a briefing from the Norman he relieved, he posted his men, instructed them on their duties and asked after their well-being and circumstances. After duties, including the maintenance of the engines and checking on the stocks of water, stones, missiles and other defence stores, he allowed them, except sentries, to rest behind the wall for a time. Guy visited the neighbouring towers, both manned by Franks: Normans and men from Flanders with whom he had felt more affinity. They acquainted him with their preparations of mangonels, ballistae and equipment for projecting Greek Fire. He was reassured by how they could support his section of wall by the discharge of bolts or fire across its front, even if the enemy managed to capture the fore-wall.

Barely had Guy sat down when Balazun came along and told him the engineer, Count Karas Selth, had asked for Jacques.

"Do you know what it's about?" Guy asked. He had come to appreciate Balazun more during the siege. The man had risen to the work and was more human for it.

"No. Some cunning scheme to do with ropes and pulleys and pickaxes I imagine," Balazun grimaced good humouredly. "Doesn't sound like much fun."

Jacques received his orders with a shrug and undertook to inform Guy what it was about when he found out himself. He slung his bundle and weapons over his shoulder and walked off.

It was hot so Guy sought the shade of a tower and sat with his back to the stones. He wondered about Irene and made many excuses for why she had not met him while he had been off duty. He brooded on their relationship for a while—their rides together, her disappearance to join Ankhialou at Archēsh, that flight from the captured city and talking until first cock-crow afterwards. Irene had seemed friendly when she, in the company of other women bearing refreshments, had visited him on the wall. Perplexed by her manner, he recalled her squeezing his hand at the strategos' speech in the square on the first day of the siege. How laced with intimacy that gesture had seemed.

To relieve his thoughts, Guy rose and walked the rampart, impressed by its strength and the commanding view it offered of the sprawling Seljuk encampment.

Balazun dawdled towards Guy. "I've only been here half a day and I'm bored scratchless already."

Guy laughed humourlessly and returned the hope that it stayed that way.

Balazun sniggered through his big, hooked nose. Looking past Guy, his countenance took on a serious demeanour. "I wonder what those bastards want?"

Guy turned and saw Reynaldus and Kamyates, absorbed in conversation, walking towards them.

"Who told you to be here?" Reynaldus spat.

"Doukas," Balazun returned disdainfully. "Take it up with him."

Kamyates stood smirking as Reynaldus, rebuffed by Balazun, switched his attention to Guy. "Where's the ugly peasant that's always with you?"

From that moment, Guy hated Reynaldus. After a long, insolent pause, he replied, "Looking down his crossbow at some evil one, I shouldn't wonder."

Reynaldus flamed and exchanged glances with Kamyates, who said, "Come on. We've important things to do."

"Well done, D'Agiles, you've made an enemy for life," Balazun laughed.

"As have you."

They stood slouched either side of a merlon for a while, looking towards the Seljuk camp, until Balazun heaved a sigh. "I must go and see if the rest of my bit of wall has changed since I last checked it."

Guy grinned as the big knight left.

Shortly thereafter, Aram Gasparian approached and offered to relieve Guy, so that he could rest before the night. Guy slept soundly for a few hours until the cool of late afternoon woke him. He sat up in his corner of the rampart near the tower and remembered it was the first day of autumn. His glance dropped to his bundle and he was glad he had brought his cloak up to the wall with him this time. He stood and looked around. Nothing appeared to have changed and Guy felt as though he had woken in a dream where danger was remote rather than immediate.

Daylight was fading. Down on the fore-wall he could make out Joaninna and a group of women with baskets of food and urns of water. It made him hungry and he thought about raiding the stock of dried meat and fruit in his bundle, but decided to wait for the meal being delivered. One could never tell when some personal reserve of food would be needed and he determined not to waste it.

The Seljuk camp was stirring to life, animals being fed and people lighting fires to squat in the dust and cook their evening meal. Guy wondered if their mounting casualties, increasingly hungry men and animals and imminent change of seasons would force the nomads to raise the siege.

He could not guess whether the defenders could hold for that long. The Christians too had suffered heavy losses in the fighting. Guy had heard figures of three hundred killed and many more maimed. No longer did Apocapes try to hold the scarp breastwork; there were not enough men and it was risky duty. Instead, the scarp merlons were used, very effectively, to shelter sorties of archers who would harass the Seljuk siege engineers and pick off those attempting to fill the ditch. The bishop's judicious administration of the food supply ensured the rations, despite scarcity of some items, were still adequate if not abundant. Most of all, there was the question of the city's fighting spirit in the face of such a formidable foe. The unknown but obviously ghastly depredations inflicted on the surrounding communities also weighed heavily on people.

Within the fortress, the squires were exercising the warhorses by walking them in strings of four around the track inside the main wall. The training kept the mounts fit without working too much condition off them. If the siege persisted, there would not be enough fodder to feed them all and many would be slaughtered. It was a melancholy thought for Guy who respected the innocence of animals. He thought of Sira and was glad that Taticus Phocas was looking after the mare for him.

Seeing the horses exercised, Guy turned his thoughts to his men. He determined to continue something he had heard Bryennius and Bessas discuss, the training of the ancients: training, training, training, so their drills were bloodless battles and their battles bloody drills. Accordingly he collected his men on the ramparts and they thrust and parried with spear, sword and shield, singly and as teams.

Just before dark, a group of nuns arrived with some women from the city. Led by the Abbess, they passed out food and drink and tended the dressings of those who had been lightly wounded. Few of the women doing this work were veiled: it was difficult enough in the heat to carry the heavy baskets and urns to the walls and up and down stairs and ladders. Guy was surprised to see Maria Taronites.

She approached tentatively.

"You're still here?" he greeted. "I thought your husband would have gotten you away at the first sign of danger."

"Would you have?" she asked playfully.

"In his shoes, yes, I would. In fact, thinking on it, I would not have brought you east of Karin. Or myself for that matter."

"Well, we're both here now," she said more seriously. "I work in the hospital with the abbess. She's a great inspiration—she and Joaninna Magistros both."

"They are," Guy agreed.

The married woman seemed friendlier now, as though the siege had broken down the usual social taboos. Guy wondered if his acquaintanceship with Irene had made Maria more relaxed with him. He was enjoying her standing close, with her brown eyes and quick smile, the cool air causing goose bumps on her soft neck above the collar of her thin dress. Guy was struck by how differently she looked clad in cheap linen instead of the rich riding habit she had shown off when he had first seen her at Karin. For a moment he wondered whether it was wiser for a woman to be richly clad or poor, beautiful or plain, married or unwed, during the sacking of a city. With a blink, he stopped the line of thought.

Maria's maid, Vartanoush Norhadian, approached Guy and offered cold roast lamb and bread from a basket. "There is a soldier over there whose bandage needs attending."

Seemingly embarrassed, Maria smiled and excused herself to go to the man.

From their first meeting on the track, Guy had thought this middle-aged, stout woman with the greying hair disliked him. Thus he was a little surprised when she praised him for rescuing Irene Curticius from Archêsh and his work on the walls since.

He protested modestly that Irene and he had fled together and everyone on the walls had tried their hardest. "All I did was run like hell and ..."

"Have you seen her, the lady Curticius, these past few days? asked Vartanoush.

"No," Guy replied reluctantly and perhaps a trifle harshly, wondering if the maid had been speaking to Joaninna or Irene herself. "Is the lady well?" he asked uncertainly.

"In body, yes. In spirit, perhaps not so."

"Why not?" He felt a wave of concern wash over him.

"Some damned fool told her they had seen her friend from Archêsh with the Saracen army. That sort of thing upsets a woman who thinks that love is ..." Vartanoush's voice trailed off.

Ankhialou again! Guy's spirits sank, his face with them.

"Be patient. She knows you are posted to the walls," Vartanoush said to his eyes. "Stay alive and stay true." The servant glanced towards her mistress, and looking back suddenly, saw Guy's gaze had followed the direction of her own. "Too flighty! At least we know what Irene Curticius is made of." Touching his arm briefly, she left with a sweep of her long black dress to continue her work.

"Do we?" Guy said under his breath, looking after the two women as they made their way along the battlements.

Dusk came and it grew cooler. Cloaked figures paced the rampart, speaking in low voices. There was no moon. Forward of their merlons they could see dim lamps here and there marking the fore-wall. Parts of the Seljuk camp were shrouded in darkness as the disciplined ghulams conserved fuel and sought rest, but campfires twinkled as the tribesmen gathered to drink and tell stories.

It was a long quiet night through which Guy was puzzled by lanterns in the small churchyard behind them. People came and went. In the early hours when the world was still, he could hear the faint sound of digging. He sent a runner to Bryennius with the information.

Seljuk Camp at Manzikert,
Morning, 2nd September 1054

Derar al-Adin woke in fright and lay still, his right hand closing on his sword hilt. Fighting the stupor of sleep and the exhaustion from want of it, he disciplined his mind to take stock of his surroundings. Outside it was barely light. The tent of woven black goat hair was shaking as one of the stake lines fouled. Comprehension and relief came quickly when Qurmul thrust his richly maned head inside and roughly nuzzled Derar's cheek, as though to say, "Good morning. You're lying on my breakfast." These days all the animals were hungry. Somehow Qurmul had broken free of his picket and had been nibbling the wisps of grass at the side of the tent. Now he wanted Derar to move off the rest.

Farisa woke. Qurmul acknowledged her with a sociable sniff. The woman rose on her elbow and stroked the horse's forehead. "What are you doing, silly?"

Derar waved the horse away, in case he pawed as they do when hungry. "Be gone! We'll find something for you directly." He lay back down and pulled his cloak over his shoulder. The ground was hard. Even in the dim light, he was aware of the dust and how they were unwashed and grimy from riding and living in the dirt. Like nomads, he thought.

Farisa sat up with her tousled hair. She had on a white cotton tunic, which hung open at the front as she searched for the little bottle of ink and quill beside her. Then she marked the parchment pinned to the tent. It was the fourteenth day of the siege.

Derar was glad she did this. They had been here for half a month. For him, the days were all marked by sameness: riding, councils, hurried meals, dirt, furious attacks and the never-ending fear of discovery. He knew he had to be more careful in his consideration of time. If he did not, he was apt to make a mistake; where wrongful advice to the Romans could cost his nephew's life. They rose and went outside to where Zaibullah boiled water over a little dung fire. The day was cool and they hovered over the embers. Farisa and Derar had coffee. The lean bulk of Zaibullah partook heartily of camel's milk, unleavened bread and spicy meat patties he had saved from the night before. Eventually Zaibullah pressed some food on them.

"Today," Farisa said, "I need to take our horses and camels and try and find some grazing in the foothills."

Derar recognised both truth and danger in this. The animals needed grass, but Armenian irregulars lurked in the most inaccessible terrain, falling on small parties or the herd guards. Still, these Armenian elements were operating mostly between Manzikert and Archēsh, or well to the south near the great lake. "Very well," he said. "You may find something in the hills to the west, downstream. Take Zaibullah with you and be vigilant. I know there's grain in the camp of the ghulams. I'll try and buy some today, though it's expensive."

Emren Dirse approached and sat. He called often, enjoying the company and conversation. Zaibullah poured him a small silver cup of scalding coffee.

Emren swallowed and screwed up his face, juggling the hot metal in his hands. "Devil's work. How d'you drink this stuff?" Nevertheless he gulped more and proceeded to relate news of the northern column, swearing to the truthfulness of his source, the Persian scribe, Ames. "Koupagan Bey had led his host northward, bypassing Kars to its west, proceeding thence to the river called Chorokh. Pillaging as he went, he followed this river downstream northeastward towards the sea. Believing himself too far from the army, he then turned about and raided back up the valley, taking slaves and booty to a collection point near where they had entered. Then ..." Emren Dirse swallowed the last of his coffee with a grimace and made to continue his tale.

Derar was listening with interest, but allowed himself to be distracted by Farisa suppressing a smile at the way Emren juggled the hot cup as he spoke.

"More," she asked.

The emir held out his cup with a knowing grin. "Then they pillaged further up the Chorokh River to the town of Baberd," he continued. "But near that place, unbelievers from a mighty fortress caught Koupagan Bey's men in a trap. The unbelievers—axe-wielding Vrangs, they call them—killed whoever led that detachment of Koupagan Bey's horde and many of his followers. The unbelievers then mounted their horses, pursued our men for some distance, rescuing all the prisoners and booty. Then they returned to Baberd." Emren looked at them expectantly.

"Thank you, Emren. It's good to know how the wider campaign unfolds. Crafty fellow—that unbeliever from the fortress of Baberd," Derar said.

Thus encouraged, Emren Dirse continued, tracing a rude map in the dust at his feet as he did so. "Koupagan Bey's main body then fell back to near Kars, but was attacked by Armenians led by the princes of their king. Many Seljuks tumbled to the dust. Koupagan Bey sent for help and a wing of the Sultan's column was despatched to help. They caught the Armenians in a pincer. Our men killed thirty of their wealthy freemen and a great many of their followers. The Armenians retreated to Kars, but not before we had seized one of their freemen, a very great fighter, Tatoul Vanantzi, the one who struck down the son of Arsuban."

Derar became even more interested. It was new intelligence to him that the Armenians could still mount a formidable army on the old caravan route from Tabriz to Karin. The news of the battle was something he might pass on to the Romans to keep them happy.

"T'was the very next day," Emren recounted, "when the main Seljuk army came up and Tatoul was brought before Tughrul Bey, who said to him, 'If Arsuban's son lives, I shall free you. Otherwise, should he die, I will order you made a sacrifice for him.' But this Tatoul is a bold fellow and replied, 'If I struck him, then he will not live, but if somebody else struck him, I cannot answer for his health.'"

"That," Derar observed wryly, "is one way to bring trouble upon yourself."

Farisa understood the structure of the campaign but was bored by the details. She was however, intrigued by the story of this formidable Armenian warrior. "I should like to see this Tatoul."

They looked at her in surprise. "So you shall," Emren said after a pause. "For the Sultan's army returns here and shall fetch him in chains, as they bring on a litter, Arsuban's wounded son."

"When will they get here?" Derar asked.

"They say tomorrow," said Emren as he swallowed more coffee and then obliterated the dirt map with the handle of his whip.

All this Derar relayed to the Romans that night. After shooting his message, he visited many campfires, so men would recognise him as having been in the camp. Over wine and roasted mutton and beef, the tribesmen boasted of their plundering rides, great deeds of fine horses, killing and rapine, of the rich booty and bound captives' stumbling in long trains to the slave markets. They spoke of the dark-haired beauty who fled Archēsh and was now surely beyond the walls where some were certain she had shot at them with a bow. Others related of another in the city, a lovely maiden, golden-tressed with porcelain skin and ruby lips. They debated, after mention of the strange new star, whether the fair woman be mortal or an angel sent to protect the city. Thus they drank and talked, thinking aloud on the ways of the perfumed women of the cities and bragging of what they would find and do when they broke into this place they called Malazgird.

Manzikert, Before dawn,
2nd September 1054

Jacques returned to Guy some time later, whispering that a countermine was being dug in the church. He then moved along the wall handing out bowls, telling the men to fill them with water, place them on the ground by the walls and watch for tell-tale movement of the liquid that would betray enemy digging. Count Doukas had similar precautions taken around the circuit walls of Manzikert. By doing this, he maintained the secrecy surrounding Bryennius' precise intelligence about the location of the Seljuk tunnel, while guarding against surprise or deception.

Guy had heard of mines being pushed forward under walls. Enemy miners would tunnel to a point where the breach was planned. Large caverns were hollowed-out under the walls and reinforced with beams. The holes were then filled with brushwood and other combustibles, and then set alight. As the supporting timbers burned, the wall collapsed into the hole and an immediate assault into the breach would take place over the hot stones before the defence could reorganise.

Guy reasoned that if Count Selth was digging in the nearby church, this section of wall was not as safe as he had at first thought. After a struggle with his conscience, he decided not to tell the men yet, lest he alarm them and compromise Bryennius' spy in the enemy camp. Jacques, he reasoned, would not allow them to be at risk without warning. Nonetheless, he walked softly along the wall and encouraged the men to be still and keep a close eye on the bowls.

At first cock-crow, Count Bryennius arrived at Guy's post and asked him to report, instantly by runner, any unusual activity in the Seljuk encampment. Bryennius was particularly concerned with the return of large numbers of tribesmen and the Sultan himself. He said Guy should be able to tell the former from their numbers and the latter's party from their finery and destination.

Mid-morning, Guy reported the arrival of many horsemen; Seljuk tribesmen, he thought. They came from the south, with others appearing to return eastward along the Arsanias Valley. He wondered how the inoffensive little village of Sashesh had fared, becoming depressed at the thought.

In the late afternoon, peering into the blinding glow of the low afternoon sun as it filtered through the dust and smoke of the Seljuk encampment, Guy could faintly discern large numbers of additional riders entering the valley of the Arsanias from the north. He sent another runner with the news.

By the time this man had found Bryennius and brought him with his scouts, it was almost dark and little could be seen. Guy joined them.

Simon Vardaheri observed quietly, "That's more fires than they've had for about ten days. They're back in large numbers and will be celebrating with lots of wine, food and storytelling. They'll have brought back all the food, drink, fodder, firewood and women they could carry. I would say tomorrow, or the day after, will be good for what you have in mind."

The church bells started ringing at sunset and this night did not fall silent. Priests trod the ramparts, chanting and saying prayers. Many who were not on duty went to church and prayed earnestly. Few in Manzikert slept well. Throughout those dark hours, Guy noticed the men engaged in the little chapel were busy again at their doings. As day broke, the bells still tolled.

With the shadows short in the forenoon, Guy observed a colourful group of horsemen ride into view from the north and sent a warning to Bryennius. Then, sensing something was going to happen, he rested his men after first satisfying himself that all was in readiness to repel a major attack.

Throughout the day most of the strategos' council walked the main wall opposite the Seljuk encampment. They looked over the sprawl of humanity and animals and spoke to each other in murmurs. Guy did not know whether he imagined it, but the tension within the fortress was palpable as people assumed the tolling of the bells was somehow connected to the swelling of the Seljuk encampment and increased entreaties by the city fathers for the Lord's help.

In the late afternoon of that day, the fifteenth of the siege, Balazun came along and ordered Guy to pick twenty good men, go to the chapel and report to Count Selth. As he left, Guy heard Balazun tell Charles to find all the Norman mounted men and report to the military stables.

Guy waited outside the small chapel yard, which was guarded by ten Varangians. Finally a tough little Georgian miner—dirty, smelling strongly of rank sweat and faintly of naphtha—led him inside the yard to the smell of freshly dug earth, clay and chipped rock. Tools were neatly stacked beside a collection of bronze vessels and mechanical pumps. Heavy pottery urns contained the terrible Greek Fire and nearby several pairs of large blacksmith's bellows had long hoses of waterproof oilcloth attached to them. Around the yard were the bundles, water skins and swords and spears of the men engaged in the mining.

Guy's attention was drawn to a small stand three handbreadths in height. From its crosspiece, silken threads suspended light and finely wrought metal tubes. He touched one and they tinkled softly. A miner told him the device was to detect the vibrations caused by the enemy's digging. There were also caged birds which would be taken into the tunnel to warn if the air was turning toxic. The uncomfortable thought occurred to Guy this new task he had been given might entail going underground. He had a vision of himself in a cramped, dark tunnel, engaged in a face-to-face fire and knife fight with a Saracen sapper. The thought did not appeal to him.

Karas Selth might have read his thoughts, for the cheerful Roman engineer emerged from inside the gutted chapel, grinned and walked over, wiping his hands on a piece of sacking. Guy was always impressed by the way engineers became absorbed in the technical details of their work. It seemed to overcome emotion, fear or doubt: Selth seeming as unconcerned now as if he had been laying plumbing in Phanar or setting flagstones along a street in Trebizond.

"Good to see you, D'Agiles. Don't worry, you're not going into the hole. We think we've found the Seljuk mine. They're still outside the fore-wall—had further to dig than we did—so once we found out the general direction of their tunnel..."

Guy nodded.

"We heard voices and saw a light," Selth continued. "So we've gone quiet for the moment, but plan to give them a nasty surprise in the morning. But, to make sure they don't use our tunnel for an unintended purpose, you and your men are here to guard this end. Not a difficult task—but one requiring diligence and silence."

Selth looked around the tiny church yard before speaking again. "Jacques has given splendid service. Seems to have done it before." The engineer bent over, examining the bronzeware and iron tools at his feet.

"Jacques seems to have done everything before." Guy was in equal parts proud, envious and astonished.

"Anyway," Selth straightened to look at him. "In the meantime, wait. Have your fellows take their rest here. It only needs a couple at a time to guard the hole while we're down there."

So they waited impatiently through the night. Guy, wishing the bell ringing would cease, emerged restlessly from the candlelit churchyard hours before dawn. Many men were moving, cataphracts and knights walking purposefully in little groups towards the stables. He looked for a face he knew who might have knowledge of what was happening. After a short time he saw Bessas.

"Centarch Phocas, what's happening?" Guy asked. "I should be with the mounted men. Why am I in the churchyard when others are saddling?"

The centarch wore a severe expression Guy had never seen before. Bessas paused in his stride and turned to regard him sympathetically. "Jacques is risking his life down that hole and especially asked for you to be at the top to get him out if need be. It's nothing anyway; we shall be done by noon."

"Done what?" asked Guy with a rising feeling of apprehension.

"The dance under arms," Bessas murmured, as he turned and walked on, shield over his shoulder, spear in his hand.

The dance under arms? All done by noon? A breakout and escape? A desperate attack on the Seljuk camp? Or tunnel? Guy wondered irritably about the riddle. He returned to the chapel yard intending to complain to Selth. He found the Roman engineer sitting on a pew in the yard, drinking water from a grubby silver goblet and chewing on a thick crust of bread and cheese that Joaninna had brought. Selth was shaking his head while the woman was stubbornly refusing to leave, as a red-faced, grey-bearded man looked on.

Joaninna hissed at Guy. "Don't you even think of deserting your post and going out there, Guy D'Agiles. Jacques wanted you here and here you'll be, with me." She glared defiantly at Selth, who in turn looked at Guy and shrugged helplessly.

The grey-bearded stranger looked at Joaninna with a bemused air. He introduced himself to Guy as Araxie Bagradian. This was his chapel.

Guy entered the dimly lit church, sat on an overturned pail and sulked. The place had been gutted, flagstones torn up and pews taken outside. Dust coated the frescos of the saints. Steps hewn out of rock led down into an ancient hiding place. The entrance, large enough to fit four men standing abreast, looked like any timber buttressed mine site. It had a curtain of heavy felt draped across it. Talking and noise were forbidden.

Joaninna joined him, offering food, and water scented with lemon juice.

After a time, Jacques emerged without his armour. He was covered in dust and around his neck was a scarf that looked like it had been stuffed with cotton wadding to guard his mouth and nose against dust, toxic smoke and heat. The dirt on his elbows and knees indicated the tunnel was not high at the other end. He acknowledged Guy and accepted a little food from Joaninna.

Selth came in. Jacques moved closer to murmur, "They're still digging, I can hear them."

"Good," uttered Selth in the harsh whispers of command. "It'll soon be time. Don't forget the Sultan's own father-in-law is supposedly in their tunnel party. The cavalry are assembling now. Much depends on all of us this day." He grasped Jacques on the shoulder.

Turning to Guy, Joaninna said, "Go and see them."

He knew she meant the horsemen, so they should know he neither sulked from pique nor skulked from fright. He turned to Selth who nodded. Thus, Guy strode to the military stables as the horsemen assembled. The emotion in the air reminded him of the feeling before the cattle raid. How long ago that seemed. Yet now many more men were saddling up and finding their places, the distant-sounding clamour of church bells masking the noise of their movement. They had dressed with care this day. Proud plumes nodded on burnished helmets. Horses and equipment were similarly groomed. In the pre-dawn, torch-lit blackness, Guy found Bessas. "I've come to see you off and bid you good luck."

Bessas, saddling dun Diomed, turned. "Thank you, Guy." After a pause while the centarch inspected by feel some part of his horse's equipment under the belly, he continued, "The tunnel is most important. Our object is to kill the miners and close the tunnel from Tughrul's end while you take care of this end. The Kelts under Balazun will feint towards his pavilion, to draw the Seljuks off by making them think we mean to have their Sultan. Count Bryennius is in overall command. Lascaris leads the Sixth Schola to destroy the engineers' camp and those in it, closing the tunnel as he does. I take three hundred irregulars and leave by the north gate to fire the enemy's fodder and drive off their animals—to draw the enemy off while our men get back inside the walls."

It all made sense to Guy—the meticulous watching to know when the tribes and their Sultan had returned, allowing them sufficient time to crowd the camp with distracted, unconcerned people—the garrison would strike hard when the Seljuks were least able to react effectively. It would be a bitter day for the Sultan if all went well. At once taken aback and admiring the audacity of the scheme, Guy asked, "Bessas, where is the count? I must wish him well also."

Bessas pointed through the gloom. "He rides Zarrar this day."

Guy pushed through the press of men and horses towards where he could see Bryennius. On the way he passed Reynaldus, giving emphatic instructions to Balazun, driving one fist into the other open hand to add force to his point. Balazun did not look happy.

Guy reached Bryennius, who was busy with a myriad of last minute details. The count wore heavier battle-armour: a polished horn lamellar cuirass over his mail hauberk. His helmet and boots gleamed from the attention Taticus Phocas had given them. Zarrar's face was protected under the iron chamfron[67] while an expensive, breathable, mail bard armoured his body. The horse was standing tall, looking this way and that in eager excitement. Guy noticed and wondered about the sleeve of a blue shirt under the count's hauberk. He had never seen it before.

---

67 Chamfron—defensive armour for a warhorse's head.

A cock crowed loudly from the loft of the main stable building. There was a sudden silence, followed by the urgent hiss of a tribune, "Form up. Form up. It's time."

Bryennius, surrounded by men pressing final questions, saw Guy and nodded to him. "Good luck, D'Agiles. Much depends on your end going well."

The awful finality of the moment struck Guy. "When we're done, I'll watch you all and cheer from the walls." He swallowed the unease within.

Bryennius grinned before mounting. "Don't get in our way when we come back in. I rather fancy we will be in a hurry."

"One thing," Guy pressed on Bryennius. "Whatever orders you've given to Balazun, I'd restate them before you go. Reynaldus is in his ear as we speak."

A worried look crossed Bryennius.

Guy raced back to the chapel as it grew light, his breathing laboured from the weight of weapons, armour and emotion. He entered to see Jacques, grim faced and intent, enter the tunnel with six others, all wearing felt hats, rude masks and jerkins against the likely flames. Guy marvelled how men could go into the earth like that. Then he took his spear and stood guard at the tunnel entrance and would not have budged had the devil incarnate emerged.

Guy did not know how long he remained there. The sky outside was slightly paler now: deep blue instead of black. Suddenly there were muffled shrieks and shouting from the depths of the tunnel. Taking his helmet off and moving closer to the entrance to hear better, he felt a rush of hot air brush his cheek.

The other tunnel guards and Joaninna exchanged anxious glances.

Selth burst from the entrance like a madman. His hair was singed. His jacket reeked of burnt wool, sulphur, resin and smoke. Blindly feeling his way to the cool air, Selth ripped the makeshift mask from his face. By an extraordinary effort he forced his singed eyelids open and stumbled to the door. "Now! Now!" he cried. "Fire the signal arrow."

A Varangian in the chapel yard dipped a naphtha-soaked clothbound arrowhead into a small brazier and shot the flaming shaft against the western main gate tower. An answering signal arrow immediately streaked low inside the fortress, as the sun touched the eastern horizon.

"They've prisoners in the hole," Selth choked. "There may be others, but we filled their tunnel with fire and toxic smoke, pumping it their way with the bellows. Surely no man could live in it. Jacques and the others will be coming back now." The stocky Byzantine engineer swallowed water and tipped the rest of the pail over himself. Wiping his grubby face with his shirtsleeve, he replaced the mask over his nose and mouth and darted back into the awful hole, from whence hot air, dust and reeking smoke now issued so that the tunnel guards themselves coughed and covered their faces.

Guy made to follow him. A Varangian and Joaninna both stopped him by grabbing at the sleeves of his byrnie. "Don't," she said. "They know what they are doing and do not need to fall over you or go back in for you."

After a seeming eternity, they emerged dragging prisoners with them. All were hot to touch and reeked of fire and sulphur, with their hair and eyelids singed. Quick hands grabbed three bearded prisoners, forcing them to their knees where they begged for mercy in a strange tongue.

With racking coughs bending him double, Selth, utterly spent, eventually got his breath back and lay supine on a dusty pew. One grimy forearm covered his eyes. Guy looked at him anxiously, wondering whether the engineer was all right. "The Horse-archer," Selth coughed, "has some good ideas, but this time he's nearly killed me." He thought for a while, then asked Jacques, "Did you manage to collapse the mine?"

"Some. They were still tunnelling and had not yet dug a cavern under the fortifications." He was sitting with Joaninna carefully sponging his face with cool water: his face and hands blistered from heat and his hat blackened and smelling foul.

"Jacques nearly didn't get out for doing it," said one.

"We got most of the gear out," spoke another.

"When it clears, we'll go back in and collapse it properly," Selth said to his grimy band.

Guy saw they were now bound by the private, closed hell they had created underground. This extended, it was plainly evident, to their prisoners.

"I wonder which one is Osketsam," Selth mused aloud.

One prisoner moved his head slightly lower at the sound of the name. They assumed he was the one.

Selth coughed again and then wheezed, "Come on. The strategos wished to see Osketsam as soon as we caught him."

Chapter Fourteen

The Dance Under Arms

*Manzikert, Before first light,
4th September 1054*

As the fight in the tunnels raged, a thousand horsemen waited behind the gates of Manzikert.

As he swung into his saddle, Leo Bryennius was perturbed by what Guy d' Agiles had just told him about Balazun and Reynaldus. He adjusted this helmet, feeling the light mail coif into place over his shoulders and lacing the face-cover into place leaving only his eyes exposed. Leaning forward, he stroked Zarrar's neck through the protective bard. "Good luck this day, old man," he said to the horse.

The indicators of Seljuk engineering and the information from Derar al-Adin had convinced the strategos that the greatest threat was Tughrul's ability to tunnel under the walls. Seljuk stone throwers had been relatively ineffective, due to their limited size and range, but their tunnel posed an immediate threat.

Days before, Leo had sent Togol and Maniakh to scout the Seljuk encampment and verify the information he received from Derar. They had wandered unchallenged through the enemy camp, returning two nights later to inform him of the precise location of the tunnel entrance and overconfidence amongst the Sultan's followers. A tight group within Basil's council had planned the coming battle to destroy Tughrul's capability to undermine the walls, so that lack of sustenance and grumbling amongst the tribes would sap his army's resolve. Derar had informed them when The Falcon would strike. Apocapes was now pre-empting the Sultan by a day.

After the scouts returned, Togol had confided to Leo that Maniakh had spoken with the dancer, Hurr, in the Seljuk camp and wished to escape with the woman.

After the first explosion of anger, Leo had asked, "Will he go over to the enemy?"

"No. It's love."

"Love? What the hell does he mean by that?"

Togol grinned. "Love? Everyone is their own—how do you say—sage. Hurr and Maniakh both risk everything—Isma'il and Dumrul will hunt them to the ends of the earth. I suppose they know what they are doing!"

Although dismayed at the loss, Leo had caved in. "Maniakh has my blessing, but must see me before he goes—the Emperor owes him a little back pay. And," Leo had grumbled, "tell him to take the Sultan's damned horses, not mine." At that, Togol had laughed and clapped Leo on the shoulder.

A thousand horsemen awaited their fate with almost unbearable unknowing. The priests moved among them, "Lord Jesus Christ, our God, have mercy on us, come to the aid of we Christians and make us worthy to fight to the death for our faith and our brothers, strengthen our souls and our hearts and our whole body, the mighty Lord of Battles, through the intercession of the immaculate Mother of God, Thy Mother, and all of the saints, Amen."

Leo leaned towards Bessas. "Are Kamyates and Cydones taken care of?" he asked. The two bureaucrats were too powerful and too untrustworthy to be allowed any latitude before such a critical undertaking.

"I beg to report," Bessas replied, "that Maniakh, deploring their calling him an unlettered barbarian—which they did—has in a drunken binge kidnapped Kamyates and Cydones both, and now holds them at spear point in a cellar somewhere. David Varaz plays the role of bumbling rescuer, who can only save their lives if they do exactly as they are told. Serena is the lookout."

"Maniakh does not drink," Leo observed dryly, glad the conversation was distracting him from the fear lurking under the surface.

"No plan is perfect," Bessas shrugged. "I told Maniakh to let them go as the attack starts. It'll be too late for them to alter its course by then and the longer we delay their release, the more difficult it will be to make it look like one of life's silly little things."

"Like betraying your country. As for plans ..." Leo knew how many things could go wrong this day, but they had few options to defeat the grinding Seljuk attacks.

He saw Balazun look his way and beckoned him over. The Norman reined in his black Castilian horse, Charles Bertrum with him. Lascaris moved his horse a few steps forward to join them. They had been over the plan before.

"Any questions?" Leo asked.

Balazun shook his head, his helmet gleaming gently in the first light. "I leave with my four hundred, straight out the main gate and ride directly for the Sultan's tent. I'm not to press the attack, but draw off the ghulams and anyone else, to buy you and Lascaris enough time to kill the engineers and destroy the tunnel. If I happen on the Sultan and can kill him without jeopardising the plan—I do so. Your Bessas Phocas will feint against their transport lines to cover our withdrawal."

Balazun had the facts all right, but Leo doubted something in his manner and was still concerned about whatever Reynaldus had said to him. With sudden doubts gnawing, Leo emphasised the plan. "For the Seljuks, the flow of the battle should be thus. First they should be surprised, and it will take them some time to react to you, Robert, which they will do by swarming to stop you reaching the Sultan. When the Sixth Schola hit the engineers at almost the same time, many of Tughrul's men should leave you and come against us. Some disorder should set in on them. By this time, your Franks should be disengaging. That, Bessas, is just when you should hit them to draw them away from us. You should be so far to our right that you ought to be able to withdraw before they bring any real weight against you."

"As agreed," Leo continued, "I will signal the stratego in the western main gate towers when the engineers are dealt with. He'll have trumpets sounded. That is the signal to withdraw. There will be a lot of dust, smoke and noise, but that should work mostly for us. The plan will unravel if anyone misses a signal, or goes flat-footed and gets caught out there. Remember, Lascaris this day commands the Sixth and the assault on the engineers' camp. I am in overall command and will have a small escort and standard-bearers with me."

They murmured understanding and obedience and turned to join their troops.

Waiting for the signal to attack, Leo thought of Martina, missing her but at the same time glad she had left Manzikert before destiny closed upon it. He reached down and touched Zarrar's neck for comfort before a flaming arrow struck low against the main gate towers and was answered by another as the gates swung open. Leo shortened the reins with his shield hand and grasping his spear tighter in his right, cantered out of the gates and swung sharp right into the space between the walls. As he rode by, he noticed townspeople jog to their places on the ramparts to support them, as the infantry reserve assembled between the walls.

Leo and Zarrar passed through the dark cavern of the fore-wall gate towers, over the wooden bridge and into the lonely plain. Like a rumble of iron thunder, the dense column of Franks followed him. Leo eased Zarrar to a halt and pointed with his spear in the direction Balazun was to charge. The Sultan's pavilion was about a mile away with its banner just visible on a low knoll by the river. At a glance, nothing seemed unusual in the Seljuk camp.

There was a minute's delay on the flat as the Franks formed into two flying wedges; one behind the other, one hundred and forty men in each. With the still bells still masking the sound of their manoeuvre, they halted for a moment as the riders braced themselves for what was to come. Then, with Robert Balazun three horse-lengths to their front, they set out trotting silently through the dawn, withholding their great Latin shout until they were seen.

Behind the Franks, the Sixth Schola trotted out the gate and over the bridge. Some horses broke into an agitated canter in the ranks, tossing their heads and fighting the bits. Lascaris ordered, as though on parade in the shadow of the imperial palace, "Sixth Schola, right wheel," and three hundred horsemen, spears vertical, trotted parallel to the ditch. On command, they halted their excited mounts. "Into line, left turn!"

Followed by his escort, Leo galloped to Lascaris and pointed with his spear to their objective. "Ride with, you?" he asked courteously.

"Of course," Lascaris replied, proud of his command of the regiment in battle this day and grateful for Leo's acknowledgement of it before the front rank.

Leo's escort, commanded by Aspietes, fell in around them. To a man, the cataphracts braced themselves for the furlong charge at the camp of the engineers, where alarm was spreading with the Sultan's men taking up their arms and looking uncertainly toward the horsemen forming by the fortress.

Lascaris said sideways to Leo, "Well, they now know we are coming." Then the centarch lowered his spear point to the horizontal tierce point. On command, from the right in the front ranks, one man after the next snapped his spear down to tierce point; creating that parade ground rippling fan-of-spears. A terrible exhilaration ran through men and horses.

In Manzikert, the bells fell silent.

Lascaris, waving his spear, started forward. Two hundred of the front ranks, led by Sebēos, leapt into a hand-gallop behind him. After them, a knot of twelve men carried clay grenades of naphtha while others nursed in their saddles the torches and fire arrows that would be used to ignite the incendiaries.

Behind Lascaris' front ranks, he kept another hundred cataphracts: the tight wedge of the reserve squadron, Bessas' men, commanded this day by Tribune Joshua Balsamon, riding in his first battle. The youth was clean-shaven and wore a pointed iron helmet, richly inlaid with silver, a trophy taken by a barely remembered forbear from an unknown Muslim prince in some long-forgotten fight. Balsamon's reserve squadron moved forward at a walk, dressing their ranks, spears upright, the horses stepping short with high heads, wanting to gallop joyfully forward with their fellows.

Boot to boot, Lascaris and Leo galloped, controlling the pace so the charge could halt on the camp and start the grim work. An undisciplined, headlong rush would only carry the regiment straight through their objective and founder, making them vulnerable to Seljuk counterattack while trying to reorganise. Dust from the Norman assault was drifting across their front. As it stung Leo's eyes, the decreased visibility made control harder, as he had foreseen and planned for. He swept past a running figure in a rough tunic and boots and knew they had reached the camp. As the cataphracts behind him came upon it, they screamed in unison as their charge smashed through the thin line of sentinels and into the scrambling engineers. "Scholae. Scholae! Manzikert. Manzikert!"

Leo saw that the plain on this side of the nomad camp was empty and surmised the enemy had not yet had time to react. What he feared most was a trap, where a seemingly surprised Seljuk camp suddenly became a hornet's nest.

"Steady, Zarrar. Steady, boy," Leo soothed, checking the bay horse in a stride and looking around. Zarrar's ears moved back to listen, spear and quiver rattling against him. The horse slowed instantly, but with a toss of the head and snatch at the bit, told Leo he was ready for anything. Turning in the saddle, the horse spinning instinctively with him, Leo saw the work of killing the fleeing engineers had been the work of a minute.

Lascaris was thinking with Leo. "You men," the centarch bawled. "Back into the camp and destroy it. Kill anyone you find there." Setting his horse to a canter, Lascaris shouted to another tribune to ride with his troop and screen them from the Seljuk camp. "Turn your horses sideways and hold your spears high, to make it look like there are more of you. Engage with bows as soon as they draw into range."

Leo could see the beginning of uproar in the Seljuk camp, discerning a few riders darting around on light coloured horses. As yet there was no sign of an organised counterattack. Where the Franks had ridden, there was a lot of dust, the first black horsemen of the Sultan's ghulams, galloping towards the gritty cloud. There was no time to waste. Leo rode back into the engineers' camp to check that the destruction was complete.

Cantering cataphracts were loosing arrows into the engineers who had hidden by the mantelets, under the beams of the engines or beneath carts. Others rode down the enemy who tried to run. Seljuk engines and carts were set alight in bursts of naphtha pots, and figures ran screaming from them. One stumbled blindly towards Zarrar, but the horse barely shied as Leo deftly turned him out of the way. Leo trotted towards where he thought the tunnel entrance would be. A dozen dirty, twisted figures, one woman among them, lay there and he somehow knew they had barely escaped from the inferno underground when his men had killed them. Their faces were dirty, blistered and screaming silently with the horror and unfairness of it. Leo felt sorry for them.

Cataphracts galloped up around him and throwing reins to the horse-holders, dragged anything combustible—ropes, tools, baskets, shields—far inside the tunnel entrance. Dousing these with naphtha, they set them alight with fire-arrows. From safely outside the evil-smelling, flame-belching hole, they hurled in more pots of naphtha to make sure of the work. Lascaris, satisfied the tunnel was ablaze, gestured the fire party to use the last of their pots on a nearby mangonel and ballista. Then they sprang to plunging horses and looked around for their decarchs, to form up and face the onslaught that must surely come.

Leo judged the tunnel beams were well alight and his main objective of killing Seljuk miners and destroying their equipment had been achieved. Eager to disengage from battle and withdraw into the fortress, he trotted off to assess how the wider fight had developed and begin the withdrawal. How he loved Zarrar. The bay was alive with the exhilaration of battle and Leo felt indestructible on him. The horse was quick and responsive, darting hither and thither at the lightest touch when asked, galloping full stretch, to slide to a halt in his own length and spin around on his hocks to tear full tilt the other way.

As he trotted up out of the shallow depression where the mouth of the tunnel was located, he saw a group of about fifty ragged figures kneeling, making the sign of the cross and lamenting piteously as they regarded him with terror. "Who are you?" Leo yelled, his question seeming like a distant sounding accusation. He was vaguely conscious that he must have appeared apocalyptic in the eyes of the freed prisoners.

One came close and shouted up to Leo, "Have pity on us. We are Christians and have been taken by the Persians as slaves." He was thin, dirty and ragged with misery over his face and fear in his eyes.

Leo, relieved his men had been cool enough in the fight not to ride them down, pointed through the tumult to the fortress gates. "Run. Run. That way!" he indicated with his spear. "Make the sign of the cross as you go."

Leo cantered up to Lascaris who was already re-establishing order amongst the regiment: shouting officers collecting their men, thrusting them into heaving ranks on their excited horses. "Well done, Scholae," Leo called to the soldiers near him and then turned to Lascaris. "Well done, Antony! Form them up. Be prepared to either fall back on the fortress, or move forward to aid the withdrawal of the Kelts."

Windrows of Turks were galloping towards them. Leo noticed that in their uncontrolled rush, most of the Seljuk riders, who had leapt to horse at the first news of the attack, rode bareback and were unprepared for battle. They posed little more than a nuisance to the disciplined Sixth Schola, now forming a strong front against them. The cataphracts of the second rank were returning an accurate archery at the Seljuks. Balsamon's reserve had joined Lascaris' main body.

Leo was relieved at seeing order established in his ranks and learning that there were few Roman casualties in the unequal fight. He hoped that the attacking Franks could now dis-engage and withdraw to the safety of the walls before the Turks recovered and brought superior numbers to bear. He cantered with his standard-bearer to a slight rise on the flank of the regiment, from where he could see the main-gate towers with the strategos' pennant fluttering above it.

"Make the signal," Leo ordered the standard-bearer.

The trooper rode several horse lengths in front of Leo so he could be seen clearly. Holding the standard aloft, he raised and lowered it several times in sharp, definite movements. There was an answering signal from the tower, followed by a series of trumpet fanfares: the signal for a general retirement to the walls.

Lascaris galloped up breathless and triumphant, the protective bard hanging lopsidedly on his black horse. He looked at Leo. "The signal?" he asked, hopeful that the fast-moving battle would soon be over. Lascaris was no coward, but an intensely practical soldier who knew to quit the fight once they had achieved their objective.

"Yes," Leo said. "All we need to do is fall back slowly and allow Balazun to return by our left flank and all should be well."

Leo looked towards the Franks but could still see nothing but dust. Then there was a great, rolling crash. He knew Balazun's charge had hit something hard.

The Seljuk Encampment at Manzikert,
Sunrise, 4th September 1054

Every instinct told Derar al-Adin that the Christians would strike this day and the engineer camp would be their main objective with secondary targets as diversions. Before first light he was up and discreetly prepared for the coming battle. Ready, he lounged by his small dung fire, drinking coffee.

The Sultan had returned the previous day, with most of the tribes getting back late the day before that. The nomads were tired and their horses jaded from the far-reaching, fast-moving raids. With them they had booty, firewood, fodder and captive women. Confidently looking forward to two days respite before the final assault on Manzikert and the plundering of the city, the huge encampment was taking its ease.

Derar had urged Farisa to rise and get ready. To mislead those nearby about his reasons for rising early, he chastised her loudly enough for the other tents to hear, that she must leave early with their animals to find grazing for them. She had flamed rebelliously at her treatment as the men of the nearby tents laughed.

Zaibullah was standing nearby when the distant attack started, the coffee dribbling unnoticed from his cheap cup as he discerned the dust cloud heading for the Sultan's tent. Derar also stood and looked as others around the camp leapt to their feet and gazed in astonishment. They had not expected the cowardly Romans to come out in open fight.

A black-clad emir of the ghulams, galloping skilfully through the throng, raised them. "To arms. To horse," he roared. "The unbelievers are attacking the Sultan. With me, with me!"

With a shout that startled the horses on their pickets, the Seljuk tribesmen around Derar grabbed whatever weapons were to hand. Some saddled, others did not: there would be time for that later when the Roman attack had been blunted and it was time to destroy them. The first wave of men rode bareback in their hundreds with this unknown emir.

Zaibullah, already saddled, armed and armoured, ready to accompany Farisa on her forage, sprang to horse and took his spear from its place near the side of the tent. He looked at Derar.

Derar turned to Farisa, saying, "Get away from the fight, Farisa, to the far side of the camp and return here only when God's will is done." She returned him a look that Derar could not fathom. A big Seljuk rushed up and pushing Farisa roughly aside, mounted her black mare. Derar seized the bridle rein and struck him forcefully in the chest with the flat of his war-axe, winding the man so that he doubled in pain. Swiftly Derar grabbed the Seljuk's long hair, pulled him from the saddle and pushed him roughly to the ground. "Thief, scoundrel," he roared over the tumult, kicking the fallen man with a viciousness that surprised him. He turned to Farisa with a sudden realisation of just how much he wanted her safely away from this place. "Go," he commanded with such authority she acquiesced as he heaved her to the saddle. Then Derar flung himself onto Qurmul.

Close by, an emir of the Seljuk tents spun his mount, exhorting his followers. Even in the haste of the moment, Derar was moved by the exquisite horse, the sumptuous saddle, black mail, black sword and the dark beauty of the rider as the youth cried, "I have seen the green-eyed girls, they beckon with white arms and fair bosoms and they make sweet entreaties. Oh! Woe to thee who does not ride well and swiftly to the battle this day." Long-haired, bearded men gathered around the youth in a mass of bows and spears. They whipped their open-mouthed, white-eyed horses, so that their maned heads rose in the air and their hooves struck the ground like so much thunder of forgotten steppe gods. "Paradise. Paradise. Fight. Fight!" they roared as one.

"Let it be done," shouted Derar to Zaibullah. "Go your way. We have our own fights this day." Derar did not wish to be closely observed by Zaibullah while appearing to participate in the battle without being caught in the press of it. Derar was no coward, but this day he had considerations other than victory for the Seljuks.

Galloping over a slight rise, he saw in an instant the unfolding battle. Amongst the splendid tents of the Sultan's camp, numbers of the *gulâmân-I suray* were racing on foot to form a forlorn front against the charging Franks. They dragged with them a bawling camel on which a standard-bearer waved the Sultan's rallying flag. Other palace guards galloped up saddled horses to spirit the Sultan and his family from danger.

Such rescue Tughrul spurned. Mounting a led-horse and taking his mace and shield, the Sultan moved towards the Franks. Mounted kettle drummers and flagmen followed him to relay his orders for the fast-flowing battle. Ranks of mounted ghulams rode around him. Others trotted into place, forming squadrons, as more troops joined the struggle.

Squinting toward the fortress in the morning sunlight, Derar could see the flames and dust in the camp of the engineers and knew with certainty that they were the main object of the Roman attack. Standards on the fortress walls were being used to relay signals, with another waved by a rider to the flank of the Roman horsemen reforming near the engineers' camp. With a glance, Derar saw that the Roman aim had been achieved and that the charge of the Franks was only a diversion.

Derar also understood that the Frankish attack was going wrong, for their feint had assumed a purpose of its own. At the very moment when they should have drawn rein, veered to the left and withdrawn back to the walls, they spurred straight towards the mass of ghulams who rode forward to meet them. One man had caused this; a black knight on a magnificent stallion rode in front of the Franks. Derar knew the knight had identified Tughrul and believed his heart's desire and his destiny could be achieved by the death of the Sultan in single combat. The black Frank and the shepherd king had spied each other, a spear-throw across the crowded field.

Derar sensed Tughrul Bey doubted he could defeat this huge Frank in a trial of arms. The Sultan paused as the flanks of the ghulams surged forward around the close-packed, galloping wedge of Christians. Thick, wafting dust obscured his view for a moment. The battlefield was becoming enveloped in this shifting, dry-powdered mix of campfire smoke, dirt and animal manure, all churned by the movement of thousands of hooves into choking clouds that coated men and horses, searing eyes and gritty in parched mouths.

In an ear-sundering crash, the opposing front ranks met in a maelstrom of fallen horses, splintered spears and torn, spitted and broken men. Some mounts tried to stop short or shy away just before the moment of contact, but were borne along by the crush of those behind them. Horses and men went down as though scythed, with the shouting, clash of arms and the screams of the stricken all around. Derar lost sight of the Sultan as a tide of loose-ordered tribal horse-archers swept past, as if they innately knew to harry the flanks and rear of the Christians.

The front of the Frankish charge was halted by the instant sacrifice of scores of ghulams on their lighter horses. But the press of armoured *gulâmân-I suray* and the Frankish horses floundering almost to their bellies in the mass of fallen mounts and riders, knocked the momentum from the Christian charge. The Franks were now fighting for their lives as the Seljuk host surged forward.

Seljuk horsemen fell like sheaves before the heavily armoured Franks. The black knight, his lance shattered, fought with his sword, cleaving around him so none could come close as his horse reared and plunged to gain firm footing. To Derar, it seemed as if the Turks' desire to capture alive the black Castilian horse, worked in the rider's favour for a while. Then a spear struck home and the black knight staggered in his saddle. Other knights fell by his side as ghulams closed around the mighty Frank's horse as both were lost from Derar's sight.

The Franks were surrounded; a third of their number killed or wounded in minutes. Some surrendered, throwing down their arms and helmets and being led from the fight on their own horses. If spared in the heat of battle, they might later hope to be ransomed, or receive an offer to change sides—anything to stay alive. In the plunging terror of the Frankish ranks, as they tried to ward off the rain of arrows, there was a discernible uncertainty. Men were looking around for a leader and finding none, more cried for mercy and made to yield.

Then there was one, riding a brown courser, amongst the Franks. Two, three ghulams fell to his sword as he cleared a space around his horse. Other knights saw him waving the weapon defiantly over his head. They took courage and the ghulams shrank from close quarters with them.

With Qurmul plunging in excitement under him, Derar looked at the Roman horse near the city and saw them formed up, but hesitant. He knew why: their leaders were attempting to learn through the dust and tumult, the fate of the Franks and determining whether to go to their relief.

"Go back. Go back," Derar cried aloud in Arabic. "There's nothing you can do."

*In the Seljuk lines before Manzikert,
After sunrise, 4th September 1054*

Leo could discern little through the dust to his front. He had seen the movement of mounted men from the Seljuk encampment towards the direction Balazun had ridden and knew a furious battle was underway, but there was no way of knowing which side fared best. He doubted that Balazun had achieved a decisive penetration by killing the Sultan and wondered why the Franks were not withdrawing. The swirling movement of Seljuks towards the Frankish charge indicated an unfolding blunder. Although some of the Seljuks had seen Leo's regiment, still forming up and evacuating some of their wounded, only a few of the enemy were moving towards him.

Leo was sweat-soaked under his armour. Perspiration dribbled down his cheeks and flying grit stung his eyes. Dust clouds eddied around as he trotted a little further away to better determine the progress of Balazun's fight. The trumpets had repeated the recall, but there was no indication the Franks were disengaging in accordance with their orders. Leo was calculating the considerable risk of moving forward to their assistance, against the very real possibility that his own men would be annihilated. By adopting one course, he risked losing the advantage won thus far, by the destruction of most of the garrison's effective horse. By returning without assisting the Franks, he risked creating a rift between the Romans and Franks inside the walls which in itself might jeopardise the safety of the fortress.

These things were on Leo's mind when a warning shout came from one of his escort. A furious fight erupted around him and the momentum of it carried his escort away. Too late, Leo saw the big Seljuk on a dun Turkmene riding hard at Zarrar's off side. Instinctively, he parried the big warrior's levelled spear with his own, but the Turkmene hit Zarrar with great force. Most horses would have gone down immediately but the powerful bay, experienced in polo and battle, had seen the attacker and turned in a half rear. Zarrar staggered and went down on his front knees. With a glancing blow, the dun Turkmene's head hit Leo and lodged before him across Zarrar's whither.

Leo, his spear useless in the close combat, dropped it and grabbed the dun's bridle, hitting the horse hard around the head with his fist to cast it off. The dun rolled its eyes in terror while Leo heard the rasp of its breath and felt the sharp edges of bit and buckles through his gauntlet. The Seljuk, momentarily blinded by the way he carried his own shield on his left arm, had not yet dropped his spear to seize a weapon better suited for close quarters.

Leo knew he had a moment. As Zarrar and he were falling, he kicked his feet from the stirrups and dropped his shield to avoid becoming entangled in them. With a swift, practiced movement, he grasped his mace from its case on the pommel. In a fearful frenzy, he hit the dun horse again and again about the head, hoping to drive it off Zarrar and make it fall, so the Turk might also become pinned and helpless.

Both men and horses fell heavily. Leo felt a sharp pain in his left foot as the bay horse went down. While Zarrar heaved up onto his forelegs, Leo thought about remounting as the horse rose, but he was too unbalanced and could not get into position. Relieved that he was not hooked-up in the stirrups as Zarrar trotted off, Leo rolled onto a knee to face his antagonist. All was terrible trained reason now, without pity or quarter: guilt and penance could come later, if he lived.

The big Turk, still holding his spear and round, silk-bound cane shield, was also struggling to his feet. Protected by his shield, the Seljuk could parry Leo's mace and still thrust at him with the spear. Leo could not see his own shield which was somewhere behind him. There was no time to pick it up anyway. Seeing his spear laying behind the big Seljuk, Leo hurled himself at his antagonist, raining blows on the man. The Turk backed off in surprise. Leo dropped the mace and retrieved his spear, seizing it two-handed like a pike.

They were together in this lonely duel on the crowded field. Adopting a bent-kneed fighting stance, Leo felt a strange calmness as the years of drilling under arms took hold. He breathed steadily and put the fall behind him. That was then. This was now. He moved forward, left foot leading, the spear point forward with his left hand. The Turk wore a corselet of fine mail and Leo was surprised that he noticed how the man's helmet dehumanised him, the spike adding to the impression of height while the low rim and narrow nasal drew attention from the flesh beneath. He glanced around, checking for other immediate threats. Horsemen were fighting near them but none were close.

He advanced aggressively on the big Seljuk, thrusting at the man's eyes with his spear point: hard and fast, once, twice, moving forward each time. The Seljuk covered himself with the shield. Again Leo stabbed with the point in an arching slash at his antagonist's eyes. The Turk raised his shield higher to better protect himself from the repeated strikes. Leo noticed the Seljuk's left leg became exposed as he lifted the shield. Leo struck again, high at the emir's eyes and saw the man's defence shift more to Leo's left. He stabbed again on the same line for good effect and was rewarded when the Seljuk unbalanced his defence further to meet the attacks.

Instantly Leo switched the direction of attack to his right by bringing the haft of his spear hard against the side of the Seljuk's knee. The man grunted in pain and fright as the leg gave way and he dropped to his left knee, thrusting out the shield arm to save himself. Exploiting the opening he had created, Leo sprang forward and plunged the point of his spear into the Turk's throat above the corselet, driving him over onto his back. Checking that his victim was disabled, Leo wrenched out the spear.

Gasping for breath after the physical and emotional demands of the last few seconds, Leo quickly looked around. He was not immediately threatened but the regiment was a short bowshot away to his right, in the last stages of driving off an attack by Seljuk irregular horse. The rush of the Seljuk charge had carried Zarrar a spear cast to his left. Leo could tell from the horse's head carriage, the way he was looking behind him, Zarrar was searching for him. In a crouching, feeling, backwards shuffle, Leo retrieved his shield and tucked the mace in his military belt, calling and beckoning to Zarrar as he did. The horse saw and turned towards him.

Four mounted Seljuks, seeing the lone, unhorsed Roman, closed on Leo with their spears aloft. He knew as soon as he faced one or two, the others would seek to get behind him. Two charged. Leo jumped aside, thrusting ineffectually at one with his spear as the rider passed. Glancing quickly behind, he saw them wrench their horses to a halt and turn back towards him.

Another flurry of Seljuk riders swept past, preventing Leo from reaching the regiment, or them from supporting him with archery, even if they could see him in the dust and confusion. He knew mobility was his only salvation and he had to catch and mount Zarrar before the battle bore the horse away. More Seljuks appeared between Leo and Zarrar. With rising desperation Leo made to run to his horse when a lone cataphract on a mail-barded chestnut rammed through the press up to Zarrar and caught the bay horse's reins.

To his mixed relief and surprise, Leo then recognised Maniakh on Speedy with the lone cataphract. The Patzinak gashed open an arm of one of the four men attacking Leo. Screaming in shock, the nomad desperately pulled his horse away. Maniakh calmly put spurs to Speedy, the big horse bounding forward and knocking over a second. The lone cataphract galloped up and passed Zarrar's reins to Leo, who swung to the saddle and was grateful and astonished to find his rescuer was none other than his youthful squire, Taticus Phocas, riding Ruksh. The three trotted to the protection of the regiment.

"Am I glad to see you two," Leo grinned in relief. "Thank you."

Maniakh looked solemn.

Leo took in the rolled cloak, water skin and saddlebag on Speedy. David Varaz appeared and passed the reins of Maniakh's blaze-faced mare to him. He looked at Leo and shouted, "I couldn't stay away—owed them for Kapetrou."

Leo clasped Maniakh's bridle hand in a gesture of understanding and gratitude. "Farewell, friend. Though it's far away, if you pass by my father's place, leave Speedy with him. He'll give you another in exchange—a good one. And tell the old man I am well."

Maniakh looked to the fight surging around them. "Tell him you're well?" the Patzinak repeated with a faintly bemused air. "Farewell, Horse-archer. Good luck to you." He turned his horses to leave and said over his shoulder, "Tell Cecaumenus I am sorry."

"You tell him!" Leo returned as Maniakh, Speedy and the blaze-faced mare melted into the swirling dust.

Leo's brief encounter with the big Seljuk emir and his rescue had occupied a few minutes. Some of his escort and the standard-bearer rode up, shaken at having been separated in the melee. Collecting his thoughts, Leo shouted to nearby Lascaris to inquire what was happening.

The centarch looked around, but could not make out the words over the din and shouting. His face clouded with concentration, Lascaris rode closer and cupped a hand to his ear.

Leo shouted again, "Antony, report!"

Lascaris, breathless and sweating under his helmet, drew alongside Leo. "I lost you, Count, and feared you dead. We're all right. The pressure from their light horse seems to have abated. Many of them are now drawing off to something on our right flank, and they haven't got behind us in strength. I'd say Bessas has struck their left."

"The Franks?" Leo shouted, as Zarrar wheeled impatiently.

"Don't know," Lascaris admitted, irritably quietening his own wilful mount as he indicated with a straight arm the Frank's location. "Cloud of dust—horses with empty saddles coming out." The centarch's description was as accurate as brief.

A glance around satisfied Leo the regiment was well formed and master of its immediate tactical environment. He turned Zarrar for a better view to the north, where dense clouds of black and grey smoke indicated that Bessas had carried the Seljuk animal-lines and baggage. As Lascaris had said, the movement of Seljuk horsemen was predominantly to the north where their leaders sensed the greatest danger now lay: the threat to their animals and precious fodder.

Leo peered once more in the direction where Balazun was most likely to be and decided that they would have to move forward to support the Franks and at least give any survivors a chance to escape. To Aspietes, he said, "Send two gallopers to the strategos, in person, and tell him I intend to move two furlongs forward—to the lava step—to try and bring out the Franks. I do not intend to become decisively engaged. I request infantry support to guard the ditch crossing and fore-wall gate as we come back in."

Aspietes repeated back the message before briefing a pair of cataphracts and sending them galloping off. Tribune Balsamon trotted up. Leo relayed his plan, to move rapidly to the front with Lascaris leading. Balsamon's hundred were to follow on in close support with bows. Thus the Sixth Schola hand-galloped forward, brushing the light opposition from the crest of the lava step where they halted defensively: trumpeters sounding the recall and standard-bearers signalling urgently.

Leo sensed a battle-moment of opportunity. Unable to disengage from the close-quarters fight with the Franks, bluffed by the brazen appearance of the Roman cavalry and fearing many more might be hidden by the crest of the lava step, the mass of Seljuks hesitated. Amongst the Franks, some seemed to sense the change in the temper of the Seljuk attack.

Leo thought he saw Charles Bertrum tear down his mail coif so he could be recognised and through the furore rally his comrades. Standing in his stirrups, Leo yelled and waved his spear high above his head, gesturing deliberately with the point for the Franks to withdraw past his left flank. Charles seemed to wave back with his sword. Then putting spurs to his exhausted horse, he charged into the surrounding Seljuks. He appeared to be in great pain, as though hit in the chest with a mace and there were two arrows caught in the back of his mail hauberk. A dozen Seljuks sought to bring him down. Thrice wounded and bleeding from other grazes and blows, he cut down two and burst through, followed by the expanding torrent of still mounted Franks who slashed their way out after him. Galloping free and turning in his saddle to check that others followed, Charles acknowledged Leo gesturing urgently with his spear. Understanding the Roman's intent, the wounded Frank led his companions in a desperate, strung out gallop past the cataphracts on the lava step and across the flat for the safety of the fortress walls.

"Let's get the hell out of here, Antony!" grimaced Leo, and to Lascaris' staccato commands, the Roman horse released a storm of arrows into the flank of the Seljuks as they confusedly tried to harry the fleeing Franks and belatedly change front to attack the regiment.

The Seljuk camp before Manzikert,
Early morning, 4th September 1054

"Oh, nicely done," Derar al-Adin murmured to himself as he saw the surviving Franks cut free and escape past the supporting Roman cavalry that was toppling dozens of un-armoured tribesmen from their horses. Before the nomads could reform and reorient the direction of their attack, the Roman horse also withdrew. Fighting all the way, the Sixth Schola retired stubbornly, showering the pursuing Seljuks with arrows and menacing any who came close with counter-attacks. Finally, still screening the rear of the Franks, the regiment reached the protection of the infantry who defended the approaches to the gates from behind portable wicker mantelets and the scarp breastworks: allowing the horsemen to enter the city without being ridden down by the numerically superior Seljuks at their backs.

Dust and smoke obscured the battlefield. Mounted Seljuks galloped towards the northern flank of their camp, Derar with them on Qurmul. After a short, unpleasant ride on his stirred-up, bounding, prancing horse, Derar saw all was destruction and confusion in what had been the well-ordered animal lines of the great encampment.

Reining into a canter, Derar saw a Christian lying on the ground and recognised him by his clothing and accoutrements as an Armenian irregular. An arrow had found its mark under the armpit of the wounded man's sword arm, a vulnerable part of his lamellar cuirass. Derar supposed it had happened as he raised the arm to strike. The Christian, his iron pot helmet fallen from his head, grimaced in pain under the beard and curly brown hair. He writhed slowly on the ground, his eyes watching Derar as he rode past. Several others lay wounded or dead nearby, but Derar knew after a quick look that the Romans had achieved this devastating blow to the army's animal transport and fodder with remarkably few casualties.

Belching clouds of acrid black naphtha smoke mixed with the distinctive blue smell of burning grass, as the army's precious stocks of hay and bags of grain glowed brightly in a crackling roar. From the intensity of the heat, Derar knew little could be saved. Camels struck by arrows ran in blind terror, smashing into groups of horsemen who even now were trying ineffectually to douse the flames. Baggage carts had been pushed together and were afire. What an hour before was the tent street where farriers, veterinarians and horse dealers had plied their trades, was now a flaming ruin.

Picket lines of horses and mules were hopelessly entangled, horses down with the lines cutting through muscle and sinew. The sight of them—white eyed, entwined in the ropes and making it worse by trying to kick and struggle free— cut at Derar's sympathies as he gave Qurmul's bit a slight tug to slow him back into a trot. Thus far the horse had been held back for the entire course of the fight. Now mad with cheated excitement, Qurmul was irritated with Derar and he in turn was vexed with the horse, as they fought against each other.

Ghulams and tribesmen galloped up and throwing reins to the horse-holders, bounded on foot into the chaos to try and cut the precious animals free and save any of the irreplaceable fodder. There was shouting and gesturing as a thousand opinions were voiced on what should be done.

Isma'il rode up roaring and bellowing on his jaded horse, trying to galvanise an immediate attack on the Armenian cavalry, still withdrawing in good order towards the fortress. Derar saw the dust, sweat and blood on Isma'il and the crazy, excited stare in his eyes. His horse, an open slash-wound in its shoulder, threw its head up and opened its jaws, trying to avoid the next, inevitable jerk on its blood-flecked, foaming mouth by the overwrought general.

It was late afternoon before any semblance of order was restored to the Seljuk camp. Derar rode back to the scattered wreckage of their tent and belongings to find Farisa already there. She knelt, close to tears that flowed freely when she looked up and saw Derar. He dismounted from the fractious Qurmul and kneeling beside her, placed an arm around her shoulders. They remained that way, until he could no longer stand the horse dancing on the ends of the reins. He rose and tied the horse to a high branch of a surviving poplar tree and knee hobbled him.

They gathered their trampled possessions and sat amongst them, silently drinking strong wine. At length, Derar gathered himself, dusted off their tent and re-erected it. Farisa found enough twigs and dry dung to light a small fire on which she cooked noodle soup and warmed some bread. Knowing Zaibullah liked it, she also boiled some of the coffee berries while Derar tended their unharmed animals. Determined to save the little barley Derar found in the sack on the cantle of Farisa's saddle, he brought it back to the fire where it would not be stolen or broken into by stray animals. Around them, people were similarly engaged, no one in the camp having had time to eat since the previous evening.

Emren Dirse and Zaibullah approached, leading their horses. Emren had found the time to saddle-up and don his iron helmet and cuirass of polished horn lamellar before joining the battle. He had been searching for his brother and sister, but having found neither, was hungry and disheartened. Farisa offered him coffee and a little of the bread she had warmed. He took it politely and sitting next to her, devoured it hungrily. Now Emren Dirse spoke of the fight against the Franks, in which he had been engaged. A glance at his worn-out horse confirmed it had been much galloped that day, for it hung its head in exhaustion and a hind shoe had come off. The suddenness and violence of the battle was at the forefront of Emren's mind. "I was looking for the Frank on my father's mare, but I couldn't see him. Nor was he amongst the hundred slain or eighty-one prisoners."

"Perhaps he didn't dare come out," Derar suggested.

"Lucky for him. I was not the only one searching. I saw Theodore Ankhialou in the fight and he looked like he was seeking someone as well."

"Did Ankhialou live?" asked Derar.

"As far as I know," Emren replied tiredly. "Unhappily for the Frank who took his woman, eh!"

The little group sat quietly in the dust for a while, staring at the few little embers and curling smoke of Farisa's fire. There was much to discuss but little said.

They watched Isma'il approach on his exhausted horse. Seeing them look at him, the haggard general stopped and asked if they had seen Hurr. They replied they had not, though Derar had indeed seen the dancer in the company of a fine looking man riding a carthorse and leading a blaze-faced Turkmene mare. For some reason Derar thought back to the fracas in Tabriz after the fire in the engineer's camp—and the subsequent hunt for a few travellers—but he said nothing, merely looking into the fire as though his thoughts were far away.

Derar glanced up to check his horse. Still saddled and bridled, Qurmul now stood quietly under the tree, boredom and tiredness combining to make his head and eyes droop as he rested one hind leg.

"Silly!" Derar said, mimicking Farisa that morning. The horse moved an ear and then turned his head to look at Derar.

"Good horse," he soothed, wondering why Qurmul had acted so strangely that day. He suspected his own indecision and contrariness—galloping around but not joining the fight—had transmitted mixed signals to the horse. He rose and walked over to Qurmul, giving him a hug around the neck. "We will be in our own lands soon."

With the sun still two hands breadths from the horizon, they heard the kettledrums summoning them to the Sultan's tent. Emren, who had been watching Derar comfort his horse, listened without moving. Then he moaned, "Will there be no end to this cursed day." With a resigned grunt, he rose and walked with Derar to the summons where they found a council of the emirs arguing and gesturing about the blame and deeds of that day.

Tughrul sat impassively, but Derar thought Tughrul Bey was seething. He initially thought the Sultan's cold rage was because the army had suffered a devastating reverse with the destruction of the tunnel, engineers, half the siege engines and much of their fodder; all in little more time than that taken over a game of polo. But there was more, for word was soon whispered around the sombre gathering that Osketsam, the Sultan's father-in-law, had been captured by the Romans, murdered and thrown from the walls.

"March out the prisoners," commanded the Sultan.

At his word, the eighty one captive Franks were forced at spear point to kneel before Tughrul. They had been stripped of their armour and weapons, but not their pride. Offered conversion to Islam, all but three declined with haughty countenances. They might have hoped for ransom or slavery. Alas fate was in no such mood this day and many of the Christians blanched when it was decreed they would be decapitated within the hour and their severed heads catapulted into the fortress.

Then the Armenian, Tatoul Vanantzi, was dragged in, one of the Sultan's courtiers saying soothingly, "Your majesty may choose to deal with this unbeliever as well this day, for the son of Arsuban has died of his wounds."

The Sultan looked resignedly at the chained Armenian. "Cut off the sword arm and give it to Arsuban with this message—your son was not slain by a weak arm."

Tatoul struggled free of his guards and made for the Sultan as if to kill him with his own dagger, but alert youths of the elite *gulâmân-I suray* sprang forth and dragged the captive to the ground. Tatoul cursed them for heathen as he was held down; an overturned camp pail used as the chopping block. It took ten men to subdue Tatoul and hold that mighty arm on the pail.

Derar, looking away from the blow, determined to inform the Romans of the fate of their ally. They would know soon enough of the fate of the Frankish captives.

Manzikert,
Morning, 4th September 1054

Barely back inside the fortress himself, Leo waited with his squire at the north gate as Bessas' men returned. Mounted on Zarrar, he counted them in like stock through a draft as they rushed past in threes and fives. A small crowd of women, Serena amongst them, were also there, scarcely able to breathe as they awaited longed-for faces.

"Well done! Well done, men!" Leo encouraged as the excited troops drew up inside the gate. Commanders shouted for their troops, trying to determine how many had been lost and who had returned maimed. Sweat ran in rivulets down horses' legs to drip on the flagstones that rang with the clamour of their shoes. Dismounting, the riders slumped against their hot saddles for support, or sank to their knees beside their horse's legs in prayer.

Anxiously, Leo looked for Bessas and was relieved when the centarch—the last man in—cantered over the wooden bridge and slid off dun Diomed, leading him through the arch of the gate towers. Bessas, walking in a sideways half-crouch, patted the dun's neck and checked for any wounds. Leo saw the arrow shaft in his subordinate's shoulder and hoped against hope it had not penetrated his armour.

Serena ran up to Bessas, threw her arms around him and kissed him through tears of joy at his return. She felt the arrow shaft and shrank back, staring at the blood on her sleeve.

"You're hurt," Leo said dismounting as he glanced at nearby Taticus Phocas who dropped Ruksh's reins and ran to fetch a medical orderly. Leo looked at Bessas' face for tell-tale signs of shock or distress.

"It'll be alright," Bessas winced to Serena.

She had tended enough wounded men in the last sixteen days to know differently. "You'll need the doctor."

Bessas managed a weak grin as he put an arm over Diomed's neck to steady himself. Then he looked around to check the well-being of the troops he had led from the walls.

"Never mind that. Your men are being taken care of," Leo said. "Just rest, until the orderlies bring a stretcher."

Bessas said nothing. He smelled of smoke, dirt and horse sweat and his grubby face bespoke the shock of battle. Dropping his shield, he clapped his free hand on Leo's shoulder in mute greeting and salute. Leo and Serena took his weight and the three stumbled a short distance and sat on the edge of a stone water trough, allowing their horses a short drink. "No more, Diomed, old friend," Bessas grunted with pain through closed teeth. "Later when you've cooled down."

Leo saw Bessas' squire approaching. "Cosmas. The centarch is hurt. We'll get him to hospital. I'll have soldiers take charge of his horse, but you see to it when you can."

"He's saved my life this day, Cosmas," Bessas said.

"Fear not I shall look after him," assured the squire, kneeling by his master. Then he looked to Leo. "Zarrar and Ruksh as well, sir?"

"Until Taticus can, thank you," said Leo. "I'll send him after you when he returns."

Leo knelt by Bessas as Serena held his hand, composing herself for the care to come. "By thunder, you've done well. Few men lost, and I saw from outside the gate the smoke and flame of your passing. The Sultan's grievously hurt this day. Just be calm while we fetch help."

"Yes," Serena echoed.

They were silent for a time. Then Bessas asked, "How did you go?"

"We've had reasonable success. Karas Selth broke into the tunnel and captured the miners." Leo removed Bessas' helmet as he spoke. "And we did well enough in the engineer's camp, but something seized Balazun and he allowed himself to become trapped in a big fight with the ghulams of the palace and imperial guards. Charles Bertrum, rallied the survivors—cut their way out."

Leo placed Bessas' helmet on the flagstones by the trough. "We went further forward than we should have to assist the Franks and came back under a lot of pressure. But Doukas was ready and led out six hundred foot to stand off the Seljuks while we got in. We lost thirty-four from the regiment."

"Who?" Bessas asked, hunching forward.

"I saw Aspieties go down on that little mare of his. Three ghulams took him on and he could not shake them off. Choniates, also, I saw with my own eyes, killed by arrows. The rest? I don't know yet?"

"Balazun himself?" Bessas asked distantly.

"Charles saw Balazun go down under a mass of ghulams, but does not know if he was killed or wounded. I am sure Reynaldus put Balazun up to it, appealed to his vanity, damn his eyes. Guy warned me something was afoot between them. I repeated the orders ... Balazun said he understood." Leo clasped a hand gently on the wounded centarch's good shoulder, trying to keep him coherent until assistance arrived.

Bessas was attempting to keep his mind from the pain. "What did Reynaldus have to gain?"

"Balazun was the only threat to Reynaldus' rising star amongst the Kelts," Leo ventured. "I do not think he, Balazun, was a fellow traveller of Kamyates."

An Armenian infantryman jogged up awkwardly in his iron lamellar cuirass and strip greaves. He had removed his pot helmet and held it by the throat-lash in his spear hand. He looked uncertainly at the crowd of dismounted cavalry and called, "Count Bryennius?"

"Here."

"The strategos' compliments, Count. He would like you to come immediately to him on the fore-wall, at the western gate tower. I'll take you."

Leo glanced from the soldier to Bessas and Serena.

"Go," she said. "I'll tell Taticus."

"Thank you," Leo said to the soldier. Then he turned to a nearby cataphract saying, "Take care of the centarch until the medical orderlies get to him please and mind our horses until my squire returns."

Leo looked into Bessas' eyes. "I have to go, but Taticus is on the way with help. Hearts up." To Serena he said, "Look after him. I fear this day is not yet done."

Leading Zarrar, he strode with the Armenian out through the main gate and handing the reins to a soldier resting behind the wall, climbed the stone steps to the fore-wall, meaning to walk along it, enter the tower and meet Basil Apocapes on the observation platform at the top. As he made his way along the ramparts, people whispered and made way.

Leo could make out Varangians ahead, guarding what he supposed were the Seljuk tunnellers. Suddenly there was tumult in the group and Leo, sensing something wrong, started to run. He saw Guy d'Agiles pulling at Kamyates and pleading with the Varangians to stop, as a welter of stabbing erupted. Then the bodies were pushed through crenelles to the concourse below.

"Stop that," Leo roared with such authority that the Varangians halted before the last two bleeding corpses were heaved from the ramparts. "What's going on?" he demanded angrily in Greek as he approached, glaring savagely at Kamyates.

"Count," the leader of the Varangian detail protested, "This man," he indicated Kamyates, "walked up and stabbed one of the prisoners. Killed him and told us to despatch the rest and throw them off the wall."

Leo's glance flickered to Guy, standing behind Kamyates.

"That's what happened," said Guy.

"He had a knife," Kamyates said evenly, "and was about to stab at me. The guards should not have been so careless. So I acted in self-defence. I couldn't do else …"

Leo noticed Guy's mouth drop open with disbelief at this lie.

"… and I have sufficient rank, as you well know, Count." Kamyates uttered Leo's rank as an insult. There was the spittle of indignation on his beard. "I have sufficient rank to have the prisoners taken care of…"

"Taken care of? Without consulting the strategos? A source of information and hostages and you decide … You!" Leo was furious enough to be intemperate.

Kamyates shrugged. "Basil can make a court issue of a dead infidel if he likes." With that threat, Kamyates and Cydones in their rich robes walked off leaving Leo seething. "What happened, Guy?"

"Count Selth caught three prisoners in the tunnel. We brought them up here and were waiting for the strategos to speak to Osketsam. As …"

"Osketsam? The Sultan's …"

Guy nodded. "As those two came close, Osketsam seemed to recognise Kamyates and was about to speak angrily with him. Kamyates just plain stabbed him in the throat and breast about four times and started screaming at the guard to kill the others. The Varangians didn't know better and followed the orders."

Basil Apocapes appeared, looking angry. "Well done out there, Count Bryennius," he said formally. Then to those around he ordered, "The council will meet in my rooms, immediately."

Guy stepped forward as if to speak.

"I saw it," the strategos said grimly, passing on.

Balazun's was the first of the Frankish heads to be hurled over the walls by the remaining two Seljuk mangonels. The priests retrieved the grisly messages of terror and tried to comfort relatives and friends.

Apocapes' council endured a long and stormy meeting. Kamyates and Cydones used their rank to rail against the attack, alleging that it had threatened the very lives of all in the fortress by sacrificing a part of the cavalry to achieve nothing more than antagonising the Sultan. Thus encouraged, Reynaldus, still covered in dried blood and fright from the battle, widened the disquiet by alleging in his petulant fashion that the Greeks had deliberately sacrificed the Franks to get them out of the way.

Leo thought Basil was close to having the three of them thrown into the dungeons. It was also a gesture, he understood, which would have long-term consequences if they ever got out of this. Given the manner in which Kamyates and Cydones had cultivated key citizens in the fortress and become well known as charming and distinguished guests; it would be impossible to act openly against them and survive afterwards. Their friends at court were powerful and had many spies.

It was the softly spoken William de Chartres who salvaged something from the tense situation. Helmet on his knee, he looked around the gathering with his pale blue eyes. He spoke to the Franks. "I followed my friend, Charles Bertrum, from the press of Saracens. What happened was no fault of any of the Romans." He had used the term deliberately, instead of the Latins' usual derogatory name "Greeks" when referring to the Byzantines. "I'll not speak ill of the dead," William shot a withering and challenging look at Reynaldus, "or the living. But I'll hear no man say that this day's sacrifice of Latin blood was the fault of the Roman Army. Had they not moved forward to support us at much risk to themselves, none of us would have got out."

All eyes turned to Reynaldus, who remained silent, glaring with hatred at William, who had just emerged as his rival among the Franks.

Basil finished by reminding them gently of the providential role of God in the battle that had allowed them, with relatively small loss, to destroy the greatest threat to their walls. Then the strategos led them to kneel while the bishop said prayers.

Leo walked with Karas Selth from the room. They were silent. He took Zarrar's reins from a Varangian sentry. The horse gave him a tired rub with his head, to ease the dried sweat itching under his chamfron. Saying farewell as Selth walked off, Leo made to mount when he heard his name spoken behind him.

"Count Bryennius!" It was William de Chartres. The Norman took the reins from his waiting squire. They mounted and rode together out of the citadel gate, stopping at the fork in the street, each motioning they were going in different directions. It was late in the day and quite still as the sun settled low and red through the dust, smoke and the distant wailing.

"Count Leo," William said before they parted, "some people don't like you or your methods. I had doubts myself at first. For what it's worth, I would ride with you any time."

"Thank you," replied Leo, touched. They parted and Leo rode down the street that led to the military quarter to speak with his men. Citizens were out and some hailed him, suspecting he may have been involved in the fight that day. Zarrar and he were both weary beyond words. The warhorse, sensing his master's distraction and day's end, walked slowly, his shoes ringing dully on the cobblestones. Leo's mind was full of the images of the battle and the weeks that had preceded it. Zarrar slowed and stopped indecisively outside the Barbarian House.

Preoccupied with his musings, Leo looked up and saw bold Greek lettering on the garden wall, "One love and one death." Without warning Martina's face came to his mind's eye. For long, introspective moments, Leo sat silently in the saddle. Zarrar's ears switched back to him, but the horse did not move.

Leo dismounted slowly. Taking the reins from around the horse's neck he said gently, "C'mon, Zarrar", and together they walked down the cobbled street.

Chapter Fifteen

One Love And One Death

The Seljuk camp outside Manzikert,
Afternoon, 6th September 1054

In the aftermath of the cavalry fight, the armies eyed each other warily: Seljuks in their camp, Romans behind their battlements. Both tended the wounds of people and horses and committed their dead. The slain emirs of the Seljuks were burned in mounds or wrapped and carried on camels to their homeland for entombment. Their perished poor were heaped on funeral pyres on the western side of the river. Within the city, the remains recovered during the chaotic battle were interred in mass graves under quicklime. Soldiers and citizens of both sides salved their maimed souls, in their churches, or on their prayer mats.

The sky became almost as black as the lava stone as the weather turned bitterly cold. Many thought it would snow. Instead it rained a steady drizzle. Sentinels on the walls drew sodden cloaks around them and watched the besieging army sheltering in their black tents.

Late in the afternoon of the eighteenth day of the siege, Derar al-Adin looked gloomily out from under the dripping goat hair of his tent at the sea of pockmarked, reeking mud that now marked the Seljuk encampment along the river. Where thousands of animals and men had trampled and eaten bare the ground, they now churned the rain-soaked soil into malodorous ooze with their hooves, boots, urine and manure. Tucked-up, hungry horses shivered on their picket lines or in restless, scrounging mobs under the care of the herd boys. Derar observed that many horses had their manes and tails chewed off by hungry neighbours and was proud of the care he and his companions had afforded their animals.

Derar lounged on a damp saddlecloth that smelled of wet wool and horse sweat, yet mitigated a little the cold ground of the tent floor. Pulling his cloak closer around him, he looked through the stripped poplars by the rocky stream bank and beyond them to the black-walled fortress. With a sigh that caused Farisa and Zaibullah both to look at him, he sank back against his saddle. Silently cursing himself for any display of emotion, Derar concealed it. "The rain—it vexes me."

Without reply, they went back to their work: Farisa preparing their evening meal, Zaibullah repairing his saddle, which had been slashed in the fight against the Franks.

Recalling the Sultan's stormy evening council after the battle, Derar felt again the cold clutch of fear. For two days his mouth had been dry with the thick taste of it. He had trouble drifting to sleep, instead lying awake and staring at the banks of clouds washing across the stars beyond. There had been recriminations that night. The Sultan had asked coldly, looking directly at Bughra Dumrul, how many more surprises the fortress of Manzikert had in store for them. Dumrul, flustered, muttered the excuse that his "spies in the fortress" had not warned him. Realising his mistake, Dumrul had corrected himself by saying "scouts", but Derar had noticed. A number of others in the pavilion had also looked sharply at the spymaster. Derar knew that Dumrul's sources in the Christian ranks posed a real threat to him. Eventually, one of them might draw the connection between Zobeir al-Adin, held prisoner in the fortress, Derar's own access to the Sultan's plans and the misfortunes in battle of the Seljuk host. Derar's nonchalant demeanour had masked his inner turmoil that night as he had gazed around the gathering. He saw the Sultan do the same and was relieved that there was fertile ground for Tughrul Bey's many suspicions: renegade Christians, Muslim mercenaries and rebellious Seljuk emirs. Many of the latter were battle-hardened, widely admired, ruthless, younger and ambitious. Tughrul also would suspect that they might wish to profit from his failure to capture Manzikert, or, slowness in doing so.

Mulling over these events in his tent, Derar watched the drizzle form lazily into droplets on the edge of the tent roof. There had been heavy showers at the start, but these had eased into the kind of light rain that is deceptively soaking. Often, as now, it came with a chill breeze.

At this introspective moment, Derar heard the cheerful voice of Emren Dirse. "Hey, desert dweller, how do you like the rain?" A pair of muddy riding boots appeared, then Emren, rain beaded on his felt cap and cloak of black wool, stooped and entered their cramped tent and lounged on a packsaddle. His sister, Burla, followed him, flashing a white smile at Farisa and Derar.

"Rain's fine," Derar rejoined, taken by surprise. "We have it in the desert as well, y'know. And snow occasionally. But not in such prodigious or untimely quantities." He had hitherto paid little attention to Burla, but felt a rising interest as she placed her weapons and mail shirt down and sat at ease in her riding clothes.

"Bah!" Emren said. "You can keep your fly-blown desert. I've served in Baghdad and around that area, stinking hot much of the time, dry, dusty and then bitterly cold with poor grazing. Keep it! We don't like it. Give us higher ground where the air is cool and the grass plentiful."

"So I see," returned Derar sardonically, recalling the Sultan's passion for Baghdad. Emren Dirse had just made clear to him part of the reason for the pressure the nomads were now exerting on the wounded Armenian nation and tottering Byzantine state. The high, cool Anatolian-Armenian plateau was much more to the instinctive liking of the Turkic tribes than the deserts where their Sultan would lead them. Thus some drifted of their own accord, to the lands of the Rum[68]—the sharp edge of their migration now backed by Tughrul's present invasion.

"Emren, why all this conquest?' he asked.

The emir pursed his lips and looked at the ground between his boots for a time. "To my mind it is because we were—are—ever more numerous and warlike, powerful enough to prey upon and subdue those around us, especially the sedentary peoples of the cities and towns of the fertile lands. All seems ours for the taking, especially as our people achieved clan identities under chieftains like Saljak, his sons—Isra'il and Mikh'ail. The last named died early in battle, leaving his sons as leaders of our branch of the Seljuks, Chagri Bey and Tughrul Bey. After being crowned Sultan, Tughrul appointed Chagri governor in the east, where he still rules keeping Kurasan under heel and the Ghaznavids at bay. Tughrul himself holds suzerainty over the western half of the Seljuk domains. The Sultan is touched by religious purpose as you know."

Emren paused, accepting wine from Farisa. "That is my view. Others have different opinions: pointing to the pitiless hardship of life on the steppes, our forefathers' persecution at the hands of more powerful Oghuz peoples and our conversion to Islam—some hundred years ago. That brought us into contact with the settled peoples who turned against us. As Mahmud the Ghaznavid did, one of his courtiers advising our extermination, or at the least cutting off all our thumbs so we could not draw the bow. Mahmud, a civilised ruler by all accounts, did not, of course, but tried to drive us from his lands. He was unable to do this, but the Seljuks were respectful of his prowess and avoided battle with him. He died, however, and it was his son, Mas'ud, we defeated at Dandanqan, thus setting us onto the path of empire. This view casts the Seljuks as a persecuted, wandering people in search of a homeland, carrying with them God's mission to protect the true believers from heretics and unbelievers."

Burla Dirse warmed to this discussion and spoke with confidence and insight on the religious pronouncements of the Sultan's vizier. She outlined the form

---

68 Rum—the Seljuk term for Romans. Thus the modern city of Ezurum (old Karin) is a derivative of "Artsn of the Romans".

of Tughrul Bey's intended secular authority over the Abbasid Caliphate, and how religious leadership would remain with the incumbent al-Ka'im. Derar had a newfound respect and liking for the woman. Before this, he had not really noticed her black hair, animated smile and laughing brown eyes. Seljuk men, Derar reflected as he listened, were fierce while their women seemed softer. Burla Dirse, captivating in this rough company, would have been breathtaking in a palace.

With the hospitality of desert and camp, Derar invited the visitors to dine with them: a sparse repast of noodle soup, flat bread and lamb, grilled over a small fire of dried dung and far-collected and carefully hoarded twigs. Without asking him, Farisa produced more of Derar's treasured wine and the five of them enjoyed a relaxed meal. Conversation ranged across different subjects, though some force kept them from discussing the campaign or its battles.

The sunset, splendid as it broke through the clouds, caused them to fall silent and watch. After dark, Zaibullah enticed Farisa and Burla Dirse to accompany him to the shops, near the lines of the ghulams where off-duty troops drifted to be entertained, or seek the companionship of other restless souls. It was a place of crowded, lively laneways, shops selling all manner of goods, touts, musicians and singers, dancers and storytellers.

After they left, and not discouraged by Derar, Emren Dirse allowed the conversation to drift to the thing that was always on their mind: the siege. "Something's up," he began. "Tughrul Bey and his vizier have been in close council. No one can get near, except I saw the emirs, Dinar and Alkan, come from the pavilion." Emren was silent for a moment, as if thinking back to the scene. "Dinar seemed pleased with himself, not at all like he had just been chastised."

"It is clear when someone has been chastised by the Sultan," Derar probed. He recalled Dinar had led the raid to the southwest, beyond Baghesh and Mush and wondered at his inclusion in the current secrecy.

"And hundreds of ghulams, with engineers as well, are making ready to move."

"Where? What for?" asked Derar with growing interest.

"I don't know, my friend. I don't know. But there is much suspicion in the camp and speculation about a spy. The Sultan and his vizier trust none."

Derar gazed out into the gathering darkness, watching the troops in their tents around their tiny, flickering fires. Aware that Emren was looking intently at him, he listened to the rain dripping from the black tent into the little puddle beside it and breathed in the mud—animal—man smell of the encampment. Derar remained silent.

The emir followed the direction of Derar's apparent interest in the glistening wet gloom. "On the first suitable night," he said, "tomorrow night, God willing, I'm ordered to attack the fortress. It would be well if you came. It would demonstrate," he paused, "your fidelity to …"

"It is a serious attack?"

Emren returned the Arab's steady stare. Even in the poor light of Derar's tiny lamp, there was a haunted look in the Seljuk's eyes. "No." There was a long pause while the two men considered his answer. "For the Sultan and the vizier, it is a diversion," Emren continued, "to wear down the unbelievers while their other plans unfold. But I must make my people think it is a serious attack or they'll be loath to undertake it. And if I can get over their walls, I will."

"I should be honoured to accompany you," Derar replied as though he meant it. "No man in this camp is more eager than I to see those inside that place get their just reward." He had no clear plan of what he would do if they did break through the defences, other than head for the citadel where he reasoned the dungeons would be. "If we break in, Emren, I want the Roman count, Bryennius, alive."

"Of course! He has your nephew."

Early the next day, Emren Dirse, Derar and the engineer, Abramas, rode a circuit of the fortress. Derar had not seen much of the southern and eastern walls and was intrigued by the forbidding bulk of the citadel on the eastern defences, and the lagoon at the south-east corner, capable of flooding the ditch along the southern wall.

Emren Dirse had been ordered by the Sultan to attack the north wall, with the aim of shifting the defenders' attention from the west. The three paused for a long time on the low spur to the north of the fortress where Emren Dirse and Abramas discussed the attack. The engineer noted the dry ditch and calculated the length the assault ladders would need to be.

Derar in his damp cloak sat silently on Zanab, as the planners conversed. He followed their conversation and made his own observations. He knew the assault force could move easily on foot after dark from the main camp and form up behind the spur line where they now rode. A crescent moon, the symbol of the Seljuks, should provide just enough light to see by, if the cloud cover was not too heavy. The troops could line up in assault formation here and wait silently on the crest while Emren Dirse gave the leaders their bearing by the stars, or on the dim outline of the fortress itself, together with the last orders for the attack. A key consideration was whether the weather would clear, allowing the use of bows.

"Your thoughts?" Emren Dirse asked his friend.

"I would beware lest the unbelievers breach that dam and flood the ditch during the attack," Derar answered.

The others looked at the defences, saw the truth of his observation and were silent for a moment. Abramas said, "A good point. But they would have done so during previous attacks—and the Sultan has ordered us."

Derar waved a hand in acquiescence. They asked, he answered: it was as God willed.

Late the following afternoon, a red sunset broke the clouds, the drizzle cleared and a cold wind mourned through the Arsanias Valley. Derar, in silence, ate little of his evening meal. At the fourth call, he prayed earnestly, then stood outside their tent and with Zaibullah nearby, started to shrug on his mail shirt and gird his weapons. He carried a marked arrow, a note tightly wound around its shaft.

He would be shooting into the wrong part of the fortress and there was little to report: simply that the Sultan had some new plan which was a closely guarded secret. He had heard a word, *baban*, but could give it no meaning or context. Lest a clue find its way back to the Sultan, he did not belabour the point that he was no longer part of the shepherd king's inner circle.

"You stay, Zaibullah. Tonight's fight is not yours," he said, joining the files from the tents of Emren Dirse, walking silently into the night.

Two thousand men moved north below the lava bank and followed the guides eastward up the low spur line. There they halted in the dim blue starlight and faced to their right, south, towards the fortress. The wind had dropped and every time a reckless scabbard clinked against a rock, or a boot dislodged a pebble on the stony rise, Derar thought the sound deafening, as if the world would awaken. They waited.

Emren Dirse emerged from the night and gave his final orders. "The wall is defended by the Vrangs," he said. "We'll move forward silently, until they start shooting. When that happens, the two mangonels will discharge fire-pots at the towers. Dumrul's spies tell us there is a sally-port in that main tower behind, with another in the fore-wall turret that we will attack. They are cunningly built and hard to see, but are there."

He paused while the information sank in, then turned to his brother. "Beyruh, as soon as the firepots hit, you must get your assault ladders up and capture the towers, and if possible the sally-ports. The Daylamis are holding the line of wickerwork mantelets protecting the siege engines in front of us. There is a party of fire-troops waiting to go with you. When we take and hold the two towers, the infidels will find it hard to dislodge us. The Sultan will bring up the rest of the army to exploit the breach. "Tomorrow," said Emren, attempting to show confidence before the forlorn hope, "we take our pleasure in Manzikert."

Derar heard the false confidence of the emir and saw the solemn figures kneeling in the dim blue light around him. They rose as one and dispersed silently to their followers. After an interval, the assault lines started forward raggedly in response to whispered commands.

The attack moved down the gentle, muddy, basalt-strewn slope. In the gloom, Derar could make out the party struggling with the battering ram, a simple tree trunk, the head of which was reinforced with iron ploughshares. They made for the fore-wall tower on which the brunt of the assault would fall. When it became wetter under foot with the mud sucking at their boots, Derar knew they had crossed the lower ground that separated the fortress from the rise. In his imagination, he could even now see the battlements. As they groped their way forward, shadowy figures loomed against the outlines of engines, black against the sky. Derar found himself among the unfamiliar accents of the Daylami infantry, where there was whispered confusion and delay as the assault passed through the earthworks and linked up with the fire troops supporting them.

Derar thought they were now well within archery range: his fears were realised when a man fell with a clatter of arms. There was a warning shout on the battlement and answering cries followed by the clamour of many men taking post on the walls. Arrows and catapulted rocks started to fall amongst the assaulting Seljuks. Behind him, Derar heard the double crack of the two mangonels being released as fire arrows were lit around him. The clay pots broke on the tower, flaming arrows readily igniting the splattered, dripping naphtha.

They ran with the ladder-parties towards the blazing tower, the men cheering and shouting now the attack had been discovered. Jogging forward with the others, Derar half slid, half fell down the counterscarp into the blackness of the ditch. He was surprised at its depth and stumbled over several bodies before reaching the other side. Groping figures in the dark assisted him up the scarp where he squeezed, encumbered by his belt and weapons, between two of the unmanned scarp breastwork merlons, to move forward across the open ground to the fore-wall. Gasping for breath, he was surprised at how high the fore-wall now appeared. Seljuks, struggling to deploy the battering ram and scaling ladders, were crammed on the narrow front between the ditch and fore-wall. Someone had misjudged the length needed for the ladders, which were now so long they reached past the tops of the merlons, to be easily pushed away by the defenders. An emir knelt over one, hacking with his war-axe to shorten it. All was shouting and confusion.

They made no impact on the walls.

Stones from above smashed the ladders and the men on them as darts and arrows plunged into the struggling mass below. From behind his shield, Derar could see Varangian reinforcements enter the threatened tower and extinguish the flames. In a far-away fashion, he heard their strange cries and oaths as they bellowed orders to each other and jeered the thwarted Seljuks below.

Drawing the message arrow from his quiver, Derar fitted it to his bow. With a cry, a Seljuk fell against him. Angrily, his aim almost spoiled and the incriminating arrow lost in the dark, he pushed the man away and was suddenly remorseful when he saw him slump dying. A stream of Greek Fire sheeted from a tower and for long moments illuminated in macabre clarity the press of assaulting warriors. The burst of orange light brought with it a renewed hail of missiles and stones from above, accompanied by screams of pain and horror, as a hissing hot stench of thrown quicklime mixed with scalding water emptied from half a dozen cauldrons.

The anguished, furious face of Emren Dirse appeared. He was shouting to the kneeling emir to get the ladder ready. In the press, Derar saw Burla tell Emren to get men shooting with their bows at the Varangians above. Hair wild under her helmet, she moved on, hitting and punching men, forcing them to lift their gaze from the chaos around them and start engaging the bearded shadows peering from the dark crenelles above.

Once more the Seljuks, with arms fully extended over their heads, forced a ladder up against the tower. Beyruh Dirse was first on the ladder. The handsome young man, with his flowing hair and brave moustaches, covering himself with his shield, clambered up followed by others. Varangians moved to meet the threat. Some carried flaming brands and by their flickering light, Derar made out the fight at the merlons.

Beyruh Dirse, shield strapped to his arm, was holding the ladder with one hand. A big Varangian wielding a battle-axe single handedly, held a merlon with the other as he leaned far out from the battlements. Blow for blow they struck. The duellists seemed as warring gods, illuminated by the torchlight against the background of stone and rolling clouds of smoke. Derar was aware of a strange hush around him as others saw it also. Then the Varangian's axe smashed through one side of the ladder, causing it to skew crazily. Beyruh dropped his sword as he struggled to maintain his grip. With a triumphant shout, the blonde Viking raised the axe and smashed it down full force into the shoulder of Beyruh Dirse, who collapsed with a cry to the foot of the wall. An angry skiff of arrows caught the Viking before he could get back behind the stones and he too fell, clutching a shaft that had entered his mouth and protruded from the back of his neck.

With an anguished shout, Emren pushed through the crowd to where his brother lay and knelt by him, oblivious to the danger from above. Beyruh Dirse was dead. Emren Dirse rose with a terrible, wild-eyed look and screamed. As if possessed, he struck madly with his mace at the blood, oil and excrement smeared fortifications, as though to smash them asunder in his terrible passion. The stones of Manzikert were unmoved and he slumped exhausted at their base.

Seeing this and knowing the attack to have failed, Derar shouted for a withdrawal and dragged his friend towards the ditch, into which many tribesmen had fled seeking refuge from the deluge of arrows and bolts.

As the attack stalled, Roman engineers, unseen in the dark, crept forth from the walls and knocked away the chocks holding the dammed waters of the moat. Water coursed down the ditch. Some Seljuks drowned under the weight of their armour, or because they were wounded and could not swim. A quick-thinking few threw lassos across for others to hold on to. Derar and Burla Dirse, dragging the grief-stricken Emren, plunged into the dark, turbulent water. With their armour pulling them down, they made their way hand-over-hand along a lasso looped around a merlon and held by a bold hand on the other side. Arrows struck the water beside them. Derar glanced back in fear to see that a skirmish line of Varangians had sallied from the fortress and was striking down the Seljuks on the open ground before the wall, shooting at those struggling in the flooded ditch. Many nomads risked their lives to pull the stricken out with them.

As they clambered up the counterscarp and beyond range and sight of the defences, sympathetic Daylamis assisted the chilled, defeated troops with hot broth, as well as improvised stretchers and dressings for the wounded. In the blue light of night, Emren's people gathered behind the siege lines while their leader with solemn dignity thanked them for all they had attempted. His followers counted the cost, the leaders moving forward to clasp his clothing, conveying the unspoken message they knew the deed was not of his making.

Derar and Emren made their way to the guard tent near the Sultan's pavilion to report. "The Sultan was resting," Isma'il, the general, said in a tone that hinted at no surprise. The two men received no thanks. To their leaders it was just another futile attack in a failing siege. "The Romans have only bought themselves a little more time, while we drain all the ditches and divert the streams that feed them," the general grunted.

They left without a word.

Not long before first cock-crow, Derar led Emren Dirse to his tent. Farisa leapt up when she saw them and bathed their hands and faces. Saying nothing, she offered them strong wine and food. Derar, who in his shock had not taken the water proffered by the Daylamis, was suddenly aware how thirsty the exertions had made him. He drank greedily of the wine and after a prayer, sank to his saddlecloth in the dark of their tent and could not stop the relief of the dry tears that racked his lean body.

The Barbarian House in Manzikert,
Late afternoon, 9th September 1054

Guy d'Agiles leaned back lazily in the hard wooden chair and savoured the moment. The sun shone warmly from the western sky while a light wind dried the ground. He was seated in the garden of the Barbarian House, nursing in his lap a crust of bread, a few slices of cheese and a goblet of red wine. It was his second day off the wall, after his second tour on it. He had shaved, bathed and changed his clothes, his washing now drying in the late afternoon breeze. The well water was pure and the apple tree still bore leaves, even if it had long been stripped of fruit. The untended garden seemed restfully remote from the fighting, even if crowded with saddled horses, piles of hay, stones, beams and other warlike stores.

Happenstance had brought many familiar faces to the garden where they now took their ease. Togol lay supine on a saddlecloth next to David Varaz. Arshak lounged close by, contributing to the conversation in his broken Greek. They looked up at the sky, occasionally rising languidly on an elbow to take more food or drink. Bessas sat near them, nursing his wounded shoulder in a sling.

There was no public shame amongst this group as they now took a few hours respite; though who could know what private humiliation any carried, or whether they alone knew of something for the common good they had failed to do, for want of time, strength, courage or presence of mind? This was each man's burden.

Guy thought there could be nothing but pride here. All had fought on the walls and in the patrolling before the arrival of the Seljuks. The scouts had entered the enemy camp to spy and spread subversive rumours. There was an easy camaraderie and trust as they recounted stories of the past few months. Guy felt at ease in their presence. None mentioned it, but Guy had won his spurs amongst these men and was accepted as an equal by them. It occurred to him then, how long he had yearned in his youth to have faced and passed this rite of passage. In his ignorance, he had been unaware of its accompanying burden of terror and guilt at lives lost and taken. He knew this feeling would wax and wane like the moon, but ever lurk beneath the surface of his consciousness.

Jacques sat in a chair nearby. At the sight of him, Guy thought of their frequent visits to Charles Bertrum, still lingering in the nun's hospital. Medical orderlies had moved quietly, with the nuns, or Roman and Armenian healers doing what they could for the patients. Many spoke highly of an Arab physician who also worked there. The scrubbed buildings of the temporarily converted monastery smelled of soap, vinegar, clean straw and the astringent and healing balms. They also smelled of fear. Strong men lay pale and silent. All must have contemplated their fate if the Seljuks broke in, and their ability in future to earn a living if they did not. Warfare and the wealth or want of Byzantium depended on the muscle power of people and animals. The disabled soldier, peasant or artisan faced a forlorn future.

Guy had first visited the hospital to see Charles, as soon as possible after the cavalry fight outside the walls. Bessas Phocas was also there with an arrowhead lodged in his shoulder. Guy had seen the centarch seated, waiting to be tended, Serena Cephala by his side, easing off his hauberk and attempting to staunch the bleeding with a cloth. Charles' arms and armour rested in an untidy pile beside the table on which he lay. A crowd of people around him had been working bare armed around a pail of bloodstained, steaming water and many discarded cloths. Flora had come towards him, dry-eyed under her auburn hair. She looked Guy full in the eyes, wordless but without reproach, then stooped and gathered up Charles' discarded clothing and equipment. "I'm in the way. I should see to his horse and clean these."

Guy knew there was nothing he could do but pray. "I'll take the horse," he had offered. So he trailed Flora Asadian outside and watched her break down. The abbess comforted her with an embrace.

Carrying his friend's weapons and armour, Guy had walked to the stables to find that someone had already unsaddled and cared for Charles' brown mare. He lingered with the animal for a little while, stroking and speaking softly to her, counting her wounds that the veterinarians had dressed.

Five days had passed since the day of the fight in the tunnel and the battle outside the walls. In that time Guy had only a few fleeting conversations, almost satirical exchanges of stoic pleasantries, with Irene, except for that occasion when he had reluctantly and awkwardly told her of her being spoken of in the Seljuk camp as a bride for the Sultan. She had blanched and become very quiet.

Basil Apocapes, leaving the Barbarian House with Bryennius, Branas and Oleg, saw the little gathering in the garden and approached the lounging men. They made to stand, but Basil bade them be still and squatted on his heels amongst them. He looked exhausted, grey bags under red-rimmed eyes, hair matted and some days since he had removed his clothes. Guy wondered how the strategos could bear his burden. Basil greeted the group warmly and praised the work they had done, especially thanking those who had ventured beyond the safety of their comrades to scout in the enemy encampment.

"How goes the battle?" Togol asked.

"All is uncertain in war," Basil replied, "But we're actually doing well—twenty-one days into it now, and the first bit is always the hardest." He looked at all of them briefly, as though wishing to make certain, before he continued, that their current ease reflected resolution, not resignation. "The first bit and the last bit. Though food and fodder need to be carefully rationed, the bishop has no fear of famine for the next two months and there's plenty of water. That said, regardless of whether the Seljuks go or stay, the winter that follows will be hard. Although afraid, the people are loyal to their duties and are brave in them. Praise God we have been able to discern the Sultan's moves and counter them, but we've no reason for complacency and must be constantly vigilant. Nor should we forget all the people who have been massacred, impoverished and marched into slavery from the lands around."

At this, they all looked at the ground.

Sensing the mood, Basil continued on a milder note. "As soon as the Seljuks raise the siege, we will pursue them most vigorously with what forces we can muster and try to rescue as many prisoners as we can, as the Varangians of Baberd are rumoured to have done."

At the mention of the Varangians, Bessas looked at Oleg and asked about the fight on the north wall the night before last.

"With the strategos' approval," Oleg began, "there was no warning that time. But I suspected something was up after three of their princes spent some time observing us from the crest the morning before. This attack was more cunning—they approached silently, until one of them fell over and we heard the clatter of his arms. Then they were on us with fire and arrows. The heathen tried to burn us out of the tower and then batter down the sally-ports. But we were too fast for them." Oleg leaned on his great axe and looked down at them.

"We need to do something about the two mangonels on that side," said David Varaz.

"We have," the Viking rejoined. "Or at least the presbyter, Araxie Bagradian is."

Daniel Branas interrupted quietly, reminding Basil they had an appointment and that he needed to refresh and rest. With the good grace that marked the man, the strategos quietly apologised to Oleg for having to move on. They all stood and watched silently as the two left.

Bryennius lingered in the yard of the Barbarian House with his comrades of the march and the siege. He took his ease, sitting on a saddlecloth, his back propped against a low wall with his armour and weapons beside him. Within a short time, he leaned his head back against the wall and closed his eyes. "Please Oleg, continue your account of the north wall. I have not yet heard the details."

They all sat or squatted around and Oleg continued. "Yes! Now, we'd been wondering at how to deal with the Seljuk stone throwers, but their rocks had little enough impact on the walls so we grew lax about them. But last night when they used them to hurl firepots at us, that was a new and dangerous menace. It turns out the priest, Araxie Bagradian, was a military engineer and understands the mechanics of war. He's been ministering to the men on the wall and they trust him, for he has a touch with common folk. He said there were still timbers in his church, the one you wrecked, Jacques …"

Guy and the others smiled at the joking reference to the tunnel.

"… Timbers stout and long enough to make a catapult of sufficient power to meet the enemy machines. There are builders and shipwrights among us, so they went to work with him and constructed an engine on one of the towers. With his first rock, Araxie struck close to one of the heathens' stone-throwers. Then, praise God, his second rock struck their stone just as the infidel's released it." Oleg laughed at the memory of it. "The two stones shattered and covered the Seljuks with dust and flying stone chips. They will be days picking the shards out of their eyes." He fell silent, looking at the ground, seeing the images of the fight once more in his mind.

"What happens now?" asked Bessas.

"This day?" Oleg asked, subtly seeking their approval to continue. "Seven rocks did the presbyter hurl at the heathen, until they ceased throwing their own rocks, to work on protecting their machines with cotton bales and other materials they have found. Now we watch them as they watch us. We offered a truce so they could get their stinking dead out of the ditch, but this was refused, so their emissary said, on the order of the Sultan."

"Hmm," mused Togol aloud. "He must be very angry."

"We've held up the shepherd king badly," remarked Vardaheri who was now regarded as an authority on the Seljuks. "He pillaged Berkri without trouble and subdued Archēsh in eight days. Manzikert has not been so easy and his people see it."

"Twenty-one days! As the strategos said, we haven't done too badly," Vardaheri looked to Bessas. "How long did your three hundred Spartan's resist the Persians?"

"Four days—a week perhaps. The Spartans and their allies—seven thousand men, perhaps, held the wall in the pass of Thermopylae."

"Against how many?" asked Togol, always interested in tales of valour. Guy had spent an evening relating the story of Roland and Oliver to him.

Bessas shook his head. "I don't know. Hundreds of thousands it's said—Persians and their allies."

They all sat in silence for a while, their curiosity aroused, trying to imagine the ancient battle.

Guy had seen sculptures and paintings of the ancients in his travels, but they seemed remote and mythical to him. "How long ago was that war?" he asked.

"About fifteen hundred years," Bessas replied.

"Seven thousand men!" Oleg exclaimed. "What we could do with seven thousand men! We started with half that many soldiers."

"It's well that many townspeople have become soldiers," answered Vardaheri.

"Were they the same Persians we fight now?" wondered Oleg aloud.

Bessas answered him. "Many use the names of other peoples imprecisely. We fight the Seljuk Turks and their allies. They overwhelmed the old Persian lands years ago, before coming upon us."

They all fell silent, each considering the context of time that this gave them. Guy recalled Charles' wondering in the mess on their first morning in Manzikert, whether anyone would remember their passing.

Simon Vardaheri broke the lull in conversation. "Somethin'll happen soon. I can feel it." There was a long silence as they all looked at him.

"So can I," said Bryennius. Despite the Roman's eyes being closed, Guy knew the Count had not been asleep, just stealing a few minutes of rest.

They pressed Vardaheri, but he could not tell more of his fears, for he did not know himself. It was some instinct deep inside the horse trader that warned him: perhaps some change in the movement and noise in the Seljuk camp that conscious thought did not perceive, but some part of his soul knew it for what it was.

Oleg recognised the return of a sombre mood and subtly changed the subject. "May I have some of your feast here?"

"Yes. Yes." David started up, embarrassed on their behalf. "It's poor manners from us not to have offered. Here's a goblet."

With the others, Guy leaned forward and took some more food, a crust of bread and some dry cheese from the blanket they had spread. He refilled his goblet with wine and sat back in the chair.

"John Curticius has done well for a man plagued with the unhappiness with his lot," Oleg started. "I must confess I doubted the man before the siege, but there's iron in him now. He's always calm when the fighting is thickest. The daughter too, is unafraid. She carries food to the wall and tends the wounded and I've seen her with my own eyes shoot at the enemy during their attacks."

Arshak, either unaware of or indifferent to Guy's feelings, broke in. "It's said the Sultan will make his bride of her if he captures the city."

Several men looked furtively at Guy as he stopped chewing and looked at the ground. He had scarcely seen Irene through the siege. Their flight from Archēsh seemed a lifetime ago, and conversation during their brief meetings was unbearably reserved. Thought of Theodore Ankhialou being in the Seljuk camp always brought a flood of unwelcome emotions. Yet again, he blinked them away. The bread felt like sand in his mouth and he was aware of others watching him.

Bryennius snorted without uncovering his eyes. "The Sultan won't get in. And that's just talk, Arshak. Where'd you hear it?"

"Kamyates," was the answer. "He's the diplomat. I'm guessing he'd know."

"Kamyates, eh?" said Bryennius, head relaxed back against the stones, eyes closed.

Simon Vardaheri steered the conversation away, if ever so slightly. "Hey, what price old Maniakh, eh? Stealing off in the midst of a battle—to look for a dancer in the Sultan's camp."

"I'll warrant he found her," Togol grinned. "Maniakh was ... is ... like that."

Bryennius' squire, Taticus Phocas, sitting on the edge of the circle, spoke up, for he too had proven himself outside Manzikert's walls. "Maniakh didn't exactly steal away. He helped us in the battle, then told Count Bryennius he was going."

"That he did. As did you, help me out of danger, that is," the count said from behind closed eyes.

Taticus Phocas blushed as Oleg clapped him on the back.

Reminded of Maniakh, David Varaz recounted the detention, before the cavalry fight, of Kamyates and Cydones. He described in uproarious detail Maniakh's feigned drunken rage and how he had stormed into the inn where the two courtiers had been whispering. "Then he grabbed them by their very clean robes," David continued with exaggerated gestures and comical expressions to illustrate his tale. "Banged their heads together and dragged them off. The mistress Serena, outside, made sure the two miscreants saw her. She screamed and said she would fetch help, while really she acted as lookout. Meanwhile I'm trying to play the part of an innocent trying to calm Maniakh down, but I can hardly stop laughing."

The men were guffawing now. Bessas, doubled forward in mirth, begged David to stop making him laugh because it hurt his wound.

"Kamyates was always complaining about not being paid enough to be out here," David related. "I was mending a bridle by that door there, some weeks ago, and he was hanging around Isaac, trying to charm information out of him and complaining about his pay while he was at it. Isaac doesn't miss much. He just said to Kamyates that he didn't deserve to be paid at all since he did not do anything, never standing guard or scouting."

Guy roared with laughter along with the rest of them, spilling some of his wine as he imagined the cheeky clerk identifying the raw parts of the haughty courtier and rubbing in salt.

"Kamyates' a fool as well," David said. "He threatened to have Maniakh's eyes and was close to being killed on the spot. But he's a damned smart fool who has charmed many people."

They laughed again, but without humour. "It would have been a good thing if Maniakh had killed him," said Togol, suddenly pensive. "I wonder if he ever found his dancer."

"Was it Maniakh," Oleg asked, "who wrote that on the garden wall—'One love and one death?'"

Images of Irene's smiling face, another of her tears at the start of the ride from Archēsh, suddenly flitted to Guy's mind's eye.

"No one knows," Simon Vardaheri said. "One of Manzikert's mysteries."

Some instinct made Guy look towards the gate, to glimpse Irene passing on foot with her mother. Looking their way, she gave a shy wave. He was certain no one else saw the two richly robed women.

Then he heard Bryennius murmur pensively beneath his hat, "T'were no shame that Trojans and well-greaved Achaeans should suffer pain long time for a woman such as she." Guy looked suddenly at the lounging form of Bryennius. He knew the count could not have seen Irene and he wondered of whom he spoke.

There was another moment of silence while the men thought on the count's words and of those on the garden wall.

In the distance, faintly from the Seljuk camp, came the human cry of the faithful being called to prayer. Jacques rose, saying, "It is time to feed our horses."

"You're right," agreed Guy, also rising.

The two Franks left. Once outside the gate, Jacques said, "I'll care for them. Go after her."

Guy jogged after the two women. He saw the swing of Irene's long dress and her shapely neck as he drew abreast of them. She smiled at him through the light veil. Thus encouraged he walked with them some little way, but the conversation seemed strained. They were dressed-up and on their way to the Orthodox Church with obvious purpose. So Guy, feeling forlorn and moved by some disquiet he could not fathom, took his leave.

Manzikert, Early evening,
9th September 1054

In the mellow light of early evening, Guy walked once more to the hospital to see Charles, hoping he would not again be ushered away. Outside the door, he met the abbess.

The woman shook her head. "I'm sorry. It is fortuitous you've come—he's called for you."

Guy found Charles white-faced on a paillasse, the angry welt of infection spreading from the cut to his neck. Flora Asadian was by his side, holding his hand, which was as pale as her own. She placed his hand down gently and stood. "You should have some time."

Guy thought Flora needed to get outside quickly, to breathe in fresh air, control her grief and compose her thoughts. He was so shocked by Charles' sudden falling away he was concerned that it must have showed on his face. As Charles looked up, Guy tried to mask his feeling with a smile. "Charles?"

His friend made to speak but no words came out. With effort, he cleared his throat. "You look terrible, Guy. You should get some sleep."

Guy knelt and took his hand. "People keep telling me that. I've slept and bathed."

"She's a good woman."

"Flora? Yes. She's nice."

"Be kind to her, Guy, for plenty of people haven't. Look after her—if you can. Don't let the infidels capture Manzikert and if you can't, get her away."

"Come! You'll be saving her yourself. Also, you had no need to ask."

"From you, that's enough. How is your heiress?"

"Irene? Well enough. Why do you smile, Charles?"

"You. And horses."

"Horses?"

Charles wheezed and was silent for a time, his eyes moving. "Yes. We were looking for a horse for you when our lives took this course. You worried about your hired hacks when you should have stayed in the inn. You went outside and ..."

"Two inns by the Golden Gate, and I chose that one," Guy said half-bitterly and half in wonder at fortune's turn. A terrible guilt hit him like a battering ram, knocking him breathless. He had chosen that inn and wanted to go on when the others would have turned back.

"Don't look so sad, Guy. We were penniless and did not know what was around the next corner. Besides, my wound was not your fault. It was Balazun and Reynaldus who got me. And Balazun's dead ... but I lost my thought. Ah, yes. Horses brought you to Manzikert and you found Irene. I came along looking for an heiress and instead found something more."

"Charles, what does it feel like?"

"When we fought our way out of the trap Reynaldus schemed us into, all I could think of, was being with her. And when I got through the gates, she was there, waiting. And now, Guy, I don't want to leave. But if I must, it was worth everything, just to feel that alive."

Guy thought Charles was going to cry. "I should have been with you out there."

Charles laughed weakly. "You were sent to your duty elsewhere—and had to be ordered to it. We haven't driven the Seljuks off, yet, so your chance will come soon enough. Anyway, what could you have done other than be struck down as well?" Charles closed his eyes, as though thinking back to the fight. He stayed that way for a long time and Guy was unable to discern if he was asleep or not. At the strains of the Muslim prayer from outside the walls, Charles opened his eyes. "Guy, it's just after sunset."

"How did you know?"

"They always have that fourth prayer just after sunset." Charles closed his eyes, listening. "Fetch me a priest, Guy. I've killed and not repented my sins, even if they were infidels."

Battle or not, killing was sinful for Christians before the notion of crusade, so Guy slipped a youth some copper coins to fetch any priest he could find, preferably a Frank; Araxie Bagradian, if not.

As they waited, Geoffrey de Rouens and Isaac entered. On seeing Charles Bertrum, they knelt by him with obvious emotion and took his hand. It was a shock to Guy. He had noticed Charles and Isaac joke when they met around the city, but he had missed the friendship develop.

Charles looked long at Isaac. "Promise me, Isaac. Swear to me that you will write what we have done here. What Balazun did. What Guy has done. The deeds the strategos has wrought. And Count Bryennius. The abbess. Togol. All who played honourable or despicable parts. People should know. We're far from home, but in our land they should know what was done by Franks and Greeks and Norsemen at Manzikert in far off but Christian Armenia."

"I swear it," vowed Isaac. "And I'll write of what you did, for that also shall be remembered. And I shall scribe it into Latin as well, for Guy d'Agiles to take back to your land and your people."

Both priests came and administered the salvation of Charles' soul. Guy went outside, for he did not need to hear the details of his friend's confession. Then Araxie Bagradian came outside and told Guy he was asked for. Guy entered the darkening hospital with its smells and flickering lamps and sat by his friend. Charles did not waken—Guy did not get to say farewell for the journey. With Jacques and Flora beside him, he held his friend's hand, willing him to awaken and praying that he would. In the small hours the abbess came, examined the still form and shook her head.

Flora howled in a grief Guy could not console. The abbess and another nun came and gently led her away. Guy rose and stumbled outside looking for a private space, but there seemed none in that beleaguered place. He walked slowly as if in a dream to the horse yards and stepped in with Charles' mare to give her a treat, passing another to Sira through the rails. Careful not to touch her wounds, he put his arms around the mare's neck and gave her a hug. He felt like crying, but no tears came to relieve the grief for the friendship and journey, the loss and loneliness.

Irene found him there. "Guy, I heard. I'm so sorry. I couldn't think where else you would be. Now that I'm here, I don't know what to say."

Guy shook his head. With Irene near, he recalled what Charles had said about how alive he felt riding back to Flora. Guy thought of the flight from Archēsh and the tumult of emotions he had felt then. "When we rode from Archēsh we should have kept going."

She looked at him in surprise.

"It was something Charles said." They stayed with the horses for a while, playing with their soft muzzles, their thoughts their own.

Charles Bertrum's friends buried him in the city before dawn, so the gravediggers and quicklime could not claim him. Jacques set Charles' sword in mortar, the cross of the hilt the knight's marker. They agreed to sell his spare horse and arms and to give the proceeds with his horse and saddle to Flora Asadian, so that she might journey to Trebizond as she had always wished. Isaac undertook to escort her. No one reminded the other that their promises to the woman depended on the outcome of the siege. Of that there was no need.

Chapter Sixteen

The Lonesome Dove

*Manzikert, Morning,
10th September 1054*

The next day dawned warm and sad after they buried Charles Bertrum. Guy trudged to the stables, carrying his armour in a roll over his shoulder, spear in hand and weapons and shield slung from his shoulder. A dry wind blew in from the southern deserts with the promise of even hotter weather. Except for a few persistent grey puddles, the ground in the city was now dust.

The siege had become a force of its own, as though the sheltering walls trapped those within. Guy felt ensnared by decisions taken months before, years even. At times he felt bitterness towards Bryennius for bringing him to Manzikert, but he knew deep inside he had come and stayed of his own accord. Wild thoughts came to mind: of taking Irene with him and going over the walls one night, thieving horses from the enemy camp and stealing away. Instead, the improbability of success and the day-to-day ordinariness of this life, bound him in his fate to the destiny of all.

Guy fed and cared for their animals as he listened to the stabler's depressing description of a high official's role in grain shortages and the black market. Guy sympathised with the elderly Armenian veteran who held his position as a stipend.

"Apocapes is a good man, but can't fix it," the stabler explained. "He's a thousand things to worry about. They have only one, themselves. Say a Greek merchant conspires with a corrupt official, and they skim off a bit. Then an honest citizen reports them to an honest official. The miscreants are confronted and deny everything. The person who reports them is reproved. The honest official is damned and will be lucky to escape blinding or imprisonment. Apocapes knows it only needs a courtier to whisper—hero and rebellion, in the same breath—and the Emperor's butter in their hands."

Guy returned to breakfast and overcome by a sense of futility, sat down opposite Bessas for breakfast. The portions of his boiled egg, crust of bread and cup of milk had grown smaller as the weeks had gone by and it was goat's milk, but better than nothing.

"I couldn't sleep," said Bessas. "This wind. It's relentless and turning hot. I heard …"

"Last night."

"I am sorry. Has everything …?"

'Yes," Guy said.

They did not talk much but the familiar company was welcome. With his arm in a sling, Bessas found eating difficult; his wound bothering him more than he was prepared to admit. Soon Togol and Vardaheri entered and joined them. The scouts had scarcely sat when there was a shout of such urgency from the western wall that they all ran to the main wall ramparts. Guy looked over the battlements, expecting to see another assault bearing down on them, but the Seljuk encampment was quiet with no discernible movement, except for two horsemen galloping in the distance.

"Patience, friend," Guy calmly commanded of the peasant who had sounded the alarm. "We don't want to scare the horses. What is it?"

"See there," the sentry pointed, "beyond the river. I've watched them hawking in the mornings. They must do it to try and catch game for their table."

Guy looked beyond the sprawling Seljuk encampment, now shrouded in the thin blue smoke of its morning campfires with ribbons of horses and camels being watered at the river. "What's so different this morning that you must call the alarm?"

"Something has stirred them up. They're different."

Guy watched the riders and then observed excitement spreading through the Seljuk camp. A horseman dashed close across their front, a bowshot away from the watchers on the walls, scarcely moving in his seat as he threw off a falcon. Silently they gazed, trying to identify the cause of the activity amongst their foes. Others of the garrison, sensing or seeing the upset, flung themselves onto the ramparts to stare. In the fortress, one might have heard a workman's cap fall upon the ground.

"Look," cried Togol in admiration. "There's a huntress for you, straight above the shop tents near the lines of the ghulams. See, two hand spans high and climbing."

Leaning his shield and spear against the rampart and thankful they had the morning sun at their backs, Guy located the shops, extended his arms to the full, thumbs together, fingers out-spaced. Sure enough, a black speck ascended rapidly. Guy thought back to the hunt and knew it for a female hawk.

"By the saints!" cried Simon Vardaheri so loudly the soldiers crowded on the ramparts heard him. "It's a dove."

"It may be from Karin," said Bessas.

Guy marked the pigeon, a white fleck against the pale morning sky with its thin streaks of cloud. The bird had been flying high and was now coming in low to her home loft in the citadel of Manzikert. But the Seljuk hunters, ever watchful for a dove, had seen the bird and cast off their raptors in pursuit.

"Come on, my beauty," roared Togol, fitting an arrow to his bow.

The dove was still three furlongs from the walls when the rising female saw her and turned, beating fast to get high enough for the plunging attack. A tiercel was behind the dove, striving to overtake the messenger. As people on the walls watched, terrified for the little bird, some sense held them in silence lest they frighten the dove. With one voice, the Seljuks cheered on their raptors. With his heart in his mouth, Guy watched the dove crest low over the merlons, and joined with the rest of the soldiers in shouting and waving their spears to drive off the pursuing tiercel. Arrows arched upward, but the brown bird was untouched.

Guy looked up while thunderous cheering broke out along the western wall. The startled tiercel, still in pursuit but distracted by the sudden fracas on the walls, veered away in alarm and lost distance. The lonesome dove still had a long bowshot to fly before reaching the sanctuary of the citadel. The falcon above folded her wings and started the long, oblique glide that became a plunging dive.

"The dove'll never do it," Vardaheri predicted mournfully. "The poor things panic when they're attacked."

The dove winged for a small window in the upper level of the citadel, the hawk all the while dropping like a stone. It seemed all of Manzikert stared silently upward at the frightful competition, while outside tens of thousands peered blindly into the sun and wondered at the outcome.

There was suddenly a great roar from the fortress. "By a hair's breadth the dove made it," shouted the exuberant Togol, jumping for joy. He turned and with the others crowding the wall, roared exhilaration and abuse at the besieging Seljuks.

Hours later, Guy searched out Bessas to learn any news. The centarch confided that the strategos at Karin had sent a message. While the large walled towns and cities of Armenia and Iberia were safe and the Seljuks had been defeated near Baberd but triumphed near Kars, the countryside was devastated with many scores of thousands killed or carried off. Such was the ruination, no cavalry could be sent to relieve Manzikert, if indeed as it was hoped, the fortress still stood.

Manzikert was alone with the host of shepherds before the gates.

Manzikert, Pre-dawn,
15th September 1054

Guy woke suddenly in the dark, cool night and lay still, listening. A wind blew: an urgent, secretive, speaking wind, pregnant with the hint of a hot day. Restlessly it rustled the leaves on the tree outside the drab grey stone of their barrack block. Slowly, Guy moved a hand under his cloak to close on the hilt of his sword.

"You awake?" Jacques whispered.

"Yes," replied Guy quietly. "Something's up. I can feel it." Guy fumbled in the dark, sliding into boots, armour and weapons. He rolled his cloak and gathered his water skin and saddlebag containing food. Tying them in a bundle he could carry over one shoulder, he waited while Jacques finished similar preparations. A curtain moved in the corner where Charles had slept. Joaninna and Flora now occupied that space and the urgent, kneeling preparations of the men awakened them, if they had slept at all. "What is it?" Joaninna asked.

"I don't know," replied Guy. "But I fear something is afoot. It occurs to me now, that we didn't notice the enemy were strangely noisier last night. Saddle the horses and take them to the churchyard where the tunnel was. It's hidden by a wall and looks abandoned, so it may not look like it's worth looting ..." Guy broke off, but they understood his meaning. "If anything happens we'll try and meet there. At least we'll have ready mounts and a little food and water for whatever comes."

Jacques and Guy then stepped into the night. "Which way?" Jacques asked.

"The north wall."

Reaching it after a hurried walk, they made to ascend the stone steps to the rampart, but were blocked by a Varangian. The dark forms of Bryennius, Togol and Vardaheri pushed past them, the count saying to the sentry, "They're with me, let them pass. Thank you."

Guy followed the three up the steep stone steps to the rampart of the main wall. Looking into the night dimly lit by the stars and a crescent moon, were Basil, Oleg, Doukas and Branas. They glanced around. Oleg, on seeing the newcomers, whispered, "All sorts of people are not sleeping this night."

"What is it?" Bryennius murmured.

"I don't know," Basil replied quietly. "But the sound of their camp has been different. For several nights since, it has been unusually quiet, as though they were resting—especially the night before this. Tonight they started being noisy again, but excessively so ..."

"Like they were trying to cover something," Bryennius suggested. "As they're noisy now."

Basil looked sharply at him. "Cover what? Have you heard from your contact?" He spoke in hushed tones so they had to crowd forward to hear him.

"Not since the arrow they shot during the attack against the north wall on Wednesday night," Bryennius answered, "when they said something was in the air, some plan. They also stated there was much suspicion in the nomad camp.

The fact the message came at an entirely different part of the wall, and during an attack, may mean my contact is under suspicion and has to play their part more convincingly." As he spoke, Bryennius' tone betrayed his concern about the pressure his spy must be under and the effect it would have on intelligence. "So far, I have not been able to determine the significance of the word '*baban*'[69] which was in the last message, with no clue to its meaning."

Baban? Basil thought on it for a moment. "Have you had your scouts out tonight?"

Bryennius answered. "No. Togol tried by different sally-ports. He's been out before, seeing what there is and spreading derogatory rumours about the Sultan's military qualities, manliness and virility. But last night he returned, saying the enemy lines were thick with pickets and he couldn't pass."

Basil held out his hands, feeling the breeze, listening, like an animal. "The wind's dried things out. It'll turn hot now and reduce their camp to dust. Surely the pressure must be telling on their army. The Sultan has to give them something." He leaned on the merlon with his rough hands. "Damn them! What're they up to? And where?"

"Listen," hissed Branas in such a tone that all were silent.

"It sounds like they have draught animals yoked up and are pulling something," Oleg ventured softly. They stood silently, mouths open slightly, heads cocked to the direction of the faint sounds, senses straining.

"In their camp from time to time," Vardaheri said quietly after a while, "they used to have a couple of elephants, for hauling their siege engines and then grain from Archēsh. But I haven't noticed them for a few days. They were normally out of sight on the northern edge of their camp. But ..." Faint noises could be heard again.

Guy listened and thought he could hear through the din of drums, horns and trumpets, the distant tinkle of chains and the crunch of heavy wheels or rollers on the hard ground. He concentrated, but could discern nothing definite and wondered if the conversation had stoked his imagination. In the dim light, he could just make out the torture of doubt and indecision on Basil's features.

Then there came the muffled but unmistakable sound of digging: earth and stone being levelled and bracing stakes being hammered in. The sounds continued.

Suddenly Basil squared his shoulders and turning to Doukas and Branas, ordered, "Stand-to! Do it silently."

"Theophanes," Basil continued. "Make sure each wall is prepared to support another, by releasing every second man. They know already, but remind them." Doukas turned to go and ensure an all-round defence was presented to the Seljuks, with plans afoot to react to any breach, or breaches. "And Theophanes," Basil hissed after him. Doukas paused and turned. "Don't let there be panic in the city."

---

69 Baban—the Seljuk name for a large stone-throwing catapult employed against Manzikert in 1054.

Doukas saluted hurriedly and continued running down the steps from the rampart, ordering a tribune to fetch the bishop and abbess and to bring them to him wherever he could be found.

"Bryennius," Basil said, turning to the count. "Saddle up and hold your Sixth in first reserve. Be prepared to plug any breach of the walls and hold it until Oleg's Varangians get there. If it all goes badly, fight your way to the citadel and hold out there for as long as you can."

The strategos turned to the big Viking standing nearby. "Oleg, have your deputy, Egin, form and command a second reserve—regiment-sized group, three hundred strong—from the Varangians still in the citadel. Their task is to move, on order, as rapidly as possible to any threatened or breached place and destroy enemy incursions. If Leo's men get there first, relieve him in-place as soon as it's safe, so the cataphracts of the Scholae can re-form a reserve." Oleg turned, grunted an order and a runner made off to the citadel.

After listening to Oleg's role in the coming fight, Bryennius turned to Guy. "Where's your post?"

"Stood down. My men have orders to assemble outside the stable shop at stand-to."

"Good. Stay with the strategos for the moment. I'll form my men in the square near the military stables. We'll be a bowshot away." With that, the count was gone.

Around them were the subdued sounds of people trying to take post without making any noise. Boots scuffed on stone and an occasional shield or scabbard bumped the walls. Men filed onto the main wall ramparts, their comrades similarly lining the fore-wall below them. Those nearby looked at Basil and Oleg, grasped their weapons and stared into the gloom.

The garrison stood to arms as the eastern sky paled beyond snow-streaked Mount Sippane. Guy knew this early light played tricks, so he looked away often from the gloom to his front, blinking to rest his eyes. By the scratches on the merlon near which he stood, he reckoned it was the twenty-fifth day of the siege and wondered whether the count of days mattered anymore.

The walls were silent now, the defenders scarcely daring to breathe. Dark shapes seemed to move before Guy, until his reason and a second look convinced him they were rocks. The hum of the night-shrouded Seljuk camp seemed to lessen behind the mask of their clamour, and then the nature of the sound changed, as though many men were moving quietly into position.

"Listen," hissed Vardaheri.

"That's a stone-thrower being made ready—that creaking sound," Basil murmured with a certainty they dreaded.

Then the sound stopped. All along the rampart men instinctively crouched lower against the wall. Starting from the low ridge to the north and rippling around to the river flats on the east, a silence descended on the unseen Seljuk host.

Dry mouthed, his heart beating, Guy peered once more into the darkness, which was receding with agonising slowness. After a long stillness, there came the grunt of many heaving in unison followed by deafening silence. Guy looked in alarm at the men around him. Suddenly came the rumble of the counterweight and whiplash report of the sling release. Guy's heart seemed to stop and he felt terror and the urge to run from the wall.

The three-hundred pound rock hurtled with unstoppable force out of the darkness, smashing into the tower on his left. The old masonry of the upper story collapsed in a spitting shower of fragments and grey dust. Screams of pain and terror came from the men maimed by splintering stone or trapped under the tumbled wall. Soldiers turned and stared helplessly at the cloud of dust in the gloom. A ripple of uncertainty passed along the line.

"Steady in the ranks," roared Basil. "Stand fast on the wall!"

In the Seljuk camp, a great shout arose as they realised the damage inflicted.

Guy joined those moved to rescue the wounded or stand in the path of the rush that might follow. A few paces and he was there, tearing with his hands at the fractured stones. Desperate clawing by a few men produced a moaning, bloodied form. "Scribones," shouted someone as orderlies carried the wounded man away. Guy knelt to listen for more sounds from the rubble. To his astonishment, Modestos Kamyates was suddenly standing against the dawn in his crisp robes.

The bureaucrat said knowingly, "The walls here are damaged internally by water and are weak. The Seljuks know it and are concentrating their efforts on it." Kamyates smiled unconsciously in his superior knowledge as he indifferently watched the men searching for others in the gloom.

How did he know? Guy wondered. It came to him suddenly; Kamyates knew and was gloating. So smug and damned superior, he couldn't help showing it to someone he thinks beneath him. Guy felt an instant, raging hatred of the bearded bureaucrat, with the cold, mocking smile. Many thought Kamyates amusing and charmingly skilled in rhetoric. To Guy, Kamyates had ingratiated himself into too many sensitive meetings, cultivated too many people and been seen too often with the sly Bardas Cydones and the ambitious Reynaldus. Now his mistrust of the man took on a hard edge, but he bit his lip and remained silent.

His brush with Kamyates occupied an instant, in which Basil Apocapes saw the faltering confidence of the men on the wall. "Oleg!" the strategos ordered quietly, "Tell the men to be steady and watch their front. Daniel, organise someone to help clear the tower and aid the maimed."

Branas spoke without any hint of unease to a nearby tribune of the garrison staff, asking him to organise the work party. The man in his helmet and corselet hurried off.

Oleg was pacing the rampart of the main wall, his great voice carrying in the languages of Vikings and Rus. "Steady on the walls." Interpreters shouted the message on to the many Armenian townsmen under arms. "Take cover, in place."

In their iron caps and mail, or quilted or felt armour and covered by their shields, the men crouched close to the merlons, their bearded faces against the grey stone. Many prayed. The leaders moved rapidly in awkward bounds along the rampart, peering through the gradually increasing light towards the enemy.

They pushed men under their shields and kicked away the little personal bundles that might impede their footing. "Take cover! Keep your heads down, men. We've repulsed them many times before. This is just one more time." Oleg was as cool as if inspecting the palace guard in Constantinople.

Gradually a dark shape took form to their front. Guy could see the outline of the terrible engine looming from the scar of the Seljuk siege lines. Involuntarily, he uttered, "My God!"

Five times the height of a man, the swing-beam counterweight mangonel was twice the size of the others the Seljuks had, or any other that Guy had ever seen. From the collective gasp along the wall, he knew its appearance had the same effect on others. It seemed hundreds of the enemy were hauling on the ropes to pull back the great arm as others heaved on the mechanism that held the counter-weighing net of stones in place until the moment of release.

Oleg saw it at once and ordered the archers to make ready. Then the Viking turned and looked at Basil. "I make it about four hundred people around that machine, many Christian slaves amongst them."

Once more Guy saw the agony on Basil's face. "Very good, Oleg. We have no choice," the strategos replied through his clenched jaw. "But, by God, I'll make the Sultan pay for this."

"At the men on the machine, in your own time—shoot!" roared Oleg, turning to coolly watch the effect.

Basil bit his lip as the first arrow showers were released then uttered to himself, "Lord Jesus Christ, our God, have mercy on us, Amen."

With a prayer for his own soul, Guy drew his bow and marking one among the crowd who seemed to be flailing with a whip, loosed the goose-feather shaft.

An answering hail of arrows clattered like hail on the ramparts where several of the rudely armoured townsmen fell. Guy jumped aside and pressed his face in the cover of a merlon and found himself looking directly at Basil who was doing the same. Guy could hear Oleg, still bellowing, ordering the archers to keep shooting. "Damn your eyes, if you cower like cowards you'll perish that way. Shoot, men. Shoot!"

Guy's eyes met Basil's. "Where did they get it from?" Guy shouted over the tumult. Another rock smashed into the tower. More of it fell with a heart-rending crash. Guy could hear Oleg still shouting.

This was Basil Apocapes' moment of self-reproach. "It's ours! Or at least is used to be. The infernal thing was left at Baghesh over thirty years ago, after Emperor Basil the Second used it against the Muslims of Her. Nasr ad-Daulah at Amida professed friendship with us—it never occurred to me that nomads would take it from his Kurds of Baghesh, or that Nasr would give it to them, nor that the Seljuks would get it working, then drag it across here. It all makes sense now, their new plan and the elephants disappearing for a few days. God forgive me. In my heart, I knew about it and I did nothing."

Guy was stunned by the oversight, and the terrifying role of chance in human affairs. What if Basil had arranged its destruction? Or if they had not had the fight at the wadi and the count had instead returned by way of Baghesh where he would surely have seen the catapult? The Marwanid Kurds of Baghesh could have destroyed it rather than be implicated in the war. How different this morning might be if the count's scouts had reported the engine, or the count had asked the direct question whether there was a big catapult around Vaspurakan. So many "ifs".

As another arrow shower clattered around them, they both winced and hugged the merlons. Then Basil rose and strode, with every show of fearlessness, along the wall in full view of the defenders as Guy drew an arrow and shot back around the side of the merlon.

Lighter Seljuk machines joined in the attack on the tower, the besiegers shouting in unison as they heaved down on the ropes of the machines to drive the defenders from the ramparts. More stones smashed into the stricken tower, pulverising the upper chambers so that they collapsed. As day grew lighter, other rocks hit the adjoining sections of the old main wall and it, weakened by the fall of the tower, cracked dangerously. Many were wounded as the deadly missile duel continued. Everywhere were the cries of the maimed, twang of bowstrings and the distinctive sound of the arrow skiffs hitting people and stone. Again and again the townsfolk braved the hail to bring bundles of shafts and bolts, water and dressings to the wall. Many stepped forward to take the places of the fallen as others helped the wounded to aid. Guy could see Egin's Varangians, back out of arrow range, waiting to be called forward. Gangs of armed townsmen, struggling with the fear and determination that wracked their souls, gathered near them under the leaders appointed by Basil.

More of the high arching, Seljuk rocks hit the section of wall near the felled tower. With a rasping groan, it too collapsed into a mound of rubble, which could be scaled by assaulting footmen.

A great cheer from the besieging engineers announced that they, after half a morning's effort, had seen the collapse of a section of the main wall. The flights of arrows from the Seljuk lines slowed to a steady harassing trickle. Guy saw a horseman race from the vicinity of the siege engines towards the Seljuk main camp along the river.

"See that?" he said to Oleg.

"I see it! They're surprised by their own success. Now they must organise a hasty assault to try and exploit their good fortune. At the moment, they are conserving their arrows to support the next attack." He turned to the men along the wall and called for them to save their missiles, except for those most skilled with the bow.

Doukas galloped up on a foaming horse. "Strategos." he cried past a cupped hand. "The Seljuks are massing to attack the south wall."

Basil did not reply immediately. Instead, he looked around at the broken north wall, the tribesmen and ghulams forming up before it, at the dust and devastation and broken stones. "Theophanes, they almost have a breach here, so this is the most vulnerable point for us. The south is probably a diversionary attack to stop us reinforcing here. There are quite a few Kelts along that south wall to stiffen the townspeople, but just in case, give Count Bryennius my compliments and ask him to detach three troops, a hundred cataphracts, to you as a reserve for the south wall."

"That is half the effective strength he has left," Doukas said.

"Very good. Give him my compliments and ask for one troop, thirty of his men."

Doukas saluted in acknowledgement and was about to gallop off.

Basil raised his hand for him to wait. "Theophanes, when you have organised it over there, find the princeps and put him in charge of meeting that attack. Then raise a third reserve of the theme irregulars, a hundred strong. Form up behind where Leo is now. Place someone in command of it, and tell them, if the Seljuks get through in either place, to go straight at it. But be alert to the rest of the town. They could be mining or just trying to bribe a sally-port guard at this very moment. Then return here."

The strategos saw Guy's look. "Tughrul moves tens of thousands around the battlefield. I meet him with scores and hundreds."

"This is it, isn't it? This is the day?" Guy asked.

Basil regarded him in silence. The strategos had borne the defence of Manzikert on his shoulders and participated in the thick of almost every fight. Already today, he was grime covered, his beard grey with dust while slivers of mud had formed at the corners of his mouth. Armoured and armed, he was magnificent in his determination and the trust placed in him by soldiers and citizens alike. "So it seems, Guy. Hearts up."

Branas, balancing himself on the tumbled stones of the collapsed main wall, called a warning. "They're about to start on the fore-wall."

One that heard Branas' warning was Aram Gasparian, who Guy had appointed deputy of his own little army. He appeared at Guy's side and after listening to Branas, said to Guy, "It's said their first rock killed three sentinels and knocked another dead into the town. What're your orders, Centarch?"

"How many men have you got?" asked Basil.

"Fifty-four," Guy answered, looking to Gasparian for confirmation.

"Daniel," Basil waved Count Branas over. "Guy and his men will defend the fore-wall breach, if the Seljuks succeed in making one, which seems likely. You get back into town. Find Doukas, who should be near the cathedral organising theme troops and townspeople, now out-of-battle, into a semblance of order. Get yourself a regiment—a short one, even fifty men if necessary—and return here as quick as you can. Go straight in to support Guy."

Basil turned to Selth, who crouched nearby. "Karas. Get work parties up here to start forming barricades on the main wall. Bring up any mantelets we have left—barrels of soil—anything. The fore-wall will go and we need something to break the impetus of their assault."

Guy heard Basil's orders and thus learned of his place in the desperate plan. He was aware of an immediate foreboding, countered by a sense of now being in so deep, he had no power over his own destiny. Reading similar thoughts in the faces of his men, he placed them in cover behind the main wall, where they made what personal preparations they could for the sudden rush into the breach. Jacques and Gasparian watched over them, but none attempted to slink away from that awful wait, even when they went a short distance away to expel their watery fear by a garden wall.

Guy stayed by the crumpled tower. He saw more dismounted Seljuks come up, but had seen enough attacks now to know that this one was fragmentary, hurriedly organised by the nomads to exploit an unexpected advantage. On an adjoining tower, the bobbing heads of the Varangians bespoke Araxie Bagradian attempting to increase the range of his mangonels, so the defenders could at least interfere with the terrible machine the Seljuks had dragged from Baghesh.

"There is a fire in the town," cried one of the townsmen behind Guy.

"Steady. Stay fast," ordered Guy crisply over the chaos and shouting as several men half rose. "Someone else must take care of it."

An ear splitting crash rent the air. "There it goes," someone shouted as a section of fore-wall collapsed under the concentrated weight of rocks hurled against it by the Seljuks. For the length of three spears laid end-to-end, it had crashed down, much of it disintegrating into a heap of shattered rubble. This impeded movement in the space between the walls and made a rough ramp leading to the breached tower. A great shout of triumph came from the Seljuk lines.

"Come on," Guy shouted without looking back as he clambered over the smashed stones of the main wall and scrambled to the breach, towards which hundreds of Seljuks were sprinting.

Manzikert, Morning,
15th September 1054

Bessas woke as Bryennius, Lascaris and Sebēos roused and hurried off. The pain of his wound had denied proper rest and he lay for a few minutes, wondering what caused his companions to leave so early. There had always had been a coming and going amongst them, but this morning had a different feel to it. He struggled up, calling for a trooper to help him don a cuirass of horn lamellar, the mail shirt being too painful to get on past his strapped left arm. As the soldier buckled on his sword belt and he stamped his feet into riding boots, Bessas heard the great crack from the direction of the north wall. He hurried towards it.

In the streets all was confusion as the worst terrors of the people rose like bile in their throats. Some rushed bewildered and half-clothed to join the crowds. Others, who had in their fears rehearsed the moment a thousand times in their minds, dressed carefully, preparing little bundles with which to seek to hide or flee, should their nerve or makeshift weapons fail them.

Bessas walked as rapidly as he could to where the regiment was assembling, squires taking the reins of the saddled horses while the cataphracts formed in ranks under the decarchs. Cosmas Mouzalon, had already saddled both Bessas' mounts. Bryennius rode up and Bessas asked for orders.

"We are saddling to fight, not run," the count said, looking pointedly at his bandaged arm. "And you cannot fight in that condition, Bessas. Seek out Doukas and support him in readying the city for the battle." Bryennius rattled off orders to Lascaris and Sebēos, then returned to Bessas. "But first, make your way to the Barbarian House and ensure Isaac has taken all his records on the enemy to the strategos' rooms in the citadel."

Bessas knew the importance of the task: the papers contained all that was known of the enemy and their scouts, spies and ways of war. They also included maps and information on the strengths and dispositions of Byzantine forces in Vaspurakan and Armenia, as well as what the enemy evidently knew of them. He left and made his way up a crowded, rushing thoroughfare, wincing as passers-by bumped heedlessly against his wound. Togol found him and taking Bessas under his care, cleared a path.

They entered the Barbarian House silently from the rear, finding Kamyates, Reynaldus and Bardas Cydones, with their backs to them, confronting Isaac. The clerk saw Bessas and Togol enter, but gave no sign.

"Pray, hand over the papers," Cydones was saying in the bullying fashion he had with people of lesser rank. "We've a task from Count Branas to take them to safety." Kamyates stood behind his manlier subordinate's shoulder.

"That may be, but I have had no such orders," Isaac replied.

"You don't need them. You'll do you're told," Reynaldus spat. His right hand, covered from Isaac's view by his shield, reached behind his waist along his belt towards his dagger. The hand stilled as a cataphract unexpectedly came downstairs holding a large, rolled skin, which might have been a map. Reynaldus made a pretence of adjusting his sword belt as the second of the two guard cataphracts, always posted to the Barbarian House, entered at the sounds. Seeing Bessas, this second trooper saluted.

Bessas stepped forward as though he had just entered the room. In a glance, he took in the annoyed look Isaac shot the well-intentioned cataphract and the expressions of Reynaldus and Cydones, as they passed from astonishment through hatred to self-control.

"What's going on?" Bessas asked, aware that his own account of the incident, even backed by the big Cuman beside him, was not sufficient proof to throw the two courtiers in the dungeons or run them through with his sword on the spot—not against the power Kamyates possessed in Constantinople and how its influence reached this far-away place.

Cydones attempted to maintain the bluff. "We've orders to take the Barbarian House papers to safe-keeping."

"Indeed," Bessas feigned surprise. "Whose?"

"Branas," the imperial courier purred.

Bessas looked at him evenly. "I hardly know about that," he countered. "I'll have to ask him. In the meantime, I have my own orders regarding the papers."

Without taking his eyes from Reynaldus and Cydones, Bessas instructed Isaac, Togol and the two cataphracts to take the bundles of notes immediately to the citadel. As they passed by him, Bessas murmured to Isaac, "Give the officer of the Varangian guards at the citadel gate my compliments. Tell him not to admit Reynaldus or any other party of Normans before the cathedral bells ring, signifying the town is lost."

As Bessas faced the three, Serena Cephala entered, calling his name and giving them a smile. With a dark blue scarf binding her hair, she wore—over men's riding clothes—an unbleached, loose cotton dress, such as a peasant woman might wear. At first they did not recognise her, but Serena's crisply enunciated Greek quickly ended their confusion. "Reynaldus!" she exclaimed in mock bewilderment, "I am surprised to see you here, so far from the fight. I am sure your troops need your knowledge and valour right now, for they are sorely pressed on the south wall."

Sensing themselves foiled, Kamyates, Reynaldus and Cydones scowled at her and left hurriedly.

Serena turned to Bessas and moving closer, scrutinised his face before quickly examining his shoulder where a circle of fresh blood stained the bandage. "I've been looking everywhere for you," she said. "A fire started at the citizen's stables. I met Irene there. She said she thought she'd seen Bardas Cydones near the stables before the fire started. She wasn't sure—it was dark."

"It is well time we flung Cydones somewhere we can keep an eye on him," Bessas said as he ran out into the street looking for the three plotters, but they had vanished into the early morning confusion of a city under attack. "Come on, we must tell Count Leo and Doukas. I'll have a section of my men search for Cydones, though there're many places he could hide in the city."

On their way, they hurried by the blazing stables. Among a crowd holding terrified horses and such gear as could be rescued from the flames, they found one of Serena's servants holding her horse amongst others, while the other searched for their saddles and other tack through the pile on the ground. Her man, recognising Bessas, explained excitedly: "We were able to rescue most of the horses and much of the tack. Some fodder was pulled out, but most of it burns as you can see now."

"Did anyone see how it started?" Bessas asked.

"No. They'd have been torn apart had they been seen."

Bessas could hardly hear Serena's man amongst the turmoil as the crowd pressed around looking helplessly at the fired stables. Seeing the signs of emerging panic, Bessas called for calm, but on foot and in pain when he tried to yell or raise his arm, he could not make himself heard.

Suddenly in the smoke shrouded light, the crowd parted before the mounted figures of the abbess and Count Doukas. Two Armenian irregulars from the Vaspurakan theme rode behind them. At the sight of the abbess, a hundred voices clamoured to tell of their fears. She held out her hand as if to speak and the crowd hushed in a moment, for the abbess was much loved in the city. "Good people, go to the churches as you have been taught, for rushing into the streets impedes those defending the city."

Much as people trusted her, so great was their fear that they looked to Doukas, for the redoubtable fighter was also well known and respected.

"Friends," he called, "the abbess is right. Go to the churches and wait. If called upon to fight, move quickly to where you're directed by the messengers. In the meantime, remain quietly in the houses of God and pray for our success." The crowd swayed uncertainly and broke up, moving off to the appointed churches. Seeing Bessas, Doukas rode over. "My God, Bessas, you'd better go to the hospital."

"Count Bryennius sent me to you."

"Good! I'm sending you to hospital."

"There's no time. We found Michael Kamyates and Bardas Cydones trying to get hold of the Barbarian House papers," Bessas said. "The papers are safe now. But Cydones seems to be in league with Reynaldus and Kamyates. And Irene Curticius has reported seeing Cydones near the stable when the fire broke out."

Concern clouded Doukas's face.

"I think we should detain Cydones awhile," Bessas suggested.

Doukas frowned for a moment. "Damn right. I just saw Reynaldus slink back to the south wall and I wondered what he had been up to. De Gaillon's dependable enough—I'll warn him to keep an eye on Reynaldus, for his own good." Doukas looked around in silence for a moment as he read the distant sounds of the battle. "Bessas, set ten or twenty of your men after Cydones. Find him and throw him in the citadel cells. Not near Zobeir, though. And go to hospital. I'll tell Leo that I've given you such orders. Are you up to it, until I can find another officer to relieve you?"

"Yes—it must be done." Bessas winced, having determined to act already but grateful for Doukas's support.

Doukas rode off towards the tumult on the north wall.

"Bessas," Serena said, taking his good arm, "I'll take you to where the regiment is. Place Loukas Gabras in charge of the search. He's a good man and true, you have said so yourself often enough."

Together they moved northward through the chaos of the city to where the regiment was formed, waiting for the order to be committed to the fight. Many of the cataphracts prayed.

Men, women and children surged past Serena and Bessas. The citizens carried stones, arrows, darts, water, food and spare weapons. Others returned from the tumult, clutching empty urns or utensils, or bearing the maimed. One woman helped a wounded Varangian who had crawled from the fight, blinded by his own blood, his mind gone. Another, a dying Rus, was propped up with his back against a wall. His face a mask, only the soldier's eyes moved as he watched them pass. From somewhere in a building close to them, they heard screams of agony. As Serena and Bessas moved on, that terrible sound was lost in the thunder at the walls and the shouting.

Manzikert, Mid-morning,
14th September 1054

Reaching the breach in the northern fore-wall, Guy found a red-bearded Rus shouting orders to the survivors to form a shield wall. Some of the stonework had tumbled onto the peribolos, allowing the attackers to scramble up. Red Beard turned to Guy. With a commanding presence and no sign of alarm, the Rus ordered him to form a second line of defence behind them. Guy waved his bowmen and slingers to his rear and the walls on either side of the breach and formed up his spearmen behind the three ranks of Varangians now being pushed into place. While the hasty Seljuk attack came upon them at a swift run, the defenders covered themselves with their shields as the darts rained amongst them.

A cheer from the tower to his right alerted Guy that Araxie Bagradian's mangonel had scored a hit on one of the smaller Seljuk engines, breaking the tie beam. Enemy figures milled in confusion around their damaged mangonel.

To Guy's front, beyond the iron lines of pot helmets covering bearded faces and hair bunched on hunched mail shoulders, hundreds of Turks charged on foot in a great mass. Behind him, Oleg was still shouting orders and encouragement. A deluge of the defenders' arrows, bolts and stones struck with crippling effect just as the Seljuks reached the far side of the ditch. The attackers were not stopped, those in the rear pushing forward and spilling around the flanks into the ditch, making for the rough scramble up to the Christian line formed above them. The sound of their shouting, clashing of weapons and the thud of their drums was deafening.

A Seljuk ballista bolt tore into the people crowded into the breach, slicing through shields and mail, killing a front-rank Varangian and another man behind him. The bodies were shuffled back into the fortress; their bloodied and holed mail shirts pulled from the dead, hurriedly rubbed in the dirt to clean them before being donned by townsmen who had none. Arrows sped into the momentary confusion in the Christian ranks and some found their mark.

Guy, who was braced on his feet behind his long, kite-shaped shield, took one look around before the battle closed on them. Basil Apocapes, having satisfied himself that the rest of the defence was in order, strode towards them, sword and shield in hand, to take his place in the breach. Oleg was forming a second line on the rubble behind them where the main wall tower had stood. Guy saw his archers and slingers maintaining their efforts against the enemy, rising to shoot, hunching a little as they fitted another arrow or stone to their weapon, and shooting again. Then he was shocked to see Irene loosing arrows from a crenelle of the main wall behind them. She wore her mail corselet and a Norman helmet over her tied-back hair. Jacques noticed Guy look and with a quick motion, angrily urged him angrily to watch his front.

Guy looked forward, just as the arrows ceased and the first wave of moustached, long-haired Seljuks arose from the scarp to grapple with the Varangians. Around him, Guy could hear the prayers and shouts of the men now facing oblivion as they braced forward to meet the shock.

The first assault wave comprised lightly armoured tribesmen, breathless from running, yelling and the steep scramble up the collapsed wall. A score of them died at the top of it, spitted on the spears of the Varangians, to then crumple backwards where their comrades trampled over them in their eagerness to grapple with the Christians. Hands reached out to grasp at the shields and spears of the first kneeling rank of Norsemen, attempting to pull them out of line. These first Seljuks died on the spears of the defenders behind. Some spears broke, the soldiers drawing swords to slash at the sea of blades and limbs, or thrust into the press of bodies coming against them.

Basil Apocapes eased into the midst of the Varangians at the breach just as the first Seljuk assault reached the Christian line on the shattered fore-wall. Guy had a glimpse of him hacking away the arm of a big Seljuk emir who grasped the fountain stump and stumbled backwards to be trampled by those behind. He lay there, covered over by others for a long time, only to be later exposed as the weight of the slain shifted and slid down the reeking, crimson slope.

It seemed as if the first mass attack would fall away repulsed. The lightly armed warriors appeared to be losing heart, knowing their attack was only to wear down the defence, before the ghulams of the *hassa ordusa* and Daylami heavy infantry were committed after the Christians were sufficiently exhausted.

Suddenly, two lassos snaked out from the Seljuks ranks. Immediately another rope with a grappling hook was thrown into the ranks of the Varangians, snaring a man of the front rank who was pulled forward off-balance and instantly killed. For a moment, the Varangians were distracted, slashing at the lassos so as not to be entangled in them. Seljuks hurled themselves at the gap from where the Norseman had been torn. A big, heavily armoured emir struck left and right with his shield and mace. As more Turks leapt into the whirling, hacking mass, three Varangians fell. A fourth was flung down across them by the violence of the assault, his shoulder stoved in by a mace, against which mail was no protection.

Basil was knocked aside and staggered against another man, holding his shield aloft to ward off the rain of blows that followed. A Varangian of the third rank stepped forward, smashing down with his axe upon the strategos' assailant. He pulled Basil to his feet.

Hundreds of Turks boiled up out of the ditch and peribolos pushing into the breach. "Fight. Fight. Paradise. Paradise!" those behind them shouted as they surged forward into the press of their kinsmen struggling for purchase on the bloody stones.

At this crisis in the fight, Guy thrust with his spear, between two Varangians, at a warrior without body armour. He felt the painful jerk all the way up his arm to his shoulder as the haft cracked badly and was then wrenched from his hand in the melee. Knowing he had spitted his man, Guy drew his broadsword and stepped forward into the blood and gore of heaped corpses, using his shield as a battering ram, slashing and stabbing around it with his sword. Aram Gasparian fought at his side.

A bolt from Jacques' crossbow tore into an emir's chest, just as the Turk's battle stare locked with Guy's. The dart sliced through mail, quilted cotton and breastbone to knock the man backwards into the ditch. The attackers lost heart then and started a reluctant, vengeful withdrawal, the covering Seljuk bowmen sending a hail of arrows to protect them.

At the sight of some of his men in their excitement making to descend the ruined wall in pursuit, Guy roared for order. "Stay in line. Re-form on me. On me! Shields up, the arrows will come now." Turning to one of his men, a minor merchant from the town, Guy bade him determine how many of them were still alive, and the condition of the rest.

Arrows came from Seljuk archers among the mantelets and engines of the siege line, as the defenders knelt behind the cover of their shields in the blood and urine-soaked mud. They drew the air with gasping sobs and held grimy hands or rags over running wounds as the shock of battle washed over them.

Guy looked around at the mounds of murdered and maimed, then towards the Seljuk lines. He reasoned that no fresh attack was imminent and knew he had a short time to prepare for the next. In that ungainly, military crouch of soldiers without cover, Guy made his way down the ranks, pushing men into place, telling them to lock shields and to reform the line the Seljuk tribesmen had almost broken. "Jacques, Aram!"

As they ran to him, awkwardly under the weight of linked iron rings, covering themselves with their shields, Guy looked behind to the main wall to see if Irene was safe. Jacques saw. "She's well. I saw her leave a moment go."

"Jacques. Take command of the archers, if you will. Tell them to shoot more deliberately. Make sure more arrows are brought up. Aram, go back to the rear and have the workmen bring up any wickerwork mantelets, palisades, or barrels of soil to be found and chain them in place." Looking behind them, Guy saw that, as the fight at the fore-wall breach had drawn him and his men forward into it, a phalanx of cataphracts of the Sixth Schola had formed along the wreck of the main wall behind them.

Led by Joaninna Magistros, men and women from the city, many wearing felt swathes as protection against arrows, were coming forward with water and a resupply of arrows and stones, and to bear away the dead and wounded. The Seljuk casualties were simply despatched and pushed forward down the ruins.

Doukas and Selth ran up and conversed briefly with the strategos behind the shelter of the fore-wall. Bryennius and Oleg joined them, after first mounting the ramparts to observe the enemy positions. Selth came across briefly, supervising the repairs to the defensive works. It was then, with Selth kneeling beside him, that Guy first looked down into the ditch.

"I don't know what tribe that was," said Selth. "To mount an immediate unplanned attack like that and press it up that slope ..." He looked at Guy. "They can fight. Let no man say otherwise"

Leon Magistros spoke up. "We didn't know how lucky we were when we had a wall to fight from."

Someone laughed uneasily.

Branas arrived, hurrying his brave, frightened sixty townsmen and peasants into line behind Guy's men.

Bryennius and Doukas crouched beside Guy. A work party had started to drag the mantelets into position; the big shields of interwoven light branches would provide reasonable protection from directly aimed arrows and some barrier against assaulting Seljuks.

"Not too close to the edge, there," Selth cautioned. "And build up a stone and earth step behind them to stabilise the barrier."

"I'll tell my men, those that are left, to spread out so the workmen can do the repairs," Guy said. "We don't need to give the Turkmen a good target."

"Very good," said Doukas. "It'll take discipline though. Take command of the remaining Varangians—they've lost their leader. That will make up your numbers."

Basil joined them. "I've just spoken to William de Chartres. He tells me the south wall was only lightly attacked, and if desired, they could spare a hundred men, twenty of whom would be armoured footmen."

Bryennius said, "We're too obvious as a group here and Guy will not thank us for the attention we bring. Let's move behind the wall." This was done and Guy motioned to join them.

"We should take William up on his offer," added Branas. "We lost too many here this morning—and all should be in the common fight at the breach."

Behind the protection of the wall, Bryennius pulled off his helmet and coif. Trails of perspiration ran down his temples. He looked at Basil as he spoke. "This is where their main blow will fall, at least while that big mangonel is out there. It seems obvious from the stable fire that they have someone, or several, on the inside. Cydones seems to be the main suspect—we are looking for him now. I believe they will keep hitting this point today and tonight, wearing us down and preventing any substantial repair of the breach. Here the slope and broken ground still present an obstacle—up the ditch scarp, onto the peribolos and then over the rubble of the defended remnants of the walls and tower, with us shooting all the time. The breach is still quite narrow, three spear-lengths broad in the fore-wall, twice that in the main wall. Thus we can concentrate our strength to defend it. What worries me most is if they attempt to make a second breach somewhere else."

"I know that's what you would do, Leo, but is it what the Sultan will do?" Basil asked.

"We cannot count on him not doing it. That counter-weight mangonel they brought from Baghesh is the centre of their strength now—we have to do something about it."

Basil looked at each in turn. "All right, everyone, when d'you think the main attack will come?"

They all looked away, good soldiers and trusted lieutenants that they were, for what a question was that? Each knew they were at the crisis of the siege, indeed the campaign—for if Manzikert fell, the Seljuks would be free to push deeper into the empire with impunity, the threat to their long lines of communication and retreat removed by the death of the defiant fortress. In their minds, they turned over the unthinkable.

Guy watched and listened to this hasty meeting. For a moment he felt again the gnawing uncertainty he had suffered before his decision to ride on to Archēsh. Now many questions flooded his mind. Should he fight as long as he could, then beg surrender if it were possible, a doubtful proposition at best? Might he rush to the citadel at the first hint of a general collapse? How could he find Irene and Flora Asadian, on whose behalf he had made a pledge to Charles? Jacques? Joaninna? Their horses and equipment, which represented all their wealth in the world?

"You've not heard from your contact?" Basil asked.

"No, Strategos," Bryennius replied. "They have proved accurate thus far and informed us the Seljuks were up to something, but were unable to find out. I would say that they, unknowingly, were referring to the stone-thrower the nomads brought from Baghesh. Now I suspect they are too closely watched, or killed in one of the assaults, or have despatched a message as they can, but we have not yet found it."

Even in this tight gathering, with its wider circle of watching soldiers, Bryennius had not betrayed the identity, gender or religion of his spy.

"Your thoughts?" Basil prompted Bryennius, returning to the matter of the major assault on the defences.

"I think the Sultan will make his main attack early tomorrow morning. It gives them the night to harass us and conduct their preparations, even widen the existing breach, or make another somewhere else to split our defence. They still have many thousands of ghulams and Daylamis who are relatively fresh. If the Seljuks start the attack early, they have all day to fight-through the town. By night, we'd have the advantage of knowing the layout of the city. In a first light assault, they can prevent people from fleeing the city, whereas by night some may slip through the net."

Basil, squatting on his heels, thought on this for some time. "Branas, Doukas, this is what we'll do. Be prepared for attacks today and this night, but rest the soldiers as much as possible. Put as many townspeople and peasants on the fore-walls as we dare. Use the professionals on the main wall. I want a first reserve based on the Scholae, one regiment of Varangians, all the mounted Kelts we have left and another of irregular foot organised today. They are to have their mounts saddled, but must be prepared to fight on foot. This reserve is to be commanded by Count Bryennius. Form a second reserve from the Kelts and Varangians—three-hundred strong, all footmen—to go straight at any breach of the walls. Man the makeshift inner enceinte with townspeople and position rubble-filled carts to close the gaps in it. Use the bishop and the abbess to encourage order amongst the populace. Doukas, double the guard on all gates and sally-ports and check them yourself, regularly. Ensure no one slips out tonight—the Seljuks would likely capture them anyway. Half stand-to everywhere tonight. Those not on watch should sleep in readiness on the ramparts. Stand-to from the end of the third watch. And you, yourselves, rest as much as you are able."

Basil saw Kamyates return from wherever he had been and fell silent.

"You've driven them off." The courtier smiled condescendingly to Basil as he approached. "Well done."

Dark looks flickered amongst the officers. Basil finished the conversation. "Think on it." Then turning his helmeted head to Kamyates, he stood with his eyes narrow. "What else would you expect, Modestos?" The strategos was not smiling.

A further two half-hearted Seljuk attacks were driven from the breach before noon. Then the day turned hot. The nomads retired to their tents to shelter, as the city also wilted in the midday heat.

From his exposed position on the breach Guy observed the enemy encampment. There was little movement amongst the black tents. Engineers rested under awnings as sentries slumped from the heat. The ghulams guarding against a sally from the fortress slouched by their horses. Guy saw many undo the girths to give their mounts some comfort through the long, boring spell of duty. He watched the scene for some time, marking the habits of the enemy. Eventually he decided that midday, when the enemy slept, would be the time to attack, or try to escape.

"A copper coin for your thoughts?" Surprised, Guy turned and was captivated by the sight of Irene. Wearing her now customary men's riding clothes and corselet with her helmet tipped back, she sat beside him.

"My thoughts were quite thick headed and not worth the poorest coin of the Romans," he smiled. With a glance, he took in the water skin over her shoulder and belt with its light sword and archery equipment. There was dirt on the knees of her trousers and her boots were scuffed. "You've been fighting?"

She looked at him with her green eyes. "Hardly fighting! I was on the wall behind you. I came to …" With a look away, Irene left the sentiment unfinished. Instead she passed him an urn of cool water and a food-laden basket. "I've brought this for you and your men. The nuns are bringing more."

"Thank you. You're kind and the men will love you for it."

"They respect and like you, I have heard." She moved closer; improperly so in the normal circumstances of Byzantine society, but the taboos had broken down for the duration of the siege at least.

"I've lost half my men this day, Irene."

"It's not your fault, and you were almost lost yourself. See! You're wounded." She touched his sword arm below the short sleeve of the byrnie.

Guy was surprised. The slight gash had stopped bleeding, but the dried brown stain from it covered his forearm. Then, to his mixed shame and relief, he saw other dried blood on him and knew it was not his own. They were silent, gazing at the Seljuk lines. Irene made to speak but stopped. They looked into each other's eyes. Guy, lost for words, remembered the food and drink and rose to carry it across to Aram Gasparian for the Armenian to pass around.

Resolving to speak his mind, he returned to her. On reaching the shelter of the wall where she stood, he pulled off his helmet and ran his hand over his head. "Jacques and I, and our friends, have collected our horses and essential belongings with some infidel clothing, in the chapel of the tunnel. It's our meeting place if all goes wrong. I don't know what will happen this day or tomorrow, but at least we know where our horses and important gear are, with a little food and water. If you," Guy searched awkwardly for the Greek words, "need to, you might join us. Together and mounted, we might be able to trick or cut our way out and ..."

Irene touched his arm again. "Thank you, Guy," she replied with moist eyes. "But I cannot. I must try and go to my father and family. And you have your hands full already."

Guy had to know. "You know Theodore Ankhialou is in the Seljuk camp?"

"Yes," Irene said quietly.

"He will want you back, if they get in. And the Sultan."

"Theodore never gives up anything," Irene murmured. "I know him. He's ruthless and has terrible rages. He'll want to kill you. You must stay away from me, for he would then know who you are."

They stood in silence for a time until Irene broke it. "I must go."

Perplexed, Guy watched her leave. He had never seen Ankhialou and could not picture the renegade.

In the late afternoon, the Frankish knight, William, and a hundred from the south wall relieved Guy and his men. After going through the ritual of pointing out significant features of the defence and the enemy dispositions, Guy wearily led his men into the city, arranged for the feeding and care of them and appointed the place they were to meet at the end of the third watch.

Proceeding to the cathedral and stepping through the silently waiting throng, he found the interior almost deserted with only a handful of people similarly intent on penance. It was cool in there, the smells and sounds of battle seeming far away as he said a prayer for Charles. At length he left and after eating with Jacques at a little inn as they had in former times, they both walked towards the abandoned church where Flora cared for their horses and gear as Joaninna, Isaac, Jacques and Guy came and went.

Passing by the military stables, they saw Taticus Phocas holding Count Bryennius' Ruksh saddled, with the bay in his yard. Zarrar was eating, taking a mouthful of his feed and walking the yard with his head up, looking at the sights of Manzikert and smelling the fear and excitement in the town.

"How now, Taticus?"

"Guy! You look awful."

"People keep saying that," Guy said with an attempt at levity. "Trying times, eh?" He walked up to the yard and looked in.

Recognising him, Zarrar, unconcernedly chewing on a mouthful of hay, approached and gave him a welcoming sniff.

"Look at him, Guy," the squire said as he stepped into the yard and placed an affectionate arm around the gelding's glossy neck. "Zarrar is not afraid."

Chapter Seventeen

Into The Breach

*Manzikert, First light,
15th September 1054*

Work parties struggled under the waxing three-quarter moon to repair the breach in the north wall, though their work was constantly disrupted by Seljuk attacks using engines, archers and sorties. So confident was the Sultan, he did not order a deliberate night assault into the gap. Despite the continual harassment, the defenders had by first light chained mantelets into place along the line of the fore-wall and cleared away much of the debris so the troops behind the barrier had a six-foot height advantage over the coming assault. The people who were killed or wounded doing this heavy work were carried by their comrades into the city.

Behind the circuit walls of Manzikert, citizens and soldiers alike spent an anxious night wondering at any sudden change to the sounds of jubilation in the Seljuk encampment, dreading the full-scale assault feared at any moment, but which daylight would surely bring. Non-combatants gathered for prayer and to await their fate in the churches and other public places. Despite his piety, Basil Apocapes had overridden the priests and forbidden the ringing of the bells, so the defenders might get what rest they could, huddled on the ramparts or the ground, for some the reins of saddled horses clutched in their hands.

Bessas and his men searched for the imperial courier, Bardas Cydones, but the shadowy figure had seemingly vanished in the dark alleys, cellars and refugee hovels of Manzikert.

With the moon going down and the palest light in the east, thousands of Seljuk tribesmen on foot assembled just beyond archery range of the north wall.

Behind them regiments of Daylami heavy infantry waited on their shields. As the light became certain, the Seljuk mangonels started to lob rocks at the mantelets in the breach. The first missile overshot, crushing a number of the Varangians. The Seljuks adjusted the range, confident this lighter engine would take care of the makeshift defences.

The third stone scored a direct hit on the mantelets, smashing one and forcing askew the night's labours of the Christians. At this, a mounted emir on the low spur line waved his sword and the long assault lines jogged forward with their scaling ladders. Turkic bowmen in the rear ranks kept up constant arrow showers to suppress the defences as the tribesmen closed with the walls. In minutes, the entire length of the northern battlements were under heavy attack, the left flank of the Seljuk assault spilling around in the drained ditch, following the line of the creek along the scarp of the eastern ditch. The densest mass of the Seljuk assault made straight for the breach, intending to batter it until they forced their way through while their comrades distracted the defenders along the adjoining sections of the defences.

Guy placed his men behind the cover of the low garden wall, instructing Aram Gasparian to watch him for orders as he went forward with Jacques and the archers. They had agreed on two hand signals: "come to me and make a stand here", a simple beckoning with a hand then pointing at the ground; and "make for citadel", by tracing a circle in the air and indicating the direction with a straight arm. Such were the symbols of one's destiny.

Lugging four quivers each, Guy, Jacques and ten men moved towards the wall. Cataphracts of the Sixth Schola led by Bryennius and Varangians commanded by Egin, were pressed behind the main wall, prepared to be committed to the fray.

"Guy!" the count called.

Guy went to him.

"They've moved it," Bryennius grimaced, his tone betraying the depth of his fears. "The big counter-weight mangonel, their *baban*. Screens have appeared in front of all the other walls—deception. It could be behind any of them!"

Guy gasped. "We've got our hands full here."

"You are right. Someone else will have to worry about the engine for the time being, but be ready to react quickly."

Guy deployed his archers along a short section of the main wall overlooking the breach. A mix of Varangians and townspeople manned these walls here, with the Franks of William de Chartres defending the breach. On the fore-wall near the collapsed section, someone had prepared a long timber arm on a fulcrum, to which a rope and closing hooks were attached. The device was designed to snare an attacker and haul them over the wall; a useful means of capturing prisoners. Guy had seen how the heavy iron claws clasped a man, who concentrating on the fight to his front, would not see the three-clawed device drop from above. The sharp points would catch on armour and belts, making escape impossible when the rope was jerked tight and the hapless victim was swung up over the battlements. The Varangians called the practice "fishing".

With a touch on his forearm, Irene joined Guy, who was at once glad to see her but concerned for her safety. His look must have been disapproving, for she responded, "They want women and booty. I will not have the fate of the Trojan women."

Guy was uncertain of her meaning; something else to ask Bessas about. "Where's your father?" he asked, mindful of her previous statement about needing to be with her family.

"The south wall."

Then battle was joined and there was no time to say more. Dipping into their quivers, drawing and loosing, Irene, Guy and the archers supporting the ballistae-men, maintained a steady rate of bolts and arrows against the attackers until their thumbs felt cut to the sinews from the bowstrings and shoulders ached from drawing with all their strength.

The storm of the first assault hit the walls. A deafening buzz like that of angry bees, punctuated by the distinctive slaps of ballistae, engulfed the fortress. Incoming arrows clattered on the merlons around the defenders, to be picked up and fired back. Hails of missiles arched both ways. Many of the poorly protected Seljuks fell transfixed. Surging up the scarp, the tribesmen pulled, hacked and cut at the mantelets. The barrier gave way with a groan and collapsed, some of the defenders falling after it to be slashed to pieces in the frenzy of the close combat.

Scores died in the stream of trampled, bloody bile that marked the breach and the scarp leading to it. Seljuks, eyes staring with fear, clawed over the corpses, their lungs gasping in the air after the mental and physical exertion of running through the assault, stepping through the bodies that paved the ditch and up that terrible climb where the dropped swords of the fallen alone were hazard enough. Those in the lead had no breath for anything but laboured, painful sobs. The supports, pressing on their comrades ahead, screamed in unison, "Fight. Fight. Paradise. Paradise."

In the breach, the levelled spears of townsmen and peasants met the nomads. The strategos had taken pains to have as many of them as possible equipped with lamellar cuirasses, pot helmets and the characteristic Byzantine iron strip iron greaves and vambraces to protect legs and forearms. They fought for their families and home, their city and religion. Having no place to hide, they struck with desperate courage, blow for blow, life for life. Despite basic training in the skills and drills of close fighting, they were not professionals and paid dearly the price of a place in the front ranks.

The fight lasted for an hour, perhaps more, with both sides locked so tightly there was no room to swing a sword. Gasping, terrified men could not even withdraw a shield to protect themselves from the short dagger thrusts. Thus they remained upright, even when mortally struck, there being no room in the press of bodies to fall, until the sway of battle bore them down, to impress its fury on their upturned faces. They bit, stabbed, kicked, and punched. In their hearts and heads they knew no choice; the invaders wanted their women, goods and lands, their lives forfeit in the age-old process. Before this fight, as over and over in the weeks before, these incidental soldiers alongside the professionals had uttered the warriors' prayer of Byzantium, "Lord Jesus Christ, our God, have mercy on us, Amen."

They believed and stayed in that inferno, killing and killed, until the tribesmen, who did have somewhere else to go, drew back to enable the Sultan's professional warriors to start forward against the beleaguered wall.

East of Manzikert, Early-morning,
15th September 1054

Within earshot of this battle, outlined against the low morning sun, Derar al-Adin sat astride Qurmul on the low ridge to the east of the fortress where he rode once more with the black tents of Emren Dirse. His friend's followers were sullen and angry that they had this lowly task of cutting off any Christian deserters or units that tried to escape or cut their way from the trap. Burla Dirse had spoken the truth when she said the probable cause of their being here was Emren's disagreement with the Sultan over the recovery and burial of their dead after the failed night attack.

Patrolling and watching in a wide arc, they had intercepted no Christian troops attempting to break out. Either the unbelievers had resolved to die in place or were confident they could hold out. "Or," remarked Emren to Derar, "they'll defend as long as possible, then those who can will try and flee in the confusion of street fighting."

"Yes," agreed Derar. "It will be difficult to keep order when the looting and ravishing start."

He turned in his saddle and thought of the miserable people they had caught during the night: two lovers barely out of their teens who had come over the wall, and a family with their aged parents and three children that had slipped out unnoticed amongst the citizens repairing the breach. The language barrier had prevented questioning until the renegade, Theodore Ankhialou, had ridden by. The man was alert to any news of his woman who fled Archēsh or the Frank on a chestnut horse who accompanied her. Ankhialou questioned the captives, denounced them as spies and ordered they should be instantly killed.

Emren had forbidden it, explaining angrily when Ankhialou had threatened to tell the Sultan of the unwarranted leniency, "Killing is simple enough when the time comes and it is necessary. But the easiest way to encourage a trickle of refugees to become a flood, out into the open where they are easy prey, is to lead them to believe there may be a way out. That is much easier than fighting your way into their lair."

Ankhialou retorted. "Their city will be trap enough when the Sultan makes a second breach this day." He had ridden off to the south, with the evident intent of completing a lap of the fortress environs back to the Sultan's pavilion by the river. After the traitor had gone, Emren Dirse released the captives into the night.

Derar was glad. He had enough debt with God already for his unremonstrative part in the killing, rape and ruin of the last months. To his surprise, he felt a sneaking respect for the garrison of Manzikert. Alone in the wilderness, hopelessly trapped with no prospect of relief, they had held together, fought every battle and shown great tenacity and skill. No doubt he had helped them. Just two nights ago, he alerted them to the plan to dig another tunnel under the southern wall. He had, seemingly long ago, ceased to hate the bay-horsed count and would not object to meeting one day to recount their experiences. Nor would he object if the Roman's pretty interpreter was also there. His lascivious feelings towards the young woman had ceased as his closeness to Farisa had grown. Nevertheless he wished her no harm and would keep his private vow to protect her if he could.

As the sun rose to mid-morning, he remembered Ankhialou's parting words about a second breach that would seal the fate of the fortress. This day was the day for which he had planned and long laboured. He had already instructed Farisa and Zaibullah to be ready to pack up their belongings and to wait for him at their campsite.

Somehow, he had to get into the city close behind the storming troops and find Zobeir al-Adin. The problem of overpowering his nephew's guards in time and thwarting Bryennius who had sworn to have Zobeir killed if the city fell, now loomed large in Derar's thinking. He needed Zaibullah close by, for while the Turk had been blindfolded when led into the city, he had been confident that Zobeir was imprisoned in the citadel which, despite the fate of the city, was unlikely to fall this day. Derar hoped some instinctive memory of Zaibullah's, the combined memory of senses other than sight, would lead them to the hostage youth.

Once the obstacle of finding the boy had been overcome, others presented themselves. Derar would not be able to stay around. Christian prisoners might confess under torture to the identity of the spy or spies in the Sultan's camp. Who knew what Zobeir would say when freed? His nephew may even incriminate him through ignorance of his plans and actions.

Derar wondered where Bryennius would be stationed in the fight. If he commanded the only Tagmata troops there, and only a few hundred at that, would he be in the thick of the fighting in the breach, or withdrawn early to the citadel? Derar thought the latter notion unlikely as the Romans had shown every indication of wishing to hold the circuit walls. He had been keen enough to ride out last night with Emren Dirse on the hunch that the mounted men of the garrison might try to flee in the dark. Nothing was lost by the deed, but now it would be foolish to remain here longer. Deciding to rejoin the Sultan's court, Derar prepared to excuse himself.

With so many imponderables troubling him, Derar looked down at his bridle hand resting on his saddle and with great weariness, closed his eyes, pressing the thumb and forefinger of his free hand against his eyelids.

"Are you all right?" asked the tireless Emren Dirse.

"Yes." Derar opened his eyes. He looked around, away from the fortress, at the vast land around him. The snow-covered peak behind seemed to reflect its own brilliance onto the surrounding landscape. Low ranges stretched away to the west, flanking the course of the river, which for Derar symbolised escape. At times, when the rescue of Zobeir seemed beyond possibility, he had scarcely been able to contain the desire to just be done with Manzikert and its perils and ride off down the valley with Farisa, following it to the Euphrates and home.

This land was beautiful in its own austere way. Brown hills, that had been light green-tinged when they arrived, were now mostly eaten bare. The bright sunlight was somehow mellow in the clear air of the distance; the lightest breeze, like the breath of a woman's kiss, pleasantly soft and cool. Whispering this hour from the northeast, it did not bear the stench of decaying corpses of men and beasts that hung heavily over the city.

He focused on the black-walled fortress with the green outline of trees inside among the domed roofs of the taller buildings. A column of brown smoke, from the smouldering stable fire of the day before, rose high into the light blue sky— with its thin, high white clouds—as though to mark for all the universe the scene of the battle. Low over the walls hung a pall of dust accompanied by the sounds of fierce fighting and the throb of Seljuk drums.

Derar had a sudden, overpowering feeling of unreality. At this place, so far from any of the famous cities of east or west, or any indispensable trade routes, such a great army had come and now fought to overwhelm ordinary people who struggled for their very lives. Just months ago he had never heard of Manzikert, long settled and venerable as it was. When he returned home, if he ever did, his family and friends would not have heard of it either. Nor would they care.

Qurmul moved suddenly, as though in response to Derar's subconscious impulse to be away. "Steady, my beauty," Derar whispered as he drew on the reins. "It'll soon be over, one way or the other."

Emren Dirse had been silent. "You're off?"

"Yes. I was hired to be a linguist and interpreter. There may soon be need of my services, therefore I must go."

So saying, Derar cantered off to the north, skirting around the low seams of exposed lava stone and wide of the thousands of Daylamis now forming up to assault the north wall. Qurmul slid on his hocks down a dusty gap in the lava step and cantered along the flat river valley bottom to camp, where regiments of dismounted ghulams waited on their shields. The counterweight mangonel, the *baban*, had been moved into a position where it threatened the western walls. The engineers were preparing defensive works around it from cotton bales and other material found in the area, to prevent the Romans engaging the machine or its crew with fire.

Riding up to their little camp, he found Farisa, expressionless, looking towards the plume of smoke rising from the city and at the dirty dust cloud over the combat at the north wall.

"They are my people, Derar. How do they bear it?" she murmured.

Manzikert, Morning,
15th September 1054

Despite heavy losses, the Seljuk tribesmen had successfully worn down the defenders of the north wall and were to be replaced by the Daylami heavy infantry. The mantelets in the breach had been smashed to pieces and the substantial casualties amongst the nomadic clans were at the cost of the destruction of the hundred led by William de Chartres and the death of that gallant knight.

To a deliberate drumbeat, the Shi'ite Daylami regulars formed up to assault. Large, brawny men they were recruited from their harsh mountain homeland in north-western Persia. Unafraid of the Turks or any other peoples, they had often brawled in Baghdad and elsewhere with the better paid Sunni Turkic ghulams, the latter receiving more than four times as much, almost forty gold dinars. There had also been ugly fights in the Seljuk encampment around Manzikert, where the unequal distribution of the coins minted by Tughrul Bey resulted in similar resentments. Well-equipped from the Abbasid arsenals with mail or lamellar corselets and protected by large round shields, their main offensive weapon was the spear. Each soldier carried at his belt, a sword or other close-quarter weapon, an axe or mace. Their own numerous archers supported them.

They started forward in long assault waves against the fortifications, with a deep column in the centre to force the breach. Heavily bearded infantry, hair curling around their ears from beneath their pot helmets, the Daylamis jeered at the Seljuks who withdrew past them. They were led by their own prince, a just and courageous man who well understood the ways of war, as he knew the cool gardens, plum trees and shimmering domes of the Abbasid capital. He could march all day on foot, ride and shoot, wield pen and sword as well as recite the Quran. Lightly he carried the heavy shield and spear as his gilded helmet flashed in the sun.

Through the ditch and up the scarp the Daylamis surged as the Varangians in the breach braced to meet them. Fifty-four Vikings and Rus fell at the first shock. Like scythed barley, both sides went down as the mound of bodies over which they battled grew. Valiant and skilled at arms as Oleg's men were, there were ten fresh Daylamis for each of them. The Norsemen wavered. Their line bent back as they were almost forced from the rubble of the fore-wall.

On the wall as he shot his arrows, Guy saw this with clarity and horror.

In the front rank leading the defence of the breach, Count Branas glanced around between blows, reading the ebb and flow of battle. Between bowshots, Guy noticed Bryennius with Togol, David Varaz and a hundred cataphracts, crouched under their shields on the wreck of the main wall and collapsed tower. Basil was kneeling next to Bryennius, judging the moment to hurl the heavily armoured Scholae down the short slope into the Daylamis.

"D'Agiles," Basil shouted, "bring your men up, now."

Guy looked around and waved on Gasparian and the others who started forward like people hunched against sleet. Guy threw his quiver and bow to Irene, who with townsmen and peasant archers, maintained a steady stream of arrows into the packed attackers. With terrible fascination, Guy beheld the murder as ranks of Daylamis and Varangians pushed and plunged at each other with spears while the arching arrows rained down on the supports. He felt something intangible first, then in a fragment of a moment, sensed Branas about to glance around again. He uttered an involuntary, "No."

"No!" he screamed, launching himself forward.

A heavy spear caught Count Branas in the throat. The honoured officer staggered, dropping his own spear and grasping the Daylami's haft in his right hand as his legs buckled. Like a bull stunned in the slaughter yard he sank to his knees with a terrible understanding flooding his eyes, like that of a gazelle seized by lions. With a triumphant shout, the Daylamis strove forward and tore at his shield. Branas, wavering on his knees, held it against them, until they tore it away, one of their champions driving a spear through the mail corselet and lamellar cuirass into his chest.

A Varangian battle-axe split the helmet, head and chest of the Daylami as Branas slumped sideways into the trampled bloody dust and shattered masonry. The Varangians gave a pace as Daylamis, surging around Branas, made to drag him away.

Ranks of cataphracts came upon them, carrying Guy and the Varangians forward. Guy was borne by the closed shields behind him and pushed into the sea of snarling bearded faces, crying to their own God in their fears. While all was lightning fast around him, it seemed his own arms and legs were as lead, unable to keep pace with the feverish demands of his fighting instincts.

A Daylami seized Branas by the harness of his cuirass. Guy saw the enemy's vulnerable arm and cut at it. As he did so, he was vaguely shocked that the Daylami—the hysteria of battle high in him—had been so intent on pulling away the fallen count that the soldier had simply watched Guy slice into his limb.

Branas' head lolled helplessly. Guy saw the fading blue eyes recognise him as Branas made to say something, but his torn throat would not work. Instead, he waved weakly towards the city. In the midst of the hacking, stabbing, screaming multitude, a decarch of the Scholae arose; taking hold of Branas by the shoulder straps of the cuirass, he made to pull him back to the Roman lines. With a great shout of rage, the Daylamis railed against them.

Standing astride the fallen count, Guy stuck blow for blow against a daunting opponent, sword blade grinding against sword blade. He noticed the eyes narrowed over the shield rim and the sun glint weakly through the dust and tumult of the combat on the burnished iron helmet, the solid brown arm raised with its bulging bicep, a hairy armpit beneath. It was unprotected: so close he could have reached out and touched it, but it was on the wrong side for him to get to with his sword.

With a sickening metallic rasp, their swords slid together so the hilts met. Guy realised how powerful his antagonist was as he felt his arm being driven back. He thought about releasing his shield to reach for his dagger, but in the press he could not disentangle from it. Grunting with effort, he strove to force back his opponent's sword arm. The Daylami's green eyes stared into his. In momentary terror, Guy was consumed by the leer of imminent success on those bearded lips.

From Guy's left, a broadsword slid with seeming ease half its length into the Daylami's armpit and he crumpled as Centarch Lascaris wrenched out his blade. Before Lascaris could recover his guard a mace knocked away his helmet and a sword slashed his forehead. Doubled over, the centarch stumbled to his right, instinctively seeking the cover of Guy' shield.

There were Greek shouts of, "Make way. Make way." Hands reached out to guide the popular Lascaris into the safety of their ranks.

"Fight on! Fight on! We nearly have him," Guy heard from close behind him.

How small the world seemed now. Nothing seemed important except to stop the Daylamis carrying off the fallen Branas: he who had ridden out to tell the Sultan to go home, and gone again to offer them a truce to bury the dead, and who was cheerful, brave and ever watchful. In all the hysteria the wider battle, even the defence of the breach itself, seemed somehow less important than saving him.

It seemed another phalanx of Daylamis, led by their prince, rose from the maelstrom and surged forward. Powerless to prevent it, Guy and the few men around him were forced back from the prostrate count. They stepped a pace back. Then two. And three.

Guy's ears rang with the din of battle and his eyes ran with dust and exhaustion. Sweat streamed underneath his helmet, stinging his eyes and tasting salt in his mouth. His tortured breath came in throat-tearing gasps and his lungs burned from the need for air. Under the heavy armour his clothing was soaked with sweat. There was blood on him and he knew it was his. He stabbed and parried with the sword but could not make a mark and felt a sudden sense of being alone.

Daylamis were bending behind their front rank to gather up Branas. There was now a growing cohesion amongst them. Guy sensed it from the way in which their shouts were becoming more cadenced and their shield wall was taking form after the chaos of the close quarters fight.

With his animal instincts racing, Guy backed another step. He saw the Daylami prince stride purposefully to the front of his men who were forming-up in the narrow space between the walls. They had conquered the awful rubble of the fore-wall and knew one more push would carry them into the fortress.

Cataphracts formed around Guy who could hear Bryennius shouting to steady their ranks and to charge on his command. Guy readied himself. Arrows arched above. Somewhere close by a rock struck the wall with a dull thud. Against the distant tumult, there was a sudden silence as the two sides at the breach looked into their enemy's eyes before throwing themselves forward once more.

Suddenly, sharp iron hooks thrown from the wall gripped the prince of the Daylamis. In an instant, the Norsemen, seeing their victim snared, jerked tight the rope while others swung on beams and pulleys to haul the hapless prince upwards. Without daring to look, Guy knew the shrieking prince was being raised over the wall to be taken prisoner.

In that moment, Bryennius and Guy screamed for the charge, hurling themselves at the startled ranks before them. With savage fury, cataphracts thrust, parried and bashed forward until with a roar of triumph, they passed over the broken bleeding form of Branas as the Daylamis broke and ran.

At the brink of the ruined fore-wall, Guy sank to his knees. There was no cheer. On seeing the enemy withdraw beyond arrow range, men pulled off their helmets and sobbed from physical and moral collapse. Guy and Bryennius looked at each other in the shocked recognition that the fight had been won for the moment and that they still lived. Then they remembered and turned to Branas.

One leaned over him and said, "Count Branas has gone to God. We can only mourn him now and bless his soul. He was the best of men and lived the life of a saint."

All seemed surreal as the soldiers stared at the ruination around them and comprehended their own survival. They heard the groans of the wounded and crossed themselves, each man wondering how long his fortunes could last. "Lord Jesus Christ, our God, have mercy on us, Amen."

Oleg, ran forward from the main wall, calling his men forward. "Leo," he cried. "My men will take over here. Get yours back. They have done enough for now." Basil, exhausted himself, nodded mutely to Bryennius. "Well seen, Oleg. We must establish order here before they come again."

Irene approached, calling over her shoulder for the orderlies to move forward and tend the wounded. She had removed her helmet. Guy could see the ring of damp, flattened hair where the sweatband had been. Without a word, she handed him a water skin.

An Armenian cavalryman rode up, dismounted and clambered to Basil, with whom he spoke quietly but urgently. In the late morning heat the strategos listened as he looked at the enemy retire to their tents. "Count Bryennius, Oleg," he said. "Leave Egin in charge here—we must attend the western wall."

Something in the evenness of Basil's tone made Guy and Bryennius exchange glances.

"You'd better come too, Guy," said the count.

The cavalryman passed his reins. Basil took to the saddle, with Bryennius and Guy hanging onto a stirrup leather each. Oleg took hold of the same stirrup leather as Guy and at a trot they made their way to the middle of the western wall.

Manzikert, Late morning,
15th September 1054

Guy followed Basil up the steps of the main wall to find many of the council already there, including Modestos Kamyates who hovered at the edges, waiting for the moment when his words might carry most weight. Cydones was missing and Guy wondered how the hunt for him had progressed.

John Curticius looked distraught. Guy shared his distress, for it was the princep's daughter the Sultan might take as his bride. He had heard Curticius, despite his shortcomings, especially the fondness for wine, had won respect on the walls as a determined and adaptive fighter.

Isaac listened in the background. Bessas, his wounded arm still in its sling, arrived looking like he had not slept properly for days.

Curticius grunted. "There it is—next chukka in the shepherd king's game."

A glance between the merlons revealed the dilemma. The concealing screens had been removed, uncovering the huge mangonel—that had wrought such destruction against the north walls—already in position to create a second breach. It was now within range of the city's defences and well protected by low berms, surmounted by cotton bales, which the Seljuks had thrown up.

Guy felt a jolt of fear when he saw it.

"You see the problem?" the strategos asked, looking at Bryennius and Selth in particular. "In the post-noon, they'll attack the breach in the north wall. At the same time, they'll create another here." He lowered his voice. "I do not believe we can defend both, for we'll be heavily outnumbered at each. Many of our men have already been cycled through defence of the first breach. All are exhausted. We're low on arrows and bolts …"

"And almost out of fire," Selth reminded them.

"We need to destroy it, now." Bryennius said.

"How?" Doukas asked, tears of failure and frustration welling in his eyes. "We can't touch it with any engine we have, nor could we build one in time. Even Araxie Bagradian's mangonel cannot reach it with a sufficient weight of rock to wreck the infernal thing." He waved impotently at the Seljuk engine. "And see, they've protected it well."

Bryennius looked long over the Seljuk camp and engine before he then turned to them. "There seem to be three choices," he said just loudly enough for the circle to hear him. "Mounted attack as we've done before. Dismounted attack as Theophanes did on the first night. Or some stratagem. They can defeat a formal mounted or dismounted attack. See, they have deployed many mounted ghulams and Daylami footmen—they're ready for that. It's what they want us to do and their sentries would sound the alarm before we left the walls and formed for battle."

They were all grimly silent.

"What do you have in mind?" Curticius asked.

Bryennius looked once more over the walls and bit his lip.

"Leo," prompted Basil.

Glancing around at the small circle of worried faces, all that was left of the council, for some had been killed or wounded, Bryennius ventured, "Someone must ride out there, as though a messenger, carrying a concealed naphtha pot, and burn the damned thing."

"Just like that?" Doukas gasped. "How'll you set fire to the mixture? We can't reach it with fire-arrows, and the Seljuks are unlikely to provide you with a flaming brand to torch it and there doesn't seem to be a cooking fire near it. Nor does carrying a pot with a smoking wick seem practicable."

Selth cleared his throat but even then could scarcely get the words out. "I've made a pot." They all looked at him. "Two—two clay pots—months ago. They have been fired in two parts. The bottom is solid and contains the naphtha. The top chamber has a solid bottom, except for a bunghole, but there are many holes in the sides to permit the flow of air. The whole is held in a rope basket with a handle. The idea is to seal the flammable mixture in the bottom chamber with a wooden bung and clay, then to put glowing coals in the top."

The council were deathly silent as they stared at the engineer.

"Brisk movement will permit the air to fan the embers and keep them alight for a short time. At the decisive moment the device is swung around, which will fan the coals to glow, then the pot is dashed against the object, the hot coals igniting the mixture as it splashes over the target. The rope basket serves as a means of delivery and also keeps the naphtha and coals together. At the time of impact, it will itself be soaked in naphtha and catch fire."

"You thought of this?" Basil asked.

"I made the pots," Selth said unassumingly. "The plan for delivery is Leo's." He looked at their doubting faces. "Might work?"

Basil looked at Bryennius. "Always thinking, eh!" He chuckled grimly then regarded Karas Selth with a long, thoughtful stare. "You say this thing hasn't been tried?"

"Once only, an earlier model. These two haven't been tried," Selth answered.

"The damned things will be dangerous enough," said Oleg, "let alone to load them on a horse, ride out there in broad daylight into the middle of the Seljuk army, and then just casually set fire to that mangonel. It's a ride to Valhalla for whoever goes."

"Oleg," Bryennius said gently, "You're right, my friend, but we've no choice, or time. The moment has come—one dies or we all do."

Basil stared over the battlements at the huge machine protected by defensive works. "Karas, you've two of these ready to use?"

"Yes, Strategos. And some naphtha pots to throw on the flames afterwards."

"And they can't put out the fire?"

"Not unless they have carefully stored a very great amount of piss and sand around it," Selth answered with somewhat more confidence.

"Which they may have done."

"Who is to make such a ride?" Oleg wondered aloud, his indifferent horsemanship adding to the multitudes of uncertainties he foresaw.

"That's the question, isn't it?" said Basil.

Guy, listening to all this, drew his eyes from the close circle of faces. Along the walls, soldiers and townspeople watched the council in silence, interpreting through their fears and hope every expression and gesture of the city's senior soldiers. Below them, hundreds looked up, pale with fright for they read the desperation in the discussion amongst the council. Many people sank to their knees in prayer, while others wept openly in terror.

Basil went to speak, but Bryennius cut in. "Strategos, we need to keep quiet about this. It's our last attempt to keep them outside the walls. We cannot afford for anyone to deliberately, or even accidentally, interfere with the plan."

It was at that moment that the corrupt merchant, Domnos Taronites, very agitated, walked up and stood by Kamyates. The merchant was wearing the same crimson gown and expensive kid shoes he had when Bryennius had shod Sira at Arknik. Like Kamyates, he was unarmed. Something about their attire indicated to Guy that they were dressed to be noticed: not as soldiers, but as rich men, ripe for capture, ready to reveal their riches, or be ransomed if the city was taken, anything to avoid being killed out of hand in the first orgy of destruction. Anything to give their sly tongues the chance to work, he thought.

Kamyates, sensing the unease of all who watched, began loudly enough to be overheard by many of the people standing below them, as well as the troops on the wall. "Apocapes! There is a fourth choice that Count Bryennius was too clever, or foolish, to bring up. Surrender the city. It's over. You must surrender the city."

Basil was speechless.

"There's no other choice," Kamyates continued smugly. "You cannot beat the Sultan. It's over. Your vanity does not matter any more. The citizens must place their trust in our Lord and beg the Sultan's mercy, if they wish to live beyond this day. I demand it."

The strategos had recovered from his shock and appeared even-toned, but Guy knew him well enough to see that this time he was dangerously angry.

Taronites, the merchant who had never borne arms, piped up, "Basil, you cannot win. Your execrable pride threatens us all. Yours, and Bryennius', and this barbarian's." He gestured towards Oleg. "And that of this foolish, greedy Frank here." With a sniff he indicated Guy. "You buffoons risk all our lives. Give the infidels what they want. Send out Curticius' daughter! She's the one the Sultan would marry, isn't she? We've all heard. And send with her the beauteous young women and men laden with gold and silver. The Seljuks will go away then, having attained their hearts' desire." The merchant looked at Curticius.

Many people looked at John Curticius. Guy watched the man visibly wither. A haunted look took hold of his face as he looked down for long moments then dolefully around. Guy thought he was about to cave in to the perceived public will, or private desire for life, no matter how timorous. Or did the father hope if the daughter surrendered herself to the Sultan's whim, she might remain alive and rise to power and influence. After all, other Byzantine girls—Qarātīs, Hubshiya, Dirār and Qurub—had borne sons who became caliphs in Baghdad— surely better that than being violated and killed resisting the inevitable in the smouldering ruins of Manzikert.

Guy, seething inwardly, despised Taronites as a wife-beater and coward. He felt his cold anger towards the man stirring, even more so given the merchant's shrill tone. Even had such a craven scheme as Taronites proposed been thinkable, the situation was too desperate now for the Seljuks to be bought off. Every person in Manzikert knew well enough the fate of Archēsh after its surrender. All understood that there would be no mercy for a city that had resisted for so long and inflicted so many casualties on the invaders. He looked around, but could not see Irene.

"Do you number your own wife, the lovely Maria, amongst those who should be thus sent forth?" Oleg exploded.

"If needs be," replied the merchant, cunning enough to know blatant hypocrisy would not wash now.

Guy had a fleeting mental image of Olga, Maria and others being forced out the gate and carried off by the infidels. He saw the angry spittle caught on Kamyates' beard and Taronites blanch as Oleg's hand gripped his sword hilt. Then Guy thought of Irene forced out of the gates by these two or borne away by some Seljuk during a sack and the idea was unbearable.

John Curticius licked his lips as if to speak.

Guy was about to cut him off, but Basil caught his eye and shook his head imperceptibly.

Kamyates added to the diatribe.

Through his anger Guy did not discern what the haughty courtier said.

There was a murmur in the crowd, an uneasy stirring, the first hint of a mass panic. In a blink, Basil Apocapes stepped forward and landed such a punch into Taronites' sternum that the merchant folded to his knees with a gasp.

"You will address me as Strategos, you petty profiteer," Basil roared, giving the quaking merchant such a tremendous kick that Taronites fell backwards down the steps. "Get off my battlements, damn your eyes. You are not fit for the walls of Manzikert, upon which so many men, women and even children have given their lives. You never amongst them I have noticed."

Now thoroughly aroused, Basil turned on the trembling Kamyates. "Stay next to Oleg and do not move, or speak, or make any gesture—because if you do, Oleg will cut off your head upon my order, given now before God and these men."

Striding to the edge of the ramparts and looking down on the crowd, Basil thundered, "Men and woman of Manzikert. We've fought great battles together. I now send a message to the Sultan—there will be no surrender here. Now go to your places and keep your spear points to the enemy. Take post!" He turned and with a sweep of a mailed shoulder, summoned his council.

With a remarkable coolness after such passion, the strategos lowered his voice, speaking only to those grouped closely around him. "Whoever is able to go forth and burn down that catapult will receive much largesse of gold and silver and many horses and mules from me and honours and high rank from the Emperor. If he is killed by the infidels and has a relative or son, all that will go to him."

Basil looked for an answer at the circle of faces around him.

No one moved or made to speak. All looked at the ground, seeking in their souls to know if they could face personal annihilation for the public good.

Guy gazed down, seeing his own worn boots in the circle of dirty footwear on the flagstones. He stole a look sideways at the Seljuk lines and the bulk of the *baban* with its guards and the groups of mounted pickets taking their confident ease. Basil asked certain death: one chance in a hundred of getting to the machine, less of returning alive from the hornets' nest that would be stirred up. Even the act of setting fire to the engine from horseback with Selth's untried device was a forlorn hope.

Guy saw Bryennius and Selth glance at each other.

Basil looked around the silent group. "T'was my mistake. I'll go myself."

"You will not," Bryennius and Selth chorused. Bryennius continued for them, "We need you—until the last spear is shattered and sword broken—we need you."

After an agonised silence, Basil acquiesced. "It need not be any man here? Is there no one who can do this?"

Guy exhausted and filthy, watched all of this. With the others he was motionless in his byrnie and helmet and shield, weapons by his side. There was silence in the group as one by one they looked up, fear in their faces. He knew these men, understanding they had wives and families and something to live for. All had risked death many times over. Not a few were at the end of their tether. Guy thought of Irene. He had come, a penniless would-be warrior to Manzikert for pay and found Irene.

"Is there no one in the city?" Basil asked quietly. "Then I must."

Guy swallowed and stepped forward. "I will."

They all regarded him as though he was a dead man already and Guy felt another deep stab of fear. "I will go forth," he said, steeling his very self, "and burn down that catapult, and today my blood will be shed for all the Christians, for I have neither wife nor children to weep over me."

Silence sealed the contract.

"You cannot ride your mare, Guy," Bryennius said, his voice the shadow of a choked whisper. "The Seljuks know her, and her former master's kinsmen will try and have her back."

"Name what horse and anything else you want," said Basil.

Guy looked at Bryennius and asked: "I'd like to ride Zarrar. He is strong and swift and not frightened."

"Take him. Is my saddle all right?"

"Yes." Guy had not given the detail of a saddle much thought. "I'll try and return it to you."

Basil smiled a secret smile. "I dare say, Count Leo will pursue you to Oleg's Valhalla and beyond if you do not return his best horse and favourite saddle. Count Selth, we'd better try out one of your infernal devices behind the stables before we let Guy go."

As they departed the wall, Basil turned to the nearby defenders and ordered defiantly, "Maintain a close watch on the infidels, men. It might look like they're having their noontime sleep, but they are damned tricky rascals. Keep your spear points to them."

The soldiers laughed with a show of boldness.

Guy did not smile with them. He was the loneliest man in the world.

Chapter Eighteen

Fairest Fame

Manzikert, Midday,
15th September 1054

Bardas Cydones' survival now depended on the swift fall of Manzikert. For a day, the imperial courier laid in the dark loft of the churchyard stable with the body of his victim. The stench of death had permeated Manzikert for so long now that even proximity to the murdered monk did not trouble him. Several times he had seen parties of searching soldiers pass by. Late on the previous day, the Cuman and Patzinak scouts with the detestable little Georgian, David Varaz, had entered the very churchyard in which he hid, but in their haste had found nothing. Instead the Armenian monk had stumbled upon him and paid the price: a cut throat.

Cydones had realised his game was up when Bessas Phocas had surprised Kamyates, Reynaldus and him at the Barbarian House. Phocas, with his tame barbarian, the meddling Cephala woman and two cataphracts, had foiled their killing Isaac and taking what papers they wished. Suspicion had been deep in Phocas' eyes and contempt evident in the crisp diction of Serena Cephala. Cydones had earlier seen her speak with Irene Curticius. He knew the latter had observed him near the scene of the stable fire, for their eyes had met. He would have killed her then, but there had been too many people around.

As the three plotters had left the Barbarian House in the dark hours of the previous morning, Cydones read the glances exchanged between Kamyates and Reynaldus. He thought that both of them would subsequently distance themselves from him, making him the lone scapegoat for any recriminations. Not having

Kamyates' highly placed friends at court, or the backing of the Norman soldiery, he was alone and hunted, unless the city fell.

His thoughts drifted as if they bore his physical being with them. He reflected bitterly how the plan had gone awry with the fight at the inn and unravelled further when he found his journey to Manzikert shared by a regiment of Scholae. The officers, suspicious of the labyrinthine nature of power and treachery in Constantinople, had been infuriatingly guarded and curious. When they had left the route-of-march and hunted down a Seljuk scouting party in the enormity of the harsh Armenian plateau, Cydones had scarcely believed either their fidelity to duty or luck in securing a prisoner. Nor had he counted on the stolid determination of a mercenary, meddling Frank, whose desire for a warhorse seemed to play some part in the trust that had emerged between Basil Apocapes, the officers of the Scholae and some of the garrison. He had not caught the couriers on the road, nor had he been able to get to them at Manzikert because they were never alone and unprotected.

Most unsettling of all had been Apocapes' closely held and exacting ability to predict what the Sultan would do next. Cydones knew Apocapes had at least one spy in the Seljuk camp. Some nights ago he had stumbled over an arrow with a message tightly bound to the shaft. He had barely concealed it in his robes before cataphracts rounded the corner as though looking for something. In his room he had read the Arabic script of the message. It had detailed the discord over the handling of the campaign among the Turkish leaders and the divisions growing between the Shi'ite Daylami infantry, Sunni professional Turkic cavalry and Seljuk tribesmen. The note related that someone, in a heated discussion between the Sultan and a gathering of emirs, had asked rhetorically and bitterly whether the bride was such a tempting trophy that the bride-price was worth the cost.

Cydones assumed that the person who wrote or dictated the note was a Turkish prince, for it described the inner circle in a direct and confident tone. He burned the paper in his room and now wished he had not spoken of its message to Kamyates, for he now knew, too late, that the bureaucrat simply abandoned those of no further use to him. Looking glumly at the limited view of the city visible from his hiding place, he remembered when he had first arrived the city had some slight appeal. Now it merely appeared beleaguered and squalid. His head slumped in despair.

"Manzikert! A dowry for the Sultan," the imperial courier sighed.

He had, on Kamyates' orders, attempted to have Bryennius slain during his return from Archēsh, but the dart launched by the killers hired by Petros Doukitzes, using Bardanes Gurgen's unknowing servant as the go-between, had found the wrong mark. Doukitzes had then disappeared and Cydones wondered whether he had been captured and interrogated. Cydones hated Bryennius and thought his planned demise no more than the arrogant soldier deserved.

The servant, Ananias, had made his way back to Manzikert, but Cydones had been able to silence him one dark night on the south-wall, making it look like just another battle death in this place where hundreds had died. Bardanes Gurgen, attracting attention to himself through his outspoken hatred of the Romans, had proved a useful distraction until killed on the walls fighting with the people he hated.

Cydones knew, if he were caught, Kamyates would denounce him as traitor or madman, if not murder him before he could disclose the courtier's own treachery. If the Seljuks broke in, Kamyates had told him, Dumrul's ghulams would make straight for the cathedral, securing anyone who wore a black scarf and prostrated themselves. Thus spared from the immediate orgy of killing, they would be taken away, questioned, offered conversion and employment perhaps, or paid and freed to make their way back to Byzantium.

In his day of forced reflection, Cydones had learned much of Manzikert: its smells, the sounds of battle joined and fading away as yet another attack was beaten back by defenders too tired to count them anymore, tattoos on the flagstones as couriers galloped with urgent messages, church bells announcing prayer and the majestic hymns accompanying them. He saw the light too, in the rise and set of sun and moon and the shadows they made.

As the clamour of the morning's fighting faded towards the noon quiet, Cydones heard a different sound, a single shod horse and a group of men in quiet discussion. He crept forward and placed his eye to a narrow window and found himself looking down on the yards of the military stables. As he recognised Bryennius, Cydones felt a surge of hatred that eased to yearning distaste as he saw Guy d'Agiles mount the count's bay horse.

Cydones quite liked the young Frank. The young man had pluck and ambition, both qualities he admired. At times, when he had encountered him in the city, Cydones had freely given advice or assisted him in learning Greek. He was aware, he remembered with rare self-awareness and a trace of shame, once suppressing a physical attraction to the Kelt that shocked him for its unexpectedness. He thought then of his wife and children, and how he missed them. A tear wet his cheek.

His thoughts turned to the fight at the inn and a Kelt with shoulder length hair who had challenged him at sword point. "Cross me again, Kelt, and die," Cydones had hissed. Constantinople was far away and he had not thought of the youth again. He dwelt for a time in his mind's eye on images of the encounter at the inn by the Golden Gate. Things had gone wrong from then on. They had escaped from Bryennius' trap only because some blundering Kelts … Guy d'Agiles! Of course! The thought hit Bardas Cydones like an axe in the gut. And Charles Bertrum and the groom, Jacques—with Bryennius all the time. How could he have failed to notice?

Cydones rolled on his back and stared at the ceiling, his fist pushed against his bearded mouth to stifle the involuntary groan. He lay there for a time feeling hatred for d'Agiles wash over him. He wormed onto an elbow and stared at the group through tears of fear and desperation.

The strategos and Selth were standing close to Bryennius and d'Agiles who were with the count's bay horse.

Perplexed, Cydones watched as the Frank mounted then walked and trotted a few laps of the small field the squires used for allowing the horses a run. The Frank cantered two laps, then a few figures-of-eight, getting a feel for the horse. Cydones knew the way riders try a new one, whether to buy as a spare at polo, or a restive post-exchange remount during a long ride.

"What the devil?" he wondered under his breath.

The Frank trotted up to the men who had been watching him closely. The engineer, Selth, took a small pan of coals from a brazier and poured them into a rope-netted vessel, gently tapping something into the top when he had finished. The Frank accepted the object and hanging it gingerly by the handle over his wooden pommel, drew his surcoat across the vessel, took up his spear and reversed it. Turning the bay horse gently, he rode two laps at a swift walk. At a command from Bryennius, the Frank collected the horse and plunged the spear point into the ground. D'Agiles grasped the rope handle and held the vessel out beside him, lifting the horse into full gallop straight at the cart. On reaching it, he pulled the horse to a halt on its haunches and heaving the rope-handled object twice around his head, dashed it against the cart on his near side. The alarmed horse leapt sideways from the explosion of flame and smoke. The Frank never shifted in his seat urging the bay to a gallop again. They made three tight turns around the fiery cart, the rider taking from his breast two more empty pots, which he dashed onto the flames.

Having completed this unusual ritual, the Frank rode the prancing horse up to the group and dismounted, the bay turning on the reins to give the fiercely burning cart an astonished stare. With a quick movement, the horse turned to his master, Bryennius, as if seeking reassurance. The count gave his blazed face a pat and slipped an arm around his neck while the horse snorted with great interest at the Frank holding his reins.

There was a discussion among the men for some minutes, then they adjusted something under the surcoat of Guy d'Agiles. Cydones thought it must have been some sort of sling to hold the pots. Interesting as the little playlet was, he could attach no significance to it. "At a time like this," he whispered again to himself. Then the Frank tied what looked like a letter to the haft of his spear. A letter? Reversed spear? Surrender? Parley? Deception! Cydones suddenly understood. The garrison meant to send d'Agiles out as though a messenger, a ruse enabling him to get close enough to the mangonel to set it alight. If they succeeded, the fall of the city was uncertain.

Alarmed, Cydones rolled over onto his back, looking at the vaulted stone ceiling a few feet from his head, turning over in his mind and discarding the first wild schemes to foil the Frank. Although the group had conducted the rehearsal with the desire of it being witnessed by as few people as possible, their obvious haste had overruled total secrecy. He deduced that the attempt would be made soon. Since it was likely the Seljuks would drag the *baban* to another point of attack to create a second breach and the western wall seemed most logical,

Cydones reasoned it would be the best place to execute the plan now forming in his mind.

Kicking off his boots, the imperial courier donned the rough sandals and black cowl of the slain priest and stole through a back entrance to the main-gate towers of the western wall. On the way, he took a basket of food and an urn of watered wine from a nun, telling her he would deliver it to the troops and she should return to the kitchens for more.

Cydones' constant poking around the defences now paid off and he planned as he made his way. He had been in the main-gate towers before where the weapon chambers were cramped to allow room for the gate and portcullis mechanism. There was a secluded ballista gallery there. Cydones knew that if he could overpower the man or two men on duty, he would have a perfect opportunity to send a dart into the Frank's back as he rode from the gates. Cydones hoped he could get away before startled bystanders worked out where the missile had come from. If he were seized, he would bluster loudly that Apocapes was trying to surrender the city and make his escape in the ensuing furore.

It proved easy to gain the tower, entering and shutting the stout wooden door after him. Inside were a Flemish mercenary and an Armenian peasant who could barely communicate with each other. They saw Cydones with the basket and as the enemy camp was quiet, moved to receive their victuals. As he passed out the bread and drink, Cydones noted with satisfaction that the ballista was already loaded with a heavy dart. The Armenian said he needed to find his relief, so he asked the priest to stay as he went in search.

The imperial courier locked the door after him, turned to the young Flemish man and smiled.

Manzikert, Early afternoon,
15th September 1054

Bessas Phocas understood that Bryennius and Selth had wanted to get Guy's ride to the mangonel underway with as little attention as possible being drawn to it. Standing in the crowd, he thought that was impossible and the time needed to ensure such secrecy unavailable. The dull throbbing in his wounded shoulder was a constant companion and he worried that it heralded an infection, but this was no time to be slinking off to hospital.

Observant townspeople, reckoning on something happening, had followed the group leading the saddled horse. More people had joined until an audience had assembled to which others were drawn.

Despite the heat, this anxious throng gathered near the gates as Bryennius, Selth and Guy led Zarrar into the cobbled area by the towers. Taticus Phocas had groomed Zarrar with loving care and even now walked behind, brushing out his tail. The bay horse, knowing something was up, nonetheless walked nonchalantly on the ends of the reins, ignoring the crowd but noticing with raised head and pricked ears, a troop of the Scholae drawn up with his mates in their ranks. Ruksh, saddled, was held by a squire. The chestnut whinnied to Zarrar who looked back with interest and recognition, but did not answer. He was like that, his own horse.

The crowd parted respectfully around Bessas, a wounded centarch of the Scholae being a figure of authority and respect in the beleaguered city. There was something else mixed with their well-intentioned looks. They sought some sign from him that this was no ending; that this night also they might sleep in their beds or whatever bower they claimed in the crowded tenements of Manzikert. Such was the restless, inquisitive, frightened crowd in which Bessas stood. Sensing this, he tried to show outward calm, wearing the uniform both as a crutch and a mask. Inwardly he was agitated and would have been more optimistic about the desperate venture to be undertaken if they had accounted for the imperial courier, but Cydones had evaded capture. Cataphracts moved through the crowd, having combed the walls and towers already that morning.

Bessas met Loukas Gabras but the decarch's glance bespoke no glad news. "The imperial courier's a cunning rascal."

"True enough," Bessas said. "Keep searching. He's running out of chances to save himself and must be here somewhere. Even the knowledge of a hunt will serve to keep him off-balance and separated from his friends. He will make a mistake and when he does, there we shall be."

"It would be better if he led us to them," Gabras said.

Bessas saw the princeps and Irene hurrying down the path towards where Bryennius was checking Zarrar's saddle and accoutrements. Guy had gone with Karas Selth into the guardroom. He turned to Gabras and smiled encouragingly. "You're right, of course. But first things first—we must make sure the Kelt's mission is not compromised."

Serena approached. She too caught Bessas' eye and shook her head. "No one has seen anything." For a time she surveyed in silence the battlements and buildings around. "He must be here somewhere."

Bessas looked at her—blonde hair under the scarf, fair skin and the bluest eyes—with tenderness he had once been unaccustomed to. This sudden realisation of the change in him was at once warming, but unsettling. The social pressures of the siege had broken down many barriers, but at a daunting price of fear and uncertainty, for the future or life itself. Serena was frightened, as they all were, but was trying not to show it.

She spoke warmly to Gabras, when many well-born people would not deign to speak to a soldier. The two had been closely engaged in the hunt for the imperial courier for a day now and the task had brought them closer together. She watched Bryennius whispering to Zarrar as the count ran his hands over the bay, telling him what a brave, clever and nimble horse he was, how he must safely bear back the Frank to the gates of Manzikert, and how from this deed he would be as famous as Bucephalus. Zarrar bent his head to Bryennius. "He's an incredibly calm horse, Zarrar, isn't he?" Serena said.

"He is," Gabras agreed. "Never was a horse better bred for the ride the Kelt must make this day."

Bessas turned as he heard a breathless male voice cry his name.

"Centarch Phocas! Centarch Phocas." It was Araxie Bagradian, the warrior monk who cried, "I've found a priest, dead a day. Stabbed—his cowl taken." He leaned forward, hands on his knees, to catch his breath. "I have not run so far since chased by a peasant for kissing his daughter—we were twelve. It still feels like yesterday."

A murdered monk was suspicious, but Bessas could not determine any immediate link to the imperial courier. "Stabbed, you say? Murdered for food perhaps?"

"Stabbed in his chapel by the military stables," explained Bagradian, shaking his head "The military stables?" Bessas' suspicions were now thoroughly aroused. "Where the killer would have seen Guy's rehearsal."

"I'm astonished," Bagradian was visibly shaken. "He was a good and pious man. I cannot understand why anyone would do this."

People jostled against Bessas who winced as one bumped his wounded shoulder.

Under the direction of Theophanes Doukas, files of archers were mounting the main wall to reinforce those already there. Against his orders, non-combatants were also forcing their way onto the ramparts to see the drama that instinct told them would be played out before the walls. "Ghoulish bastards," Doukas mumbled to Bessas as he passed, glaring at the disobedient citizens.

Serena took Bagradian's arm, saying, "You had better sit down, if you feel faint." She led the priest a few paces to the stone seat under the shade tree by the guardroom. As he sat, the rough black cloth of his habit rose, revealing ancient gnarled feet in worn leather sandals. The nails were long and aged, with dirt under them. Thick calluses had cracked around the sides of the brown, dusty foot and the instep was dried and coloured by long exposure to the sun.

Guy walked with Selth out of the guardroom and prepared to mount.

Seemingly in the vast distance, Bessas heard Basil order, "Prepare to open the gates."

There was an acknowledgement from the guard and the rasp of the portcullis being raised.

Serena stared at Bagradian's feet. She stood suddenly, looking Bessas full in the eyes. "He's here. How often have you seen priests here with soft white feet?" Before Bessas could fully comprehend, Serena had seized his arm with such force that the nails dug into his forearm. "He's there, in the tower already. Cydones! I saw a monk with soft white feet climb the steps and walk towards the gate tower."

Gabras stepped closer to her and motioned to four troopers.

Bessas heard Zarrar's shoes on the cobblestones as the horse took a step forward to brace himself while Guy swung to the saddle. "When?"

"Just now!" Serena cried, already turning to run to the steps leading to the ramparts, Loukas Gabras and four men sprinting after her.

Bessas ran after them for a few painful steps, then turned and called, "Jacques, come quick, and make ready your crossbow."

The small group ran up the steps, roughly shouldering aside several townsfolk. Serena tried the door leading from the rampart to that level of the tower. It was barred from the inside.

Bessas made a sign for silence. Seeing a heavy pole on the ground, he signalled for a party of cataphracts to fetch it, using whatever cords and straps they could find as carry-ropes. Zarrar's shod hooves scraped on the flagstones below. At last the battering-party appeared on the rampart. Bessas whispered to Jacques to enter first then waved them on.

From beneath came the echo of the guard commander ordering, "Open the outer-gates," followed by the dull rumble of the rollers as the great iron doors swung inwards on their iron tracks.

The little wooden door in the tower gave way, and the battering party fell in on top of it. Jacques stepped over them, crossbow raised to his shoulder. Nothing was said. Bessas entered the dark chamber immediately after Jacques and saw the figure in a monk's cowl crouched over the ballista. The hooded face turned towards them. In the daylight from the arrow slit, Bessas could see the scowling countenance of Bardas Cydones. The imperial courier looked startled, but not terrified as he deliberately turned his head away from them and sighted down the length of the ballista bolt, his soft fingers moving to the release.

Manzikert, Early afternoon,
15th September 1054

As he waited in the guardroom, Guy felt an enervating sense of nothingness. To his surprise he felt less physically frightened now than in the immediate aftermath of volunteering to destroy the mangonel. He had just banished his doubts, no terror, merely nagging preparation, into the pail of excrement at the back of the guardroom and refastened his dress. The old stones of the walls near him were silent and he was grateful for the privacy they afforded for this last reflective moment.

At the strategos' insistence, Guy had shaved, bathed and changed his clothes to appear as a well-rested and confident chieftain when he rode forth. Simon Vardaheri and Taticus Phocas had obtained and burnished a good mail hauberk that would cover his thighs to the knees when mounted. Guy's own helmet and a borrowed coif were also polished to a high sheen. Jacques and Flora Asadian treated sword scabbard, belts and scuffed boots by staining and polishing until the leather gleamed with a deep red-brown hue. Into these boots were tucked fitted blue riding trousers. Over a white linen shirt, Guy wore a quilted tunic held to be arrow proof when worn under the mail. Zarrar had been groomed and saddled, armoured with his polished bronze chamfron and mail bard.

At the stables, before Guy donned a surcoat of unbleached linen, Jacques had tied a broad strip of cloth crosswise around his shoulders. This had open pockets sewn into them, both at his left breast so he could reach the two additional bottles of naphtha there with his free hand, his left being occupied with shield and reins. Then they had set out on the long walk through the growing crowd to the guardroom.

In the shadows of the guardroom a circle of silently watching Armenian locals, mixed with Varangian and Norman mercenaries, witnessed his final preparations. They had fought valiantly for a month but were now beaten: one breach in the walls and another soon to be made. Guy could see it in their eyes: he was a dead man the moment he rode from the gates into the midst of the Turkish host.

He had not seen Irene since volunteering to destroy the catapult. Everything had happened too quickly. While the imminent ride should have filled his thoughts, all he could think of was her face, their early rides, the escape from Archēsh and the chill morning after with the dark memory of her former lover stalking them, when Guy had promised not to let the nomads have her.

"Ready?" Karas Selth asked in the coolness of the room, where every sound seemed deafening.

"Ready," Guy replied.

"Any words?"

"No."

"None?" Selth asked doubtfully.

"No."

Selth leaned forward and with his dagger cut a vertical slit on the front of Guy's surcoat. Taking the first bottle of incendiary liquid, the Byzantine engineer eased it gingerly into a pocket sewn inside. Then he reached in with the second. "Mind you don't knock them and blow yourself up when you mount."

Guy looked at him sharply.

Selth stood back. "Let's hope the Turks don't look too closely. If you think they suspect something, look them in the eye and act proud. The firepot is in the gate-yard. You'll pick it up on your way through."

They walked together into the bright light and growing crowd. Guy pulled the coif over his head and Selth laced it in place. Guy then set his helmet upon his head and adjusted the throatlash, feeling the unfamiliar mail against his throat and neck. The borrowed heavier armour felt hot and constrictive.

It seemed to Guy that he had never seen the world so clearly. Each face, scent and sound had a majesty he had not before noticed. He saw Serena and Bessas rush off followed by Gabras and his soldiers and thought it a strange thing for them to do. Jacques was not in sight and that concerned him too. Domnos and Maria Taronites were there; his hostile face seeming far away and unimportant. Maria stared at him, her mouth open a little.

With a show of confidence for the crowd, Basil exclaimed lightly, "Good luck, Guy d'Agiles. The message is for the Sultan."

Guy nodded and approached the horse. Zarrar snorted suspiciously and moved a step away.

"Steady, Zarrar." Bryennius spoke soothingly to his horse and turning to Guy explained, "He can smell the naphtha and knows what comes. Don't worry. The horse will do his work."

Then Irene was standing next to him, her green eyes moist and black hair bound back by a blue kerchief. She stood between Guy and the near-side stirrup, preventing him from mounting. Oblivious to the silent crowd, their eyes met.

"Don't do this for me," she murmured. "I am not worth your life." Irene took his hand in hers and for long moments she gazed at his face. "Don't."

"I'll see you soon, Irene."

They were silent until she said finally, "You lost your scarf on the Archēsh track," She took the kerchief from her hair and knotted it around his arm. "For luck."

Zarrar moved impatiently.

"All right. All right," Guy turned to the horse and mounted with help from Bryennius and Selth. Seating himself in the saddle and searching with his toe for the off-side stirrup, he felt the explosive power beneath him. "Steady, Zarrar!" He looked down at Irene's face.

"He's right," reassured Bryennius.

"Beware of Ankhialou," Irene warned. "He often rides a grey horse, a gelding with a dark mane and tail." She smiled bravely. "He knows of you and will be searching for you. He's bigger and very cunning. But you're a better rider, more skilled-at-arms, and God is with you."

They handed up his shield and spear with the letter firmly attached by a red ribbon. Irene stepped forward. Taking a light chain and its crucifix from her neck, she attached it to the throat lash of Zarrar's bridle. The bay horse, sensing a bond between Guy on his back and the woman, bent his head to her. Murmuring something no one heard, Irene Curticius kissed Zarrar lightly on the muzzle and stepped back.

Guy read the emotion in her face. "I go for you and will return for you," he said.

"I shall pray for you." She blinked away tears.

Zarrar moved again.

Guy swallowed and motioned the horse on. "What does the letter say?"

Bryennius answered. "Blessed are the peacemakers, for they shall be called the children of God. Isaac chose it."

"Go!" said Basil.

Bryennius swung onto Ruksh and fell in alongside, the two horses stepping into the shadow of the vaulted gate chamber. The strategos walked on foot with them, never taking his hand from the bridle rein of Bryennius' chestnut. In the gate courtyard, two of Selth's engineers eased coals from a brazier into the upper chamber of the fire-pot, stopping up the hole at the top with a wooden plug. They covered the pot with a piece of damp felt so the concealing surcoat would not catch fire and carefully passed the device to Guy, who slipped the rope handle over his pommel.

Zarrar tensed at this strange new ritual with its suspicious smells, his whole bunched body a question. "Steady, boy," Guy soothed, as Bryennius laid a calming hand on the horse. The three walked into the harsh sunlight outside the main wall and through the fore-wall gates.

"God is with you, Guy d' Agiles," said Basil.

Bryennius stroked the horse's neck once and clapped Guy on the shoulder. "Hearts up."

Guy nodded, urging Zarrar on a few steps. The horse snorted with suspicion as he stared with pricked ears at the wooden bridge and unfamiliar corpses, Seljuk earthworks, the sentries and saddled horses of the ghulams. Suddenly realising they were alone, Zarrar made to turn back to the fortress.

Guy straightened him with a turn of wrist and a heel. "Come on, Zarrar," he murmured, trying to conceal his alarm. The horse responded with a sudden start forward, the pot dangling unsteadily from the saddle. "Zarrar, steady," Guy whispered, thinking how preposterous he would look, bursting into flame, or worse, being bucked off before the crowded city walls. Then Zarrar relaxed and walked forward confidently, his ears back listening for Guy's voice. Feeling the horse bond with him now, Guy breathed a sigh of relief. He heard the iron gates swing shut behind him. "It's almost as lonely out here," he said, the horse moving an ear forward when his rider finished speaking.

Squinting beneath his helmet, Guy set his mind to rehearsing his course to the mangonel. The device was almost two furlongs away, a rough string of pickets with three or four men in each group marking the forward extent of the Seljuk lines. Their forward troops were dismounted, some holding loosely girthed horses. Most were footmen. Guy would need to brazen his way obliquely across the frontage of the western wall, pass through the sentries and ride up to the machine, a short bowshot beyond the pickets and protected by barricade of earthworks and cotton loads.

Dry-mouthed and heart pounding, he rode through the sentries, making sure to pass close to one dismounted group. He kept them on his left, the shield side, so the pot hanging against Zarrar's off-shoulder would not be noticed by them. Glancing down, he saw the device moving awkwardly in its rope basket. To him, it looked enormous and he dreaded that the whole Seljuk army must surely see it. He feared the coals burning the horse, causing Zarrar to buck or bolt, or setting fire to the felt and his surcoat or worse, going out altogether. Through his uncertainties, Guy searched for a sign of smoke near the machine, so that if his first plan did not work, he could dismount and throw a brand from a fire onto the engine after he had doused it with naphtha. Most of all, Guy was concerned that the Seljuks might uncover his plan before he struck at the engine and attack him in numbers he could not fight off. A thousand fears coursed through this mind.

He held the reversed spear with its letter high for the dismounted sentries to see. They were fierce, bearded men wearing round felt caps and lamellar cuirasses of laced leather or horn over black and brown homespun tunics. One of them pointed to the mangonel with his spear and smiling broadly said something Guy could not understand. He reasoned the fellow was boasting of what the mangonel would do to the wall this day. Another moved on foot to intercept him.

Guy uttered the Seljuk phrase Togol had taught him. "My patrons send me as their delegate to see the Sultan." He feigned a harmless, resigned smile and nodded back at them, thinking Latin insults. Waving his spear toward the machine, Guy indicated he intended to have a look at it. With the deference due to a mounted man of rank, the sentries allowed him to pass.

Zarrar, as he ambled by in his quickstep, gave the footmen a suspicious, disdainful, snorting glance. The horse walked swiftly, light of mouth and collected, his ears pricked, one switching back every few seconds listening for Guy's command.

From the corner of his eye, Guy could see a few ghulams tightening their girths without any appearance of urgency. Others had mounted to get a better view of him. There seemed to be no immediate menace from them and none appeared able to prevent him reaching the engine.

Through the picket line now, Guy had perhaps a furlong to ride. From the corner of his left eye, he saw an armed and armoured warrior walk towards him on a well-bred grey horse. Something about the newcomer spelled trouble: he did not look Turkic, bore an almond-shaped shield and was not carrying a bow. Another rider, a big Seljuk on a Turkmene mare, joined the stranger. The two talked familiarly with each other as they approached to within a spear cast of him. Guy thought the horseman mounted on the grey made to ride behind him and close up on his off side, leaving his companion to draw alongside Zarrar's near-side. The two strangers might look just like a polite escort, but it would severely hamper his attempt to destroy the stone-thrower if they succeeded in getting one on either side of him.

Guy pointed his spear at the grey's rider and said loudly and insultingly in Armenian, "Stay on my shield side, both of you! I have no reason to trust a brigand like one or traitor like the other." Uncertain at his haughty challenge, they drew rein, following two spear lengths to Guy's left. They were riding relaxed, insolently so—spears under their thighs.

Guy calculated half a furlong now to the engine. He could see the bulk of the mangonel coming into view as he outflanked the works protecting it and was awed by its size and power. He was conscious of only desultory movement in the sprawling Seljuk camp. It was hot and this closer view confirmed that the Turks had mostly retired to their tents to escape the midday heat.

From the walls, there was silence. He did not look back.

"You speak with an accent," the rider on the grey observed. "Latin, if I'm not mistaken. Do you perchance know of a P'rang on a chestnut horse who fled Archēsh with an Armenian woman of great beauty?"

Now certain his interrogator was Theodore Ankhialou, part of Guy was tempted to have it out there and then with Irene's past suitor. He reined-in his feelings and gave the grey-horsed rider a long, scornful look. Judging the time and space to be right, Guy suddenly plunged the spear point into the ground. With a slight move forward, he crossed himself and lunged Zarrar into full gallop, grasping the firepot's rope handle and allowing the felt pad to fall away. Glancing over his left shoulder he calculated he had several horse-lengths start on the two startled riders. He heard Ankhialou shout and saw some of the soldiery lounging under their black tents near the mangonel, crawl out and stand to stare at him. The fulcrum of the machine was five times the height of the tallest of them.

In a trice, Zarrar galloped up beside the works before the catapult, enabling Guy to see the treacherous footing around the engine. Coiled ropes, buckets and personal bundles, digging tools and a pile of large rocks littered the ground over which he and Zarrar now had to manoeuvre. He noticed dust clinging to the oil the Seljuks had painted on the weathered timbers.

Drawing abreast of the rear of the device, Guy drew on the bit and brought Zarrar's near side to the machine. Facing his pursuers he stood in the stirrups on the bunched horse, swinging the firepot around his head, before dashing it with all his might low at the bulk of the supporting beams. There was the sound of smashing pottery, an audible blast of hot air and a purplish flame burst forth, immediately followed by a rolling cloud of pungent black smoke which momentarily blinded Guy and caused Zarrar to plunge sideways in alarm.

Aware of an immediate upheaval amongst the Seljuk troops camped close around, Guy swung Zarrar on his hocks, taking the first shock of Ankhialou's sword on his shield. He spurred the bay horse out of the hide embrace, breaking free of the grey and galloping a few strides around to the other side of the machine. Drawing rein as he fumbled inside his surcoat, Guy grasped the first concealed naphtha bottle, hurling it high at the greased axle on top of the support beams. There the vessel shattered, splashing the sticky, flammable mixture over the upper part of the mangonel, causing the searching flames to leap upwards into it.

Sweat blinded Guy's eyes. The emotional and mental exertions of the last few seconds already had him gasping for breath. Both mounted adversaries were on the other side of the machine, shouting at each other, coordinating which way they would attack him. A group of footmen ran up on Guy's unshielded off-side, one thrusting at him with a spear. The others, half a dozen of them, carried pails of sand and wet sacks to try and beat out the flames. Guy pulled Zarrar back onto collected haunches, using his balance and legs to make the horse swing left, then right, and left again in little rears, confusing his attackers as to his intentions and winding the bay horse up, like a twisted rope, for the sudden lunge. In those few precious seconds, the fire took hold. Guy felt the heat as the flames started to roar up the machine.

Holding the last naphtha bottle threateningly aloft and screaming manically at them, he lunged Zarrar amongst the footmen, scattering them in disorder. As

Guy moved, so did the two horsemen. Ankhialou, wielding a sword, broke to Guy's left, forcing the grey high over the earthworks behind the cotton loads to the front of the machine. The mounted Seljuk, making for Guy's right had taken up his spear and was thus the more dangerous.

Guy spurred straight for Ankhialou, threatening him with the pot. Ankhialou shrank from the assault and his horse, hocks floundering in loose earth, went down on its knees. Seeing Ankhialou temporarily unbalanced, Guy wheeled Zarrar again to counter the mounted spearman behind him.

Guy felt a stab of terror as Zarrar stumbled, his hind legs fouled in a rope on the ground. Almost dropping the naphtha pot in an effort to stay in the saddle, he hauled on the reins to raise the horse's head. Zarrar collected himself and lashed out with his hind-legs, casting off the entanglement. Guy felt a rush of relief and exhilaration as the bay horse regained his stride.

Expecting Guy to ride past Ankhialou, the Turk halted his mount before turning it to try and block Guy's escape. In a fleeting chance, Guy saw the Seljuk, flank-on, at too awkward an angle to attempt the use of his spear. For a moment, the Turk was vulnerable. Guy felt the exhilaration of opportunity. Turning in the saddle he pitched his last pot at the machine, feeling the blast as the mixture exploded. Then he put Zarrar straight at the Seljuk horse's hindquarters. The bay sprang through the air, knocking the other horse half down with his chest. For a moment, Guy feared he would become trapped in the fall, but with his powerful hindquarters, Zarrar calmly launched straight into a jump, cleared the falling Turkman and landed like a cat, lifting immediately into a hand-gallop.

Wheeling towards the fortress, Guy looked over his shoulder at the conflagration engulfing the mangonel. "There's a wedding gift for you," he roared. Knowing his life depended on the horse, he leaned forward and patted Zarrar's neck through the mail bard while checking the horse's gait. "Good boy. Good boy. You've done it, Zarrar." Satisfied they were in working order, Guy urged the horse into a full-stretch gallop for the walls of Manzikert, while wiping the sweat from his right hand to ensure it would not be too slippery to hold his weapons.

Aware of the clamour behind him and knowing Ankhialou and the Seljuk would be hard in pursuit, Guy saw before him the line of sentries forming to try and block his way. A number of ghulams had mounted and were also galloping to head him off. Arrows arched through the air towards him. Seeing the letter marking where he had plunged his spear into the ground, Guy sprinted for it, wrenching the point from the ground as he galloped past. In a single smooth, arching movement, he brought the blade to the tilt and passed unmolested through the thin line of footmen, who moved ineffectually to try and block him as a spontaneous roar erupted from the watchers on the walls.

Twenty ghulams of the *hassa ordusa* galloped towards him in a single extended line. Guy knew he had to break through them to get under the covering archery of the walls, or be forced back into the Seljuk camp and killed or captured. He selected an emir on a black stallion as his point of attack. Magnificently armoured with a gilded helmet and mail coat of black iron, the emir rode heavily, his horse fighting the bit. This man would be the least likely of them all to be able to skip away from Guy's spear point.

"Steady, Zarrar. Steady, boy, steady." Guy checked Zarrar back from the flat gallop and was thrown forward in the saddle as the bay abruptly shortened stride, ears back and mane flying, reins slippery with sweat. Zarrar collected as he slowed to a hand-gallop and Guy could hear the grunt of his breathing, the thunder of his hooves on the ground and the mad metallic swish of the mail bard.

"Steady, Zarrar. Steady," Guy whispered as he settled in his saddle for the shock.

Borne along by their momentum, the ghulams galloped towards them. Guy judged their coming, all hoof beats and yelling, waving spears and urging their horses to full speed, trying to catch him on their points as far from the walls as possible. Three of them shot arrows towards him.

With a quick glance, he saw the renegade Byzantine and a Seljuk riding hard, a spear cast behind him and closing. He knew he could not waste a moment cutting through the line of ghulams, for the cost would be a sword plunged into his back with such force that the mail would not stop it.

Pushing Zarrar on a little, Guy made as if to ride at his right of their line. As he hoped, the big emir jerked at his horse's head to try and change course, but the black, head extended at full gallop, was unbalanced by having it tugged harshly to its left. The emir tried to wrench the horse to slow down, resulting in a few ungainly strides.

It was at this momentarily unprepared pair that Guy and Zarrar, working smoothly as one, launched a furious charge. Covering them with his long shield, spear couched along the nearside of the bay horse's neck, Guy and Zarrar punched through the hot air, the point of the Frankish lance aimed straight at the emir's eyes.

There was a heavy hush on the walls as the drum of hooves and "whoosh, whoosh, whoosh" of warhorse breath sounded loud in the still air. In the instant before they hit, the black horse hesitated. Zarrar with his boundless confidence did not. The watchers gasped at the violence of the impact as the black rider went down, spitted on the iron point of Guy's shattered spear. Thus Guy and Zarrar broke through the line of the ghulams, six of whom wheeled in pursuit. This momentary delay enabled the hard-riding Ankhialou and the Turk, both waving swords, to catch up, one either side, trying to crush Guy between them so he could neither escape nor fight.

Guy had expected their coming. Thinking he could manage the horse and fight more effectively without the encumbrance of the shield, he flung it off at the head of the horse on his left, causing it to check and fall behind two lengths. Switching the reins in his hands again, Guy drew his sword as soon as he dared after the downing of the black emir, risking those few strides to ensure he and the horse were all right. This was no time to grasp the weapon too early and lose it in a fall, or drop it because he was not firm in the saddle.

Turning to his right, Guy swung savagely at Ankhialou, the blow frustrated on the renegade's shield. They raced along the edge of the ditch, horses' heads low under the hissing swordplay, dashing over the rough ground and so smoothly jumping the slain that the riders barely noticed the motion. So close and fierce was this combat, the archers on the wall dared not shoot at one for fear of hitting the other. All was the gasping for breath of men and horses both, the fierce clang of weapons and hoof beats on the hard ground.

Guy twisted left and right in the saddle, so busy raining blows from his father's broadsword onto his antagonists that he had no time to guide Zarrar. He could see the blue of the renegade's eyes and his haughty moustaches over snarling white teeth. There was hatred between them, like fighting dogs at a country fair. Guy saw Ankhialou's blade snake out and touch his cheek. Fighting to control the horse and fend off two assailants, Guy realised that in the speed of the combat they had passed by the bridge to the gate and that he must break contact to return to it.

Sitting back in the saddle and drawing on the reins, Guy sat Zarrar abruptly on his haunches before Ankhialou could check his horse. Surprised, the renegade galloped past them a few strides before he could halt and turn. Swinging Zarrar clear behind Ankhialou's grey, Guy galloped back the other way, thrusting at an emir and two ghulams that tried to block him.

Crowding him with their horses, they delayed him for frightening, endless moments. Seeing the efforts of these three, other ghulams made to join them and there was a great shout from the Seljuk host. Guy felt the glancing blow of a mace on his helmet and reeled in the saddle. As a sword reached for his throat, he smashed the blade away with his own. Just as another struck at the chamfron guarding Zarrar's forehead, Guy slashed at the unprotected arm and heard the rider scream. He felt a Turk's stirrup grind into his leg and blood trickle down his face inside the coif. Crowded by three Seljuk horses, Zarrar stumbled. Through the tumult and fear, Guy saw Irene's face come to him as if in a dream.

Then Zarrar, kicking, striking and roaring with rage, burst from the melee.

Guy heard the cheering on the walls and sensed the arrows engulfing the Seljuks that were not close to him. Then there were the gate-towers before him and cataphracts cantering out to form protectively around him. Bryennius, mounted and smiling, was suddenly at Zarrar's head and saying something to Guy, but he could not make out the words. Exhausted and sobbing for breath, he slumped forward in the saddle, sweat streaming down his arms and legs under his armour. Twice he tried to sheath his sword but his arms trembled so much he could not match them. A cataphract leaned from his saddle, took Guy's sword and wiping the blood from it on his own horse's mane, slid the blade into its scabbard.

Brown rivulets of sweat poured from Zarrar's belly, Guy could smell it from under the bard. He wanted to be sick from physical effort and felt he would never again be able to get enough air into his heaving lungs. On excited horses they passed under the gate towers into the euphoric throng. Through the perspiration misting his eyes, Guy saw Irene weeping as she looked at him. He nodded back weakly.

Wild with relief and joy for deliverance from certain death, the crowd surged forward. Selth, Curticius and Doukas were in the forefront of it, yelling exultantly that the frightful mangonel was fiercely ablaze and the Seljuks would never be able to douse it. Frankish soldiers, claiming Guy as theirs, pulled him from the saddle and bore him shoulder high to the steps of the cathedral. There they set him down, pulled off his helmet and coif and gave him a draught of watered wine.

Young women of the city, ignoring the protesting Taticus Phocas, took charge of the reins and unsaddled Zarrar, removing the reeking bard, saddle and cloth along with the chamfron and bridle. With pale arms they gave him a mouthful to drink, sponged him with cool water and dried him with soft cloths. They covered him with a light blanket, decked him with ribbons and love knots and led him to the steps of the cathedral, where the crowd reached out to touch with love the warhorse who had saved them from the swords of the infidels. Guy fought free of the Franks and went to Zarrar, throwing his arms around the horse's neck.

While people stood to arms around the walls, Basil Apocapes, beaming at their deliverance, ascended the steps of the cathedral. He tried to speak, but his voice was lost in another round of wild jubilation as Guy locked eyes with Kamyates in the crowd, the bureaucrat's face a storm of hatred.

Basil took Guy by the shoulder and led him forward. Four times Basil held up his arms for silence before the people would let him speak. He took Guy's sword hand and held it aloft.

Chapter Nineteen

The Wrath of the Shepherd King

The Seljuk Camp before Manzikert,
Early afternoon, 15th September 1054

Derar al-Adin was dozing under their tent in the early afternoon heat. Farisa lay close to him without touching in one curtained section of the tent. Zaibullah lay under the other. The sides were up encouraging any vestige of breeze. He glanced aside and counted the days Farisa had been marking on her parchment. It was the twenty-seventh day of the siege.

Derar calculated the Sultan's army did not have much more endurance for this venture. The early capture of Berkri and Archēsh had fanned appetites for easy and profitable victories. Widespread raiding proved rich in slaves and booty for the tribesmen and an agonised bloodbath for the Christians; scores of thousands of whom were still being chivvied eastward in footsore, broken-hearted caravans.

The disparate army's morale had been dented by the impregnability of Karin, Kapetrou and Avnik, a repulse from Baberd, the sanguinary victory over the Armenians of Vanand and now the endless fighting at Manzikert. This had been exacerbated by rumours of Roman troops concentrating at Caesarea for a counterattack, discord amongst leaders, unequal pay, casualties and the lack of fodder and grazing. Cracks were showing. The Sultan needed this army to impose his will on Baghdad and Cairo; he would be foolish to have it destroyed before the walls of Manzikert.

Much depended on the *baban* hauled from Baghesh, but it seemed impossible that the city would not fall this day. With one breach all but forced and another likely that afternoon, Derar could not see how the defenders would hold out.

Accordingly, he set his mind to the details of the apparently endless task of rescuing Zobeir al-Adin, vaguely listening to the background sounds of some distant hubbub in the lines, imagining another fight between the ghulams and the Daylamis, or a dispute over fodder prices. Then he heard the distinctive sounds of urgent shouting, a few horses at full gallop and the fierce clash of swords.

Farisa rolled indolently over on her side to have a look, but sprang up, urging, "Derar. Come and see! There is a fire and the ghulams are chasing a rider to the fortress."

Mindless of his bare feet in the dust, Derar leapt up and watched the smoke rising in a dark plume from the camp. He saw too the galloping fight that overtook a lone horseman as he rode through the line of dismounted sentries.

"The *baban*, the mangonel, it's burning," Farisa exclaimed. "Who could do such a thing and hope to escape?"

Even at that range, Derar had the feeling that he knew the horse as the one ridden by the Roman count at the wadi fight. If the rider was the arrogant Roman and he was now killed, how would that complicate the release of Zobeir? "Someone who rode from the city?" Derar wondered aloud, as cheering erupted from the walls. "And they seem to have made it back."

They watched the smoke for a time until Farisa asked, "Will they be able to save it?"

"I think not."

She turned and looked up at him with her beautiful eyes. "Derar, the Sultan will be very angry. Take care."

But distance could not be kept. Derar was summoned to report with horse and arms to the Sultan's council, where he appeared a short time later hoping the mask of serenity he tried to weave was successful in covering his almost unbearable tension. Riding to the Sultan's pavilion, he fell in with Emren and Burla Dirse, also mounted and looking worried.

"What's happened?" Derar asked.

"An unbeliever rode from the city and by a ruse, got close to the *baban*, doused it with the Greek Fire and burned the thing to ashes," Burla said.

Derar had supposed this. "Why did no one stop him?"

"The Greek Fire was concealed on his person." Emren said. "He had a letter tied to his spear which he carried reversed. He rode calmly and said he was a messenger."

In the distance, the dust and din of another fruitless assault against the walls was underway. In his annoyance, the Sultan had ordered the planned attack to go ahead anyway.

It was a short ride. They were ordered to halt some distance from the council's pavilion. Emren Dirse and Derar handed their reins to slaves who stood by for the purpose. As they did this, a large group of the grim faced officers of the *hassa ordusa* shouldered their way from the pavilion. A thousand of their men stood ready, black-mailed on dark horses. There were shouted commands as the officers mounted and they rode off towards the smouldering wreck of the *baban*.

Glancing at each other, Emren and Derar walked to the council pavilion situated beside the vizier's own. The vizier's tent was distinguished by five horsetail standards: black, red, white, green and yellow, hanging limply on their staffs in the stifling air. There the two friends were made to wait outside with many others. Both were worried, Emren Dirse for speaking his mind and Derar on his own account.

"There'll be reckoning this day," Emren muttered under his breath.

Derar bade him be silent as the vizier emerged purposefully from the Sultan's tent and looked around the uneasy throng. His hard gaze came to rest on Derar and he walked towards the Arab. Derar's heart thumped and he fought the desire to run into the crowd. The certain knowledge that he would have been caught stayed him and instead he made an appropriately subservient greeting to the high official of the Seljuk state.

As always, the vizier was impeccably polite. With such power he could afford to be, as the intimation of consequential violence for disobedience carried its own persuasion. Of all things, he started to quiz Derar on the Quran and interpretations of it. Then it occurred to Derar that it was a test. The vizier was examining him to ensure he was Sunni—they were looking for Fatimid spies who might be sympathetic to the Romans. He passed this interrogation and al-Kunduri moved on to other Arabs in the group.

They waited, as the attack on the walls failed and the roughly handled Daylamis dragged their maimed away from the jeers of the Christians. Some time later, one of the Daylamis' senior princes, wounded and hollow eyed from shock, came and forlornly stood close to Derar, waiting to be summoned to the Sultan. Two Arab mercenaries Derar knew only vaguely and from whom he had taken pains to distance himself, were dragged away and not seen again.

In a cloud of proud horses and self-importance, the contingent of *hassa ordusa* returned, driving on foot before them fifty pitiful creatures who had been appointed to guard the *baban* that day. They too waited until, a short time later, the Sultan appeared. The catapult guards were unceremoniously pushed to the ground. Tughrul Bey walked the length of the line looking fiercely at them. Then he turned his back and returned to his tent. The prostrate men looked at each other in fear and bewilderment.

From the door of his tent, the Sultan simply said, "Behead them." Swords were drawn. "No!" commanded Tughrul Bey. "Away from here. I don't want to look at them."

Derar watched as the hapless men heard their fate with reactions of either fortitude or fright and were led away by the black horsemen. Meanwhile the rest waited.

After a considerable time, Derar was summoned forward with Isma'il and Dumrul. "Take the Arab as interpreter," the vizier commanded. "Convey the Sultan's message that it will be his pleasure to receive the Frank who made this ride. The Sultan admires such courage and wishes to meet this far-riding soldier and to give him gifts. Go tell them."

They mounted and rode to the western gate. There, where the parley had taken place on the first day, they halted with the horsetail standards. Derar rode forward under a reversed spear, hailing the ramparts in Persian. There was a reply in a tongue he could not fathom, so he waited. After a time, a plain Roman pot helmet appeared in a crenelle of the fore-wall and shouted in Arabic after their purpose.

"Parley, in the Persian tongue," Derar called back.

"Wait," came the response from the wall.

"How long?" rejoined Derar.

"Not long," the voice from the walls responded. "It'll take a few minutes to assemble the proper officers."

So the Seljuk party sat their horses nervously, for the day had become one of impatience and retribution in the Sultan's camp.

The gates opened and three horsemen rode from the city: a Roman officer with his arm in a sling, a peasant-looking fellow on a well-saddled chestnut gelding of fine Bedouin stamp, and a standard-bearer holding aloft the pennant of a Byzantine general.

Derar recognised the wounded officer; he had seen him at the wadi and sensed the shadow eyes under the Roman's helmet flicker at him.

The peasant opened the conversation in badly accented Turkic. "We do not have a Persian speaker available right now. We must talk in your own tongue."

"That'll do," Bughra Dumrul replied politely. "We don't have much to discuss."

"On the contrary," the peasant said provocatively. "We'd be obliged if you would again remove your dead. They foul the air."

Surprised at this deliberate rudeness, Derar thought at first the peasant was merely ignorant of the courtesies required, but there was deeper insolence that made him think the fellow knew Dumrul and was baiting him.

Dumrul replied in a similarly provocative vein. "Are you all that's left—a wounded Roman and a peasant?"

"Not at all," the chestnut rider responded. "Indeed there are many troops and horses in Manzikert and we want for nothing." Then to Derar's astonishment, the peasant started questioning Dumrul about members of his family and tribe. He sensed that Dumrul knew the man, but could not yet place him.

The Roman officer watched closely.

Suddenly Dumrul changed the subject. "We've the Sultan's business to discuss. The Sultan, Tughrul Bey, Client of the Commander of the Faithful, wishes to meet the one who rode from the fortress and burned the engine."

"Why?" The peasant could not conceal his surprise.

"The Sultan, wishes to meet him and give him gifts. He's impressed with his audacity and skill. We offer safe conduct."

The peasant and the officer conferred. "Very well. We'll ask him."

The Roman rattled off a command to the standard-bearer who walked his horse back to the fortress. They settled down to wait, the peasant astounding the four in the Seljuk party by saying, "You don't know me, do you Bughra?"

There was a long silence before Dumrul exclaimed, "Vardaheri! 'Tis you! I swear I wondered. What're you doing here? The last I heard, you escaped and fled Samarqand with a Song woman from beyond the steppes. They hunted you both and brought her back. It's said you returned many months later and burned the house of her master—with him killed inside." Dumrul had the air of a man who had met an old friend. "You weren't in Tabriz recently were you? There was a fire there as well, you know?"

Vardaheri ignored the searching jibe. "The woman lives?"

"She does, still, in Samarqand and—different master," replied Dumrul in a friendly tone with the hint of amusement about it.

"Well. Well! I may have to return," laughed Vardaheri, looking thoughtful and walking his horse forward to converse with Dumrul.

After a few minutes, the Roman spoke, in Arabic, as if practicing his command of that language and motioned his grey horse towards Derar. Both acted as if they had never seen each other before, speaking softly to avoid being overheard.

"Derar al-Adin?"

"Yes. And you were at the wadi fight where Count Bryennius … entertained … me?"

"I was. Centarch Bessas Phocas."

"Zobeir al-Adin lives?" Derar asked quietly while the others were distracted by Vardaheri, thinking he may as well get to the point.

"He lives."

"You've been hurt?"

"I am recovering quite well, thank you," Bessas said. "How is the Sultan's army?"

Derar was mildly surprised at how easy it was to hide in the open. "It has its problems, but they aren't beaten yet. They may attempt another tunnel under the south wall. I don't know where."

"It's very stony there?"

"They're following a fissure in the rock."

"Thank you," whispered Bessas.

"Your Arabic is quite good," Derar said loudly enough to be heard by the others. "Where did you learn?"

"I served some years on the southern borders of our lands—the frontiers with the Mirdasid and Noumayrid emirates," Bessas replied in similar vein.

Derar lowered his voice again. "The Sultan has several spies in the city, but I have been unable to find out who they are." He leaned forward as though checking a buckle on his bridle. "They speak of being frustrated in their attempts to learn your governor's battle plans."

"Indeed?" said Bessas with evident interest and a hint of pleasure.

"In the Sultan's camp they suspect some," Derar continued. "Two Arabs may have been executed this day because the Seljuks feared they were working for the Fatimids. The Sultan also suspects members of his own extended family whose ambition overrides their prudence."

"Power and glory are wonderful destroyers."

"The Horse-archer, he is well?"

"Very well. I'll tell him you asked."

"Good. His interpreter, is she well also?"

The Roman looked blankly at Derar, then recalled. "She's long gone."

Derar feared for the woman. "Gone? Away?"

"Yes. Away. Before you got here," Bessas said.

"Safely?" asked Derar.

"Yes. Safely."

Derar reflected gratefully on this. "She is well away from this place. Was that the Horse-archer's mount ridden today?"

"It was."

"Did he ride it?"

"No. Another."

"Another? Most skilled, as though the saddle was his throne," Derar said, looking at the walls. "But what would move a man to take such a risk?" Derar asked.

Bessas shrugged.

"On the subject of horses," Derar continued, "the chestnut mare that was stolen by your Frank and ridden from Archēsh, she's precious to a friend, a good man. Can a trade be arranged?"

"The Frank is a friend and a worthy man also. I will ask."

"Is the Frank that has the horse and escaped from Archēsh, the same man that was your decoy at the wadi fight and has now burned the mangonel?" Derar asked, having a warrior's interest.

"Yes. The same."

"Aiee! He's caused the Sultan big trouble," Derar said. "But what moved him to such a deed. It must be duty or great love?"

Bessas smiled. "A detail of our fight here—a story for the ages. I will also ask him, one day."

The Roman standard-bearer returned and spoke to Bessas and Vardaheri. Bessas turned in his saddle to listen in silence, merely looking at the Seljuks as the peasant interpreted to them. "The one who rode forth this day thanks the Sultan, but must regretfully decline, as he has many duties to attend to."

Dumrul and Isma'il did not seem surprised, but were dismayed. With trepidation, they returned to Tughrul Bey who reacted to the snub with quiet anger, ordering the second tunnel to be pushed forward.

Manzikert, Midday,
17th September 1054

Guy woke in fright from his nightmare in which the second Seljuk tunnel had led to the fall of the city and to his and Irene's imminent capture. He was in his sleeping space in their room in Manzikert. It was daylight and all was quiet. With effort he rose to an elbow. Jacques was sitting on a stool looking earnestly at him. Guy heard the sound of water and looking to his other side saw Flora Asadian wringing out a cloth into a pail of water. He realized then she had been bathing his face and grazed temple.

"You had a bad dream," she said in her accented Greek, soft rays of the autumn sun slanting through the open door and playing in her auburn hair.

"The tunnel? The city?" Guy asked, feeling weak. "What day is it?"

"What do you remember?" asked Jacques.

"I rode from the fortress and burnt the catapult. Then we went to the cathedral where there was a great deal of celebration—and wine. The Seljuks attacked again. Then the Sultan wanted to see me. Bessas found out there was another tunnel. I had dinner at Curticius' place—the princeps was very friendly. After that I must have slept."

"Slept!" exclaimed Jacques. "You came back swaying on your feet last night. And you left out several important things. First, you're a hero. Second, you're rich, for the strategos had promised gifts, gold and largesse and an audience with the Emperor. But to answer your question, it's Saturday and twenty-nine days since the infidels arrived and invested the city. The fortress is safe. The counts, Doukas and Selth, found the infidel's tunnel this morning. They gained its direction from the tapping of picks on rock. Just this morning they broke into it, dragging out the enemy with iron hooks and killing them all."

Guy looked at Jacques, while trying to imagine through his headache how the tunnel fight had played out in those dark spaces under the ground.

"My head hurts," he said limply, sinking back.

"I'm not surprised," said Flora. "You took a hard knock and should rest awhile."

Guy rose on an elbow, looking around their cramped quarters with its armour and weapons, saddles and cloaks and little bundles of spare clothes. Irene was not there. He slumped back.

"Irene's gone for food," Flora said quietly. "She'll be back soon."

"I must get up," Guy moaned, struggling to rise.

Irene entered carrying a basket of food. The fold of her black dress gathered as she knelt near him, placing the basket on the swept floor. She said nothing at first, but her eyes sparked with affection as they roved over him.

Flora and Jacques stood back and turned away.

"You've awoken at last," Irene smiled.

Guy could not take his eyes from her. "It were no shame," he whispered to himself, "that Trojans and well-greaved Achaeans should suffer pain long time for a …"

Irene blushed. "I didn't know you had read Homer?"

It was Guy's turn to flush. "I haven't. At least not yet."

"You heard the words?"

"Yes. Count Bryennius spoke them one day."

"He was quoting from Homer. Who was he looking at when he spoke?" Irene asked, caressing Guy's forehead with a light touch.

"No one," Guy said, thinking of that day in the garden of the Barbarian House. "He was laying down taking his rest and had his hat over his eyes. He could see no one."

"Count Bryennius?" Irene mused to herself looking at the floor with a far-away expression.

"What of him?" Guy asked, trying to sit, his curiosity aroused by her tone. "I have sometimes wished I were like him, without feelings."

Irene looked away. "I should have listened to him when he tried to convince me to leave Archēsh." She fell silent then, staring pensively at the hem of her dress and biting her lower lip softly in recollection.

"Did he?" Guy watched her for a while. "A copper coin for your thoughts?"

"They're not worth one," Irene replied, looking up quickly with a smile. "He mystifies me, that's all. When the last dove came from Karin, Count Bryennius was in the room when they brought its message to the strategos. There was a cryptic note at the end of the despatch. No one could fathom its meaning. But I saw the slightest smile on the corner of the count's lips."

"What was the secret message?" Jacques asked.

"It said," Irene recalled, "something like, 'Cattlelifter well. On. Take care.'" With a searching stare at each of them in turn, she asked, "What did it mean?"

Guy and Jacques looked blankly at each other. "Another one of Manzikert's little mysteries," Jacques mused.

Guy laid back, looking at Irene and feeling at ease. She smiled at him and touched his forehead lightly. "You'd better eat and drink something."

"Goat's milk for you, wine for me," Jacques grinned, raising his goblet. "Would that Charles Bertrum was here," he added seriously.

"Would that he was."

The Seljuk camp before Manzikert,
Afternoon, 17th September 1054

Derar al-Adin could taste the stench of defeat in the hollow looks in the soldiers' eyes and the sullen undertones about the Sultan's generalship. He was sitting in the shade of his tent, taking in the scene and dreading another summons. In this moment of private tension, he was glad Farisa and Zaibullah were off tending their horses and camel—he did not wish to have to explain again the headaches and loss of appetite. He looked at the marks Farisa made on the tent wall—denoting the twenty-ninth day.

The previous evening he had barely slept, spending much of the late afternoon with the Persian scribes who had accompanied the raiding columns. They had, in the manner of bureaucrats everywhere, calculated the amount of booty and

Christian dead. Taken aback at the toll, Derar had undertaken the nerve-racking crawl in the early hours and despatched another message arrow into the fortress.

Fear had stalked the Seljuk army from the moment of the mangonel's destruction. Such was the mood that some people of influence feared for their lives. Derar looked at the distant walls standing defiantly on a canvas of handsome terrain and early autumn sky. It was a dangerous time for him now. Should he avoid the orgy of blame that inevitably follows defeat and now steal away from the Seljuk army to secure the release of Zobeir al-Adin?

His melancholy was interrupted by the approaching voice of Emren Dirse. "Hey, desert dweller," the Emir greeted in a quietness Derar had not heard before.

"Emren. What brings you?"

Accompanied by Burla, Emren stooped under the tent and sat cross-legged next to Derar. "We're beaten." They all sat in silence for a while before Emren ventured, "I need you to write something for me the Romans will understand. Will you do it?"

"Of course." Derar looked hard at his friend.

"There are two things I must do. First I must retrieve the remains of Beyruh Dirse from the ditch. And then I will give to the Frank who has my mare, a copy of her pedigree, so it is not lost to her." Emren looked long at the fortress, then at Derar. "Do you think he would care about the mare's breeding?"

"I would normally say not," he paused. "But this Frank could be different. One never knows."

A cavalryman of the *gulâmân-I suray* cantered up on a dappled-grey horse. Leaning from his saddle, the youth informed the two men they were required at the Sultan's court. "Now, please," the young man ordered with polite authority before riding off to summon others.

With a resigned glance at each other, they rose and taking up their weapons, walked towards the Sultan's pavilion. A disturbance on the walls made them pause. They could make out between the merlons many heads moving with an obvious air of excitement. Then there was the distinctive squeal of a pig and they could see the swing beam of a catapult arm being hauled back.

Derar had an inkling of what was about to occur. "Don't do it," he said under his breath. "Take your victory gracefully, lest you never be forgiven."

Emren looked at him, but said nothing.

There was ragged cheering on the walls as men heaved sharply down on the ropes of the engine, catapulting an object from the sling into the dusty air. High in the air it shot forth, landing with a dull thud away from them. They made towards it, shouldering through the outraged crowd that had gathered. In the middle of the throng a bound pig lay dying in the dust, dirt in its mouth and a dulled eye staring at them.

From the walls came a ragged chorus. "O Sultan, take this pig to wife and we will present you with Manzikert as her dowry." Twice more the chant was repeated.

When they got to the court, it required only a glance to see just how offended Tughrul Bey was. Derar could scarcely breathe as the ghulams made in his direction, passing him to seize another. Isma'il was dragged forth, as was Dumrul. The Persian scribe, Ames, was also flung before the Sultan.

Isma'il stood resolutely, touched by the gloom that had dogged him constantly since he failed to capture Manzikert by *coup de main*[70] on the first night and by the despair caused by Hurr's leaving. The prolonged siege had deepened Isma'il's agony. A blow with the haft of a spear sprawled him full length on the ground. The disgraced general lay looking hopelessly at the dusty ground before him, the unfairness of it writ large in the silent language of him.

The spymaster, Dumrul, tried bluster and pleading, reciting how much he had done for the Sultan in the past and at what personal cost. He also was pushed roughly to the ground.

Heedless of his crisp white robes, Ames prostrated of his own volition, all the while praying, either to prove his fidelity or assuage his fright.

Two Christians were also shoved forward. Theodore Ankhialou stood in his characteristically arrogant manner of dealing with other men, staring back at the Sultan as if his defiance would spare him. A kick to the back of the knees brought reality. The other, by his dress and the cut of his hair and beard, was an Armenian rural landlord. Deliberately, this man shook off his guards and slowly prostrated himself.

The vizier walked to the centre of the circle of silent soldiery, looking with exaggerated contempt upon the line of prostrate men. After a disdainful interval, he turned and faced the Sultan's pavilion, the signal for Tughrul to theatrically walk forward.

Sensing the fraught period of selection had now passed, the crowd murmured. Under cover of this, Derar whispered to Emren Dirse, "Who's the last man?"

Emren leaned slightly towards. "Tigran Zakarian, the landlord of a place called Arknik. We rode by there on the way back from Karin. He's supposedly well connected to Apocapes' council and escaped over the wall the night after the mangonel was burnt. It's said his wife remains inside."

At the thought he might yet be exposed, fear stabbed the very heart of Derar, but he held his nerve and muttered back. "Supposedly! Not well enough connected!"

The vizier spoke. "The Sultan, Tughrul Bey, Lord of the Land of East and West, Client of the Commander of the Faithful …" At the sound of his clear tones, the crowd hushed.

Derar scrutinised Tughrul Bey, who stood a spear cast from him. Despite the defiance and anger, Derar had never seen Tughrul Bey look this tired or old. The Sultan glared at the circle of faces, his stare lingering long on his relatives standing together at the front of the crowd.

---

70 *Coup de main*—an overwhelming surprise attack.

Tughrul Bey walked along the line of condemned men, pausing over Theodore Ankhialou. "Oh conquering Sultan," he mimicked, "go and take the town of Manzikert, then we and all Armenia will submit to you." He paused there, looked down, then turned on his heel, saying crisply to the commander of the *hassa ordusa*, "Place their heads next to those who failed to guard the *baban*." The Sultan paused by Zakarian, "Except this one."

Realising he was being addressed, Tigran Zakarian twisted his head and awkwardly looked up in terror.

"You may yet be useful," murmured Tughrul Bey, as if to himself, "if you can talk your way back into the Roman camp. If they take your head, it's no loss to me."

The Sultan and vizier looked at each other with that knowing way they had. Watching them from the crowd, Derar was certain the Sultan's lips formed the words, "Tabriz." They left at this point, Prince Alkan from Chorasmia hurrying after them.

Later Alkan came to see Derar in his tent. "Before he died, was murdered, Osketsam told me you're a literate man, a poet."

"I don't know where he got that idea," Derar protested vehemently, remembering the frightening encounter with the Sultan's father-in-law in the guard tent when he had thought capture was imminent. He was concerned that getting him to write something the Romans understood might be a trap. Derar observed the air of excitement that accompanied the black beard and clear eyes of Alkan. "Why do you need a poet? If I knew a poet, that is."

"I don't need a poet. I need a witness that can write."

Derar's brow furrowed.

"Don't be perplexed. The Sultan has decided to give up the siege ..."

Derar's heart leapt. The release of Zobeir and an end to this misery was at hand.

"... but I am honoured with his authority to make one more attempt on the walls. The army will give the appearance of withdrawing and, in doing so, will move the siege engines to the eastern wall. I think the gate between the citadel and the lagoon is the most vulnerable to attack, as we have drained the lagoon."

"I don't advise it," Derar said sincerely. "Indeed, I counsel against it. The unbelievers will not be fooled for long and will know the weak spot themselves."

"We'll use wheeled crawlers to get to their walls. Anyway, I can do no other, and I ask you to be on the ridge to the east, with the other notables, to witness our deeds."

"As you wish," Derar sighed deeply as Alkan walked away.

Farisa watched. "Why do they do it?"

"In war, Farisa, there is always someone to offer up more death. The best offer themselves, as that Frank did. The worst offer the lives of others."

That night Derar sped another message to the Romans.

*Manzikert, First light,
18th September 1054*

Before dawn, the defenders were prepared. The other walls were lightly held with the main fighting strength of the garrison concentrated out of sight and under cover in the citadel and along the eastern wall. The cautious strategos had a strong reserve ready in case the spy's intelligence was incorrect or duplicitous, but Manzikert was ready for Prince Alkan.

Jacques woke Guy before first light, informing him the Seljuks had moved their engines to the eastern approach overnight. Stiff, sore and still fatigued, Guy struggled after Jacques to where Basil Apocapes was quietly directing the troops into place. The strategos saw Guy. "You've done your bit," he said. "No one will hold it against you if you stay out of this one."

Guy shook his head. "My men are here."

"You're right."

"Where is Count Bryennius?" Guy asked.

"His regiment is in reserve," Basil explained, "out of range of their stone-throwers, behind the citadel. Doukas is in the citadel. They, like you, have stretched their good fortune. This is the Sultan's last gasp—it's my job to meet it." Basil stood and peered between the merlons towards the growing light. "They're silhouetted against the dawn. See the standards on the ridge. All their chieftains are up there watching the fun." He turned to the nearest soldiers. "Keep down everywhere. Don't show yourselves or shoot back until I give the word. We want them to think we're done for. Pass the word."

Basil glanced back at Guy. "Every engine they have—except the one you burned—is out there. This'll be the most intense flogging we have had. It appears they are going to try and smash the gate. This Lord Alkan knows his stuff—if they'd concentrated like this early on, we'd have had trouble."

"We did have trouble," Guy reminded him.

"Watch out," commanded Basil. "Here it comes, like the flood."

A storm of rocks and darts hit the old fortifications like hail while others arched high overhead to wreak havoc amongst the townspeople waiting behind the walls with loads of rocks, arrows and water. Dust and flying fragments filled the air and people screamed as a score or more were killed or maimed in minutes. There was a ripple of near panic and people looked uncertainly at the strategos. "Stay down! Stay down," Basil gestured as his shouts were lost in the din.

Then there came a remorseless rain of arrows, clattering between the merlons to drive the defenders from the walls and skiffing over them to seek out those in support.

Guy, crouching next to the strategos, chanced a look. He saw the formidable assault force moving forward behind four-wheeled and roofed mantelets, thickly covered with fresh hides as protection against fire. Each sheltered between forty and fifty soldiers who heaved the machines forward.

The strategos looked for himself. "Five of those machines. 'Crawlers' they call them. The Turk means to push them right up to the walls. The ditch is shallow there because of the rock, so they'll probably fill it in while we're pinned down. This time we'll let them."

Count Selth approached, hunched under his shield. "When?"

Basil shouted to be heard. "I think we should let them come on so we can hit them hardest at close range, as we discussed last night."

Selth looked doubtful, but nodded. He peered quickly between two merlons, ducking back as a hurled rock exploded close by. "We can let them come close to the wall between the towers. I've rigged up heavy beams, one end sharpened, so we can swing them low and hit the crawlers from the side, hard enough to overturn them, I pray, or at least puncture the roofs so we can get the last of our fire in."

Basil, crouching in the debris, shifted his weight. "All should have been told. We will make a seemingly ineffectual response with a couple of engines and a few archers. That should stop them from thinking we're up to something." He called over two tribunes to reinforce the orders.

Alkan's barrage was relentless. As planned by Apocapes, the desultory Christian response seemed to cease altogether. There was a discernible thrill amongst the emirs on the ridge as Alkan's crawlers approached the fosse where his troops erected protective mantelets from which they commenced to fill the ditch with rocks and spoil. Further back, a large reserve was readied to exploit the entry made by the assault troops.

As hours passed, the bright sun grew hotter.

Under the furious punishment from the Alkan's engines, cracks appeared in the fore-wall and the gate towers were so badly damaged the outer gates hung crazily on their hinges.

Taticus Phocas, Loukas Gabras and a cataphract appeared at Guy's shoulder and addressed the strategos. "Count Bryennius' compliments. He sent me to find out what's happening," the squire shouted. "It looks like the inferno here."

"They've filled the ditch in places, and five Seljuk crawlers are close to the walls," Basil shouted back. "Their engines and archers have slackened their effort for fear of hitting their own men. We're about to engage. Tell Count Bryennius to hold firm where he is."

The strategos and his chief engineer crawled to a crenelle and peered out. "Now's as good a time as any," Selth said.

Basil stood and with his great voice boomed as he waved his sword, "May Christ be with us."

Archers, slingers, javelin throwers and ballistae-men sprang to their posts and delivered a storm of destruction to the Chorasmians below, as the city's mangonels heaved full slings of rocks into their midst.

Selth waved his arm, and the great beams were cast from the towers, swinging wildly on their chains until smashing into Alkan's crawlers. Three were knocked over outright, the occupants quickly despatched by archers on the walls. A fourth had a large hole pierced in its roof, into which a pot of Greek Fire was thrown. The fifth stalled beneath the gate towers, disabled by a broken wheel. The men in the towers hauled up the heavy beam for another attempt, sending it smashing into the wall of the crawler, throwing it sideways and crushing many of the men beneath it.

Loukas Gabras ran to Guy begging permission to rush to the threatened gate. Sending the cataphract back to Bryennius with news from the fighting line, Taticus Phocas sought Guy's approval to go with him.

"Let them go," urged Jacques. "It is not your place anyway, since you do not command them. What they ask is something men with fire in their belly cannot be held from, like a good horse."

Guy looked down at the slaughter in the ditch and on the peribolos, as the remnants of the Muslim attack tried vainly to carry the fractured gates. He had faced many attacks now. This one did not have the same fearful intensity: instead it had the shameful aura of desperate failure and murder. He turned to the two ardent young men. "I cannot stop you. Take prisoners if you can. There's been enough killing." He watched them bound down the rubble to join the assault team forming inside the gates under a tribune of the local Armenian troops.

The hail of missiles from the wall broke the attack, forcing the survivors to fall back. Few moved amongst those sprawled obscenely below the fortifications. Apocapes strode along the wall, calling on the soldiers to cease shooting. A ragged cheer rippled along the walls as the sortie ran from the gates and despatched or captured the few survivors cowering under the remnants of the crawlers.

From his vantage point on the wall, Guy saw Taticus and Loukas run towards the wreck of the closest crawler, dragging from it a wounded leader, judging by the richness of his armour and weapons. He watched them bend over the prostrate figure as if examining his wounds. They then half-dragged, half-carried him inside the gates and onto the main wall where Apocapes was watching the Sultan and his emirs turn their horses away.

"They're leaving, God damn them," the strategos spat bitterly. "So much murder and mayhem, and they just ride away as if it is nothing." His voice was lost in the rising crescendo of cheering and abuse from the Christians on the walls.

Tacitus and Loukas dragged their prisoner to Guy. "It's Prince Alkan himself," announced Taticus.

Guy looked at the Chorasmian nobleman, proud and foolhardy, defiance in his eyes and blood on his gilt armour. "Get his wounds treated and put him in the dungeon," Guy ordered.

"Wait!" snapped Basil, stepping down from a crenelle and glaring at Alkan whilst jerking a thumb towards the departing host. "This was your idea, was it, this last attack?"

"Yes," retorted Alkan.

"Well, you can join them," Apocapes raged. "Cut off his head," he said to the soldiers nearby, "and return it to the Sultan."

Guy was speechless, a nausea creeping to his stomach.

Alkan, resisting furiously and grunting in his exertions, was thrust to his knees, his neck stretched over the framework of a mangonel.

"No!" cried Guy, to a glare from Basil.

A Varangian's axe did the deed. Prince Alkan's severed head with its silent screaming protest was catapulted over the littered peribolos and bloody ditch to roll over and over, unnoticed in the trampled dust far behind the departing emirs. The walls rang with the cheers, celebrations and insults of the Christians as their deliverance and triumph became apparent. Guy watched the sanity return to the strategos' demeanour and regret to his eyes.

"Shall we send the infidels another pig as well, strategos," asked a nearby soldier.

"No," said Apocapes turning away, his head bowed. "We—I—have insulted them enough. Now we must tend our wounds. Nor is their apparent departure to be trusted. Stand down. Sentry posts manned. Summon the council to my rooms in the citadel."

Seeing the city through a blur of tears, Guy stumbled away, into the standing figure of Modestos Kamyates who had witnessed everything, including Guy's distress. The courtier's countenance revealed a revulsion equalling Guy's. "That was badly done," he murmured sadly. "You see, we Christians have no higher claim to righteousness."

Guy nodded mutely and dragged his spear and shield away, shaken by the strategos' lapse and the unexpected humanity in Kamyates. As if in a dream, he returned to the little room in the barracks and threw himself down on his paillasse.

The following morning, Guy woke to the sight of Jacques excitedly entering their room. At first he was alarmed and instinctively rose to a knee, reaching for his sword. A second look revealed there was no disquiet in Jacques' manner. Guy felt refreshed after a good night's sleep. His headache was gone and while the covered slash on his cheek itched a little, he was confident it would heal quickly. Sitting on his bedding, he gingerly touched the wound on his head and was mildly surprised by the rough feel of a scab, but pleased it did not hurt much.

"You'll live," Jacques said breezily as he squatted in his loose trousers and a mail corselet he had acquired from somewhere. He wore a leather military belt with the sword of Sira's former master in its scabbard. "The infidels are still leaving."

"I thought they left yesterday?"

"They can't all go at once. We've won," Jacques smiled as he rose and began to whistle a country air from home as he tidied up around their room.

Disbelieving, Guy sat on a stool looking up at him. It seemed so long ago that he watched the Seljuk army ride into the valley. So much had happened since then. He brooded over the terror of battle, struggling against a fatigue that he could never before have imagined and of what seemed like the strategos' final betrayal of all they had fought for.

Irene entered. Wearing a gown but unveiled, she was also flushed with excitement. "I wanted to tell you …" she started, but saw at a glance that Jacques had already passed the news. So she just flung herself across the room and hugged Guy, burying her face in his tunic so the tears of relief could not be seen.

Guy held her for a little while, smelling the perfume of her hair and feeling her body against him. At length he said, "Let's go and see." He took up his military belt and they set off.

Jacques swept up Guy's felt hat and placed it on his head, and carrying a water skin, walked behind them into the uncertain early light of the thirtieth day of the siege.

They reached the northwest tower where the door sentry, a Frankish footman, recognised them and permitted entry. Along the walls the garrison remained stood-to, as they had in the early mornings for over a month now. The people lining the walls watched silently, each wrapped in their own thoughts. Guy looked at the faces: Frank, Rus, Norse, Roman, Armenian with a few Kurds and Arabs. The armoured professionals stood under arms next to ragged peasants and townspeople. Many wore bandages and all were gaunt from the physical and emotional drain. Many prayed silently as they watched the Seljuk host depart.

Bryennius and Lascaris were lounging on merlons next to Basil Apocapes with Togol and Simon Vardaheri slouched against the wall nearby. Though bareheaded, all were armed and armoured, their helmets in a pile on the flagstones. The group saw Guy and his friends and gave a silent acknowledgement. He noticed the long locks of the Cuman contrasting with Vardaheri's bald scalp, remembering how infrequently he had seen them without their caps or helmets on.

"The Daylami tribe are leaving already," observed Lascaris, a clean bandage around his head.

Long columns of them were riding their camels, or marching away, across the crest to the north; from where they had launched so many fierce attacks. Beyond them were long windrows of tribal horse-archers already saddled up and making eastward, with their pack camels and donkeys trailing them. Even at a glance, there was an obvious difference in the enemy dispositions. The siege lines were abandoned. Beyond them a mounted picket still guarded against a surprise attack from the fortress, as the Seljuk host in their camp struck tents and loaded their carts and pack animals.

"What do you think, Count Bryennius?" Basil asked.

"It certainly looks like they're leaving, but they are a crafty lot, and determined. They might just as well make it look as if they are leaving and double-back when we have relaxed our guard."

"They'll need two days at least, to clear a camp that size," Lascaris stated with professional calculation, "or they'll simply clog up the road back past Archēsh. And if they attempt to withdraw too quickly, their main body will draw beyond their prisoners and booty."

"Antony is right," Bryennius remarked, turning to the strategos. "I suggest we give them a couple of days to get clear and then we follow up, to make sure they have gone, hurry them up a bit and rescue anyone we can."

A thoughtful Basil gazed over the departing host. "We can mount about two thousand here?"

Bryennius and Lascaris glanced at each other. "Close enough," Bryennius replied.

"There has been no word from Artzké," said Basil. "I fear much of the enemy may withdraw that way to free up their route from here. I have not noticed significant smoke from that direction, which might indicate it has gone up. So Artzké may provide more troops for us—could join us at Archēsh, or have a detachment meet us here, or both."

"We could only have half of the Artzké men to follow up the enemy on the Archēsh track," Bryennius said. "We'll need to screen any withdrawal of the Seljuks on the southern route, along the north coast of the Sea of Bznunik. The Artzké troops would need to do that—half of them at least. We might also get a courier off to Taron, to see if they can send a contingent."

A lone rider on a chestnut horse approached at a slow walk from the Seljuk encampment and distracted Lascaris from the discussion. "What is this fool doing?" he asked.

"Another looking for a relative to take and bury, I shouldn't wonder," said Basil. Then he turned and shouted, "Steady on the wall. Let the Turkman be."

Guy recognised the rider as the one who had walked his horse along the edge of the ditch on the first day of the siege, asking after Sira. "It's Emren Dirse," he said, surprised as much by his memory of the name as by the perplexed looks from the men around him.

Sensing the interest of the group in the tower, Emren Dirse halted and looked up.

"Who goes there?" challenged Vardaheri in the Turkic language.

"The Emir Emren Dirse. We've spoken before, I think," the rider called back.

"How come you?" asked Vardaheri.

"In peace," the Turkman replied. "I seek the body of my brother and to speak with the Frank who rode with the woman from Archēsh."

Vardaheri looked at Guy, saying with a grin, "Everyone wants to talk to you all of a sudden."

"I'll go down and talk to him," Guy volunteered, his curiosity aroused. He heard Irene catch her breath and winced inwardly. "It'll be all right," he said.

"Go," said the strategos. "Take Togol and Simon with you, if they agree. See what you can find out."

Simon Vardaheri, who had been watching them keenly, turned to the wall and called down to Emren Dirse: "Where do you believe your brother is?" In answer, the Seljuk pointed with his spear to the ground between the ditch and northern fore-wall.

Basil spoke to Vardaheri. "Tell him to go there. Our party will pass through the sally-port and meet him there."

Irene went with them, only her promise of remaining in the tower overcoming Guy's objections. They walked between the double-walls to the place where, on Lascaris' order, Varangians opened the sally-port by a tower. Guy, Togol and Simon Vardaheri made their way onto the peribolos, down the corpse-strewn scarp and out of the ditch to where Emren Dirse waited with his skittish mare.

The emir said nothing as the three approached. All held their hands on the hilts of sheathed swords. As they came close to him, Emren Dirse looked at Guy and said, "It is you?"

Togol interpreted.

"What do you want?" Guy asked, looking closely at the Turk and listening to Togol's interpretation. From its length, Guy thought Togol's introduction was more polite than he had been and he was again grateful for the big Cuman's tact.

"First the body of a relative," Emren Dirse asked.

"The strategos has directed that you may search," answered Togol.

Emren Dirse thanked him and made to lead his horse into the ditch, but she uncharacteristically baulked. The emir tried twice to lead her in, but the mare still refused. Shortening the long reins so he had more control and something to strike her with, he got alongside her shoulder and flicked the leather ends against her flank, trying to make her go over the edge with him. The mare threw her head up and stumbled backwards.

His overwrought nerves failing him, Emren Dirse went to strike her harder, but Vardaheri stepped forward saying: "We'll hold your mare. It is not a pleasant task. It'll be easier …"

Surprised at the Roman speaking the language of the steppes, Emren Dirse soothed the mare, which then came to him. "Thank you. What happened to the man I spoke with on my first visit to the walls, the one who asked after the dancer, Hurr?"

"Why do you ask?"

"The woman disappeared on the day of the mounted battle outside the walls. I have often wondered about him and her." The emir did not miss the exchange of glances. "You needn't worry. Anyone interested in chasing them is dead, having paid the price of leading the Sultan here."

"What is said of it?" Vardaheri asked without disguising his interest.

Guy with unbearable curiosity listened to the Turkic conversation before him. Then his heart leapt as Togol explained, "He said that on the day of the battle, Hurr, for that is her name, could not be found by her consort, Isma'il, one of the Seljuk generals. After the fight, Isma'il wore out a horse searching the camp for her, so everyone knew something was amiss. The talk then was of a stranger riding a carthorse and leading a hack, who some saw with the dancer. Neither the stranger nor Hurr were ever seen again after that day. Their spymaster sent a party to look for them, but they returned empty handed weeks later."

"Fancy that," Guy breathed aside. "Maniakh, stealing the mistress of an enemy general, right in the middle of a battle and getting clean away with her. What stories old Speedy could tell, eh?"

"The less said the better," said Vardaheri.

"You've fought well," Emren Dirse said as he took a rolled kilm from the back of the chestnut mare and followed the horse trader on foot into the ditch. Togol stood near Guy, interpreting what they said.

"So did you," replied the horse trader politely.

"Apocapes still leads you?" Dirse asked.

"Yes. A good soldier and a pious and just man," Vardaheri answered.

"Pious? Until yesterday! Was there a real need to separate Alkan's head and defile it so?"

"Apocapes had lost many of his people."

Still conversing, the pair drew away from Guy's hearing. Togol went after them, leaving Guy with the mare at the edge of the ditch. He could see Irene standing in the highest floor of the tower and he gave a restrained sign of reassurance.

The three figures knelt by the fore-wall, Guy guessing they had found the object of their search. Soon they rose and struggled back towards him with the body rolled in the strong fabric, tied at the ends and in the middle. Breathing heavily, they hauled their burden out of the ditch towards the mare. She rolled her eyes in alarm but stood obediently as they gently lifted the burden across her back and tied it in place.

They stood looking silently at each other until Emren Dirse spoke. "I ask—beg—once more for the return of the chestnut mare."

As Togol interpreted, Guy looked at the Seljuk in his boots and fine mail, the silver inlaid iron helmet and long moustaches. The blackness of the Turk's long hair and the depth of the brown almond eyes fascinated him. There seemed to be no threat in this enemy now; merely sadness without self-pity.

Togol was looking at him and Guy realised he had to give an answer. He hesitated, unexpectedly torn in his feelings. At length he said slowly, "Alas, I cannot part with the mare. She has become too precious to me."

"I feared as much," said Emren Dirse. "What's his name?"

Vardaheri looked at Guy who whispered, "Tell him."

"Guy d'Agiles from the far off land of …" Vardaheri looked once more at Guy. "Provence."

"From Provence, in the Frankish lands," Vardaheri interpreted.

"Guy d'Agiles," Emren Dirse repeated. With a deliberate movement, he thrust into his belt pouch and drew forth a piece of folded parchment, which he passed to Vardaheri, asking him to give it to Guy.

It was done. Guy looked blankly at the diagram, which comprised the neatly annotated lines of a tree-diagram, headed in many places by Arabic script. "What is it?"

"It is a great honour. It's Sira's pedigree, so it is not lost to her," the horse trader answered solemnly.

Guy was deeply moved and for a moment almost offered to return the horse, but he saw Togol's hard brown eyes looking at him and remained silent.

Emren Dirse saw the softening expression on Guy's face, knowing it for what it was. Saying farewell, Emren Dirse started to lead his laden mare back to the Seljuk lines.

"Wait!" called Guy.

Emren Dirse hesitated, then turned to look at them.

Guy glanced at Vardaheri. "Where can he be found? It might be possible to provide him a filly, if I know where to send it."

After Vardaheri interpreted, the emir looked long at them, saying, "My father's sister lives in a white house, near the market in Tabriz. It has five palm trees behind the garden wall. They'll know where to find me. I would be in your debt. Peace be with you." Then he returned to the Seljuk lines.

The three watched the retreating figure for a time. Togol eventually saying, "Now that you've given your word, you must keep it." Clapping Guy on the shoulder, he declared, "It's too hot here, let's go."

They reached Irene who had descended from the tower and was standing near the sally-port with a question in her eyes. Guy told her what had happened.

"I'm glad. I know he chased us from Archēsh, but you did a good thing."

As they re-entered the fortress, Guy lingered, looking back towards where Emren Dirse had gone. "It feels like it is over," he said.

"Not yet," said Togol. "It's not over yet."

Manzikert, Late at night,
19th September 1054

In the bright light of the full moon, Leo and Lascaris removed their weapons and armour, leaving them in the cleft of the roof and climbed to the highest place they could on the cathedral. Leo eased himself onto a flat space near the top and heard Lascaris breathe a sigh of relief as the centarch sat down beside him.

"How did you happen on this place?" asked Leo in awe of the view, surpassed only from highest tower of the citadel. The night air was crisp and a breeze had cleared the air a little. He gazed over the now deserted river valley and the roofs and streets of the city.

"I noticed it soon after I got here," said Lascaris. "Often through the siege, I would wish to be up here—as if away from it all. Look how the moonlight plays on the snow of the mountain."

Leo glanced across, then at his companion. The normally neat Lascaris had unkempt hair and beard beneath the bandage gleaming so white in the moonlight. Below them in the city the last revellers were unsteadily weaving home from the wild celebration that had shaken Manzikert. The circuit walls remained fully manned, but most posted there slept in their cloaks. Sentries peered out into the night. Through the day, Doukas had work parties clear corpses from the ditch, dragging them away by mules fitted with collars and traces, to burn or bury downwind. The work was far from complete.

Looking at Lascaris, Leo reflected on how many people had some secret place where they went in order to seek some private respite from the horror of the siege. For Basil it had been the citadel tower, where Leo had on occasion joined him. Others took solace in a corner of a church, the lonely crowd of an inn, madness, prayer or the creeping, restless sleep of melancholy.

For Leo it had been at the stables with his horses. He smiled now at the thought of them nuzzling him, showing their loyalty and concern in the amusing little habits they had: like Ruksh always following him to the gate as if for the last time. Or the day Leo, running breathlessly past to some threatened point with a troop of cataphracts at his heels, glanced over to see Zarrar looking at him and trotting impatiently along the yard rails with his head over them.

"What are you thinking?" Lascaris asked.

"Just that I would go to the stables when I could—to get away."

Lascaris, digging into the satchel he took from his shoulders, produced wine and two goblets. "This will get you away," he said mischievously. "Red."

"Son of Bacchus! I've enjoyed about as much water as I can stand."

He saw Lascaris smile back in the moonlight as they raised their goblets to each other.

"Bessas should be here," Leo said.

"That he should," replied his companion. They were silent for a time while each thought of their friend's plight as an infection of his wounds took hold.

They sat talking and drinking quietly, as men do who have been through much together. The town fell silent around them and the moon rose higher.

Memories came flooding back to Leo: of long rides, touching stirrups and a winsome smile under a crumpled hat; of the nights waiting for a message from Derar al-Adin; the desperate cavalry fight on the plain and constant Seljuk assaults. He regarded the walls of Manzikert where they stood, pitted and scarred in the eerie light cast by the bright moon. "If the stones could talk," he murmured. "Do you remember how pretty it was when we rode in, with its trees and gardens?"

Lascaris took in the present shabby appearance of the city, the untidy stacks of war stores pillaged by the defenders as they struggled to feed the people, repair walls, haul away their wounded and bury the dead. "And the lovely fountains and orchards. The strategos will be a long time cleaning up the district after this raid." He took another long gulp and looked at Leo staring thoughtfully into the distance. "What will happen now?"

"Now? The strategos sent a courier to Taron, today, asking them to send any spare cavalry they have. If they arrive some time tomorrow, we will let them spell their horses a few hours, then get after the Seljuks. I had a last word from Derar this morning. He said there is a column of prisoners being driven towards Archēsh. We'll harass the Seljuk rear guard to the point of panic and rescue the prisoners if we can. Derar said he'll meet us just this side of Archēsh."

"It's not a trap?"

"I doubt it. We will be very damned prudent in any case, and we still have his nephew. Most importantly, the Sultan has been defeated—for the time being. Derar can hardly confess to him now and expect to get away with it."

"The Arab never did find out the identity of the Sultan's spy within the fortress, did he?" Lascaris asked.

"If he learned their identity, Derar isn't telling. Bessas and Serena caught Bardas Cydones just in time. The imperial courier was about to discharge a ballista bolt into Guy's back as he rode from the gate. Jacques had no choice but to shoot him with the crossbow. Even Joaninna Magistros couldn't keep Cydones alive." Leo paused. "Damn it! I needed him to live, and talk about Kamyates."

"It is quiet, isn't it?" Lascaris sighed. Turning, the centarch saw the strange new star that had formed before the siege. "It is still there," he barely whispered.

Leo followed the direction of his gaze, thinking of the time he had first seen it, supporting the wounded Tzetzes during the dark night on the Vaspurakan steppe. Recalling the ambush in which Tzetzes was hurt, Leo said, "For a while I was half-sure Bardanes Gurgen was up to something. He and his man, Ananias, both died on the walls."

"Gurgen? He drew attention to himself through pride," Lascaris said.

"He did. I'll always suspect Ananias was somehow connected with Cydones, but both are dead and we'll never know now."

"Very convenient for Ananias to get himself knifed on the walls one night," said Lascaris.

"Very—for Kamyates and his cronies! Tigran Zakarian, I'm certain was one of theirs, the Seljuks I mean." Leo took another sip from the goblet and moved his weight on the hard seat. The breeze grew cooler and he pulled his tunic closer around him.

"Zakarian? He's disappeared," Lascaris said. "Vanished."

"Gone over the wall when the game was up, I should think."

For a while there was a comfortable silence between them.

Lascaris broke it. "I couldn't bring myself to hate either Gurgen or Zakarian."

"Me neither," Leo agreed. "Gurgen simply said what he thought. Zakarian? Well, in a land where the old Armenian aristocracy cleared out years ago with twenty thousand of their followers, Zakarian was just trying to hang onto his ancestral ground by accommodating each new master as they happened along. First us, then the Seljuks. It's the scheming, treacherous, smug bastards in Constantinople I can't stand. They will yet sell the empire down the drain from their curtained chambers."

The distant night noises of Manzikert intruded into Leo's thoughts. He listened, hearing a few drunks still wandering the cramped streets. A dog barked somewhere. In the heavy silence of its absence, the Seljuk camp seemed almost as oppressive now as had been the constant hum of its past life, punctuated by outbreaks of distant laughter and the strains of their unfamiliar music. A horse whinnied from the military stables.

"That was some ride, by D'Agiles," said Lascaris. "I've never heard of such a thing. He should be a dead man a hundred times over. Lucky he had Zarrar."

"More than the horse I think." Leo smiled to himself as he thought of some of Zarrar's quirks. "Did you see Zarrar fight his way out of that melee? I'm glad he doesn't do that when I'm tacking shoes on him. No, I must say Guy d'Agiles had more than one good ride, as a decoy before the fight at the wadi and escaping Archēsh with Irene. He certainly knows how to get the best out of a horse."

"Still—makes you wonder …" Lascaris said barely audibly, as though hushed by the majesty of the night and heroism of Guy d'Agiles' feat against the mangonel. "I couldn't have done it."

"You don't know until you try, I suppose. I've wondered, especially about that last ride when he knew what he was going into. With hindsight though, he didn't. He thought he was going to certain death, which makes him even braver."

"You're right," said Lascaris.

Leo stared unseeingly into the bright night. "Selth and I had talked about going together when we thought up the mad scheme. I'll always wonder if I would have been up to it, desperate or brave enough to force my body and horse through the ordeal. And to my shame, it's not lost on me, I did not volunteer when the moment came. We all thought that whoever went was a dead man. D'Agiles stepped straight forward—and not in the heat of battle either! It was a thought-out decision and he did not shrink back once he had spoken. He went out there by himself. He did it for the princeps' daughter, Irene. And not even to possess her. For with his poor station—a wandering mercenary—he held little hope of winning her. That much you could read in his face. He made that ride to save her from …"

Both men were quiet. For the first time in months, Leo consciously noticed the breeze whisper through the trees. It reminded him of the night Martina had left Manzikert with despatches and the memory awakened the crushing emptiness now enveloping him.

Lascaris tried the bottle again, but it was empty. Disappointed, he looked at it, then at Leo, who returned his gaze. "For men who drink little, we have done commendable damage."

"Yes, I fear," answered Leo absently. He was silent for a minute, his mind tracing the intermingled steps of those whose paths had crossed his in the months since leaving Constantinople. He looked over the city, the valley and mountain, still under the moon. "So many memories here, Lascaris. This has been a good end to it."

"Is this the end?"

"It's the end of the siege—tomorrow—another chukka. It's cool, and late, and we will probably have a long ride after sunup." Leo looked at Lascaris. "Now, how do we get off here without breaking our necks?"

Lascaris got to his knees with a puzzled expression, and in a careful, ungainly crawl looked down. "Good question," he chuckled.

Chapter Twenty

A Draught of Cool Water

Manzikert, Early morning,
20th September 1054

It was still dark on the thirty-second day since the siege began. Guy, restless and beginning to feel his strength return, was up by lamplight, attempting to put into order the pile of tack and accoutrement his friends had placed in a corner. Jacques, also working by lamplight on the step outside, was repairing a worn strap on his saddle. Guy, without taking much notice, heard Jacques talk to some passer-by. Beyond that, there was the unmistakable feel of men and horses moving.

Guy, sensing someone in the room behind him, turned and saw a tall, handsome stranger in a corselet and cavalry boots. Straight and dark-eyed with curly black locks framing his youthful face, the newcomer looked at Guy for a moment, then broke into a broad smile, "It's you."

Guy remembered Irene saying the same words on the day of their first ride outside the walls. He grinned back. "Damian? I have heard much of you."

"I hope it wasn't all bad," Irene's brother laughed. "I thought you'd be older. You're recovering well?" He looked doubtfully at Guy's injuries.

"I am thank you. They look worse than they are."

"Oh, you look quite heroic, but I'm sure you're lying. I've come through without a scratch. People will think I have done nothing—close enough to the truth. That must've been some ride into their camp. It'll enter the folklore of the Kelts. Justly so, I say."

"There didn't seem to be much choice at the time," said Guy. "Were you attacked at Artzké?" Guy asked.

"I haven't been there," Damian admitted solemnly. "They looked at us and there was half-hearted probing. I was sent out with three hundred men to find out what was going on, but we were cut off and couldn't return there, or get through to here. So we made our way to Mush. I was told when I got here last night that Artzké is now under great threat, since much of the Seljuk army withdrew by that way."

Damian looked around the little room. "You've had a fight of it here. I've never seen such destruction. I was sick with worry about my parents and sister. Many times we sent scouts to try and find a way through, to see if we could assist or form a co-ordinated plan, but the entire area was always thick with Seljuk patrols. I came myself once and heard the sound of battle by night but couldn't get through." Damian fell silent for a moment. "I fear the devastation of Vaspurakan and Armenia has been widespread and severe."

"So fear I," agreed Guy. Then, seeking a more pleasant subject he enquired, "Are you looking for Irene? She isn't here." As an afterthought, he asked, "What are you doing here in Manzikert?"

"Irene's sleeping at home," Damian said. "I wanted to meet you. I never liked Ankhialou, though it should have been a most successful marriage—they were both in love with the same fellow!"

Guy grinned at the joke.

"Too full of himself—and his own wellbeing—to be of use to anyone else. I'm here because I brought despatches from the strategos of Taron. In answer to Basil Apocapes' request, he has deployed mounted troops as a screen to follow up the enemy withdrawal along the shore of Bznunik. I've guided a regiment of Taron horse, to join your forces here, to pursue the enemy to Archēsh. I return to join our screen approaching Artzké as soon as my squire has arranged a change of horses."

Except for the attack led by Alkan, Guy had been left out of things for four days to recover. As Damian spoke, Guy realised that Togol had been right, the campaign was not yet over.

When Basil Apocapes rode out in the first light of the following day leading fifteen hundred horse, Guy trotted close by him on Sira, at his right Jacques on brown Arzema. With Basil was his command-group comprising: an escort of a hundred Armenian irregulars, gallopers, duty-tribunes, scouts, clerks and his standard-bearer. Behind them rode the lead files of the Sixth Schola, Zobeir al-Adin amongst them on an indifferent garrison remount. Sallow from his months in captivity, the Arab was closely watched by Simon Vardaheri and David Varaz.

As soon as the force left the close environs of the fortress and crossed the low crest of lava country to the east, a tribune from the Manzikert garrison cut away and cantered south-east with Damian Curticius to join the troops from Taron. They bore the message of Basil Apocapes' intent: that the Taron troops harass the Seljuk withdrawal along the northern shore of the lake and rescue any Christian prisoners without becoming decisively engaged. The two dispersed Roman groups would link-up on the steppe west of Archêsh.

All had seen the pall of smoke that rose in the direction of Artzké.

On command, Bryennius' Sixth Schola cantered forward as the screen, each troop riding widely dispersed in arrowhead. The horsemen were soon lost to a lazy eye in the undulating folds and stony-rises that marked the countryside along the road to Archêsh. Basil kept the remaining thirteen hundred, Franks and Armenians, deployed in a diamond formation so they could quickly change front to meet any threat or opportunity. Alternately walking and trotting, the Manzikert horsemen followed the dust cloud of the withdrawing army.

In the mid-morning, a galloper on a sweating horse reined in alongside the strategos and spoke rapidly in Greek punctured with the army phrases Guy had come to know so well. "Strategos, Count Bryennius' compliments, he's halted on a rise four furlongs distant, from whence the barbarian's rear-guard can be seen, as well as a column of prisoners. The count requests you move forward to his position."

"John," Basil summoned the princeps. "I'll take half my escort. Bring up the main body steadily." With a word to the closest of the duty tribunes, Basil motioned his big grey into a hand-gallop and shouted for Guy to accompany him.

Sira had seen the excitement of the galloper's arrival and Basil's horse collect itself in anticipation as half the escort wheeled out of column and cantered forward. When Guy gave Sira a signal, she stepped into an easy canter to clear the column. Guy urged her to a hand-gallop and they were soon moving with Apocapes across the hoof-pitted and denuded steppe to the rise ahead, with its lace of tiny cavalry waiting just this side of a crest, where they were able to peep over without being obvious.

Riding boot to boot with Basil, Guy saw the man. Straight in the saddle of the reefing iron-grey horse was Apocapes of Manzikert. Pious in his beliefs and usually his conduct, kind towards widows and orphans, loved and respected by those he commanded, Basil rode in a plain pot helmet with leather strips of neck protection, a mail shirt with drab cotton trousers tucked into riding boots. A mace nestled at his pommel and a sword by his side as he carried a spear at an oblique angle across his mount's wither. On his bridle arm, he held the almond-shaped shield as easily as a letter and Guy noticed, in a caught memory, the way it rose and fell with the motion of the horse.

Guy beheld he who had defeated the shepherd king. Yet why did Basil Apocapes murder Alkan in the manner he did? Revenge? A calculated insult or outburst from a usually suppressed temper? An ordinary man driven to a mistake? Who was qualified to judge?

With glances towards the smoke plume in the south, they rode past the corpses of Christians unable to keep up with the forced pace of the Seljuk withdrawal. Enemy stragglers on foot, or leading broken-down horses, tried to steal away. The ground was littered with discarded bundles, armour and weapons. Here and there a cart had been pushed off the track because of a broken wheel or axle. Guy got the distinct impression of an army now hurrying away. It was not broken and in panic, but the evidence of a hasty withdrawal was more prolific than the tell-tale signs of a few dropped cloaks and scabbards left by a disciplined force feigning flight in order to draw their pursuers into a trap.

As they approached Bryennius' advanced position, Basil and Guy saw the Scholae standard-bearer signal to them and they changed direction to rein-in next to Bryennius. Now the bulk of the snow-covered crest of Mount Sippane was behind their right shoulders. Guy drew rein below the rise and looked ahead into the lower ground, forcing from his mind dramatic images of the hunt with hawks, his lonely journey to Archēsh with despatches and the racing ride away from the doomed city with Irene.

"Report," rasped Basil.

Bryennius began. "By the dust and smoke, most of the Seljuk army seems to have passed through Archēsh already. The city has probably been subjected to another sack on their way through. If you look into the middle ground where the dust is thickest along the track there, you can make out a column of Christian prisoners, guarded by infantry. To their southern flank and behind them, is a rear guard of lightly armoured cavalry, *sipahiyan* horse. I make it about a thousand. They'd probably think that sufficient as a rear guard against us."

"I see them," replied Basil, studying the distant dust. "You've seen the smoke over Artzké."

"I have," said Bryennius, at times brutal in his assessments. "It started soon after first light. I fear the city has fallen and was fired as the shepherds departed. All the more reason for us to crack on. We've pressed them harder than they thought possible and their order is starting to break. D'you see the ridge with a knoll on it, a handbreadth to their northern flank?" Bryennius had time to study the ground and did not waste it.

Apocapes followed the count's tactical descriptions and assessment.

Guy, listening, held a clenched fist out at arm's length to identify the feature Bryennius had described. Basil grunted assent that he also had marked the ground.

"If we move rapidly around the left flank," Leo explained, "and occupy that higher ground, the enemy rear guard might fear being surrounded and cut off—especially if pressed from behind at the same time. Our object would be to get their cavalry, in an attempt to flee the perceived trap, to desert their infantry. Our men on that high ground would secure against counter-attack on your left flank, while our main body disperses their infantry and rescues our people."

Basil watched the withdrawing army on the lower ground and asked, "Is there no chance the prisoners could be bait, that what you propose is what the Seljuks want us to do?" The fate of Artzké so soon after the deliverance of Manzikert had obviously shaken him.

Guy could see the weight on Apocapes' shoulders and the agony in his face. What if he had realised the threat to the lakeside city and pursued immediately?

What if the Sultan had then turned and counter-attacked, with his full army, the small Manzikert force in the open?

"I've considered it," Bryennius replied, "but I don't think so. The Sultan withdraws because he has other priorities, with the caliphate most important. Affairs at Manzikert had collapsed to the point where Tughrul Bey was having trouble keeping his army together. It looks as though he has salvaged his vanity by threatening to return next year, and delivered some booty to his army at Artzké. I'd say his aim now is to get away in good order. His rear guard is expendable, as are the prisoners."

Basil studied the situation, tugging at the ends of his moustache as he grappled with the doubt and decision that mark the loneliness of command. "Salvaged his vanity, eh? How many souls has that cost us?"

Guy considered the scene and stared intently at the strategos, thinking as he did, that Bryennius was right—go with him.

"It's a risk," Basil said, "but we'll take it. As you say, possession of that higher ground is vital. Hold here and give your orders while the main body comes up."

"There's something else," Bryennius said. "I'm supposed to find my, ah, friend, out here somewhere. We need to ensure he's not killed when he approaches."

"I'd not forgotten. Word's been passed, but I'll remind the other officers," assured Basil.

Guy sought the strategos' permission to ride with the Bryennius, receiving it on condition that the count was happy to have him. Guy and Jacques dismounted with the others while the centarchs assembled around Bryennius for orders.

As the advance guard of the main body began to arrive and deploy, the remnants of the irregulars commanded by Seranush Donjoian rode in from the north. He nodded towards Guy in recognition and reported thus to Basil Apocapes. "Praise God you've held Manzikert. I have lost a third of my men in running fights over the past month, but in return we have ambushed their patrols in the foothills, killed their couriers on the road and destroyed as many of their supplies as we could. I have a hundred dead and another fifty maimed. I bring a hundred. What d'you want me to do?"

Basil listened to Donjoian's account, thanked him and his men, then bade them retire to Manzikert with their wounded. They had played their part.

Guy joined Bryennius as the troopers were tightening their girths, leading their horses into ranks then mounting. "The Seljuks will be looking at us into the low sun and through their own dust—that's good," Bryennius said, as he placed his helmet on his head and fastened the leather throat lash.

The Sixth Schola moved forward at a smart trot, armour clinking, horses champing the bits and iron shoes striking the scattered lava stones that lay upon the trodden earth. The ranks were thinner now than when they had marched into Manzikert. All had cropped their hair and shaved away their beards on account of the heat of the season and filth of the campaign. Their faces were gaunt with strain and under the helmets, eyes that had seen much, took in all before them with experience and calculation.

Squadrons of the Seljuk rear-guard, had discerned the intention of the Romans and were forming up to seize the decisive knoll before the Sixth occupied it and threatened the road to Archēsh. There was no time to lose.

"As flying wedge," Bryennius roared, "gallop, march!" Zarrar sprang forward and was already four lengths ahead of the first rank.

Breaking into a hand-gallop, the well drilled cataphracts re-organised into the flying wedge, the most heavily armed lancers and horses in the lead ranks, mounted archers behind ready to shoot over their heads.

"Charge!" signalled Bryennius.

Couching his spear and shield in the front rank of eight men, Guy saw Bryennius draw his bow. His shield already hung from the high wooden pommel and his spear was slung behind his right shoulder. For two furlongs they flew with reefing horses and wild yells. Sira pulled and snatched the bit, so that Guy's world was filled with the flying chestnut mane and grunting breath of the mare's head in front of him. "Steady, Sira. Steady, girl," he spoke as he drew back on the reins to keep his interval in the knee-grinding, stirrup-grazing pace.

Before them, Zarrar's powerful rump bounded up the side of the yellow-grassed hill, Bryennius drawing his bow on something the other side. Then both horse and rider were lost to Guy's sight. Togol went over with Bryennius.

Guy let Sira race on reaching the top of the hill and plunging down the other side. Perhaps a hundred ghulams were there, flogging their mounts up the slope towards the crest to where the Romans had just beaten them. Guy noticed a Seljuk dead on the ground, an arrow in his throat just above the lamellar cuirass. Sira jumped the corpse with Guy scarcely feeling the action.

Five ghulams were down before the bows of Bryennius and Togol when the charging front rank of cataphracts reached them and racing past, cut down another six before Tribune Balsamon bellowed for the racing horsemen to rally. The Seljuks, now at the tactical disadvantage, shrunk back from the iron avalanche.

Guy joined in the chorus of, "Steady—whoa, there," that sounded around him as the cataphracts controlled their excited horses.

Bryennius bellowed for them to fall back and reform. "Get back up to the crest line, men. Stand your horses side-on to the enemy and hold every spear up straight. Make it look like there are a thousand of us."

Guy, with Jacques close by, kneed Sira back to the crest. He sought out Bryennius who was watching the action unfold on the lower ground where Basil led the main body of Christian horse forward against the rear of the withdrawing army.

In the valley, ribbons of dust rose from the officers riding in front of the charge. One led by a half a furlong, the horse's head and tail stretched out flat, charging straight for the straggling Daylami footmen who were starting to run in panic across the steppe. Guy could see Seljuk horsemen of the *sipahiyan* start to group in squadrons to counter the charge, but these men also hesitated before melting away to the east.

Guy watched—with an impassiveness that perplexed him—the charging horsemen sweep past the abandoned carts. Christian prisoners making the sign of the cross threw themselves onto the ground. The horsemen rode over the straggling Daylamis, cutting them down without mercy and racing among the fleeing Seljuk cavalry, hacking left and right with swords or spitting on their spears those unable to flee fast enough. With audible whoops and shouts, the rolling dust cloud enveloped those on foot.

"Pull them up. Pull them up!" Bryennius cried. He turned to Guy. "That's the useless thing about cavalry. They get too excited and go chasing after things—scatter to the winds—ripe for the counter-attack which they are too disorganised to resist."

They watched in silent relief as the dust slowly cleared. The charging regiments halted and reorganised, two of them forming a strong front to drive off any Seljuk threat. Cataphracts were dismounting and freeing the prisoners. Even from the crest, Guy could hear the weeping and lamentations as those saved when almost beyond hope broke down and wept on the armoured chests of their rescuers.

A dust-caked, sweating Thracian on a dun horse, rode up and relayed an order from Basil. "The strategos' compliments. He requests you to screen to the east of the main body and form an outpost line for the night, on advantageous ground short of Archēsh. Tonight we'll start back the people rescued. Tomorrow, we re-occupy Archēsh."

"Tribune, any word from the right flank column out of Taron?" Leo asked.

"Some. During their withdrawal along the shore of the Sea of Bznunik, the infidels came upon the city of Artzké. The people had placed their faith in the waters and wall around them and were unconcerned, but the infidels found a shallow way to the city and put their swords to work, killing almost everyone."

"It's that bad?"

"So it's said," replied the tribune, "but I didn't see it with my own eyes. It's also reported the two Seljuk columns have joined around Archēsh."

"Thank you," said Bryennius.

"Was there someone dear to you, at Artzké?" asked the tribune.

"No one. But all. Thank you. You should return to your post. Kindly tell the strategos we move off within the hour." He clapped the tribune on the shoulder by way of an apology for his usual curt manner. "You might suggest, having now seen the ground, that he replaces us here with a flank guard before we move off."

The regiment rode forward in the early evening and before dark had trotted to a position along a low crest. From there a few sharp eyes could make out, amongst its trees in the growing darkness to the east, the taller buildings of Archēsh. They loosened their girths a hole and fed a little grain to their horses. A rivulet ran behind them. It was one of the unforgettable sights of Guy's life, to see the lines of saddled, unbitted horses with their heads down, a foreleg bent for most, as they drank greedily of the clear, stony stream.

At last light a picket challenged two strangers. A decarch informed Bryennius that a small party of Saracens had approached under a reversed spear.

"How many?" Bryennius asked, sitting on the ground, his helmet on one side, Togol on the other.

"It looks like a man, a boy and three horses," the trooper replied.

"Did they say anything?"

"They asked after a blind man on a pale horse."

"Very good. Bring them here," said Bryennius.

Guy saw the count glance at Zobeir al-Adin, who sat in the churned dirt watching a slender Arab in his late thirties approach leading a warhorse of Bedouin type.

"We meet again, Horse-archer," Derar greeted in quite good Greek.

"How now, Derar al-Adin? So you speak Greek after all?" replied Bryennius, getting to his feet.

"I thought it necessary to keep something back—I didn't have many chess pieces in hand at the wadi." Derar did not acknowledge Zobeir's presence, although the nephew's relief at his uncle's presence was evident.

"Still, it seems to have worked out in the end," Bryennius said warmly enough.

Derar recognised Guy and acknowledged his presence, "Are you the one who rode with the woman from Archēsh and destroyed the Sultan's mangonel at Manzikert—and his heart with it."

Guy glanced at the ground, then up, to notice the beautiful youth looking at him with dark eyes.

"It's him," Bryennius said. "Please sit everyone."

Derar looked long at Guy. "My compliments—a feat worthy of record." He turned to Zarrar to give the suspiciously snorting gelding a pat. "And on your fine horse, if I am not mistaken."

Zarrar, at such familiarity from a stranger, gave Derar one of his quizzical, "Who the hell are you?" sorts of looks, which so amused Guy. Since the stranger was talking amicably to Leo, Zarrar did not seem to mind Derar after that and the tough warhorse positively bent his head to the Arabian youth who stepped near, caressing softly with fine fingers under his jaw and whispering in his ear.

"Thank you," Guy said. "But there were many deeds worthy of record at Manzikert."

Derar turned from Zarrar. "On both sides. I befriended the Seljuk emir, Emren Dirse, through all this strife, a brave man and good."

"We know him," Guy replied as they all sat on the ground around the fire.

Derar paused politely. "He was able to save two children, a brother and sister, from slavery. They've been taken to his aunt's house in Tabriz for safety. Emren Dirse appreciates your offer of a filly. It'd be well if you are able to keep your promise one day soon and return the children to Christian lands." He was silent for a time, looking down. Finally he gazed into Bryennius' eyes. "All war is horrible, but in my days, I've never seen the like of this campaign. And I have no wish to see another."

"Are you certain of the numbers killed and carried off?" asked Bryennius.

"As certain as the scribes."

Guy wondered if the Arab mused on the personal cost of trying to rescue just one such life, tossed around in the maelstrom of the shepherd king.

Bryennius was silent and pensive as he looked searchingly at Derar.

"What happened to your Turk?" asked Guy.

"Zaibullah? We lost touch in the confusion of the withdrawal today. He rode ahead with our camels to find a campsite for us." Derar glanced at Zobeir, sitting away from the fire.

Bryennius stared at Derar. "Will he come looking for you? I hate loose ends."

Derar shook his head. "He was well paid and was owed nothing. He's also a practical man who will attribute his good fortune to the vagaries of war and get on about his business. Moreover, he has two camels and their baggage to profit by it."

"Perhaps," admitted Bryennius. "Did the Sultan ever tumble to your, ah, game?"

Derar thought on it. "No. There were plenty of people in the camp upon whom suspicion might fall. I don't particularly fear being hunted." Then he rose and walked to Zobeir, rattling off something in Arabic.

Guy, Bryennius and Togol looked at each other.

Simon Vardaheri interpreted. "Derar said that when Zobeir gets home, he should say nothing to anyone of his adventures and seek a quiet life as a scholar or healer."

Togol suppressed a laugh. "It's good advice for everyone, except wanderers and horse thieves, eh, Simon?"

Vardaheri merely looked into their little fire and said nothing.

"Is there anything else you need to tell me before we move on to more pleasant conversation, Derar?" Bryennius asked as the Arab resumed his seat.

"One thing only," Derar responded. "The Sultan has sworn to return to Manzikert next year. It is not over for you, though some of his advisors are encouraging him to move on Baghdad instead—to his destiny."

"Destiny." repeated Bryennius, as if far away.

"The Sultan was furious about the pig ... his ... umm ... dowry ... catapulted into the Seljuk camp. That was a mistake by your strategos."

Bryennius rose and walked a few steps along the crest, to stand looking away from them to the sunset, his outline dark against the redness in the west. "The spark was the Sultan's intention to take as a bride the most beautiful woman in the city. But, it was not Apocapes who ordered it," Bryennius said over his shoulder. "The deed was inspired by a rabble-rousing courtier named Kamyates." The count turned sharply on his heel to see if the name had provoked a response from the Arab.

Derar al-Adin arched his eyebrows. "A name to remember I suspect, though I haven't heard it before. I'm glad it was not Apocapes."

After another penetrating stare at Derar, Bryennius asked, "Do the names Cydones, Gurgen or Zakarian mean anything to you?"

"Cydones? No, nor Gurgen. Tigran Zakarian was working for the Sultan. He narrowly missed execution a few days ago and was kicked out of the camp immediately afterwards."

"Ah ha," acknowledged the count.

Guy wondered why he did not ask about Ankhialou.

Instead, Vardaheri asked on Guy's behalf. "Theodore Ankhialou?"

Derar looked to Guy. "Executed, for encouraging the Sultan to besiege Manzikert."

"Did you see it?" Guy asked, aware of conflicting feelings: empathy for the renegade's misfortune and a desire to be free of his revenge.

Derar looked at the dirt.

"Guy needs to know if he has to sleep with an eye open," Bryennius explained.

"I didn't see it. But I have no doubt." Derar looked at Guy. "I know he hunted you over a woman. I don't believe you need fear." Derar switched his gaze to Bryennius who was still standing. "Did this Kamyates order the beheading of the Sultan's vassal, Prince Alkan?"

"No. That was a mistake."

"A mistake?"

"Have you never made a mistake?" said Bryennius in the curt manner of command.

"Ahh!"

"Anything else we can assist you with?" asked Bryennius.

Derar paused, his brow furrowed as if in doubt. "There is—a somewhat delicate matter. My companion, here, is one of you, a Roman, a woman ..."

Guy looked in surprise as the youth suddenly stood and regarded Derar, wonder in her eyes.

'... Farisa was captured as a child in the 1048 raids by the Taghlibi Arabs out of Resaina—captured I think from near the city you call Mush. I bought her at the slave market at Amida and have promised her freedom if she helped me in this quest."

Derar rose also. "Farisa, though it seems long since I regarded you as a slave, I made a promise. It is often easier to stay with what you know, or have become accustomed to, but when I returned to camp the day the *baban* made the first breach, you said whilst looking at the dust and smoke of battle—'They are my people, Derar. How do they bear it?' You said, my people. Thus you are free and I will give you gold and a horse. You must go with these Romans, whom I believe trustworthy and find your home and heart."

Farisa made to speak, but Derar held up his hand. "If you should wish to return, you will always have a place of honour in my house, a free woman." He turned to Bryennius. "You can see to it?"

Farisa looked uncertainly at the count as he spoke to Derar. "I shall furnish an escort for her to the abbess tomorrow, and from there to wherever near Mush she wishes to travel." He turned to the woman. "Welcome home, Farisa. You are among friends."

There was a pensive silence for a time, until Bryennius said in a lighter vein, "Derar, Farisa, you must stay with us tonight. There're too many stragglers, freed prisoners and excited Roman troops behind us. You'd not get through and even a written safe conduct might not be enough protection with patrols of illiterate men around. Tomorrow, Derar, I will send an escort with you to the Arsanias River beyond the battlefields, then you can make your way downstream towards Amida and thence to your home. Now, we have more pleasant things to discuss."

Derar thanked him.

"I must check my posts," said Bryennius. "Then you may wish to carve a soldier's scant meal with us."

"It would be our honour. Perhaps we can share. Farisa has some bread, cheese and lamb. Do you drink the wine of Shiraz, Count Bryennius?"

"Yes, we do!" boomed Togol.

Thus the former enemies spent the night on the steppe.

Archēsh, Mid-morning,
21st September 1054

The following morning, Basil Apocapes' tiny field force entered unopposed the devastated city of Archēsh. The Seljuk maimed had been left at a church to the clemency of the monks. Basil's men could find no sign of the turmarch in the city and none of the survivors could tell of his fate. Some swore he had been killed after being horribly tortured, finally confessing where the city's gold was hidden. Basil appointed John Curticius to remain with most of the troops to restore order in Archēsh and Artzké, with the promise that Manzikert and other cities would send what aid they could. The surviving stragglers of the Seljuk army who had been captured the day before, mostly Daylami footmen, were set to work repairing the defences and cleaning the debris from around the public buildings. Lascaris' squadron of the Sixth Schola was tasked, for the time being, to assist with the restoration of order to the town. Basil ordered the mounted screen pushed forward to maintain pressure on the retreating enemy. Another party set out by fishing boat to make contact with the garrison and theme commander at Van.

Guy, Bryennius, Togol and ten cataphracts rode for Kavadh's smithy. Guy wished to meet the man that saved Irene during the sack of the city. Bryennius thought to offer him assistance as the blacksmith was a Muslim in a Christian town. Now that the Seljuk army had gone, prejudice and vengeance would come to the fore. Riding around the corner of the back lane leading to the shop, they saw an angry group of perhaps two dozen townspeople. These shrank back from the armed party.

A veiled figure in drab riding clothes, sword in hand, guarded the entrance to the structure. At Guy's approach the figure lifted their veil and he was astonished to be looking into the green eyes of Irene Curticius.

"What are you doing here?" they asked of each other in unison, Guy looking down at her from Sira.

Irene recovered first and explained, "The local people have lost virtually everything. In their pain they have attacked Kavadh. I arrived just in time."

Just in time to nearly share his fate, Guy thought. Instead he said aloud, "The road isn't secure."

As though reading his thoughts, Irene explained. "I quickly caught up with the rear guard, so I was quite safe—except from the dust. I came to reassure myself that the man who saved me would in turn be unharmed. I see Count Bryennius had similar thoughts. But, Kavadh is hurt." She motioned to the farrier and moved towards him. "You guard the door while I see to him."

Guy rode inside the building and saw the farrier sitting with his back to a post. He was holding a shoeing rasp as long as a man's forearm. Guy knew it was the first thing the Persian farrier had been able to pick up to defend himself with. A bloodied gash on Kavadh's forehead marked where a thrown rock had momentarily stunned him. Shahryād was in a corner loosebox, dried sweat on him from the long ride, the saddle equipped for a journey and reins tied to the near stirrup.

Dismounting, Guy tied Sira up well away from the stallion that whinnied in greeting to the mare. Sira pricked her ears at Shahryād for a moment, then turned her head to look at the noisy crowd outside the doors. "You women are all the same," Guy grumbled under his breath to the mare. Sira gave him a quick nudge of acknowledgement with her forehead.

Bryennius dispersed the gathering, telling them Kavadh was under Roman protection and that public vengeance would not be tolerated. The four stayed with Kavadh a short while, breaking their meagre bread and taking cool water from the well in the yard. Guy wondered at the bond forged between the young woman and the man who shod her horse, as she stayed in this far away outpost under the spell of one whose name Irene now never spoke. Perhaps Kavadh also loved her a little, he thought. He pictured in his mind's eye, Irene coming to the smithy and sharing her troubles as the blacksmith shod her horse.

Kavadh recognised Bryennius and Togol as the countrymen who had visited his shop the day before the brightened star in the sky. He remarked on it and asked after the imperial courier. "I never liked him and often wondered about you two showing up." The farrier was silent awhile, his gaze drifting with workmanlike interest to the way in which their horses had been shod. "And those two fellows who passed through, weeks before you, having me shoe their horses in the manner of the Persians?" He looked around at them, saying as though thinking to himself, "These have been strange times indeed. What became of the courier? I always wondered if you hunted him—or whether he hunted you? Or whether each hunter was in turn hunted?"

"It's said that he died on the walls of Manzikert," Bryennius replied. After a moment's reflection, he asked Kavadh whether he knew any of the imperial courier's associates in the town, or had heard of an insignificant fight on the Manzikert road the day before the first sighting of the new star.

A shiver ran down Guy's spine as he thought of the ballista bolt aimed at his back by Cydones as he had ridden from Manzikert's gates. Guy remembered Togol talking about the two attackers who had escaped from their attempt on Bryennius' party as they returned from Archēsh. He wondered, as he had no doubt the count wondered, who they were and what became of those two.

Kavadh had not heard.

After a time they rose to go, said their goodbyes to the Persian farrier of Archēsh then rode to the citadel to find the strategos.

Basil Apocapes established himself in the turmarch's former quarters, still being scrubbed clean of filth by Daylami prisoners under guard by Armenian cavalrymen.

Guy could only imagine how it felt for Irene when she had been here before, or what feelings touched her now. Seeing her stand in the place where she had loved another only to be betrayed, he felt that familiar sense of solitude. Irene glanced over and saw the look on his face, which he attempted to cover with a smile. He knew the attempt failed and his mouth had only twisted into a grimace.

In the background, the strategos was explaining how Bryennius was to return with his men to Manzikert. Curticius would restore order. Basil himself intended to move on with a flying column to shadow the Seljuk army east to Berkri, the first Armenian town to be sacked in this campaign of 1054. "So many dead," Basil murmured. "And so many wounded, and carried off and ravished. Stock destroyed. Dwellings wrecked. Gold and silver stolen. All the feed burned away or consumed by friend and foe alike. It will be a hard winter and I don't know how we shall survive without famine and misery."

Irene, sensing Guy's thoughts, held his gaze. Gently she walked to him and took his hand to lead him outside. Guy looked at the strategos who waved him away.

Downstairs, where troopers of the strategos' escort held their horses, Irene asked, "What irks you, Guy? Are you worried about him, Ankhialou? You need not. I love him no more. Nor have I since before I left this place."

Guy thought of Ankhialou. Imagined visions of the man with Irene vied with sharp images of the snarling face of the one he fought outside Manzikert. Suddenly he was aware of Irene looking intently at him. "Derar al-Adin says he is dead, but didn't see it!" Guy said.

Irene blanched and he wished he had remained silent. "It vexes me," he said. "We'll need to be ever watchful."

She moved a step closer and took his hand. "We are assured he is no more, but if that is not so, perhaps he's gone to the Persian lands with their army. There'll be no safe place for him in Vaspurakan now."

They sat on the step together, waiting for the others to come out. Changing the subject to a more cheerful one, Irene asked Guy, "What will you do now that you are rich?"

"The strategos has said I must return to Constantinople to receive largesse and perhaps an office from the Emperor." He had come into her life as a penniless mercenary and ridden against the catapult out of love for her and through desperation at the plight of all in the city. How he had profited by it sat uncomfortably with him, given the despair and penury, but he had little desire to test his finer feeling by returning to his former hardship. "It seems I am favourably mentioned in despatches and the strategos has made certain undertakings on behalf of the empire."

"Your good fortune seems to bother you, Guy?"

"In part it does." He turned to look in her eyes. "I have only done what seemed worthy. Many others have done right and lost everything."

"Others have done wrong at every turn and profited by it. What about Taronites? And Kamyates? How they have grown rich at the suffering of others." She looked at him intently. "You saved Manzikert. You have risked your life and earned your reward. Take what you are comfortable with and give what pleases you for the public good."

"There's only so much I can cart all the way back to Constantinople," he joked.

Excitement sparkled Irene's eyes as she listened. "Constantinople! It is the one place to be in the entire world. You will ...," Her voice trailed off as she saw the look on his face.

"Will you come with me?" Guy asked. "As my wife?"

Irene flung her arms around him, whispering damply into his neck, "You must ask father." She drew back and looked at him. "He's upstairs with the strategos."

Guy stood, having asked the impossible question and received the answer that once seemed beyond hope. He rose and strode past Bryennius and Togol towards the steps.

They looked after him. Togol shrugged.

To Guy's mixed relief, delight and frustration, the princeps' approved of his suit on the face of it, but raised the issue of the incompatibility of their different faiths. It was agreed between them that Guy would escort Irene and her mother to Constantinople and the care of the extended Curticius family, where some contract might be reached on who would convert. Guy knew such a breathing space might be prudent, but certain of his feelings, was impatient at the delay. He relayed this to Irene who professed to be satisfied with the arrangement, if equally impatient and suspicious of her father's designs for the family's influence.

Derar al-Adin assuaged Guy's nagging doubts about Ankhialou later that day during the long ride back to Manzikert. "While I did not myself see the deed or the lifeless body, there is no doubt of the fate of those who brought the Sultan to Manzikert."

The Sixth Schola spent another night on the steppe. Traumatised peasants and refugees out of hiding approached, begging for food and, though it was less apparent, for reassurance from the trauma. The soldiers shared what little they had. Recognising it was cold comfort to the terrified citizens, the cataphracts affirmed the Seljuks had withdrawn beyond Archēsh and were unlikely to return during this season.

"That would be right, sirs," an old peasant had muttered. "There is nothing left for them to take and few left for them to kill."

That night was cool. Guy awoke in the small hours, lying for some time looking at the near-full moon high overhead and the new star in Taurus. From his cloak, he could see the huddled figures of the soldiers, the pacing sentries and horses on the picket line, their heads bowed from hunger and work. He thought back over all that had happened since he had watched the moon over Arknik on the march from Karin. Thinking of Irene, curled in her cloak a discreet distance from him, he felt a deep sense of hope for the future.

The regiment rose before dawn and resumed the march, by evening the footsore men leading their weary horses through the long sunset shadows of the circling mounted patrols and into Manzikert.

As they entered Guy looked towards the breach where the fighting had been so bitter. Now the foundations of the smashed wall had been excavated in preparation for permanent repair. Piles of cleaned, cut stone for the facings were stacked nearby and workmen were toiling in their shirtsleeves, collecting rocks for the mortared rubble of the filling. Masons were already setting the first stones in place.

"Look there," said Jacques in such a tone of astonishment that Guy turned quickly to see.

"Where?" asked Guy, who could see nothing worthy of such a remark.

"No. I'm mistaken," joked Jacques, "for a moment, I thought I saw Kamyates getting his hands dirty doing something useful."

Guy glanced at Jacques striding along on one side of him as Irene walked on the other. The peasant was now excellently horsed and furnished with fine armour and weapons. Remembering the times he had seen Jacques with Joaninna, Guy reflected that his man had also prospered and found comfort for his soul. His comrade of the siege now counted as a friend.

"His hands are grubby alright," Guy said, before turning to happier thoughts. "If only my father could see us now, Jacques."

"For my money," Jacques replied, "I think he should. We've done well enough. But you can tell from the way people talk, that the frontier's unstable. So I think, with your approval, I'll be back off home to Provence with Joaninna. You should also return, having made your fortune. Charles' family should know of their son's fate and courage. Know it from you."

Guy thought that a tempting, if complicating, thought. The bereaved family would have nothing to thank him for. Looking around, he could see the garrison and citizens had been industrious during their three-day absence. The environs of the walls had finally been cleared of corpses and work parties were burning the debris from the ground formerly covered by the Seljuk encampment and siege lines. It was as though the townspeople wished to expunge the memory of it from their souls. Around the fortress, people had already herded out livestock in search of grazing. Peasants were scratching furrows in the grounds to plant barley; the hardy, quick-growing cereal crop which was the mainstay diet for people and animals alike during the freezing winters. Others mixed, dried and stacked the dung-cakes that would provide fuel through the winter.

Count Doukas met the returning column inside the north gate and had a long conversation with Bryennius after he dismounted. Guy, standing nearby, learned with a jolt that Centarch Bessas Phocas had sickened from infection and died.

Bessas, dead?" Bryennius said barely audibly, moving a pace and grasping a stirrup leather as if to steady himself.

Doukas looked closely for a moment. "I believe that Kamyates may have had something to do with it, for the cunning courtier has left for Karin with the avowed intention of returning to the palace in Constantinople and reporting on events here. The scoundrel will have gone to cover his tracks, paint his own part as significant and everyone else as being at fault in some way."

Silently, Bryennius undid the throat lash and pulled the helmet from his head. "Who went with him?"

"He took his servant and that creature, Reynaldus."

"Did he now? When?"

"Three days ago. As soon as Apocapes and you were out of the way. They've a good start," Doukas answered.

"Basil will be furious," said Bryennius, turning away. He approached and addressed Irene who was standing by Guy. "Mistress Curticius. Serena Cephalus is your friend ..."

"Of course," she whispered. "I will go to her." With a quick touch of Guy's forearm she mounted and was gone.

"I am very sorry," said Guy not knowing what else to say.

Bryennius nodded understanding and stood by his horse for a little time, looking across his saddle as if far away. At length he turned to Lascaris. "Antony, we have services to perform."

A month later—Manzikert,
Early morning, 30th October 1054

Basil had been outraged on his return a week later when told of Kamyates' flight to the capital. The strategos seemed as much exhausted by the Herculean task of repairing the physical and moral wounds of the district, as by the fight to drive off the nomads. He simmered over the escape of Kamyates, his mood somewhat improved by despatches from Constantinople informing him that troops of the Macedonian theme, commanded by another Bryennius—an illustrious general close to the inner circle of that famous military family—would be sent to the eastern frontier, to be in a position to defend it by the following spring.

Guy was there when Basil passed the news to Bryennius.

"Militarily," Basil had told him, "I think we'll be all right here through the winter, until your distant namesake arrives with the Macedonian legions, which, so they tell me, will drive the Persians before them as did Alexander."

Bryennius had grinned at the strategos' sarcasm.

"Leo, I'm sending you and your men back to Constantinople—you've done your bit. Tell Cecaumenus what has happened here, that a hundred and thirty thousand Christians were sacrificed to the indulgence of the shepherd king." Basil looked long out of the window at the circuit walls of Manzikert. "The shepherd king! One man caused all this—these paths and destinies to intertwine, some with horror and death, others with hope and—what chance this life? And for what purpose?"

Basil had been quiet for long moments, staring out, as though at the horizon. He returned to Bryennius. "Beware of Kamyates. He'll be spreading poison as soon as he gets back to Constantinople. When he hears you've returned," Basil had gripped Bryennius' shoulder, "well, watch your eyes. Kamyates will try and have them out, especially if you openly contradict what he says—that this was a minor battle and the Seljuks are no threat to the empire and that the incompetence of the eastern armies was to blame. Take Guy with you. Kamyates will be unable either to counter his well-deserved fame, or deny what he relates of events at Manzikert. And speaking of events, have you heard any more of your Arab friend?"

"Not since we set him on his way with his nephew and a certain amount of gold and silver. The Roman woman that was with him we sent to Mush with a nun and a few of my men as escort."

"Good! Another soul saved. How much gold and silver?"

Bryennius had hesitated. "Adequate, I would say."

"Hmm!" Basil had grinned. "Well. It's no more than he deserved. And one never knows—he may be useful at some stage in the future."

After the immediate hard work of commemorating the dead, repair of the physical damage started and crops planted, there had been a public feast accompanied by merriment and dancing. Many said was the most heartfelt in the city for years. In a way, it was this celebration that really marked the end of the siege and the first occasion on which the ordinary people were able to rejoice at what they had achieved.

A month after the raising of the siege and before the autumn weather turned too bleak, Guy and Irene accompanied the Sixth Schola as the regiment departed Manzikert.

They formed up in the early morning, each man mounted and under arms, the gaps in the ranks partly filled by the squires promoted to their places. Their gear was easily strapped and roped onto pack mules, for the men had sold or given away much that they no longer required. Squires, assisted by hired citizens, drove their spare horses including ten fine animals now belonging to Guy—gifts from Basil Apocapes. Guy and Irene rode behind Bryennius as the regiment paraded in the square and trooped down the barren avenue to leave the city by the western gate. The citizens turned out in a throng, cheering them to the echo. Varangians, Norman and Armenian troops lined the way, crashing their spear hafts on the flagstones in salute to their comrades-in-arms of the siege.

It was a time of turbulent emotions for Guy. So many faces and places were familiar. He turned in his saddle, hoping to see Jacques so they could share this moment with a glance, but the groom was somewhere back in the column with Joaninna, Isaac and Flora Asadian. Guy looked at Irene, beautiful in her green riding habit. She had drawn back her veil and Guy could discern a tear in her eye.

As the procession left the walls of Manzikert, they heard urgent whinnies. Hector and Diomed, who had been grazing loose in the river flats, galloped over and searched for their places in the ranks, shouldering in, looking for the man who would no longer ride them.

"Let them in," said Bryennius. "We will take them back to their master's family."

A standard-bearer turned his horse to make room. As they took their usual places, Serena Cephala, veiled for the journey, rode alongside and touched Diomed's dun neck with a gloved hand and stroked Hector's grey forehead as he nuzzled close to her.

Basil rode awhile with Bryennius at the head of the column. They passed along the track through freshly sprouting crops where peasants tilled the earth. The recent rains had brought on new growth and the day was rich with the shooting barley and the scent of new life.

Guy watched one woman, bowed down from terror and toil, usher her small children to the track and close to Zarrar, who bent his head to them. This nameless poor woman of Vaspurakan stroked the horse's neck and made to kiss the boot leg of Bryennius, but the rider stooped down and took her hand as she held up her children to kiss his. Guy reached down also, and looked back as he passed, to see the children reaching up to the outstretched hands of Lascaris and those who rode behind.

Basil saw them off at the bridge where the column crossed the river and rode up the escarpment on the other side. As Guy and Irene paused with them, the strategos and the count exchanged a few parting words.

"You'll be alright?" Bryennius asked.

"Between you and me, Leo, I don't know if I can do that again."

"How long will you stay?"

"For a time. But when I last spoke to my father, he had much praise for the country around Edessa. Perhaps I'll travel there one day."

"For the way you defended Manzikert, there will be rewards and high office in Constantinople," Bryennius said.

"Perhaps. We'll see." Basil paused and looked at the ground, then into the count's eyes. "Leo, say a prayer for me in Saint Sophia, for I took a life I shouldn't have, even in battle."

Bryennius nodded.

Then they said farewell and the count trotted after the regiment as it moved up the rising ground, most of the riders looking back for a last glimpse of the fortress as they passed over the crest.

There, Bryennius peeled off, cantering to a low knoll. It was the place, Guy remembered, from where he had his first glimpse of the city. The count reined-in and sat his horse, looking back.

Guy glanced at Irene and they followed, drawing up alongside him.

Bryennius said without turning his face to them, "Much happened here and now it belongs to the ages." He motioned to the faces in the column. "And now some ride forward to their futures, others back from whence they came." With that, the count drove his spear point into the earth, the upright haft lonesome in the clear morning air, as though to leave some sign of his passing.

Guy's stirrup touched Irene's.

She spoke quietly. "I'll never forget the moment that I first saw you. I somehow knew you would be important in my life. And I'll never forget your riding out that gate on Zarrar. It was the loneliest and most frightening time of my life. Even that ride from Archēsh was less terrible."

Guy leaned over and squeezed her hand. Then he looked at Bryennius. "What moment do you remember most, Count?"

"There were so many," the Roman answered after a pause. "Good, bad, indifferent, pleasant, terrifying. Not many when I was filled with devotion to church or empire, I must say."

"The moment you would live again and again if you could?"

Bryennius beheld the valley and the snow-capped mountain beyond. At length his gaze rested on the fortress. Zarrar moved impatiently, as if to return to the column. With the touch of a heel and rein on the horse's neck, Bryennius stilled him. "The moment I would live again?" he mused, looking at Guy as if he had never considered it that way before. "It was a draught of cool water from a well in Manzikert." With that, he looked long at the fortress and turned Zarrar to the road ahead.

THE END

CHARACTERS

Plain text denotes real historical characters
# denotes real historical figures, of whom I have invented or assumed much
* denotes fictional characters

Main Characters

Guy d'Agiles *#	Frankish mercenary. His real name is unknown.
Leo Bryennius*	Byzantine officer.
Derar al-Adin*	Arab mercenary with the Seljuks.
Basil Apocapes #	Byzantine general.
Bardas Cydones *	Imperial courier from Constantinople.
Bessas Phocas*	Byzantine officer.
Irene Curticius*	Daughter of a Byzantine officer.
Martina Cinnamus*	Byzantine courier.
Modestos Kamyates*	A high ranking official from Constantinople.
Tughrul Bey#	Sultan of the Seljuk Turks.

Minor Characters

Arabs

al-Ka'im	Sunni caliph in Baghdad.
al-Asfar al-Taghlibi	An Arab raider and slave trader.
Derar al-Adin*	An Arab mercenary with the Seljuks.
Farisa*	A Roman captive, the servant of Derar al-Adin.
Zobeir al-Adin*	An Arab mercenary of the Seljuk army.

Armenians

Ananias*	Servant of Bardanes Gurgen.
Aram Gasparian*	Citizen of Manzikert.
Araxie Bagradian*	Priest of Manzikert.
Armine and Theodore Vosganian*	Associates of Togol.
Arshak*	Scout for the Byzantines.
Bardanes Gurgen*	An Armenian patriot.
Kavadh*	Muslim blacksmith of Archēsh.
Gagik-Abas II	Bagratid king of Armenian Kars (1029–1064).
Joaninna Magistros*	Healer from Manzikert.
Ruben*	Scout for the Byzantines.

Seranush Donjoian * — Irregular officer of the Byzantine Army.
Simon Vardaheri* — Horse trader.
Tatoul Vananttzi # — Also T'at'ul. Nobleman of the Kingdom of Kars.
Theodore Ankhialou* — Irregular officer of the Byzantine Army.
Tigran Zakarian* — Landlord of Arknik.
Vartanoush Norhadian* — Maid of Maria Taronites.
Yūryak* — Courier for the Byzantines.

Byzantines (Romans or 'Greeks')

Aaron Vladislav — Former Governor of Vaspurakan.
Agatha Bryennius* — Wife of Leo Bryennius.
Anna Curticius* — Wife of John Curticius.
Aspietes* — A *cataphract* of the *Scholae*.
Athanasia* — Abbess of the monastery Manzikert.
Bardas Cydones* — Imperial courier from Constantinople.
Basil II ('The Bulgarslayer') — Byzantine Emperor 976—1025.
Basil Apocapes# — Commander at Manzikert in 1054.
Bessas Phocas* — Byzantine officer.
Catacalon Cecaumenus — Byzantine general. Governor of Iberia and Ani in 1048.
Constantine Monomacus — (Constantine IX) Byzantine Emperor at the time.
Antony Lascaris* — Officer of the Scholae.
Cosmas Mouzalon* — Squire of Bessas, Lascaris and Sebēos.
Damian Curticius* — Byzantine officer. Irene's brother.
Daniel Branas* — Basil's Military Secretary.
Domnos and Maria Taronites* — Merchant from Karin and his wife.
Eirene Prodromos* — Serina's maid.
George Drosus. — Governor of Iberia and Ani in 1054.
Irene Curticius* — Daughter of a Byzantine officer at Manzikert.
Isaac* — A clerk.
Helene Cephalus* — Serina's mother.
Joshua Balsamon* — Junior officer of the Scholae.
John Curticius* — Princeps of the Manzikert garrison.
Karas Seth* — Army engineer at Manzikert.
Leo Bryennius* — Count of the Scholae.
Loukas Gabras* — Trooper in the Scholae.
Maniakh* — A Patzinack scout for the Byzantines.
Mariam Branas* — Wife of Daniel Branas.
Martina Cinnamus* — Courier.
Michael Cerularius — Orthodox patriarch in Constantinople.
Michael Psellus (1018–1081) — High-ranking bureaucrat.
Modestos Kamyates* — Senior official from Constantinople.
Maro Atticus* — Trooper of the Scholae.

Nicholas Italos*	Serina's servant.
Nicetas Pegonites	General.
Peter Stoudios*	Soldier of the Scholae.
Petros Dourkitzes*	Citizen of Melitene, the servant of Bardas Cydones.
Pholos Cephalus*	Civil official in Manzikert
Sebēos*	Officer of the Scholae.
Sergios Atticus*	Soldier of the Scholae.
Serena Cephalus*	Daughter of a Byzantine official in Manzikert.
Taticus Phocas*	Leo's squire.
Theodore Vladislav	Strategos of Taron, son of Aaron Vladislav.
Theodora	'Empress Elector' of Byzantium.
Theophanes Doukas*	Officer at Manzikert.
Tzetzes*	Trooper of the Scholae.
Togol*	Cuman scout.

FRANKS

Charles Bertrum*	Frankish knight.
Guy d'Agiles *#	Frankish man-at-arms: real name unknown.
Hervé	Mercenary for the Byzantines.
Jacques*	Guy's servant.
Reynaldus*	Norman mercenary.
Robert Balazun*	Norman mercenary.
Raymond de Gaillon*	Commander of the Franks at Manzikert.
Geoffrey de Rouens*	Norman knight, a friend of Charles Bertrum's
William de Chartres*	Norman knight of Balazun's group.

GEORGIANS

Bagrat IV	King of Georgia
Ch'ortuanēl	Soldier.
David Varaz *	Count Leo's Iberian scout.
Liparit Orbelian	Nobleman—pretender to the Georgian throne.

KURDS

Abu-Nasr Iskander	Shaddadid ruler of Dvin.
Abu Nasr Ahmad Nasr ad-Daulah	Marwanid ruler of Diyar Bakr (Amida).
Wahsudan ibn Mamlan	Ravvadid emir of Tabriz.

PATZINAKS

Galinos	Warrior who rescued Cecaumenus after Diacene.
Tyrach	Khan of the Patzinaks.
Maniakh*	Scout for Count Bryennius.

Characters

Seljuk Turks

Abu 'Ali ibn Kabir	Representative in Constantinople.
Abramas*	Persian siege engineer in the Seljuk army.
Abimelech	Seljuk emir, brother to Kutulmush.
Lord Alkan	Commander of troops from Chorasmia.
Alp Arslan	Seljuk emir, nephew of Tughul Bey.
Ames*	Persian scribe of the Sultan's court.
Amid al-Mulk Muhammad al-Kundur	Vizier of Seljuk Sultan Tughrul Bey.
'Amr-Kāfūr	Emir of the court of Tughrul Bey.
Arsuban	Emir of the Seljuk army.
Asan	See Crown Prince Hasan.
Beyruh Dirse*	Younger brother of Emren Dirse.
Bughra Dumrul*	Sultan's spymaster.
Burla Dirse*	A Seljuk woman.
Çağri Bey	Brother to Tughrul Bey.
Crown Prince Hasan	Seljuk nobleman, killed at Stragna.
Dinar	Emir from the Court of Tughrul Bey.
Emren Dirse*	Seljuk Emir, a friend of Ibrahim al-Adin's.
Hurr*	Dancer with the Seljuk camp.
Ibrahim Inal	Foster brother to Tughrul Bey.
Isma'il*	Seljuk general of the advance guard.
Kijaziz	Emir of the Court of Tughrul Bey.
Koupagan Bey*	A Seljuk Emir, a relative of the Emir Samuk.
Kutlumush ibn Arslan	Senior Seljuk emir, the cousin of Tughrul Bey.
Osketsam	Tughrul Bey's father in law.
Osman*	Seljuk Emir.
Samuk	An Emir of the Court of Tughrul Bey.
Seljuk	Sometimes 'Saljak'. Founder of the Seljuk Turks.
Tughrul Bey	Sultan of the Seljuk Turks.
Zaibullah*	Seljuk tribesman.

Varangians/Rus

Flora Asadian*	Rus-Armenian woman: companion of Charles.
Oleg*	Viking/Rus commander at Manzikert.
Olga*	Oleg's wife.

AFTERWORD

I first came across the story of an unnamed Frankish mercenary's ride at Manzikert, during 1992 while reading J.C.F. Fuller's *Decisive Battles of the Western World*. This man's single handed attempt to save a doomed Armenian city immediately struck me as an extraordinary feat of military derring-do and superb horsemanship. The wider story of the sanguinary Turkish raids into Byzantium's reluctant Armenian provinces and old hatreds lingering for a millennium was given immediacy by the war then being fought between Armenia and Azerbaijan over Nagorno Karabakh. Thus I became interested. Who was this remarkable Frank and what was he doing there in 1054? What prompted him to undertake such a suicidal act? Matthew of Edessa's record of his words, "today my blood shall be shed for all the Christians, for I have neither wife nor children to weep over me," was little more than a hint. His story deserved more than the couple of lines in a few history books.

The historical records are sparse and often biased, a challenge exacerbated by what Christopher Beckwith describes, in his preface to *Empires of the Silk Road*, as a Western, especially Anglo-American, apathy about Central Asia.

This is reflected in the general indifference to the 2015 centenary of the Armenian Genocide, one of the first great crimes against humanity of the ugly twentieth century. In a sense the paucity of readily available sources is liberating. The storyteller is freed from conjectural "history"—this might have happened, or that—to imagine what it might have been like for ordinary people to live through those times.

There are of course different views on what happened in eleventh century Asia Minor and why: the Seljuk Turks and other Muslims cast as aggressors; or the Sultan seen as responding defensively to Byzantine moves into Persarmenia and Azerbaijan. While Edward Gibbon in Volume Six of *The Decline and Fall of the Roman Empire*, describes Tughrul Bey, after his initial conquests in Iran and Iraq, as the guardian of "justice and the public peace"; Alfred Friendly is doubtless correct to note in *The Dreadful Day*, while "Armenian chroniclers were not driven to understatement …the carnage must have been ghastly." One of a growing number of scholars interested in this period, Osman Azis Basan from the University of Edinburgh, in his PhD thesis, *The Great Seljuks*, notes Tughrul stating "world dominion" was not possible without Seljuk unity. Similarly, depending on bias, the 1048 battle at Kapetrau is variously described as a hard-fought draw, or Seljuk victory.

John Julius Norwich's *Byzantium* trilogy brings that oft forgotten empire and its colourful characters alive, with sympathy and insight into the personal strengths or failings—"the smug intellectualism and obsessive personal ambition"—of key figures. Historical Byzantine perspectives can be read in *Fourteen Byzantine Rulers* by the eleventh century Byzantine bureaucrat, Michael

Psellus, and in Princess Anna Comnena's *The Alexiad*. For the Armenian story, Ara Edmound Dostorian's translation of *The Chronicle of Matthew of Edessa* and Robert Bedrosian's translation of Aristakes of Lastivert's *History* are essential sources. The American historian, Paul A. Blaum's closely researched and detailed series of monographs—*An Armenian Epic-The Siege of Manzikert, The Dawn of the Seljuks, Diplomacy gone to seed—a history of Byzantine foreign relations, A.D. 1047-57*—amongst his other works, are vital sources. Warren Reed's novel *Hidden Scorpion*, draws on experience in the Middle East to vividly portray some of the pitfalls of diplomacy and espionage which, given human nature, seems to have changed remarkably little in a millennium.

While there is a great deal of information available on medieval warfare, the following titles provide a useful starting point. *Byzantine Armies 886-1118* by Ian Heath and Angus McBride; *The Armies of Islam 7th-11th Centuries* by David Nicolle and Angus McBride and *Armies of the Caliphates 862-1098* by David Nicolle and Graham Turner, are detailed and well-illustrated. Warren Treadgold's *Byzantium and its Army 284—1081*, provides a wealth of information on doctrine, organisation and administration which, in the way of armies, was in constant change. Sir Charles Oman's *A History of the Art of War in the Middle Ages* is also a most useful reference. For notes on Seljuk history, culture and military organisation, the two volumes on the Seljuk period, from *A Cultural Atlas of the Turkish World*, by Metin Eriş et al, published by the Turkish Cultural Service Foundation, are essential sources. The representation of the Manzikert defences draws on the diagram in Jacques de Morgan's *The History of the Armenian People: From the Remotest Times to the Present Day*. The city's triple walls are mentioned in Alfons Maria Schneider's 1937 study, *The City-Walls of Istanbul*.

Manzikert is better known for the 1071 epochal defeat of a Byzantine army near the city, the Empire's "terrible day" from which it never recovered. The story of the siege in 1054 is little known, though if valour and impossible odds are the measure, it stands as a Greek and certainly Armenian epic. The fortitude of ordinary people bought the tottering Byzantine Empire a seventeen year respite which was wasted by those in power in Constantinople. In this, the siege is a story for all time.

I undertook a field trip to Malazgird in eastern Turkey in 2002. Remnants of the fortress were still there—not romantically perched alone, weathered but intact like some more famous sites—rather largely lost and forlorn, buried in the sprawl of an untidy Turko-Kurdish town. The feel of Kurdish rebellion lingered and while Turkish officials were friendly and local workman restoring some of the defensive walls, both interested in and informative about their work, the landscape had the air of remoteness and hardship. To visit this once flourishing region was a lesson in the impermanence of human affairs.

With this in mind, I have sought to inform and entertain, hoping to do justice to the players in the story of those turbulent times.

Lance Collins 6th January 2016

GLOSSARY

Abbasid Caliphate The Sunni Islamic caliphate based in Baghdad. An objective of the Seljuk Turks, Baghdad was occupied by Tughrul in 1055.

Armenian Church Founded in the 4th century, the Armenian Church recognised the single divine nature of Christ in contrast to the Orthodox and Catholic beliefs. This was the reason for religious persecution by Byzantium.

Artsn (Place) Variously, Ardzen, Artsen. An un-walled city some ten miles northwest of Karin, overrun and pillaged by Seljuk Turks in 1048. It survived in Turkey as the hamlet of Khar Arz (literally ruins-of-Artsn) until renamed Kahramanlar in the 1980s.

aventail Part of a helmet arrangement, the aventail is suspended from the back half of the helmet to protect the wearers neck (and occasionally, shoulders). Mail was preferred, but either a stiff single piece, or strips of leather were also used. Common in Eastern and Byzantine armour, it was seldom used in Western Europe.

Azaz (Battle) Battle in August 1030 near Aleppo in Syria where the Byzantines were defeated.

baban Seljuk name for the large stone-throwing catapult, possibly an early form of trebuchet, of Byzantine origin, employed against the walls of Manzikert in 1054.

ballista See siege engines.

banda (plural) or *bandum* (singular) Byzantine cavalry tactical formation of 300 men commanded by a count. It is roughly equivalent to a 19th Century cavalry regiment commanded by a lieutenant colonel. For ease in the novel, the more modern terms have been used: regiment (300 or more men), squadron (100) and troop (30).

bard Horse armour, worn like a horse-rug, of mail, iron or horn lamellar, or glued felt to protect horses, especially from arrows.

bezant The Latin term for nomisma, the gold standard of Byzantine currency.

byrnie A mail shirt, short-sleeved and reaching the hips. From the 8th Century on, it was replaced, for those wealthy enough, by the knee-length or lower and longer-sleeved hauberk. It was probably still retained by poorer soldiers in western armies.

Byzantine Army Although wily diplomacy was a factor, Byzantium, under constant attack on several fronts, owed its long survival to a remarkable military system. In the first decade of the 11th Century, under the Emperor Basil II (the 'Bulgarslayer'), the Byzantine Army was virtually unparalleled in discipline, equipment, tactics and success. By 1054, although depleted by war, usury and mal-administration, the army remained sound in strategic doctrine and battle tactics. Cavalry was the dominant arm, but was supported by infantry, artillery, engineers, medical and logistics units. Depending on the skill of its commanders, it performed creditably if not flawlessly against the huge Patzinak invasion of Thrace. By 1054, much of the army available for eastern service—Aristakes puts the order of battle at 60,000 men—was concentrated at Caesarea (modern Kayseri). It seems few were deployed forward on the frontier before the campaign of 1054. Broadly, the army comprised:

The Tagmata. High quality professional troops quartered in and near Constantinople. Although structures changed, the *tagmas* can be considered as:

- **Scholae**—3000 strong, equivalent to a modern brigade, divided into 300 strong *bandum*, or regiments commanded by counts.
- **Excubitores**—a brigade of cavalry.
- **Watch**—cavalry—emperor's bodyguard.
- **Numera**—infantry garrison unit to guard Constantinople.
- **Walls**—infantry garrison unit to guard Constantinople.
- **Optimates**—a logistics unit, assisting with the baggage on campaign.
- **Hetaeria**—imperial bodyguards.
- **Hicanti**—cavalry.
- **Immortals**—cavalry.
- **Varangian Guard**—an imperial guard unit comprised variously of Vikings, Russians and after 1066, many Englishmen. There is some doubt about when it was formed, but it was certainly in being by the time of the disastrous Battle of Manzikert in 1071.
- **Byzantine Navy**—The navy was considered part of the Tagmata.

The Themes. These were the 46 regional military commands, of mostly irregular troops of varying quality, commanded by a military governor. Once the backbone of the Byzantine state, their military capability had been seriously depleted by 1054. It is estimated only some 5,000 troops defended Vaspurakan in 1054. They included cavalry, infantry, artillery, engineers, baggage and the like.

Allies and mercenaries. Byzantium made full use of these, particularly from the early 11th Century. Franks, Varangians, Rus, Uze, Patzinks and later, Turks, are all mentioned.

Ranks. These were bewilderingly bureaucratic, constantly changing and still argued. Warren Treadgold's *Byzantium and Its Army, 284–1081*, covers them in detail. For the purposes of the story, the following are used.

- **Domestic**—these were the senior army commanders, a modern field marshal. The Domestic of the Scholae was often appointed as overall commander on campaign.
- **Strategos**—a general. For command of a theme, the term dux or catepano was sometimes used. Basil Apocapes was evidently a subordinate district commander, albeit of some influence and ability and hence, for the purpose of the novel, accorded 'strategos' as a courtesy title.
- **Turmarch**—a subordinate fortress/district commander, subordinate to the strategos commanding a theme. A modern equivalent might be a brigadier.
- **Count**—the commander of a regiment or similar level of responsibility; a modern lieutenant colonel.
- **Centarch**—the commander of 100. The modern equivalent would be a regimental second in command, or a squadron or company commander, a major.
- **Tribune**—a commander of fifty man, roughly equivalent of a modern lieutenant or junior captain.
- **Decarch**—a commander of ten, a modern corporal, a section commander.

cantle The raised rear of a saddle seat behind the rider.

cataphract Byzantine medium cavalry trooper. Not light cavalry, nor as heavily armoured as the fully-armoured *klibanophoroi*.

centarch See Byzantine Army—Ranks.

chamfron The defensive armour for the fore part of a warhorse's head.

chukka A time division, or 'quarter', of the game of polo.

circuit walls The extensive walls surrounding and protecting the circumference of a city or town.

coif Mail armoured hood for the head and neck.

corselet Body armour, generally short-sleeved or sleeveless, reaching the hips or below.

coup de main An overwhelming surprise attack.

crenelle An embrasure, in a parapet or breastwork, to shoot through.

Cumans A pagan, nomadic East Turkic people, coming from NW Asian Russia who conquered southern Russia in the 11th Century. They both warred with and were employed as mercenaries by Byzantium. In the latter part of the 11th century they conquered the Patzinaks.

curtain-wall A curtain wall was a relatively thin wall, depending for its strength on the enfilading towers spaced along its length: commonly used in circuit walls, where strength was sacrificed for length.

decarch See Byzantine Army—Ranks.

Daylamis Also referred to as the Delmic Tribe. Mountaineers from south of the Caucasus, employed as infantry by the Abbasids. Daylamis were Shi'ite Muslims and predominately infantry.

destrier Frankish name for a European warhorse. Not the heavy great-horse of the later medieval period, but a lighter hunter type.

Diacene (Battle, 1049) Site in the Balkans of a disastrous Byzantine battle against the Patzinaks.

domestic See Byzantine Army—Ranks.

donjon A tower keep, the last bastion within the citadel.

enceinte The wall or ramparts which surround a fortress; the area thus enclosed.

Excubitores See Byzantine Army—Tagmata. .

Fatimid Caliphate Shi'ite Muslim empire based in Egypt from June 969 AD.

fief de hauberk A military fief, or landholding, held by a knight in return for armed service to an overlord. It was a cornerstone of the feudal system in Western Europe.

foot Collective noun for infantry.

gallery wall A gallery wall was a strong defensive wall in which covered or partially covered galleries were constructed, allowing defenders to operate engines of war from protected positions. The ruins at Manzikert indicate that at least some of the defences were gallery walls.

ghazis Islamic border raiders, equivalent of the Byzantine *akritai* (borderers), especially on the frontier with the invading Turks.

Ghaznavid Dynasty (AD 977–1186) A successor state to the Samanid Empire, this Turkic dynasty held power southwest of the Oxus River in Khorasan,

Afghanistan, and northern India. The Qarakhanids, other successors to the Samanids, controlled the lands to the immediate east of the Oxus River. The Ghaznavids reached their zenith under Mahmud in the 1030's, his son being defeated by the Seljuks at Dandanqan in 1040.

ghulams Turkic professional soldiers of the Seljuk state and the Abbasid caliphate's elite corps, roughly equivalent to the Byzantine *tagmata*. Forerunners of the Mamluks, they were a slave army of heavily armoured and armed horse-archers, who wielded considerable influence in Baghdad politics, not unlike the Praetorian Guard of imperial Rome.

hand-gallop A quick gait, faster than a canter but rather less than a full, headlong, racing gallop: a collected, balanced pace where the horse is kept 'in hand', ready for any stopping, turning or jumping.

hauberk Long military tunic of mail, either ring (iron rings sewn on a mostly leather backing) or, more commonly, chain mail split front and back for riding and marked by head and neck protection. From the early medieval period in the West, only knights were privileged to wear the hauberk. It was the armour *de rigeur* of Norman and Frankish knights of the late 11th and 12th centuries, superseding the earlier byrnie.

Hetaeria See Byzantine Army—Tagmata.

Hicanti See Byzantine Army—Tagmata.

horse Collective noun for cavalry.

Immortals See Byzantine Army—Tagmata.

Kapetrou (Battle) Fortress near which was fought a battle in Armenia in 1048 where Byzantine (including Armenian) and Georgian troops intercepted but could not defeat a Seljuk raid withdrawing from raids, including the sack of Artsn) in 1048 CE. It is generally given as Pasinler in modern Turkey.

keffiyeh Flowing fabric headdress of the Arabs.

khutba Friday prayers in mosques.

Kinik The tribe of the Ozguz in which Saljak/Seljuk, founder of the Seljuks, was born.

knight See *milites*, *miles*.

Kurds Kurdish dynasties arose during the six hundred years after the Arab invasion and Kurdish conversion to Islam. Most significant for the period of this story are the *Ravvadid* (also Rawwadid) Kurds who were based around Tabriz from 955 to the Mongol invasions in 1221. The *Shaddadids* ruled a predominately Armenian population in the Gandja districts but were not a significant influence in 1054. Other Kurdish dynasties were the *Marwanids* of the Diyarbakir region (990–1096) and the *Hasanwaihids* of Dinavar in the Kermanshah area (959–1015). The *Marwanids*, though professing friendship with Byzantium, proved to be decisive allies, or vassals, of the Seljuks during the campaign of 1054. There is evidently some disagreement whether the Marwanids were Kurds or Arabs.

lamellar Form of body armour comprising overlapping plates, of iron, horn or leather, held together by leather or silk lacing. Very common in Iran and Central Asia, it was also popular in Byzantium. A number of sources illustrate lamellar cuirasses being worn over mail as additional protection.

Latins Western Europeans. It was a reference to both the use of Latin language by many of those people, and their allegiance to the Catholic Church of Rome.

line/lines A row (of soldiers), normally facing the enemy, for example, skirmish line or siege line. Or, as a direction, for example, a line of retreat, or lines of operations/communications. Or: soldiers' accommodation (normally in the field), tents arranged in rows, horse lines and so forth. Also used to denote the extent of an area occupied by troops, for example, forward edge of siege lines.

loosebox In a stable complex, an enclosed stall in which a horse can move freely about, lay down and so on.

mangon/mangonel See siege engines

mantelet A kind of shield or shelter for soldiers or sailors in war, a screen to cover besieging troops.

majra An arrow guide, a piece of grooved timber held in the bow hand so a short dart could be drawn back against the string and released as an arrow. An ideal sniping weapon when the sniper did not want the telltale, long arrow shaft giving immediate warning of missile attack.

merlon In fortifications, that raised part of battlements that separates two embrasures or crenelles.

miles/milites The Latin singular/plural for a knight, specifically armoured horsemen. Dating back for some time, the term came into wider use in the 10th Century, later having linguistic variations such as knight or chevalier.

money The currency and coinage of Byzantium changes over time, but the standard coin of the Byzantine empire was the gold *nomisma* (or *solidus*, the coin identified by the Crusaders as the *byzant*). There were 72 *nomisma* to the pound weight of gold. Leo's salary would have been 206 *nomisma* (three pounds of gold) a year. This currency began to be adulterated in 11th Century. Silver coins included the *miliaresion* valued at one twelfth of a *nomisma*. Copper coins of lesser value were the five, ten, twenty and forty *nummi*, the 40 *nummi* coin being one *follis*. While the currency was into a long period of decline starting from about this period an everyday cloak would have cost about one *nomisma*.

Moors North African Muslims of mixed Arab and Berber descent, who occupied southern Spain between the 8th and 15th centuries.

naffatin A corps of specialist troops of the Abbasid infantry. These were armed with fire projectors and naphtha grenades.

nakhara An Armenian landlord from one of the great landowning families.

near side The left side of a horse, the side from which they are customarily mounted, due to most early riders being soldiers and because swords were usually worn on the left hip.

off-side The right side of a horse, the opposite to that customarily used for mounting.

Oghuz Turks Nomads from east of the Jaxartes River, they were in turn forced to westward migration into Islamic lands by the Kipchaks (later Polovtsi or Cumans). The Seljuks were a branch of the Oghuz, led by Seljak after whom they were named.

paillasse A bed of straw, usually encased by a mattress cover of hessian or other cheap material.

peribolos In the land defences of Constantinople, the stretch of ground between the ditch and fore-wall.

Patzinaks Also known as Petchenegs. A powerful pagan sub-tribe of the Oghuz Turks and cousins of the Seljuks. The Patzinaks from southern Russia raided Constantinople through the Balkans, posing a significant threat to the Byzantines during the mid-11th Century.

P'rang Armenian term for 'Frank'.

prick spurs Early form of European spurs, having no rowel, merely a point.

princeps Byzantine Army appointment title for the chief of staff.

Qarakhanid (or Karakhanid) A Turkic tribal confederation from Central Asia. After the collapse of the Samanids at the close of the 10th Century, the Qarluq confederation of tribes established the Qarakhanid Dynasty as the ruling force in Transoxiania (between the Oxus and Jaxartes Rivers).

razzia Turkish/Islamic raid/raiding. Also *ghazwa*.

Rum Turkish and Arabic term for 'Romans' and Byzantine Empire.

Rus People from around of Kiev, a district by then showing strong Viking influence. Modern Russian culture originates from the Viking interrelationship with the surrounding population and Orthodox Christianity gained from Byzantium.

Saracen Generic Latin and Byzantine term encompassing the peoples of the Middle East: Turks, Arabs, Persians, Egyptians and others.

Scarp The interior wall of a ditch of a fortification at the foot of the walls. Counterscarp is the outside wall of the moat or ditch.

Scholae See Byzantine Army—Tagmata. The oldest and most famous of the Byzantine imperial *tagmata* cavalry regiments. They replaced the Praetorian Guards of the ancients after the battle of the Milvian Bridge when Constantine (306–337) won control over the Roman Empire, making some concessions to Christianity.

Seljuk Turks Descendants of the Oghuz, the Seljuks emerged as a distinct Turkic tribal group in the early 11th Century. They converted from paganism or animism to Sunni Islam.

Shaddadids See Kurds.

Seljuk Army *The Cultural Atlas of the Turkish World* published by the Turkish Cultural Service Foundation, provides some insight into the organisation of the Seljuk Army. Basic organisation comprised:

- *Gulâmân-I suray* ('youths of the palace') palace guards. Well turned out and equipped with responsibility for the safety of the sultan and high standard of ceremonial duties.
- *Hassa ordusu* (imperial guard). Professional cavalry with a weight of armour comparable to the *tagmata* or West European knights of the time. By the end of the 11th Century there were said to be 20,000 of them. The corps was probably based on the *ghulams* of the Abbasid Caliphate.
- *Sipahiyan* (knights). These were cavalrymen who supported themselves off their private fiefs, comparable to the theme soldiers of Byzantium.
- *Haşer.* Ordinary people drafted into the army and paid a wage.
- *Gaziyân* (raiders). These were professional troops used for cross border raiding—a state sponsored continuation of the Muslim ghazi tradition.
- **Infantry.** The Daylamis provided the backbone of the professional infantry.
- **Turkoman tribesmen.** Overwhelmingly the famous horse-archers, these were the clan followers of the emirs who only loosely obeyed the Sultan's direction. By their migrations, raiding and participation in major campaigns, they were a major if unreliable source of Seljuk state power.

- **Specialists.** These included: physicians, veterinarians, armourers, judges, siege engineers et cetera. The sophistication of Seljuk siege operations at Manzikert bespeaks the increasing sophistication of their military force.
- **Allies.** It seems a number of allies joined the Seljuk campaign of 1054 and those before and after it: Kurds, Daylamis and troops from Chorasmia (an old Persian satrapy south of the Aral Sea) being mentioned in the sources.

The size of the Seljuk army during the Manzikert campaign is difficult to gauge. A very large field army for the time would have been 50,000 troops of all arms, though Armenian sources list Tughrul Bey as having 100,000 men at his disposal for the invasion of Armenia. Given that the campaign of 1054 was the major military effort of the Seljuk empire at that time, Tughrul Bey's assumed total deployed forced is about 50,000.

siege engines In warfare, mechanical and chemical devices used to overwhelm the defences of a fortified place by weakening the physical defences, injuring personnel or driving them into cover so they were unable to fight effectively, or by protecting besieging/attacking troops. The same weapons could in many instances by used by the defence. Volumes have been written on the subject and there is a good deal of information online. Anti-materiel engines were used to attack the physical defences. These included a variety of stone throwing mangonels (which could also hurl clay pots of naphtha), battering rams, a variety of tools for prising out stones, scaling ladders, tunnelling equipment, mantelets to protect besieging troops and wheeled shelters to protect assaulting troops. Movable towers, common in siege warfare to get soldiers over the walls, are not noted in the sources on this siege of Manzikert. The most common anti-personnel weapon was the ballistae, a bold-shooting "crossbows" of reasonable accuracy. Combined with archery and fire, they were employed to sweep defending troops from the walls so they could not effectively defend them. Anti-personnel "chemical" weapons included fire, and toxic smoke. Attempts to cause disease, such as plague, in a besieged city by hurling dead animal carcasses over the walls, have been noted often throughout history, but no sources mention it in relation to the 1054 siege of Manzikert.

semissis See Money.

Shi`ite* **Muslims** Followers of 'Ali, husband of Fatima, daughter of The Prophet, Mohammed. There was a schism between *Shi`ite and Sunnis after the death of Mohammed (632 CE).

Smyrna (Place) A Byzantine city on the Mediterranean coast. Modern Izmir.

solidus See Money.

strategos Byzantine general. See Byzantine Army—Ranks.

Stragna River (Place/battlefield) Now the Great Zab River, it was the scene of Cecaumenus' and Aaron Vladislav's decisive defeat of the Seljuk Prince Hasan in 1047.

Sunni Muslims Sunnis respect the memory of the four caliphs: Abubeker, Omar, Othman and Ali, assigning last place to Ali, the husband of Fatima. The split between Shi'ite and Sunni Muslims occurred after the death of Mohammed and concerned the question of succession. Ali argued he was the natural heir. Othman reasoned there should be no dynastic succession.

tagmata The collective name for the central Byzantine army of professional troops: roughly equivalent to a modern corps, for a total of about 30,000 men, mostly cavalry. The *tagmata* might be likened, in organisation and function, to the Household Division of the British Army.

Theme Byzantine regional military districts commanded by a *strategos* or military governor. Geographically based, there were 47 of them at the death of Basil in 1028, extending from southern Italy to Armenia. Depending on size, wealth and population, they contributed army contingents of from 4,000 to 15,000 before the mid-11th century decline beginning in 1028. In 1054, Vaspurakan had some 5,000 theme troops: the neighbouring themes of Iberia-Armenia and Taron, 15,000 and 3,000 respectively.

tremissis See Money.

vambraces Byzantine strap-on armour for the forearm, to provide protection below the mid-length mail sleeve of the hauberk or byrnie. Usually made of iron strips riveted to two straps. Greaves to protect the shins were of similar construction.

Varangian Guard See Byzantine Army—Tagmata. A *tagmata* unit of the Byzantine Army from [disputed] 988. Its ranks were filled with, variously, Rus, Danes, and Scandinavians and after the battle of Hastings, Englishmen. It is likely they were mounted infantry, riding to battle and dismounting to fight.

Varangians See Varangian Guard. As a people, Danes and Swedes.

Vaspurakan (Place) Once a separate Armenian kingdom Vaspurakan was peacefully subsumed into the Byzantine Empire, under Basil II, in 1021 CE. A Byzantine military district (theme) of southwest Armenia. The capital is variously given as Van or Manzikert and seems to have switched between the two.

Vikings As a people, Danes and Norwegians.

About the Author

Lance Collins grew up in rural Australia and was educated at La Trobe University in Melbourne. He joined the Australian Army in 1979, graduating into the Intelligence Corps. After a variety of army appointments, Collins was promoted to lieutenant colonel in 1995 and was appointed as the senior intelligence officer for the International Force East Timor between September 1999 and February 2000. He has a master's degree in international relations and maintains a lifelong interest in horses, history and literature.

His previous published work is, with Warren Reed, the non-fiction *Plunging Point: intelligence failures, cover-ups and consequences*, HarperCollins, Sydney 2005.